Complicated

Kristen Ashley

NEW YORK TIMES **BESTSELLING AUTHOR**

KRISTEN ASHLEY

This book is a work of fiction. Any reference to historical events, real people, or real places are used fictitiously. Other names, characters, places, and incidents are products of the author's imagination. Any resemblance to actual events, locales, or persons, living or dead, is coincidental.

Cover Image: Pixel Mischief Design

Chapter 1

Later

Hixon

Hix rolled to his bare ass on the side of the bed, putting his feet on the floor.

Damn.

What was that?

Not good.

Not *good.*

Because it was good.

It was unbelievably *good.*

On this thought, he felt her move in the bed. Heard her low mew. Smelled her damned perfume.

Powdery, flowery and sweet, but it wasn't any of that that got to him.

There was a musk to it that made all that sexy.

Add that to the scent of sex in the room. The trace of her on him (that being more than just her perfume). The dark that surrounded him cut only with moonlight and a distant streetlight, so he could see practically nothing. This meaning he only had his other senses at his command, Hix felt his stomach tighten, his shoulders, his jaw.

All this to beat back the draw of her.

He had to get out of there.

He pushed up to his feet, mumbling, "Gotta go."

There was a quick beat of silence before he heard her soft, surprised, "Sorry. What?"

He reached for his shorts, pulling them up his legs, repeating, "Gotta go."

The mood of the room changed. The sluggish, warm feel of post-really-freaking-great-coitus shimmered to nothing as something heavier started seeping in.

"Go?" she asked.

God, she could unravel him with a syllable.

So, yeah.

That was right.

Go.

He had to *go*.

And do it before he smelled more of her. Heard more of that voice any way it came at him—the way it was before and for certain the way it sounded just then with hurt trembling through it.

He definitely couldn't look at her.

Not in her bed, the sheets rumpled because they'd made them that way, their clothes all over the room because they'd thrown them there, her mass of hair a mess because his fingers had been in it.

Not any of that.

But also just not looking at her *at all*.

"Go," he grunted, locating his trousers five feet from where his shorts had been and tearing them up his legs.

He heard her movements in the bed, sensing she was sitting up in it, not getting out of it, which was good. If the woman did more than that, and all he had to do was visualize it in his head, he'd turn back.

"I...well, uh..."

That was all she said.

But it was too much. Now each syllable seemed to coat his skin, sing to him, luring him back.

Jesus.

What was that?

And damn, it'd been a long time.

But as long as it had been, he'd never been that guy.

The guy he was right then going to be.

How did that guy play crap like this?

"Thanks," he muttered.

Another quick beat of silence before she said in a voice that was low and stunned, "Thanks?"

"Yeah." He shrugged his shirt on his shoulders and didn't bother with the buttons. He just glanced her way without really looking at her even as he bent to tag his shoes and socks from the floor, thankful they were all in a messy pile, not thankful her lacy bra was tangled with them. "That was great," he finished.

Lame, man, lame. And total dick, he thought.

The feel of the room went stunned, and sluggish again, this time with something that didn't feel good at all.

"Yeah," she said softly to his back. "Great."

He turned her way, skimmed his eyes up the bed, noting in a forced-vague way she was up on a hand, holding the sheet to her chest, her hair falling down her shoulders, the rich, honeyed, sunshiny blonde of it made dark in the marginal light, even as her other hand was lifted, pulling the front of her hair out of her face.

Yup.

Not good he looked at her.

"Later," he said.

"Right." There was a bite to that. Bitter and barbed. "Later."

That made Hix pause, hearing that in her tone.

And it made him make a mistake.

He looked through the shadows into her eyes.

He couldn't quite see but he felt they were bitter and barbed too.

"Don't worry about locking the door behind you," she said, now each word that came out of her was ice cold. "As you know, there's no crime in this town."

Oh yeah.

He knew that.

But it didn't change things.

"You need to lock up," he said quietly.

She tipped her head to the side sharply. "And it's my understanding you need to go."

"Greta—"

She dropped her hand from her hair and a long, thick lock fell into her left eye, further shadowing her face in a way it felt like she'd taken a huge step back from him.

Nope.

He didn't need to see that either.

"Bud. Please."

Her words weren't an entreaty.

They were scorn.

And yup.

He had to get out of there before he did any more damage.

Even so...

"Lock up behind me," he ordered.

"Roger that, Sheriff."

"You got a way to get your car back from the club?" he asked.

"Don't worry about me, darlin'. I got a way to do a lot of things," she drawled.

All right.

She would be good. She'd move on.

Now he could be done.

He made the turn to go but twisted right back and again caught her gaze.

"It was great, Greta," he repeated the truth in a tone that, this time, it couldn't be missed he meant it.

"Yeah, Hixon. Brilliant." Her words were clipped, and even

though he knew without a doubt she agreed with what he'd said, her tone didn't share his sentiment.

As he hesitated—in the shadowy dark he couldn't see her eyes narrow, but he would swear he could feel them do just that—she finished, stressing just how much she was done as she gave him her, "*Later.*"

He lifted his chin, turned back to the door and walked his ass out.

He put on his socks and boots just inside her front door and buttoned his shirt before he walked out.

No one would be awake at that hour, but it didn't matter.

In that moment, Hix wasn't thinking about what would run through people's minds if they saw him come out of a house in the very early morning with his shirt undone.

In that moment, Hix was only thinking about what would run through people's minds about Greta if a man came out of her house in the very early morning with his shirt undone.

He sat in his truck at her curb and waited until he saw her form, shadowed from the minimal light filtering through the sheer curtain over the window in her front door and he knew she'd locked herself safely inside.

Only then did Hix drive away.

Chapter 2

Tedium

Hixon

On his way to work on Monday, Hix's phone rang.

He pulled it out of his chest pocket and glanced at the display.

He immediately wished he didn't have to take the call.

But even if she was no longer his wife, they had three kids. Those kids were coming to his place after school that afternoon for their week with him, so he had to take the damn call.

"Yeah?" he answered.

"Nice," Hope replied acidly.

This annoyed him.

It had always annoyed him.

Even before.

But seeing as this was far from the first time he'd answered a call from her that way (when he was driving, mostly, but also when he was in the thick of shit, even before she'd divorced his ass) since she'd divorced his ass, it annoyed him now a good deal more than it had before.

Though, he'd known for a long time Hope liked things how she liked them.

Only how she liked them.

So she didn't much care how often she had to relay precisely how she liked them.

He just hadn't cared when they were together, because he'd been taught by his parents that in marriage, to earn the good, you took the bad and you found a way to deal with it.

With that said, there'd been a time, a very long one, when he thought that trait was a good one. His woman knew what she wanted and didn't back down.

He didn't think that way anymore.

"In the car on the way to work, Hope," he told her. "You know I'm not big on talking on the phone and driving, and you know why." And she did. Back in the day when they lived where shit happened, he'd seen a variety of unpleasant results when people were more interested in what was happening in their ear than what was happening on the road. "The kids okay?"

She ignored his question in order to note, "You *could* get a car that has your phone connected right to it so you have a better shot at doing the impossible. That being multitasking."

On his salary, how she thought he could do that and set up a house where he could finish raising his children the time he had them, he had no clue.

Hope got the new cars.

Hix had had his Bronco since his senior year in college.

In other words, he'd had the thing for twenty years.

This hadn't bothered him either. It still didn't. The Ford Bronco was the best vehicle ever put on the road. He'd switch her out when she died a death he couldn't bring her back from, and not a second before.

Hope didn't give him a chance to respond, even if he had no intention of doing that.

She announced, "We need to talk."

Fabulous.

This had been her refrain now for weeks.

Three of them.

In fact, it started about an hour after they sat in that fucking room with their fucking lawyers and signed those fucking papers.

"Repeat," he bit out. "The kids okay?"

"They're fine," she returned. "But we need to talk."

"Is it about the kids?" he pushed.

"No, Hix. It's not. There's stuff to talk about that doesn't involve the kids."

She was very wrong.

"Not anymore."

"God!" she snapped. "Why are you being this way?"

"I don't know, Hope," he replied, making the turn into the parking lot at the side of the sheriff's department. "Maybe, considering I signed divorce papers three weeks ago, I get to be whatever way I want."

Like always, Hope persevered. "There are things that need to be said."

"Think you said them all when you signed your name on the line next to mine."

"Hix—"

He finished parking and cut the engine, saying, "Probably see you at the game tomorrow night."

"I can't talk to you about this at Corinne's game."

He stared out the windshield at the red brick that was the side of the department and asked, not for the first time, therefore he did it on a sigh, "Wanna clue me in on what 'this' is?"

"I'd like to. In person," she answered, also not for the first time. Then suddenly, her game changed. He heard it in her voice when she coaxed, "Lunch today. My treat."

"Unless there's something up with the kids, we're not talking, Hope. So it goes without saying we're not gonna have lunch."

"How long is it gonna take before you get over this and let me back in?"

Hix felt his chin move slowly back into his neck at the same time his eyes blinked just as slowly.

Get over it?

Christ.

And let her back in?

Seriously?

"You divorced me, Hope," he reminded her quietly.

"I remember, Hix."

"Do you remember the part where I shared repeatedly over the year we were separated that I didn't want that?" he asked.

"Can we *talk* about this? Face to face?"

It was Hix ignoring her now.

"I didn't want it. Not for the kids. Not for our family. Not for me or you. Not for *us*."

"Hixon—"

"We were good. We were happy."

"I wasn't happy," she said softly.

"You made that clear enough," he returned.

"Honey, can we—?"

Honey?

Oh hell no.

"You got something to share about the kids, we can talk. Over the phone. Unless you catch Mamie injecting heroin. Then we can talk face to face."

"Oh my God! She's thirteen years old!"

She was.

Jesus, how did his baby get to be thirteen years old?

He didn't ask his ex-wife that.

He stated, "Now I gotta get to work."

"I cannot *believe you*."

"Take care of yourself, Hope."

With that, he hung up wishing that would be the last time he had to deal with a call like that from his ex-wife but knowing it would not.

He was unsurprised when this thought came true as she called him back while he was putting his hand on the handle of the front door to the department.

He declined the call, opened the door, stepped inside, stopped and took in his department.

His office was at the back, a big window to the room.

Dispatch was to the right, behind bulletproof glass that was put in before he got there for reasons unknown, since practically everybody in that county had a gun, but the zombie apocalypse would have to hit before anyone would use it in a police station. The only things more sacred for Nebraskans were churches, cemeteries and Tom Osborne Field at Memorial Stadium.

Most likely it had been because they had a surplus in the budget.

One woman working in that room. Reva. She did weekday shifts.

In front of him, a long, tall, old, nicked, battered wood counter that still gleamed with care and age.

Reception. No one working that. Any deputy who saw someone walk in would take it.

Beyond reception, past a freaking swinging half door, just like in the TV shows, four desks. Two by two, side by side and stacked.

Behind the wall to the right, past dispatch, their one interrogation room, their one observation room, the locker room, the secure vault, which was the munitions room, and their processing area where they did fingerprinting and took mug shots.

The two cells they had were at the back, opposite his office, mostly open to the room. Open, of course, not including the bars.

Not surprisingly, the one deputy at her desk looked like she had nothing to do.

This was because there was nothing to do.

That county lived in a throwback bubble that made Hix wonder why all the girls weren't wearing petticoats under their poodle skirts, bobby socks and saddle shoes, and all the boys didn't have pomade in their hair and their jeans turned up at the hems.

In that county, people left their keys in their cars and their house doors unlocked.

In that county, most businesses closed on Sunday because that was when you went to church and then went home for family time, Sunday dinner, and if it was the season, football.

It was a county of Cleavers.

It was eerie.

Hix had felt that way about Hope's hometown since the minute he'd stepped foot in it twenty years ago to meet her mother and father.

He hadn't wanted to move there from Indianapolis, but she'd wanted to raise their kids there (and also wanted her mother close so she could foist the kids off on her when she wanted to do something else). So once they started having them, she'd started in on him. And in pure Hope style, she hadn't let up.

On that, Hix had held out.

It took nine years.

Then, before Shaw could get too entrenched in school and the friends he'd make, and Hix had seen the way things were going in public schools in the city and he didn't like it much, he'd given in.

That was seven years ago.

His boy was seventeen now. Corinne, his second child, his first girl, fifteen, sixteen in January. Mamie, his baby, thirteen.

Hope had been thrilled with the move.

Hix and his kids had been bored out of their minds. No Children's Museum. No Colts. No 500. No Monument Circle lit up for Christmas. No Eagle Creek Park. No special occasion dinners at St. Elmo Steak House. No weekend trips up to the Dunes or rental cottages on Lake Shafer, or family treks up to Chicago to catch a Cubs game and then hork down the best pizza known to man.

Just a whole lot of Nebraska filled with farmland sprinkled with farmhouses, or ranchland with ranch houses and the occasional town that wouldn't ever get uppity enough to consider declaring itself a city.

That place was where city cops went after a bad case that twisted their shit in a way they couldn't face even the possibility of another one.

Or where metro cops went to lose their minds.

Of tedium.

There were a few drunks who did stupid shit because they were drunk. There were some kids who did stupid shit because they were kids. There were whisperings of domestic violence or child abuse that not a soul would report because "that doesn't happen here," but if it got out of hand, the concerned parties went to their pastor, not their sheriff.

There was pot.

That was it.

The last death that was suspect ended up being a suicide, and that was twenty-three years ago.

And the only criminal element there was a man who had a crew who operated a meth lab that Hix couldn't find any legal reason to raid. Not to mention the former sheriff had had a good-ol'-boy arrangement with him that he could make his shit in their county, but he couldn't sell it in their county.

An arrangement that criminal held true to, to that day.

Reason one why Hix couldn't find a legal excuse to raid his lab.

And when that sheriff retired two years into Hix and Hope moving back, and Hope didn't let up on pushing him to run, he'd run for sheriff unopposed, thus won.

He'd been opposed the last election. A deputy from the next county over moved in and tried to *move in* on Hix.

Hix had taken ninety-eight percent of the vote.

This was because McCook County didn't like change. The last sheriff had held his post for thirty-three years. He'd endorsed Hix his first election, when he didn't need to, and his second one, when he only kind of did.

And Hix might have been born and raised a Hoosier, but Hope was Cornhusker to the bone, even if she'd finished fucking up her degree (thus not graduating) at Purdue (her third and last hope).

Nebraskans just played it that way if your momma pushed you out on their soil, but definitely if both your parents, and all their parents, hit Lincoln for their higher education.

And Hope's kin had, and so had she, the first try.

But when Hix was grown enough to quit wanting to be a superhero, then a fighter pilot, after which he thought he'd settle for an astronaut, he got serious.

This was precisely at that time when he was eleven years old, sitting in that parking lot in the car with his mom, and that gaunt, jittery man had knocked on the window.

She'd gone all funny, telling him to lock his door, locking her own just in time as the guy went for the handle, and she got them away with the man shouting after them.

He'd never forget how pale her face was or how tight she held on to the steering wheel as she drove them home, saying repeatedly it was all right. She'd only fallen apart behind her bedroom door with his dad after his dad got home, and she did it not knowing Hix sat outside, listening.

After that, all Hix had ever wanted to do was be a cop.

It wasn't about making a difference. It wasn't about righting wrongs.

It was about finding bad guys and making them pay for forcing women, or anyone, to be that damned scared.

But now, Sheriff of McCook County, Nebraska, he didn't do dick.

If his deputies threw a drunk in the tank, he dried out and they let him go. He screwed up and got behind a wheel, Hix sat in a courtroom months later while their county judge gave him or her a lecture in responsibility and a slap on the wrist, even if that lecture was repeated...*repeatedly*.

This being because that judge was always related one way or another to the drunk.

It just wouldn't do to make Thanksgiving uncomfortable.

Forget about it with the kids messing around. They were all far more scared of their parents than Hix and his deputies.

Then again, it wasn't about kids in his county driving new cars, having the latest smartphone, wearing designer clothes and looking to score ecstasy or Rohypnol to better enjoy their night on the town.

If they got in trouble, they might not be home to help work the fields.

So they'd get laid out by Dad, or Mom, in a way that Hix never saw them again unless it was at a school event where they would mind their manners, all "yes, sir," and "no, ma'am," and he'd see them open their date's door so she could get in the car.

He understood it was unhinged that it seemed like he missed crime.

But it wasn't that.

He missed feeling relevant.

He was forty-two years old but he felt like an ole timer with nothing better to do than flip the sign on the door so it didn't say OPEN. It said, GONE FISHIN'.

There were a good many places to fish in Indiana, and if you wanted to make a thing of it, you'd go up to Wisconsin and get the really good shit.

Hix hated fishing.

He didn't share that in those parts, or the fact he wasn't a big fan of hunting either.

He watched his son play football. The school year wore on, he'd watch his son at first base for the school's baseball team.

He also watched his daughter play volleyball then take a break before soccer season hit.

And his baby he watched dance.

Other than that, now that he no longer had a wife and only had his family every other week, he sat at his desk and listened to his deputies ask him how to deal with Mrs. Schmidt accusing her neighbor, Mr. Christenson, of stealing the tomatoes out of her garden. He worked out at the gym. He hung with his boys at the Outpost to catch a game or three. And he watched a shit ton of TV.

And last Saturday he'd gone to the Dew Drop out on Country Road 65, and he'd listened to Greta sing.

Between sets, after he bought her a drink, they'd chatted.

After she was done, he'd taken her home.

And after that, he'd made love to her.

He hadn't fucked her.

He'd made love to her.

It started off differently, hot, heavy, wet, desperate.

Then for some reason, it had changed.

No, not for some reason.

He knew the reason.

He'd nipped her ear with his teeth and she'd turned her head, dislodging his mouth, and in the light of the moon, he'd seen her face.

She'd looked turned on. It was hot and he got off on the fact he made her look that way.

But she'd also been smiling.

She liked what he'd done, how it made her feel, *all* he'd done and how it felt.

But she also just liked *him*.

And he'd liked that.

He hadn't had a woman since Hope had told him she wanted him to leave, and when he argued that she was making a massive mistake, for her, their kids, their family, him, *them*, and she didn't let up, he'd left. Through a year's separation, the whole time he thought he'd get her back and he wasn't going to screw that chance any way he could.

But even if it had only been his hand and a lot of good memories he could make even better in his head, with Greta, no matter how long it had been since he'd been inside a woman, he'd taken it slow. He'd taken his time. And he took them both where he'd been with only one woman in his life.

His wife.

And it had been better than it had ever been with Hope.

Far better.

Beyond anything he knew could happen.

He knew why too.

Because Greta with the great voice, great hair, beautiful face and ample curves knew what she liked too.

But what she liked wasn't about getting what she wanted.

It was about giving.

And Hix had never had that. Not like that. Not unadulterated. Pure. It being about her getting off on giving to him even as he got off giving to her.

Not once in his marriage. Not once in any relationship.

He gave.

He didn't get.

Except from his kids and they gave him everything he needed by simply breathing.

He was down with that too. He loved his wife and he was the kind of man that thought that was his job, to pull out all the stops to give his wife what she needed, what she wanted, what made her happy.

He knew no other way mostly because he'd have it no other way.

Until he had it another way.

"Boss?"

When Bets called him, Hix realized he was standing just inside the door not moving.

Shit.

He moved to the swinging half door and swung through it, and as usual with Bets, dealing with her the only way she forced him with her crap to deal with her.

He held her eyes only as long as was necessary to say, "Mornin'."

He walked down the center aisle between the desks as she replied, "Mornin'. Have a good weekend?"

He walked right past her, muttering, "Yup."

And he had, for the first time in about a year and three weeks.

Or at least he'd had a good Saturday night.

Until he'd screwed it up.

He went to his office, then to his desk, tossed his phone on it and rounded it, hitting the button to boot up his computer.

His desk was at the side of the room, his back to the wall beyond which were the cells.

He did this because he didn't want his desk facing the window. It would imply to his deputies he was keeping an eye on them. He also didn't want his back to the window, not because he didn't want his back to the door, that window was bulletproof too. Because he didn't want his deputies to see his computer screen or watch him when he wasn't aware.

So to the side it was. They had their privacy of a sort, as did he.

He was standing behind the desk, about to sit his ass in his chair, when Bets's voice came from the door directly opposite him.

"Heard you hit the Dew Drop."

Another thing he didn't like about small towns in not-very-populated counties.

Without much else to do, everyone got up in everyone else's business.

And without much else to focus on, everyone's business was easy access.

But with him, for some reason, even before he became sheriff, everyone thought he was their business. Him and Hope and their kids.

It was worse that it was Bets hitting his door first thing on a Monday morning sharing this.

Shit.

Here we go, he thought.

She walked in and Hix beat back a sigh.

"I've been there a couple of times. It's pretty cool," she noted.

He'd been there only once before last Saturday, years before, on a night out with Hope.

And Bets was right. The Dew Drop was cool. Out in the middle of nowhere, plenty of parking because everything around it was a field, the building looked like a shack.

This was because, back in the day it was a shack where the few

African Americans in McCook County and its surrounding ones, and the few other people who inhabited them who knew cool, could go to listen to jazz or blues played and sung by traveling artists who'd never miss the chance to do their thing in hopes of making their names.

But also, they'd never miss the chance to give the management of the Dew Drop an opportunity to earn a cover charge.

There were a number of people in McCook County who had the respect of its citizens.

But there were only a handful who had the respect shown Gemini Jones.

The man was the fourth generation in his family to own and manage that shack.

And it might have been a shack back in the day, but now, you walked in, you got classy pink and blue lighting, plush semi-circle booths, tables in front of the small, intimate stage with tiny burgundy-shade covered lamps and long rosy-pink tablecloths on them, drinks served in stemmed glassware or heavy lowballs set on thick marine-blue cocktail napkins. Beer was served draft only. And the second you sat down, a small bowl of warmed almonds and cashews was set on the table in front of you.

If that club was in any city in any country in the Western world, it'd be cool as hell and popular to boot.

Instead, it was in the middle of nowhere in Nebraska, and it was cool as hell. But clientele was thin on the ground, so even though it was popular as best it could be, the crowd was only healthy, not what that club deserved—heaving.

"Yup, it's cool," Hix agreed, not sitting, just looking into Bets's eyes.

She made a movement with her body that, if she'd allowed its fullness, would have had her drawing the toe of her boot across the floor.

Hix sighed again.

Bets spoke.

"Hear they have a new singer."

Okay, it wasn't even eight in the morning and he was having a bad day.

But even if he wasn't, this shit had to end.

That shit being Bets having a crush on him.

She'd had it before his wife divorced him. But the minute she'd heard Hope had kicked him out, it went into overdrive.

Even before, she wasn't good at hiding it. When she'd convinced herself she had a shot, she didn't bother.

She got razzed about it by his two male deputies—one in an affable way, one in an asshole way—and she was so deep in the throes of the possibility of something that was impossible, it bounced right off her.

His other female deputy, Donna, didn't think much of it.

She didn't razz. She threw glares, then took Bets aside and had chats, and when that didn't work, she took every opportunity presented her to share however she could that Bets was doing the sisterhood in law enforcement no favors.

Hix had been hoping that Donna, a veteran to Bets's mostly rookie, would get through. And in the meantime, he made things very clear in every way he could without being an asshole.

That wasn't working.

And now Bets knew he'd gotten himself some from Greta, which meant others knew as well, which didn't make him happy.

But her walking into his office first thing on a Monday morning to bring it up in her irritating way made him less so.

All of this pushed him to declare, "Right, Deputy, we need to get this straight."

He watched her body go still as her focus on him went acute.

"Been tryin' to make things clear in a way that wouldn't cause harm," he shared. "Since you're not getting that message, I'm afraid I'm gonna need to be more direct."

"Hix—" she started, beginning to look panicked.

"Right now, I'm Sheriff," he interrupted her.

Her eyes got wide and he watched her swallow.

He knew why, all of the reasons.

One of them being the fact that he was the sheriff, so he didn't feel the need to force that down his deputies' throats. They called him Hix. He called them by their first names. Unless it was an official situation where they needed to communicate they had their shit tight to the citizens they served, that was the way it was. They were a team. He was their leader. They knew that and didn't need reminders.

Until now.

He kept at her.

"Three things are happening here that make the one thing you want to happen something that is not ever gonna happen."

He lifted a hand, finger pointed up, and he flicked it out before dropping his hand and continuing.

"One, you're twenty-seven years old. You're closer to my son's age than mine. I've lived that part of my life. Had the wife. The kids. The house. Don't know where my change in circumstances is gonna take me, I just know it's not gonna take me back there. I've done that. What's next will not be that. Not settin' up house again to make another family. You got that ahead of you, and if that's what you want in life, you gotta find a man who's up to giving it to you."

"I—"

He spoke over her, lifting his hand again with his fore and middle fingers pressed together and up, and he flicked it out before dropping it.

"Two, and this is more important, Bets, so listen clear to this. I'm your boss. I'm this county's sheriff. You're my deputy. That shit is *not* gonna happen."

"If—"

He did the finger thing, indicating three, and again talked right over her.

"Three, mean no offense, none at all, but even if you weren't my deputy, I wouldn't go there. As I said, you're too young. There are men who're into swimmin' in a pool they should have vacated a decade before, but that man is not me. Regardless, again, no offense, you just aren't my type."

And she was not, even though she was a pretty woman. Dark-blonde hair. Nice brown eyes. Had a perky look that reminded him of an ex-cheerleader.

She was not a perky woman. She could be a badass when the situation warranted, which was something he liked about her. She was diligent and detailed, something else he liked. She did her job, was usually in a good mood and didn't bring shit into the department, if she ever had any in her life. But he didn't know if she did because she didn't bring it in.

She could have had the respect of her colleagues, if she wasn't panting after her boss, this being the only shit she brought into the department.

But she was never perky.

And right then, she was less so when her eyes got squinty and her face got mean.

This didn't surprise him. She could get that way and it came easy.

Jesus.

Bets.

"So your type is an old, fat, washed-up, part-time lounge singer and most-time hair dresser?" she asked snidely.

Greta, fat?

He nearly busted out laughing.

He didn't.

He thought about the fact he didn't know Greta did hair.

Not to mention the fact that Bets had been annoying him.

Now she'd pissed him off.

"What you need to get is the fact that what I'm into is not your concern," he returned curtly.

She shifted her shoulders in a defensive way, losing the hold she had on his eyes and muttering, "Not sure why you're sayin' this shit to me, Sheriff."

"Yes you are," he replied quietly.

She glanced under her lashes at him and again looked away.

Hix decided it was time to be done.

"Now we're done with this and I mean done, Bets. I know Donna has had a word with you. You ignored it. I been givin' you no signal you should keep up with this shit, you ignored that too. So right now, you walk outta my office havin' this straight, Deputy. You do that, we're good. I get *any* hint you're not movin' on, we're gonna have to have another conversation, and this one wasn't that fun for either of us. The next one will be less so."

She made no reply and didn't move.

"Are we clear, Bets?" he pushed.

"Clear, Sheriff."

He had an inkling they weren't clear.

That forced another sigh.

"Good, anything I need to know about the weekend?" he asked, moving them to where they should be.

"No clue," she bit off. "I wasn't on call this weekend."

With that, she was done and she shared that knowledge with him by walking out.

He watched her then blew out another breath as he sat in his chair.

He looked to his computer, lifted his hands to the keyboard and typed in his password.

He did this thinking, Bets knew he'd been to the Dew Drop and left with Greta.

If Hope knew that too, their conversation this morning would have gone a lot worse.

But Sunday was a day to rest, maybe including resting the gossip.

That meant he'd give it a few hours before Hope heard.

The thing that freaked him was, as her very recently ex-husband who had never wanted that title, he thought he should care.

But for some reason, he didn't.

Not at all.

Chapter 3

Acceptance

Hixon

At the end of the day, Hix drove home, for the first time in a week looking forward to what waited for him there.

Or, more accurately, he drove to the shithole apartment he'd rented that he thought would make do until he got Hope's head straight and went back to his real home, but it was now the only thing he had to give his kids.

Something he had to change and fast.

He'd made that trek every day for over a year, going the opposite direction from the house he put his family in that was in one of the few (there were only three) slightly sizeable old neighborhoods in the town of Glossop, McCook's county seat.

He'd left his ex-wife and three kids in a big, graceful old home that had been built just before the turn of the twentieth century. A house Hope had wanted before she even left to go to college. A house she kept at him to get after they'd moved there, even before they could afford it, but regardless, it wasn't for sale.

When it was, it had been a pinch, but Hix bought it for her.

It was perfect. Four bedrooms, two and a half baths with another half in the basement, a big kitchen, a big dining room. The basement done so the kids had a place to call their own. Close to work for him.

The day he'd moved them in had been the fifth best day of his life, behind the day he'd married his wife and the ones she'd given him their children.

Greta lived in a house like that, thankfully in one of the other neighborhoods.

Hers was smaller, the area she lived in not as old, not as affluent, home values not as high. But it was just as graceful, settled in among wide streets and tall trees and established houses that had been built before any post-war housing boom so they were all different, distinct and had their own style and charm.

It didn't suit her, a gorgeous woman in a sequined dress singing torch songs in a classy shack. That kind of woman lived in a bohemian loft or makeshift warehouse, though Glossop had none of those.

But it was a great house.

On that thought, as he drove, for the first time taking that trek going home or anytime, his head turned so he could look into Lou's House of Beauty.

He then looked ahead, not only because he didn't want to drive into the oncoming lane.

Because he saw her there, working on a woman in the chair closest to the window.

Lou's House of Beauty, owned by Louisa Lugar, was the only game in town.

Corinne went there. Mamie too. Also Hope's mother.

And Hope.

"Shit," he muttered under his breath. His eyes filled with the road and the businesses that lined Main Street in front of him.

But his mind was filled with seeing the back of Greta, her hands raised to work on the woman in her chair, her big mess of hair tumbling down her back.

While driving, Hix felt that hair in his hands, on his shoulders, chest, stomach.

"Shit," he repeated.

He kept driving and swung into his apartment complex that did its best not to be the shithole it was. Four buildings, two side by side and across from each other, four units in each building, two by two up and down.

It was clean. Well-kept. But not attractive.

Hix's was a top unit, two bedrooms, stairs to reach it at the side so as not to obstruct the bottom unit. His parking spots were to his side and open to the elements, which was a bitch in the winter. The parking spots to the unit under him were at the front of their house.

In the inside parking spot was Shaw's silver Toyota Camry with its Glossop Raiders sticker in the back window that Hope had graduated from two cars ago, and they'd kept for when Shaw could drive.

The kids were home.

Hix focused on that and not Greta, Greta's hair, the feel of it, her working in the salon his wife and daughters went to, or the fact that his kids were up in a shithole apartment where his son had his own room, but his girls had to share his bed and he had to sleep on the couch when they were there.

This would end soon. He had a real estate agent looking into things for him and he'd be introducing that notion to his kids that night.

He could live anywhere in the county.

He also could not.

His older kids went to school at Glossop High and Mamie to Glossop Middle School.

So it was going to have to be Glossop.

He parked the Bronco, got out making sure to lock her up and jogged up the steps.

He barely got through the door before Mamie was on him.

"Dad!" she shouted, her arms going around him in a tight hug.

He put his hand to the top of her dark hair.

His kids were all him, all of them. Dark hair. Blue eyes. Tall, lean bodies with long torsos, proportionate legs. None of Hope's strawberry blonde hair or green eyes, or shorter torso with long-ass legs for any of them, and none of her curves for the girls.

Mamie tipped her head back and demanded, "Guess what?"

He grinned at her, standing in the still-open door. "What, baby?"

"Madam DuBois says I get a solo at the next recital!"

Madam DuBois, real name Margaret Leach. She was one of the many full-blown characters in town and she ran one of only three dance schools in the county, the most popular one, likely because she was the most dramatic, and likeable, teacher.

No one called her anything but Madam DuBois, and Hix suspected no one even knew her as Margaret Leach since she'd moved there eighteen years ago after her husband died in a car accident on I-65 outside Chicago, and to put that tragedy behind her, she'd taken his life insurance money and reinvented herself.

Hix only knew because, before he put his baby in her class, he'd ran her.

"Why are you excited about that?" Hix asked.

His little girl's eyes got huge.

"Why am I excited about *a solo*?" she asked back, like he was a moron.

He shuffled her in so he could close the door, saying, "It's not surprising to me the best dancer in the troupe gets a solo."

That was when she gifted him with her smile coming at him huge.

"Yo, Dad," Shaw called from his place sitting at the dining room table that was in the miniscule space off the equally miniscule kitchen, a space that could loosely be called a dining area.

His son.

Otherwise known as Mr. Cool.

"Yo, kid," Hix replied.

"Hey, Daddy!" Corinne yelled, moving from the master at the back into the bathroom in the hall and closing the door.

Corinne had a love affair going on with the bathroom, mostly because the mirror in there had the best lighting and she was perfecting the art of painting her face and doing her hair in as many arrangements she could dream up, or watch how they were done on YouTube.

"Hey, honey," he yelled in return, seeing as she'd closed the door.

Mamie let him go and danced to her brother, asking, "What's for dinner? Chicken tenders from the Harlequin?"

Translated, Mamie wanted chicken tenders from Harlequin Diner and wouldn't be happy with anything but.

Now *that* she got from her mother.

"Thought I'd cook," he told his girl and grinned as he watched her nose scrunch.

"You're not the greatest cook, Dad," she replied.

"He is, Mame," Shaw clipped, zoning right in on ticked the second he always did, right when he thought either of his sisters were giving their dad shit.

This was new. Or new-ish.

It had been going on about eight months.

"Shaw," Hix said low, moving to the kitchen.

"Your cooking rocks," Shaw shot back.

That was a lie.

He sucked at cooking.

"All he can make is hamburgers, waffles and tuna casserole," Mamie butted in, looking at Shaw then turning her attention to Hix. "You make good hamburgers, Daddy, and waffles. But your tuna casserole is kinda *ick*."

"Mame," Shaw bit out.

"She's right, son, it *is* ick," Hix put in.

"She doesn't have to say it," Shaw returned.

"Maybe not, but she didn't say it mean. I think it best we all feel cool with sharing whatever honesty we got, just as long as we don't do it mean," Hix replied.

Shaw gave him a look that said he agreed but didn't like doing it before he turned back to his books on the table.

Hix went into the kitchen.

To say his children had run the gamut of emotions since Hope asked Hix to move out would be an understatement.

Shaw had started off this period of their lives pissed...at Hix. Surly and combative, for months, he barely spoke to Hix and never looked him in the eye.

As things wore on and Hix fought for their family, his son, not stupid but instead attentive and protective, clued in.

He'd then become Hix's champion and his relationship with his mother deteriorated.

Hix tried to step in on this and found to his surprise his efforts were rebuffed.

But Shaw was the oldest brother of two girls and he saw them both mirror the same emotions, going from shock, to fear, to desperation, to game playing and finally sadness.

Not to mention he watched his father run through all of the same.

Shaw had been so ticked about all that, and it being clear his mother was the driving force of causing it, he'd missed Corinne and Mamie hitting acceptance.

Maybe because he'd noted his father never got to that last part.

Hix needed to do that, for his son. For his son to rebuild his relationship with his mother.

He just needed to do that, for all his kids.

And for himself.

Tonight was the night to start doing that.

A new home.

Settling in to what they had now.

Acceptance.

And moving on.

He and Mamie got to work, not on tuna casserole but on Tuna Helper, with peas, which was a vegetable all his kids would tolerate, and garlic bread, because Tuna Helper was decent but garlic bread always rocked.

And he made them sit down at the dinner table because now he only had half the time he should have with them to know what was going on in their lives, so he felt the need to concentrate the time he had and make the most of it. This meant no more eating in front of the TV, like they'd done when their mother and father were together.

The only exception to that was Sunday, when they did nothing but hang in front of the TV or go out together to see a movie then come home and hang in front of the TV. It was about junk food and laziness and comfort in each other's company.

Hope hated this new tradition and had confronted Hix repeatedly since she'd learned of it in order to share she wanted it stopped. She was not a big fan of laziness. Or junk food. Not even for a day.

It could just be said, Hope didn't care if the kids tolerated whatever green she put on their plates. They ate it because she said so and that was that.

Hix had always hated watching her force their children to eat shit they didn't like. Shaw had even once sat at the dining room table until ten at night, facing a cold bowl of homemade potato soup that until he finished it, she wouldn't allow him to get up from the table.

In the end, he'd forced it down, retching after every bite.

That was when Hix had had enough.

But they'd had a deal that they didn't argue about parenting in front of the children. And regardless of the fact he'd shared not only after the potato soup incident, but often, that he was not a big fan of this tactic to encourage their children to eat healthy, she pulled it when they were in front of the children.

So since his wife wasn't big on playing fair with that, not long after Shaw and the soup, no matter it drove Hope up the wall, if one of the kids put up serious resistance, Hix would take up their plates himself, scrape whatever shit was on it that they didn't want to eat onto his plate, and then he'd eat the stuff.

At that point, Hope had shared repeatedly she wanted him to quit doing it.

When he didn't, she'd started to cook things they all tolerated.

According to Shaw, she'd slid back to her former ways after their dad left.

That was up to her.

At his place, such as it was, they had Sunday junk day.

His mind heavy with memories of how Hope could be, much of it not all that great but at the time he'd accepted it and now he was wondering why, as well as filled with a lot of other crap that had been coming at him for a little over a year, it was Shaw who broke the silence after they started eating.

"Can I go on a date on Wednesday night?"

Dating on a school night?

He looked to his son. "No."

"It's a study date," Shaw informed him quickly.

"It's a pretend-to-study-and-instead-make-out-because-Wendy's-parents-let-you-study-in-her-room date," Corinne teased.

Oh Jesus.

"Then hell no," Hix stated.

Shaw quit glaring at his sister and looked to his father. "Don't listen to her, Dad. Wendy's cool."

"I've met Wendy. I know she's cool. I've met Wendy's parents. They're cool too. Apparently *too* cool," Hix replied. "But just pointing out, you do know we're the same gender, right?"

Corinne giggled.

Mamie giggled with her and Hix hoped like hell his youngest didn't catch his drift because he was already having trouble with his older girl catching it.

Shaw, unfortunately, didn't catch it.

"Of course I know," he gritted.

"And I also figure you know I wasn't born your father."

Light dawned and Shaw looked to his Tuna Helper.

Corinne giggled again until Hix shot her a look and she swallowed it back, barely.

"You want, you can have her over here. Study at this table," Hix allowed.

"Fabulous," Shaw mumbled, but what he didn't do was decline that invitation.

This meant Hix best take another look at Wendy.

And her parents.

"I can't wait to date," Mamie declared, and Hix lost all interest in Tuna Helper.

Even though he'd wanted to make his oldest girl wait until she was sixteen, Hope didn't mind she started at fifteen, and Corinne *really* didn't want to wait.

So she'd had her first five dates over that past summer, with three different guys.

Hix was counting in a way he knew he always would.

So now that he'd passed the time where he had to endure her having her first date, as well as the ones after it, he was looking forward to the time someone he approved of slid a ring on her finger so he could stop enduring the dating portion of her life.

"It isn't all it's cracked up to be," Corinne informed her little sister authoritatively.

At that, Hix's stomach almost lost the little Tuna Helper he'd fed it.

"Why would you say that?" he asked.

"Because boys are stupid, Dad," she answered casually.

"How are they stupid?" Hix pressed.

"Because they talk about themselves all the time," she replied. "What movies they like. What music they like. How *sick* some skateboard is. Blah, blah, blah." She scooped up Tuna Helper, muttering, "Ask a girl a question about herself once in a while, why don't you?"

That made Hix grin.

But he saw now that Shaw was looking sick.

"You could just talk yourself without him asking you questions, you know," his son began to defend his half of the juvenile gender, or more likely, the fact he hadn't asked a girl a question about herself.

"And sound like an up-myself douchebag?" Corinne asked.

"Not a big fan of that word, honey," Hix noted quietly.

Without skipping a beat, Corinne altered her statement. "And sound like an up-myself idiot?"

"It's called conversation, Cor," Shaw educated her.

"No, Shaw, conversation is, 'I really liked that *Avengers* movie. I thought it was rad. I seriously liked the fight scene in the city. The Hulk is *da bomb*. Hey, Cor, how did *you* feel about that *Avengers* movie?'" Corinne returned. "Instead of forgetting the last part and going on to say, 'But whatever, I think Mr. Galveston is a jerk. That pop quiz was uncool. I totally tanked it. My dad's gonna be so pissed.'"

"Mr. Galveston *is* a jerk and that pop quiz sucked," Shaw retorted.

"Is your dad gonna be pissed?" Hix put in, aiming this toward his son.

Shaw looked to him and gave a cool-guy shrug. "Maybe."

"Son—"

"Pop quizzes are for teachers who are sneaks," Shaw declared. "And anyway, we've been in school for two weeks. He didn't even wait two weeks. He gave it in the *first* week. What teacher gives a pop quiz the first week?"

Hix had to admit, he agreed.

Just not out loud.

"Best the sneak next time and be prepared," Hix advised.

"What do I care where Uzbekistan is?" Shaw asked, sounding like he genuinely wanted to know.

"You wanna become a marine, you better care about a lot of things," Hix told him. "World opens way up, you earn a uniform."

Shaw saw his point and shared that by jerking up his chin.

His son had wanted to be a marine now for three years. He wasn't giving up on that, talked about it all the time.

This made Hix proud.

And it scared the fucking shit out of him.

"May be good too," Hix went on, "you ask Wendy if she liked that *Avengers* movie."

Corinne busted out laughing.

Mamie joined her.

Shaw studied his dad's expression until he saw Hix was funning with him and only then did his face crack in a smile.

Hix let them put down more food, and did it himself, before he launched into it.

"Right, kids, want you to know, I called a real estate agent."

All eyes came to him.

He kept giving it to them.

"She's gonna be finding us places to live and I'll arrange it so, when we go see them, we all go together so we can all decide together where we're gonna move."

"What's wrong with this place?" Mamie asked.

Hix took his baby in, wondering where that came from.

She was still a little kid.

But day by day, she was growing out of that.

She didn't have her own space in his old house because Hix wanted his girls to share a room, and share the closeness that would bring. Hope agreed because she'd wanted a guest room.

But his baby had to know that sleeping in her father's bed with her sister and cramming her stuff into one drawer and a third of a closet wasn't optimal when her dad was sleeping on the couch, and they all shared a bathroom.

"This is close quarters," he said carefully, wondering if her question stemmed from the fact she thought, when he finally moved, he'd be moving back in with their mother.

"I like close quarters," she replied, took a bite of garlic bread and kept talking while chewing it. "We all gotta be together and Cor can't hog the bathroom all the time because we don't have another one to go to."

"You think Dad might not wanna sleep on the couch, Mame?" Shaw asked, not ugly, just pointing things out.

"Oh yeah," Mamie murmured.

"Can I have my own room in our new pad, Daddy?" Corinne asked.

He shook his head. "I'm thinkin', no. Sorry, honey."

"You're gonna be in it for, like, two years, Cor," Shaw pointed out and looked at Hix. "You should get one of those townhomes they built when I was in junior high, out on County Road 12. Lev's dad lives there and it's way cool."

Moving from a graceful, old, three-thousand-square-foot home to a shithole apartment to a three-bedroom townhome a twenty-minute drive from town.

It was still in the school's district.

It was also still a step down.

"Someone's selling, we'll look, Shaw," Hix allowed. "But just sayin', they aren't very big and they're not close to town."

"I'll be gone next year. Corinne two years after that. Mamie not long after that," Shaw stated.

"Don't remind me," Hix muttered.

"What I'm sayin' is, Dad, you don't need a huge pad," Shaw replied. "We'll be cool with whatever you get and not just because we're all almost grown."

"I'm gonna live with Daddy forever," Mamie declared and looked at him with a big smile. "I'll make my husband move in with us. That way you can have tickle wars with our kids and we can still have Junk Sundays."

At the thought of his baby having babies, Hix was in danger of losing his dinner again.

"Your future husband would *so* not be down with that, Mame," Shaw murmured.

"Like, *so not*," Corinne agreed.

"Yes he will," Mamie shot back. "Everybody likes Dad. I even heard Mrs. Turnbaum say he's the most likeable guy in the county, *way* cooler than the old sheriff, who she said was a big blowhard." She looked from her siblings to Hix. "What's a blowhard anyway?"

"It's not a nice word, baby," Hix told her.

"Well, I like Sheriff Blatt," Mamie announced. "Though, I'm glad he's not sheriff anymore because he's got a really big belly and it looked funny in his uniform."

"I like that you got rid of the uniforms, Dad," Corinne put in. "Everyone thinks it's cool you only make our deputies wear the sheriff shirt and then they can wear jeans and boots. That whole sheriff gear thing is stupid and *so* yesterday. I mean, *hello. Smokey and the Bandit* came out in the last *millennium*."

It far from sucked his kids were hilarious.

"I'm thrilled you approve of my wardrobe choice for the department, honey," Hix said on a grin.

He was grinning because he was teasing his girl.

He was also grinning because he'd talked about getting them a new place, a place where they'd settle, leaving the in-between place, this stating plainly that life had changed in a permanent way none of them could do anything about.

He had no idea how Hope was with them. Outside of sharing such things as their mother made them eat stuff they didn't like, the kids didn't give him much and he didn't pry. They came to him good, not moody, broody, acting out or out of their normal self in any way that was alarming, so he figured she was holding up her part of the job.

Which meant they were all moving on, not as he'd want—together—but they were moving on.

And Shaw's point was valid, as much as Hix hated hearing it.

If his son stayed on his current course, he was going to enlist right after high school, which was around nine months away.

If Corinne stayed on hers, she was going to go pre-Law at the University of Nebraska in about two years.

And Mamie wouldn't be far behind.

This meant Hix had to prepare to really move on.

In a variety of ways.

Greta

"Jesus, it's two hundred dollars," my mom groused. "Bitches up in this burg act like keeping up with the Kardashians is their only goal in life, even though there's fuck-all to impress. You're booked solid every day and you got your weekend gig. You can give your old lady two hundred dollars so she can pay her fuckin' cable bill."

"Yeah, Mom, I could if I didn't give you fifty dollars to cover your water bill last week. And a hundred last month to cover your cell phone bill, that along with buying you a new oven because yours somehow got busted in a way your landlord refused to pay for its repair. And remind me, how much did it cost to pump your septic tank in July? Something, I'll add, your landlord should be seeing to too."

"I kept you fed and clothed and a roof over your head for eighteen years. Figure I got at least that for you to help your momma take care of shit."

"Mom, I'm thirty-eight. If that washed, which it doesn't, your time was up two years ago," I retorted.

"You keep me fed and clothed and a roof over my head and all that, you'd be right. Since I only need a little extra here and there, you ain't."

I drew in breath and stared from my spot in my pretty wicker chair on my cute front porch at my sleepy street, sleepy even though it was only nine o'clock.

Not a car. Not a noise. Not a blaring radio.

Quiet.

Peace.

Except in my ear.

I changed the subject, asking, "You seen Andy recently?"

My mother went silent.

I was a fan of her silence, but right then, not the reason for it.

"You told me you moved here after I moved here because I moved Andy here," I reminded her. "And as far as I know, the five months you've been here, you've seen Andy once."

"I got shit going on," she retorted.

"Like what?" I asked.

"Like shit that's *my* shit and none of your business. But I'll be up in *your* shit, my cable gets turned off."

Okay, after all the times I'd put up with it, this time, me in my pretty chair on my porch by my sleepy street where Mom was not supposed to be, but she was because she'd followed me after I'd finally tried to make a break from her, it was safe to say I was really, *really* done with this crap.

"Do it," I taunted.

"Say what?"

"Do it. Get up in my shit."

Mom was silent again.

I couldn't rejoice in it because of what she said after she broke her silence.

"So rumor's true. You fucked the sheriff."

I straightened in the chair and felt the unpleasant sensation of my throat closing.

All day at the salon I'd worried.

No one had said a word.

Now it was coming at me from *my mother*.

"Sorry?" I pushed out.

"Girl, you ain't in Denver anymore," she informed me. "You fuck the county sheriff, get right in his I-don't-have-to-try-to-make-you-believe-I-got-big-balls-through-my-fancy-ass-ride Real Man with *Real* Big Balls Bronco outside a fucking nightclub at two in the morning, this little burg, people are gonna talk. 'Specially since Soccer Mom Barbie kicked out her GI Sheriff Joe. Soccer Mom Barbie's gonna reel that boy back in, mark my words, girl, soon's he comes to heel. Ain't no way GI Sheriff Joe's gonna go all in with Trailer Trash Barbie when he's got sweet, strawberry pussy waitin' for him."

I looked to my lap where I was sitting cross-legged and where I'd rested my cup of tea against my angled thigh.

God, people were talking.

Even Mom had heard!

"I'm not trailer trash," I said softly.

"Greta, told you all your life, guess I gotta tell you again. Don't be stupid. You can take the girl outta the trailer but you can't take the trash outta the girl. You are what you are. You got fancy ideas with that asshole husband of yours and what'd he do when your Farrah Fawcett to his Lee Majors turned in his mind?"

She didn't wait for my response.

Then again, Mom never did.

"He dumped your ass and went out and got himself the real thing."

"Why are we talking about this?" I asked.

"'Cause you think, you give our handsome sheriff a little somethin'-somethin', you got game. You don't got game, girl. You got shit. You don't want me to get up in your face. And just sayin', you don't want that sheriff to get himself in the middle when I do. Won't get you a second trip home from that shack in his Bronco. That I know for certain."

Oh, I'd learned how Mom could make the men in my life feel.

I'd learned that lesson very well.

"I wasn't threatening you with Hixon."

"Hixon?"

"That's his name."

"His name is *Sheriff Drake*, and don't you forget that, Greta," she suddenly snapped. "You wanna moan that out when he's givin' it to you, you do that. I bet he'd get off on that. But he ain't no *Hixon* to you, girl. Don't think, no matter your *Playboy* bunny with a few extra years look, he's gonna stick around and fight your battles for you. What he's gonna do is take, and take more until he's got his fill and then he's gonna *go*. Men don't stick around and they don't do jack when they *are* around. The more you expect from them, the more reasons they got to get up and go. He's no different, I don't care he has a badge. He just ain't. They never are. And you can't be stupid about that because you saw all the jackasses that left your momma swinging. And girl, you're all that because I *gave you all a' that*. Was even more of a looker than you in my day. And just sayin', I can pull me in some dick even now, whenever I get lonely."

Oh yeah.

I'd seen that.

All of it.

I felt my lip start to curl but stopped it in order to demand, "Can we talk for a second about why there always has to be battles between me and my own mother?"

"Because you won't give me two hundred dollars. Yeesh. That bleach you use soak into your brain or what?"

"You visit Andy, I'll give you the money," I haggled.

"I'll see my boy when I see my boy, not when you tell me to."

"Then you don't get the money."

"So you *want* me to cause a scene at that House o' Beauty place you work? All those uptight bitches who never miss church on Sunday but probably moan real pretty when their hubbies take 'em up the ass Sunday night after their kids are asleep seein' your momma in all her glory?"

"God, do you always have to talk like that?"

"I am who I am. Ain't changin' for nobody."

I looked again to the street, feeling tight around my mouth.

Hell, in my whole face.

In fact, it was a wonder I didn't look Botoxed to within an inch of my life with all my mother shoveled my way.

I reminded myself I was done with this crap.

"No, you're right. You are who you are and there it is. There's where it's always been. But here we go, Mom, big news item. Perk up and listen. I didn't move Andy out here just because the home is better, it's quiet, they're great with him, it doesn't cost as much, and I needed to get away from things that reminded me of Keith. I moved us both out here to get away from *you*. And I wasn't real thrilled when you followed. What I am is finally, after way too long of not getting it, realizing that if you cause a scene, that's about you. People know me here. They like me. It's a good place. I've been around longer than you. So if you come to the shop in all your glory, they'll think you're trash and they'll feel bad for me because I've got a momma who's got no problem throwing her trash around."

"See I haven't made a scene in a while, you forgot how good I can do it."

"See you don't get that I can warn Lou about your upcoming antics, and share with the clients too, so if you feel like getting up to something, they'll be prepared and can just sit back and enjoy the show."

"Fuck, sheriff shot his wad in you, he shot in too much badass so now you think you got balls."

I totally *hated* when she talked like that.

Which was pretty much all the time.

I was *her daughter* for God's sake.

"No, wait," she went on. "My prissy, fancy-pants daughter probably made him go in gloved."

I did.

And when he beat his retreat, he hadn't even taken the time to see to that particular business.

He hadn't even offered five minutes of cuddling.

He'd given me mine, got his, I heard his breath even on my neck, he'd pulled out, rolled to his ass on the side of the bed...

And then he'd rolled right out.

"Again, I'm thirty-eight, not eighteen. You'd never acknowledge it, but I have a brain in my head, so yeah. Of course he used a condom."

"*Used a condom*," she mimicked. "Like she's a nurse or somethin'. Girl, real people call 'em rubbers."

I'd had enough.

Actually, I'd had enough when I was thirteen. And sixteen. And eighteen, nineteen, twenty.

And when her crap made me lose Keith.

I could go on.

But really, in Pleasantville where it was actually *pleasant*, I'd definitely *had enough.*

Mom wanted to play her games?

I hadn't been able to stop her in thirty-eight years.

I wouldn't be able to now.

The only thing I could do was change how I reacted.

Keith had told me, but did I listen?

Nope.

Now he was with Briefcase-Toting Lawyer Barbie and I was here.

Alone.

Talking on the phone with my trash-mouth mother.

And by God, I could change that too.

"We're done talking."

"We ain't done until I know I haul my ass out there, you got a check waiting for me."

"Don't waste the gas, Mom."

"God, you're a pain in my ass and have been since I pushed you out."

"Love you too."

On that, I hung up.

That felt good.

For a whole second.

Shit.

She was going to do it.

Shit!

She was totally going to show at Lou's and cause a scene.

I pulled in a deep breath and tried to let the calm of the quiet, dark street soothe me.

I couldn't.

Because my mom was going to cause a scene at my place of business whenever she worked up the energy to do it. Which, if her cable was imminently going to be turned off—and it was, seeing as she never made the call for a handout until that threat was real—would be soon.

I'd lost jobs because of her in the past.

Lou wouldn't ask me to leave. She knew all about Mom. She actually couldn't wait to meet her. Not to make friends, to see what she'd get up to.

Lou was like that.

She probably wouldn't be so excited for the possibility after she experienced the real thing, though.

However, I couldn't muster up all my usual horror and despair after my mother's version of a loving phone conversation.

Nope.

Since he left, and I didn't sleep a wink then I dragged around all day Sunday licking my wounds, even during my visit with Andy, and *then* I'd tried to keep myself together, worried it would come out in the salon all that day, my mind was filled with Hixon Drake.

I wished it could be filled with all he'd done to me, all he'd made me feel, how damned good it was.

Respect.

Care.

Time.

Attention.

Not to mention talent.

God.

It had been amazing.

Better than Keith by about ten thousand miles, and Keith was excellent in bed.

Better than *anybody*.

Yeah, I wished I could think about that, even if it had ended with him sharing with me indisputably I was only what I was. Something that had been shared with me way too many times before.

This being a piece of ass not worth any more of his time than it took to get what he wanted out of me.

And I wished I could think about what an asshole he was for sharing just that with me.

Especially after I felt...

After I'd thought we'd had...

Whatever.

I didn't feel it and we didn't have anything but near-simultaneous orgasms.

But no.

I couldn't think of that either.

All I could think was what a complete and utter fool I'd been.

He'd bought me a drink, stared in my eyes (not at my breasts, a nice switch) while he chatted with me between sets like he gave a shit about what I said, and *BAM!*

I forgot all I'd learned.

All my momma taught me.

All the things all the guys in my life had taught me.

All Keith had taught me.

That being the only good man in the world was my little brother Andy.

And as ugly as it was to think, that was probably only because he'd had a traumatic brain injury that had essentially arrested him at the age he'd sustained it.

Fifteen.

Forever.

And ever.

No therapy.

No relearning of skills.

No readjusting life expectations, so instead of Andy going for being an architect, he worked as a janitor.

No nothing.

Except keeping him safe, and those around him the same, while he lived his life reading comic books, watching movies, experiencing terrifying seizures, occasionally having episodes that were totally forgivable because big chunks of his brain had been damaged beyond repair, but the rest of the time he was so damned sweet, he was a constant toothache.

And him being the only real, sustained light in my entire life.

Yeah.

The only good guy in the world, or at least in my life, was my Andy.

But I'd forgotten that.

However, that wasn't what filled my head after Hixon left.

Nope.

It was the fact that he may never have seen me, not in the eighteen months I'd been living in Glossop. Then again, in the beginning, he'd had no real reason to look. And after things went down, he'd had other stuff on his mind.

But I knew Hope and the girls from the salon.

And I'd seen him.

Him and Hope.

Unreasonably handsome Hixon Drake with his cool, pool-blue eyes, powerfully-built body and natural swagger that wasn't eye-roll-worthy, but drool-worthy. The tall, beautiful Princess of Glossop Hope. And their three equally beautiful children.

Lou had a girl on the same soccer team as Sheriff Drake's girl, and I was close with all of Lou's family (except her husband Bill, who was likeable, but did things that were really not-so-likeable), so it wasn't rare I took in a home game.

And I had a client who had a daughter who thought I walked on water so she asked me to her dance recitals, and I went.

Sheriff Drake had a daughter who danced.

So I'd seen them. All five of them, together, in various groups, separately.

The perfect family.

Tall. Strong. Proud. Gorgeous. Happy.

Glossop's royal couple, hell, royal family—the sheriff and his brood.

When they fell apart, the town was agog. They couldn't credit it. They couldn't *believe* it.

It was unbelievable.

No.

Unthinkable.

Everyone thought it'd last a few days. Then they decided it might take a few weeks. After that, a few months.

When the divorce went through—and I knew exactly when it went through, it was the talk of the salon all day (this making me an even bigger idiot, can anyone say rebound?)—everyone was freaked.

If it could happen to the perfect family, it could happen to anybody.

The townsfolk had been split down the middle.

At first.

Men and catty women said it was all about Hope being Hope, thinking her shit didn't stink and her female parts were coated in gold, wanting to bust the balls of a man who would allow that to keep peace in his family.

Until the time came when he was done allowing that.

Women and men who wanted to get into Hope Drake's pants said it was Hixon who was an asshole, probably had someone on the side, or several someones, and she was best shot of him. Because look at her, she's Hope Drake. She could get anyone.

Time wore on and Hope sat in Lou's chair and let her mouth run, and probably did it other places besides, thinking women would feel her pain (when, with what she had and the games she was playing endangering that, we did *not*) and the mixed looks Hixon Drake was getting started to be not so mixed anymore.

The tall, beautiful Princess of Glossop thought she was just that.

So when my mom said Soccer Mom Barbie would get her GI Sheriff Joe back when he came to heel, she wasn't talking out her ass.

Everyone knew Hope was pitching one helluva fit to get her man to do what she wanted.

The thing was, it wasn't only his Bronco that declared the kind of man he was.

How the woman who'd shared nearly twenty years with him didn't clue in made everyone think even less of her (and her waning popularity, especially in the last three weeks, was running out, so not many thought much of her already—not anymore).

Someone's tiara was tarnished, and unless *she* got *her* head out of *her* ass and came to heel, broken perfection would not get fixed.

And it was my experience that a good way to make a woman come to heel was show her she could be replaced.

Even with a Trailer Trash Farrah Fawcett who had a few too many years on her, it would work.

Don't get me wrong. I didn't think Hixon took me to bed to get his wife back.

At least not consciously.

I just knew if nothing else would wake her shit up, that would.

So if my mother had heard, Hope Drake definitely had.

And the thing of it was, even though I wasn't Hope Drake's biggest fan even before it became clear what kind of woman she was and how that had affected her family (and it went without saying also before I slept with her ex-husband), there was a part of me that thought it best that happened.

They fixed what was broken.

Maybe not for him.

Definitely not for her.

But absolutely for those three kids.

I knew better than most that the perfect family never existed, but the slightly-imperfect perfect family that still worked was on the endangered species list.

So if there was a shot, everyone should do what they could to protect it.

That was what I'd been thinking the past two days.

That I hadn't done that.

I'd been charmed by a handsome man who made me forget I was supposed to have hardened my heart against men who might look at their wives like she was the first female created and God had outdone himself (and that was how Hixon had looked at Hope), but me, he'd treat like dirt.

And then he made me remember.

Now...

Well, now, if my mom had heard about what had happened, I was likely going to be thrown right in the thick of it.

And I had a feeling that wasn't going to go well for me.

I had that feeling because nothing ever did.

And dammit, I'd taken more than my fair share of lickings.

I'd had enough.

But it was more.

After the one Keith had delivered, then me finding the first moments of respite in my life and thinking it might finally go okay, that being before Mom followed Andy and me out here and blew that all to smithereens, I didn't know for sure, if I got another one, that I'd be able to keep on ticking.

Chapter 4

The In-Between

Hixon

Hix felt it the minute he walked into the department the next morning.

He saw the cause when he looked beyond Donna, Bets and one of his other deputies, Larry, all of them at their desks in the bullpen, and he aimed his attention to his office where Hope was pacing.

Goddammit.

He swung through the swinging half door, and it was Larry who moved from his desk, close to the aisle to say, "Mornin', Hix. And sorry, man. We asked her to wait out here. She refused. And she pitched a fit when Donna said she was gonna give you a call, so Donna thought it best to put her back there and maybe she'd cool off before you got here."

He knew from having seen that pacing before, that hadn't happened.

"Not your problem," he growled, tipping his chin down to Larry, lifting it to Donna and noting that Bets was avoiding him but doing it looking under her lashes toward his office.

Once he'd greeted his deputies, Hix just kept staring into his office as he prowled there, seeing Hope had noticed he'd arrived and was standing smack in the window with her hands on her hips like it was *her* damned office and she was waiting for a naughty boy to show up and receive his chastisement.

He didn't need three guesses to know that word had reached her about Greta.

What he didn't quite get was why that drove her here.

Surely the woman could share what was on her mind on a freaking phone, not dragging his staff in as witnesses to whatever she'd worked herself up to dole out.

He moved down the side hall that led to the door to his office as well as the one at the back that led to the alley.

He turned right through the one to his office.

He hadn't even closed the door when she launched in.

"You're fucking *unbelievable*! How could you *humiliate me this way*!" she shouted.

He closed the door and ground out, "Calm down."

"*Calm down?*" she screamed, advanced quickly and lifted a hand to shove his shoulder.

It rocked back and he felt his face turn to stone.

And he was way too pissed to fully experience it, but still, he distractedly felt something else turning to stone, and where that was happening was in his chest.

"You do not put your hands on me," he warned low. "With what we are now, not ever. But not in anger. Never in anger, Hope."

She rolled up on her toes and spat, "Fuck you. You fucked a fucking *hairdresser*."

"I can see you're pissed, I don't get it, but I can see it. So can three of my deputies and Reva. I get you don't care what that means to me as their sheriff. But they can also see *you* acting like a crazy woman."

After a quick eye flare, Hix was not surprised Hope, who cared what people thought of her and went to pains to keep up a variety of appearances, backed off two steps.

Hix moved into his office, and after the shove, he felt it prudent not to go to the blinds at the window and lower them.

Instead, he walked behind his desk, putting distance and furniture between them.

"You don't get why I'm pissed?" Hope asked when he'd stopped.

He lifted his eyes to her to see she'd also moved to stand four feet in front of his desk between the two chairs there.

"No. I don't."

"Are fucking *insane*?" she demanded to know.

It sucked but she was even beautiful like this.

Angry as hell.

It flushed her cheeks. Made her green eyes bright. Made her chest heave, bringing attention to her full tits.

She'd also often plant her hands on her hips or hitch out a foot, taking your attention to those areas, reminding you she had a great ass, fantastic, long legs, just how perfectly your hips fit into hers and just how good it felt to have those legs wrapped tight around your ass.

And she would sometimes toss her long, wavy hair that, at forty-one, she now had to dye back to its natural flawless pink champagne (her words for the hue), but even aided to that color, it was no less magnificent.

These were several of the reasons why Hix had always found it difficult to argue with her. Seeing her that way, it would make him impatient to get to the part of the fight that would end it.

That being having angry sex, something at which they both excelled.

Then again, normal sex with his ex-wife hadn't sucked either.

"Nope. Not insane," he answered her question.

"You fucked a hairdresser *at my salon*," she informed him.

"Hope, I can't imagine you didn't know it would happen eventually. And in a town like this, it could be your salon, the grocery store, a teacher at one of the schools, whoever, you'd hear about it and likely know the woman. You know everybody. Everybody knows you. It's unfortunate but it was going to happen."

"It was going to happen?" she snapped. "I cannot believe you fucked a stylist at my salon, but what I really can't believe is that you fucked *anybody*!"

Since she unfathomably wasn't noting the obvious, he pointed it out.

"Me doing anything is not your concern."

"It's not...it's not...it isn't..." she stammered irately and finished on a high pitched, "It isn't my concern?"

"It's not your concern," he affirmed.

She shook her head in brief, concise shakes. "I can't...I cannot believe you'd say that or even *think* it. Especially about something like *this*."

Right.

Hix had to admit, he was confused.

How could she not?

"We're divorced," he pointed out.

She leaned forward and on a near shout declared, "For three *weeks*!"

"That doesn't negate the fact we're divorced. But seeing as I'm reminding you of things, I'll also remind you that we may have been divorced for three weeks, but you kicked me out a year ago."

"And so this is my punishment?"

He felt his brows draw together. "Your punishment?"

"My punishment. You making a point."

Hix stared at her.

Then he gave her the honest truth.

"Not one thing that happened between me and Greta had shit to do with you."

Again she leaned forward and this time hissed, "Do not say her name in my presence."

Okay.

Right.

What the hell was going on here?

"You do get the concept of divorce," he noted curiously.

"Don't be an asshole,' she shot back.

"I'm not. I'm genuinely wondering at this point if you do."

"What I get is the fact that I've been asking you to have a *conversation* for the last now *more than three weeks* and you refuse *to speak to me*," she returned, leaning forward each time she put emphasis on her words.

It had not been the prevailing reason why Hix was overwhelmed with happiness when he'd married Hope nineteen years ago. That reason being from that point forward he'd only ever have one woman in his life he'd have to try to figure out.

But he couldn't deny it had been a relief.

The prevailing reasons were that she had a great sense of humor. She was more into watching sports than even he was, the same with action movies. They'd both wanted the same things out of life, including the number of children they'd had in the exact order and gender they'd miraculously been given them. She could often be generous with her love, affection and time. She was spectacular in bed. And she was gorgeous.

Now, he realized, after all their years together, he didn't get her.

He didn't get Bets.

What he did get was that their bullshit pissed him off.

"Okay, seems I gotta expend the effort to make something else straight this week," he began.

"Oh, so sorry, Hix. Is your wife and the mother of your three children taxing you with her demands?" she cut in sarcastically.

His voice dropped to a whisper. "That's not right. You got it in you to get that or not, the simple matter of fact is that that is *not* right."

His tone went normal, but steely, when he kept on.

"You're not my wife anymore, Hope. That's something *you* wanted, not me. Like you have a way of doing, you got what you wanted. And getting that, you don't get to call me over and over again to demand my time. You don't get to storm into my place of business and pitch a fit. And you do *not* get to act like I wounded you when

I'm living my life, a life *you* disconnected, legally and emotionally, from yours."

"Hix—"

Like Bets, even though his mother had taught him differently, especially when speaking with a woman, he talked over her.

"Now I see when we made arrangements for custody and decisions on who was going to get the house and all that other shit, we should have made it clear how this was going to go from now on. Since you're here, we'll take that opportunity."

She stepped forward, her expression beginning to soften as she noted his mood and the fact it wasn't shifting, so her game began to change. "Honey—"

He leaned into his fist in his desk and growled, "Do not ever fucking call me that again, Hope."

He watched the color drain out of her face as her eyes widened.

He ignored that and declared, "Now this is the way it's gonna be. You got a father and two brothers who live in this county who can help you out if you got a problem with your car, the house. Unless it affects my children, I don't want to hear from you. You find someone you wanna date, I don't care. Date him. I don't wanna hear from you. I find someone I wanna see, that's my business. I'll do it. And I won't be giving you a courtesy call to share that intel."

He drew in a breath but continued speaking before she could get a word in.

"But if you need to change arrangements with the kids for any reason, you text me. It'll be rare I won't be able to take my kids so that won't be a problem and we won't need discussion. We have an issue to discuss about the children, we talk on the phone unless it's serious. Other than that, Hope, you didn't want to be in my life, you are no longer in my life. You wanted us done, we're done. And listen to that, Hope, because I'm not gonna repeat myself, and having a lot of time to think on it, doing that like I've been doing now for years. When I say we're done, we. Are. *Done*."

Her eyebrows were up, her eyes blinking rapidly, before she whispered, "You can't...you can't mean that."

He felt his head dipping to the side in mystification.

"I loved you," he told her.

She moved another step forward, lifting her hand, her face again warming. "Hix."

"I loved the family we made. I loved the life we created."

She stopped in front of his desk and put her hand on it, her mouth beginning to curve up.

"And you tore that apart," he went on.

Her lips parted as her face went slack in shock.

"You broke us," he reminded her. "You broke *me*. Then you ended us. You wanna be friends now, that's not gonna happen. You think you can do that and still depend on me to be there whenever you need me, that's not gonna happen either."

"I—" she whispered but he didn't stop speaking.

"I wanted to grow old with you, Hope. I wanted to drive around the country in an RV or buy some bungalow in Arizona to spend the winter months, or whatever we decided we were going to do. But I wanted to do it with you. Hold your hand when our son stood at the front of a church waiting for his bride. Turn right into your arms when our daughters safely brought grandchildren into the world. Sign the cards you gave me for our grandkids' birthdays, graduations, whatever we could celebrate, until the day I died. I told you all this before when I tried to find a way to fix whatever you thought was broke. But you didn't listen. You didn't even share with me what you thought was broke so I could try to fix it. You just took all that from me. And it hurt like fuck. So I am not gonna be your friend or the man you call when the toilet gets backed up. This time, you pushed for what you wanted, it's you that lives with the consequences. You don't push even more to make it the way you now want it to be."

"We really need to talk, Hix," she whispered urgently, almost pleading.

His voice shared exactly how much he meant it when he stated,

"You know my answer to that, and I will not answer that request again."

They stood staring into each other's eyes until he watched it happen.

Bets could get mean.

Hope could get ugly.

And right then, she got *ugly*.

"You want it that way, Hix, you got it," she bit out.

He pushed off his fist in the desk and crossed his arms on his chest, deciding not to remind her, *again*, that *wasn't* the way he wanted it and point out that was the way she'd made it.

He'd said his piece.

They were done.

And *he* was done.

"Now I know another election won't be coming around for a few more years, but don't think, you treat me like shit this way, it'll be that easy to win when the other two times you won was because of my dad, my mom, my brothers and *me*." She jerked a thumb at herself. "*We're* McCook and I'm not thinking it'd be hard to remind folks you're *not*."

Was she serious about that bullshit?

For Christ's sake, the first time he ran unopposed.

He opened his mouth to speak but she wasn't done.

"And I hear your slut does good hair, though thank God her hands have never been in mine. But thinkin', her movin' in on you the way she did, she might find herself losin' clients. And fast."

He felt all the muscles in his body get tight and started, "Hope, don't you—"

"Nope," she shook her head, moving away but not losing eye contact with him. "You stood there telling me the way it was, Hix, now you get to know the way it is. And part of that way is that you don't get to tell me what to do anymore."

Like he'd ever told the woman what to do.

He rounded the desk and followed her, warning, "You don't wanna play it this way."

She put her hand on the door handle, turned to him and spat, "Wanna bet?"

He made it to her just as she'd half-pulled open the door.

He slapped a hand on it above her head and shoved it closed.

She jerked her head back to look up at him with narrowed eyes.

He tipped his chin down to look at her, right up in her space and not moving.

"Shaw is going into the military, but we got soccer camps, dance classes, college tuitions, then weddings to pay for, Hope," he informed her. "Not certain the Schroeder name holds the sway you think it does, but regardless, I just wanna see if I have this clear. Your play to hurt me because you're not getting your way is to threaten my livelihood and take away my ability to see to my children?"

"You're a good cop, Hix. You'll find another job in another county or some city, where you always really wanted to be anyway."

He could not believe he was hearing this.

"So your play is to try to take *me* away from my kids?"

She gave a casual shrug but her eyes were flashing with fury.

He was hearing this.

He just couldn't believe it.

"And you don't even know Greta, but you know Lou, and you're gonna try to throw them under the bus to have your tantrum?"

"*Greta* should know better than to jump on a man before the ink is dry on his divorce papers."

"Greta didn't pick me up, Hope. That was me."

"I don't need the details," she hissed, coming up on her toes to do it. She rolled back and continued, "But like you said, she got what she wanted, she lives with the consequences. She's probably been panting after you since she got into town, lying in wait."

"I've never seen the woman before Saturday."

"Maybe not, Hix, but for sure she's seen you. *All* the women have seen you. And she's a woman, she saw her shot, so don't be stupid.

You didn't pick her up. You didn't do anything but be Hixon Drake, which is all you ever needed to be."

He had no idea what that remark meant.

And he didn't give a crap.

"Leave Greta alone," he warned.

Her face twisted, and suddenly, she wasn't beautiful at all.

"Kiss my ass."

She turned to the door and yanked on it so Hix removed his hand and stepped away.

He turned and watched through the window as she stormed out of his department.

"Goddamn shit," he muttered when she slammed through the front door.

He took his gaze from the window not meeting any of his deputies' eyes and stalked to his desk. He turned on his computer but didn't enter the password.

He didn't even sit down.

He stalked back around the desk and only stopped when he saw Donna in the door.

"Got somewhere I gotta go, Donna," he told her.

Instead of nodding and getting out of the way, she walked in and closed the door quietly behind her.

Christ.

Was he having to repeat himself with a woman *again*?

"Donna," he clipped.

"Think you should let Hope have some time to get her head together."

"I'm not worried about Hope."

Without hesitation, she continued, "Then I think you should know Lou opens at eight, but on Tuesdays Greta doesn't start seeing clients until ten. She does late hours so ladies who work can get to see her. Being a lady who works, and seeing as she's my stylist, I know her schedule."

Hix ground his teeth.

"I see you're not in a good mood," she said carefully. "But I know you're a man who doesn't like to be blindsided, so I'm gonna say it even though I think you probably already know. Everyone in town is talking about it."

"*Shit*," he hissed between his teeth.

She took a hesitant step forward, her eyes sliding to the window before they came back to him.

"And, uh, we didn't say anything about it because we were all pulling for you. We thought, up until, well...you know, um..." She didn't finish that but she did go on, "It's just that, we had hope. We didn't say anything because we thought it would all work out. But now, well, I think you should know that the town's been talking about it since 'round about the time you stood in your own driveway and threw your suitcases in the back of the Bronc."

Hix drew breath into his nose, tipping his head back to look at the ceiling and lifting his hands to rest them on his hips.

"But I figure you probably knew that too," she said quietly.

He again looked at her.

"For what it's worth," she went on, "I'll say, at the beginning this time, Greta's really great."

"Nothing is happening with me and Greta," he ground out.

She looked him right in the eye, hesitated a beat, then whispered, "That's a shame."

"My divorce was final three weeks ago," he pointed out.

She nodded. "Unh-hunh."

"She doesn't need the shit I got in my head right now," he shared. "But it's way too soon for me, my kids, and because of that, it wouldn't be fair on any woman."

"Right," she said softly.

"We just had a thing."

She again nodded. "It happens."

Hix dropped his head and looked at his boots, muttering, "Hope is gonna grind her to ash."

"Jep and Marie Schroeder are salt of the earth," Donna declared, and Hix lifted his head to look at her again. "Cook and Reed too. Everyone likes 'em. Hope's family has that from the town and they also got a lot of respect."

Her gaze leveled on his in that way of hers that got attention even from the drunkest drunk or the most punkish kid.

And she kept talking.

"But none of them held Krissy Schultz's hand until the fire department got there with the Jaws of Life to get her out of that car, Hix. And none of them was seen having a word with Lyle Koch at the side of the church when his wife turned up at work with a black eye for about the fifteenth time. And none of them treated old Mrs. Olson like she was perfectly sane to think her house was haunted and went to it every night. Driving all the way out to that old farm, thirty miles, before he went home to his family, just so he could do walkthroughs to give her peace of mind that some poltergeist was not gonna spirit her to another realm. All this until her kids got her sorted in a nursing home. None of them did any of that. But you did. And everybody knows it."

"You heard," he murmured.

Her face changed in a way he'd never seen it.

But only for an instant.

Then she shook her head and said, "I grew up in this town. Grew up here just like Hope did. I know her, Hix. And she's a great gal. That's getting lost in all this, but she just plain is. I know that because I grew up with her. But even if I didn't, I'd know it knowing you and knowing you're not a man who would put up with a woman who wasn't. We all know she's a great gal."

She pulled in a breath, kept her eyes trained on him and kept going.

"Except when she doesn't get her way. She's always been like that, from way back. And right now she's not getting her way and everyone who knows her knows how that goes. The point I'm trying to make is, don't let her get into your head and give you even more to worry about. It's not just your deputies that are rooting for you, boss. And it's not just us who wanna see you happy again."

He acknowledged that with a short nod of his head.

"This will pass, for all of us," he told her.

"It always does."

"Thanks for comin' in here, Donna."

She gave him a small grin and said, "Always around, you need me, Hix."

She was.

He had his boys in that town, but now that he was thinking on it, the person he was closest to was Donna. She hung out with him at the Outpost before Hope asked him to leave, but she did it a lot more frequently after. She was his most veteran deputy, so in the rare instance anything went down, she was his number one. He counted on her to keep the others focused when he wasn't around, and she never let him down.

She was a good deputy. A good woman. Her husband knew it. Her kids. The town.

And so did Hix.

"Thanks," he murmured, turning back to his desk.

"Right, boss, that's outta the way, you should know, Peters's cows got loose again. They're blocking County Road 16, and traffic, such as it is, is backing up. Which, through the report, is all of three cars. He's not answering his phone. Should I send Larry and Bets out there to deal with it?"

Peters was probably still passed out from drinking alone in front of his television like Hix suspected he had every night since the mean sonuvabitch's wife came to her senses and left him two years before.

His fields had been fallow those two years and Hix had no idea how his cows hadn't wasted away.

But his fences had, seeing as the man wasn't a good farmer even before his wife took off.

"Send 'em with the message that this is the third time, and McCook County Sheriff's Department gives more than three strikes, but less than five. So he best get onto sorting out that damned fence or county fines will have to be deducted from his whiskey budget. And if the drivers are still idiotic enough to be waiting for cows to pass when our deputies get there, tell them to thank whoever called it in and divert the drivers. This county is on a grid system, it shouldn't be difficult for them to find an alternate route."

Her lips ticked on her, "Gotcha."

And with that, she took off.

Hix turned to his computer, thinking, if Greta wasn't going to be showing up at work in less than two hours, he'd have gone to deal with Peters himself.

A banner day for the sheriff. That meaning there was something to do.

However she needed a heads up. And it should come from him.

But the last time they'd dealt with Peters, they'd had to wedge open his door and throw a glass of water in his face to wake his ass up. He might not have time to deal with Peters and get to Greta in time to warn her before she faced her day at the salon.

What should not be was him showing at her front door unexpectedly, invading her space after he'd exited it the way he had.

It wasn't better he'd be showing at her work, but he figured it was better than invading her home, even to stand on her porch.

So work it was.

And until then and after that chore was done, he just had to hope he was right.

That this would pass.

And do it without any more of Hope's casualties piling up.

At five to ten, Hix pushed through the door at Lou's House of Beauty, and seeing as he'd been there before to drop off or pick up Corinne and Mamie when they had their appointments (albeit infrequently since Hope normally went with them), he didn't have to take in the décor.

It was, like pretty much everything in Glossop, suspended in time. The women there could be wearing those dresses with shoulder pads and having their hair rolled in the way they did during World War II, or they could be how they were right then. The woman in Lou's chair getting a hot-pink lock of fake hair what looked like Velcroed to her roots.

"Uh...well..." He looked to Lou when she started stammering and saw her wide eyes cut to the back of the salon even if her face remained pointed to him. "Um, hey, Hix."

"Lou," he greeted, skimmed a glance through the woman in her chair who he didn't know and looked back to Lou. "She in the back?"

He knew he didn't have to say who "she" was.

If any crime ever happened in that county, he'd have Lou on his confidential informant list.

That's the way it was everywhere.

From rumor to speculation to hard facts, if they were to be had, the first place they were had was at the local beauty parlor.

"Yeah," Lou answered.

"Thanks," Hix muttered, and without invitation, moved that way.

He did it wondering if Greta had been in that salon any of the times he'd been there for Corinne and Mamie and he just hadn't noticed her.

Then he pushed through the door to the back, saw her standing at some shelves filled with bottles, boxes and tubes, and she turned to him, the visual of her right there, a few feet away, live and in person smacked him in the face, and he knew there was no chance in hell he hadn't noticed her.

He loved his wife. When they were together, his mind had not once taken him to another place, not even to wonder how it would be with another woman.

But he was still a guy.

And Greta was tall and she was built. She had a few pounds on Hope, but they'd settled in all the right places.

On Saturday night, she'd been wearing a tight black dress that hit her knees. It had one shoulder bare, material swooping over the other, and it was covered in sequins with dangling spangly bits that moved when she did.

Now she was wearing a pair of faded jeans that had a wide cut at the hem and a cream, slouchy, collarless shirt that almost looked like a man's, except for the silky material it was made from and the fact the long tails were cinched loosely at her waist in a knot. The shirt's arms were rolled up near to her elbows and its buttons undone at the chest to the point cleavage was a given.

And Greta had fucking great cleavage.

There was a mess of thin gold necklaces coming down her chest to flirt with the opening in her shirt, long thin hoops that tangled in her hair and brushed her shoulders, and peeking under the hems of her jeans he could see a pair of spike-heeled, tan suede sandals that, across the foot, had a load of thin straps.

Her toes were painted a wine color.

As were her nails.

It was far from good she not only looked great in a tight black dress, she looked seriously great in just a pair of jeans and a shirt.

But it was her hair, face and eyes that had him standing silent, staring at her.

Eyes a light blue that was almost gray. They were big, wide set, making her seem open, approachable, friendly. And she had a lot of hair that had a lot of big curls, feathering and waving away from her face, a mix of honey and sunshine in the tendrils.

And he remembered she'd had a great smile, big teeth that were so white, if the healthy whites of her big eyes and mass of her big hair didn't accompany them, they might seem unreal.

But when she smiled and really gave it to you, her pretty, rosy lips spread wide, exposing two rows of the most perfect teeth he'd ever seen, that smile could blind you.

Though, she wasn't smiling then.

She looked frozen in time.

"Greta—" he started just as the door clicked shut behind him.

At the sound of his voice, she jerked out of it and took two wide steps, right into his space.

Tipping her head back, she whispered heatedly, "What are you doing here?"

"Something's happened and I need to share."

Her head tipped angrily and her mass of hair went with it.

It lasted less than a second.

And it was a spectacular show.

"Yeah, like your ex calling Lou and telling her to erase all her and your daughters' appointments from her books forevermore and to be ready because her posse are going to be calling in and doing the same?" she asked tersely.

He looked to her shoulder and whispered, "Shit."

"Lou's not friends with your wife, she's friends with me," she went on. "She'll hold strong. But I reckon, your ex follows through with what she isn't hiding is her plan, only so much Lou can take. What with the fact that Bill sometimes forgets that marriage is a partnership and his part of the partnership includes letting his family share in his paychecks instead of them going right to the Outpost to pay his tab every month."

Fantastic.

"I'll have a word with Bill," he told her.

Or another one.

"Don't have a word with Bill, Sheriff, have a word with *your wife*."

"She isn't my wife, Greta."

"Not sure she's been fully notified of the status change."

"She has, and if she hadn't, we had words this morning."

Her brows drew together as she slid an inch back. "Words that might drive her to make a few calls to her posse so all of them could check off their to-do list canceling those pesky hair appointments?"

"Words like that, yeah," he ground out.

She stepped a step away and looked to the floor at her side, murmuring, "Damn."

"Greta."

She looked to him and he had to take pains to ignore the fact that one look from those eyes in that face made his entire focus center on the itch in his hands urging him to touch her.

And the feel of his crotch.

"Have your clients been canceling?" he asked.

"Not yet but it'll happen and that won't be too good. But now it's happening...*to Lou*. And she needs asses in her chair, Sheriff, not cancellations seeing as she has two daughters to feed, and oh...I don't know, she might want some ramen noodles for herself and maybe to be able to throw some scraps at Bill every now and again."

"This will blow over," he said.

And he hoped like hell he was right.

She studied him saying a dubious, "Right."

"It will and you and Lou will be good," he assured. "It was a one-time thing, people will see that and then someone else will do something that'll take their attention and they'll forget all about it."

He powered through her wince when he said it was a "one-time thing" and she powered through the rest of it, declaring, "You clearly don't know women very well. When the sisterhood gets activated, they'll train their daughters to pile bitch hatred on their mark to insure it won't die when they kick the bucket."

His gaze moved to her hair before it went back to her eyes. "Don't know, but my guess is, you're talented. Closest hair salon is twenty miles away and someone might make that trek once or twice to make a point, but then it'll get old. But regardless, Hope has an elevated idea of her pull in this town. You do your job well, I'm sure your clients will be loyal to you."

"Well, I'm glad *you're* sure."

He moved into the space she'd put between them.

It was a mistake.

Added to all the rest that was her, her perfume hit him.

He did his best to ignore that too and murmured, "It's gonna be okay, Greta."

She held her ground even if she did it holding her body stiffly and returned, "It's not gonna do the cause of communicating 'it was just a one-time thing,' you showing here, Sheriff."

It hit him then she was calling him "Sheriff," not Hixon or Hix.

He didn't comment on that or think about the fact he didn't like it all that much.

He said, "I wanted to give you a heads up."

"Well, thanks. You've done that. You have another heads up to give me, come in disguise or better yet, try smoke signals."

Shit, she was going to make him laugh.

He couldn't laugh. He had to get this done so he wouldn't experience something else that drew him to her.

"While I've got you—" he started.

At that, she moved back two steps into the cramped space, nearly running into the shelves, rolled her eyes to the ceiling and declared to it, "Oh boy, here we go."

He felt tightness hit his neck. "Here we go with what?"

She looked to him. "I jumped the gun, sorry, bud." She circled a hand at him. "Carry on."

"Here we go with what?" he repeated.

"You want the multiple choice?" she asked.

He rocked back on his heels and crossed his arms on his chest.

As he did, she watched him do it, her gaze dipping to his chest, and something came over her face that looked a lot like she'd looked the first time he'd touched her hand resting on the table between them at the Dew Drop.

She wiped that clean when she refocused on him.

For his part, he took pains to ignore that too.

"A, you can try to make yourself feel better for treating me like a piece of ass by apologizing again."

Damn, that was what he'd been about to do.

"B," she went on, "you can treat me like the piece of ass you think I am by angling for a little nookie in Lou's back room, or perhaps showing me to the alley."

Okay.

Right.

He'd been a dick, but even so, he was there, she knew why so she had to know that shit was not on.

"Greta—" he began on a growl.

"Then there's C," she rolled over his word with some of her own. "You starting the conversation that you think might win you a piece of ass whenever you get the itch by ascertaining if I'm open to be your booty call."

He closed his mouth and felt his lips thin.

"Or D, a combination of the above," she concluded.

"A," he bit off.

"Right," she mumbled.

"I'd also like to offer you an explanation," he continued tightly.

"Well, I'd say I'm all ears, but *hopefully* I have a client coming in T minus right about now."

Damn, she was infuriating and hilarious *at the same time.*

She hadn't been hilarious at the Dew Drop.

She just sang like a dream, looked like a wet dream, and listened while he talked like she gave a shit what he had to say.

Christ.

And dammit, he hadn't asked her a thing about herself.

Christ.

"I got divorced very recently," he informed her.

"Considering I'm learning the hard way that you're a public personality, Sheriff, I know that. But just to say, I've been in Glossop awhile now so I knew it already, which makes *me* the idiot."

"You aren't an idiot."

"I am," she whispered.

All of a sudden, Hix grew still.

And he did because just as suddenly, she'd changed. The whole of her changed. Hell, the air in the room changed.

"You're not an idiot," he whispered back.

She said nothing.

"It was good, all of it, not just what happened in your bedroom."

He watched her swallow but she didn't reply.

"I've been married for nineteen years. I signed my divorce papers three weeks and three days ago," he finally shared.

"You're counting the days," she said softly.

"Yeah," he replied the same way. "And now I think you get me."

She nodded, lifting her hands to cup her elbows in a defensive posture that, strangely, Hix felt a trace of pain just at witnessing it.

"If it had happened in a few months..." He trailed off.

"I get it."

"It didn't."

"No."

"So, the time isn't right, for me, I got kids, for them, so also for you."

She nodded again.

"And now I've screwed it up," he said. "Acted like a dick. Made you feel—"

"It's okay."

"It isn't."

"It's okay, Hixon."

She called him Hixon.

The tension went out of his neck.

"I didn't mean to make you feel what I made you feel and I'm sorry for that. So sorry, Greta. I had a lot messing with my head. Too much. So much I shouldn't have taken it there between us. You got no reason to believe me but I'll say it any way. I'm not that guy."

"I believe you."

He studied her. "Yeah?"

She nodded.

And it was then she started unraveling him.

She did this letting her face get soft.

"You've been married nineteen years. Unless you stepped out on her, it's impossible for you to be that guy."

"I never stepped out on her."

"I believe that too," she whispered.

And she did. He saw it in her eyes, in the softened line of her body.

Jesus, she was a woman who could communicate with every inch that was her.

No figuring out Greta.

She gave it all with everything she had.

He had to ignore that too.

"Right, good," he muttered but held her gaze. "But it isn't okay. I was the ass in all that. You didn't deserve that. I should have explained it then. You were...you *are*...great."

"Thanks," she said quietly.

He drew in breath and said gently, "I'm glad we got that sorted, Greta. With the way I treated you, I don't deserve it but it means a lot you took the time to listen so I could give it to you."

"Well, uh...thanks for taking the time to give it to me."

He wanted to smile in order to see if she'd give him that back.

But he didn't deserve that either.

"Now you've got a client," he prompted.

She lifted her chin. "Mm-hmm."

"So I'll let you go."

She unhooked her hands from her elbows to throw an arm toward the door at the back. "That leads out into the alley."

"I'm walking through the salon."

She stared at him.

"We didn't do anything wrong," he stated. "We're adults. We connected. We enjoyed each other. I'm not attached anymore. You aren't either." He lifted his brows. "I assume."

She shook her head, her hair brushing all over her shoulders, something Hix had to avoid watching.

"I'm not."

She wasn't.

A woman who could sing with that honesty, listen with it, talk with it and make love with it, of course she wasn't.

He forged past that too and carried on talking.

"So we have nothing to be ashamed about. Nothing to hide. Hope can get ugly. That's her prerogative. We don't have to give people reason to believe she has that right because she doesn't. She's a forty-one-year-old woman throwing a tantrum. The folks in this town are close-knit and loyal. They're also sensible. They'll see things as they are and move on. If Hope doesn't, it's not my problem anymore, and it sure as hell isn't yours."

"Okay, Hixon."

He looked into her big eyes.

And he wanted to ask her to lunch at the Harlequin.

He wanted to see if she was free some evening next week to take her to a movie.

He couldn't do that.

Because his ex-wife was who she was, and things were how they were, Hope was giving him reasons to fall out of love with her.

But that was where he was at now.

Falling out of love.

He knew Greta intimately. He knew she was funny and honest. And he knew there was a vulnerability to her the cause of which it wasn't his right to have.

That was all he knew.

Except for the fact that he knew without doubt she didn't need to be like his apartment.

The in-between while he was sorting out his life.

She deserved more.

He just wasn't in a place he could give it to her, and with the wounds Hope had inflicted, at that time in his life, he wasn't sure he could give it to anyone again, at least not for a long time.

In that time Greta could find her more and she didn't need a man with his head a mess standing in her way.

"I gotta get to my client," she said.

He stepped out of the way and jerked his head to the door. "Go."

She moved to it and put her hand on the handle but turned to him.

Then she ripped his heart clean out of his chest, her big, beautiful, blue eyes staring right into his as she said, "She's a complete fool."

With that, she opened and walked through the door.

Hix pulled air into his nostrils.

And smelled hints of her perfume.

Shit.

He gave it a beat.

Three.

And after that he followed her, dipping his chin to the women in the salon, a number that had grown more than double to when he'd walked in, murmuring, "Ladies."

But he caught Greta's eyes, tipped his head to the side, his lips up, and then without looking back, he walked out the front door.

And he did it not having that first clue that, with a tip of his head and a small curl to his lips, he shifted the axis of Glossop, Nebraska in a way anyone who knew either of them, which was most, started to believe dreams could come true.

Chapter 5

All I Need

Greta

The door to the salon opened and Lou called out, "Greta is *not* talking about Sheriff Hixon Drake!"

I sighed and looked from the sink, where I was doing a rinse, to the door to see my next client, Shari, hurrying through, her gaze on me, eyes huge.

She was twenty minutes early.

She was usually ten minutes late.

"So it's true!" she cried.

Wonderful.

This was what it had been like all day.

To say I was relieved that the salon hadn't been firebombed after word got out the Princess of Glossop's ex-husband had slept with its resident easy-trick hairdresser-slash-lounge singer (that being *me*) might be a high-drama understatement, but it was true.

To say that relief was tempered by the fact I'd learned Hixon Drake was a good guy, he just was never going to be the guy for me, was just an understatement, but a sad one.

"Greta has enough to worry about without every female walking in that door asking her for the lowdown about our sheriff," Lou declared.

Shari kept her eyes on me. "I know. I've heard. I think Hope Drake activated the PTA phone tree to rally the girls to come to your house tonight, drag you out and tar and feather you."

Wonderful.

"Stupid woman does that," Joyce, sitting in Lou's chair with Lou's shears working at her head, chimed in. "I'll get Jim's shotgun, sit on Greta's porch and offer the medical professionals opportunity to explore the concept of finally extricating her head out of her behind by aiming some buckshot at it."

"Me too!" Mrs. Swanson, who had her head back in the sink, shouted out.

Mrs. Swanson was eighty-two and sadly had such bad arthritis, her weekly wash and set wasn't a luxury. It was a necessity since she couldn't do her own hair.

She certainly couldn't pull the trigger on a shotgun.

She might not even have the strength to hold one.

Though Joyce did and she was also ornery enough to do exactly what she said.

"We're not talking about Hope Drake," Lou announced. "Greta's got problems comin' out the ying-yang, starting not with Hope but with the fact her momma threw down."

Shari's still-huge eyes turned to me and she pushed out a long, "*No.*"

I nodded to her then turned back to finish up Mrs. Swanson.

"Oh my gosh!" I heard Shari exclaim. "I hope she comes today. I want it to be a day I have an appointment. I don't want to miss out on Greta's mom making a scene, cursing and blinding. All this town's been talking about is Hix and Hope Drake *for months.* It's getting boring. We need something new to talk about."

We really did not.

Especially if it was about me and my mother.

"She really say the F-word out loud and in public?" Mrs. Young called out from under the dryer.

I hadn't only told Lou about my mom. You did hair, you chatted. So my regulars knew too.

So did Lou's.

I grabbed a pink towel off the shelves behind the sinks, shook it out of the precise roll Lou and I folded them in and started to wrap Mrs. Swanson's head in it, saying, "The F-word, B-word, H-word, D-word, and she'll probably sprinkle in the P-word and even the C-word."

Mrs. Young, rightly, looked horrified.

"That's it," Joyce stated. "She strolls in here and does any of that, it's gonna be me goin' to your momma's house and dragging her out to take her to one of Pastor Keller's revivals. He'll dip her in the river and hold her down until she sees Jesus. And if she doesn't, he'll hold her down until *she sees Jesus.*"

I helped Mrs. Swanson to sit up with my gaze on Lou, both of us visibly trying not to bust a gut laughing.

"I know we're talkin' about your momma now, Greta, but just to ask, are people cancelling because of Hope?" Shari queried worriedly from where she'd sat herself in one of the dryer chairs with its bonnet turned up.

"Hope cancelled her and the girls' appointments with Lou. And Julie Baker cancelled her appointment with me next week," I answered, walking Mrs. Swanson to my chair. "But other than that..." I shook my head.

"Well, that's good," Shari mumbled.

"Julie Baker would tear her own fingernails out by the roots before she'd miss a chance to do something mean," Joyce shared. "But she'll haul her behind to Styles and Smiles all of *once* before she puts her tail between her legs and comes back to you girls."

"Yup, I'm not bothered," Lou declared nonchalantly, running her fingers through Joyce's painfully short hair to distribute the product that only Lou put in to make it look cute since Joyce was a wash-and-go type of woman. "I lay witness to no less than *five* terror attacks on hair that came to me from Styles and Smiles. Francine never mastered the art of foils to the point it's nearly criminal she keeps on trying."

This was true.

I'd had two women come to me after their hair had come off *with* the foils put in at Styles and Smiles.

This made me think I never should have worried about Lou and her House of Beauty. Some women budgeted not only for the style, but for the gas that would take them across the county to see Lou or me. They'd take a floozy sleeping with their sheriff and having a foul-mouthed momma working there in order to get good hair, no sweat.

And I'd met Francine. She was a nice lady. But unless you wanted a straight-up dye, bleach, set or cut from the era of Shirley Jones to Dorothy Hamill to her most contemporary look, the Rachel from *Friends* circa the first season, your best bet was to go to Lou's House of Beauty or the Cutting Edge, which was miles away in Morsprings.

We weren't only the only shop in town. We were one of the only choices in the county.

While Lou whisked off Joyce's drape, Mrs. Young's dryer binged and she pulled up the bonnet, doing this talking.

"Hix'll bring his girls back to you, Lou. Hope might not be level-headed enough to understand her girls'll lose their minds, they go somewhere and get bad hair. But Hix adores his daughters and he might be a man, but he's also the father of two girls, so he'll understand it. Not to mention, he won't be too fond of wastin' the gas money to get them to Yucca to see Francine."

"I hope so," Lou replied, taking cash from Joyce for her cut and style. "They're good girls and they've got great hair. I'll miss having my hands in that."

"And anyway," Shari put in, "he won't dis the salon where his girlfriend works."

I felt a heavy weight hit my chest as my eyes shifted from combing out Mrs. Swanson's hair to Shari.

I felt Lou's attention on me and I had a feeling she was about to say something.

But I beat her to it.

"I'm not his girlfriend, Shari."

"But I heard—" she began.

"We met and we..." I slid my glance to Lou then back to Shari. "It's too soon for him. He's a nice guy and I'm glad I met him, but it was a one-time thing."

"Has he lost his marbles like his ex?" Joyce asked incredulously and my attention shifted to her.

"It's too soon for him."

"Too soon, shmoo-soon," Joyce snapped at me. "Hixon Drake never struck me as stupid. In fact, the opposite. And everybody knows, good drops itself in your lap you don't shove it off and say, 'Now's not the right time. I'm dealin' with the fact my addled wife didn't see the good thing resting his head on the pillow beside hers.' No. You snatch up that good and hold it close and process all that dealin' while life reminds you, you survive the bad, good always comes slidin' back in right after it."

"That's a nice thing to say, Joyce," I told her quietly.

"I'm not bein' nice," she retorted. "What do the kids call it today?" She didn't pause for an answer. While hefting her tall, strong, sturdy, farmer's wife body out of Lou's chair, she declared, "I'm bein' real."

That was when I looked right at Lou.

Lou didn't need me to look at her.

She was already ordering, "Okay, let's stop talking about this."

Joyce walked up to Mrs. Swanson and me at my chair.

"Have a mind to stroll right into the Sheriff's Department and share some of it with Hix," she informed me.

Mrs. Swanson made a frightened peep, likely because Joyce wasn't only a wash-and-go type of woman. She was no-nonsense, ballsy and known not to care if you had a problem with her speaking her mind, in which she had a lot of opinions she felt the need to let out.

I whispered, "Please don't do that."

"I won't, girl," Joyce stated. "Have a mind to do it but I like you too much to meddle. He's got his head planted in his keister like his ex-wife, he has to sort himself out. And if he misses out on a good thing doin' it, that's his problem." She leaned into me. "But just to say, don't you worry about Hope. Known her since she was a little thing. She can get up to some antics, but the minute she realizes it's makin' her look bad, she'll back down. Everybody in this town knows that, and most everybody in this town knows you, so you won't have any problems. Not a good girl like you. Just ride it out, Greta. It'll be over before you know it."

"Thanks, Joyce," I replied on a smile.

"Whatever," she muttered and turned to Lou. "Six weeks, Lou."

"You're in my schedule, Joyce," Lou returned.

On that, Joyce walked out.

"I hope he changes his mind about it being too soon," Shari said, and I looked from rolling a thin rod in Mrs. Swanson's hair to her. "Even my Rich says something's wrong in the cosmos, you don't have a man. I always told him I wasn't sure there was a man that was man enough to be good enough for you."

At that, my chest warmed.

"Wow, Shari, that's so sweet," I told her.

"Maybe, it's also true," she replied. "I heard about you and Hix, I thought, there it was. I shoulda thought of that the minute I heard Hope'd kicked him out."

That didn't make my chest warm.

It made it feel heavy again.

"My great-nephew, Owen, just moved back into town, Greta," Mrs. Swanson said to me from her chair, and I looked down at her. "He's a good boy. His dad's gettin' on and needed help with things.

His wife had her head in her bottom too. But she messed things up at least three years ago. It won't be too soon for him."

"I'm not looking for a fixup, Mrs. Swanson," I said gently. "But it's nice of you to think of that."

Her eyes turned to the mirror as I used the pointed end of my teasing comb to separate another bit of hair to roll, "Well, you just say the word when you're ready, sweetie. Be my pleasure to introduce you two."

I again looked to Lou to see she was unravelling Mrs. Young's curlers but doing it watching me.

We had a hectic day seeing as we always had hectic days. Because of that, I hadn't had the opportunity to share the fullness of what happened with Hixon in the back room with her.

Lou and I had met years ago when she had to come out to Denver for her cousin's wedding and the salon I'd worked at had sent stylists out to do the bride and her bridesmaids' hair. Lou had sat in to keep an eye on things, we got to talking, and I knew she was my kind of people within minutes of meeting her.

She didn't hide she felt the same.

We kept connected through email, texts and occasional phone calls, and not long after Keith ended things with me, she told me about Sunnydown, and the fact her stylist was moving to Omaha because the man she met online was there and things were getting serious.

I'd then taken vacation out in Glossop, stayed with Lou and her family, looked into Sunnydown for Andy and found it was cleaner, nicer, the people were great, and it cost a whole lot less than where he was at in Denver.

So I'd moved, and as his guardian, I took Andy with me.

And Lou, with her long history of living in Glossop (she'd moved there from Yucca when she'd married Bill sixteen years ago) and all her connections through her work, had settled me right into that town like I'd been there since birth.

So we hadn't known each other since forever, but we worked

together every day, she'd looked out for me from afar, and she meant the world to me.

In return, I gave great hair at her joint, treated her daughters like they were my own, and didn't point out Bill was an asshole when she was at my place, drinking whiskey and telling me all the reasons Bill was an asshole.

In other words, we were tight.

And looking at her right then, I knew she was worried.

Worried that word had gotten out about Hixon and me. Worried that my mom had thrown down. Worried that Hope Drake had declared war. And worried that Hixon had walked into the salon and talked to me in the back room about things I hadn't yet had a chance to process through with my best bud.

So I set Mrs. Swanson's hair and put in Shari's foils while Mrs. Swanson was under the bonnet. I then finished with them both while Lou took care of her clients that wandered in, got their hair done, had their say about Hope, Hixon, my momma and me.

And when we had a lull with one of Lou's appointments flipping through a magazine waiting for her dye to set, and I had a break to go out and get us a late lunch, she cornered me in the back room while I was getting the stuff I was going to need for my next client.

"One-time thing?" she asked.

I turned to her. "Lou—"

"Got three calls last night about what happened at the Dew, you know that, told you when you got here. Not ten minutes after, Hix strolls right in like he comes to visit you every morning before you start work. Then he leaves and smiles at you like he smiled at you. And it's a one-time thing?"

I stared at her. "How did he smile at me?"

"Girlfriend, he aimed it *right at you*. How'd you miss it?"

What was she talking about?

"I...he...we..."

How did he smile at me?

I shook that question out of my head and spit out what I needed to say to Lou.

"It's his idea that it's a one-time thing. He just came this morning to share that Hope was on the warpath. I...he...we..." On that, I just shook my head then whispered, "He was just being nice because what happened with us..." I sucked in a big breath and finished softly, "It was good, Lou."

She leaned back and threw out both hands. "Of course it was good. God can be a jokester but He wouldn't play a joke so cruel as to make a man that fine and not give him the talents to see that concept *all the way through.*"

God had definitely done that.

"How did he smile at me?" I repeated.

"Like he didn't want to walk out that door, leaving you behind, but instead he wanted to drag you out right along with him."

I started breathing hard.

She was right.

How did I miss that?

"Always liked Hix and Hope together," she announced, and I again stared at her. "They looked good together. Both of 'em love their kids like crazy. Both of 'em loved each other like crazy. She can be a spoiled brat, and he's a man, no escaping any man having his moments of being totally clueless, not even a man like Hix. But he loved her. Way he looked at her stated plain he didn't care everyone knowing just how much. Thought it was a shame, them going through that rough patch."

As much as I never really liked Hope, and I hadn't known Hixon at all, I'd felt the same.

"Until I got my first call about what happened at the Dew," she went on. "And then he walked out of my place and smiled that smile at you. Then I thought, God works in mysterious ways. He looked at his wife the way he did for years and now it's been proved she didn't deserve it. But one night with you has proved he has it goin' on, seein' as he realized what he'd found with the way he looked and smiled at you."

I again shook my head. "He was...what happened...it was just a mistake. Not a mistake, exactly, but bad timing. Nothing's happening. He just divorced her a few weeks ago."

"I don't care if he divorced her yesterday," she retorted. "He may be in denial, Greta, too much coming at him too soon. Got no idea what it takes to rebuild your life after a marriage of near on two decades falls apart. Don't wanna know. But even a good guy like Sheriff Drake doesn't hear his ex is on the warpath and then walk his ass to the local salon to warn his one-night stand to batten down the hatches. He gets on with things and lets the sisterhood work out their issues and the chips fall as they may. At best, he sends his deputy, who's one of your clients, to give you the warning. What he doesn't do is take his time to have a private moment with you in the back room of your place of business, then walk out after sharing with you it was what it was and now he's moving on by looking at you and smiling at you the way he did."

"I can't believe that," I told her.

"I can since I saw it with my own two eyes. And just sayin', I wasn't the only one."

I couldn't think on that.

She had to get me.

And I had to get me too or I might do something dangerous.

Something I never did.

Hope.

"No, you don't understand what I'm saying. I can't believe that in the sense I *won't*."

She shut up.

I piped up.

"Listen, Lou, he made things clear, now twice, that it was what it was and it's done. You may be reading it a certain way because you love me and you like him and you like the idea of him with me. But what you saw wasn't what you saw. Even if it was and he's got things screwing with his head, I can't believe it was what you saw because I've got enough on my plate, and I can't take on all of that and how it might play out."

"Greta, girlfriend—"

I stepped closer to her and gave her a small, not-happy smile.

"He's a good guy and that's the reason he came himself. And there was another reason, that being him explaining where he's at. And I appreciate that, Lou. Because there *was* something between us and it was good. I felt it and I think he did too. But at this time in his life, he goes there, taking me with him, with Hope being the way she is and him being put through the wringer by her, he's trying to save me from being put through that wringer too with things up in the air with how that'd play out. He's protecting me from that. And we only had one night, I don't know him all that well, but that says a lot about him."

"I know how it'd play out," she declared.

"No you don't. And I don't. And he doesn't either," I replied. "You said yourself, and I saw it too, how he feels about her. It's too fresh and they'd been together a long time, they have three kids, they live in a small town, anything could happen."

"Are you saying you think they'll patch things up?"

I shrugged. "Maybe."

Her brows knitted. "Are you saying he told you he wants that?"

I shook my head. "I don't think so. She didn't seem like his favorite person."

"Well you know what?"

Oh boy.

I knew some whats.

I also knew sometimes I didn't want to hear Lou's variety of what.

She was worse than Joyce.

"Lou—" I tried to waylay her.

"Hope Drake is gonna be a lot less than his favorite person when someone stops keepin' their mouth shut, waiting to see how it'll play out between them, now that those papers have been filed. Someone is gonna share that the reason she put him through that wringer is because she wanted him to use the inheritance he got from that uncle of his to buy her a twenty-five thousand dollar twentieth anniversary ring instead of what *he* wanted to do with *his* inheritance."

I tried again. "Lou—"

And failed.

"That being save it in case of emergencies. But if those didn't come around, use it to put his girl through law school and maybe have a little extra to help his other girl with whatever she wanted to be in this life, and use what they'd saved for both of those things to give his daughters the best weddings they could dream up."

Yeah.

I had a feeling Hixon wasn't going to be too happy with his ex-wife when that someone got around to sharing just that about Hope.

Lou kept on.

"Probably the person in this town who was most freaked Hixon signed his name to those papers was Hope. She thought he'd cave. He didn't cave. And now she's scrambling. She screwed the pooch, and huge. And she's not as stupid as she seems. She needs to get him back before Hix is the wiser to her bullshit. If they're back together, no one will say a word. He finds someone worth his time in the meanwhile, she hasn't just screwed the pooch. She's plain old *screwed*."

"This doesn't have anything to do with me," I pointed out.

"Honey, you're wrong. I don't know what happened at the Dew, or after it, I just know he walked in somehow knowing the time you were on today and arriving at that time so he was the first person you saw, besides me. And he did all that with one thing on his mind." She leaned into me again. "*You*. That doesn't say one-night stand. That says *protect your woman*."

Protect your woman.

Your woman.

His woman.

"Please stop," I begged.

She leaned back.

"It isn't that," I reiterated.

She looked at me for a second then advised, "Greta, sometimes to carve some good in your life, you gotta work for it and even fight for it."

She might be right.

She was still wrong.

"It isn't that," I said yet again.

Her voice got gentle. "Love you, honey. You know it. Never doubt it. But you let life happen to you and sometimes it's a good thing to fight back."

"You're right. Definitely. You're right about that. But this isn't the time for that."

"I think—"

"Keith was it for me."

She closed her mouth.

I felt my eyes sting but pushed through it. "He was my everything."

"Greta, girlfriend—"

"He was a good guy. He treated me...he was with me..." I couldn't finish that. I just said, "And I lost him."

"Did you fight?"

I couldn't go there.

"It doesn't matter," I told her. "I lost him. Now this man...he's a good man, Lou, you know it. Everyone does. What happens to me if I go for it and I don't win?"

"What happens if you do?"

I couldn't go there either.

"That doesn't happen for me a lot."

"Maybe it would if you fought."

"And maybe it would just leave me that much more beaten."

"I gotta admit, you've endured more than most," she muttered.

"You think?" I asked, trying to be funny.

She didn't laugh.

She suggested, "Maybe you're in for a change."

Okay.

I had to end this.

For both of us.

"You know, I was fourteen when Mom had Andy, and then completely forgot she'd had a kid."

"Honey," Lou whispered, her tone quieting, her face gentling.

She knew.

"So it was me who changed his diapers and fed him his bottles and got up when he was crying. And it was me, when he got big enough, who made him his breakfast and got him to school and made him do his homework. And it was me, even after I'd moved out, that got up early to go there every morning to do the same. It was also me who never missed any of his football games and attended his parent-teacher conferences."

Her eyes started getting misty, but I had to nip her hopes and dreams for me in the bud before I got talked into letting her sweep me along right with them.

I'd become a mother at fourteen to a child I didn't carry, and I didn't mind because I'd fallen in love with Andy the minute I laid eyes on him. He was something to love and I'd never had that, not in all my short life, and I gave him all the love I had bottled up and all the love he had coming.

Which was a lot.

But even before that, with the mother I'd been given and no father to speak of, I'd never had any dreams and I'd never hoped for anything, except to spend the rest of my life with Keith from the minute he'd kissed me after our first date.

I couldn't start now.

"But it was *her* who was driving when Andy's body got crushed and his skull got fractured right along with it. And the only thing good that came out of that was that she was incarcerated for eight months for drunk driving and I could get myself declared his guardian. So I know what life is like. I know what's worth fighting for. And I know from what I've learned that I should just take the good of a nice guy looking after me when I get caught up in his life drama at the same time he offers me the best thing he can right now. Keeping me out of that drama."

I lifted a hand and touched her arm before dropping it.

"I love that you want good for me, Lou," I said softly. "What you need to get is that I've got the only brand of that I'm ever gonna get, and after all that's gone before, I'm good with that."

"Maybe you should meet Mrs. Swanson's Owen," she muttered.

I grinned at her. "How about I just keep hold on what I've got. My mom and whatever this is with Hix and Hope Drake notwithstanding, I like it. A great job. A great house." I gave her a big smile. "Good friends. It's awesome here. A quiet town. Good people in it. Peaceful. Nice. Folks look after folks. Things are simple. This Hope thing will blow over and those two will move on however they're gonna move on. And I've already decided I'm done with Mom. She may be more stubborn than I expect, but I figure, the Greta Money Bank dries up, she'll slither out just like she slithered in." I lifted my shoulders in another shrug. "And then it'll all be just peaceful, quiet, nice. Simple."

"Want more for you, babe."

At that, I laughed a little bit and kept smiling at her after I was done.

"I wasn't being funny," she told me.

"I know, sweetheart," I replied. "The thing is, what I have *is* more. It's the best I've ever had. Yes, even better than when I was with Keith because that was always shadowed by what he wanted that I couldn't give him, all he was giving me that I couldn't give back and me terrified when he'd figure out that I wasn't worth it. I'm happy. So you don't have to want more for me, Lou. I've got all I need."

"I still want more for you."

"Of course you do, you're my friend. That's your job," I returned. "But right now, *I* want chicken tenders from the Harlequin, and if I don't get them soon, they'll get cold while I'm doing hair. They're good cold, but they're better hot."

Lou, being Lou—that was a really good friend—let it go because she got that I needed her to.

"That's my order too. And curly fries."

"Like you have to say that," I muttered, turning back to the shelves.

Lou turned to the door.

As I grabbed what I needed, she called my name.

I looked over my shoulder at her.

"I know you won't like hearing it, but the life you're willing to settle for being so much less than you deserve, it breaks my heart, Greta."

My heart thumped hearing her say that.

Then she walked through the door and it closed behind her.

AT SEVEN THIRTY THAT NIGHT, I rolled my black, boxy, traveling beauty case with its steel edges up Mrs. Whitney's front walk.

As always, she had the door open and was standing in it, waiting for me before I had to heft the case up the five cement steps that sat halfway up the path and led to the short walk to her door.

"You always have the prettiest outfits," she told me when I got close. "You even make a shirt and jeans look like it's walkin' down a New York City sidewalk."

"And you always have the sweetest things to say," I replied.

Her eyes dropped to my feet. "But I have no idea how you wear those heels, standin' on your feet all day."

"Practice," I shared.

"Come in, darlin'," she invited, moving out of my way as I pulled open her screen door. "You had dinner?"

And she always asked if I'd had dinner.

So I gave her the answer I always gave her.

"I'll get something when I get home."

"Got chops and mash," she said. "They're still warm."

"Thanks, Mrs. W, but I eat heavy at lunch and light at dinner."

"All right, Greta, come in, come in." She scooted me in through her foyer but stopped us right there. "Just gonna go look in on the mister." Her faded blue eyes caught mine. "And I'll have to do it again after the set, darlin'."

"I know, Mrs. W. It's all good. I'll go in and get set up."

She gave me a small smile and headed up the stairs.

I headed into the kitchen.

She came in and I washed her hair while she leaned over her kitchen sink then I sat her in a chair at the table and started my work.

"So, what's happening in Glossop that I need to know about?" she asked.

She was probably the only woman in town who didn't know just what that was.

This was because "the mister," her husband, was upstairs on life support and had been since he'd had a heart attack three years ago that stopped oxygen from going to his brain.

They'd revived his body.

They couldn't revive the rest of him.

And she didn't have the heart to pull the plug or the insurance to keep him in a hospital bed.

She also loved him so much, she refused to leave him, terrified he'd slip away when she wasn't around. She went to the grocery store once a week. And Pastor Keller came to her on Sunday afternoons to pray with her.

And every two weeks, I did a wash and set.

She had other friends who visited here and there.

And she had a sleeping husband who would never wake and she'd never stop taking care of him in a bed upstairs.

It was beautifully sweet. It was tremendously sad.

It was life.

I gave her the lowdown on what I knew, including my mother, not including Hixon and Hope Drake.

"I sure hope your momma doesn't bring her trash into the House of Beauty," she murmured when I was done.

"She will, Mrs. W. But I'm learning that's her way and it doesn't have to change the way I do things."

"She did what she did to my brother that she did to yours, darlin'," she started quietly, "don't think I'd be givin' her money all these years."

I thought about the man I'd never seen upstairs and whispered, "Yes, you would."

She thought on that a second and whispered back, "Reckon you're right."

I felt the need for a subject change, for both of us.

"You want, week after next, I'll get you an appointment with Lou at the salon. You can go on in and I'll clear my schedule to be here for the mister," I offered, not for the first time.

"Oh, child, that's sweet. But maybe it ain't right to leave Burt with a stranger. I'm sure he'll like the look a' you, say he wakes up. But once he gets over that, he'll still be wondering where I am."

He wouldn't wake up, couldn't. His brain was more gone than Andy's.

Yet more evidence it was futile to hope.

Even so, for the first time, I pushed, "Maybe Pastor Keller will come sit with him."

"I don't think so, Greta. But you're a good girl and it sure is nice you'd offer."

I shut up about that like I always did.

When she was walking to the bonnet dryer she'd set up herself in her kitchen after it all happened, I asked, "While you're cooking, you want a polish change?"

Her eyes came to me and lit. "You bring your polish, darlin'?"

I smiled at her. "Don't I always?"

She smiled back. "You sure do. And I'd love to get some of that pearly peach you had last spring. I know we're headin' into fall, but I'm not a fall. I'm a spring. Had my colors all done up professional-like when ladies were seein' to that kind of thing. But I figure, spring color in fall, that'll still be like havin' pearly pumpkins on my fingernails."

"Sounds perfect," I told her, heading to my case to pull out another compartment.

I changed her polish. I set her hair. And I gave her a hug before I left, when she always stuffed a twenty in whatever pocket I had available to her, this on top of paying me and the tip she handed me, face to face.

Lou had a family to look after so she couldn't swing an evening home appointment. Her old stylist was young and had a life after work so she'd declined doing it. Which left Mrs. Whitney with Francine hauling herself from Yucca, and charging her double to make up the gas money.

I'd said yes the first time Lou asked me.

Mrs. Whitney didn't get much company and went out even less.

But that didn't mean she didn't want her hair looking nice.

She appreciated me taking the time to come to her place, which meant I got home late after a very long day.

Appreciated it enough to want to give me an extra twenty dollars.

I never said a word about it.

It wasn't necessary.

She needed to do it.

So I let her do it.

After that, I drove home, and as I drove home, I called Andy.

The staff got him on the phone for me and I listened to him chatter away while I drove, and then while I made myself a spinach salad with diced hard-boiled eggs, sliced red onion, dried cranberry, slivered almonds and some sprinkles of cheese.

He had to go so I let him go before I ate it.

I cleaned up after myself and made some tea.

Then I walked out to my porch and sat in my wicker chair.

There was a bit of a nip in the air sharing summer was saying its farewells. Soon, when I sat on my porch, I'd have to wear a sweater like I had to last fall.

But right then, I didn't need one.

I just sat cross-legged in my chair and picked up the book I'd left out there.

I balanced it, closed, on my lap and lifted my tea to my lips and my eyes to the street.

And I let the peace and quiet of Glossop sink into me.

It had been quite a day and a long one to boot.

But the thing I liked most about living there was, no matter I'd met a man who I knew, in another life or with the right timing, might be able to wring miracles and balance my world, a world that had always been unsteady, at the same time making me happy. No matter his ex-wife was undoubtedly going to shake things up in a number of unpleasant ways for the foreseeable future. No matter what my mother would dream up to torture me to get what she wanted out of me.

No matter what anything.

I always had that spot right there on my porch in Glossop to remind me I'd made it to the exact right place I needed to be.

I might never have had any hopes and dreams.

But with the life I'd led, I'd always craved just what I was right then experiencing.

Calm. Peace. Simplicity.

For me.

And for Andy.

So I could take the bad and take the good.

And end every day's rollercoaster having everything I needed.

Serenity.

In other words...

Glossop.

Chapter 6

Speeding Tickets

Hixon

Saturday night, Hix sat on his couch, his eyes on the TV that was playing a late night movie, the volume set low since his girls were asleep in the back.

His mind was not on the movie.

Like it had been awhile, it was on the shitty mess of things that had consumed his life.

Shaw was out on a date that night with Wendy.

That was two dates that week.

So Hix was also up waiting for his son to get home by a curfew he knew Shaw wouldn't push. His boy never did.

His curfew on Saturdays was midnight.

He had ten minutes.

As he waited, didn't watch the movie and thought about the shit of his life, Hix held on to the fact that the week hadn't started out great, but it had surprisingly settled in.

He hadn't heard again from Hope. He also hadn't seen Greta

(which meant he hadn't had to fight the temptation of her). He further hadn't had to lay it out for anybody else.

And no one had said boo to him about anything.

Except for Pastor Keller walking right up to him while Hix was eating lunch with Donna at the Harlequin.

The good pastor did this to state, "Hope to see you and Greta in a pew real soon, Sheriff. Greta can forget her duty to God on occasion, which for her is understandable. But I haven't seen you there in some time, son. Although God frowns on one of His children not understanding the concept of the sanctity of marriage, He has His way of seeing right comes from wrong. So bring your new woman to the Holy Father's house so He can see what He's wrought in all its glory."

Keller hadn't given Hix the opportunity to say a word. He'd said what he felt needed to be said and walked away.

When he did, Hix hadn't been ticked at what he'd said or that the man had the damned nerve to walk right up to him and say it.

All he was thinking was wondering what was understandable to a deeply religious man like Pastor Keller (and in Hix's opinion he was even more deeply religious than his occupation had call for him being) to make him think Greta could miss church on a Sunday.

This was not his to know, so he forced himself to let that go and just be happy that nothing else reared up about Greta.

Including the news that he'd hooked up with her clearly hadn't filtered down to the kids.

They'd had an evening where they went to see a couple of houses that none of them liked, but that was the only shift in the norm.

So that was all good.

But the rest was not.

It was shit.

And it didn't just fill his mind and take his focus off a late-night movie.

It had been filling his mind all week.

Hell, all year.

And obviously all this shit had to do with Hope.

But right then it was centering on the fact that, since before she'd asked him to leave, when he'd pressed to get to the bottom of her issue that was making her so unhappy, she'd just clam up, give him a look full of hurt and say, "You know, Hix."

He didn't know.

He had no clue.

He just knew he'd asked repeatedly, demanded, threatened, then even got down to begging for her to let him in on it.

She hadn't done that.

All he got was more, "You *know*, Hix. *You know*."

And now he wasn't only pissed at how she was behaving, he was pissed she'd never had the courtesy and respect for the life they'd built together to give him a straight answer about why she'd torn it apart.

He was also uneasy about the fact that he might be pissed, but he wasn't infuriated.

His frustration was about courtesy and respect, not love and loyalty.

It wasn't about the fact that she'd broken his heart.

It was about the fact that he simply had the right to know why she had.

Through this, he was trying to hold on to other things about Hope. Things he'd need when she eventually snapped out of her snit and became the woman who, for the rest of his life, he'd have to deal with in appropriate ways that wouldn't make his kids uncomfortable.

Things like how she was whenever Shaw would get one of his many scrapes climbing trees, falling off his bike, skateboarding—taking care of their son and adjusting her mothering from cooing and babying to soothing and reassuring the older his boy got.

And the way her relationship changed with Corinne after she got her period. How they started to become not mother and daughter, but mother-friend/confidant and daughter, having their quiet talks in the kitchen together, giggling like best friends.

It was also how she sat beside him in that small hall with tears falling silently down her cheeks when Mamie performed in her first dance recital.

Mamie had been so little, and the girls up there were all over the place, some of them just standing and waving to their parents.

But Hope had been feeling so deeply, it spilled out on her face.

Pride, probably (because Mamie went through the routine, badly, but she was one of the few who did it).

Though he figured Hope was also realizing that was an indication that their baby was growing up and the next recital would be different, and the next, and the next, until Mamie was driving herself to dance class right before the time she drove away to meet life, and, like Hix, she loved that future for their daughter at the same time she dreaded it.

He also thought about the fact she'd never bitched that she did all the cooking.

He hated cooking, she knew that. She liked to do it up once in a while, but most of the time it was a chore.

He (and then Shaw) never gave her reason to have to take out the trash and he saw to the tending of the cars, the lawn, or if something was broken, he fixed it. But Hix knew none of that made up for her having to be in the kitchen every night. Even after she'd started working part-time for her dad when Mamie went into second grade, going full-time when their baby hit middle school, she did all the cooking.

But she never did any bitching.

Then there were their Christmas mornings.

Hope never opened her presents until the very end. Not to manipulate attention to herself, but because she was so enthralled by watching her family enjoy what they got, the holiday she always took pains to do up big for all of them, she forgot people wanted her to know she was loved too.

And there was how close she was with her mom. How she managed to still be the little girl her dad needed without making that nauseating. How she razzed her older brothers but was the first to show when someone was needed.

That had been his wife.

That had been the woman he loved.

That had been her part in the life they'd had.

He didn't know who she was now.

But that was the woman he needed to hold on to so his kids didn't have to negotiate awkward times at graduations, weddings, family gatherings.

He just didn't know if she kept up with the shit she was dishing out, if he'd be able to hold on to that.

And this was no longer about what she'd done to him and their family for reasons still unknown.

It was about the fact she had no problem dragging Greta into it.

I am, Greta had said, asserting her idiocy.

Like it wasn't his to know why she missed church, it wasn't his to understand what change came over her in the back room of Lou's salon, no matter how much it disturbed him.

He'd already picked her up, taken her home, slept with her, and left before he'd even walked to the bathroom to get rid of the condom she'd given him to use.

He was not that guy.

And she was not that girl.

She didn't need any more of his shit.

He didn't have the right to get up in hers.

But damn, on his couch, his kids under his roof, trying to get to sleep, he'd think of her mouth on him. Her hands. The feel of her hair. The hot, tight slick that had closed around him when he'd slid inside. The noises she'd made. The look on her beautiful face, her eyes staring right into his as he moved inside her.

He'd think of it and go hard.

On his couch.

His kids under his roof.

And not a day passed when not once, not a few times, but dozens of them, he'd think about her. How bad he'd wanted to laugh when she'd been so hilarious in her tizzy. How she let him in on everything just looking at him. How much it sucked things weren't different and he couldn't ask her out on a date, ask her about herself that time, be able to laugh when she was funny, get her to smile at him again.

And what her parting shot had meant to him.

She's a fool.

Hope had thrown him away. Their family. Their life. He'd taken that hit, and at the time thought he'd never recover because that hit had landed in his heart. Absolutely.

But it had also shaken his manhood.

She's a fool.

And with that, like a miracle worker, he'd recovered.

He was a trained investigator and he had been a loving husband. As both, in his mind for months he'd torn through everything with Hope to try and figure out where it'd gone wrong.

There was no evidence, no trail to follow, not one fucking thing.

She's a fool.

Except that.

Because that was the only thing the minimal evidence there was, was leading him to.

They'd had a good life.

She'd thrown it away without fighting for it, finding some way to make whatever was going wrong, go right.

Like a fool.

So maybe that was where he was now. Where Greta had put him. Pissed he didn't understand but no longer torn up about it.

And more, beginning to feel unsure he gave a shit anymore.

On that thought, the door opened and Shaw came through it.

"Hey, Dad," he greeted quietly.

"Hey, kid. Fun date?" Hix asked.

"Yeah," Shaw answered, walking in and stopping at the end of the coffee table. "Girls asleep?"

"Yup."

"You want me to help you pull out the couch?"

"Nope."

He watched in the light from the TV, the only light in the room, as his son's head turned to the set then back to his dad.

"You're watching *Smokey and the Bandit*?" Shaw asked.

Hix grinned up at him. "Your sister reminded me I haven't seen it in a while."

Shaw grinned back. "You should start using your middle initial like Sheriff Buford T. Justice. You can be Sheriff Hixon T. Drake."

"Actually has a ring to it," Hix joked.

Shaw chuckled, noting, "Good your middle name is Timothy and not William. Sheriff Hixon W. Drake would sound stupid."

"Son, I called myself Sheriff Hixon T. Drake, the stupid would start there."

Shaw chuckled again and began to move past the coffee table.

"You goin' to bed?" Hix asked.

"Yeah," Shaw answered.

"Right. Sleep good. See you in the morning."

"Junk Sunday," Shaw mumbled.

Hix took his gaze off his son and grinned at his TV.

"Dad?"

Hix looked back to his boy, now standing in the mouth of the hall, turned again to face him.

"Yeah, kid?"

"I'm here."

He felt his brows draw together. "See that, Shaw."

"I mean, I'm home. Nothin' will happen, but if one of the girls needs anything, I'm home, you wanna go to her."

Hix felt a burning in his chest.

"Sorry?" he forced out.

Shaw stepped one step from his place into the room.

"Wendy and her mom go to her at the salon. Her mom heard from someone, and Wendy heard her mom talking to a friend about it. I don't think the girls know, but Wendy told me just in case someone said something to me about it."

Shit.

"Shaw—"

That was all he got out before his boy hurried on.

"Wendy says she's super cool, Dad. Says she's funny, and she's like you, she's old, but not *old* old. And she wears really cool clothes that Wendy says a lot of girls at school try to copy. But her clothes aren't like trying-too-hard cool. Like she's old but she doesn't get that she's old so she still tries to be young."

"She isn't old," Hix said low.

"I know, I mean she's old*er*, like you," Shaw said quickly.

So maybe things with Greta had filtered down to at least one of his kids.

That was unfortunate.

But thank Christ the one it filtered down to was the oldest and his boy.

He still wasn't going to have this conversation with Shaw.

So Hix shook his head. "Shaw, I don't think we should—"

"I went by the salon. Stood across the street so she wouldn't see me. Looked at her. Dad, she's real pretty." He paused then whispered, "Even prettier than Mom."

That sent Hix to his feet and he slowly walked to his son, stood close and put a hand on his shoulder.

"I know you're angry with your mom—"

"It's not that."

"It probably is, kid."

"I just...just..." Shaw couldn't finish.

"You just what, buddy?" Hix asked quietly.

"I just...well, I like Wendy. She's cool too. But I think...well, what I think is, I like who I am when I'm around her."

Oh yeah.

He had to have another look at this Wendy.

"And you are...I'm you," he went on.

"You're me," Hix stated, not quite getting it.

"You're better if you have a woman to look after."

Hix drew in a breath and took his hand from Shaw's shoulder.

"It's like, well, like...like..." Shaw kept on. "Like you're a little lost, not havin' that."

Yeah.

He was.

He was not that guy who got off and took off.

He was also not that guy who built a life with a woman and a family but did it always wondering if the grass would be greener with some other woman, living some other life. And he was not that guy who was about making his woman look after him, take care of his needs.

He'd never been any of those guys.

He'd been what his father had taught him to be.

A man whose reason for being was to look after his woman and his family.

He'd lost half of that and he didn't know how to be that guy—the guy who didn't have that half.

He just hated that his boy had noticed it.

"Son—"

"Wendy's dad is sick, Dad."

"Shit," Hix whispered.

"She doesn't want anybody to know. There's some treatment he's gonna try. They don't know how it's gonna go but they think maybe it'll be okay. But she doesn't talk about it. Not to anybody. Not to any of her crew. But she does talk about it to me. And I *like* that."

"You should, Shaw. Says a lot about the trust she's got in you. And you should take care of that, son. It's maybe the most important thing you've ever had to do."

"I know."

After his boy gave him the weight of that, Hix felt Shaw's attention intensify.

"Should I not have told you?" he asked, sounding concerned.

"No. It's between you and me and it'll stay that way."

"Right," Shaw whispered. Then he said, "I know she sings at the Dew Drop and I'm just sayin', you should go."

Hix beat back a sigh. "I'm not gonna go."

"You should."

"I'm not."

"Okay, but you should, and you shouldn't not do it because you think you're protecting us or something. We get it." He lifted his shoulders and when they fell, they fell farther than he normally held them. "It's the way it's gonna be now."

Hix didn't like the look of that shoulder droop.

But he couldn't cure that. That was one of the many things only time could cure.

So he had to focus on what else was on his boy's mind.

"I hope you understand that I'm not showing you disrespect because I don't wanna share with my son what happened between me and Greta," Hix said. "But what I will share is that I think what you think happened is not what happened."

"Okay."

"So you can stop thinking about it."

"Right."

The way Shaw said that made a slither of something unpleasant drift down his spine.

So he asked, "What?"

"Nothin'," Shaw muttered, looking like he was going to make a turn back down the hall.

"Shaw, we share honesty, remember?" Hix pushed.

He stopped moving and looked to his dad.

"You hooked up with her," he stated.

"Again, kid, I'm not gonna share—"

"And that's it?" Shaw cut him off to ask.

"Sorry?" Hix asked back.

"So, you...what? You meet a pretty lady and get yourself some then scrape her off?"

That burning sensation came back to his chest.

"Shaw," he growled, thinking the way he said his son's name said it all.

He thought wrong.

"So, like, Corinne, Mamie when she gets old enough...Mom when she starts dating again, it's okay some guy hooks up with them and then just blows 'em off?"

"We're adults, and I'm sorry, Shaw, but this is something you don't know about."

"Everyone says that. But then everyone says you learn all you need to know about life in high school. I get that. I get that it's all real concentrated, all the cliques and unfair teachers doing crap that's not cool and you gotta put up with it, and losing at football games and learning how to live with that, and breaking up with girls or having them break up with you and beginning to have to worry about your future. I'm almost through all that and you don't think I get how it is?"

He had a point.

"It's more complicated than that," Hix informed him.

"People say that when they're trying not to see how simple stuff really is."

Shit.

He had a point there too.

"Greta understands how it is," he told his son.

"Really?"

Hix's body locked.

"God, you're the sheriff, Dad," Shaw said low. "You're like, the president of McCook County or somethin'. People, they..." He hesitated then forced out, "Know about you. About us. They pay attention and would even if you weren't the sheriff. But it's more because you're sheriff. And her? You just..." He did a quick shake of his head. "Whatever and then scrape her off? Folks think you're like a god or something. And you're a dude and dudes get away with that crap. But her? She does hair. She's pretty and dresses cool, but she does hair. It isn't nice, the way it is, people givin' guys a pass on stuff like that, but it's not the same for girls. It's still the way it is. Wendy's hair is awesome so I know she's good at what she does. People are still only gonna think she does hair and Mom is who she is 'cause a' Gramps and Gran and Uncle Cook and Reed and you. And *you're* the sheriff. So they'll think you work, bein' with Mom. They'll also think, you hook up with her and scrape her off, she's nobody. She just does hair."

"I'm not sure it would help matters, and it wouldn't be cool to her if I made her or anyone else think what happened was something it wasn't," Hix explained.

"Okay, so...go listen to her sing. You don't have to take her home and bone her. Just be her friend. You're her friend, folks'll get how it is and everyone will just settle into that. Not think she's just a hairdresser but also some slut or something that maybe other guys can have a go with and treat her the same way."

Hix drew in breath through his nose slowly and let it out just as slow, wondering if he was more troubled about the conversation he was having with his son or the fact his son somehow got to be so damned smart it was a little scary.

"You should take care of her, Dad. I know it's totally not fair, but girls at school that put out..." He again hesitated before he muttered, "I hope Mom's up in Corinne's face about not putting out. It isn't pretty."

"You hear other boys saying shit about girls, you shut that down," Hix ordered.

And he himself would have a word with his girl, no matter that he was looking forward to that a lot less than he was enjoying his current conversation, and he'd pretty much rather be anywhere than right there talking about what he was talking about with Shaw.

"Uh, duh, Dad."

And his son had respect.

He was glad of that but he wasn't surprised.

He'd learned that from his dad.

But now what was Hix teaching him?

Shit.

"I'll go. Have a drink with her between sets. But then I'll be right back, Shaw."

"Okay, or you can stay. I'm here. It'll all be cool you wanna go out and do something for yourself for once. I've got it covered."

"You're lucky you're such a good kid," Hix muttered. "If you weren't, I'd probably be more ticked at whatever your geography grade is gonna be."

"Brains come in a lot more forms than being able to call out the country when you see the flag for every team that comes out in the opening of the Olympic ceremonies," Shaw replied glibly.

"Whatever," Hix murmured, feeling his lips twitch. "Go to bed."

Shaw, obviously relieved at how their conversation had gone, faked a salute then turned down the hall.

He didn't get to his room before he called quietly, "Have fun, Dad."

Hix wasn't going to the Dew Drop to have fun.

He was going because his son was right, and Greta was too about Hope being on the warpath and he had a statement to make that should be declared to a larger audience than just Greta in the back room of the salon.

She was not a piece of ass. She was not open to be played with and speculated about.

She'd had his cock but she also had his regard.

He was not going to try to make her his friend. It had been a long time but he knew enough about his reaction to her, and had already had a taste of her he knew he wanted more of, that that would last about a second before he'd be trying to find ways to get her back into bed.

But people didn't need to know that.

They just needed to know he thought she was what she was.

A beautiful, funny lady who could sing really freaking great and could make jeans into a fashion statement and should be shown respect.

"Go to bed," he said to his son who was hesitating in his doorway.

"'Night, Dad," Shaw replied.

"'Night, kid," Hix returned.

His boy's door closed behind him.

Hix turned and rested his shoulders against the wall.

Then he pushed from it and walked down the hall to his room in hopes of getting a change of clothes and not waking his girls.

When Hix hit the Dew Drop, he didn't select a table like he did the last time.

He took a seat at the middle of the bar.

This made him still visible, but when he spoke with Greta, the intimacy of one of those little tables with their shaded lamps would not be there nor would it be communicated to anyone watching them.

Nor to Greta.

It wasn't lost on him he had a lot of attention as he made his way to the bar.

But that was why he was there so it also didn't bother him.

He was just glad Greta was obviously between sets, because soft jazz was playing in the background and the stage was empty. It gave him a chance to continue the effort he'd expended on his way there to get his shit together so he'd be able to hold it together when the time came they had their chat.

After he took his seat at the bar, he glanced at the bowl of hot nuts the bartender set in front of him, ordered a beer and surveyed the scene.

It was Saturday night, all the tables taken, all the booths, most of the stools at the bar, a few folks standing and talking, but no one at the bar waiting for a drink. This was because Gemini Jones kept plenty of servers on hand so his patrons could relax in their seats without worrying about when their next drink would come.

Hix also noted what he'd noted the first time he was there years ago with Hope.

There weren't a lot of places or occasions in McCook County that made you give up your jeans. Church. Weddings. Graduations. Anniversary parties. Jameson's Steak House in Dansboro.

And the Dew Drop.

So he, along with most of the other men, was wearing nice trousers and a dress shirt. The men not dressed like him wore suits.

That was the respect you showed the Dew Drop. There wasn't an official dress code. Then again, no one would ever dis the Dew or Gemini Jones by showing up in a way that would be frowned upon.

"Sheriff."

He turned his head and saw Jones himself standing beside him, looking at the bartender and lifting his chin at him for some reason.

"Gemini, I'm off-duty, but even if I was on, most times folks just call me Hix."

Gemini turned his attention to Hix and slashed a white smile at him.

"Then...Hix."

Hix didn't need to take Gemini in. Even with Hix not a regular at his club, Gemini wasn't a stranger in town or in the town's business. He went to Town Board meetings. He had kids at the school. He was involved.

He was also short, had his hair cut close to his scalp and a precisely groomed, thin mustache over his top lip. Even though he couldn't be more than five six, he was burly, had wide shoulders, sturdy legs and a stomach that protruded but didn't give any indication the man wasn't fit.

That said, his height or build didn't matter.

Not with Gemini.

With Gemini, it was about presence.

He had that, not just in his place, a place he'd inherited from his momma, who'd inherited it from her daddy and so on. A place he grew up in that was just him, every inch of it.

He was also that anywhere he went.

Why he had it was something you couldn't put your finger on and Hix had learned with that kind of thing, you didn't try. He was who he was to the Dew Drop, the town, the county, and since that was a force of class and intelligence, you didn't question it.

"She's in back, touching up perfection," Gemini told him, and Hix held back a sigh at his comment and what it shared he knew about why Hix was there.

"Like to have a word with her," Hix replied.

Gemini looked to his club but did it shaking his head and speaking to Hix. "She's back on in a few." His eyes went to Hix. "I'll get word to her for her next break."

"Thanks," Hix muttered.

"Always like repeat business, but 'specially glad to see you here," Gemini noted. "Word around town..." Gemini shrugged. "Started off good enough, then nothin' more juicy to gnaw on happened, things began to turn."

It didn't surprise Hix that Gemini was giving him indication he not only liked Greta, but looked after her.

And with the other info he shared about things beginning to turn, something Hix had not heard, now he knew it was good he'd taken his seventeen-year-old son's advice.

"Had my kids this week," Hix murmured.

"Mm-hmm," Gemini murmured back.

Hix shifted on his stool to face the man closer on, this regaining him Gemini's focus.

"You're makin' it clear she's your business, and I understand that. But with respect to you and the same you obviously give to Greta, just to say, we connected. She's a good woman. But we're not goin' there and she gets why. I'm here as a friend and 'cause I like to listen to her sing."

Gemini didn't break eye contact when he repeated, "Mm-hmm."

"That's all I'm gonna give you, man," Hix said low.

Gemini's head tipped to the side, but all he said was, "I'll get word to her you're here."

With that, he glided away, melting into his club with an ease borne of being born to it and a coolness that no one could imitate no matter how hard they tried.

The bartender had served his beer through this and Hix took a sip, watching the piano player come out before Greta made her return.

But when she did a minute later, he had to suck in breath.

She had a different dress on. This one a shiny dark-red satin that had gathers all around her middle and hips. The deep vee of the front dipped low to show cleavage, her arms were bare, the hem cut above her knee.

Her hair was pulled back in a huge mess of curls at her nape, fat curls falling around her face, the ends of some brushing her collarbone.

She also had big, rhinestone earrings dropping from her ears, more of that bling on a wrist, and a pair of spike-heeled sandals with big chunks of bling encircling her ankles and gold straps across her toes on her feet.

And her beautiful face was made up like it had been last Saturday.

Dark and bold.

Shit.

Fuck.

She was gorgeous.

So gorgeous, it took a beat for him to realize she was scanning the tables in front of the stage nervously as she gracefully, even in those heels, but also very quickly made her way to the piano player as subdued, respectful applause broke out at her appearance.

She bent to the piano player and said something. He shook his head. She put her hand on his arm and kept talking. He kept shaking his head, saying a few words, and then he was scanning the crowd.

Hix saw the piano player's glance linger slightly on him before he looked right in Greta's eyes and spoke very briefly.

She stiffened and paled before she turned away from him and walked equally stiffly to the mic set up at the end of the baby grand, center stage.

"Hey, ya'll," she said in it, and the applause that came after that was louder. "Thanks for hanging. Time to give you a bit more."

She barely finished saying that when the piano sounded and the clapping stopped instantly.

Not because she didn't deserve more.

Because they were glad she was back and they wanted silence so they could experience fully what she was about to give them.

And right then, what she gave them was Rihanna's "Stay."

It was also then he got why she'd had her conversation with the piano player.

She hadn't wanted to sing that song. A song he'd heard in passing but the words coming out of Greta, her piano player taking the mic above the keyboard to accompany her when the time came, he heard every fucking word.

He also knew, since she didn't want to sing them, just what they meant.

And each word beat into him as he watched her stand in front of that club and lose herself in the song, her eyes closing, her body not swaying an inch, her fingers staying wrapped loosely around the mic stand without budging, just her lips moved as she poured her yearning all over them.

All over him.

Shit.

Fuck.

She ended the song, smiling and not looking anywhere near the bar in a way he suspected she guessed that was where he was, while the patrons showed their approval and as the rest of the band—a drummer, two guys taking up guitars—walked up and took their positions on that small stage with her.

Once the band was ready, she immediately went into "Come Away with Me" by Norah Jones, and Hix heard it, he liked it, she sang it beautifully. But mostly, through that and the songs she sang after it, he sipped his beer and retreated back to where he had to go to pull his shit together so he'd have it tight when she walked up to him in that dress, those shoes, with her hair like that, her face like that, after she sang that first song.

When she completed the set, she said in her sweet voice through the applause to the audience, "Thank you. Gonna take a little break but I'll be back."

The applause ran deeper as she smiled, lifted her hand slightly in a lithe gesture of thanks and farewell-for-now and walked off the stage.

After she disappeared, Hix fought ordering another beer. It wouldn't make him drunk but that didn't matter. In his position, he had to live his life as an example.

Normally, this wasn't taxing.

But right then, he needed another freaking beer.

She came through some dark curtains hanging over a door to the left side of the room, and her eyes hit him briefly before she made her way to him slowly when someone stopped her, having to touch shoulders, say some words, bend over to listen to a few.

She finally broke free of her admirers and took the final steps to him.

"Hey, Hixon," she said softly, her chin tipped down a bit so she was looking under her lashes at him.

This didn't last long, but it was affective in a way he knew she didn't intend by the nervousness she couldn't quite hide she was holding her body, and then she glanced at the bartender.

"On it, Greta," the bartender said.

She finally looked fully at him from where she was stopped at his side.

He turned his stool to face her and said low, "Hey, Greta."

She looked surreptitiously side to side, noting the stool to his left was empty, the one behind him had a man's ass on it, but Hix knew even though his back was to him that that guy was turned to his date beside him.

Her attention came back to Hix as she stepped a step closer.

Different perfume this time. Deeper.

Sultry.

Damn.

"Uh...this isn't exactly a smoke signal, darlin'," she murmured.

Hix couldn't stop his smile.

Her eyes dropped to it then immediately looked away.

"Yeah," he agreed.

She smiled politely beyond him, and even polite, he felt that hit his gut. Then she reached beyond him and he felt that hit his gut too as she took up what looked like sparkling water on the rocks in a tall, thin glass with a curved, dark-blue straw and looked again at him.

"So, what are you doing here?" she asked, put the straw between red-painted lips and sucked.

Him being there was the right thing to do.

But her looking like that, right there with him, sucking on a straw with those red lips, that right thing was killing him.

"Met this woman who sings here. She's talented. So I thought I'd take in the show."

"Unh-hunh," she mumbled, staring into his eyes.

He leaned closer to her and watched her brace.

Yup.

Killing him.

"Maybe some other time I'll explain shit a lot more fully to you. But had reason to think on things, and what I thought was that things might not be what they could have been but that doesn't mean I can't enjoy your singing. It also doesn't mean this can't be cool between us. You're smart. You're funny. No one on this earth can have too many friends, they're the good type of friend. So there's no reason why we can't have that even if we can't have the other."

This made her surprised, and as he was learning was all Greta, she didn't hide it.

"You want to be my friend?"

That made Hix go still.

Shit, he hadn't thought how that would sound.

"I didn't mean—" he started quickly.

But he stopped when she tipped back her head and busted out laughing.

Christ, even that sounded like a song.

She looked back at him, and still chuckling, stated, "You crack me up."

He felt his lips give a relieved twitch as he replied, "Noticed that."

"Might be good to have the county sheriff as a friend."

He grinned flat out and jokingly warned, "A friend doesn't ask a friend to fix their speeding tickets."

She chuckled again but he got serious.

"Hope give you any more shit?"

She got serious too.

"Nope."

With that, she slid onto the stool beside him and rested her arm and her drink with her fingers around it on the bar.

This time, her nails were painted gold.

But her toes were painted red.

He turned on his stool toward her.

"You?" she asked.

"Not yet."

A look of concern came over her face. "Has she…?"

She said nothing more so Hix prompted, "Has she what?"

"None of my business," she muttered to her glass.

He leaned into her again and said quietly, "Friends don't ask friends to fix speeding tickets but they do ask questions if they give a shit."

She lifted her gaze to his.

"Is she dragging your kids into this?"

He leaned away and shook his head. "No. Not yet and hope to God not ever. She does that, the girls'll have to be married in a church the size of a football stadium for her to be far enough away from me in the front pew."

She smiled at him, he liked it, buried that, but her smile slid away.

"Sucks, you have to think about stuff like that," she noted gently.

"Yeah," he agreed.

"I don't know her real well," she shared. "And I reckon you know there's been a lot of talk."

"Yeah, I know that," he muttered.

She gave him a somewhat sad but understanding smile before she continued, "But everyone says she's a nice lady. Divorce is tough. It takes its toll. But things'll get better."

He tipped his head to the side. "You know about divorce?"

She lifted her drink and put her straw to her lips, sucked up some and put it back to the bar before she said, "Yeah."

"Kids?" he asked.

She shook her head.

"How long were you with him?"

"Nine years."

Interesting.

He knew by the look of her that she wasn't twenty-two. But he also figured she wasn't close to Hope's age.

But married with no kids in nine years?

He didn't ask. Their "friendship" all of five minutes long, it wasn't his place.

He decided to change the subject.

"How long you been singing?"

"Since choir in junior high. Won the state competitions a couple of years going in high school. Knew I didn't have it in me to make the big time but I like doing it. It's extra money which never hurts, so I'd get gigs here and there like this one. Friday and Saturday only, when they don't have an act that's come into town." She shot him another smile. "Bonus, I get to do up my hair and wear a pretty dress, even in the fields of Nebraska, so it's fun."

"Get that but not sure about you not having what it takes to make the big time," he noted.

"Is our sheriff A&R for a hot record label on the side?" she teased.

"Nope. But my ears know what they're hearing."

"That's sweet," she whispered in a way she told him plainly it also meant more to her. She straightened in her chair, took another sip from her water, and stated, "But life has a way of telling you where you're supposed to be and what you're supposed to be doing. Had someone once tell me after a gig in Denver he wanted me to try out to be a backup singer for a big act. But..." she lifted her well-formed shoulders, "the time wasn't right."

"Time is always right to chase your dreams."

At that, she gave him a full white smile, lighting the space around him, making him fight back a blink.

"Born with a nice voice, a great head of hair and a good hold on common sense," she declared. "And don't think I'm bragging, I'm just saying it like it is. Promise you, if I could belt it out like Céline or Christina, I would not be sitting here with you. I'd be ignoring your ass as I swanned by you at a club with a hundred times this capacity surrounded by my bodyguards. But I just don't, Hixon. And honestly, I'm cool with that."

And honestly, she was. Nothing about her said she wasn't. No hesitance in tone. No rigidity in her frame. No shadows behind her eyes.

"Well, then that makes McCook lucky since the Dew Drop got you," he replied.

"And that's sweet too." She shifted in her seat and tilted her head. "Sorry, but I probably need to get back. You stayin'?"

"Got my kids, Greta. Might catch some of the next set but should get home to them."

"Of course," she murmured then reached out and touched his

wrist fleetingly before she whispered, "I'm real glad you came, Hixon."

"Me too, Greta."

She gave him another blinding smile before she slid off her stool and glided away with much the same skill as Gemini had done, but with a far more attention-grabbing sway of her ass.

He decided to take in a couple of songs to make things even more clear to the folks who were no doubt watching and then he'd get home to his kids.

And maybe, he might come again next Saturday.

It hadn't been easy, at first.

Then Greta made it not hard.

So maybe they could be friends.

These were his thoughts when his eyes left her ass and went to the back of her head as she abruptly stopped moving to the curtained door.

What he saw instantly made his entire body grow tense.

She was talking to a man in a way that she held her expressive frame in a posture of detachment. Her head turned to the side and he saw her profile was guarded.

He then saw Gemini swoop in and put a hand on the small of her back, saying something to the man even as he guided Greta to the curtains.

She disappeared through.

The man stared at the curtains even after they'd closed behind her.

Gemini positioned himself to the side of them, providing presence and making a point.

The man moved back to a table.

Hix watched him and he watched how his gaze fixed on a stage that didn't have a soul on it.

At that point, Hix ordered another beer.

And settled in.

This time Hix's attention being on the man at the table at the edge of it, he found when Greta returned to the stage that his instincts, as usual, weren't wrong.

He'd been so caught up in Greta, he hadn't noticed.

Now, he noticed.

So he did not leave a couple of songs into her set.

He didn't leave at all.

Chapter 7

Ten-Four

Hixon

After Greta's final set (which had been the second one he saw), Hix waited outside in the big graveled area around the Dew, his back to his Bronco, shoulders leaning against it, arms crossed on his chest, while the patrons drove away.

He was not alone.

One of Gemini's men stood outside the front door, eyes to the lot, manner alert.

Hix still didn't move.

The cars thinned until Hix figured the ones left were staff, Gemini's...

And Greta's.

Except a Mercedes sedan that Hix could see the head of the man in the driver's seat, the back of the car to him, undoubtedly his eyes on Hix through the rearview mirror.

So yeah.

Hix didn't move.

What he did was see Gemini come out and stand in the front

door next to his man. Gemini's eyes went from Hix to the Mercedes back to Hix. It then seemed he took his time coming to a decision.

When he came to it, he strolled to Hix at the back of his Bronco.

"Hix," he greeted when he stopped a couple of feet away.

"Gemini," Hix replied.

"With respect to you, just to say, we take care of things like this ourselves at the Dew."

He took the respect but he still didn't feel real great about the rest of what Gemini had to say.

"Things like this happen frequently?" Hix asked.

"No. But it's a club. And since she came to us, I'm thinkin' you get more than most that Greta is Greta."

Oh, he got that.

"We haven't had problems," Gemini continued. "But we've had to make things clear on an occasion or two."

Right.

"I'll see her home," he announced.

"Hix, my man, she'll be good and he won't be back."

"I'll see her home."

They locked eyes.

They did this awhile.

Hix broke it, jerking his head toward the car. "He been here before?"

Gemini turned to the side to swing his gaze also toward the car.

Asshole knew he had company and was still goddamned sitting there.

Gemini swung his attention back to Hix.

"He was a regular even before Greta. She showed, got the vibe immediately, though it was contained." He paused before he gave Hix what was needed. "Vibe changed last Saturday. You didn't know it was fizzling, caught up in other things you didn't catch it when the change came. But I did. So he's showed tonight, made his approach, it tweaked Greta, he won't be back."

"Man's got some balls, you out here, your man right there, me out here, sittin' in his car makin' plain his intentions. You know who he is?"

"I know he won't be back and I know Greta will be good."

"I know that last part too."

They did battle with their eyes again, and it was Hix who broke it again.

"You take him. I'll take her. I'll also take a phone call on Monday, you lettin' me know all's good."

With a sigh, Gemini said, "And I'll take that deal."

"Either I go back in or I want one of your men walkin' her out here. Sayin' that, I'd rather stay right where I am and have one of your men walk her out here. He's makin' it clear he's ignoring our message, that doesn't mean it shouldn't keep coming."

"I see that play," Gemini murmured. "She'll be escorted to you. I gotta make arrangements to get her car back to her again?"

So Gemini took care of Greta's car last Sunday.

"I'll follow her home."

Gemini nodded and apparently that was that.

He said not another word before he moved back to the front door of the club.

Staffers hit their cars and took off.

No one approached the man in his car.

This communicated to Hix that whatever Gemini did to "take care of shit like this" he didn't want the sheriff watching.

That didn't make him all that comfortable, but he couldn't focus on that then.

This was due to the fact that a big, black man came out, his hand on Greta's arm.

She still had on her dress, her heels, and he reckoned her car was not the Navigator left in the lot, or the Camaro, the Charger or the Lexus.

It was the blue Jeep Cherokee.

The man didn't lead her to the Cherokee.

He led her to Hix.

And she made it plain from top to toe this didn't make her happy.

So not happy, she only shot a glare at the man who dropped his hand from her arm when he stopped her at Hix. She didn't express gratitude or say good-bye as he turned without a word himself and walked back to the club.

"Another smoke signal I missed?" she asked irritably.

"Man in the car over there is an admirer. So I'm walkin' you to yours then I'm followin' you home then I'm makin' sure you're locked in safe and sound."

Dread chased the annoyance from her face as she looked toward the car.

Yeah, she'd read the guy and what she'd read had tweaked her.

"God, totally knew that guy was a creep."

"You get a lot of creeps?" he asked, but he suspected he knew.

For a woman like Greta, a man could turn creep real easy he had even an inkling of that in him.

"I don't know," she murmured, slowly shifting her gaze back to Hix. "If Gemini reads it, he takes care of it and doesn't share."

He felt his mouth get tight. "That's not doing you any favors, Greta. You should know when you gotta keep your eyes open."

"I do that all the time anyway, Gemini knows that," she replied. "So I reckon he just doesn't want me freaked."

Hix couldn't fault that at the same time he could.

But it was late. She was probably tired and he had kids sleeping under his roof. Now was not the time for that debate.

"You the Cherokee?" he asked.

She nodded.

He moved, pushing from the Bronco, dropping his arms and taking her elbow.

He walked her there and stood beside her as she opened the door and folded in.

She did that thing only some women do, not putting one foot then the other in the car, instead aiming her ass at the seat, pulling herself up and lifting both legs in like a lady.

Christ, everything about her called straight to his dick.

She looked up at him.

He issued orders.

"You can reverse out, but don't start on your way until my headlights are behind you. Phone out of your bag, on the seat, in reach. Your car probably locks automatically. Don't care. Lock it manually. You with me?"

She nodded but asked, "Do you think he's *that* much of a creep?"

"I think I don't wanna find out, but you'll want that less."

"Right," she mumbled.

"Curious," he continued. "Gemini have someone escort you to the car after every gig?"

She nodded.

He nodded back. "Good. Now after every gig, you lock your doors immediately and ride home with your phone like that. Then you walk to the door of your house with your phone in your hand."

"You're creeping me out, Hixon," she shared.

"It's after two in the morning, you're a woman alone, and if you don't get me, I'll give you a copy of *In Cold Blood*."

Her eyes got big but her lips muttered, "I've read it, message received, say no more."

He grinned at her and waited until she opened her bag, got out her phone, put the bag on the seat beside her with the phone on top, all of this she did with her door open.

When she went for her seatbelt, he closed her door and moved purposefully slowly to his truck.

He swung in, watching her Cherokee move in the lot through windows and mirrors as he belted up, started up, circled in the now-open lot and got up on her tail where she was idling.

She drove and he followed.

When they made it to her house, she slid up the drive to the side and stopped in front of the big detached garage that sat at the back.

Unlike the Saturday before, when he'd parked at the curb, he drove up the driveway right behind her.

He got out with eyes to her, watching her come out unlike she gone in.

One heel attached to a shapely leg down then the other, and she was out.

He pulled in a breath as he moved to her.

She closed her door, beeped the locks and let him take her elbow as they moved to the side door he figured led to her kitchen.

She opened the screen door she'd already put the storm windows in even though they were in Indian summer. She unlocked the kitchen door, moving through, switching on the lights.

Hix followed her.

He had not paid any mind to her house the last time he was there. This mostly because he kissed her the minute she'd let him in the front door, and he kept doing it as they made their way up to her bedroom. He hadn't had it in him to take anything in on the way out.

But right then, he saw the kitchen he was expecting in that house, but not a kitchen he would expect of her.

Totally redone but still looking old, the green of the cabinets and center island was a shade of soft mint. The countertops all butcher block. Drop porcelain farmer's sink. Flagstone floors. Long, spiked, old-fashioned brass hinges on cupboards, brass cup grips on the drawers, simple brass handles on the cabinets.

She had plants decorating the space here and there. Modest but decorative wreaths arranged nicely on the walls. Bright pottery on shelves. Some wicker. Pots and utensils on display on hooks. And oddly, but it looked good, a little lamp with a tall, thin base on the edge of a counter.

The high windows over the sink would make it sunny, but to give privacy, sheer white shades were down, starting a ways from the top so nothing obstructed the sun there, even sheers.

It was a country kitchen in a home in a sleepy county in Nebraska, and she looked like she belonged nowhere near it in that red satin dress, those shoes, her bling, with her hair arranged like that at her nape.

"You redo this?" he asked after he'd looked around.

"Old owners. This, the porch and the bathrooms did it for me," she answered.

He verbalized his thoughts. "You in that dress don't seem to belong here."

She studied her surroundings like she'd never seen them before.

Still in her perusal, she murmured, "Funny, the minute I walked into this place, I knew I didn't belong anywhere else."

That said something about her with all that was happening with Hix in that moment he couldn't afford the headspace to decipher.

Without him telling his mouth to do it, Hix shared, "Last place I wanted to be from the minute I hit Glossop was here."

Her attention came to him. "Where were you before?"

"Indy."

Her pretty lips tipped up. "That's not exactly cosmopolitan, Hixon."

"More than here."

"You got me on that," she muttered and tilted her head. "Are you saying you miss the city?"

He twitched his shoulders. "Guess I like things complicated."

"Yeah," she whispered.

Shit.

She put a hand to her island, moving slow, tentative, like she didn't know where it was or if her aim would hit it, and noted, "Gemini would have seen me home."

"I know, he shared that with me."

Just as slow, but not as tentative, she ran her teeth over her lower lip before she repeated with one addition, "Gemini would have seen me home, Hixon."

That time, Hix didn't reply.

"Taking care of your citizens, Sheriff?" she whispered.

He replied to that.

"No, Greta."

He watched her chest move as her breathing escalated.

Then he watched as her lips parted to let more air in.

And finally, he watched her mouth move as she said quietly, "You need to go."

"Yeah."

He didn't move.

She didn't move.

She just stood there in that damned dress and those damned shoes with all that great freaking hair around her beautiful face and breathed.

"This isn't smart," she whispered.

She was totally right.

He said nothing.

"We're gonna do it anyway, aren't we?" she asked.

He looked into her eyes and knew it was not at all smart.

But they were going to do it anyway.

"Yeah," he whispered.

She took in a big breath and her chest heaved with it, the fullness at the insides of her breasts exposed at the vee of her dress pushing against the material.

She took in another.

And then with a low noise that came from deep in her throat that he felt score straight to his cock, she took the first step, the second, third, and she was in his arms.

She did that, came to him. It was him that dropped his head and his lips bore down on hers.

Hers opened. He swept his tongue in and instantly pivoted her, walking her backwards toward the hall door.

And the stairs.

He had her zipper down in the hall.

She had his shirt untucked at the foot of the stairs.

He had her dress down to her waist by the middle of them.

She had his belt undone by the top.

All this they did with their mouths attached, tongues dancing.

He shimmied the dress over her hips at the side of her bed while she fumbled with the buttons of his shirt.

Her dress had fallen to her feet and she'd gotten enough buttons undone he could slip the ones through at his cuffs and tear it over his head. He did this as he toed off his shoes.

The second he dropped his shirt, his hands went to her ass, lifted her up and her legs circled him. Hix put a knee to her bed and then both of them in it.

He kissed her and took the kiss deeper, made it last, and only disengaged to bend down to pull off his socks.

He only got that done before she reached to him and tugged him back to her.

He didn't fight it.

Hands all over her, everywhere he could get them, he whispered in her ear, "You got another condom?"

Her hands diving in his trousers and shorts, skin to skin at his ass, in his ear she whispered her answer. "One left, Hix. But, baby, as hot as you are, take this sister's advice and slide some in your wallet."

His mouth went back to hers, his eyes looking in hers, seeing them sparkle even through the shadows.

"Thanks for the advice," he said, his smiling mouth moving against her also smiling mouth.

She nipped his bottom lip telling him she was done chatting.

He got her message and kissed her again.

Just like when she was fully clothed, something he didn't comprehend the last time he'd had her, when she was in bed, Greta communicated with everything she had. The sounds she made. Her movements. Arches. Stretches. Touches. Tastes. Nibbles. Scrapes. Squeezes.

It was all too good, sweet, hot, wet, he had to escape before it went out of his control.

And he did that making his way from working her breasts over her lacy bra, down her belly to between her legs.

He gently opened them.

"Hix," she whispered.

He put his mouth to her over her panties and then he put pressure on by pressing in his tongue.

"*Hix,*" she moaned, her fingers diving into his hair.

Right.

With that, he was not going to take this slow.

So he rolled away, dragged her panties down her legs, his cock jumping when they caught at one ankle on the bling of the shoe she was still wearing, and as he rolled back, she opened herself to him.

Jesus.

Shit.

He lowered to her, and with just a touch of his mouth, she pitched up into him and filled it.

He did not let that invitation slide.

Tossing her legs over his shoulders, he ate her, his hips uncontrollably grinding his cock into her mattress at the sounds she made, the taste of her on his tongue, the wet seeping into his mouth, the feel of her legs tightening around him, the points of her heels digging into his flesh.

He took from her and more and more until her hand fisted in his hair and she gasped, "Condom."

He turned his head, ran his lips along her thigh and murmured, "Not done, sweetheart."

Then he went back at her.

Jesus, so damned sweet, her fist in his hair shoved him deeper even as it seemed she wanted to pull him away, and she squirmed under him, pumping against him at the same time evading, until she forced out, "This...I'm...*baby.*"

She was on the edge.

Only then did he lift up and over her, catching her eyes, hers focusing on his with difficulty.

"Condom," he growled.

She rolled to her side immediately, reached and opened a drawer in her nightstand.

He pushed up to his knees between her legs and practically tore the packet out of her hand when she rolled back.

As he opened it and slid it out, she knifed up, got on her knees, opened his trousers and pulled them down his hips.

It was a huge fucking relief when his heavy, hard cock bounded free.

It was sweet, fucking torture when her hand wrapped around it.

He shoved her hand aside, rolled on the condom and grasped her hips.

Like she knew his thoughts, her fingers curled around his shoulders and she surged to him as he lifted her up. Her legs wrapped around. He let her go with one hand to grasp his cock and guide the way. Feeling her slick on the head, finding her, he drove her down.

Her fingers gripped his shoulders, her head fell back, her spine arched and her legs tightened around his ass as she ground into him, a long, low moan ripping up her throat.

Jesus, God, she was amazing.

He drew out, sunk in, again and again, and her head snapped forward, her forehead falling on his, one hand sliding to clutch him at the back of his neck, fingers up in his hair, the other arm rounding his shoulders as she bounced into his thrusts, her heavy breaths clashing with his.

"Need more?" he grunted, meaning did she want him at her clit.

"Hell..." she puffed. "No," she bit off her last as he filled her again.

He grinned and drove deep, pounding her down on him as he did it.

"Don't look so pleased with yourself, Sheriff," she huffed.

"Baby, buried deep in you, no other way I can look."

"Stop turning me on when I'm about to come," she demanded.

"Stop makin' me wanna laugh when *I'm* about to come," he returned.

Suddenly, on a downward movement, her body bucked in his

arms and her hold grew tighter, her voice lowering, going even more breathy as she whispered, "Hix."

He dropped her to her back and fully took over, thrusting hard, the wet sleek of her convulsing around him, and he wrapped his hand around the bottom of her jaw, hoping like all hell she was as close as she seemed.

"Greta," he grunted when her eyes stayed closed even after he positioned her to look at him.

Slowly they opened as she rocked under him, held on to him with every piece of her.

She'd done that the week before, and Christ, but he loved how she did it.

"Want you lookin' at me when you give that to me, sweetheart," he told her gruffly.

"Okay, Hix," she whispered, her nails digging in at his shoulder.

"Fuck, baby," he growled.

Her nails felt great.

Her hold felt better.

But her tight, wet pussy contracting around him...

The best.

"Hix."

"Stay with me, Greta."

"*Hix.*"

"Stick with me, sweetheart."

"*Can't,*" she breathed, tightened her hold on him and arched into him.

Her lips parted, her head took his hand with it as it turned slightly to the side, tipped slightly back, and the mewling rush of audible breath slipped out of her as she came.

He forced her head farther to the side, ran the edge of his teeth down the line of her neck and then rooted himself in her, sinking his teeth into the soft skin between neck and shoulder, her perfume filling his nostrils, his groan deep and long, his orgasm un-fucking-believably *tremendous*.

It took until he'd mostly recovered before the feel of her penetrated.

She still had a hold on him, she hadn't moved, but her intimate embrace felt somehow slack even as her body, which should be loose and soft under him, seemed braced.

He lifted his head and looked down at her.

Her eyes were open and her head was still turned to the side, but she seemed to be staring at nothing and not just because of the dark.

His fingers were still wrapped around her jaw so he used them to right her and bring her focus to him.

"You doin' okay?" he asked gently.

"Yeah," she murmured, lying right under him, but still removed.

"Greta—"

"That wasn't smart."

Hix traced her jaw with his thumb. "Maybe not, sweetheart, but it was good."

"Yeah," she agreed quietly but not convincingly.

"It wasn't good?" he asked.

"It was good, Hixon, but—"

He moved his thumb from her jaw to rub it along her lips.

"How about, when I'm still inside you, we not talk about how stupid that was and just be good with how good it was?"

"Okay," she mumbled.

She gave him that easy, he pressed his advantage. "And how about, I'm no longer inside you, we still don't focus on how stupid that was?"

She pulled in a deep breath and let it go.

He dipped closer to her and kept hold of her jaw. "We're allowed to do this, Greta. And we're allowed to feel how good it is."

"So when we talked earlier, when you said you wanted to be friends, what you meant was friends with benefits?"

Stung she'd even think that, much less say it, he lifted away and slid his hand from her jaw.

"No, that wasn't what I meant."

She made no reply.

He looked above her head and muttered, "Apparently I do like it complicated."

"It would seem that way."

He looked back down at her. "It's too soon."

"You've said that already."

"I'm not in a place where I can know for sure I'd do right by you."

"You've pretty much said that too."

"But I've never had better."

He heard her swift, stunned gasp.

"And you make me feel good in a lot of ways, including feeling good about bein' me, and I don't mean I feel that just from sleeping with you."

He felt the colossal shift in her mood even as he heard it in her whispered, "You don't feel good about you?"

"Sweetheart."

He said no more, not about to inflict a conversation that included mentioning his ex-wife on her while he was still semi-hard and inside her.

"Okay," she said quickly. "We'll not go there."

"Thanks," he murmured.

"But, uh...Hix, you're hot."

That made him grin as he repeated, "Thanks."

"No...like, really."

Shit, he was going to start laughing.

"Like I said, thanks."

"No," she repeated, lifted her hips slightly and stated, low, firm and *hot*, "like...*really*."

He couldn't help it, his body started shaking.

She kept talking.

"I mean, baby, you lifted me up and planted—"

"I was there."

"That was hot."

His body kept shaking. "I know, I was there."

"I have no idea how you got me upstairs, me walking backwards, the whole time kissing me and taking my dress off me," she declared. "That only happens in movies, and they have choreographers for that kind of thing."

His laughter became audible with his chuckling.

"Though," she carried on, "you know, there are other things that are good about you, not just how hot you are appearance-wise and how good you are in bed. I'm just not in the position to point them out seeing as my mind is still a little scrambled from the huge, honkin' orgasm you just gave me."

He kissed her quick and murmured, "Shut up, Greta."

All of a sudden, both her hands were framing his face.

And just as sudden, her voice had changed when she shared, "I get where you're at. And part of that is understanding you're trying to protect me. That means something to me, Hixon. A big something. So this time, we both know what this is. And it was good. We have that again with a far less confusing ending. Now it was what it was, life is what it is, and we're still friends. Right?"

Jesus.

Was she for real?

He sure as hell wasn't going to ask that question and get the wrong answer.

He was going to take what she gave him.

"Right, baby," he whispered.

She ran her thumbs along his cheekbones and noted, "You probably need to get back to your kids."

"I do. I'm sorry, Greta. I wouldn't—"

"Hix, shh," she shushed, one of her thumbs moving to his lips. "I get that too."

She was for real.

Real and sweet and everything he needed right then, willing to take it and give it and not expect anything in return.

"Move your thumb," he ordered against it.

She complied.

He dipped down and kissed her.

He continued to do it as he pulled out but ended it by lifting up and pressing his lips against her forehead.

With his lips still there, he asked, "What do I say right now to make you know how fuckin' great you are?"

"I think...that," she answered quietly, her arms she'd slid around him during their kiss giving him a squeeze.

He looked down on her. "Got a robe?"

He heard her hair move on the pillow with her nod.

"Where?" he asked.

"Hook on the back of the door to the bathroom."

"Stay here," he commanded.

"Okeydokey, smokey."

He was again chuckling when he rolled off of her, taking the corner of her comforter and throwing it over her when he got to his feet on the side of the bed.

He hitched up his pants, made his way to a door that was open, blackness inside, and found when he hit it that he'd guessed correctly. It was the bathroom.

He got used to the shadows, did what he had to do, fully righted his trousers, grabbed the robe and walked back out to her.

He bent over her when he got to her and hooked her around the waist.

Her hands flew to him as he lifted her out of bed and put her on her feet.

He handed her the robe.

She shrugged it on and took off her shoes while he found his things and got dressed.

Then he grabbed her hand and tugged her out of the room, holding it all the way to her kitchen door.

"Don't care there's no crime in this town, Greta, lock this behind me."

"Ten-four, good buddy."

He busted out laughing, hooking her waist again with his arm and pulling her to him for a kiss.

When he ended it, he lifted away just an inch and said, "You're really fuckin' great, Greta."

"Thanks, Hix. You are too."

He gave her a squeeze, a touch of the lips, then he let her go, opening the door and moving through.

He looked back as he did to see her standing in it, watching him go, the curls that were a mess at the nape of her neck were now still a mess at the nape of her neck with a bunch of them falling down her shoulders and chest.

She looked magnificent.

It was all her.

And what he gave to her.

Real and amazingly unreal.

Theirs.

For a really good night, a damned fine memory with not even a hint of shit attached.

"Lock,' he ordered.

"I know," she said, the words trembling with humor. "Yeesh. You can take the smokey out of his late seventies cop car and slap him in a late nineties Bronco, but you can't take the smokey outta the smokey."

He didn't think how her commentary oddly, but awesomely, fit with hints of what was happening in his life at that time.

He just shot her a grin, lifted his hand in a low wave, and walked to his truck, hearing her door close and the lock go.

He was in his truck, starting it up, when he saw her kitchen light go out.

He reversed from her drive and scanned the streets both ways to see if the Mercedes that was in the Dew's parking lot was anywhere to be seen.

He drove away, rounded the block three blocks down and drove back, riding down her street, still scanning for the car.

When he saw it wasn't there, he headed home to his apartment and his kids.

He had no idea what it meant, all that had gone down with Greta and him that night.

He just knew he felt a whole lot better driving away from her this time than he had the week before.

And most of that had to do with the fact he knew he'd left her feeling a whole lot better too.

But part of it had to do with the fact that he felt good. Plain, straight-up good for the first time in a really long time.

And he had Greta to thank for that too.

Chapter 8

Not Yet

Greta

Late the next morning on my way to Sunnydown, my dashboard told me I had a phone call.

I took it and didn't even get out a "Hey," before Lou said, "One-time thing?"

I grinned at my windshield.

"I take it that means Glossop's gossip mill is running a lot quicker than last week," I noted.

"I told you!" she hooted.

I shook my head, still grinning but also saying, "Don't get excited. He likes to listen to me sing. And he's a good guy. Funny. Sweet. We enjoy each other's company. We enjoy other things about each other too. And that's all there is. It's not going anywhere unless it goes somewhere, and I'm not expecting it to do that. I just like spending time with him and dig the fact he likes the same from me. That's where we are. That's it. So don't go planning any bachelorette parties."

"Girlfriend, I hear you. I don't *believe* you because my guess is, even if Hixon Drake doesn't think he's doing something with a purpose, he doesn't do dick without a purpose. But whatever. I hear you. You gotta live in that place in your head, you just do. And I'll make you wear a T-shirt at the salon that says 'She told me so' with an arrow pointing to my chair when that time comes."

If that time came, I'd gladly wear that shirt.

I just wasn't going to hold out for that time.

If Hixon Drake wanted to be friends and that friendship turned out it came with benefits, I was not going to say no. He was easy to be around. I felt like crowing at the top of my lungs any time I made him burst out into that gorgeous, deep laughter. He was spectacular in bed.

And he looked out for me, *me*, not a citizen of McCook County, but *me*.

So no.

Hell no.

I wasn't going to say no.

"And just to say," Lou's voice kept filling the car. "If this keeps going and next month you find the homecoming king and queen shoved right off their float with the ladies of Glossop slapping crowns on yours and Hix's heads and installing you on those thrones, don't be surprised."

"I'm sure that warning should bother me, but I'm not in the mood to care," I replied.

"I bet you aren't," she chortled. "Now give your girl something. On a scale of one to ten, how good is Hixon Drake in bed?"

Seven thousand, one hundred and twenty-two.

The lift-me-up-and-plant-me-on-his-cock thing?

Forget about it.

"That's for me to know and you never to find out," I answered.

"You suck."

I started laughing.

Lou kept talking.

"Though if *he* sucked, at the good stuff that is, I figure you wouldn't allow there be a take two and convince yourself you guys are taking it slow. You'd find your sweet way to say *sayonara*."

"We're not taking it slow, Lou. There's nothing to take slow. We're just friends."

"Friends who do the nasty."

I laughed again. "Yeah, that kind of friends."

"You got that hair, those eyes, those teeth, that rack and that ass, so I already hate you. Now you're *friends* with Hixon Drake, I'm not sure I can stand to look at you."

Please.

She was tall, willowy and had a body that bore no testimony to the fact she'd had two kids.

She also had a face free of lines even though she was forty-four years old, had had her fair share of life stressors and then some. Not to mention she had that pixie look with the bow-shaped lips *á la* Janine Turner circa the *Northern Exposure* years, except her short hair had thick bangs that brushed her lashes.

She was gorgeous.

I didn't tell her that because she knew that's what I thought since I'd already told her that *ad nauseam*.

"You'll get over it by tomorrow," I told her.

"I'll try," she replied then asked, "You headed to Andy?"

"Yeah."

"Give him a hug from me and the girls."

Andy loved Lou.

And the girls.

Then again, Andy loved everybody.

"Will do."

"Have a good day with your baby bro, Greta. And see you tomorrow."

"See you, darlin'. Later."

"Later."

We disconnected. I kept driving. And I did it singing to a Sarah McLachlan tune on the radio without a care in the world.

This was because Hix was right. We were adults. We could have whatever the hell we wanted, however the hell we wanted it.

So what, Glossop had more churches than it had bars (one of the latter, three of the former)?

Somewhere else, not a small town in the Bible belt, no one would blink.

He had kids but no one would make us their business. I suspected even Hope wouldn't sink that low to score one on her ex.

So it was what it was and I *liked* what it was. I'd only dated two guys since I'd hit Glossop and only slept with one. He'd been nice, a farmer that lived too far out to make it a problem after I ended it, and I'd ended it because he wasn't all that interesting and he was terrible in the sack.

I didn't want kids and I didn't need a husband.

But friends.

You always needed friends.

So I'd take that.

I drove into the parking lot of Sunnydown seeing what I always saw when it was my day to spend with Andy.

My brother standing out front with a male staffer waiting for me.

I smiled at him and waved through the windshield as I found my parking spot, seeing Andy wave enthusiastically back.

I had two days off a week and essentially worked two jobs, so I didn't have a lot of time.

But anyway, Andy felt safer in the home, had been living in one for as long as his brain could competently remember, so it was a different kind of home to him.

Even so, I liked to get him out of it. Give him something else. New scenery. A shake up of his routine that wouldn't freak him out. So I tried to get out there one or two nights a week to take him out to dinner or bring some to him.

And we had our Sundays.

I always took him out on Sundays, and that day, while the weather was still good we were going to have a picnic on the river then go to my house to watch a movie and after that hit Tony's Pizzeria in Yucca. Once we'd had all that excitement, I'd take him back home.

Occasionally, he spent weekends with me, but since I sang Fridays and Saturdays, that was only when Gemini had another act in town.

All this worked for Andy. We talked on the phone in the evenings, he got to take some adventures and he was good where he was all the rest of the time. It would also be good if he got a work placement. He liked people, he liked variety in the people he saw, and if it was steady and he knew his schedule, he settled in pretty easily.

But now he was good with the way things were.

Since it worked for Andy, it worked for me.

He was in my door the minute I opened it after I'd parked.

"Hey, buddy," I greeted, jumping down.

He just wrapped his arms around me and twisted his neck so he could rest his cheek on my shoulder, facing out.

He was a big guy. At least six feet. And at twenty-four years old, obviously, he had the body of a man.

If life had been different and he cared about things like keeping in shape, he'd also be different. Maybe his shoulders would be broad, not sloped. Maybe his little belly not there, but flat.

But things hadn't been different. He hadn't gone on to be that football player that started for the varsity team his sophomore year (he was that good), his dedication to his sport building his body into the man he'd become.

He was this Andy.

I hugged him back and he jumped away, grinning big at me and saying, "Comics."

I turned to the car, reached in, grabbed a plastic bag thick with comic books off the passenger seat and turned back to him.

He snatched them from me.

"Candy," he stated.

I grinned up at him, did the turn and grab thing and he snatched that bag from me.

He opened it, looked inside, and his face lit up when he turned his gaze to me.

"Snickers."

He was excited. When he was excited, he'd have word-finding problems.

He could speak full sentences and communicate well, unless he was excited, scared or having an episode.

"Of course, Snickers. They're your favorites. And Reese's and Butterfinger." I socked his arm. "I take care of my baby bro."

He nodded and jumped into me, giving me another hug where he put his cheek to my shoulder.

I rounded my arms around him, closed my eyes and took him in.

Not yet, my brain reminded me. *Not yet, Greta.*

When he pulled away, I ordered, "Take those to your room, buddy. I gotta stop at reception real quick. Then we'll go. That good for you?"

"Yeah, Ta-Ta."

Ta-Ta.

He'd called me that from way back.

It had been his first word.

When that became uncool, it was shortened to Ta.

It was bittersweet having Ta-Ta back.

He loped off three steps before he turned back to see if I was following.

I looked him over when he did.

I had no idea who his father was, like I had no idea my own, and the simple matter of that fact was that Mom probably didn't either, on both counts (or at least I'd trained myself to think that way instead of her actually knowing and never telling either of us, something she'd flatly refused to do to the point I'd quit asking).

But unlike me, who looked a lot like Mom, Andy had dark hair and dark eyes, a strong jaw and great cheekbones.

He also had a scar that puckered his skin from his right temple, separating at the side of his eye like a bolt of lightning, one end going up and over, obliterating the outer edge of his thick eyebrow, the other end going down and carving into his cheek all the way to his upper lip.

That scar ran into his scalp under his hair too, what with it being where his head had slammed into the side window, shattering it and going through.

Though just as much damage had occurred when his head was bounced violently around on his neck, his brain slamming back and forth into his brainpan as the car lifted and rolled, only for the other car to hit them, stop them rolling, but making Andy crash his head into the front windshield.

The side impact had ripped open his skin and fractured his skull.

The front impact had just added insult to injury.

His right side had been crushed, so I knew, under his clothes there were a bevy of scars I couldn't see.

Mom, on the other hand, had sustained a severe concussion, a fractured wrist, and seven broken ribs.

It didn't help matters for Andy that it had taken firefighters almost an hour to cut him, unconscious, out of the wreckage.

Once they'd gotten her out, Mom had walked away on her own two feet. Gingerly, I was sure (I wasn't there, just there for the aftermath).

But she'd done it.

His smile at me took my attention from my thoughts, and when he saw I was following him, he loped to the building and went through the door.

I did too, pulling an envelope out of my purse.

As I made it through the doors, I saw the staffer who'd been outside with Andy walking down a hall but doing it turned to me.

"Hey, Greta," he greeted.

"Hey, Sean," I called back. "Thanks for waiting with him."

He gave me a, "Never a problem," with a brief wave and kept

walking.

I went to Renatta at the reception desk.

"Hey, Greta," Renatta said.

"Hey, girl." I slid the envelope on the shelf above her desk to her. "This month."

"Cool," she replied, reaching out to take it. "We'll get this processed. Thanks."

"Thanks back at cha." I went on as she made a move to get out of her seat, "Have a good one."

"Will do, and enjoy the picnic with Andy," she returned, getting up and moving to the office at the back with my envelope that had in it my monthly invoice and the check to pay it. "He's been talking about your picnic all week."

"Awesome," I replied. "Glad he's looking forward to it."

"He always looks forward to his big sis," she said on a smile and disappeared in the office.

I looked down the hall where Andy's room was.

It was clean, wide, well-lit and had nice pictures on the walls, bulletin boards covered in notices on bright paper and stuff the tenants had made.

I couldn't have this, if not for Keith. If it wasn't for him, I could likely never give anything this good to Andy.

Keith and I had been dating for eight months when Mom had nearly killed my brother.

And from the impact of that car right into Andy's door then after, Keith had taken care of everything. Hospital bills Mom's shitty insurance didn't fully cover. Physical and occupational therapy her shitty insurance also didn't fully cover. Then his first home.

He'd asked me to marry him two months into Andy's recovery and two months after that we'd had a small affair in Vegas that was quick, classy (or as classy as Vegas could be) and led to a four-day honeymoon that started there and ended in a cabin by Lake Powell.

That had been my decision. Keith was taking care of Andy, I didn't have the money for a big to-do, I wasn't in the mood for it with what had happened to my brother, so I didn't want Keith spending the money even though he said he didn't care. He just wanted me to have what I wanted.

That had been Keith.

He always just wanted me to have what I wanted.

But he was the hotshot, genius house flipper who'd made a mint from the first house he bought, gutted, renovated and turned over when he was twenty-two and kept doing that to more and more houses with bigger and bigger teams until that very day.

I was a hairdresser.

He was great with Andy, before and after the accident. He hated my mother with every fiber of his being (also before and after the accident).

And he loved me.

But I felt it. How much he could give. How much I couldn't.

He kept giving and giving.

I knew I'd use him all up.

And I did.

But it was Keith who'd felt guilty about it. Guilty enough, he forced a divorce settlement on me that I didn't want, at first refused, but after he sat me down and laid it out, I knew not only did he need to do it, I needed to take it.

This meant my house in Glossop was paid for. The furniture in it was paid for. So was my Cherokee.

And I had enough to pay for Andy's home for a good spell.

In the meantime, I had so low overhead, if I was careful, and with the extra I got from Gemini, I could keep that balance healthy and therefore keep Andy safe for a long time. Not only doing that, but having a decent life for myself in the process.

So Keith looked out for me even though Keith was gone.

And he looked out for Andy the same.

In fact, he'd been out three times since I'd moved there, leaving behind Lawyer Barbie, coming to visit with Andy and check in on me.

He'd also arranged with staff to pay the monthly bills all three times he'd come and had taken Andy out to buy new clothes.

That had upset me. He was already paying those bills even no longer married to me.

But that was Keith. He got annoyed when I confronted him about it so I shut up because the least I could save him was that.

Andy came out of his room, taking me from my thoughts, and we walked out, both of us calling our good-byes to Renatta as we went.

We climbed into the Cherokee, buckled up and headed to the river with me telling Andy what was contained in the picnic in the back.

He approved.

Then he said, "Football."

I glanced at him. "Football?"

He looked from out the windshield to me. "Football, Ta-Ta. It's on TV."

"Yep," I said. "'Tis the season."

"Can we go and watch a game?"

My heart lurched, my hands on the steering wheel tightened, but I forced my voice to light when I asked, "You wanna go to one at the high school?"

He'd never asked me to do that. Keith had taken him to Broncos' games, just the two of them, but Andy had never asked me.

And I'd never gone with Keith and Andy because I couldn't. I couldn't hack it. I hadn't been to a football game since the one I'd watched my brother play in the day before my mother picked him up from a party, drunk out of her brain, and shot into a dual carriageway she should have stopped at, getting hit by a car that was probably going about sixty miles an hour, only to fly into the oncoming lanes and get hit there too.

"Yeah," he answered excitedly. "Can we?"

"Sure, honey," I said softly. "I'll find out the schedule and talk to Gemini."

"Okay."

I glanced at him again and saw he was looking back out the

windshield.

He spoke when I aimed my gaze the same way.

"Can we go see Gemini again?"

On an outing, I'd taken him to the club so he could see where I sang. He'd met Gemini. And at Gemini's invitation, we'd been back several times.

Gemini was almost as good with Andy as Keith.

Then again, that was Gemini.

"Sure. I'll sort it all out."

"Okay."

"I forgot to give you Lou and the girls' hugs," I told him.

I felt his gaze when he replied, "You can give them to me at the river."

I grinned. "Will do, buddy."

"Give them back," he ordered.

"I will."

"Okay."

And that was that.

I kept grinning, only part of it forced, as I asked, "You want me to get you a Glossop Raiders sweatshirt to wear to the game?"

More excitement, this time a lot of it, from his, "Oh yeah!"

I stopped grinning in order to smile at the road and marked on my mental to-do list to go by the drugstore that had a section of fan gear at the back.

Maybe it wouldn't be too bad.

Because I'd be there with Andy.

"We'll eat hotdogs and nachos and drink big Cokes," Andy continued.

"Yup, baby bro, we'll do all that."

"And Lou and Snow and Maple can come with us."

Snow and Maple.

Lou's daughters.

Bill's names.

Lou had just been glad her husband had been so involved with wanting to name his daughters that she didn't fight too much what, exactly, he'd wanted to name them.

And in the end, as these things do, Snow and Maple became Snow and Maple. Snow, with her smile that sparkled like glitter, and Maple, who was sugary-sweet.

"Definitely."

"It'll be fun," he declared.

"Absolutely."

"Okay."

My brother fell silent.

I drove.

I did it not thinking about the fact that he'd started to drive, got his learner's permit, but he'd never handled a car on his own.

And he never would.

But the life he'd been supposed to lead had ended in one.

I did it thinking the fried chicken in the back that came from the deli at the grocery store in town was Andy's favorite.

And he was going to love it.

WE HAD OUR PICNIC.

Then we went home and watched *The Man from U.N.C.L.E.* on my TV.

After that, we went to Tony's Pizzeria, got a big pie and Andy got a huge bowl of spumoni ice cream that was triple the regular bowl but at the same cost, what Tony always sent out for Andy.

I took him back, got him sorted in his room, gave him a big hug, got one in return, and he had dug into his comic books before I'd walked out of his room.

He'd always been a reader and liked writing too. His grades in English Lit and Comp had been top-notch.

Now, he had some problems reading and writing but comic books were perfect. Thus he'd be through that huge pile before Tuesday, even if the staff kept their folks occupied with a variety of things, with Andy pitching in to help out because he was a lot more functional than many of them.

I walked out of Sunnydown, got in my car, and for some reason, I wasn't even at the town limits (way earlier than normal) before I had to start chanting.

"Not yet, Greta."

I hit the Glossop town limits.

"Not yet, girl."

I hit my neighborhood.

"Not yet, baby."

I drove up my driveway, switched off the car, jumped out and walked to the side door.

I let myself in, whispering, "Not yet."

I turned on the light on the counter in my kitchen that made the space seem so cozy.

Then I went into the living room and turned on the light dimmed low by the side of my couch.

I moved back into the kitchen, right to the stove, set the gas going and put on the kettle.

Only then did I turn to the island, brace my hands on the edge and let it happen like I always allowed myself to let it happen so I could deal.

In other words I let myself think of Andy's sloped shoulders and how he'd look if he'd been able to be the man he'd been becoming.

I let myself think of the fact that Andy had never, nor would ever drive a car by himself.

He'd also never read *In Cold Blood*, not because he couldn't, but because much of it he wouldn't remember even after he'd just read it and the going would be so tough, it would only frustrate him and send him into an episode.

He wouldn't ever have a girlfriend.

He wouldn't ever make love.

He wouldn't fall for someone, marry her, make babies with her, giving me nieces and nephews to spoil. Giving all of us big, crazy, loud holidays.

My brother, my baby, my Andy, he'd never realize a dream. He'd never even feel the despair because he hadn't realized one.

He might not even remember what happened that day.

I hadn't been right when I'd told Lou I'd never hoped for anything, dreamed anything.

I had.

For Andy.

From the moment he'd been put in my arms, I'd hoped and dreamed that he would have everything he could ever wish for. And I'd wanted to do everything I could to give him a life where he'd have the smarts and the strength to make that happen.

I'd wanted him to have all I'd never had. I'd wanted to make him feel he was never missing a thing.

I'd done all I could and he was on that road.

He was on the road to being *magnificent*.

Then she'd taken it all away.

From Andy.

From me.

Now he was a different kind of magnificent.

But that wasn't what I'd wanted for my Andy.

My eyes were shut tight holding the wet back when the kettle whistled.

My time was done.

I opened them.

I sniffed.

Then I turned around and made myself some tea.

I took it to my porch and picked up my book.

That night, I didn't take in the calm of my street.

I opened my book, and after the time it took me to force my mind to concentrate, I started reading.

I wouldn't let myself think again about all Andy had lost.

Not until next Sunday.

Chapter 9

It's Not That

Hixon

Hix walked into his department Monday morning to see Hal at his desk.

"Yo, Hix," Hal called and smiled a smile that Hix didn't like all that much. "Good weekend?"

Clearly, from his read on Hal's smile, news that Hix had been to the Dew and had waited outside for Greta had made the rounds.

"Yeah," he grunted, moving down the aisle toward his office.

As he got close to Hal's desk, the man unsurprisingly (considering it was Hal) had the balls to ask, "This hairdresser the reason Bets is acting like she's perpetually on the rag?"

Hix halted and turned only his head to his deputy.

He liked all his deputies—in their jobs and out of them—including Bets when she wasn't being a pain in his ass.

Not including Hal.

He was a good enough deputy.

But he was an asshole.

His voice said things Hix wasn't going to verbalize, but he still made them clear when he replied, "How 'bout I leave your private life to you, you let me have mine, and you don't say shit about Bets like that at all in anything owned by this county, like this building, your cruiser, during your time earning a paycheck or to anyone who's also on the county's dime."

What Hix hadn't verbalized was that Hal's private life included the fact he'd been a cop in Kansas City until his wife had become fed up with him chasing skirt.

She'd given him an ultimatum: they changed their lives in order to assist him in changing his ways or they were done.

Instead of cutting her loose, what he should have done, he'd changed their lives. They'd moved up to Glossop and he'd moved into his position as a deputy.

But he hadn't changed his ways.

He had a steady woman on the side and a couple of other not-as-steady ones he also saw.

Who he banged, and so many of them not being his wife, was unfortunately not something Hix could release him for.

Hal did the job, had a number of years on it, was as good at it as he could be, considering nothing ever happened, so Hix was stuck.

Therefore Hix put up with him.

But Larry only tolerated him.

And Bets tried to avoid him because he razzed her about Hix, also about being a rookie, and lastly she avoided him because he was an asshole.

Donna detested him and was professional enough to work beside him without hurling, but that was the extent of it.

This last came to a head after they'd solved the burning mystery of the farmer whose chickens were getting stolen (the farmer's daughter's boyfriend said farmer wouldn't let her date was doing the deed).

Donna and Hal had worked that, and after they sat in his office reporting on it, Donna had turned to Hal and declared, "If I have to sit in a squad and listen to your trashy sex talk with one of your floozies again, Hal, I'll forget about the protect-and-serve brotherhood and share with Ashlee you can't keep your dick in your pants. Don't test me. This is your only warning."

She'd gotten up after that and walked out.

Hal had turned to Hix, clearly feeling the brotherhood he didn't consider Donna a part of because she had a badge but not a dick would commiserate, but Hix just stared at him until the man spoke.

"I just—"

Hix had lifted a hand. "Not my business. But Donna's right. That shit does not happen on county time. You got life stuff with family and friends you need to deal with on the job, that's not an issue. You wanna talk like that with one of your women on the county's time, we got a problem. Now, you want my counsel, I'll tell you to keep your dick in your pants for anyone but your wife. You want my opinion, I don't like how it reflects on this department that you don't. Since you didn't ask my counsel or my opinion, I gotta keep my mouth shut about both. I won't, I find any more of your shit happens on the job."

"Everyone takes personal calls on the job," he'd defended.

"And right now I'm tellin' you, my deputies don't take *that* kind of personal call on the job," Hix returned.

Hal said nothing.

So Hix did.

"Feel we got that straight. Now, out."

Hal had slunk out and Hix had made a point not to schedule Donna on weekend call with Hal, nor had he put them on a case together.

It was working.

Just.

"Sorry, boss," Hal muttered.

Having been reminded of his place, something, thankfully, that Hix didn't have to do often, Hal looked that mix of chastised and pissed he pulled off so well.

He then cleared his throat and asked, "Larry phone in about the weekend?"

"Accident on 28," Hix told him. "Lots of damage to the cars, thankfully minimal damage to the people. He says his report is on my desk."

Hal nodded.

"Outpost had a thing but Betty-Jean handled it before Larry and Donna could hit it," Hix went on. "That's it."

"Right."

"Yeah," Hix said, dipped his chin and then walked the rest of the way to his office.

He didn't look at Hal as he settled himself and he also didn't think of Hal.

He'd had Junk Sunday with his kids. It had been great. Now was the not-so-great part, since they were off to Hope's after school and practices that day.

But also now he could turn his mind to something else, something his, and what he was turning it to was Greta.

He should have gotten her number before he left her.

He didn't.

He'd rectify that.

But that morning, after Lou's opened and he was sure Greta would be around, he was going to call down to the salon and ask her to meet him at the Harlequin for lunch that day.

He didn't care what that would say to anyone but Greta.

And what he hoped it would say to Greta was that Hix wanted to spend time with her in a place they couldn't lock lips and things would then get out of control.

Not that he didn't want that. Greta out of control was a very good thing.

He just wanted to get to know her better.

He liked looking at her. She made him laugh. There was stuff about her he was curious about and he wanted to know.

And she knew where he was in his life and his head, and she didn't care.

She was uncomplicated, the only thing in his life that had been in a long time. She gave him that freely, when he wasn't acting like a dick.

He liked it.

And he wanted more.

He could give it headspace, overthink it, fuck it up.

There was no reason.

She was just Greta. She made him laugh. She made him feel good.

So he wasn't going to make something simple, complicated.

He was just going to have lunch with a woman he liked to spend time with.

What came after that, he wouldn't give it headspace either.

His son had been right. He'd been living so long with trying to hold together his family his only focus, he forgot to look after himself.

That wasn't teaching his kids good lessons.

If his two girls found out about Greta, he'd deal with that if or when the time came.

But Corinne may give her brother guff, she still looked up to him and listened. Mamie adored him and would follow his lead.

It might end up in disaster.

It might be great.

It didn't matter right then. He wasn't bringing her into his children's lives right then.

Right then it was two people getting together for lunch.

That was all Hix was thinking about.

And for the first time in a very long time, he was looking forward to something.

This lasted all of ten minutes, when the deep chill that came from the bullpen hit his office.

He looked from the report he was reading out the window to see Bets had arrived and she was avoiding Hal at the same time doing that to Hix.

If he was there before her, she came in and said hey.

This time, she was at her desk, staring at her computer like the impossible had happened and something interesting was on it.

She'd been like that all last week.

He'd give her that week.

Then he'd find some way to snap her ass out of it.

He was finishing up reading the report when another feel came from the bullpen.

He looked out the window and then he fought closing his eyes and tipping his face to the ceiling.

He just drew a breath in through his nostrils.

Letting it go, he got up and moved to the side of his desk, standing there but leaning his thigh into it as he watched his ex-father-in-law, Jep Schroeder, finish walking by the window to disappear down the back hall.

Hix aimed his eyes at the door and saw Jep walk through.

Jep had a thinning head of gray hair and a thick mustache over his top lip, and the only thing about it that had changed since Hix had met him was the color.

He also had a way about him that said plain he was a good ole boy in the right sense of that—he was a good man and he was not young.

"You got a minute, son?" Jep asked.

In all likelihood, he had all day.

And it had been setting itself up to be a good one, if Greta agreed to lunch.

Now?

Not so much.

"Jep, not sure this is a good idea," Hix said by way of answer.

Jep gave him a look that lasted a few beats before he replied, "Won't take much of your time, Hix. Promise. And I won't be much of a pain in your patoot. That's a promise too."

Hix sighed before he tilted up his chin.

Jep closed the door behind him and walked in. He stood behind a chair and put a hand on it when Hix didn't move from his place, leaning against his desk.

"We got a situation with Hope," Jep announced.

Well then...

Right.

He had to make this clear as best he could without hurting feelings or damaging a relationship that meant something to him.

And he had to pull that off now.

So Hix shook his head. "Love you like a father, you got that and always will, no matter what papers I've signed. I hope you knew that before I just gave it to you. That being so, I also hope you get you got my respect even as I tell you whatever situation you have with Hope has nothin' to do with me."

Jep held his gaze as he nodded slowly.

"That's the situation we got with Hope, son," he said quietly.

Not a surprise. She probably went straight to their ranch after her conversation with Hix in that very room last Tuesday.

"I know it'll take time," Hix replied. "I know it won't be easy. And I know in this town, it bein' so small, that'll make it even harder. But that doesn't negate the fact I'm tryin' to move on from all this and I'll ask you to help me with that by not bringing this kind of thing to my office. But also, Jep, not bringing it to me anywhere at all."

"You're done with her," he whispered.

"She divorced me, so yes. I'm done with her, Jep. I'm sorry but there it is."

Jep swallowed, looked to the side, sniffed loud and Hix gave him time.

The man was sixty-two and he had more land than Hix figured took up the whole of the town proper of Glossop.

He was a rancher, not a farmer, as his father (this happening twice over) had been, all of them expanding the ranch and the head of cattle on it to the point they didn't see lean years like other ranchers sometimes had to endure. His sons worked with him as well as both owning their own small farms. His daughter worked for him too, doing the books, dealing with the auctions, making the sales of steer sperm, overseeing her brothers' individual accounts, their farm business, and all the rest that was required, which was a lot with an operation that large.

For the men, the work was honest, but hard and never-ending.

Even so, Jep looked his age, not a day younger, but not a day older either.

Except right then.

Right then he looked about a hundred.

"Jep," Hix called.

His ex-father-in-law turned his eyes to Hix and requested, "Can I ask one thing of you, Hixon?"

"Hate to say it how I gotta say it, but it depends on what that thing is."

Jep accepted that with a nod.

"What it is, is that I know it's none of my business, wasn't when you were with my daughter, isn't now. But can I ask if you're needin' to use that money your uncle gave you to buy you a new place?"

Hix straightened from the desk, surprised this was something he wanted to know.

Surprised, but there was no reason not to tell him.

"No choice," he shared. "Had to use some of it on a lawyer and setting up the apartment too. Why?"

Jep's eyes went even sadder and he shook his head. "Just... guess..." He pulled in breath, looking like he was struggling, and Hix hated watching a man who was always so sure of himself going through that. Finally, he got where he needed to go. "Wanna know you're covered, son."

This wasn't surprising.

Hix had a great dad.

But Jep still was like a father to him and had always treated him not like a son-in-law, but like a son.

Not to mention, Hix had Jep's grandchildren half the time.

"I'm good, Jep. Kids're good. We're lookin' at houses. We'll be settled soon."

"Unh-hunh," Jep mumbled.

"We're okay and it'll get better, time passes," Hix assured him quietly.

Jep nodded.

Then he lifted himself up, faced Hix dead on and declared, "We spoiled her. Our last. A girl. Marie wanted one so bad. I didn't admit it, but I did too. Let her have her way until it was time to stop doin' that, then she set about makin' things her way and we shoulda nipped that in the bud too. We just didn't, and now—"

Hix cut him off. "Jep, now she's an adult and she needs to bear the consequences of her actions, not you. Not Marie. This isn't on you. Or Marie. And further, no need to find a place to lay blame. What's done is done. It's over. We just gotta find our way to move past it and settle in."

"Reckon you're right," Jep muttered.

"No choice but to be right about that," Hix told him.

His shoulders slumped, the light in his eyes dimmed, and Hix wished he'd found different words or not said anything at all.

"We'll miss you at our Thanksgiving table, Hixon," Jep told him.

"And I'll miss being there, Jep," Hix replied.

Jep brightened. "Maybe one day, you all get settled in, we'll all—"

"Jep," Hix said carefully.

"Yup. Yup," Jep replied, catching his meaning and nodding. "You're right, Hix." He took his big, calloused hand from his chair and lifted it Hix's way, pressing it toward him a couple of times, saying "Best be leavin' you alone. No need to follow me out, know my way."

Hix stood where he was and watched Jep walk slowly to the door.

He stopped in it and turned.

"End this the only way I can," he stated. "And that's to tell you the God's honest truth. Me and Marie, we want you to be happy. Cook and Jessie do too. Reed, he spoils his sister more than any of us ever did, he's not handlin' things well, but he'll come around. His Molly's already there." He gave a grin he didn't even try to make Hix believe was real. "But she's always been the sharper tack between those two. Smartest thing Reed's done is make that woman his wife, and you know I've said that to his face so you don't gotta keep it under your hat, mostly 'cause Reed agrees with me. But we all...just to say, we all..." He smacked his lips, held Hix's eyes, and finished, "Don't care what no papers say. You'll always be family, son. Not my grandbabies' daddy. *Family*, Hixon. The real kind. Always."

Hix found he had to clear his throat before he replied, "Same."

Jep nodded quickly and repeatedly and murmured, "Let you get to work." And on that, he opened the door and walked out.

Bets walked in.

Damn.

"Bets—" he started.

She interrupted him.

"The Mortimers called. They just got home from a weekend in Lincoln. Home game. Made a thing of it and cashed in some freebie they'd won for a double-night stay at a Best Western. Got back this mornin', found someone painted graffiti on their barn. They're ticked. They want someone out there. I'd say I'd go with Hal, but, don't get pissed, he's being more of a dick than normal and I'm fed up with his crap. So just wanna ask, can I go alone?"

Butch Mortimer was born in a bad mood and he was big as a house.

His wife Louella didn't come straight from the loins of her momma. She came straight from the loins of Satan.

No way in hell he was sending Bets out there to deal with those two alone.

And this would take some time. Time to listen to Butch shouting. Time to listen to Louella bitching. Time to ask the questions that might give them answers that possibly might pinpoint the actual person who graffitied their barn rather than the dozens of suspects who disliked them enough to be moved to do it.

Shit.

Apparently, he'd have to ask Greta to lunch tomorrow.

He moved from his spot, saying, "We'll both go."

She looked panicked.

She'd have to get over it.

He was her boss. They had to work together so she had to find a way to make that work.

She might as well start now.

THAT NIGHT, after they did not narrow down the suspects of the barn taggers, and after Hix had gone to the gym to work out, he sat at a stool at the bar of the Outpost between his buds, Toast and Tommy, watching Monday Night Football on Betty-Jean's eighty-inch TV.

His gut was full of wings and pop and his mind was full of football and the lunch he hoped to share tomorrow with Greta.

In other words, he was feeling good.

Until his phone rang, he lifted it from the bar and the screen said HOPE CALLING.

Toast made a grunt, but then again Toast had had his own bitter divorce from his wife two years previously. Tommy just shifted on his stool, giving Hix a half-grimace that said he felt Hix's pain even though he was a confirmed bachelor so he couldn't even come close to doing that.

They'd seen the screen.

For Hix's part, she had his kids, he had to take the call.

"Be back," he muttered, sliding off his stool and letting the phone ring until halfway to the door of the bar where he took the call. "Hope."

"Hixon," she replied shortly.

He pushed out the door. "The kids okay?"

"Yes," she bit out.

He pulled a deep breath into his lungs and stopped on the sidewalk, looking unseeing at Main Street.

When she said nothing, he prompted, "Right, you wanna let me in on why you're callin'?"

She did because she launched right in.

"I know you dislike me repeating myself, Hix, however, it's important enough to me to make one final attempt to ask you to stop this Junk Sundays thing. It seems lost on you that I've been trying since they were born to teach them healthy habits. They have to live in those bodies for what I'm sure we both hope is a long time, so it's important that they take care of them."

"Hope, it isn't lost on me. What also isn't lost on me is both Shaw and Cor play sports, so the entire school year they're training and conditioning. Mamie is in dance year round. In the summer, they all like to go and help your dad out on the ranch and that work is heavy. They aren't sitting around playing videogames all the time. It's one day and they don't eat so much they puke. They just have a day to relax and let loose."

"Well, I don't like it," she shot back.

"You've made that clear."

"They need to be shown what's right, Hixon. Not shown what's right but there are exceptions. Right is right. There are no exceptions. And they need a solid foundation for that when it's their turn to make good choices."

"Hope, they're not five years old," Hix returned. "No offense, but it's weird, a momma tellin' her seventeen-year-old son what he can put in his mouth. Or her fifteen-year-old daughter. Or even Mamie. We gotta loosen our hold and let them make those choices. We can't treat them like first graders until the second they take off for college."

"Shaw has a man's metabolism," she retorted. "But it would not be good for the girls if they got heavy."

Hix tried to hold on to his temper.

"Neither of our girls are heavy, they don't have the build or the habits to go that way, but that said, I'm not a big fan of you giving them ideas that they'd be anything but perfect however they are."

"Society is not kind to fat girls," she snapped.

"Unfortunately, you're correct. But how about we worry about that if either of them gives us any indication they're going to put on too much weight?"

She said nothing, and since they were on the phone, Hix couldn't tell if she was seething or scheming.

He'd find out it was the former.

"So this is your play."

Hix blew out another sigh and replied, "I'm not playing at anything."

"Yes you are. Making it more fun to stay at Dad's than put up with Mom expecting them to make the proper decisions about important things in their lives."

"I don't let them throw keggers at my place, Hope," he clipped. "We have donuts and chips and dip and watch movies and football for *one day*. Christ, it's not a big deal."

"It is to me."

"Yeah," he bit out. "And you've shared that. I've listened. I don't agree. So we're not talkin' about this anymore right now and we're not talking about it again."

"Hix—"

"Later, Hope."

With that, he disconnected, and since he was on call, he not only had to drink pop with his wings rather than beer, he couldn't turn off the phone but he could turn off the ringer.

So he did that, put his ex out of his head and walked back into the bar to continue with friends, football and shit food.

It didn't occur to him as he did that for the first time since she'd kicked him out, he had no trouble putting her out of his head.

It also didn't occur to him that he would not have to go home to her after football with his buds and listen to her bitch about the fact he put down so many nachos and wings.

By the time he sat his ass back on the barstool, he just ordered a plate of nachos and didn't think of her at all.

The next morning, after going out first thing to the Mortimers to take their shit that he hadn't yet figured out who'd graffitied their barn, Hix hit the department.

The instant he did...

No, the instant he saw the back of the rounded woman sitting in the chair beside Larry's desk, he went wired.

Hal was not to be seen. Donna was probably out in a cruiser (the woman liked a desk about as much as Hix did, which was to say not much at all). Bets was at her desk.

Hix looked to Reva in the dispatch room and gave her a chin lift before he moved directly to Larry.

Larry looked up at him and straightened in his chair, murmuring, "Sheriff. This is Mrs. Calloway. Mrs. Calloway, this is Sheriff Drake."

Hix was no longer paying attention to Larry.

One look at young, pretty Mrs. Calloway, he was also no longer wired.

He was tweaked.

"Mrs. Calloway," he murmured.

"Sheriff," she whispered.

"She's in reporting her husband didn't come home last night," Larry put in. "She last saw him yesterday morning before he went to work. I've been explaining that protocol for a missing—"

His gaze cut to Larry as he cut him off. "Deputy, a quick word."

Larry looked surprised, but Hix didn't spend time taking that in.

His attention returned to Mrs. Calloway.

"We won't be long."

She nodded.

Larry got up and Hix walked him to the back. He stopped them at the mouth of the hall that led from the cells to the back rooms.

He turned in a way that Larry had his back to the room and he kept his face expressionless.

"Take her statement," he ordered under his breath. "Get everything you can from her. When she last saw him. How he was when he left. His mood and manner the evening before. Where he works. Where he hangs. Who he hangs with. His normal schedule. If anything has seemed unusual about his behavior or routine the last few weeks or months. Get his cell phone number. The make and model of his car. License plate number. Get anything she can give you."

"Boss, a missing person isn't a—"

Hix allowed himself to lift his brows. "You got somethin' better to do?"

"See your point," Larry muttered.

"It's not that."

When he spoke those words, Larry focused more fully on him.

"That woman takes care of herself," Hix explained. "Nails are polished. She does somethin' to make her hair that way. She's got weight on her but she's also wearin' stylish clothes. Those clothes she's wearing, though, Larry, she wore yesterday. She might not have taken 'em off, she's been so worried about her husband not showin' last night. She mighta just been so freaked her man didn't come home by the time morning arrived, she took off her pajamas and picked those clothes right up off the floor to put 'em back on to come see us. She has the remnants of yesterday's makeup on. She hasn't done anything to her hair, not even brushed it, just shoved it back in that ponytail before she came here. And her eyes are dilated, which is an indication of panic or anxiety."

He got closer to his deputy and laid it out.

"Her husband comes home, Larry. She's not here because he's in the Dansboro Motel with his piece on the side and she's fed up with putting up with it and wants to make a point. She's not here because they've been having serious issues, he's over it and he took off. She's here because her husband comes home every night and last night he didn't come home."

"Right, boss," Larry whispered.

"Go get everything you can out of her."

"Right, boss," Larry repeated on a nod, turned and took off.

Hix watched him and then he moved to Bets's desk which was behind Larry's.

He bent slightly to her and said quietly, "Listen in. Take notes. Be alert. You don't have to hide it. We want Mrs. Calloway to know we're taking her concerns seriously. Then be ready. We got a man to find."

She stared up at him with wide eyes and nodded before she grabbed her notepad.

Hix didn't want to. He wanted to listen in. He wanted to make sure all the right questions were asked, no time was wasted, the interview was thorough and concise. And he was torn about the decision he made.

But he not only had to let his deputies know he trusted them when serious shit hit, he had to let his citizens know he trusted his deputies.

So he went to his office. Powered up his computer. Put in his password.

Then he watched covertly as Larry talked to Mrs. Calloway.

HE'D CALLED Donna back by the time Larry escorted Mrs. Calloway out the door and to her car.

Hal, who was out at Babycakes Coffee House getting himself an espresso drink that, not unusually, he didn't ask his colleagues if they also wanted one, had returned before she'd left.

So he had all his deputies in his office fanned out in front of him with Hix leaning against the front of his desk while Larry reported what Faith Calloway had given him.

"You were right, boss," Larry said. "He comes home. If he's gonna be late, he calls. According to Mrs. Calloway, he's a family man. He's foreman on old man Grady's ranch down in Grant county, so he's got a long drive to work, gets up early, leaves early, gets home late. But likes to eat dinner with her, have some time with his kids before they go to bed. She says he's in a fantasy football league and he and his boys got a thing where they rotate houses every Sunday and watch the games, but that's usually all he's away from them. He works so much and is on the road so much, when he's got time, he likes to spend it with the family."

"She report anything weird about him the last few weeks?" Hix asked.

Larry shook his head. "Not that she's noticed."

"Their story?" Donna queried.

Larry looked to her. "He got her pregnant when she was seventeen, he was nineteen." Larry turned his attention to Hix before he said, "She blushed when she said that. Seemed embarrassed."

Hix nodded.

It was a good catch. Didn't give them anything they needed but it gave them insight into Faith Calloway.

Larry turned back to Donna and went on, "He married her and Mrs. Calloway says folks thought they wouldn't work, but they did. They got a little girl, firstborn, she's eight. Little boy came three years after. Mrs. Calloway works in the county clerk's office part time and her husband's ma looks after her boy while she works." Again he looked to Hix. "She says it's for 'play money.' She says he started as a ranch hand for Grady, worked for the old coot even before they hooked up, but even though he's real young, he works real hard so Grady promoted him to foreman. They aren't rollin' in it but they also aren't hurtin'. But she says, kids're gettin' older, they wanna start to take 'em for trips to Disneyland and stuff like that so they're savin' up. That's her idea of play money."

Another good catch.

Play money wasn't nice clothes or new cars.

Play money was something for the family.

"No behavior changes," Hix gave his question as a statement.

Another shake of Larry's head. "She says nope."

"Finances, who does them and is there anything funny?" Hix asked.

Larry tipped his head Bets's way and told him, "Bets asked that. Mrs. Calloway does the finances, and no. She hasn't noticed anything funny."

"What about Grady? Did Nat Calloway get to work yesterday?" Hix pressed on.

Larry nodded. "When he didn't come home, Mrs. Calloway called him. Grady told her Calloway came, did his thing, left at around six, which was usual. She called Grady around nine. When her husband still didn't show around ten, she started calling around the hospitals. Said she didn't wanna do it before that because she didn't wanna think anything happened to him. She was still hopin' he'd just walk in the door."

"She call any of his buds?" Donna asked.

"Yup," Larry told her. "All of 'em. None of them had seen or heard from him."

"Why didn't she call us?" Hal asked.

Larry looked to him. "Said she figured he was in a wreck or somethin'. Said, after she called the hospitals, she actually put the kids in the car and drove the drive down to Grady's to check herself. She didn't find anything. Didn't think to call us until she got home from her drive and made her second round of calls to the hospitals early this morning. That still got her nothin' and she heard nothin' from nobody. That's when she decided just to come in."

Hix had been right. She'd come to them in the clothes she'd worn yesterday, clothes she hadn't yet taken off.

And she didn't suspect her husband of wrongdoing. She didn't suspect he'd been arrested. She didn't suspect he'd been caught in a prostitution sting or a drug deal.

She just suspected he'd been in a wreck.

Nothing else occurred to her until her worry overwhelmed her and she came in but did it only to get reinforcements.

"Drugs? Drink? Gambling? They been fighting?" Donna asked.

Again, Larry shook his head. "No drugs. No gambling, unless his football league constitutes that. She says she'd know. They're comfortable with money but they wouldn't be if he was doin' anything like that. Drink, yeah, but she says it's the normal kind. A coupla beers after work. He likes bourbon but doesn't like to drink the hard stuff around his kids. And she was real honest about what it's like between them. Said it was a bumpy road at first, bein' young, settin' up house, havin' a baby to look after so soon. But they ironed it out. She said they aren't perfect, they argue some. But they're in a good place now."

"Friends who might drag him into something?" Hal put in.

More shaking of Larry's head. "Not that she knows of."

"So there's nothing?" Hal asked disbelievingly. "This loving family man just didn't show up home one night?"

"Apparently," Larry answered.

"She give you his phone number?" Hix asked.

Larry nodded.

"Right." Hix looked to Bets. "Want you to see if you can track down that phone. If it's got GPS, wanna know where it is. Also want you on the line with Dansboro Police and the sheriff departments in Grant, Hooker, Cherry and Sheridan counties. Give 'em info on Nat Calloway's truck and a general description of the man. Tell 'em it's not an official missing person's case but we got cause for concern so if they can keep their eyes peeled for that truck, we'd appreciate it. Then I want you on the line with all the hospitals in all those counties, see if they got Nat or a John Doe of his description in a bed. The county coroners too. And then I want you to call all the hotels and motels in McCook and those other counties, Bets. Find out if Calloway is registered or his truck is registered. If not, ask 'em if they'll do you a favor and do a walkthrough of their lots to look for it."

"Isn't that a lot of effort for a guy who's probably pissed his woman let herself go and is likely off with someone who does it for him?" Hal asked.

Everyone looked to Hal, including Hix. "What makes you say she let herself go?"

"Saw her when I got back from Babycakes. She's fat," Hal answered.

Christ.

"You're a tool," Bets muttered.

She was right.

Hix decided he wasn't going to bother responding to Hal's remark.

"Larry, you and me are gonna go down, talk to Grady and see if he'll let us talk to his hands."

"Right, Hix," Larry replied.

He looked between Donna and Hal. "Bets is staying here, want you two in cruisers, eyes peeled for that truck. Parking lots. Camp grounds. Wherever you can think to look."

"On it, boss," Donna murmured.

Hal said nothing.

"Okay, everyone, let's move," Hix ordered, pushing up from his desk.

They were all moving, Larry in step behind Hix.

They walked through the department, and except for Bets who hit her desk, they all went out the front door and made their way to the side lot.

The county had money, and not much to spend it on, but they felt law enforcement was a priority even if not much happened.

That meant each deputy and Hix had their own cruisers, if you could call them that. They were big, double cab Rams painted white with gold and brown stripes down the sides on which it said SHERIFF with a star in front of the word, and under which it said McCOOK COUNTY. The SHERIFF was across the tailgate and the hood too.

He and Larry went to Hix's cruiser and angled in, but the minute Larry's ass was in his seat, Hix said, "I gotta make one stop. It's only gonna take a couple of minutes. Then we'll get on our way."

"Okay, Hix."

With that, Hix drove the two blocks to Lou's House of Beauty and parked in front of it.

He didn't look at Larry as he folded out of the truck. He looked through the window where he saw Greta's back to him as she worked on someone in her chair.

He also felt attention from the women in the salon and from Larry in the truck.

He ignored it, opened the door and shoved only his torso through.

Greta turned to him and her eyes got big.

She was beautiful. Funny. Sexy.

And now he saw she could be cute.

"Lou," he said to a Lou who was smiling so huge, it looked like it hurt. "Ladies," he said generally. His eyes hit on Greta. "Greta, don't mean to interrupt but need a minute if you can spare it."

She looked to him at his place half in, half out the door. She looked out the window at his truck with Larry in it.

Then she looked down at the woman in her chair. "You okay here? I won't be long."

The elderly woman, who Hix had seen around but didn't know, nodded enthusiastically. "I'm okay. I can wait all day. You take all the time you need, darlin'."

"Thank you, ma'am," Hix said to her and lifted his eyes. "Greta?"

Greta moved on pale-pink, high-heeled pumps his way.

Today, she was wearing a white, slouchy top with a low vee neck, jeans that hugged her legs to her ankles, where they were rolled up, and some kimono-like thing over her top that was black with big gray, white, green and pink flowers on it.

She looked like a movie star out for a casual stroll, the sole reason behind it being having great photos snapped of her by the paparazzi.

He got out of the door but held it open for her. She glanced at him as she walked out, also shooting her gaze toward Larry in the truck before he took her elbow and stopped her just outside one of Lou's windows, in full view of the salon.

"Don't have a lot of time, Greta," he told her when she looked up at him.

"Okay, Hix."

She wasn't hiding she was guarded, but also curious.

"I didn't get your number, was gonna call down to the salon yesterday, wanted to have lunch with you. Somethin' came up. Was gonna call down this morning. Something else came up and me and Larry gotta drive down to Grant County."

He fished in his jeans, got his wallet out, flipped it open and pulled out a card.

He shoved the wallet back as he handed it to her.

She took it.

"Hopefully," he continued, "what we're lookin' into will sort itself out today. So maybe we can have lunch tomorrow, you can fit that in your schedule. Don't have time to program you in my phone right now. You text me, I'll program you in when I got a second and then I can call you direct."

She was staring up at him, lips parted.

"Now I gotta go," he said.

"Right," she whispered.

"Lunch tomorrow if we can, yeah?"

She stared some more, seemed to pull herself out of it and a small smile hit her face.

"Yeah, Hixon. Definitely."

He nodded to her, wanting to smile back, pleased as hell she was clearly into that idea, but he had other shit on his mind. Shit he had to focus on, not doing it thinking Greta may be wondering, after what had gone down between them, why she hadn't heard from him or seen him.

He was not that guy who got off and took off.

He also wasn't that guy who played games, liked you, but felt the need to play it cool and waited days to connect so you wouldn't know he did.

"Later, sweetheart," he murmured.

Her smile got bigger and nearly blinded him.

He'd take that and keep it as the next hours unfolded because he had a feeling deep in his gut he'd need it.

"Later, Hix."

He shot her a small grin, turned and walked to the truck.

He was starting it up, looking out the windshield at Greta walking back into the salon, doing it half-turned, arm up, waving his way, looking over her shoulder, still smiling that smile.

He lifted up his chin to her, and as the door closed, his eyes moved to the rearview mirror and he started backing out into Main Street.

"Don't get pissed at me when I point out that woman is *fine*," Larry remarked.

"Mm," Hix replied.

There was silence as Hix put her in drive and started them on their way.

Three blocks in, Larry said quietly, "Good for you, man. Good for you."

"We're just friends."

"Like I said, good for you, man. And I don't mean that snarky, Hix. She's pretty. Looks sweet. Great fucking smile. Friend or whatever, after what you been through, you deserve a smile like that aimed your way. So good for you."

Hix didn't reply.

But Larry was right.

More than just Greta's smile was good for him.

Now he'd connected with her, she had his card, his number, she knew where he was at.

So he could clear his mind and focus on finding Nat Calloway.

"Not thinkin' Nat Calloway is gonna walk in those doors, Hix."

Hix took his attention from where it was aimed through the windows of dispatch to the outside windows facing the street and looked at Ida who took over for Reva doing the nighttime dispatch shift, three to eleven.

Dispatch wasn't McCook County Sheriff's dispatch. They didn't have enough going on to have their own dispatch.

It was McCook County everything dispatch. Sheriff, fire, emergency, and a couple of hotlines (suicide and sexual assault). The county's 911 number ran through that room so even Dansboro Police, the only town in the county that was big enough to have their own force (albeit there were only three people on that force) used that dispatch.

But the county was sleepy enough, five days a week, it was only operated from seven in the morning to eleven at night, the weekend shift going all the way to one in the morning mostly just because. The 911 calls were redirected to a service for the midnight hours due to the fact that no one called in during those hours because most the county was asleep, but it was still willing to pay for cover.

Hix had spent the day getting more of what Faith Calloway said about her husband, Nat.

Good guy. Hard worker. Family man. Loved his wife. Loved his kids. Might miss church on Sunday but only because that was one of the few chances he got to sleep in, though Faith didn't miss it and took the kids.

He was liked.

Hell, Flynn Grady was beside himself, and not just because his foreman was missing, but because that foreman was Nat.

Hix had call to know Grady after Hix's deputies had been called in by the sheriff of Grant County to assist with some cattle rustling mess that had happened a few years earlier.

Grady was a decent man, but he was crotchety. The kind of man you would know he liked you when he kicked the bucket and put you in his will.

But he liked Nat. So much, he'd suspended operations that day to set his hands on the roads to see if they could find him.

Not one of those men had protested or dragged their feet. They set out for their trucks practically before Grady finished giving the order.

That said a lot without using a single word.

Hix didn't argue with this interference.

Mostly because he wanted that man found.

They'd also learned that no one thought Nat and Faith would work out, but he'd loved her at seventeen, and according to everyone they asked, he loved her now. He wouldn't cheat. Worked too hard to get caught up in anything—another woman, booze, drugs, gambling. But it wasn't the fact he didn't have time, it was the fact he loved his wife too much. When he wasn't working or on the road, he was with his family or his football league buddies.

Simple man. Simple pleasures. Simple life.

And now he was missing. No clues. His truck was nowhere to be found. They couldn't locate his phone so it was either turned off or destroyed. Last person who saw him was one of Grady's ranch hands and that man had seen him get in his truck and drive away.

Still, it was nearly eleven and Hix was at the station. He'd gone over his notes and copies of all his deputies' notes and he'd done that repeatedly. He'd then gone out to the Harlequin and brought in dinner for him and Ida.

After that, he'd hung out with her in the dispatch room, his eyes often straying to the windows, his mind filled with Nat Calloway.

"You got a bad feeling," Ida noted.

"Yup," he agreed.

She nodded.

"You know the Calloways?" he asked.

She shook her head. "Think they go to the Methodist church."

For some in that town, what church you attended was the social divide. Ida was a Baptist. She was one of Keller's flock. She was a fine woman but her social stratum wasn't all that layered.

"We don't have much in the way of this kinda thing in this county, 'less a man or gal gets itchy feet," she remarked. "Reckon in the big city you saw more of this. So I reckon your bad feelin' isn't a good thing."

She was very right.

"Nope," he agreed.

She leaned to him. "It's late, Hix. Go home. Get some rest. It's as bad as you're thinkin', you're gonna need it. It isn't, then you got a decent night's sleep."

It was good advice.

So Hix nodded, took the sole of his boot off the chair he'd pulled in front of him and his ass off the one he was sitting on.

He looked down at Ida.

Round, red cheeks, hair going gray and she wasn't about to do a thing about it, something he knew because the "going" part of gray had almost went. If she dissed Lou's House of Beauty and trimmed the long ends herself, Hix wouldn't have been surprised.

"Your shift's over in twenty minutes, Ida. Could wait. Walk you to your car."

"You need company to keep your mind off things, Hix, you're welcome to stay. But I'm used to the solitude and I like it. Got four kids at home who fight more than my husband and I did before he pulled on his boots and took off, and that's saying something. Quiet does me a lot of good."

Her four kids were actually four adults still living with their mother. Hix couldn't figure out if they were sucking her dry or loyal to the bone after their daddy left her with them when they were a whole lot younger. This was mostly because she fought with them as much as she said they fight with each other.

There was love there, though, and Ida seemed content.

Not to mention, it wasn't any of his business.

"Right, Ida. Catch you tomorrow."

"You will, Hixon. Try to sleep good."

He lifted his chin. Gave her a low wave. Went to his office, shut it down, shut the bullpen down, leaving the lights over reception on for Ida.

He gave her another low wave before he left, got in his Bronco and drove to his apartment.

He threw back a beer watching late night TV and trying to unwind, clear his head, find tired.

But he was still wired.

Even so, Ida was right.

Until they figured out what had become of Nat Calloway, he'd need to have his shit together so he needed his sleep.

He picked up his phone first, going to texts and finding Greta's.

Now you got me. Hope things went ok with what you were looking into. That means hope I see you tomorrow.

That was Greta. She didn't play games either.

For his part, Hix hadn't texted a woman not his wife, one of her friends, Donna, Bets, or one of his daughters in nineteen years. He had things going but he'd felt a reply was needed and he didn't have any damned clue what to say.

He'd gone with, *Good to see your text. Things aren't going great but call you tomorrow.*

She hadn't replied and Hix suspected this was because she was giving him space to get done what he needed to do.

Greta on his mind, he hit his shower before hitting the sack, because he didn't jack off in the bed his daughters slept in.

So he did it in the shower, thinking of Greta.

Then he hit his bed, closed his eyes, and it took a while, but finally he found sleep.

While he slept, the rain came.

Chapter 10

Really, Really Bad Day

Hixon

When his phone rang, waking him up, the first thing that hit Hix was that it was raining.

The second thing that hit him was seeing from his alarm clock it wasn't quite yet six in the morning.

And grabbing his phone from the nightstand, the last thing that hit him was that it was Bets calling.

He felt a compression in his gut, an acrid taste in the back of his throat as he got up on a forearm, took the call and put it to his ear.

"Bets."

"Hix, I found him."

Hix pushed up, the covers falling off, and he swung his legs around so he was sitting on the side of his bed, doing all this asking, "Where?"

"Game trail some hunters use. Hix...boss...shit." She paused before she hit him with it. "He's dead."

Hix closed his eyes for only a beat then he pushed up and started moving. "It's raining, Bets."

"Yeah," she said. "Ran to my car before I called you. Have a tarp in the back. It's a new one, Hix. I was gonna do some painting, so I bought it this weekend and thank God I did. It was in a packet. It won't screw with the scene. I took a bunch of pictures best I could in this light and then threw it over him."

"Good," he grunted, dragging on some shorts. "Now, we end this call, text me directions to exactly where you are. Then you get on the line and you call Donna. You tell her where you are, you tell her to bring a tent and you tell her to get her ass there fast. Then you get on with Larry. Tell him to bring lights and get his ass there. After that, you get on with Hal and you tell him to get his ass there and do it bringing a shit ton of coffee."

"Right, boss," she replied.

Hix kept talking, phone wedged between his ear and shoulder as he did up his jeans. "You get done with that, I want you to get on the line to the forensics boys up in Cherry County. Tell them to come down and do it fast. I'll call Lance on the way there."

"Okay, Hix."

Hix took the phone from his ear long enough to pull on a clean undershirt then he put the phone right back.

"His truck there?" he asked.

"Nope."

Goddamn it.

Where was that truck?

"You up all night lookin?" he went on.

"Yeah."

"Good job," he said. "Now make those calls."

"You got it, boss."

"See you soon."

"Yeah."

He hung up, tossed his cell on his bed and went to his closet to grab a clean sheriff shirt. He shrugged on his shirt, buttoned it up, tucked it in, wasted precious time transferring his badge from the shirt that was on the floor to the shirt he was wearing. He hit his closet and grabbed his sheriff slicker then went back to his bed. He sat on it, put on his socks and boots, shoved his wallet in his jeans, tagged his cell and the slicker and hauled his ass out through the rain to his Bronco.

Hix stood under the big marquee tent they'd set up over the body and stared down at the man who was now on his back. After Lance, the county coroner, had done his thing and Hal and the forensic boys had taken their pictures, they'd turned Nat Calloway, who'd been on his stomach, to his back.

He'd seen pictures Faith had emailed Larry so he already knew. And what Calloway had, even death and rain didn't do much to dim it.

Pretty wife. Good-looking husband.

They fit.

Perfect match.

He tore his gaze from the body as Lance approached him.

"Right, Hixon," he started, cleared his throat and launched in. "Man's been dead 'round about thirty-six hours, give or take. Got a gunshot wound to the back, right shoulder, another to the back of his neck, which unfortunately went through and through and part of what it went through was his jugular. Bled out fast. Reckon you figured this out already, but that didn't happen here. This is the dump site. Crime scene is somewhere else and," he looked to the ceiling of the tent, indicating without words how unlikely what he said next was now going to be before he aimed his eyes back at Hix, "there'll be a goodly amount of blood."

Hix nodded.

Lance kept going.

"Gunshot isn't at close range. My guess, this man was running away from the shooter, and the shooter was either a good shot and was aiming to kill or he got lucky or seriously unlucky, depending on what he wanted to go down. Shoulder hit and a rip in his shirt at his right biceps that looks like a bullet went through it but didn't hit flesh says it's the last. No other indications on the body how many shots were fired, but right now it's lookin' like at least three."

Hix nodded again and told Lance something he knew, "Man's wallet is in his jeans. Money in his wallet. This wasn't a robbery, unless he desperately wanted a cell phone, which our man has but he doesn't have on his person."

This time, Lance nodded. "Nothing to give indication he was tied up or there was a struggle either. No obvious defensive wounds, may be some I find after I cut his clothes from him, but nothing I can see so it doesn't look like there was a fight. He's got abrasions on the heels of his palms with dirt and small rocks dug in, probably from falling forward once he was hit. My best guess right now, it's from goin' down on concrete. Other than that, don't know what it is at this point except the obvious, it was a shooting."

Hix looked back down at Nat Calloway.

"Can't know more until I get him on my table, but forensic boys are done with the body. Gonna get him into town and get down to gettin' you some answers right away," Lance went on.

"Right," Hix murmured. "Thanks."

Lance gave him a look, clapped him on the arm and moved to spread out his body bag.

Hix walked to the leader of the two-man forensics team from Cherry County.

"Anything you can give me to go on?" he asked even if he knew the answer.

He got that answer right away when the guy shook his head. "If there was anything, the rain fucked it up. Got no footprints. Got some cigarette butts and litter, but all we got of that's been out here since maybe 1977. We still bagged it just in case. This being the dump site, minimal blood." The man's chest puffed out with his big breath before he concluded, "With this rain, this spot is what this spot was before a body was dumped in it. It's just a spot on a game trail with a man's body in it. We got dick for you, Drake. But we'll keep lookin'."

"I'm leavin' Hal with you to help do that," Hix told him.

The guy tipped up his chin.

"And you need anything, he's your man," Hix continued.

"'Preciated, Drake."

"Nope, it's appreciated you boys comin' down here to help us out."

The guy dipped his chin and lifted a hand.

Hix held his eyes a beat then walked away, turning his attention to his deputies, Bets standing to the side watching, Hal the same but not close to Bets, as Larry and Donna were in squats, helping Lance transfer the body onto the opened body bag.

Hix waited until they had Nat Calloway zipped in and had lifted the body onto the hand stretcher. Something Lance could carry a quarter mile through tall grass and mud, but he wouldn't be able to carry it back loaded with a body.

"You can hang tight for five, Lance," Hix called out, "wanna give my deputies direction and then we'll help you get 'im out."

"Thanks, Hixon," Lance called back.

His team took their cue and moved to form a loose huddle under the tent.

Hix didn't waste time.

"Hal, you stay here, help the forensics team to comb this place and all around. From here all the way back to the road and don't be stingy about the distance you check the perimeter of this site. That said, this is a dump site. Unless you happen onto where the crime was committed, I doubt the perpetrator spent a lot of time here. If he went to the trouble of dumping a body in a place like this, he's not gonna move a man's body just a half mile away from where he shot him to death. There's a lot to do. Be smart about the time you spend here."

Hal jerked up his chin.

Hix kept at him.

"Those boys need anything, you get it for them. Mouth of this trail, such as it is, has enough vehicles at it, one of them our coroner's van, folks are gonna be curious. Keep alert. While you're searchin', you see anyone is curious enough to come lookin', you send them right back to their vehicle and on their way. Forensics team finishes up, you get back to the department and you get all the pictures printed out. Yeah?"

Hal nodded. "Yeah, boss."

Hix looked to Donna. "Want you back at the department. You call all the sheriffs of the adjoining counties and give them a brief. Tell them where we're at." His gaze grew intent on her. "Donna, I want that fuckin' truck found and I want the crime scene located. From what we got with time of death, whoever did Nat Calloway didn't have a lot of time to take him somewhere far. But that truck could be anywhere by now. And I want it."

"You got it, Hix."

"You get done doin' that, and don't take a lot of time doin' it, you tell Reva to watch over reception and I want you to start combing every inch of road between Glossop and Grady's ranch. Ask the boys down in Grant to help you out seein' as there's a chance the crime happened on their patch. You won't find the truck, but you might find the crime scene and we need that."

She nodded.

"Not gonna be anything to find," Hal put in, throwing an arm out to indicate the steady wet that was falling around the tent. "Man was probably done outside, seein' as he was hit runnin' away. It's been raining since the middle of the night. Whatever there was is probably washed away."

"We're still looking," Hix told him.

"We should be knocking on doors and it's Grant County Sheriff who should be doin' it," Hal returned. "That's dusty road from here to Grady but it's got houses on it, farms, ranches. Gunshots are loud. People hear them."

Hix's jaw felt tight. "Yeah, and anything left of that crime scene we can find before this rain takes it, we'll bust our balls to find it,

Hal, *before the rain takes it*. Not goin' house to house, some of those houses miles apart, chattin' with folks while rain washes away a crime scene. We got no cause to believe Nat Calloway was anywhere but on the road between Grady's ranch and his house, only about two miles of that being Grant County's patch. Got no idea what happened, but my gut says whatever happened was on that road. Regardless, abrasions on his palms tell Lance he fell to concrete, so if we gotta focus our search, we're doin' it on the concrete that makes that road."

Hix kept Hal pinned with his gaze as he took a breath and went on, annoyed it was taking time to point out the obvious to one of his deputies.

"He didn't bleed a little, he bled a lot, Hal, and it was eighty-six degrees yesterday. That blood had all day yesterday to bake into wherever it poured out. I'm not feelin' all that lucky right now, but we get a stroke of it, we might find a huge-ass stain. That said, the rain won't wash away anyone's memories. We can canvass once we've exhausted our attempts to locate where Nat Calloway was shot runnin' for his life. And that's what *you'll* be doin' after you're done helpin' the team, finding out if someone heard something, saw something, then you can help Donna pinpoint the site."

Hal gave him his chastened, pissed look but Hix ignored it when Bets spoke.

"You want me on that too, boss?" Bets asked, and Hix looked to her.

"Nope, Bets. I want you to go home and get some sleep."

Her eyes grew big then squinty.

"I found him. I should be able to—"

He cut her off. "You been up all night and a man's been murdered. Your dedication to finding him has been noted, Bets, and it means a good deal to this case that you found him and he wasn't out here for days, weeks, before someone bumped into that body. I appreciate it. This team appreciates it. But now I need all my deputies fresh and alert and you been up all night. You need to go home, unwind, try to relax and get some sleep. I don't want to see you for six hours."

When she opened her mouth, he leaned an inch toward her and lowered his voice.

"I'm not cutting you out of this case, Bets. We need to find the person who did this and I'm gonna need all of you to help do that. But we gotta go about it the right way, clearheaded and smart. I'll give you your duties when I know you can perform them the way I already know you can perform them...doin' shit right."

She looked about to argue but then she ducked her head and nodded.

He turned to Larry. "You're with me. We're goin' to talk to Faith Calloway. Then we're goin' back to Grady. After that, we're helpin' Donna and Hal."

Larry looked sick a second before he hid it.

Hix got that look.

Larry had not ever had to tell a woman her husband and the father of her young children had been murdered.

Hix himself had only done it once, back in Indianapolis.

To say the experience sucked was an understatement, and to say that he remembered every second of it like he'd just walked out of that woman's house was not an exaggeration.

"Wanna help Lance carry him out."

Bets's words took Hix's attention from Larry back to her.

"Sorry?" he asked.

She lifted her chin. "I found him. You're right. I'm tired. Been up all night. I'm also hyper. So I'm good for now. And I found him. I want to help get him out of this fucking place."

She wasn't dainty. She didn't have Hix, Larry or Hal's power.

But she could help them carry the deadweight of a body out of there, and even if she couldn't, right then she'd do it if she had to will it to be done.

Yeah, Bets was still mostly a rookie.

But she was a good deputy.

"Larry, front end," Hix ordered then looked back at Bets, "You take the foot. Lance and me'll take the sides. Donna, you lead the way and go at a good clip. We got company at the road, I want you pushing them back." He drew in breath and finished, "Let's get him out of here."

They moved. Hix sent looks to Hal and the forensics team then he took his position at Nat Calloway's left side.

They hefted him up, and by the time they started out from under the tent, Donna was twenty yards down the trail.

They fortunately had no onlookers watching as they got him in the back of Lance's van (though a number of cars slowed as they drove by).

The coroner didn't waste time taking off. Donna and Bets didn't either.

But Larry approached Hix at the side of his Bronco.

"It's gonna freak her out," Hix said. "But this is an official visit so we need to hit the department and get a Ram before we go to her house."

Larry nodded but started, "Hix, I've never—"

"I know," Hix interrupted. "And it's gonna be one of the most shitty memories you'll hold on to for the rest of your life. But she needs to know as soon as we can get to her. And we need to give her what she needs to put the worry to bed and start her mourning."

Hix got closer to Larry and stood in the gently falling rain with his hand on his deputy's shoulder.

"You go in her house, you are not her friend," he said quietly. "You're a sheriff's deputy. You're sorry for her loss. You make no promises we're gonna find who did this. You make no assurances that it's gonna be all right, because it's not. Even if we find who did this, for her, it's never gonna be all right. She's gonna get on with her life eventually but this will be a black spot in it and that is never gonna change."

Larry nodded and Hix kept on.

"You can tell her we're gonna do everything we can to find who did this. And you're gonna watch her to see if there's anything we mighta missed yesterday. This is not the time to grill her or ask more questions seein' as you did a thorough job of that yesterday. We can ask her to get in touch with us immediately if she thinks of something. We'll make certain she understands she can contact us at any time if she has questions, and we'll make certain she knows we'll keep her as up to date as we can on the investigation as it unfolds. Other than that, this is the time to tell her she's lost her husband, her babies have lost their daddy, we make sure she's got someone with her and then we leave and get on findin' the person who ripped that family apart."

Larry stared him in the eyes before he swallowed and mumbled, "Yeah."

Hix gave his shoulder a squeeze, let him go and watched as Larry walked to his truck.

He swung up into the Bronco.

They drove to the department and switched out to a Ram.

Then they drove to Faith Calloway's house.

"Was not wrong about the hands. It was concrete. He went down forward, did it hard, also has abrasions on his knees," Lance stated, going through the motions of starting to fall, hands lifted in front of him, but not finishing that.

Hix and Larry were standing in the coroner's examination room with Lance, Nat Calloway's dead body on a table, all of it covered but his head and his feet, his toe tagged.

It was late evening after a really shitty day.

"Like I said at the scene, neck hit did him in," Lance continued. "Bullet went through his neck, don't have that. Got the bullet out of his shoulder. Both wounds came from the same caliber of gun, which I'd hazard to guess was the same gun. Put that bullet in the system, it comes back with a hit, you'll get the notification."

When he paused, both Hix and Larry gave him nods, so he kept going.

"No drugs in his system. No alcohol. Last meal was a ham and cheese sandwich and chips." Hix watched as Lance's manner changed. "Nothin' else, boys, 'cept the man had sex sometime the day he died. Got vaginal secretions and sperm on his genitals. He was dumped face down, wet did seep in but not enough to wash that away."

"He was married, Lance," Hix told him.

Lance nodded. "Then sorry to say, you gotta ask his wife if they had relations before he took off for work but after he had his morning shower, if that's when he cleans up."

Fucking great.

"We'll do that tomorrow," he muttered and glanced at Larry.

Larry's mouth was tight.

"The only other thing I can give you is I reckon you're right," Lance declared. "This was done on a stretch of road, maybe, outside guess, a parking lot. Those abrasions and debris I found aren't from somethin' like a sidewalk. There's too much debris, abrasions too rough. Besides that and the two holes in him, man was fit. Healthy. Young. No defensive wounds under his clothes. Nothing that gives indication he was held captive or bound. Nothing under his fingernails but dirt and not a lot of it, but foreman on a ranch is gonna have dirt under his fingernails after a day on the job."

"So outside of the fact he had sex, had this shitty-ass last meal of a goddamned ham sandwich and got shot on concrete, we got nothin'," Larry said.

"Sorry, son, but yeah," Lance muttered. "That's all we got."

Larry blew out an audible breath.

Hix turned to him. "First thing tomorrow, want you to take Bets or Donna to Faith Calloway's house. You're there because she talked to you first and you're her point person on this because of that. She needs to know you're on it, you're her man, you're following through, and she can count on you. You give her the minimum you can to update her on our progress. Don't get bogged down, just assure her she has all of the department's resources devoted to solving her husband's murder. But if she blushes tellin' you she got pregnant at seventeen, want Donna or Bets to ask her about any activities she and her husband got up to before he went off to work the day he died. You with me?"

Larry nodded.

"He didn't have time to have a quickie in his truck on that stretch of road, Larry," Hix told him in a lame effort to make what wasn't going to be easy a little easier. "And no woman dragged his body from where she shot him and then carried him to the dump site. Nat Calloway made love to his wife before he went to work. It won't be fun she has to share that with a female deputy, but she's not gonna be gettin' bad news that her husband cheated on her coming on the heels of her hearing the worst news she'll probably get in her life that her husband's dead. What she will get, if she gets to the point she's thinking rationally at all, is that we're being thorough."

"Right," Larry mumbled.

Hix took him in, noting the frustration and exhaustion written plain all over him, before ordering, "It's been a long day, man. Go home. After you get back from Faith's in the morning, we'll have a team brief and get back on it."

"Yeah," Larry replied, looked at Lance and said, "Thanks, bud."

"My job," Lance murmured.

He glanced at them both and took off, his shoulders drooping, the weight of the day weighing visible and heavy.

Hix and Lance watched him go, and when he disappeared, Lance spoke.

"You get anything?"

Hix turned back to the coroner. "Nothin'. No one saw anything. No one heard anything. No lock on the truck. No crime scene found. Rain stopped, still couldn't find dick. Talked to his boss. Talked to the men who worked under him. Talked to his friends. Canvassed that road. Canvassed his neighborhood. Outside of everyone bein' anything from pissed as shit a good man's dead to dissolving into tears a good man's dead, we got dick."

"Forensics get anything?" Lance queried.

Hix shook his head. "No footprints. No tire tracks. Can't even tell a person walked out there carrying a body, rain beatin' down the grass and game goin' through that area. Might not be lookin' for a criminal mastermind, but my hunch says it's someone who knows the area, since they took him to that spot. That still doesn't give us shit. Any hunter or outdoorsman can spot a game trail in his search for a dump site. There's no motive. No witnesses. My only guess is, we can't find that truck, someone wanted it. But it was a five-year-old Ford F150 that wasn't top of the line when Calloway bought it. Not a pimped-out ride that would garner attention or envy. So if he was done for that truck, the person who did it was either desperate, whacked out or just an asshole."

"No truck, you reckon you got two people to look for?" Lance asked. "Person would have to have their own vehicle and you haven't mentioned another set of wheels. That road is dusty, but someone'd notice an abandoned vehicle, and then they'd notice Calloway's truck if the shooter had to leave it to go back and deal with his own car."

"Either that or we got a drifter with a gun who knows the area and is strong enough to heft around a five foot eleven, one hundred and seventy-five pound body."

Lance's attention to Hix turned into scrutiny.

"He had sex, Hix. Could be the woman lured him, her man got him, one took his truck, the other took their car."

"I've learned anyone can get up to anything in this world, Lance. But I'd be out-and-out shocked Nat Calloway scored himself some, got murdered after he did the deed, then got his cheating ass dumped in his own town. We spent all day yesterday essentially investigating that man and there wasn't even a hint he had that in him. And we checked all that road, but if I had to wager, he was done close to Glossop, so for the sake of time and convenience he was dumped just outside of Glossop. But bottom line, there simply wasn't enough time for him to get his rocks off and then get himself dead. So he was murdered close to home, unless the killer knew him, and out of some act of remorse, dumped him close to home. Or the murderer didn't mean to kill him, and again out of an act of remorse, dumped him in a place he'd be found. But I'd stake my badge on the fact no woman was involved."

"That happens," Lance noted. "That kind of act of remorse."

"Yup. And since we got nothin', we've got nothin' we can rule out."

Lance looked to the table and back to Hix.

"This man a man who'd stop for someone who looked like he needed some help?" he asked.

"Yup," Hix answered.

"So you gotta find that truck," Lance said quietly.

"We gotta find that fuckin' truck," Hix replied.

Lance tipped his head to the side. "Wife hold it together?"

Hix clenched his teeth before he forced himself to release them but still had to bite out his, "Nope."

"This guy's twenty-eight, how old's she?"

"Twenty-six and they got two kids, eight and five."

"Shit," Lance muttered.

"Yeah," Hix agreed.

"She got kin close?"

Hix nodded. "Her sister, his sister and brother, all their folks. Before Larry and I left, his mother was there. As we were walkin' out, the rest were descending."

"Least she's got support," Lance muttered.

"Least she's got that."

Lance held his eyes. "Somethin'll break, Hixon."

Hix had worked as a detective for two years in crimes against persons at Indianapolis Metropolitan Police Department.

He and his partner had a good close rate.

They also had cases they couldn't solve.

And from that first look he had of Faith Calloway's face while she was sitting next to Larry's desk yesterday, Hix knew the sour feeling in his gut was not only about what they were going to find when they found Nat Calloway.

It was the feeling that this was what they were going to get.

What appeared to be a random crime on a lonely stretch of road, the only reason behind it being stealing a man's truck.

They had that rain that likely washed away evidence and time was not on their side.

Unless the person who did it felt compelled to walk into his station and make a confession, Hix had the very bad feeling that nothing was going to break in this case. He had four people on it all day, five when Bets came back to them, a forensics team, a coroner who'd already done his autopsy, and they didn't have a single lead. They had no crime scene, no shell casings, no witnesses, one bullet, a dump site and a victim that it would seem no one had one single reason to want dead.

"Somethin'll break, Hix," Lance repeated into Hix's thoughts, doing it more firmly this time, and Hix focused on him again.

"We'll work to that," Hix told him.

"Know you will. Now like you said to your deputy, it's been a long day. Go home. Face this head on tomorrow," Lance replied.

Hix gave him a nod, a low wave, and murmured, "Thanks, Lance."

Lance nodded back.

Hix went out to his Ram, drove it to the station, parked it next to his Bronco and went in.

Ida was in dispatch.

He greeted her by lifting a hand and flicking out two fingers before he went right back to his office.

He'd ordered all his deputies home for a good night's sleep so the place was deserted, lights on in his office as he'd left them, the rest of the lights were out, outside the ones they always left on over reception.

He sat at his desk, opened the file on it and spread out the photos Hal had printed out.

He looked them over. He looked them over again. He studied each one from corner to corner. Then he stood up, bent over them, unfocused his gaze and stared at them all at once.

Nothing jumped out at him.

They were just photos of a man, clothes and hair wet, face down, head turned to his left, right arm cocked and up, left arm caught under him, both legs arranged haphazardly like he'd fallen, put a hand out to stop his fall, but hit his head and went unconscious.

But he hadn't fallen and he wasn't unconscious.

He'd been tossed and he was dead.

Maybe the person carrying him had Nat Calloway's right wrist held by his hand, which was why it was flung out.

He couldn't know unless he had the man who did it in front of him to ask.

And if he had that man, that wouldn't be a question he'd ask.

"Know pictures like that tell stories to men like you," Ida said quietly from the door, and Hix lifted his gaze to her. "But you been in here an hour, Hix, so I reckon, they aren't talkin', maybe you need to give them some time, look at 'em in the morning, and maybe they'll be ready to tell their tale."

"That's my hope, Ida, but my concern is they wanna keep their secrets and I gotta find some way to pull them loose."

"Maybe you should do it when you don't look like you've been hit by a truck," she suggested.

More good advice from Ida.

"Yeah," he replied.

She tipped her head toward the bullpen. "Gotta get back."

"Before you go," he called as she made her start to turn. "Town talking?"

She nodded. "Word's definitely out. Shock. Whispers. Sadness, even if they don't know the family. We're not used to this here in Glossop. Terra from the *Guide* called, twice. Me and Reva been puttin' her off. Blatt came and went this afternoon. Said he'd catch you later."

The editor of the paper and the ex-sheriff sniffing around was not a surprise and town talk was unavoidable.

Even so.

"We gotta do our best to keep gossip contained," he told her. "They can and will talk, but my team needs to be free to do the work they gotta do, not deal with people flipping out. Nothing indicates this is anything but random. Nothing fitting this MO has happened anywhere in the state. What we know right now, we got a one-time deal and we gotta figure out who did it. That's all."

"I'll do my part in that, Hix, that's a promise," she assured.

She would. You didn't work dispatch that included suicide and sexual assault hotlines, which meant the training to do all of that, without having a head on your shoulders.

"Let you get back to it," Hix replied. "And I'll say my goodnight now."

"Right. 'Night, Hix. Try to get some rest."

He doubted that would happen.

He still gave her what he hoped was a reassuring smile.

She went back to her desk. He shut down and headed out to his Bronco.

He needed answers.

He needed bourbon.

But as he drove, what he gave himself was not heading to his apartment.

He headed to Greta's house.

It was after nine at night, but as he pulled up to the curb in front, he saw she wasn't inside, watching TV or painting her nails or shit like that. She was sitting on her porch, the porch light on, and she had a laptop in her lap.

She also had her eyes on the Bronco.

She shifted them to Hix as he rounded the hood, made his way up her walk, the steps to her house, her porch, and as he moved to stand in front of the wicker chair beside her.

But once he'd stopped, her eyes dropped to the chair and then came back up to him.

He took her invitation and rested his weight in the chair, slouching right into it because he didn't have the energy to do otherwise, aiming his gaze to the quiet street.

"You need a beer, darlin'?" she asked quietly.

"You got bourbon?" he asked the street.

"Yeah."

He didn't say anything else but he didn't need to.

He heard her setting her laptop to the side and he saw her walk across his line of vision as she went into the house.

He stared at the street and then lifted both hands, rubbing them over his face.

Damn.

He was tired.

He had his arms resting on the arms of the chair when she came back out.

He lifted one hand to take the healthy dose of bourbon she held in front of him.

He took his gaze from the street to see she had a big, stylishly-shaped wineglass in her hand filled with red wine and she was folding herself in the chair next to him, legs crossed under her.

As he was noting, this seemed like pure Greta. Courtesy so ingrained, she wasn't even going to make him drink alone.

Once she'd settled, her attention came right to him.

"Faith is one of my clients," she said softly.

"Right," he muttered.

"So, I've seen some cop shows, and my guess is you can't talk about it," she noted, still giving him the soft.

"No, Greta, I can't talk about it."

"Don't need to, baby," she whispered. "Written all over you that you've had the definition of a really, *really* bad day."

"Yeah, sweetheart," he confirmed. "I've had a really, *really* bad day."

She leaned toward him, reaching out and wrapping her fingers around his biceps, giving them a comforting squeeze before she let him go and sat back.

When she moved away from him, abruptly, he announced, "Told you I didn't wanna move from Indy."

"Yeah, you told me that," she replied.

"This is a good place to raise kids," he shared.

"I can totally see that."

"Man like me, the job I do, though, it doesn't offer much."

She twisted in her seat so she was faced more his way, kept her gaze on him, all this telling him she was listening.

"I don't want crime. No one wants crime," he stated.

"No," she said. "No one wants that."

"But this is what I do. It's what I know. It's what I wanted to do since I was a kid."

She nodded encouragingly.

"And here, it didn't feel like I was doin' much to help. Not anybody. Not anything that was worthwhile. 'Cause I gotta admit, I don't really give a shit who graffitied the Mortimers' barn. They aren't gang tags. Those two make a habit outta pissin' people off. They're mean as snakes. Hell, coupla months ago, Louella shot her neighbor's dog when he got loose and made his way on their land."

"Oh my God," she breathed.

"Dog survived," he told her. "But the vet bills were astronomical. They refused to pay 'em. Nothin' I could do about that. Their land. They got chickens. That coop is more fortified than Fort Knox and the dog was nowhere near it when she shot it, but she defends herself by sayin' she's defendin' part of their livelihood by discharging a firearm, I got no recourse. But that's who they are, and you're like that people in these parts aren't gonna feel a lot of kindness for you. What they're gonna do is maybe get up the nerve to piss you off right back by spray painting unflattering stick figures of you on the side of your barn while you're away for the weekend."

"Mm-hmm," she murmured.

"But that's my job in these parts," he told her. "Finding who did it and takin' it as far as the Mortimers use the law to make me take it, which with those two will be as far as the law will allow me to go."

"Hix," she whispered, but said no more.

So Hix kept right on talking.

"Felt now for years that I was irrelevant. Experience I had. Skills I got. And my job is about bein' up in some man's face for spendin' too much time with his bottle of Jim Beam and not enough keepin' track of his cows."

"You're not irrelevant."

"No. And now a man's dead and his five-year-old son is probably not gonna remember him much when he grows older and it's been made clear in the ugliest of ways that I'd sure as fuck rather be talkin' to owners of stores across the county about spray paint purchases. I'm also a dick for not seein' that as relevant, no matter I don't like the citizens I'm doin' it for."

"You're not a dick either, Hixon."

Hix looked to the street and did it belting back half the healthy dose of bourbon she'd poured for him. The burn made the muscles in his jaw bulge out as he gritted his teeth to fight it. But not long after, the warmth hit his chest and gut and it was worth it.

"You didn't will Faith's husband to get murdered because you were bored, darlin'," she said carefully.

Hix's only response was to throw back the rest of the bourbon.

"How can I help?" she asked.

"You're doin' it, lettin' me sit with you and bitch."

She let that sink in then she offered, "Can I get you more bourbon?"

"Gotta drive home, Greta, so no."

"You don't have to drive home."

He turned his head to her again.

"This," he started, lifting his empty glass to indicate the two of them on her porch, "is about a friend comin' to a friend after a shitty day. It isn't about me showin' at your place to bury that day in something sweet."

She smiled at him. It was small, sad, sympathetic, but entirely genuine.

"Okay. Though...uh, the 'something sweet' remark totally bought you that option if you want it open to you."

He couldn't believe it after the day he'd had, but what she said made his lips tip up.

"Good to know," he muttered.

"You can think on that over another glass of bourbon," she returned.

He looked at her a couple of beats then he looked to his glass.

He didn't answer her before she slipped the glass out of his hand and she was again walking in front of him to get into the house, this time carrying her closed laptop with her.

She was back, he had another healthy dose of bourbon in his hand and she was settled in beside him, sipping wine, when he asked, "What were you doing on your laptop?"

She glanced over his shoulder into her front window like she could see it from there and then back at him.

"Trolling eBay and discount designer sites for new cocktail dresses." She shot him a big grin. "I have a guest room closet full of them, due to my history." She lifted up her hand, thumb and forefinger half an inch apart before dropping it, all the while talking. "And I'll admit the barest *hint* of an addiction to pretty, shiny dresses. That said, I haven't bought one in a while and I figured it was time to treat myself."

"You find anything you like?"

"Seven hundred anythings. I should say, more precisely, when you showed, what I was doing on my laptop was narrowing that down."

He tipped his lips up at her again before he looked to the street and threw back more bourbon.

"Sorry I didn't call today," he said to the shadowy quiet beyond her porch.

"Word travels fast, Hix," she replied, back to soft and gentle. "I got it."

"Not thinkin' I can take you to lunch anytime soon."

"I get that too," she told him. "But, just sayin', I'm on my porch practically every night. Like the quiet. It's restful. Sets me up for a good night's sleep. So, seein' as my porch doesn't have a door, it's safe to say it's open for you anytime you wanna share it with me. That said, even if I'm in the house, my door is open to you, even if first I gotta unlock it after you ring the bell."

Hix looked to her again and his tone laid testimony to the truth of his, "Means a lot, sweetheart."

She nodded.

He lifted his glass and again shifted his attention to the sleepy street before he took another drink.

He felt her attention drift from him and they sat in the quiet for a while, both of them putting back bourbon or wine.

After some time, she asked, "You get any food in you today?"

He hadn't.

"Not hungry."

"I bet," she whispered, then offered, "I can make you a sandwich or something."

Nat Calloway's last meal was a sandwich.

"Think I'm good," he declined.

She kept at it.

"You wanna go in? Relax in front of a movie?"

He looked to her. "Thanks, babe, but no."

Her face grew soft as her gaze grew concerned. "Is there anything I can turn your mind to to help you take it off your day?"

"Probably not."

The concern deepened. "You gonna be able to sleep?"

"Probably not," he repeated.

She studied him for a few beats before a playful smile hit her face. "Just guessing on this, but seeing as you've been busy, you probably haven't bought any condoms."

That shocked a short bark of laughter from him and he shook his head through it, answering, "That guess would be right."

"Damn," she whispered, still smiling at him.

He twisted his torso in the chair and leaned into the arm toward her. "Again, Greta, I'm not here for that, and just to say, me wanting to have lunch with you is about communicating that to you too. It's safe to say I like what we've shared in a big way but I'm not here to get that from you and that's not all I want from you. It hasn't swung my way to find a time to prove that to you so I'm takin' that time now. I'll finish my bourbon. I figure you won't share wide I had two before I got in my car, unimpaired, mind you, and drove the five-minute drive home. But that's what I'm gonna do."

"I want you to stay," she blurted.

He stared into her eyes.

She leaned into him too. "I want you to stay, Hixon. I want to be with you, but more, I don't want you to be alone. Not after today. Not with what you've gotta face tomorrow. I heard you and I appreciate what you've said. But there's not much I can do to help you out except look after you. So how about you let me do that."

"Baby," he murmured.

She said no more and didn't wait for him to say anything.

She unfolded from her chair, got up, transferred her wineglass from her right hand to her left and came in front of him. She bent to him, wrapped her fingers around his free hand resting on the arm of the chair and she gave it a tug.

He resisted.

She tugged harder, her eyes locked to his.

Hix quit resisting.

When they were both standing and doing it close, she tipped her head back and whispered, "Let's go to bed."

Looking in her beautiful face, hers filled with soft concern but also traces of anticipation, Hix didn't bother attempting more resistance.

He followed her into her house, watched her turn off the porch light and locked her front door himself.

NAKED, his back to her headboard, his knees cocked, up and opened wide, his fingers gentle in her hair, Hix watched Greta suck him off.

He could come just watching how deeply she got off sucking his cock.

But she was seriously good at it. Lots of suction, lips tight, excellent use of tongue.

But no woman could do that forever, unfortunately. So when he started to rock up, meeting her movements, his fingers going from gentle to twist in her hair, and the noises she was forcing out of him came faster and got lower, she drew him out.

She wrapped her hand tight around him and came up to her knees between his legs, bracing herself in a hand beside him on the bed, her face close to his, his hand still in her hair as she started jacking.

"Good?" she whispered.

Good?

Not quite.

Great?

Absolutely.

"Yeah," he grunted, staring in her eyes.

She stared back, then her gaze started wandering his face, and in a voice that sounded like half a whimper, half a moan, she said, "God, you're so damned handsome."

He took his hand from her hair, wrapped it around hers pumping his cock, lifted his other one to curl it around the back of her neck to hold her right there, and he tightened their grip on his dick, quickening their movements.

"Oh my God," she breathed.

"Yeah," he agreed, beginning to thrust up into their hands.

She tipped her chin down to look at him and when she again gave him her gaze, he felt as well as saw through the dark around them it had gone from hot to fiery.

"Okay, baby, I kinda like this," she admitted huskily.

"I do too," he growled the obvious.

He just caught her turned-on smile before he yanked her to him with his hand at her neck, starting to kiss her hard, but he lost it, groaning into her mouth as he shot, his hot cum landing on his stomach.

She was kissing him when he began to power down their strokes but he kept their hands moving on him as he took over the kiss.

Finally, he released his hold on her hand on his dick but only to reach out, still kissing her, to cup her pubis and draw her gently closer to him.

She broke the kiss, took her hand from his cock, put it to his chest and whispered, "Hix."

"Straddle me."

"You don't—"

He released her but only to dive into her panties at the front, going deep, encountering what he felt on the outside, that she was drenched, and filling her with his middle finger.

Her back arched, a gust of breath hit his lips, and she scrambled up as he dropped his legs to give her access to come astride him.

He cocked them again and watched her face from close as he finger fucked her, felt her warm breath get heavier against his mouth, her hips begin to sync with his movements. He slid another finger in to join his other and kept at her.

"Yeah?" he asked.

"Oh yeah," she whimpered.

"Clit?" he asked.

She didn't answer that time. Just nodded and did it fast.

He grinned and slid his fingers out to move to her clit.

Once he put on pressure and started circling, she emitted a sexy, quiet cry and lifted her hand from his chest to clamp it around the side of his neck.

"Yeah?" he asked, even though he knew.

She ground into him.

Yeah, he knew.

"You got a toy, baby?" he queried. "Somethin' I can slip inside you while I work your clit?"

"I...the night—" She cut herself off as she mewed, bucked, pressed her neck against his hold there, and damn, this was almost hotter than her sucking him and jacking him. "Yeah, in the—"

Again she didn't finish because all of a sudden her head dropped. She dug her forehead in his neck where it met his shoulder, moaned, and her body trembled over him, her hips grinding her clit into his fingers as she came.

He took her through it and cupped her when it was leaving her.

He also twisted his neck to tell her what he wanted.

She lifted her head, met his mouth, letting him have hers for a deep kiss.

When he was through with her, he used his hand at her neck to press her forehead back into his shoulder and they both stayed right where they were as he listened to her breath even out.

"You're gonna be busy, I'll go buy condoms," she declared.

He felt his body get tight.

"Greta."

She pushed against his hold still at her neck so she could catch his eyes through the dark. "I know, Hix. I know. Message received. And that was hot. Like, serious hot. But, you know, just in case we get bored of the idea of handjobs."

"You're not my booty call," he said low.

"Again, message clear."

"Not sure I can make it that, naked with my cum dryin' on my gut, my hand still in your panties, which is all you're wearin' except that sweet bra."

He saw her eyes sparkle through the shadows. "Right. I can see your dilemma."

"This is serious to me, Greta."

The sparkle died and she slid her hand down to his chest and pressed in but not to pull away.

"What happened before that made you feel like a dick, that's over, Hix. You're not gonna have to pay for it as long as whatever is happening with us is happening. Stop kicking your own ass. The only person who has the right to do that is me and I'm over it. Let yourself be over it too."

"Babe—" he started, withdrawing his hand from her panties and gliding it around her hip to the small of her back.

"You had a bad day and I like you." She pressed into his chest again. "I *like* you, Hix. I like talking to you and listening to you, and what I like most of all, tonight, even after what just transpired, which was awesome, I liked that you came to me after a bad day. I'm not reading anything into it and I'm not feeling used. I led you up here because I wanted to give you what I just gave you and it was a conscious decision. I'm delighted beyond measure you returned the gesture, although it was unnecessary. Just let it be what it was and *relax*."

Jesus.

There was no other way to put it.

She was just freaking *great*.

"All right, sweetheart," he muttered, trying not to smile.

"Now, just to say, your Bronco has been at my—"

"Babe, I'm spending the night."

She fell silent.

"Unless you don't—" he started.

"I do," she whispered.

"Then get off me, Greta. I gotta wash up. Then I'm beat and I need some sleep."

He caught her grin before he caught the brush of her lips against his and she pushed away.

He rolled off her bed and watched her as she sat on the side of her hip, hand in the bed, eyes on him as he went to the bathroom.

He turned the light on this time and understood why the bathroom was one of the reasons she bought the house.

Tongue and groove all the way up the walls painted white. Big, claw-footed tub. Wide-plank wood floors. Broad, spindle-leg sink. Built-in, window-front cabinets. Toilet open to the room but the shower discretely tucked away so the bathroom had one but it wouldn't mess with the old-fashioned look of the room.

He pulled a thick washcloth that was a soft beige color and rolled up in an arrangement with a bunch of other ones out of a steel pail and cleaned his stomach. He rinsed it, draped it over the edge of the sink, turned to the door, switched off the light and walked back into her bedroom.

She was down, moon and streetlights coming through the windows to show her on her side, body pointed to the bathroom, head on a pillow, legs curled up, arm in front of her over her breasts, and Christ. Even seeing that through the shadows, he wished he could sketch so he could have that image, frame it and look at it whenever he wanted.

She reached out the arm at her breasts to yank down the covers, pushing up as she did to get under them herself.

Hix hit the bed, stretched out on his back and hooked an arm around her waist to pull her into his side.

He slid his hand up, encountered bra and asked, "You sleep in this?"

"Not usually."

He unhooked it, and with a few deft movements, had the straps down her arms.

He tossed it to the floor then curled her into him.

"Well, uh...all I can say about that is that you should teach classes on how to do it," she remarked. "I don't think I've ever been divested of a bra that expertly."

Hix chuckled.

He'd started the day on the news a man had been murdered.

And in bed with Greta, he was ending it chuckling.

"That was a pretty one, sweetheart, but they're always better off than they are on."

"Mm-hmm," she mumbled against his chest, pressing her now-bared breasts to his side.

As with everything he was discovering with Greta, it felt great.

He stroked her up her spine, over her shoulder and down her arm as far as he could reach since she'd curled it around his middle.

"You good?" he asked.

"Yeah, Hix," she answered, underlining that by snuggling closer. "You need me to set an alarm?"

"I won't sleep in."

"Figure not," she muttered.

She was worried he wouldn't sleep at all.

He gave her a squeeze. "Just...it's good. Don't worry about anything."

"Okay, darlin'."

He held her close, smelling her hair, hints of her perfume.

She cuddled closer.

"Greta?"

"Yeah, Hixon."

He lifted his head, twisted it and kissed the top of her hair.

"Thanks, baby," he said there.

Her arm gave him a squeeze but she didn't otherwise reply.

He relaxed.

Her weight melted into him.

He stared at her ceiling, felt her softness, her warmth, smelled her, and finally, his eyes drifted closed and Hix slept.

Chapter 11

Headway

Hixon

Hix woke up to a dark room.

The first thing he noticed was that he was in Greta's bed.

The next thing he noticed was that he was alone.

The next was that he felt refreshed.

After that, he saw from her bedside clock it was before six in the morning. He also saw her wineglass and his bourbon glass were no longer where they'd set them the night before.

Last, he smelled bacon cooking.

Having woken on his side facing Greta's side of the bed, he rolled to his back, did a stretch then rolled again and threw his legs on the floor.

He went to her bathroom, flipped on the light, used the facilities and then headed to the sink.

He washed his hands, splashed water on his face and dried it with a fluffy, white hand towel.

A quick survey of all her cabinets told him she didn't have a spare toothbrush but he found some mouthwash in her medicine cabinet.

He rinsed with it, spit it out and headed back into her bedroom where he got dressed, all the way down to his boots.

He found Greta and the bacon in the kitchen.

She had her hair in a messy bun at the top of her head, tendrils floating down, and she was wearing a simple, short robe in gray T-shirt material.

A robe that clung to her hips and ass in a way Hix was going to have to expend a goodly amount of effort in order to ignore.

The bacon was in a frying pan on her stove and she had her back to him, tending it.

"Babe," he called.

She turned to him, looked him up and down and smiled.

It was lucky he'd made it to the island which gave him an excuse for the fact her smile made him stop dead.

Not to mention, the robe clung to her tits almost better than it did her hips and ass.

Fortunately, she took his mind off of this by announcing, "If you think you're leaving my house without a good breakfast in your belly, Hixon Drake, think again."

The good of her smile shifted away as he replied gently, "This is not what you want to hear. And it's brutal, sweetheart, so I hope the indications you're giving me that you can take it mean you can actually take crap like this. But as much as I appreciate you lookin' out for me, I know Nat Calloway's last meal from getting the coroner's report, which included the contents of his stomach. I'm grateful for your concern but stuff like that makes a man's appetite not what it used to be." He hated to see her pale so he finished, "It'll pass."

"You need to eat, darlin'."

"I'm not hungry, baby."

"I don't mean to be flippant in the face of certain tragedy, Hix, but I simply cannot believe even murder beats the smell of bacon."

On her words, he felt his stomach rumble.

She might have heard it, she might not and just was bent on her need to look after him when she repeated on a tender push, "I get what you're saying, Hix, darlin', but you need to eat."

"Right, I'll let you feed me, Greta, but not to be rude, please, God, no biscuits and gravy."

Her brows shot up. "Are you telling me *you*, a *Hoosier*, do not like stick-to-your-ribs biscuits and gravy?"

"White gravy should be smothered over a chicken-fried steak and that's its only use."

"How weird," she murmured.

"Not weird, just my opinion," he replied.

"No, Hix, it's weird because I agree."

He stared at her.

No one in the entire state of Nebraska agreed with that.

She shot him a grin. "So, rest assured, no biscuits and gravy. Just eggs as you like 'em, bacon, toast, and ranch-style beans, you're in the mood."

Suddenly, he was starving.

"Beans sound good," he muttered.

She tipped her head to a full coffeepot and said, "Mugs in the cupboard. Creamer in the fridge. You want sugar, it's in that canister on the island, spoons in the drawer by the dishwasher."

He moved to the coffee. "Gotcha."

"Egg order?" she prompted.

"Fried, over medium."

"Toast order?"

He was pulling down a mug and looked to her. "Toast order?"

"Light, medium, toasty, burnt," she explained.

"You do toast to order?"

"It's not hard. There's a little dial to the side, you see," she teased. "You want burnt, I'll turn it all the way to ten."

He shot her a grin. "Medium."

She gave him a brief nod and he made his coffee while she moved around, dealing with bacon, eggs, beans, toast, butter.

He took his mug to the end of the counter closest to her where the sink and dishwasher were, catty-corner to where she was at the stove in the middle of the back wall, and he leaned a hip against it.

"You always get up this early?" he asked.

"I do when I have a good-lookin' hunk of man in bed who has to wake up and face another shitty day and I know he didn't eat the one before." She looked over her shoulder at him, eyes bright, and he could see the happy there was partially forced to hide her worry for him. "Though, just saying, I'd do it even if you ate yesterday."

"This is my job, Greta, you don't need to worry about me," he informed her quietly.

"Someone has to do it," she returned in the same tone.

"No they don't."

"Okay then, *I* have to do it, so please let me."

He held her gaze as he ignored how that made him feel too, lifted his mug to his lips and muttered, "Knock yourself out." He took a sip, but when he was done, he saw her mug by the stove was half empty, so he offered, "Want a warmup?"

"Yeah, darlin'. Just a splash of creamer." He got her a warmup, slid the mug by the stove, and she requested, "Stools by the door, I pull them to the island when I eat in here. They get in the way otherwise. Could you bring them over, please?"

He looked to the two half-Windsor-back stools, side by side next to the door then back at the kitchen.

It wasn't a small space and there was plenty of room around the island.

"Okay," she went on, and he turned his attention back to her to see she was looking like she was trying not to laugh as she watched him. "So they mess with my aesthetic."

"Right," he replied, his word shaking with his own laughter.

"I'm dishing up, get on those stools," she demanded.

"She's bossy in the mornings," he mumbled, moving to put down his mug on the island in transit to the stools.

"Just like to eat my food when it's hot, snuggle bug," she retorted.

He stopped, turned, stool in hands, and asked, "Snuggle bug?"

She awarded him with another big smile. "You snuggle."

He did?

"No, I don't."

"Uh...you were there," she reminded him.

"You snuggled me."

"You hooked me around the waist and put me there."

He did do that.

"We fell asleep that way because a man does that after he's bedded down with a woman as good as you are with your mouth..." he paused, and finished, lips twitching. "And hand."

She planted that exact hand on her hip. "Woke up with *you* wrapped around *me*."

Come again?

He'd never wrapped himself around Hope. He moved around in sleep. She did too. It was go-to-sleep cuddles and then they went their separate ways.

"You did not," he declared.

"Okay," she was still smiling and turning back to the stove, "tell yourself that...snuggle bug."

He set the stool down and asked, "That stool placement work for you, gum drop?"

She whirled around, spatula in hand. "Gum drop?"

He headed back for the other stool. "Not sure you want the meaning of that."

"Try me," she dared.

He brought the stool to the island, setting it beside the other one, and shot her a different kind of grin. "You taste sweet."

Color rose in her cheeks, it was more indication she could be cute, and she turned back to the stove.

"You're right. Maybe I didn't wanna know," she muttered.

"Better than the alternative," he pointed out.

She faked horror with her, "Ohmigod."

"Can't say I'm wrong," he noted.

"Ugh," she pushed out.

"Could call you donut," he said to her back.

"Blech," she said to the stove.

"Cupcake," he suggested, sliding his ass on a stool, enjoying the hell out of this.

"Gag," she declined.

"How about pumpkin?" he offered. "That wouldn't give anything away."

"Please, no," she said, bending down with an oven mitt on her hand and pulling out one of the two plates she was heating in the oven.

Greta heated plates.

Jesus.

"Gum drop it is," he stated, forcing his mind from heated plates.

She shot him a look, her face severe, eyes amused, and straightened.

She dished up. He got off his ass again to get cutlery for both of them.

He sat down, she set his plate in front of him and went back to make her own.

He didn't give her any more shit as she grabbed her mug and sat opposite him.

"Babe," he called and her eyes went from picking up her fork to him.

"That one works," she declared. "You go with another one, I'll have to bounce from snuggle bug to stud muffin, depending on the occasion."

The day after Hix stood, near to that very hour, next to a dead man, he sat on a stool in a country kitchen next to a beautiful woman who'd made him breakfast and he busted out laughing.

Still doing it, but while it was diminishing, he reached out, caught her behind the neck and pulled her to him.

"I was just gonna say, thanks for goin' all out to make me breakfast."

She stared into his eyes close up and whispered, "You're welcome, Hix."

"Now I'm gonna say thanks for making me laugh after a shit day and facing another one."

"You're welcome, baby."

He touched his mouth to hers, let her go and tucked in.

After a few bites of crispy bacon, perfectly toasted toast and exceptionally fried egg, he said with mouth full, "Relieved to know the woman who forces breakfast on me can cook...sprinkles."

Her big eyes came to him, she gulped down the coffee she'd been drinking then it was Greta who busted out laughing.

"S-s-sprinkles?" she asked through it.

"Take that however you want," he offered.

She kept laughing.

Hix went back to eating but did it smiling.

"You name a dog Sprinkles," she informed him.

"Then we're back to gum drop."

"Please, God, deliver me."

Hix chuckled and kept eating.

He got done when she was half done, and he hated to say it but he had to.

"I'll clean up while you finish up and then I gotta go."

Her eyes came to him and the cheeriness was gone, the worry was back.

"I'll clean up, darlin'. You gotta go, just go."

"Need to get home, shower, change—"

"Hix?"

"What?"

"Shut up and get outta here."

He grinned at her, picked up his plate, cutlery and mug and took it to the sink. He rinsed them all and came back to her, close to her side.

She tipped her head back.

He dipped his, running his hand along her neck at the back and curling his fingers around the side as he touched his mouth to hers and pulled a couple inches away.

"Thanks again, sweetheart."

"You're welcome, Hix."

He smiled at her, traced his fingertips along the soft skin at the side of her neck then let her go.

He was at her front door and about to open it when she called out, "Catch ya later, stud muffin!"

He bit back laughter but couldn't quite stop his smile as he opened the door, lifted a hand, gave her a flick of the wrist and walked out.

Hix wasn't smiling when, two and a half hours later, he turned his eyes from the whiteboard timeline case profile he'd drawn up that was butted to the wall across from his desk—a whiteboard that had way too much white—to watch Bets and Larry come through the front door to the department.

They both looked to him but only Larry walked back to his office. Bets went to her desk.

Hix got up from behind his and had his ass leaning against the front of it when Larry walked in, coming to stand in front of him.

"Faith has been updated and you were right. It was her Calloway had sex with the day he died. She told Bets they...he..." He cleared his throat and pushed through it. "She likes to get up with him. Get him breakfast. So after he showers, he wakes her up and they...take care of business."

"Right."

"Doesn't rule out another woman," Larry pointed out.

"Lance didn't say he found vaginal fluid from more than one woman, but I'll call him later and make sure of that."

Larry nodded.

"Do me a favor, man, and call the others in," Hix requested.

Larry turned to the door and walked out.

Hix stayed where he was and watched the progression of his team as they filed into the office.

Donna was last in and she closed the door behind her.

They fanned out exactly as they'd done the day before. Donna at one end, Bets beside her, Larry beside Bets, Hal on the other end, like Larry was playing buffer for Donna and Bets against a colleague they both despised.

In the rare times he had a briefing with them all, this was always the way they positioned themselves.

He'd never noticed it.

Now he did and Hix's high estimation of Larry rose higher.

"Right, unless anyone else had ideas since yesterday, I want us to start adjusting our focus and broadening our scope. We're lookin' for drifters. Homeless. And partners. We got nothin' so nothin' is out of bounds. Two men, man and a woman, even two women. Ask around. Hit the bars, diners, cafés and shelters in the county. New faces. Known folks. People actin' hinky. People givin' a bad vibe and gettin' attention. Work as partners, Larry and Hal, Donna and Bets. Work it out amongst yourselves who's going where. We struck out finding a crime scene, we have to focus on finding a suspect."

"So you think it was about the truck," Bets noted.

"Only thing missing is that truck," Hix replied.

"That's the only thing I can think too. Figured, maybe he picked up a hitchhiker or something. Maybe a fugitive who needed a ride but not one he had to share."

That was a good idea, but unlikely. Unless the kill freaked him out, that brand of perp would take Calloway's wallet, or at least the fifty-three dollars in it, especially if he took the time to move the body from the crime scene.

Even so.

"Run with that," Hix ordered. "Anyone recently jumping bail who's desperate enough to go to those ends to get his ass out of Nebraska. Do a search on that before you and Donna head out."

"We got a BOLO on that truck, Hix, and no hits on it," Donna pointed out.

"He might be layin' low, Donna. I'll start reaching out to law enforcement outside the adjoining counties at the same time hitting park services. Rangers get police alerts, gonna make sure they're on the ball as well as get folks to put a bug in the ear of anyone they know in Wyoming, Colorado, Kansas, Montana, South Dakota, doin' the same myself."

"What about Iowa and Missouri?" Hal asked. "Not like roads don't lead those places."

"Great stretches of nothin' in the states I named, Hal," Hix returned. "This man is on the run, he wants a lotta nothing. Not to hit a state where he'll be nabbed by highway patrol or a town cop faster 'n he can say his own name. But bugs in the ear means be on the lookout same as BOLO actually *stands for* be on the fuckin' lookout, so right now, havin' dick, we gotta light some fires under people in hopes they'll get motivated to lend us a hand. We also gotta go with hunches, attempt to create a focus of efforts and see if we can find a needle in a goddamned haystack then pin motive and opportunity on the damned thing."

Hal looked to his boots.

Hix cut his gaze through his team. "Time to get moving."

They didn't hesitate but Hix turned his attention to Hal.

"Hal, a minute." He looked to his door where Bets was the last to file out. "Close the door, Bets. Yeah?"

She couldn't quite fight back her grin as she muttered, "Yeah," and closed the door behind her.

Hix looked to Hal.

"I'll make this short because there's shit to do," he began. "You waste time sayin' stupid shit during a briefing one more time, Hal, you're suspended. I'm not fucking with you. We got a dead citizen and his grieving widow and kids in this county and I don't need to be explainin' to you how to do your job or the decisions I make. You got a genuine question or suggestion you wanna add, I'm open to it. You wanna bust my balls for whatever reason, shut it down."

"You're threatening to suspend me during the first murder investigation in McCook County in fifty-two years?" Hal asked incredulously.

"Yes, Hal, I am."

Hal straightened his back and puffed out his chest. "You're giving preferential treatment to the other deputies."

"Are you kidding me?" Hix asked, now he was incredulous.

"You told Bets to tell me to bring fucking *coffee* to a crime scene yesterday."

"It was six in the morning, settin' up to be a long day since we had the first murder victim on our hands that the county's seen in fifty-two years, so yeah. I want my deputies alert and that means I want them to have some damned caffeine, and to get that not every one of 'em stoppin' by Babycakes on the way to check out a body dump."

"I coulda brought the tent," Hal pointed out irately.

Hix could not believe what he was hearing.

"You're bustin' my balls and wastin' my time," he warned low.

Hal was and it would seem he couldn't stop himself from doing it.

"You're handlin' Bets with kid gloves 'cause it's clear you got fed up with puttin' up with her dewy eyes, obviously laid it out, and you gotta expend effort to kiss her ass and snap her out of it 'cause she's a girl and not a man who first, wouldn't give you dewy eyes and second, you could just say it like it was and he'd take it like a man. Not to mention, you left me behind as forensics' errand boy while the rest of you started the investigation."

Hix couldn't even think of his first point without physically getting in the man's face.

So he focused on the second.

"Those Cherry County boys treat you like an errand boy?" he asked.

"No," Hal mumbled. "You did."

"Hal, I left you behind because you have experience at a murder scene so you'd know more what you're lookin' for working *with* forensics at a dump site. And I told you to show them McCook hospitality because those boys aren't paid by our county and they coulda told us to go spit rather than hauling their asses down to another county to investigate a crime scene. It's called interdepartmental relations and that leads to interdepartmental *collaboration*, somethin' right now we *need*."

Hal opened his mouth.

Hix lifted his hand.

"Listen to me, Hal, and listen good. Your balls are so big you can't bring coffee to your team and you got a problem handling orders or doin' the job you're paid to do for this county, then we have a bigger problem and that's to do with your continued employment. From the very beginning, you wanted to blow this off. When my hunch this was serious played out, you've questioned nearly everything that's come out of my mouth. Just now, Bets had an idea that, frankly, mired in the utter *lack* of shit that surrounds Nat Calloway, didn't occur to me. She's now workin' that, and who knows, it might help us catch a killer. I can't believe with your years on the job I gotta tell you this, but you're either with us or you're against us, and that *us* includes your superior officer and the two females we have in this department. My advice is, make your choice. Don't make me make it for you."

"I want this guy found much as you, Hix."

"Then welcome back to the team."

Hal glared at him a beat before he asked, "We done, boss?"

Since they were into it, he wasn't.

"No," he answered.

"What else?" Hal bit out.

"I gotta partner you with Larry because he's the only one who can work with you without lettin' his feelings for you get in the way of that work. That doesn't say anything about Bets and Donna. Watchin' you alienate yourself from your colleagues, that says a lot about you and none of it is good. We need to find who killed Nat Calloway and we need to work as a functioning, healthy unit to do it.

Again, with your time on the job, thought you'd sort yourself out with your fellow deputies, but you didn't do dick to do that. So now I'm forced to share with you, you need to expend some effort, Hal. You razz Bets and you take it too far. You avoid Donna because she gave you some honesty you didn't like to hear and you need to get over it. They don't have to like you so much they ask you to Sunday dinner. But they *do* have to like you enough, trust you, know you got their back, to work with you on a job that in this place may seem like it don't matter much, but we've got a dead man in the morgue proves that wrong."

Hal didn't reply.

So Hix asked, "Are you understanding me?"

"Yeah," Hal gritted.

"Good."

"Now we done?" he asked.

"I hope so, Hal."

Hix would swear he could hear the man actually grinding his teeth before he stalked out.

He drew in a big breath and went back behind his desk.

He put Hal out of his mind and picked up his phone in order to start first with park rangers to make certain they'd seen the BOLO and maybe motivate them to get some of their rangers out in their vehicles to search their parks for Calloway's truck.

He'd graduated to calling county sheriffs when his cell on his desk beeped and he looked to the screen to see it was from Reva, who was just across the way.

It said, *Terra Guide.*

His eyes went out the window and he saw Terra Snyder, editor of the town's paper, the *Glossop Guide*.

He lifted a one-minute finger to her through the window, noted she'd caught it and then set about tying up his phone call.

He did this trying to think of Terra's arrival as a boon. Their paper came out only once a week, on a Tuesday, that day had passed, and Hix hoped they had this solved by that day next week.

However, they also had a website and if she could get word out that they were looking for anyone who saw anything on that stretch of road around six o'clock on Monday night, maybe they'd catch a break.

In reality, this would probably just buy them a bunch of phone calls from people giving them crap they couldn't use in an effort to be helpful or insinuate themselves into the situation in order to find out what was going on.

But Terra was a good woman. She ran the paper practically by herself, was serious about her job even if it was mostly reporting on bridge club tournaments and high school sports, getting student interns from the high school or home for summers from college, and that was mostly it.

So Hix pushed up from his desk, exited his office and walked out, calling a greeting to her when he entered the aisle between his deputies' desks on the way to reception where she was standing, watching him.

"Hey, Terra."

"Hix," she replied, studying him closely.

He didn't talk to her over the reception desk. He moved through the swinging half door and went to stand close to her, resting a hand on the desk.

"Heard you came by, sorry, been busy," he remarked.

"I bet," she said. "Got anything for me?"

Openly, he gave her what she needed to know, only what she needed to know. The victim's name. Age. His occupation. The fact he was a family man. And that he was now sadly dead.

"Got any suspects?" she asked, her head down, the fingers of one hand tapping away on the screen keyboard of a tablet she held in the other.

"I can't comment on an ongoing investigation, Terra," he told her.

She lifted her eyes to him. "Come on, Hix. Don't shut me down like that. This isn't Indianapolis. But it *is* the juiciest piece of news Glossop has had in near on two centuries."

All of a sudden he didn't feel like this was a boon.

"How about you go to Nathan Calloway's widow and describe it like that?" he suggested.

She looked instantly contrite and Hix was relieved he hadn't been wrong that she might be a reporter, but she was a good one as well as a good woman.

"That was out of line," she muttered. "Sorry."

"Forgotten," he replied. "Now you could do us a favor, you're willin' to help out."

She perked up and asked, "What's that?"

"Anyone who saw anything on County Road 56 from Glossop to the Grady ranch down in Grant County. Broken-down car. Hitchhiker. Sometime between the hours of five and seven Monday night. They saw something, they can call this department. Also lookin' for a truck, it's Nathan Calloway's. White Ford F150, can shoot you the details on that through email."

"I can put somethin' up on the website, Hix."

"We'd be obliged, Terra."

She stared hard at him, remarking, "Could read from that you don't got a lot."

"Read whatever you want," he returned. "But I'll tell you we've got all our resources at work on this, and we're doin' everything we can to find out who did this to the Calloway family."

She nodded, dropping her head to tap on her tablet before she looked back up at him. "Gotta know, citizens of this county have anything to worry about?"

Hix shook his head. "Nothin' leads us to believe that's the case. Everything points to this being a random, one-time incident. But that doesn't mean I won't say what I say when I do my yearly talk at the middle school. Always be alert. Lock your doors. Let loved ones know where you're at and when to expect you home. Though, again, sayin' that only because it's smart and should be routine for every citizen of this county."

"That's good," she muttered, tapping away. "Spin this also as a PSA, remindin' folks they should look after themselves."

He didn't like the idea of spinning a murder any way, but if there was a way it had to be spun, Hix would pick that one.

The front door opened and Hix looked to it to see Henry Blatt, McCook's last sheriff, strolling through.

"Hope you ain't talkin' to the press, boy," he declared loudly, his gaze swinging from Terra to Hix.

Terrific.

"Sheriff Blatt, what's your take on what's happened to Nat Calloway?" Terra called out as Blatt sauntered right to the swinging half door and also right through it.

"My take is no comment," he stated and kept talking and walking. "Drake, wanna talk to you. Office."

Hix watched him go, sighed and looked to Terra.

"Just to say, off the record, which is not something a reporter usually throws out there, but thank God you're in that office instead of him, this happened in this town, Hix," Terra murmured, lifted her tablet his way and said, "Thanks. You shoot me the details of that truck, I'll have some text to you to look over before I post it on the website. Work for you?"

"Yeah, Terra, thanks."

She nodded, moved, waved to Reva and walked out.

Hix turned to the half door and saw Reva in the door to dispatch.

"That pompous ass messes things up for you and the Calloway family, Hixon, you'll have another shooting on your hands," Reva announced.

Reva was a petite, very round, older version of Ida but with short, dyed-brown hair teased into a helmet style that oddly suited her.

However, whereas Ida was a sage who was relatively mellow, regardless that her family might or might not be significantly dysfunctional, Reva had the wisdom of her years and was a ball-buster, which might be the reason why her son was a heart surgeon in Omaha and her daughter flew jets for the Air Force.

"It'll be all right," he told her.

"It better be," she shot back, turned and flounced to her desk.

Hix went through the swinging door and right to his office, relieved to see Blatt at least had it in him not to be sitting in Hix's chair.

He was standing, staring at the whiteboard, and the second Hix hit the room, Blatt turned to him, clapped his hands, rubbed them together and asked, "Right, run it down for me."

"Henry—"

Blatt lifted a hand his way. "Don't give me that. This is serious. You need all the help you can get."

"We got it covered."

Blatt's eyes narrowed. "I'll repeat, don't give me that shit, boy."

Hix let his deputies call him by his first name and he'd never, maybe even with a gun to his head, though he hoped that was never tested, refer to one of them as "boy," "son," "girl," or "gal."

Until he'd retired, Hix had never called Blatt "Henry," but Hix had been called "boy" almost exclusively, unless Blatt was feeling soft-hearted, then he'd call Hix "son."

Hix hated it.

But right then, the priority was stopping a retired sheriff who'd never investigated a murder in his entire career interfering with a murder investigation. It was not telling the man how he felt about being forty-two, the elected sheriff and being called "boy."

"Due respect, Henry, I understand you wanna help but the best way you can help is let us get on with this case."

"I know every inch of this county and practically every soul in it."

The first was true. The second, even with a county that unpopulated, it was still large in land mass, so it couldn't even come close to being true.

"You happen onto a five-year-old, white, Ford F150 with McCook County plates that shouldn't be anywhere but the Grady ranch or a house on Emerson, not much you can do," Hix told him.

"You run it down for me, maybe I'd have other ideas," Blatt returned.

"Henry, I got some calls to make and then I gotta get out there and see if I can make some leeway in finding out who killed the father of two little kids. Again, respect, but I don't have time for this."

"I'm here to help."

"And I'm tellin' you, best way you can do that is let me get on with doing my job."

Blatt gave him a scowl. "That isn't respect."

"And just to point out," he tossed out his hand to indicate the both of them in that room having that conversation, "this isn't respect."

Blatt blew out a breath, broke eye contact, lifted a hand to squeeze the back of his neck, dropped it, then looked again to Hix.

"Faith is my wife's sister's great-niece. My sister-in-law is married to Faith's great-uncle."

Damn.

It was true that Blatt was a blowhard, but outside of liking a bit too much his position of authority, he'd always given indication he was also about serving his citizens.

He just did it in a pompous-assed way.

"Then how you can help is keep an eye out for Nat's truck and look after Faith. She's gonna have a lotta people in her space thinkin' they're helping when they're probably not. If you can shield her so she can get on with her grief without playing hostess to half the town, you'll be doin' a lot."

Blatt didn't look like he liked it, but he did look like he was considering it, then he came to a decision.

"Yeah. Maybe I'll spend the day on Faith's porch. Make sure she's got quiet to take a nap or somethin'."

Hix bit back a sigh of relief.

"I'm sure she'd be grateful."

Blatt nodded.

Hix got out of his way when Blatt started toward the door.

The man stopped when he was in line with him.

"Find this fucker, son," he ordered, fire in his eyes, wearing his sixty-eight years on his face.

He knew Faith and he cared for her.

He also knew Nat and he wanted the man who ended his life to pay for it.

"We're throwin' everything we got at that, Henry."

Blatt nodded, drew in a big breath and walked out Hix's door.

Hix was back at his desk, making his last calls, approving the notice Terra sent to him after he'd emailed her the details on Calloway's truck, fielding other calls from papers in the county, when his cell on the desk beeped again.

He looked to it and it was another text from Reva. This time it said, *Hope.*

His eyes went to the window but Reva texting him because she couldn't phone him seeing as he was on the phone had taken too much time.

A knock came at the door and his gaze turned there to see Hope standing in it, her face soft.

Shit.

He did what he could to make the call he was on short and then ended it.

The minute he put the handset in the receiver, still in the door, she called quietly, "Hey."

"Hope, whatever this is, I really can't do it now," he returned.

Unsurprisingly, he said that and his ex-wife walked right in.

Hix rose from his seat.

"You doin' okay?" she asked.

"I'm working."

"I know," she said, again quiet. "I heard, Hix. God." She shook her head coming to a stop right across the desk from him. "I'm so sorry. So sorry. It's had to have been rough."

"I wasn't married to him, Hope."

"I know, but you..." She looked to the windows before she came back to him. "You never liked the murders in Indy."

"Not something you like."

"I think you get me, honey."

He felt a muscle tick up his cheek.

"I'm fine, Hope. Thanks for stoppin' by but I got shit I really gotta see to."

She nodded. "Yes, I...yes...well," she stammered, looked back to the windows, and when he got her attention again, he clenched his hands into fists at the hurt he saw stark there. "I just...I know now's not the time but I heard you were, well, last night you went to..." She paused then said like she had to force it to come out, "*Her.*"

It sucked that, after all her recent behavior, he totally could believe she came there not to see how he was doing but to share in her way she didn't like it he was spending time with, not to mention doing, someone else.

But they were not going to get into this and not just because it was none of her freaking business.

"Hope—"

"You know," she started quickly, "that I know that I made it that way. That was my fault. But now I'm here to say that I'm here, Hix, if you need me. You need someone to talk to. You can come to me."

"Thanks for the offer," he pushed out.

"I know we haven't been getting along real great, but that offer's genuine, Hixon."

"'Preciate it."

"Seriously."

Christ.

"Hope, I got *shit to do.*"

Her body gave a small jerk and she whispered, "Right. Yeah. Of course. Of course, honey. I'll just...get back to Mom and Dad's. They say they're thinkin' of you and the team, and of course that poor family."

"Right."

"Well, better go," she muttered.

"Yeah," he agreed.

She looked into his eyes, sucking his time, making it clear the effort she was expending to force a smile his way at the same time still not hiding the hurt she felt he'd gone to Greta and not giving him a hint of the concern she was pretending to feel for him, which was the lie behind the reason she'd come there.

"Talk to you later?" she asked.

He didn't know what to say to that without saying something he shouldn't so he decided just to keep his mouth shut.

"Okay, well...later."

"'Bye, Hope."

She nodded, hesitated, and when he said no more and gave her nothing, she turned and slowly walked to the door, giving him ample time to call her back.

He did not.

He also didn't look out the window to watch her go.

He sat down, texted all his deputies to let them know the notice would go up on the *Guide* website within the hour, walked out to Reva to give her that same news, went back to his office and got back on the phone.

He was into his final call when his cell beeped again.

He bit back a curse as he listened to the sheriff of Wheeler County telling him he'd keep his crew sharp in keeping an eye out for Calloway's truck.

But he felt himself relax when the text displayed faded away.

He got off the call, picked up his cell and engaged it, fully reading Greta's text.

Folks at the Harlequin say you got a thing for their Reuben so I'm bringing you one even if I have to drive it all the way across the county. So text me your whereabouts, smokey.

He grinned as he texted back, *Office, babe.*

I'll be there soon, she replied.

She didn't lie and ten minutes later Hix caught her coming in.

He got up and moved out to go and get her.

"Hey," she called when she saw him come out of the back hall.

"Hey," he replied. "Come on back."

She glanced to Reva, smiled that way then came through the swinging half door.

He met her halfway down the aisle and turned. Taking the plastic bag with the Styrofoam box flattening the bottom from her hand, he put his other hand to her elbow and led her to his office.

He let her go and went right to the whiteboard, flipping it around so the timeline and the photos taped to it were not facing the room. This was not so she wouldn't see confidential details of an investigation, but so she wouldn't see disturbing photos of a dead man.

"Is this okay?" she asked as he turned to her, her eyes to the now blank board.

"What?" he asked in return.

She looked to him. "Coming here." She lifted her hand to indicate the bag. "Bringing you lunch."

He smiled. "Hell yeah."

She smiled back.

Hix looked down and opened the knots to the bag, seeing inside there was only one tray.

He raised his head. "Nothing for you?"

"It's my day off," she told him. "And I've got a ton to do so I'm just dropping that off to make sure you eat something and then I have to get to doing it."

"Right," he replied, having a ton to do too but thinking he wished part of it was being able to spend fifteen minutes eating a sandwich with her.

"That ton to do includes buying another bottle of bourbon," she shared. "I'm running low."

Hix smiled again. "Right."

"And, well...um, buying other things," she went on.

Hix started chuckling. "I get a say in priority of these two items, bourbon would come in second."

Greta started laughing.

It died away, she gave him a close look and what was behind her eyes was not about her, it was about him.

"You doin' okay?" she asked softly.

"Yeah, babe."

"Okay," she whispered.

"Though one thing I'm not doin' okay about is that I'd really like to kiss you to say thanks for the Reuben. But Reva wouldn't share shit that happened in this department that had to do with sheriff business, even if she was waterboarded. Gossip does not hold that same level of confidentiality. Not even close."

She was back to smiling when she said, "I understand."

He wasn't far away from her but he got closer. "Tonight, meet you at your porch."

"Okay," she replied.

"Don't know when, it might be late, but I'll text you before I show."

"Sounds good, Hixon."

"And thanks for lunch, Greta."

She swayed to him, her eyes to his, but didn't touch him. "My pleasure, snuggle bug."

He chuckled again.

She grinned, reached out and touched a finger to the back of his hand and said, "Later."

He knew the response to that.

"Yeah, sweetheart, later."

She kept grinning at him even as she turned and walked out the door.

Hix watched her leave his department, doing it waving again at Reva.

Then he went back to the whiteboard, flipped it back around, pulled the Styrofoam out of the bag, set the bag aside, opened the box and ate, standing up and staring at the board in front of him.

Half the sandwich gone, pickle decimated, one bite into the second half, Hix froze, and mouth full, he mumbled, "Shit."

He closed the Styrofoam, went to his desk and nabbed his cell.

He shoved it in his breast pocket, and still carrying the sandwich, he took off out the door, going to Reva and only saying, "You got reception," before he hauled ass out of the building.

He ate the rest of the sandwich in his Ram between phone calls.

"You got this from scrapes?" Donna asked.

They were standing on the shoulder of County Road 56, seven miles up from Grant into McCook County, only distant farmhouses dotting the landscape, the rest just field, both the men of Cherry County's forensics team squatted in the tall grass about six feet from the road, digging in the turf.

"Concrete's graded," Hix said, watching forensics, Donna standing close to him, Larry, Bets and Hal all out in the grass in different directions, heads bent, walking slow, swishing with their batons through the grass.

"And?" Donna prompted.

He looked to her.

"Heels of both his palms had bruising come up, not dark, didn't catch it because of that, but it was there. Once I noticed that, it delineated scrapes that would indicate they cut in on the diagonal. Grading of the road goes side to side to allow water runoff. If he was runnin' *down* the road and took a header into his hands, that bruising and those scrapes would be horizontal. But they were diagonal, which meant he was running off the road."

"And that?" she tipped her head to where forensics was digging.

"We were lookin' for a bloodstain and shell casings on the road yesterday, Donna. Drove down to Grady's, drove back and did it slow. Took me nine miles and I saw that grass depressed, broken grass on the way to it that could seem beaten down by rain yesterday. That depression looks natural, unless you're lookin' for it. And that grass bouncin' back in the sun today, the broken grass not doin' that, you can see the path that leads to the depression. Yesterday, figure it didn't look like that. Today, didn't have to look hard to find it."

He jerked his head to the bullet in an evidence bag weighed down by a rock on the hood of his truck, which was one bag amongst many that mostly contained cigarette butts and their bonus find: three shell casings. Two they'd found in the turf not far from the road, one had been knocked, probably by cars, to the opposite side of the road where yesterday they didn't look.

"He went down on the road when he took one in the shoulder," Hix told her. "Got up, kept running. Shooter followed him. Got off two more rounds while he was in the grass, going after him. The one that hit his shirt, the one that got him in the neck."

"So guy did him, carried him out, and did it in a hurry, not bothering to clean up after himself," Donna noted.

"Not a high traffic area, houses not even a little close, but he killed a man and folks around these parts stop, they think someone's in trouble. He got that body, put it in Nat's truck, and got the hell outta here."

She looked from the grass to Hix. "No other vehicle? No partner?"

"Got nothing on this road or the shoulder, such as it is, to give us tire impressions, rain took that, and obviously no skid marks to say he'd been run off the road." Hix shook his head. "Donna, gut tells me the man stopped to help someone out. I'm thinkin', guy pulled a gun, my guess, he wanted Nat to drive, but Calloway thought his best bet was to get his ass outta his truck and run. The man tried to steal his truck, Calloway saw his face, man panicked."

"You thinkin' fugitive like Bets said?" Donna asked.

"I'm thinkin' a fugitive that would do something fool enough to jump bail or run from the cops after he'd committed a crime would know that what he'd get for stealin' that truck would be a whole lot better than what he'd get for shooting a man and definitely killing him."

"Tweaker," she murmured.

"Blatt saw to the fact no meth was sold in our county and I gotta admit a good byproduct of that deal is, since McCook's meth man doesn't sell close to home, he's not a big fan of someone else's product hitting his county, so he shuts that down before we gotta lift a finger."

"Man could be from outta town, Hix."

"Then how would he know about that game trail?"

She nodded. "Yeah. True."

Hix looked back to the grass. "Least we got a crime scene."

"Yeah."

"And meth isn't the only shit that could string someone out."

"Yeah."

His cell rang and Hix pulled it out of his breast pocket to see it was the chief at Dansboro Police.

"Gotta take this," he muttered.

"Gotta help out," she muttered back, then waded into the grass.

Hix took the call, hoping he'd get word on a Ford F150.

Instead, the fact they'd found the scene of the crime got out and he found himself giving an update.

He gave it, waded in the grass a different direction than any of the bodies out there, and helped out.

Hix pulled out, rolled off Greta, tagged her around the waist and hauled her up and around until she was on her knees in front of him, her back to his front.

He took her hand, planted it under his in the headboard, positioned behind her, guiding his cock with his other hand, then he drilled inside.

Damn.

So sweet.

Her head flew back and hit his shoulder and she lifted her other hand and braced it into the wall above her headboard, rearing back into his thrusts.

He slid his hand from her belly to her tit, rolled the nipple then pulled it.

"Hix," she gasped, dropping her head forward and taking his cock.

He brushed the hair at her nape aside with his chin and then rested his lips there, grunting against her skin as he fucked her.

They'd never fucked.

She got off on it.

He did too, including the fact she did.

She tipped her ass up and slammed back into him harder.

Hell yeah.

She got off on it.

"Yeah, Greta," he growled into her skin, pulling her nipple.

She whimpered and drove back into him faster.

"Fuck yourself, baby," he encouraged.

Her head fell back again and she puffed out, "Yeah."

He left her nipple, slid his hand down between her legs and pressed in at her clit.

Her body jerked against him.

"*Hix.*"

She was pounding into him now, no rhythm, no control, panting and reaching for it.

He pulled out again.

She cried out, "*No!*" but he turned her, walked into the headboard on his knees, lifted her up and slammed her down on him, this getting him a breathy, "*Yes,*" right before she shuddered in his arms, her limbs wound around him going tight, and her pussy convulsing around his dick as she came.

He rode her against the headboard, trying to focus on the beauty of her face as she gave it to him.

But he lost focus when the pressure built in his balls and he grunted, pounding fast and hard, his eyes closing tight, white exploding behind them as he shot into the condom inside her, coming spectacularly.

Her lips were working his throat when he came down, and he bumped his chin gently against her head to tell her where he wanted that.

She gave it to him, tipping her head back and offering him her mouth.

He took it, kissing her hard then softer until they were mostly brushing and nibbling lips.

Only then did he mutter, "Gonna clean up."

"Okay, darlin'."

He touched his mouth to hers, slid out, moved back, laid her in bed and then exited it.

He got rid of the condom and washed up in a dark bathroom before rejoining her in bed.

Hix didn't have to hook her around the waist to pull her into him that time.

She cuddled right in after he'd settled on his back and as he was yanking the covers over them.

"Who's snuggling now?" he teased.

"Shut up, Hixon."

He grinned to the ceiling, curled his arm around her and drew circles on her hip as she pressed her naked body into his side, snaking a hand along his gut, curving it around his other side and holding him close.

"You're in a better place tonight," she noted.

Earlier, on her porch, he hadn't had bourbon, he'd had beer. He'd also had some cold fried chicken he found out she'd bought for him just in case he came early enough to eat, or late but without dinner.

It had been the last.

She'd also shown him the three dresses on her laptop that she'd bought that night (all three he'd given his wholehearted approval). She'd told him the salon was on fire with talk about Calloway's murder. And she'd assured him that everyone had faith in him and his crew finding who did it.

She'd also said, "A beauty salon is not a confessional, but you know, it wouldn't be good to lose a client. So it was a little bird that told you that the Mortimers' neighbor's son loved his dog a whole lot. Not to mention, he's got a paper route he does for spending money, thus the means to buy spray paint his parents didn't know about, as well as a grudge his dog was shot and his parents were forced to use the money they were saving up to buy him the latest Xbox for his birthday in order to save that dog's life. Insult to injury, he mighta acted on that. And his folks mighta found the paint cans. And they mighta reamed his ass even if they still thought it was pretty damned funny. So they might be comin' in to share their son acted unwisely in his anger or they might not. Just act surprised if they do and don't give me up if they don't."

"Talked to them already, Greta, and they told me their son would never do that," he'd replied.

"Well, after they did that, they checked to make sure the statement they gave the sheriff was indeed correct and found that it was not."

Even though he was grateful for the knowledge and amused she was so funny in the way she provided it, he shared gently, "You're not my booty call. You're also not my informant, sweetheart."

She'd just smiled back. "I know. What I am is the chick who's cool with ratting out one of her clients' sons if it takes a least a little something off your mind."

After that, with no will to fight it, he'd dragged her ass off the porch then nailed it in her bedroom.

"We made headway today," he replied to her mentioning he was in a better place.

She gave his middle a squeeze. "Good."

"Yeah."

They both let that settle before Hix spoke again.

"Think that Reuben had magical powers, eating it, I saw somethin' I hadn't noticed from the photos we got and I'd been givin' those a lot of attention."

She lifted her head from his shoulder and looked at him through the dark. "Then no more bitching about me feeding you."

He lifted his hand and cupped her cheek, grinning at her and murmuring, "No more bitching, baby."

She gave him a flash of a smile and settled back in on his shoulder.

Hix took his time drifting his fingers along her cheek as he slid his hand away.

She snuggled closer and muttered, "Pancakes okay for breakfast tomorrow?"

"Hope to God I close this case but now hope to God I do it without packing on fifty pounds."

She gave him a warning shake. "What was that we agreed about no more bitching?"

"Right. Sorry," he mumbled then spoke distinctly, "Pancakes will be good."

"Excellent."

The hour, the dark and the sex settled in, so Hix did too, relaxing and feeling sleep coming when Greta asked, "You talk to your kids?"

"Shaw called tonight after football practice, heard what happened, checking in. He handed the phone off to his sisters. So yeah. They're worried about their dad but think they're all old enough to get this is part of the job. At least that's what they gave me. I'll know better when I got 'em back."

"Good."

Hix hadn't shared with Greta about Hope's visit that day.

Since Reva had been there when Hope showed, Greta might already know if that news had hit the salon and she just wasn't mentioning it. Or she could not know and he wasn't going to bring his ex into her bed.

What he was going to do was carve out some time where his mind was not centered on a murder and consider what was happening with Greta.

He had friends. He had female friends. He'd never had a friend with benefits, he was thinking that might be nice, but it still wasn't what this was.

No, he was thinking that wasn't what he *wanted* this to be.

It was too soon but he was also beginning to think he didn't give a shit.

She was great and it might not be the best timing, but he'd be a fool if something that gave every indication it was just that awesome walked into his life and he didn't work with her to discover where it might go.

That conversation would have to happen after he found a murderer.

But it was going to happen.

So as Hix fell asleep feeling Greta's warm weight pressed to his side, along his stomach, smelling her, he found he had another reason to catch a killer.

And fast.

Chapter 12

Really Fuckin' Simple

Hixon

The next morning, Hix woke up again before six, alone in Greta's bed.

He hauled himself out and went to her bathroom, flipping on the light switch and seeing poking out of her pail, with its bouquet of rolled washcloths, a toothbrush in its packaging with a blue bow stuck to it that was five times the size of what it was stuck to.

He grinned, did his thing, including brushing his teeth with a new toothbrush, went back out and got dressed but carried his boots with his socks stuffed into them down the stairs, dumping them at the foot and smelling sausage as he rounded the steps to head to the kitchen.

She was standing at the sink in her robe, body facing her windows that now had the sheer shades drawn up, a coffee cup held aloft in front of her, but her head was turned, eyes to him.

"Thanks for the present," he said, strolling into the room.

"You'll learn I'm bountiful with my generosity," she joked.

He stopped close to her side, dug his fingers in her hair and held her in position as he bent and took her mouth in a morning kiss that shared far more gratitude than any toothbrush was worth.

When he broke the kiss and lifted slightly away, he watched her slowly open her eyes and breathe, "Today, I'm totally buying you dental floss."

He started chuckling, doing it dipping in to touch his mouth to hers before he let her go and went to the coffee.

She went to the stove to turn sausage links.

Once he made his mug, saw hers was still mostly full, he rested the side of a hip against the counter, turned to her.

"I catch this guy, I'm taking you to dinner."

Slowly, she pivoted to face him.

"Dinner?" she asked.

With the look on her face, Hix knew she got him.

"Dinner," he confirmed.

"Hixon—"

"Not now," he whispered. "Not now, baby. I need this, what you're givin' me. Need it to be easy. Need it to be uncomplicated."

"Okay," she said softly.

He said what he said but he still held her gaze and made sure she understood him.

"At dinner, you're up for it, we'll complicate things."

Something lit her eyes, her face, making her early-morning, makeup-less beauty awe-inspiring.

Hope, maybe.

Excitement, absolutely.

"I'm up for it," she told him.

He smiled at her.

She smiled back.

And there was the hope.

Christ.

Yeah.

Awe-inspiring.

"Since that's gonna happen, sweetheart, feel at this juncture it's not takin' it too far to ask your last name," he remarked.

She stared at him before she busted out laughing.

He was smiling at her because he liked her laughter and it *was* funny they were where they were and he didn't know her last name, but he was just glad she also found it amusing, when she quit laughing and shared, "Dare. It's Dare."

Greta Dare.

He liked it.

"Bonus, my middle name is Kate," she went on. "Not Katherine. Just Kate. Apparently my mother wasn't into too many syllables."

"It's pretty," he murmured.

"Thanks," she whispered.

"Timothy," he told her.

"Sorry?" she asked.

"Your bonus."

She grinned then her eyes went strange and her body started visibly shaking. "Ohmigod," her voice was shaking too. "You're Sheriff Hixon T. Drake. You totally need to start going by that handle on your CB."

He liked the fact she shared his and his son's sense of humor, not to mention got in on a joke she didn't even know was their joke.

"This has been suggested by my son," he noted.

She gave him a blinding smile. "Well, that's two votes."

He shook his head. "Not gonna happen."

"Shame," she muttered, still smiling and turning back to the stove.

"You need help?" he asked.

"Nope," she told the sausage. "Just need you to pull over the stools and sit your behind on one. You probably won't be relaxing for a while. You do it over breakfast, get your belly full, you'll be able to face the day."

He stared at her back as she moved from the sausage to the

counter by the stove, grabbed the handle of a spoon in a big bowl and started beating what sounded like batter.

Then he moved to her. Right to her, right into her space, fitting himself to her back and putting his hands to the edges of the counter on either side of her.

It was batter.

Pancakes.

Like she'd promised.

He dipped his head and set his lips to the skin at the side of her neck.

"Night before last you told me you liked me, and I didn't share you got the same. But I'll share more. It's about pancakes. It's about the way you sing. It's about how amazingly beautiful you are, so beautiful, sometimes, if I don't brace myself, it blinds me. It's about you knowin' I really need another bourbon and gettin' me one when I'm tryin' to do the right thing. It's about you knowin' better what the right thing needs to be. It's about how hot it is when you fuck yourself on my cock. And it's about how gorgeous you look when you come. It's about stud muffins and gum drops. It's about a lot of things, Greta."

"That all sounds really complicated, Hix," she replied softly, her voice breathy.

"No, sweetheart, all that is really fuckin' simple."

On that, before it did get complicated, he kissed her neck, moved away and got the stools.

He was ass to stool, sipping coffee, and she was pouring batter on a heated griddle when she commented, "I noted you chose stud muffin and not snuggle bug."

Hix started chuckling.

She turned to him with happiness, playfulness and a little heat in her eyes, "I'll admit, I prefer that one too."

He busted out laughing.

Greta grinned as she set aside the batter.

She didn't feed him pancakes.

She fed him big, fluffy buttermilk pancakes with sausage links and warmed syrup.

She ate beside him.

She was only halfway done when he'd finished, rinsed his plate, and got himself a syrupy-sweet kiss.

"Meet you on the porch?" she asked after he'd pulled away.

"Definitely."

"I've gotta sing at the Dew tonight, snuggle bug," she reminded him.

"I'll see you there too."

Her eyes gave him a smile.

He moved away but brushed his finger along the smile at her lips.

Then he moved out of the kitchen, sat on a step to pull on his socks and boots, and called out, "Later, gum drop," on the way to the door.

"Later, stud muffin," she returned.

He shot a grin over his shoulder at her as he walked out her door.

Mid-morning, Hix, with his ass leaned against the edge of the desk, his ankles crossed in front of him, Larry standing to his left, Donna and Bets to his right, Hal farther away but close to the whiteboard, stared at that damned board.

All their eyes were to it.

Larry had called Faith yesterday with the news they'd found the crime scene and he'd given her a call that morning just to check in.

They'd sifted through a variety of messages Reva and Ida had taken from folks calling in after seeing the website, none of them having anything to do with what happened on 56, none of them pertinent, so they'd also moved on.

They got their report that the slug and the shell casings were from the gun that killed Calloway. They also got their report that there were trace amounts of blood the rain hadn't soaked away in the soil forensics took from the crime scene and that blood was Calloway's.

So they had more.

They still had dick.

The slugs were not in the system.

None of the team's legwork the day before got them much of anything. They didn't have hardly any homeless problem in McCook so any homeless anyone noted were known, not drifters, not the kind to shoot a man down while stealing his truck, not even the kind to be out on that road, and definitely not being in the position to own a gun.

Regardless, his department couldn't be seen rousting homeless and harassing them without reason—say a witness who saw them wandering 56 at any time, especially the day of the murder.

They didn't have that.

No one had seen any drifters.

There were a number of fugitives to look into and Donna and Bets were on that. But unless they could nab them there was nothing they could move on, and they couldn't deem them a person of interest unless they'd been spotted at least in the county, but better, around the place of the murder or dump location at the time of either.

Other than that, his crew had come up with zilch.

"I need to pay a visit to our meth man," he said into the quiet room. "He doesn't deal here but he probably knows who uses and may feel compelled to keep our relationship copacetic by helpin' out."

Donna looked to him. "A snake eats a rat, he doesn't rat on a rat."

He lifted his brows to her. "Got another idea?"

"Pissed to say I don't," she muttered.

The phones rang throughout the department but Reva was catching calls so the team just turned their attention back to the board.

The ringing stopped.

Seconds later, Hix's line rang.

He reached across, picked up and put the handset to his ear, his eyes to the lights on the phone telling him he was getting a transfer from Reva.

"Yeah?" he answered.

"Call for you, Hixon, and you'll wanna take it," she said with urgency.

He unhooked his ankles and straightened, turning toward the phone. "Send it through." He heard a click and said, "This is Sheriff Drake."

"Drake. Miller. Ranger at Fort Robinson," a man replied. "We think we got your truck."

Hixon lifted a hand and cut his gaze through the room, snapping his fingers. He hit a button with his other hand and put down the handset.

"You're on speaker, Ranger. Got my deputies with me."

"Right. Found a Ford F150 this morning. Like you asked, we did a number of patrols so it wasn't there yesterday. Found it on a patrol this morning. Seems dumped, no one around, engine cold, so whoever had it's been gone awhile. Your plates but even if they'd switched 'em out, won't matter. Back cab is filled with blood."

Hal prowled out, yanking out his cell.

"It'll take a while, but we're coming with lights on, Miller," Hix told him. "You call your locals?"

"Figured you'd want the news first, but they're my next call."

"Great. Thanks. It'll be a trek to get up to Dawes, but we're on our way. You got my cell in case you need to call?" Hix asked.

"Got it. See you when you get here."

They disconnected while Hal walked back in.

"Forensics is on their way there," he announced.

"Good, Hal, thanks," Hix muttered then looked to Larry. "You're with me." He turned his attention to Donna and made sure she read his look that she wasn't going to like what he had to say for a variety of reasons, but she was going to have to do it. "I'm on the road, we still gotta talk to our meth man. You're gonna do that with Hal."

Her eyes shared she didn't like it but she just said, "Got it, Hix."

Hix looked to Bets. "Bets, want you goin' over any calls Reva takes. Do it while runnin' names of known fugitives anywhere in the U.S. that have ties to McCook County."

"Needle in a haystack?" she asked.

"Yup," he answered. "Also, the McCalls don't turn in their boy for spray painting the Mortimers' barn after school today, you take a ride out there and have another chat with them."

"Bryce did it?" she asked, eyes crinkling.

"Louella shot his dog," Hixon answered.

"Art I'd paint on their fuckin' barn'd be a lot more colorful, those assholes shot *my* dog," Hal muttered.

Bets set her crinkle to Hal, muttering back, "Totally."

Hal looked surprised she shared this with him, but Hix didn't have time to feel relief it seemed his uncomfortable chat with his deputy yesterday might bear fruit.

He turned to Larry and said, "Let's roll."

"With you, boss," Larry replied.

And they rolled.

Hix and Larry were standing next to Ranger Miller as the Cherry County forensics boys went over the truck when his cell rang.

He dug it out of his pocket, saw the call was from Donna, took it and put it to his ear.

"Yeah?" he asked.

"Kavanagh Becker is a dickweed," she answered.

Kavanagh Becker, their meth man.

Hix blew out a sigh before he asked, "What?"

"Won't talk to anyone but you," she told him. "And that would be you and only you, not you and another one of your deputies there for backup."

He could strangle Blatt for leaving him this shit.

"He give any indication it's worth my while to make that effort?"

"I don't know. Think he's scum but that's not the only reason I wouldn't play poker with the man."

Damn.

"This gets done, I get back, I'll take care of that. Anything else?" he asked.

"Sadly, no. There?"

One of the forensics men was heading his way so he said, "Not yet but I gotta go."

"Right, Hix. Later."

"Later."

He disconnected and jerked his chin up to the guy as he shoved his phone back in his pocket.

"First, the good news," the man started.

Which meant there was bad news.

Shit.

"Let's have it," Hix said.

"Guy didn't have time to run a vacuum, so we got hair, we got some fibers, we got mud. Your vic took care of his truck so it's tidy but not clean as a whistle. This may narrow some shit down."

"Right, good, what else?" Hix pressed.

"Well, obviously, he couldn't clean up that blood and reckon he knew it because he didn't try. Also, your vic's cell is in there. It's stomped to shit but it's his model. It's not much but at least that mystery's solved."

Hix nodded.

"Now, the bad," the guy said. "Whole damned thing is wiped down. Steering wheel, dash, handles, windows, even the exterior. Hood to tailgate, thing's been gone over with what looks like Windex. Streak free. Not even a partial fingerprint we could pick up."

"*Fuck*," Larry bit off.

"Larry," Hix murmured.

"I'd say this is a fuck moment, Sheriff," the guy put in, sounding frustrated himself.

Hix gave him a nod and turned to Larry. "On your cell, man. Call

Faith, ask her if her husband happened to keep a bottle of window cleaner in his truck. He didn't, get on to Bets and get her on the phone to every gas station and convenience store between Glossop and Fort Robinson to see if any of their clerks recall a man in a white Ford truck buying glass cleaner in the last three days."

Larry nodded and stepped away.

Hix looked to the ranger. "We'll arrange for this to be towed to McCook."

"You got your hands full and I got a brother-in-law with a towing business. You want me to take care of that for you?" Miller asked.

"Be obliged."

Miller nodded and stepped away.

Hix looked to the forensics guy whose name he now knew very well was John.

"We find this asshole, you come to the pig we're gonna roast in celebration and I'll have your favorite bottle waiting for you."

"Cherry's a big county, Sheriff, but can't say we've had anything this interesting in a while, no matter how much what we're investigating sucks. That said, never turn down a hog roast or a bottle."

"Me either," the other forensics guy, named Jay, called.

"Hope the next call you get from us is sharing the details of when you can roll up for that and not another request for you to roll out," Hix replied.

"Me too, brother," John muttered, turned and headed back to the truck.

Larry returned and immediately shared, "Bets is on it."

"Right," Hix said, staring at the truck.

"You figure his prints are in the system and that's why he was so methodical about wiping that truck down?" Larry asked.

"I figure anyone with a TV set or who can read knows their prints in a truck owned by a man who was murdered would be methodical about wiping down the truck they transported his dead body in and then stole."

"Yeah," Larry mumbled.

"We're out," Jay said as he and John moved from the truck. "We'll call we got a report."

"Thanks," Hix replied.

"Tow's comin'," Miller said, joining them.

Hix turned his attention to the man. "Thanks to you too, Ranger."

"Skeeves me out, knowin' that trash was in my park. But still, hope this gets you a step closer in catching him," Miller returned.

Hix did too.

Larry was with Bets running down a lead at a convenience store in Alliance, where a man shared he'd sold a bottle of Windex to a man in an older model, white F150, and Hix was in his Ram heading out to their meth man's fortress when his cell went.

He dug it out, saw the call was from his girl and took it, answering, "Hey, honey. How you doin'?"

"You have a girlfriend?" Corinne asked in accusation.

Fuck.

"Cor—"

"I can't believe you have a *girlfriend*. You broke up with Mom like...*a month ago*."

Not even close.

"Corinne," he growled.

"She says we should prepare because you're movin' on and we're gonna have to do it with you," Corinne declared furiously.

But Hix felt a burn hit his gut.

"Who?" he demanded.

"What?" his daughter snapped.

"Who said that?"

"*Mom*, Dad, who else?" she retorted.

Hope.

Hope probably knew his Bronco was in Greta's drive last night, and in retribution she'd told his daughter he was seeing Greta.

"She tell Mamie?" he asked.

"Just me and Shaw. She doesn't want Mamie upset. And anyway, Mamie's at dance. And by the way, not cool you told Shaw about it and not me."

"I didn't tell Shaw."

"Well he knew and he was all up in Mom's face about sharin' something with *your kids* about *their dad*."

As much as that had to suck for Hope, she'd bought it, and now she'd bought the fact that Hix was not going to do fuck all to help her rid herself of it.

"We'll talk about this next week," he told his girl.

"Will you be marrying her by then?" she asked snidely.

"First," he bit off, "you do not talk to your father that way. Second, you need to calm down and think about this. Your mother and I have not been apart for a month. We've been apart a lot longer than that. And last, Corinne, we'll talk about this next week."

"So I'm *sure* you want me to keep it from Mamie like you kept it from *me*."

"Yeah. That'd be nice," he returned. "Seein' as I would have told you myself if there was something to tell and I'd do it when it was the right time to tell you. I'd appreciate it if you let me at least do that with your sister if that time comes."

"Whatever, Dad."

"Again, you do not talk to me that way."

She said nothing.

So he said, "I'm ticked at you but I love you and now I gotta go."

"Right, later, *Dad*."

He didn't understand the emphasis on "dad" but he wasn't going to ask and it wouldn't matter. She hung up on him.

Hix drove and did something he didn't like to do for two reasons, the new one—speaking to the woman at all—being the one he most disliked.

He called Hope.

She answered on the first ring.

"Fancy *you* phoning *me*," she said sarcastically as greeting.

Like that wasn't what she'd been angling for.

At least one thing was clear. She was over her urge to be there for him when he needed her.

"I told you we were done."

"Yup, remember that, Hix. Vividly."

"We weren't. You're the mother of my children. I was intent on finding a way to keep hold on that and find something good we could still share through it. But now, Hope, we're done."

There was a pause before, "What's that mean?"

"That means you're the mother of my children and that's all you'll ever be in a way I seriously hope you consider reclaiming your maiden name."

There was a moment of stunned silence he actually felt was stunned through the line before, "Hixon, if you're pissed I told Shaw and Corinne—"

"Yes, I'm pissed. And the way I'm pissed means you just broke the last straw, Hope."

"Does she mean that much to you?" she snapped.

"No. Not yet. But my children do."

On that, he disconnected and threw the phone on the passenger seat.

She called back four times in the six miles it took him to turn into the long drive that was on an immense plot of land where he had to ignore the man hanging at the opening of the fence, a walkie-talkie and a SIG Sauer on his belt.

He drove up to the massive, sprawling ranch house that had been built last year after Becker had scraped off his last not-quite-as-massive, sprawling ranch house and replaced it.

When he did, his phone rang again, and since he had to pick it up to take it with him, he saw it wasn't Hope but Shaw.

So he took the call.

"Shouldn't you be getting ready for the game?" he asked in greeting.

"Yeah, Dad, but we need to talk."

"Shaw, sorry, son, but I'm in the middle of something."

"I get that, Dad, and I gotta be quick anyway 'cause Coach'll be ticked he sees me on the phone. But just to say, I'll talk to Corinne after she cools down and I want you to think about me livin' exclusively with you."

"Shaw—"

"She's a bitch."

Goddamn it. He had to defend her.

"Don't say that about your mother."

"Okay. Right. Sorry," he clipped out each word. "I still wanna talk about livin' exclusively with you."

"We'll talk later, Shaw. Keep your cool too, look after your sisters, have a good game tonight and we'll talk, kid. Promise."

"Okay, Dad. Be safe, yeah?"

"Always."

They disconnected, Hix swung out of the Ram, rounded the hood and walked up the steps with his eyes on the man standing at the top, also with a walkie-talkie and a gun on his belt.

"Mr. Becker is waiting for you," the guy announced when Hix's boot hit the top step.

Mr. Becker.

Like he was a genteel landowner.

Priceless.

Hix lifted his chin and the guy turned, opening a hand-carved door that had to cost thousands and guiding Hix through it.

Hix didn't bother looking around. The wealth and opulence enjoyed by a man who destroyed lives was of no interest to him. The man in front of him who was armed was.

He was led down a hall and then through a door to the left.

He'd barely cleared it and noted he'd hit a well-appointed study before Becker was moving to him, arms out, smile wide on his face, crying out, "Hixon!" like he was a beloved son returning home from war.

"Becker," Hix replied, briefly taking him in.

Tall. Lanky. Aged fifty-eight but looking maybe forty-five, tops.

He didn't look like a wealthy rancher rolling in it.

He didn't look like a respectable meth-dealing businessman who was killing it (which was unfortunately what he was).

He looked like an aging rock star who was past it.

Faded jeans. Washed-out rock concert tee (Mötley Crüe). Salt and pepper hair heavy on the salt brushing his shoulders.

Hix never knew if Becker wanted to blend into the scenery of Nebraska and/or his clientele or if he wanted it known he might live in a house that cost over a million dollars, but he was true to his roots of being raised in a trailer in a trailer park on the outskirts of Dansboro.

His glance wasn't so brief on the woman sitting like she belonged there in the chair behind Becker's desk.

If Becker looked the aging rocker, she looked the aging groupie. It didn't take intense scrutiny to see, shave a couple of decades off her, she'd be a knockout. But it was clear she still took care of herself and held on to as much as she could of beauty that had once been immense.

It also didn't take intense scrutiny *or* her proximity to Becker to understand she was bad news.

Her eyes were sharp on him.

He turned his attention to Becker who stood three feet away, pretending to be miffed Hix had dissed him on a hug.

"Congratulations in order?" he asked.

Becker gave him another ridiculously large smile.

"This is Tawnee. My new babe."

He was a fifty-eight-year-old man describing a woman at least in her late forties as his "new babe."

And again.

Priceless.

Hix turned only his head to her and dipped his chin. "Pleased to meet you, ma'am."

For some reason she smiled at him like she'd just heard an in-joke that Hix didn't understand, and she liked the idea he was on the outside.

"Sheriff," she purred.

Hix fought his lip curling.

"Tawnee, Hixon, *Tawnee*," Becker stressed, like Hix should know who she was, and with that name, maybe she *was* an aging groupie. A famous one. Maybe an ex-rock-video-vamp. "Tawnee Dare," Becker went on.

Hix grew still.

"That's why you're here, only you, Hix," Becker shared and faked looking sad. "Sorry to say, I don't know anything about this horrible story of the young ranch hand cut down in his prime leaving his family widowed. But Tawnee wanted a word with you, and I figured you'd want her to have that privately."

"He was a foreman," Hix forced out.

"Say what?" Becker asked.

"Nathan Calloway. He was foreman at the ranch where he worked."

"Well, that's impressive," Becker remarked, but did it like he didn't mean his words.

"And I'm here to talk about him." He glanced through Tawnee Dare, obviously—her last name, her beauty so extreme years only dimmed it, they didn't fade it—Greta's mother. "Sorry, ma'am."

"Already told you," Becker started, "I don't know anything about this *foreman*. But," he swayed his upper body back, wrapped an arm around his middle, resting his other elbow on it and his chin on his upraised hand, "seein' as you're fuckin' Tawnee's daughter, she thought she'd have a few words with you."

"Yeah, Sheriff," Tawnee said, gaining Hix's focus. "Now, I figure you know my girl is a good girl, and you goin' back for more, you know just *how good*. But thought, way I look out for my daughter and all, you also best know she's connected here in McCook. She's got family." She smiled a smile the opposite of what her daughter could achieve. It did nothing to the rest of her face and eyes. It was just a movement of her lips she didn't come close to meaning. "Family who looks after her, say someone thinks he can fuck her and then fuck her over."

"So you wanted me out here so you could threaten me," he said, and her eyebrows shot up feigning shock.

"Now, I wouldn't do that. Though, won't be no reason to, you don't fuck my girl over."

Hix looked from Greta's mother to Becker. "You don't have anything for me on Calloway I have no reason to be here."

He gave Hix another massive smile. "Reckon not, since Tawnee said what she needed to say."

"You've yanked my chain," Hix stated.

"Say again?" Becker asked.

"You've yanked my chain."

The roguishness sweeping clean from him, Becker studied Hix shrewdly and was wise enough to read Hix's demeanor and keep his mouth shut.

They'd had barely any contact at all. Blatt had made it that way while Hix was his deputy and Hix had inherited that when he'd become sheriff. Becker didn't really know him. Therefore, Becker didn't know not to play games with him.

He'd just assumed since Hix had no choice but to fall in line with Blatt's deal, this only because Becker never stepped over a line Hix could use to pounce, that Hix was someone who'd take a few not-so-friendly jabs aimed his way just for a meth man and his moll to enjoy some shits and grins.

"Friends don't do that," Hix educated him.

Becker got all business.

"Now, Drake—"

"Think on that, Becker," he ordered, turned to Tawnee, dipped at the waist in a phony bow and capped it by touching his forefinger to his forehead and flipping it her way. "Ms. Dare. Pleasure."

Then he turned on his boot and walked out of the room, out of the house and into his Ram.

He'd cleared Becker's land and was driving down County Road 21 when he pulled out his cell and called Greta, eyes to the dash clock seeing it was after six at night.

"Hey, good timing. Just got done with my last client, everything cool?" she said in greeting.

"You gonna be home soon?" he asked.

"Yeah. You gonna be done early? Want me to pick something up or cook? Just to say, I have to leave for the Dew at around eight, but I might be able to push that."

"I'll be there in half an hour."

"Okay, Hix, but is everything okay?"

"I'll be there. Half an hour."

It was hesitant this time when she repeated, "Okay, Hix."

"Later, Greta."

"Yeah, later, darlin'."

Hix hung up and drove.

HE DIDN'T PARK in her drive.

He parked at the curb.

He walked to the door that she had open by the time he hit her porch, her eyes to his Bronco at the curb before they came to him.

She pushed open the storm door for him but stepped back into the house the minute his hand went to it, her gaze never leaving him as he entered.

The storm door swooshed shut on a well-oiled hinge.

He didn't fuck around.

"Met your mom," he announced and watched the blood drain from her face.

Oh yeah.

"I think you can understand I can't have any ties to a criminal element, Greta," he stated the obvious.

She shook her head. "Hix, she has a record, but—"

Of course she did.

"You should have told me."

"I didn't think that—"

"During our conversation at the Dew. After one of the times you let me fuck you. Over breakfast. Your mother's the moll of the only known drug pusher in the county. That's somethin' I need to know."

Her eyes were huge. "Hix, I didn't—"

"Now I got him callin' me out to his fortress, thinkin' he can fuck with me, standin' there smilin' as your mother threatens me, I don't treat you right."

She looked like she was going to move to him, saying, "Oh my God, Hix, I'm so—"

"This is over."

She went solid and snapped her mouth shut.

"I can't do it," he continued. "Shouldn't 've done it. Shouldn't 've started it. Shit has a way of gettin' complicated real quick, but Greta, babe, gotta admit, even with all Hope's bullshit, you take the cake."

She unfroze her mouth enough to start, "Can we—?"

"Nope." He shook his head. "No. Your mom, she's a real gem, Greta. Pure class."

"God," she whispered, her expressive face filling with dismay.

Oh yeah.

She knew.

She knew all along.

Fuck him.

"Coulda saved me from that," he told her. "Coulda at least given me a heads up so I wasn't blindsided like that. Walked in there, no clue. Just an evening's fun for an asshole and his piece."

She winced.

"Yeah, it went like that," he bit off.

"I'm so sorry, Hix. Let me—"

"I am too, Greta. But now I know so I can untangle things before they get too messy."

To explain what he meant by that, Hix was only a step in the front door, so he only had to turn and reach to the handle to open it.

He looked over his shoulder at her.

"I'd say take care of yourself, but it was made clear to me you got an army to do that so I won't bother."

He gave her that.

Then he walked out the door.

Greta

I SAT on my ass on the floor by my front door with my phone in my hand and I called her.

"Well, hello, my doting daughter," Mom answered jovially.

God, I hated her.

Hated her.

"He was the best thing that's ever happened to me," I whispered.

"I'm sorry, baby girl, Momma can't hear you," she sing-songed.

"Better than Keith."

"Is that so?" she asked happily.

"Yeah," I pushed out.

"Well, sounds like someone should have paid their mother's cable bill."

"Actually, sounds to me like someone's got herself a sugar daddy," I returned.

"Greta, Greta, Greta," she chanted with fake disappointment. "You just never listen to me. Like I told you many times before, a girl has to play *all* her angles."

"Scratch this one."

"Say what?"

"Scratch this one," I repeated.

"Hmm..." She pretended to consider it then stated, "Maybe I don't want to."

"You're dead to me."

"Now it's drama," Mom muttered in exaggerated exasperation.

"You're dead to Andy."

That got me silence.

"I've already called," I informed her. "Taken you off the visitor list. If you try to see him at Sunnydown, they're going to call the police."

"So you think Sheriff Drake will come after me?" she scoffed.

"I think, after whatever you did to him today, he'd enjoy that immensely."

She'd obviously chewed him up, something I already knew, but she gave that to me too because her voice went nasty and threatening.

"You think you can keep me from my boy—"

Her boy?

He'd never been *her boy*.

I cut her off.

"You're dead to me. You're dead to Andy. Your reign of terror is over, Mom. Long past due. Now, I hope this one lasts a while because if he doesn't, you...are...*fucked*."

I drew in breath as she snapped, "Greta."

"Goodbye, Mom."

I hung up.

I then blocked her calls.

Hixon's words invaded my brain.

No, sweetheart, all that is really fuckin' simple.

"Guess you were wrong," I murmured to the darkening room.

And it was then, silently, I started crying.

Chapter 13

Last Straw

Hixon

"Blood's Calloway's, no surprise," forensics' John told Hix the next morning over the phone. "Fibers, carpet, already talked to Larry, says from what he's seen of Faith Calloway's home, they're from there. Also says he'll get samples just so we can check."

"Right," Hix muttered when John paused.

"Hairs," John went on, "we got some that look like they're probably Nat's and seven long, light-brown ones we got off the driver's and passenger's sides that Larry says could be the wife's, though he thinks she gets hers dyed and we know these aren't, but we gotta run 'em. That last, Hix, think you know but sucks to remind you, it takes weeks to get DNA run, even on an active investigation. Sometimes months. Seein' as this is so crucial to where you're at in yours, I'll try to see what pull I can get but everyone's tests are crucial. So my suggestion is, see if you got county money in your budget to get private tests run. It'll go a lot faster."

"I'll send a deputy up to get samples," Hix replied. "It'll be Bets. You met her. Elizabeth Rowe. She'll be there sometime today."

"Gotcha. Any luck with the convenience stores?" John asked.

"Maybe. Got a sketch artist going to Alliance today. I'll be expediting that since the guy reports the man he saw was not only twitchy, he had long, light-brown hair."

"Fuckin' A, hope we nail this fucker," John muttered.

"Yeah," Hix replied. Something coming from the bullpen that set his eyes that way, and when he saw what it was, he set his jaw. "Gotta go. We'll keep you informed."

"Great, thanks, brother."

They disconnected as Lou hit the door with Bets on her heels.

It was a busy day for a Saturday at McCook County Sheriff's Department, and obviously not just because he and all his deputies were putting in overtime to catch a killer.

"Sorry, boss, I tried—" Bets started.

"It's okay, Bets," he said, eyes to Lou but he turned them to his deputy. "And since you're here, need you to find time today to go up to Cherry and pick up some samples from forensics."

"On my way to Alliance yesterday with Larry, I didn't get a chance to deal with that other case and they didn't come in," she replied.

"Cherry first."

She nodded, glanced at Lou and took off.

Hix didn't even get up from his desk when he said to Lou. "This shit does not hit my office."

"You'll see," she said quietly.

"Lou, seriously, I don't think it's lost on you—"

"You'll see last night you made the biggest fuckin' mistake in your *goddamned* life."

Hix shut his mouth.

She turned to leave, and Hix started pulling in a big breath to alleviate his frustration but he stopped in the middle of it when she turned back.

He didn't like the look on her face. It was worse than the pissed-off disappointment she'd been wearing before.

So he braced.

"Hear you're lookin' for a house," she noted.

He didn't respond.

"Probably gotta use that inheritance your uncle gave you."

Hix grew alert.

That was the second time someone had mentioned that.

She shook her head then finally lost the control she'd been holding, if only by a thread.

"Poor, stupid, *stupid* Hope," she spat.

And with that, she stormed out.

He didn't watch her go.

He picked up his cell, went to Recent Calls, touched the name he needed and put the phone to his ear.

Greta's answer was hesitant. "Hey."

"Our shit is done. It doesn't come to my office. It doesn't exist in my life at all. Next person you run your mouth to, Greta, you let them know that."

"Lou," she muttered.

"Yeah," he bit out.

"Listen, Hix, I didn't know she was—"

"I said what I had to say."

There was silence and then, "Yeah, you're good at that."

He shouldn't ask. He didn't even want to freaking know.

He still asked, "What's that remark mean?"

"It means you're good at talking and you're not real good at listening. I've never been interrupted so much in my whole damned life. But it's not even that. It's just all about you. You think you escaped narrowly, I'm clueing into the fact that maybe the one who escaped was me."

"Then we're both good with where this is at," he clipped.

"Yeah, we are. Goodbye, Sheriff."

He was going to share his farewell but he had dead air.

Hix tossed his phone down, got up and walked out of his office, calling to Donna, who was, strangely, standing and talking to Hal like she didn't hate his guts.

She turned her head his way. "Yeah, Hix."

"You get a second, wanna see you in my office."

She nodded. "Give me a minute."

He jerked up his chin and walked back to his office.

He went to his phone, snatched it up and called Larry.

"Yo, boss," Larry answered.

"You on your way to pick up the artist?" Hix asked.

"Yup."

"Use lights. John called. They found long, light-brown hairs that haven't been chemically treated. Bets is goin' up to Cherry to get samples. We're carvin' money outta the budget to run private DNA tests. I want that sketch and I want it soon. You with me?"

"Hell yeah. Lights on, Hix."

He was in the middle of what he had to say to Larry when Donna walked in and he ended the call quickly after Larry affirmed he'd got him.

"Close the door, would you?" he said to Donna.

She closed it, turned to him and said, "I can't read your face."

"This is personal. Not business," he announced.

"Uh-oh," she mumbled.

They had shit to do so he wasn't going to waste any more on this than he had to.

"Two times, people have mentioned my uncle's inheritance to me..." he trailed off, seeing her go wired before she blanked it. "Tell me," he bit out.

"Hixon, I'm thinkin' maybe we should do this over beers."

"You said you all kept your mouths shut, all that went down with Hope and me," he reminded her. "Something else you didn't share?"

"Hix, seriously, beers," she replied.

He stood at the front of his desk and stared into her eyes.

She blew out a breath, walked to him, put a hand on the back of one of the chairs in front of the desk and said quietly, "Think you'll get, when I tell you, why we thought this all would blow over."

"Tell me," he repeated.

"It was about the ring."

Hix closed his eyes and shook his head.

He opened them and demanded, "Say again?"

"The twentieth anniversary ring."

Hix felt his body turn to stone.

"She thought you'd...I think she thought you would..."

"Cave," he whispered.

He saw it then, Hope staring at him the way she did over that damned table, the papers on it, their lawyers present.

He knew it then, how she'd seemed almost paralyzed in shock after he'd lifted his head once he'd signed his name.

Now he knew it, how she'd started calling an hour after they left that table, begging him to talk.

You know, Hixon, you know.

After he got that inheritance, she'd asked him to buy her that ring on their twentieth anniversary, smiling, excited, showing him the photo of it in a catalog.

All he'd seen was the price, and he had to admit he didn't hold back his laughter that she'd even suggest he get her something that pricy when they were on the verge of putting kids through college.

He'd also admit that maybe that was not the right reaction to have.

That said, she'd given him a tremulous grin once he was done laughing so he thought she'd gotten where he was at, where he thought they both should be at.

And saw the light.

Obviously, she hadn't.

But he never in his life would think she'd wage war over a ring. A war that would destroy their marriage.

And he never in the life he'd led with her thought she was a woman who'd do such a despicably selfish thing.

"Hixon, if I thought for a second she'd actually go through with it, I would have said something," Donna assured him quickly. "And then when she did, I thought...I know it wasn't my place, but I thought you were better off without her."

"It wasn't your place."

He watched her watching him carefully.

"It wasn't your place to be in the position to tell me," he explained. "It was hers."

"I saw Lou was in here, was it her that said something?" she asked, beginning to look ticked.

He shook his head. "This dies right now."

Her eyes grew sharp. "Know you're seein' Greta, that going okay?"

"It's over."

She swung back a bit and murmured, "Right."

"This dies here, Donna. Lou coming in here. What happened with Greta. Hope's bullshit. It's just done. Life is now just what it was before, except now I know well and truly I'm good bein' shot of Hope. Greta's the Greta you know. Lou is just a good friend and she'll calm down. We put who killed Nat Calloway behind bars, it'll all just go back to normal."

"Okay, Hix," she agreed dubiously.

"I'm not pissed you told me," he assured her. "I'm not pissed you kept it from me. I'm not anything but maybe a little troubled how easy it is to get over the woman I spent nearly half my life with."

"Yeah," she said quietly.

"That's it."

"Okay, Hixon."

"Beers would not be unwelcome tonight, though, you can get away from the ball and chain."

She gave him a smile.

"I'll call Herb and ask Larry to take call. Then I'll call Toast and Tommy and one of us will pick you up so you can get slaughtered."

That wasn't going to happen.

But he'd be glad to have as much as he wanted and not have to worry about taking call or driving.

"Thanks, Donna."

Her eyes got sympathetic. "I'm sorry, Hix."

"That's the troubling thing," he returned. "I no longer am."

"Healthy," she murmured. "Healing."

"Yeah."

"Good."

He nodded.

She shot him an uncertain grin, gave him a long lookover.

Then she walked out.

He watched her go and wondered if, through salon gossip, Greta knew about the ring.

After that, he wondered why that would be the first thing he wondered.

You'll see last night you made the biggest fuckin' mistake in your goddamned life.

He forced his mind to Tawnee Dare and he wanted to doubt the truth of Lou's words.

But, damn it, since he threw back the first half of his beer after he got back to his apartment, that being after laying into Greta, he'd felt that doubt start nagging.

It didn't matter.

He had a killer to find and the woman he'd been seeing had direct ties to the only known criminal in the county.

So yeah.

It didn't matter.

The hell of it was he could tell himself that.

But that drag in his gut wouldn't stop nagging.

"Boss."

Hix looked up from his computer with the picture of the sketch the artist had drawn of a man who looked like a lot of men but with a goodly number of lines on his face and long hair.

It wasn't much. Then again a convenience store clerk in a large-ish town saw his fair share of people, so it was better than nothing.

Which meant it was something.

And now Hal was at his door.

"Yeah?"

"Gemini Jones here to see you."

Goddamn it.

Greta.

"He says he might have something on the Calloway case," Hal continued.

Surprised, Hix looked to the windows, saw Jones standing by Hal's desk, then he looked back to Hal.

"Would you bring him back?"

"Sure thing," Hal said, disappeared from his door and Hix closed the email on his computer, minimized everything he had opened, got up and had just flipped the whiteboard when Hal brought Gemini in.

"Thanks, Hal," he said and went to Gemini, hand out. "Gemini."

"Hix, or do I call you Sheriff now?" he asked on an upturn of his lips and a firm shake of Hix's hand.

"Hix is good."

The man was in trousers and a dress shirt, no tie, but looking dapper, which was his way even out of the Dew Drop and in rural Nebraska.

They let go but Hix kept his hand up and motioned to the chairs. "Have a seat."

Gemini moved to a chair. Hix moved behind his desk.

He sat, Gemini was already folded in.

"You want some coffee?" Hix offered. "Or you wanna just share why you're here?"

"I know we're both busy so let's just get to it, yes?"

Hix nodded.

Gemini got to it.

"I know a young woman who had cause to drive through Grant County Monday evening on the way to see her momma in McCook."

Hix felt his neck grow tight.

Gemini kept talking.

"Now, you see, her momma read the *Guide*'s website when word started getting out and mentioned what she read around her daughter. Her daughter then mentioned something to her momma. And they immediately realized their moral dilemma."

"Gemini, please just give it to me straight," Hix requested, speaking evenly and trying to hold on to his patience.

"All right, Hix, you see, the dilemma is, this girl, she's out on parole and that parole is contingent on a variety of things, including her not leaving her local area, which happens to be in Kansas. So if she comes forward sharing what she saw, she might do damage to all that good behavior she showed. And since she's trying to find her way to a righteous path that would be a shame."

"If she witnessed Nathan Calloway having his life ended in a violent way and she's sitting on that—" Hix started.

Gemini shook his head. "No. But she did see a man in a white truck pull over for a man who was walking along 56. She says that man didn't look all that good, drifter, vagabond. She'd had that truck trailing her for several miles after it had pulled out from a ranch behind her. The man on the road saw the oncoming cars, lifted his arm to flag them down, she drove by. She saw in her rearview the truck slowed and stopped."

Christ.

They had a witness.

"She needs to make a statement and she needs to look at a sketch."

"Hix—"

"I'll personally talk to her parole officer if you can assure me she's here only to see her mother."

"Her momma's got diabetes, had a spell. She's okay now but it's been a while since they've seen each other and she felt it worth the risk to make a visit. So yes, Hix, I can assure you she's here to see her mother." He lifted both hands and dropped them. "She's a good kid. She makes stupid decisions and spends time with people who aren't worthy of it. But she's trying to get smart about that and she's had a helluva lesson to teach her that's the way to go. She does right, comes forward, it bites her in the ass, this could be a catalyst for very bad things."

"I'll print out the sketch we have. Give it to you. If it looks like who she saw flagged Calloway down, please just confirm that to me. But if she's willing to come in and make a statement, I'll do everything in my power to see she doesn't get hooked back into the system. I'll even drive down there and talk to her parole officer myself. And if she can improve on this sketch, I'll buy her mother flowers."

Gemini smiled. "I'll take the sketch."

Hix turned to his computer and set it to printing.

As it did that, he looked back to Gemini. "She said Calloway pulled over, was it, in her estimation, a Good Samaritan-type of thing?"

Gemini nodded.

"This man on the road, was he alone?" Hix pressed.

Gemini nodded again. "Alone. Tall. Brawny. Dirty clothes. Haggard. Sunburned. Leathery. Carrying a canvas duffle on his back. She says she wouldn't have pulled over, but she also says, at the time she passed them, she thought God was good, making men like the man in that truck who had the kindness to do it."

At his words, Hix couldn't stop himself from lifting his arms, putting his elbows to the edge of his desk, linking his fingers and resting his forehead to them, such was the weight of that statement not coming true.

"I know," Gemini said quietly. "Tests your faith, shit like this. Putting that young man there. Putting my girl in a bad position. How an act of kindness that leads to an act of what might be desperation or even insanity could tear like a tidal wave through so many lives."

Hix lifted his forehead, put his chin to his hands and gave him an understatement.

"Yeah." He sat back and rested his arms to the arms of his chair. "She give you more?"

Gemini shook his head but said, "Just what he was wearing. Jeans, beat-up canvas jacket, even though it was hot outside, long, brown hair."

And they had their suspect.

They just had to find the fucker.

He turned to the printer on the credenza behind him, nabbed the sketch and got up, walking it around the desk to where Gemini had also left his seat and was standing.

He handed him the sketch. "I hope she does the right thing and I'll again give you my promise I'll do right by her if she does."

"Charity's a good kid, she'll do right," Gemini replied, dropping a name and doing it on purpose.

She'd be coming in.

Hix wanted to howl with relief.

"If she doesn't," Gemini kept on, "she'll have to break more laws getting away from her momma who'll tan her ass."

And that was the rest.

Her mother had already solved this dilemma. Charity had always been coming in. Gemini had just showed first to broker the deal to make it safe for her to do it.

Hix gave him a small grin, this time, the way Gemini did it and why, not bothered in the slightest he'd been played.

Gemini lifted the sketch. "I'll be in touch."

Hix tagged a card from the holder on the outer edge of his desk and gave it to Gemini. "My card. Call direct."

Gemini lifted the card too, smiled and walked out.

He'd barely touched the front door to push outside before Hal and Donna were in his office.

"What was that?" Donna asked.

"Possible eye witness who saw Calloway pull over for a drifter with long, brown hair."

"*Fuck yes*," Hal hissed enthusiastically.

"The sketch sucks, but the minute Larry comes back with it and scans it so we got a decent copy of it, I want it out on the wire. We might be able to sharpen up some of the rough edges soon, this witness comes forward. Pray for that," Hix told them.

"We'll be all over that," Donna returned.

"Need you two on the line with homeless shelters in Omaha, Lincoln, bigger cities. I'll email the description. We have hair, face, now clothes. And he was carrying a big duffle. Convenience store guy said our guy could be anywhere between forty and sixty. I get now why he gave that range, seein' as Gemini's witness says he was leathery, haggard. Wanna know if any shelters have any regulars who went walkabout and haven't been seen in a while."

"All over that too," Hal stated and walked out.

"We gonna get him?" Donna asked.

"He's had days to get away and the wheels to do it and only got a couple hundred miles. Convenience clerk says he's twitchy. Witness says he was a man she wouldn't stop for, but at the time she saw Calloway do it, she was glad God made a man who would. Even so, somehow the man had a gun and the cognizance to wipe down that truck. Regardless, I figure we got someone who's not firing on all cylinders in a way it's more than he'd put two bullets in a man. That could work in our favor. That could screw us totally."

She nodded. "I'll get on those shelters."

Hix nodded back, rounded his desk and got instantly pissed.

And he did that because his first thought was that they were closing in on him, so Hix was in a much better place than he was yesterday or the day before and definitely the day before that.

And he couldn't share it with Greta.

"You KNOW how they're gonna play this, Bryce."

It was late afternoon and he had Bryce McCall and his two parents in his office, Bryce in one chair, his mother in the other, his dad standing behind his son's chair.

They'd brought him in.

"It was stupid, I know," the fourteen-year-old mumbled. "Mom and Dad already laid into me."

"I'm sure they did," Hix said. "And most folk would listen to reason. The Mortimers won't."

Bryce ducked his head, scooted a foot on the floor and muttered under his breath, "She shot my dog."

"She did."

Bryce lifted his gaze to Hix's.

Hix held it and carried on.

"So, in light of the fact that I think this town has been reminded in an ugly way about what's important, if you write a letter apologizing to them, I'll take it out to them and then share I won't be taking this further. If you apologize, I'm satisfied you saw the error of your ways and feel remorse. This is not to say I condone what you did or vandalism in any form, Bryce," he warned, waited for the kid's nod then kept going. "However, considering the extremity of the extenuating circumstances, although your response was not right or even justified, it was understandable."

"Yeah," the kid whispered. "And I'm, like, totally grounded so I'm already kinda in jail."

Hix bit back a smile and continued, "They can, of course, push it. That's their prerogative. But they'll have to do it in civil court. I won't be pushing anything. If they have an issue with that, they can vote for my opponent in the next election."

Bryce grinned. "Too bad I won't be old enough to vote then."

"Yeah, kid. Too bad," Hix murmured.

The door opened and Larry swung his upper body in, hand on the handle.

"Sorry, Sheriff...folks, wouldn't interrupt but gotta say," his gaze leveled on Hix, "Kavanagh Becker is here to see you."

Hix turned his head to look out the window and he saw Becker and one of his goons studying the mural of the sheriff shield painted over a depiction of Nebraska pastureland at the side of reception.

Hix felt his lips thin and he lifted his chin to Larry. "Thanks, Larry."

"Not a problem." Larry's gaze went through the room, he murmured, "Again, sorry," and backed out of the door, closing it behind him.

"I think we're done anyway," Hix said, rising and moving around his desk.

He shook Bryce's hand. He had to hold firm and lock arms to share he couldn't accept the hug his beaming mother seemed intent on giving him when he shook hers. And he felt his shoulder nearly get dislocated when Bryce's father pumped his arm then knew he'd have a bruise after the man clapped him on the back.

He walked them to the door then he looked through the windows and gave Larry the high sign.

He was only five feet in and facing the door, arms crossed on his chest, when Becker came through.

"You don't have to close the door, Larry, he's not staying long," he said to his deputy.

"Right, boss," Larry replied and disappeared.

"You have one minute," Hix told Becker, who'd stopped only a few steps in because that was as far as he could get or was welcome.

"It would seem, perhaps, things didn't go as I'd intended during your visit yesterday."

When he stopped talking, Hix prompted, "You have fifty seconds."

"Drake," Becker bit off.

"Forty-five seconds."

"It was just a joke," Becker shared. "Tawnee and her daughter play it that way. Getting one up on each other. She wasn't actually threatening you. But she does worry about her daughter. Apparently Greta's last man ended things with her in a way Tawnee didn't like. It might not be the usual way a mother would deal with her daughter finding another man and sharing her concerns with that new man that she was keeping her eye on shit, but Tawnee's not your usual woman."

Hix felt something unpleasant slither through his gut at learning Greta's last man ended things in a way a woman like Tawnee Dare wouldn't like, but he wasn't going to discuss that with Kavanagh Becker.

"Greta and her mother close?" Hix asked.

"They're mother and daughter."

"That's not really an answer," Hix pointed out. "You met Greta?"

Becker stared him in the eyes. "No. Seen her. Got the best of her momma. You probably get me, if she gave more talent than just looks to her girl. Learned a long time ago, you can tag the pretty, young ones, but you also gotta expend the effort to train 'em, seein' as they got no earthly clue how to use their mouths."

Hix's stomach turned.

"Okay, we're done," Hix declared, moving toward him to show him out.

"Drake, you don't want this deal we got to fall apart," Becker warned.

And there was the reason for the visit.

Hix stopped and asked, "I don't?"

"Don't be stupid," Becker snapped.

"Not me who hauled the sheriff's ass all the way out to his place just to play a joke. I'm investigating a murder, Kavanagh, but even if I wasn't, I would hope you'd treat my time as more valuable than that."

Becker tried a winning smile. "You know how it is, first blush of finding a woman who gives a really great blowjob."

Now he was going to vomit.

"*Now* we're done," he stated and moved to stand by his door and hold his arm out of it.

Becker moved to stand in front of him. "It would be a shame, somethin' like this messed with a good thing."

"Far's I can see, the only one who's got it good is you," Hix remarked, dropping his arm.

"Now, I obviously wouldn't know anything about it but I do live in this county and I'm very aware of the incredible job you do keeping illegal substances at a minimum. Probably wouldn't buy you good returns in the next election, such things flooded our towns."

"Nope. Probably wouldn't. Then again, I sent people who pushed them to the Nebraska State Penitentiary, that might make me real popular."

They had a preposterous staring contest that Becker lost, stating, "It appears we're at a stalemate."

"Nope again, 'cause if you don't get your ass out of my station, it'll be in a cell. Told you twice we're done. Now I'll make it clear. We're done. You remain, you're trespassing. And, well, not sure how much of a crime that is, might have to look a few up more to see how long I can detain you, but I wouldn't mind havin' you as a guest if I get to see you in our accommodation."

"Don't be a fool," Becker hissed.

"Not me standin' there when the sheriff asked me to get the fuck out."

Becker glared at him then moved only to be yet another person to stop in his door and have something else to say.

"One last thing, you should talk to Greta. Tawnee's beside herself. Appears Greta didn't think the joke was funny either and cut her momma out. She was a might hysterical when she was relating things to me but it would seem she's made some other bad choices in regards to her daughter in the past and this was the last straw for Greta. Tawnee doesn't have much family. She needs her girl." He assumed an expression of contrition. "She can be a wild one and she got a wild hair. It wasn't the right thing to do, Hixon, and she sees that now. If she didn't think it'd make things worse between her and

Greta, she'd be here herself. But askin' you, man of a Dare woman to man of a Dare woman, Greta's the only kid Tawnee's got, and Tawnee's Greta's only momma. We fucked up. Don't let Greta take that too far, and just sayin', Hixon, *don't let Greta take that too far*. For her and her momma *and* shakin' up the way other things should be."

Hixon had no reply and Becker didn't wait for one.

He took off.

Appears Greta didn't think the joke was funny either and cut her momma out.

She's made some other bad choices in regards to her daughter...this was the last straw for Greta.

He'd experienced just that the day before with Hope.

Right before he lost his shit on Greta.

What were the straws that came before?

He had no idea.

He hadn't asked.

He hadn't even known she had a mother in town.

Because he hadn't asked.

Hell, he didn't even know until yesterday morning what her surname was.

Because he hadn't freaking *asked.*

It could be they had a screwed-up relationship that was a vicious cycle of this kind of shit that he'd just get caught up in.

It could be, Greta and everything about her being the exact opposite of the nominal he'd experienced with her mother (but it was more than enough), this was a long time coming.

Again, he had no idea.

He hadn't asked.

He'd just laid her out and walked out.

Walked out on her.

Again.

But this time, he'd done it ugly.

"Fuck," he whispered.

You think you escaped narrowly, I'm clueing into the fact that maybe the one who escaped was me.

He stared at his opened door in front of him and repeated a whispered, "Fuck."

He lifted his hands, rubbed them over his face, and since he couldn't do dick about that now—he needed to catch a killer, deal with his daughter, try to decide if it was right or would cause World War III if he backed his son's play to live with him exclusively, come to terms with the fact his wife had divorced him over not buying her a goddamned ring, and he needed to let Greta have some time—he'd sort it out later.

However that needed to be.

You know how it needs to be, asshole, he thought. *And this time, you're fucked.*

These thoughts occurred to him when he made it to the front of his desk, so he leaned into his hands on it and dropped his head.

That all sounds really complicated, Hix.

No, sweetheart, all that is really fuckin' simple.

It was simple.

It was.

And he'd complicated it again being a dick.

"Fuck," he whispered.

It was good it was beers with Donna, Tommy and Toast that night.

He was going to need them.

Chapter 14

Lock This, Baby

Greta

"That was fun, we won! Now pizza!" Maple cried, dancing in front of Lou and me, holding Andy's hand, Snow on his other side, walking so close to my baby bro that their arms were brushing.

Andy, in his Glossop Raiders sweatshirt, turned and grinned at me.

He'd had a blast at the game. The Raiders won. And it hadn't been the torture for me I'd thought it would be.

It was the Friday after the Friday that Hix had walked into my house and gutted me.

I wanted to say I was over it.

I wasn't over it.

I wanted to say I was glad for Faith but not for Hixon that a sketch had been in this week's *Guide* of the man who killed Faith's husband and rumor around town was that the sheriff had everything he needed, including a witness who saw Nat pick up the guy who killed him, they just needed to find that man.

But I was happy for him.

I wanted to say that I hoped like hell they found the guy so Faith could have some closure and not so Hixon could also put this behind him.

But I hoped like hell they found this guy—for both reasons.

I also wanted to say he hadn't looked amazingly handsome in the picture the *Guide* printed of him and his deputies in full uniform standing at the gravesite at Nat's funeral last Sunday (fortunately, they'd printed that picture, not one of Faith or her kids).

And he didn't.

He'd looked *devastatingly* handsome.

And I knew he'd looked devastatingly handsome before I'd even seen the picture because I saw it firsthand seeing as I'd been at that same funeral.

I'd also gone to pains to avoid the spear of his eyes I caught twice from where I was sitting and he was standing with his deputies at the side of the chairs set up for funeral-goers.

And, even though Lou had used her magical powers to put the hush on any talk about Hixon and Hope Drake around me, I still heard my fair share. And I wanted to say I wasn't skimming the range of emotions between interested and concerned when gossip reported that Hixon had instituted a veritable freeze-out of his ex-wife, and it was a known fact his son was angling to live solely with his father (thus giving rise to speculation both had learned why Hope had divorced her husband).

But I absolutely was skimming that range of emotions.

What I wasn't doing was seeing, speaking to or sleeping with Hixon Drake.

This regardless of the fact that he'd called on Sunday after the funeral, a call for obvious reasons I did not take, however he'd left a message in his lovely, deep voice that said simply, "Greta, we need to talk."

I had not replied.

I'd blocked his number too.

I was learning.

I was learning I didn't need my mother's malicious antics and I didn't need some man I barely knew treating me like dirt.

So I wasn't going to have either.

I was going to have Andy. Lou. Her girls. My work. My singing.

And the rest could go to hell.

Now I had Andy for the weekend. When I'd told Gemini my brother wanted to catch a Raiders game, he'd found an act to take my place.

I'd also cleared my client schedule for Saturday.

So I had a full weekend with my brother to look forward to and the Raiders winning to start that off was indication it was going to be a good one.

"Race you to the car?" Snow asked Andy.

"Yeah!" Andy yelled.

She took off.

Maple let him go and took off too.

Andy, knowing he could beat them by a mile, shot another grin over his shoulder at me, this a goofy one. He gave it a few beats to give them a head start, then he took off after them at a sedate lope.

"He's *da bomb*," Lou said from her place striding beside me as we walked out with the rest of the town from Raider Field.

She was right.

I looked up to her then back to where we were heading, watching the girls and Andy weave through the crowd, the girls just going for it, Andy stopping every once in a while to say, "Hey, sorry," and "pardon," and "gotta keep up with the girls."

In other words, they were going to beat him by a mile.

I watched them start to pull away in a break in the crowd and did it noting, "It's weird, you know. I get so pissed...I still..." I shook my head. "I grieve for the life he could have had. Then, I realize, if he'd had that, I wouldn't have this Andy and I don't know whether it's right or wrong to feel blessed I have this Andy when he could have had so much more."

"It's never wrong to love someone just as they come," Lou told me.

I glanced at her before again looking ahead. "You're right. I know that. But I'm not sure it's healthy I'm still holding on to some of that, Lou. It happened nearly a decade ago."

"My grandma died when my mom was twenty-two. And to this day, on Grandma's birthday and the anniversary of her death, you handle Mom with care and don't mention her red eyes. That was over four decades ago, Greta. I think what would be unhealthy is if you tried to stop yourself from feeling grief. The life he could have had that your mom took from him will always be something he lost. So it'll always be something you wished he had. Just feel what you feel, babe. And...shit."

I looked up to her after she said that last word to see her gaze narrowed on something in the distance.

"What?" I asked.

"Hixon," she hissed.

My eyes flew to where she was looking and there he was. Standing talking to a bunch of people just inside the chain link fence that ran around the field, wearing a navy V-neck sweater with a T-shirt under it and faded jeans—making that simplicity look awesome. His younger daughter was not too far from him looking like she was doing a pirouette with two other girls who were doing the same.

Shit!

"We have to get by him without him seeing me," I said under my breath like he was standing one foot away, not thirty, doing this grabbing Lou's arm and getting close to her. I gave it a yank. "Move to my other side."

"Why?" she asked. "He *should* see you. You look *fine*. You always look *fine*. But with that pink in your cheeks and that cute jacket and those jeans that make your awesome ass look even more awesome, he should get a load of what he's missing."

"Lou," I snapped.

"No," she returned calmly, moving a half step away, forcing my hand to fall from her arm. "Screw Hixon Drake."

Fabulous.

I kept walking, giving in, but ordered, "Don't look at him."

She said nothing.

We carried on and I hazarded a glance up at her.

She was looking right in his direction and I knew by the way she was skewering something with her eyes, it was him.

"You're not helping," I told her.

"He's not looking at me. He doesn't even know I'm here." Her attention came to me. "He's looking *at you*. And I'm *glad*. Because right about now he's probably missing a little of that action and I'm not just talking about the fact you are *fine* and he was tapping that. I'm talking about the fact pretty much everyone knows *he* now knows Hope is a spoiled-rotten bitch and pretty much everyone knows, after he escaped a *full* lifetime of *that*, he let a great thing slip right through his fingers."

It felt like my heart skipped a beat after the first part of what she said, and that skip was more like a walloping *thump* so I kinda didn't hear the rest of it.

"How lame would it be if I raced you to the car?" I asked.

"Super, double, extra lame," she answered.

Ugh.

We made it through the gate without incident, and then I stepped it up in my high-heeled boots to get to the car.

I didn't run. I didn't dilly-dally.

I wanted to be able to say this was because I wanted to make sure Andy and the girls had made it safely to the car.

But it totally wasn't.

IT WAS the pounding that woke me up.

But when I was awake, I heard the rain.

Shit!

Rain.

I tossed back the covers and raced out of my room, across the hall, to the room I thought of as Andy's, even though he didn't sleep there very often.

I threw open the door, heard the source of the noise but didn't see Andy, so I closed it, and there he was on the opposite side of the door, standing, hands to the wall, slamming his head against it.

"Sweetie," I whispered, rushing to him, putting my hands on him. "Shh, just rain. It's just rain," I soothed.

Fingers curled tight around his biceps, I pulled back.

He kept slamming his head against the wall.

"Andy, darlin', please, stop doing that." I pulled harder. "Come away from the wall."

He didn't stop even as he resisted my pull.

"Andrew!" I snapped. "Come away from the wall!"

I tightened my hold and gave his arms a yank, only for him to give my hands a powerful shirk at the same time his body jerked forcefully to the side.

I lost hold, falling back a step, and when I went to move forward and regain it, he lifted an elbow and drew it back sharply, catching me in the eye.

I cried out and fell backward. Tripping on the edge of the rug under the bed, I fell further, hitting the end of the bed, sliding down it and falling to my ass on the floor.

"Ta-Ta."

I blinked the stars out of my eyes and looked up at him.

He was turned, arms crossed, hands cupping his elbows, swaying and looking at me, and I didn't know if he understood he'd put me where I was and felt bad or if he was still freaking about the rain.

"Ta-Ta, Ta-Ta, Ta-Ta," he chanted then lunged forward, coming to his knees, putting me in a tight grip and yanking me to him as he fell to his ass, burrowing into me as I slid my arms around him. "Ta-Ta, Ta-Ta, Ta-Ta, Ta-Ta, Ta-Ta."

"It's okay." I ran a hand over his hair. "It's okay. I'm here. You're okay. I'm okay. It's all okay."

I didn't know it was forecast to rain.

If I knew, I'd have taken him back to the home.

He wasn't good in the rain.

The doctors didn't think it had to do with the damage to his brain. Not in that way.

They thought it had to do with the fact it had been raining hard when he'd had his accident and this was the way his mind dealt with that psychological trauma.

"Let's get you to bed, yeah? Let's get up in bed," I cooed.

It took a while for me to get him up but I did, got him in bed, and then I slid in with him.

He rocked as I held him in my arms, shushing him and fussing him until he fell asleep.

I kept doing it until the rain stopped.

And I continued to do it until I felt certain it wouldn't start again.

Only then did I slide away, tuck him in then go downstairs to grab some ice for my eye because it hurt like hell.

I took the ice in a Ziploc bag wrapped in dishtowel with me when I returned to bed.

I did it with my door open, Andy's open, but even so, I didn't get much sleep.

Andy was up, sitting at a stool at my kitchen island, scooping up a spoonful of Trix from one of the huge bowls I used for ice cream during my PMS times (and other times besides, if I was honest) when I walked down in the morning.

I kicked myself for oversleeping but was relieved like crazy he just got himself a bowl of cereal and didn't do what he sometimes did before I learned (or more accurately Keith and I had learned) not to oversleep.

That being walking out the front door and taking a stroll.

My relief didn't last long when he turned to me, dropped his spoon into the bowl with a plunk and a splash of milk and stared at me.

I knew why.

I had a shiner.

Crap.

"Andy—"

"Me..." He straightened from his slump over the bowl, his anxiety chasing away his ability to find words. "Bad. Me bad."

Unfortunately, since it was random what he would remember and what he wouldn't, he remembered last night.

I moved to him and put my hand on the island. "It's okay."

His eyes were riveted to my black one. "Bruise."

"It's okay, darlin'. It doesn't hurt," I lied then gave him a huge smile. "And it makes me look badass." That wasn't a lie, but unfortunately it didn't make me look, say, Chuck Norris badass, and not just because Chuck Norris was so badass, he'd never get a black eye. It made me look trailer-trash-had-a-rougher-than-normal-night badass.

His head twitched, he looked to me, his gaze moving over my face then his lips tentatively curled up.

"Put up your dukes," he joked.

I did, punching him lightly with one on his biceps.

He started laughing.

Crisis averted.

I moved in and gave him a kiss on the side of head.

Then I moved back, leaned against the island and asked, "What are we gonna do today? You wanna go shopping for some new clothes?"

He'd turned back to his cereal but he twisted his neck to frown at me. "No shopping."

Just like a man.

"Wanna go to the shelter and play with the dogs?" I suggested.

He liked that and they liked when we came. Those dogs needed love and attention and Andy had the capacity to give a lot of both.

But he frowned. "They won't let me take one."

This was new.

And it was true.

Maybe I needed to get him a dog.

Of course, that would mean me taking care of said dog while Andy only had visitation.

Next idea.

"*Parks and Recreation* marathon?" I tried again.

His face lit up. "Yeah!"

He loved that show. We'd seen every episode at least four times.

"Thank goodness I got the stuff to make pulled pork so it can cook all day while we laze in front of the TV," I replied.

"Pulled pork, Ta-Ta, cool. Thank you."

He loved my pulled pork.

"Right. We have a plan. I'll get that in the Crockpot while you finish your Trix, and then get a shower. I'll get cleaned up and we'll spend the day with Leslie Knope and Andy Dwyer."

"Awesome," he muttered, turning back to his Trix.

I moved around the island to get the Crockpot out of the cabinet under it.

Andy ate his Trix and got a shower as I put the pork shoulder in the Crockpot with the rest of my secret ingredients (secret to the extent Andy didn't know them but the rest of the world did since the recipe was on the side of the spice packet).

We watched *Parks and Rec*.

When the time came, we pigged out on pulled pork, homemade macaroni salad and waffle fries. Not long enough after, we scooped up ice cream in my special ice cream (and Andy-cereal) bowls. Some time after that, I went to bed feeling like I weighed a ton and having a dull throb in my head from watching too much TV, not being active enough and eating *way* too much.

I didn't care even a little bit.

On Sunday, Andy was feeling the pull to play with the dogs at the shelter.

So we did that after I got a latte and Andy got a hot cocoa at

Babycakes, during which Andy, as was his norm, charmed the pants off of Babycakes Watson, the owner, who had that moniker for reasons unknown to me.

She also had a history of dogs she named the same thing, one after the other that replaced one when it had died. They were all poodles and she was currently on Babycakes IV (who was in attendance during our visit at the coffee house, then again, they always were), a standard red who had replaced the sadly departed Babycakes III, a standard blue who had died last year.

After playing with the dogs (and cats) at the shelter, we came home and watched movies.

After that, I took him for ribs at Po-Jack's barbecue place in Morsprings to finish up our barbecue-themed weekend.

Then my weekend with my brother was done.

So I took him home, went back to my place, made myself tea, gave myself my moment and finally went out to my porch.

Alone.

Just as I'd done every night since Hix ended things.

It was Monday night and I was in the produce section at the grocery store when the first thing happened.

That being Shari walking her cart up to mine and crying, "Ohmigod! Your eye!"

This, or a version of it, had been the refrain all day (and from the workers at the shelter, Babycakes, and the folks who saw me at Sunnydown).

I was learning that a black eye didn't start out black. It started kinda faded purple.

It got a deep, ugly, horrid black that defied concealer after a few days.

"Andy winged me with an elbow accidentally," I told her, also a constant refrain that day (though I didn't share that with others in front of Andy). "It looks worse than it is."

That last was true. It hurt the first few days but now it was just a dull ache I barely felt at all.

"Oh, you poor thing," she murmured, studying my eye before she brightened. "Did you hear?"

I heard a lot of things. I worked in a salon.

So my reply was, "I don't know."

"About Hal."

Hal?"

"Sorry?" I asked.

"Hal...uh, what's-his-name. I don't remember his last name. I kinda don't want to, he's kinda a jerk. But I've met his wife Ashlee in passing. She's nice. Not sure you know her, I think she gets her hair done at The Cutting Edge."

She was rambling and I was tired, in heels and hungry so I cut in to say, "I don't think I know him," in a hopefully not rude effort to get her to move this along.

"He's one of Hixon's deputies."

Oh boy.

"He found the gun that killed Faith's husband," she declared.

I stood still and stared at her.

"It's really good he did that. Apparently, he spent ages workin' hunches on his free time, out with metal detectors with a couple of his buddies on game trails, hiking trails, roadsides. And he found it on a stretch of road over in Sheridan County."

"That's excellent," I told her.

"Yeah." She grinned. "One step closer."

I hoped so, for Faith (and, damn it, Hixon).

"And, well..." Shari's look turned cautious, "you probably heard Shaw moved in with Hixon. Permanent-like."

Uh-oh.

"Yeah?" I murmured.

"Is it okay to talk about this?" she queried. "I mean, I know you two aren't an item anymore but it didn't last a long time and...hey, by the way, you gonna go out with Mrs. Swanson's Owen? She's telling everyone she's gonna set you two up."

Crap.

"I'm just kinda...doin' my own thing at the moment," I replied.

She nodded like she, a woman who was now thirty-six, hadn't been married to her husband since she was twenty and she had any concept what "doing her own thing" as a single gal really meant.

Then she kept talking.

"Well, as you can imagine, Hope is beside herself. But think she's finally gettin' smart, 'cause, see, everyone knows this wasn't Hixon's idea. It was Shaw's. He's real mad at her." She leaned in. "*Real* mad." She leaned back. "I thought, when I heard, that she'd be spreadin' it around that she blames Hix. But apparently, Shaw threw such a fit at havin' to go back to his momma's yesterday, Jep had to get involved. He came into town. Sat down with his girl. Told her the way of things and the girls went back. But Shaw didn't. And all day today, all Hope's sayin' is that her boy needs his daddy at his age and she thinks it's good, Shaw havin' time with his father, learnin' to be a man before he goes off to be a marine."

"Well, I hope that all works out," I said, and I did, but I'd rather not be talking about it.

"Girls won't be far behind, I reckon, they learn the full truth about their momma," Shari predicted.

"Well, I hope with that they never do," I shared, and I hoped that too, a lot.

"Me too, but," she shrugged, "things got a way of gettin' out and Hope's on the back foot now. She's scramblin'. Losin' Hix like she did. Losin' her son like that. Folks knowin' why and they're bein' nice enough, but she's also feelin' the cold shoulder. She's got a lot to make up for, pain she's caused. So now she's got Julie Baker spreadin' around how proud she is of Hix, this sad business with Nat Calloway and how far they got when they started with a whole load of nothin'. Julie's spreadin' it wide how Hope always knew what a good policeman he was and how she isn't glad how he got the reason to prove it, but she's still glad the county knows for certain we're in good hands."

God, Hope Drake was a piece of work.

"Mm-hmm," I murmured.

Shari gave me a close look that shifted to a horrified one.

"You aren't okay with talkin' about this," she said, aghast at what she thought was her insensitivity.

She was sweet and she was right in what she'd said earlier.

Hixon and I weren't an item anymore. We never officially were. It was just me who was an idiot bent on proving that fact repeatedly with all men.

So she shouldn't feel bad.

"It's just that I've been on my feet all day," I lied, twisted from my cart and lifted up a foot to show her one of my pumps that I could run a marathon in, even right then (okay, maybe not right then but if pressed, I could maybe walk a 5K). "And I just wanna get my groceries, get home and get these off. But Andy ate me out of house and home so I have to restock or go hungry. And from what Andy and I put away this weekend, I can't put that off and just buy some fried chicken at the deli. I need something green or my body is gonna shut down."

"I hear you," she replied and smiled. "Though I don't because I only wore heels to my prom and my wedding, but those were enough. So I also do and I'll let you go."

"Thanks, babe. And it was good to see you, Shari."

"You too, honey. Give that brother of yours a hug from me when you see him again, and you should bring him for another day in the salon sometime. I wasn't there any of the times you've brought him but all the girls say he's great and I'd love to meet him."

"Good idea. I'll talk with Andy about that."

"Great. Get done with your shoppin', get yourself home and I'll talk to you later."

She raised a hand, gave me a wave, put it back to her cart and motored off.

I grabbed my salad fixins, fruit and wheeled my cart into the small sea of aisles that were half the number of any King Soopers in Denver, but still managed by some miracle to have all the stuff.

I did this trying to put all Shari had shared out of my mind.

And failing miserably.

They got the gun.

Good.

That meant at least that crazy drifter wouldn't shoot anybody else (I hoped).

Also, Hixon's son had turned his back on his mother.

I had no idea if that was good or bad, but in one way or another, no matter the reason, any child doing that was bad.

And Hope was back-peddling.

I had no idea how that would go.

All I knew, and I knew it well, was that Hixon Drake had one hell of a temper, so if he reacted the way he did to spending time with my mother, him discovering his wife ended a two-decade-long marriage over a piece of expensive jewelry, well...

She was screwed.

I was in the coffee and tea section when the next thing happened.

And it was a lot worse than Shari gossiping about Hixon and Hope Drake.

I also had my mind filled with what she'd said, much of it about Hixon, so my mind was filled with him.

Therefore I was not prepared for the man himself to make an appearance.

But this he did, saying from close to my side, "Greta?"

I turned my head from perusing the tea selection and stared up at him standing right there.

At my side.

God, that thick, dark hair with its minimal, but awesome, silver flecks, his height, those broad shoulders, his pool-blue eyes.

It was hateful he was so beautiful.

He didn't stare at me.

His eyes narrowed on my shiner and his face turned to granite.

"What the fuck?" he whispered.

"Hixon," I whispered back.

Suddenly, and honest to God I didn't know how it happened or how it happened so fast, I didn't have hands to my cart and head turned to Hixon Drake.

I had my back pinned to shelves and Hixon Drake in my space, his thumb curved around the bottom of my jaw, fingers splayed along my cheek, tilting my head back, his face in mine, his eyes sweltering, his voice an enraged (loud) rumble.

"*What the fuck?*" he near-to bellowed.

"I—"

"Who did this to you?" he demanded to know.

"It was just a—"

His hand slid from my jaw to clamp, firm but still surprisingly gentle, around the side of my neck. "Why didn't you report this to me?"

My head twitched in confusion.

"Report...what?" I asked.

"I'm the sheriff, Greta," he bit out. "A man takes his fist to you, you call the fuckin' *sheriff*."

"A man didn't—"

"Who did it?"

"Hixon, it was just—"

He got nose to nose with me. "Who fuckin' touched you?"

God!

It was infuriating how he never let me speak.

"Step back," I demanded.

"Greta, tell me who did this to you," he growled.

"Take your hand off me, Sheriff, and step back!" I yelled.

He stared into my eyes and didn't move.

"Back!" I shouted.

He stepped back and took his hand from my neck but he did it putting his other one to my cart and holding it steady, angling his body, me imprisoned by the cart, his frame and the shelves.

"Talk to me," he ordered.

I was at that moment very aware we had an audience.

I didn't look from Hixon.

"It's not your business."

"A man harms a woman in my county, it's my business," he forced out between clenched teeth.

"It's not what you think."

Now he was letting me finish sentences, but he still didn't listen to me because he didn't refer to that with his next, he just continued on with what he had to say.

"And I'll make this clear to you right here, I don't give a shit you've blocked my calls, any man harms you, Greta, *you*, you tell me and I deal with it for you first as a man *then* as the sheriff."

Um.

What?

No. No. No.

He wasn't going to put his dibs in to look after me after he stood in *my house* and *gutted me.*

"Step away," I ordered.

"Talk to me."

"Step away!" I yelled.

He dipped his face in mine and roared, "*Talk to me!*"

"My brother did it! All right! He doesn't like rain, freaked out, elbowed me in the face."

He slid back an inch and stared at me in surprise.

"It's fine. I'm fine. He's fine. Now *step back!*" I screeched the last.

"Your brother?" he asked a whole lot more calmly.

I wasn't so calm.

He didn't get to pin me against shelves like some alpha-male run amuck and ask me questions he should have asked me when he was sleeping in my bed and eating breakfast at my kitchen island.

"My brother," I bit out. "Now, Sheriff, you don't get to do this. You made things clear in my living room and, I don't know, say *just now*, jumping to conclusions I'd be stupid enough and also slutty enough to get myself another man about a week after you dumped me before we even had a date and then letting that man hit me without turning his ass in to the cops."

"That's not what I thought."

"What'd you think?"

God!

Why had I asked?

I needed to *get out of there*.

"Your mother is connected to Kavanagh Becker and he's not a nice guy but he *is* a guy who has a posse of equally not-nice guys."

"I've never even heard that name in my life."

"Okay, sweetheart, but it doesn't make that fact any less true."

Sweetheart.

Oh shit.

I was going to cry.

I hadn't cried since it happened.

I couldn't cry.

"Step back, Hixon," I whispered.

"Greta."

"*Step back!*" I shrieked.

He stepped back.

I snatched my purse out of the seat of the cart, turned and ignored the onlookers we had (especially the sheer number of them) as I ran out of the grocery store, leaving my groceries behind, leaving my cart behind, probably leaving a healthy dose of my dignity behind, thus focusing on the fact I had leftover pulled pork in the fridge.

I probably couldn't eat it without throwing it up.

But in case I managed to pull myself together, at least I wouldn't starve.

The ringing of the doorbell came first.

When I ignored that, the knocking came.

When I ignored that, with only intermittent spurts of respite, it just kept coming.

Finally (and by "finally" I meant this lasted probably five minutes, but that was a *long* five minutes) , I moved and stood on the opposite end to the door at the picture window at the front of my house and peeked through the windows.

From my angle, I couldn't see who was at the door.

But I could see a Bronco in my drive.

Not at the curb this time.

Oh no.

He wasn't trying to share with anyone who saw it that he was there for just a visit and not for an all-night booty call by parking casually at the curb. He also wasn't intent on sharing with me that he was going to do what he had to do and get the hell out of there and he wanted to do it without the bothersome effort of reversing out of my drive.

Nope.

He'd parked in my driveway like his badass and supercool (it sucked, but it was true) Bronco belonged there.

He wanted to push this?

Fine.

I had a few things to say to make things clear too.

And maybe he might allow me to finish a few sentences for once so I could say them.

But after I did, we'd be done.

For good.

So I went to the door, unlocked it, pulled it open and glared into Hixon Drake's devastatingly handsome face.

"What?" I snapped.

"Can I come in?" he asked gently.

Fuck him.

And fuck his *gentle.*

"Be my guest," I declared, stepping back and moving away, far away, putting the couch between me and him.

He walked to the back of it, his eyes never leaving me, and stopped.

"Greta—"

"I let you in here because this time *I* have a few things to say and if you don't want to listen, you can leave right now."

He just held my gaze and said nothing.

He also didn't move.

I took that as indication he was going to listen so I launched in.

"Not that you deserve an explanation, but it'll make," I jerked a thumb at myself, "*me* feel better to share with you my relationship with my mother is nonexistent. From the moment she nearly killed my brother in a drunk-driving accident, *her* being the drunk, she became nothing to me but a nuisance I had to throw money at way too often to stop her from interfering with my life. Something, I'll also share because I'm feeling in the mood that has stopped very recently. She wasn't liking that all that much, even though apparently she's found another meal ticket, so she took that out on me and did it through *you.*"

Several moments after I quit talking, Hixon asked, "She almost killed your brother?"

I jerked up my chin. "That record I told you about. She served eight months. However, if it was up to me, after what she did to him, she'd still be in prison, rotting."

Again several moments after I stopped, he asked, "And your brother?"

"He's at Sunnydown. He has a TBI. Severe issues with recall. Deficits in attention and concentration. Problems reading and writing. Lack of motivation. He has episodes. Sometimes they're seizures. Sometimes they're aggressive. He also has regressive behaviors that the doctors think have nothing to do with the TBI and everything to do with the trauma of having our mother be a mother who was okay being shitfaced and picking up her fifteen-year-old son from a party in the rain. And that also explains the rain. He gets agitated and sometimes harms himself when it's raining. It rained Friday night. He was spending the weekend with me. He had an episode. I tried to stop him from hurting himself, he caught me with an elbow."

I pointed with my whole hand, fingers out straight and pressed together, to my eye and then offered my conclusion.

"That's it. So we're done. Finished. As you said...*over*. Thank you for listening and have a nice night. Don't worry. I'll lock the door after you leave."

Again with the gentle when he replied, "There's more to say."

"You're right, there is," I agreed and then gave him exactly that. "Even if we were together, it would not be your right to pin me against shelves in a grocery store or *anywhere*. It would also not be your right to detain me in *any way* if I didn't so wish, especially after I repeatedly asked you to step back."

"I mentioned this the other night, but as I unfortunately conveyed, I wasn't in a space to be as forthcoming as I should have been since I also unfortunately assumed incorrectly that you already knew. But Kavanagh Becker cooks meth. A lot of it. In this county. And he's tight with your mother."

I stared at him.

God.

God.

My mother.

"He's a dangerous man," Hixon carried on. "He cooks it and distributes it out of this county, but he doesn't deal it in this county. Regardless, to do what he does and to get as wealthy as he is doing it, he's good at it but doesn't keep great company. After your mother and Becker had their fun with me, Becker paid a visit to me at my department the next day and shared your mother is not happy you've cut her out. It isn't a leap, baby, with the games they played with me, the way they both were during that, to think that something broke with that and they came after you."

Okay, well.

Damn.

That made sense.

And damn again.

Mom had a really bad guy in her corner.

I hadn't thought of that at the time, what with losing Hixon taking precedence and all.

But I thought of it now.

I bit my lip and looked away, considering the many atrocities she could inflict on me with these new resources.

And Andy.

Shit.

"I'm sorry."

When those words came from Hixon, I looked back at him.

He continued talking.

"I saw your eye and I've not been in a good way about what I said to you, how I left it between us, you blocking my calls, me worried that they might be affecting your life and how that might be, and I didn't curb my reaction. I should have, in a grocery store, in your living room, it doesn't matter. But you have a black eye, Greta, and I've had a coupla those. They don't feel good and there's never a good way to get one. I just jumped to what I hope you get now are valid, if erroneous, conclusions about how you got yours."

Crap.

That made sense too.

And crap again.

If something like that was swirling around someone I cared about and I saw they had a black eye, I might pin them against some shelves too to demand their story, and I wasn't even a six-foot-one, built, badge-wielding alpha-male.

I didn't give him that.

I snapped, "Fine."

"I still shouldn't have pinned you in like that and forced a scene."

"You're right. Thank you for your apology. Now you're free to leave."

"Greta—" he started, his body moving like he was going to make a move to come to me.

"Don't," I whispered and he froze. "Not again, Hixon. Just don't."

"Corinne knows about us."

And another time that night, my head twitched in confusion at his sudden, bewildering announcement.

"Sorry?"

"My daughter. Corinne. Hope told her about us. She's...not pleased. She sees it as a betrayal of her mother. On the other hand, Shaw already knew, talk in school, his girlfriend filled him in so he wouldn't get surprised if kids said something to him. He's cool with it. But he wasn't cool with his mother sharing news he knows I would have shared when the time came to share it. He's been having issues with Hope for a while, with what she did to our family, those came to a head, and right after Corinne blasted me, he called and asked to live with me. All this happened on the way to Becker's. I actually hung up with Shaw getting out of my truck at the foot of the stairs to his house. Then I walked in and got hit with your mom and Becker's form of fun. I took that out on you—"

I interrupted him to confirm, "You did."

"And it was wrong," he carried on.

"It was," I agreed.

"And I regretted it almost as soon as it happened."

"And you show this by calling me the next morning and telling me what I should do when I run my mouth?"

"Then I was pissed at Lou."

"I see." I nodded. "And you took that out on me."

He bent and leaned into both hands on the back of the couch, his head tipped back to keep hold on my eyes, and I lamented the fact he looked amazing doing that too.

"Right," he started, "I get this doesn't look good for me and I get why. I totally get that, sweetheart. But I'll point out, I don't usually have a nineteen-year marriage ending because my wife didn't get a promise from me I'd buy her some fancy-assed ring for our twentieth..."

He trailed off and studied me, not moving from his position.

And I knew I gave it away.

"You knew," he said quietly.

I pressed my lips together but they unpressed themselves to blurt, "I'm sorry, Hixon. Everyone knew."

"Right," he muttered, oddly not looking pissed out of his brain, as he should be. "Whatever," he kept muttering.

Whoa.

Whatever?

When he spoke again, he wasn't muttering.

"I live in a shithole apartment not big enough for my kids when I have them, and I don't like it much even when I don't. My daughter feels I betrayed her mother, and her, by seeing another woman, and I wasn't with her or in a position to have the time or anything close to it to explain things to her how they should have been explained. My son is setting himself up to despise his mom until his last breath and I'm struggling with the fact I know I should do somethin' about that and the understanding, with the harm she's willingly inflicted on our family, I have no motivation to help her repair things with her boy. I was investigating a murder where every second is crucial in the days closest to the event to find as much as we could to catch the killer, and I'm driving twenty miles out to Becker's place for him and your mother to play with me. That was all happening and I lost it. With you. I regret it. Because it was the wrong thing to do. But mostly because you didn't deserve it and I know I hurt you."

He was calm.

He was apologetic.

He was making sense.

He was taking his time in what was his busy, crazy, messed-up life to explain this to me.

He was beautiful, all tall and dark and leaning into my couch.

But I couldn't do it.

Because when he'd said he wanted to complicate things with me, I'd never wanted anything more in my life, except Andy to have a happy one, and of course, the time I sat in the waiting room with Keith while Andy was in surgery, wanting Andy to get out of that surgery room alive.

I hadn't even wanted Keith that much and I'd loved him with what I'd thought was every part of me.

But with Keith there was always the knowledge that he gave, I took, and the guilt I carried with me constantly because of that.

With Hixon, I got to give. I got to take care of him. I got to be the one he came to when he needed to suck back bourbon, not able to share anything but wanting to try to unwind from serious business after an incomprehensibly ugly day.

He gave too. He teased me and made me laugh and looked at me in a way that made me feel beautiful, and he not only showed, but verbalized that he appreciated what I gave to him and that it meant something.

He also didn't hesitate to take all that away.

I couldn't do it again.

Maybe from the beginning he'd been right.

Bad timing.

We should have waited. Waited for his life to calm down. Waited for him and his kids to settle into a new life.

Just waited.

We didn't.

And now it was broken in a way it couldn't be fixed.

I hated it that he knew he broke it and he was there trying to fix it.

And I hated it that I had to tell him it couldn't be fixed.

"I can't risk it again, Hixon."

He kept his place but dropped his head.

God, I hated that too.

"I'm sorry," I whispered.

He tipped his head back and again gave me those blue eyes.

I didn't hate those.

God.

"What we have is good," he said softly.

"It's not the right time."

"Then we'll give it time."

I shook my head.

And I'd thought he'd gutted me the last time he was in my living room.

But I was wrong.

He gutted me right then.

"Greta, you're the finest woman I've ever met. We work together. We fit together. I know you feel it the same as me. And we'd be fools not to see where that would lead, and I don't give a shit all that's swirling around me, or you. If we can make it through what I did to you, I can earn your trust again, and we can get beyond all that's happening now, I got a strong feeling where it would lead."

"I had a good man like you who left me because of my mother, Hixon. She's not going anywhere."

"I wanna know that story, but I don't care about your mother."

"Trust me, I've had thirty-eight years of it, and she's been quiet for a week. She's just sharpening her knives. Eventually, you'll care."

"Babe—"

"It hurt too much, what you did to me," I whispered.

He shut up.

"It had only been days," I explained quietly. "What happens when I have more and you take it away?"

"What could happen if that never happens?" he returned.

"That's not the life I lead."

He pushed up from the couch, kept looking me straight in the eyes, and declared, "I'm stronger than that other guy."

"You can't know that."

"I can because I know this, if you wanted a twenty-five thousand dollar ring for our anniversary, I'd take a second job to get it for you."

I gasped.

And I stared.

"And that's because in two days you gave me more than my wife did in nineteen years, notwithstanding our children and the fact she's got issues, but she's a good mother. That's an uncomfortable realization, sweetheart. And she had her way of doin' nice things. But she wasn't you."

"You can't know that either."

"I can. I do."

Oh my God.

"Hixon."

He lifted one hand and dropped it.

"You need time. I'll give it to you. I need time too. Corinne is still pissed and Shaw's not in a good place. But Greta, I leave, it's not my right to ask this of you, but I'm gonna do it anyway. Think about it. Unblock my fuckin' number. And after I give us time, take my call."

"I don't want to hurt you but I have to say at this juncture I don't think that's smart, and I say that for the both of us."

"You seen the *Avengers* movie?"

And again my head twitched.

"Sorry?"

"The *Avengers* movie. You seen it?"

"Which one?" I asked stupidly because I'd seen them all. Andy liked them.

"Whatever one."

"Yes...uh, all of them."

He nodded. "I was a selfish fuck. I get you. I get that guilt you carried in your marriage. I don't know the story. I just know in my way, I did that to you. I took from you and I didn't give back. I did that because you came into my life in a time I needed to take. And that'll happen again. But that's not all there is to me. I just need you to think about whether you'll give me the shot to prove it to you."

That was incredibly sweet.

Still.

"Why did you ask about the *Avenger* movies?"

He smiled at me.

And I wished he hadn't done it.

"Because my daughter says boys are stupid. They talk about themselves all the time, don't ask girls questions, don't let them talk, don't listen. And I've unfortunately proved grown men who should know better do that too."

Goddammit.

Now he was making sense, being sweet and now kinda cute.

"I wanna know all about you, Greta," he said in a voice that sounded like velvet and felt that way too. "So I'll give you time to think about it. And after you have that time, I hope you give me that privilege, 'cause before the season ends, I wanna go watch my son play ball and have you there, walking out of Raider Field with me next to you. Not Lou."

After delivering that, he turned and strolled to the door.

He opened it.

Stopped.

Looked at me.

And smiled.

"Lock this, baby."

Then he disappeared.

Chapter 15

Dive Under

Greta

"You are not getting back together with that man."

It was the next morning and I was standing in the back room of the House of Beauty getting ready for my first client, with Lou, who was also getting ready for hers and apparently feeling like she could tell me what to do.

Needless to say, after she'd shared she'd heard about the grocery store incident, I'd shared what came after.

"No, I'm not, Lou," I replied. "But you have to admit, he's had it rough. And that was before some random, crazy drifter shot a twenty-eight-year-old father of two after he did nothing but stop to help out said random, crazy drifter, and it being Hix who's the guy who has to find some random, crazy man that's crazy enough to shoot to death a man with a kind enough heart, he'd stop to help him out."

Lou looked away and muttered, "I gotta admit, that's way worse than any day Julie Baker sat in my chair and stared at herself in the mirror after I'd done her hair like she'd allowed a small child with learning disabilities to do it and wondered at her own sanity." She looked back to me. "Before, of course, she moved to your chair and did that shit to you."

One could say I wasn't too torn up Julie Baker was no longer my client.

"I'm kinda glad we had it out," I declared.

This was a lie.

I was not.

Before, I was hurt, mad and sad.

Now I was confused, scared and wondering at my own sanity if I didn't think on it like Hix asked me to do.

"And at least this is a better way to leave things than they were before," I went on.

And at least that was true.

"But when Keith told me we were over and I asked why, he said he couldn't live with Mom in his life anymore and he wasn't going to ask me to choose between him and her because he knew I'd choose her. And he was so done with it, he didn't let me have the opportunity to prove him wrong," I reminded her.

And that was also, sadly, true.

I kept going.

"He loved Andy and would lay down his life for him. I believe that to my soul. He loved me the same way. But he hated her with a passion that was equal to those two things combined. We would argue, but we'd only fight about her. Any time she asked me for money, he'd get angry. But when I gave it to her, which was too often, I knew that then, I know it better now, he'd lose it. Totally. He got tunnel vision about it. That was all he could see eventually when he looked at me. My weakness about her. The fact he used his hard-earned money to look after Andy, and I used mine to look after her. It just got worse and worse until it consumed everything, including us. And she's already played with Hix in ways he clearly didn't enjoy."

"We're in no doubt about that," she cut in to say irritably.

We certainly weren't, me especially.

"So I don't need that threat hanging over me, falling in love with a new man."

She stared at me hard and asked, "Falling in love?"

I lifted a shoulder. "He's great."

"Babe—"

I interrupted her before she could get started. "He didn't end it in a good way. But that was the only thing bad about it." I fought my lips curving up as I said, "He called me gum drop."

"How ridiculously sexist," she decreed.

"I called him snuggle bug."

Her eyes bugged out. "You called Hixon Drake *snuggle bug*?"

"It was a joke. Both of them were."

She pulled herself together after receiving that news and did it ending up looking hesitant.

The next thing she said explained the look.

"I always wondered why you kept helping that woman out."

I looked to the boxes of hair dye and replied, "She's my mom."

"Greta—"

I looked back at her. "You don't get it. You have a great mom. You don't understand. But even how she was with me growing up, if she'd died when I was twenty, I'd still feel it on her birthday. The anniversary of her death. It's just how it is. It's just the connection. It's there and there's no getting rid of it. Even cutting her out of my life that connection is still there. It makes no sense. It just *is*. And maybe I was a slow learner with that, Lou. But also maybe if I had stopped helping her out, she would have gotten herself in trouble, sick, in prison, out on the streets, dead. Who knows? And then it would have been guilt that I wasn't the kind of person who had the fortitude to look after my mother even if she is how she is. I couldn't win either way. Keith didn't get that and I understand why he couldn't. But the bottom line is...she's my mom."

"Are you gonna let her back in?" she asked.

I licked my lips, rubbed them together and lifted a hand to pull out the box of dye I'd be needing.

"I don't think so."

"And it was what she did to Hix that pushed it too far?"

I looked to her and gave her a smile that even felt sad on my mouth.

"She didn't do that to Hix. She did it to me. She just *used* Hix. So yeah. Definitely. That she would go out of her way to find new ways to harm me and do that without compunction hurting some innocent person just out doing his job, with her knowing that job was a really not-fun one at the time. It had always been her manipulating me, using me, lashing out at me. She didn't hurt Andy because she wanted to hurt me. She did it because she's stupid and weak. It was an avoidable accident but I think I still let her stay in my life because it was that. An accident. This wasn't. She planned what she did to Hix to get at me. She went out of her way, got others involved, and that kind of malice is too extreme to ignore."

"You know, Hixon is right," she told me. "Everyone's heard of Kavanagh Becker. He's kind of our Voldemort. He's the one you don't speak his name. People try to forget he exists, talk about him in whispers. He's not a good guy."

Yep.

That sounded like my mother's type.

"Marvelous," I muttered.

"No matter what happens with you two, babe, Hixon Drake is a good sheriff. Bunch of people saw him up late, in his office, while that whole thing with Nat started going down. Even before they found Nat's body, word spread he was all over finding him. Everyone talked about how single-minded he was about doing what he could for Faith and her kids. The man even put on a uniform he *never* wears and made his crew stand at his side at Nat's funeral to make it known to Faith he has her back. He'd lose his mind if Kavanagh Becker hurt you." Her lips twitched. "And I reckon, what he said to you, he'd really *lose his mind* if that guy hurt you. You'll be okay and maybe your mom will slink away after a time of not being able to get anything out of you."

"I hope so."

But I didn't actually hope so and not because I never hoped for anything important.

I knew she wasn't done.

But I did think she'd eventually give up if I had the strength to continue going my own way.

She played all her angles but she wasn't a big fan of expending too much time and effort getting blood from a stone.

"Toodle-loo!" someone called from the front room. "Y'all here?"

"That'd be mine," Lou murmured and moved to the door, shouting, "In the back, Agnes! Coming right out!"

She stopped at it and looked back at me.

"I never said this because it was too fresh but you really should know it. Keith messed up, girlfriend. I never met her but just your stories make her sound like Tawnee the Hun. I know with things the way they are with Bill that if you love someone, you put up with *all* the shit that comes with them. I know a lot of people wonder why I put up with his shit but the answer is simple. I love him. And I'm sure Keith loved you. He just didn't love you enough."

"Thanks, darlin'," I whispered.

She wasn't quite done.

"One thing Hixon Drake is right about, you're worth getting a second job to buy you a big-ass ring if that was what you wanted. Although I'm pissed at him for what he did to you, at least we agree on that." She gave me a smile. "And I know that mostly because you're the kind of woman who'd never want that. You'd like getting it. But that isn't what's important to you."

She was right.

I liked diamonds.

But I had a sneaking, confusing, scary suspicion I'd move into a trailer if Hixon Drake lived in it, and after I'd moved out of my mother's when I was twenty, I'd sworn I'd never go back for any reason.

"Don't make me cry," I ordered. "I didn't wear my waterproof mascara."

She grinned. "Okay, I won't. I'll just say I no longer hate you because you're gorgeous and have a great ass. I hate you now because you get to have a scene in the grocery store with a hot guy pinning you against the Celestial Seasonings, getting all wound up on your behalf, shouting in your face then calling you sweetheart. As I've said, I'm pissed at Hix. But I wasn't even there, I just heard it from seven sources, and I still know that was *hot.*"

"It wasn't hot," I shared truthfully. "It was kinda scary and more than kinda annoying."

"Yeah, I get you thought that then. But now..." She shook her head. "I'm pissed at Hix but I might find my way to unpissed if that gives any indication of how much that man feels for you. And not to give you reason to forgive his badass self for acting like such a huge dick, but I've known Hixon Drake for years and I've heard more about him than is healthy for anyone outside Brad Pitt, and he's not the man to cause a scene in a grocery store, Greta. If he lost it in the manner half the women of this town are tittering relentlessly about at this very moment that says something I don't wanna hear about Hixon Drake right now. That man isn't sheriff. He *lives and breathes* the responsibility behind that badge. So pinning a woman against the tea selection in a grocery store is not the way he'd go."

She paused.

I braced.

Then she gave me the rest of it.

"But he saw you with a shiner and he went that way. Yeah," she said contemplatively. "That might help me find my way to unpissed."

"Now *you* are being scary and annoying," I returned.

She rolled her eyes, puckered her lips in a kiss my way and walked out the door.

Gah!

Lou.

THAT FRIDAY NIGHT, through the applause after I sang Billie Holiday's "He's Funny That Way," I murmured, "Thank you," into the mic.

Billie, by the way, was one of the artists I didn't like to sing because you just didn't sing her songs, seeing as you could never do them justice. These, in my estimation, included Barbra Streisand, Dolly Parton, Tina Turner, Céline Dion, Whitney Houston and Adele (but that wasn't an exhaustive list).

However, my pianist, Elvan, the man who set my set lists—lists that would be crowd pleasers for Gemini—made me.

It didn't hurt too much.

But he always gave me something after he gave me a toughie.

And this time he rewarded me, leading the boys into Annie Lennox's "Cold."

I loved that song. It fit my voice perfectly. And I loved to wrap it around the icy-hot beauty of the lyrics.

So I was smiling when I felt my eyelids get lazy as the drummer did his thing and the others came in and I fell into the song, standing at the microphone, swaying, my hands suddenly weightless, floating around my hips as my head drifted, the only constant being aiming my lips to mic.

I was finishing the first verse when something caught my attention and I focused slowly on it, seeing with some surprise Gemini standing close to the stage, something he never did. He didn't sift through the crowd while anyone was performing. It wouldn't do for the host to interrupt a performance in any way.

But as I caught sight of him standing right there, blocking people from seeing the stage, his eyes shifted.

I followed their direction and saw Hixon sitting at the end of the bar, his eyes locked on me.

And somebody kill me, the minute my eyes hit his, they were caught.

Trapped.

Captive.

I couldn't look away. Even as I sensed some members of the audience shifting, twisting in their seats, turning to look to see who I was singing to.

But I was singing words about a woman who wanted to swim in her man's eyes.

And I wanted that.

I wanted my shot at that.

I wanted my shot to swim in the blue of Hix's eyes for the rest of my life.

What I didn't want was for him to know that.

But I couldn't look away.

Fortunately, as they had wont to do, the song ended, I tore myself out of his spell and forced a smile at the audience who were clapping somewhat more enthusiastically than usual. My mind hazily attempted to try to remember what song was next, hoping it wouldn't get me into more trouble.

Unfortunately it was the nature of the beast for a lounge singer like me that the next song wasn't much better, but at least it didn't have lyrics about swimming in someone's eyes.

It was Eva Cassidy's "Fields of Gold."

And I managed to sing that and the next four songs of my set without once looking at Hixon.

I exited the stage concealing my haste (I hoped), expressing my gratitude and saying I'd be back. And I sat in my tiny dressing room backstage (yes, hiding) terrified that Gemini was going to come back like he had just a few weeks before to tell me Hix was out there waiting for me.

When the knock came and Gemini swung in, I was holding my breath.

"He left, beautiful," he said softly. "Spoke with me briefly. Said he enjoyed the show but was concerned he was making you uncomfortable. So he asked me to tell you that you look gorgeous and then he left."

I blew out a breath but it wasn't a complete relief.

No.

Because Hixon might have gone but he'd left only to be thoughtful and only after saying something sweet.

"Not my place, you didn't ask, heard about the grocery store incident," Gemini began.

Of course he did.

Everyone had.

"So I don't know what's happening. I just know you could do worse. And what I know about that man, not sure you could do better," he finished.

I wasn't sure either.

"It's complicated," I whispered.

"It always is," he replied kindly. "You're fabulous out there, as usual. Keep it coming, Greta."

"For you, always, Gemini."

He gave me a small smile and ducked out.

I looked to the mirror.

Drew in a breath.

And then I went out to get a sparkling water and work the crowd.

LATE THE NEXT MORNING, I hustled to the door as the doorbell sounded.

I opened it and stopped dead seeing a man standing there holding a huge vase filled with roses the extraordinary color of deep blue with creamy calla lilies and dreamy baby's breath tucked tight amongst the azure petals.

"Greta Dare?" he asked.

"Uh...yeah," I answered.

He shoved the flowers my way. "Delivery."

I took them.

"Enjoy," he muttered, turned and jogged to and down the steps of my porch.

I stared after him then slowly backed out of my door, closing it.

It felt like I wafted to the kitchen island where I set the flowers down, and it felt like it took a year for me to lift my hand to nab the small envelope poking out of the arrangement.

I slid my finger under the flap, holding my breath.

And I withdrew the card.

It was a plain white card that said two words and nothing else.

Dive under

I looked back at the arrangements and stared at it.

Those blue roses.

I'd never seen blue roses.

Dive under.

The lyrics to "Cold" hit me and I started trembling.

God, Hix could be hot and sweet and classy and...and a lot of things quoting two words of a song called "Cold."

I snatched up my phone, engaged it, touched the screen until I got to where I was going.

UNBLOCK THIS CALLER.

"Shit, shit, damn, damn, shit, shit."

He survived the surgery, but I'm sorry, Ms. Dare, he sustained significant head trauma during the accident. We've induced a coma until the swelling in his brain goes down and then we'll have to see. However, it's my sad duty to inform you that you should prepare. With the trauma he sustained, it's my opinion that the young man you knew very well might not be the young man who wakes up.

I switched off my phone, it emitted its weird electronic click, and I threw it with a clatter on the island.

I walked out of the room.

But I did not throw away those flowers.

It was the next Saturday.

Which was, like it always was, the day after Friday.

It had been a home game for the Glossop Raiders.

A home game I did not take Andy to.

Also a home game I did not walk out of with Hix at my side.

I had not unblocked him.

I had also not received more flowers.

And he had not been sitting in the audience that night (or the night before) as I sang wearing a dress he'd seen on my laptop and had approved of with a look on his face that made me wish I'd had it right then so I could model it for him.

They had not found the drifter that killed Faith's husband and things had settled in to the point that no one was even talking about that or Hope and Hixon anymore.

Now, Hixon and I were still a topic of conversation after I sang that song to him at the Dew (after which, for days, that was all anyone had to ask me about, except Lou, who just kept rolling her eyes at me, and I hadn't even told her about the flowers).

I'd just arrived home from singing. It was late. I was tired. I loved my house but I was wishing for the first time since I got over Keith that I wasn't coming home to it with it being dark and empty. And I was wondering for the seven-millionth time if I should not only unblock Hix but do it and text him that the flowers were beautiful and I had a hankering for chicken tenders from the Harlequin.

I let myself into my kitchen, automatically moving toward my island to throw my purse and keys there before I would go back to switch on the light and lock the door when someone grabbed me from behind.

My entire body went chill as I opened my mouth and screamed.

A hand clamped over it and then I was forced forward, fast and hard. The hand left my mouth and became a fist caught agonizingly in the back of my hair right before my face slammed into the edge of the counter of the island.

I grunted at the impact and blinked, shaking my head, feeling my limbs loosen as my brain struggled to stay conscious, and that fist in my hair pulled me up.

I felt the arm fixed around my middle and I heard a man say in my ear, "I just wanted to listen to you sing."

I cried out as down I went. My face slamming full-frontal into the top of the island this time, I felt and heard a terrifying crunch, and I was yanked backed up.

"That's all I wanted," he ground into my ear. "I just wanted to listen to you sing. To tell you I like how you sing. To get close to the lips that make that sound. And who're you? Who're you to act like you mean something? Who're you, but an aging lounge singer in a club in the middle of nowhere, acting like a diva? Acting like you *matter*."

He started to take me down again but I twisted at the same time I brought my foot up and aimed as best I could.

I stomped it down. I was wearing high-heeled sandals, and it seemed my heel caught his toe because he made a high-pitched noise and his arm at my middle loosened.

I yanked viciously free of that hold, but he still had his fingers in my hair so I was reeled back when I tried to dash away. I whirled around, my neck bent to alleviate the pain of his hand still in my hair, but my eyes found him.

I clenched a fist, aiming up.

I planted it with everything I could muster in his throat. He made a foul gurgling noise and his fingers slipped out of my hair.

I was terrified out of my mind, acting on instinct that was a drive, its sole purpose being to incapacitate him, and I got close. I put my hands to his shadowy shoulders, seeing it was the creepy guy from the Dew Drop.

I lifted a knee with all my might and slammed it between his legs.

He emitted a tortured moan of agony and coasted down to his knees, falling to the side, and I vaguely heard a *thunk* that might have been his head hitting the leg of my island.

But just then I realized I still had my keys in my hand.

So I *took off*.

I bleeped the locks on my car as I flew across the kitchen to the door he'd left open and turned my ankle in my damned heels when my feet connected with the concrete of my driveway.

I didn't go down and I didn't waste time closing the door behind me. I kept right on sprinting so I hit the door of my car with too much momentum and the rest of my body collided with it.

I just pulled back, my hand slipped off the handle once, I caught it the next time, got it open, hauled myself in, closed the door, hit the locks, and then fumbled around turning on the car and putting it in reverse, actually hearing the tires squeal in the drive as I backed out.

My head was bouncing around on my neck as I cut the wheel at the end of my driveway. I threw my Cherokee in drive and tore down the street, heading straight to the sheriff's department.

But my stomach sank when I caught sight of it and saw the lights on at the front but nothing else. No one beyond those big windows.

And it came to me this was Glossop, not Denver. The police stations didn't stay open all night.

They didn't need to when only one man got dead not of natural causes or by his (or her) own hand in over fifty years.

"God!" I shouted, swinging into the side parking lot and coming to a jolting halt when I slammed on the brakes, staring at the lineup of five Ram trucks looking parked precisely and ready for action but with no one around to activate them.

I looked stupidly down to my passenger seat then my lap and realized I might have kept my keys but not my purse, which held my phone.

But I'd left a *creepy creep* in my house.

I've heard more about him than is healthy for anyone outside Brad Pitt.

Lou's words came to me and they came with the fact that not only did I know Hixon had moved to those not-so-great-not-exactly-the-projects apartments on the west side of town, something everyone knew.

He was also the sheriff.

Not to mention the man who'd put in his bid to look after me.

On these thoughts, I reversed out, put my foot down and drove like the woman possessed by fear and adrenaline that I was.

I entered the apartment complex and saw his Bronco right away.

So I parked with the hood of my car butted up against a small stand of trees next to it, got out, ran behind my car, the Bronco, some silver car and to the side stairs that surely had to lead to Hixon since his car was parked to the side, not to the front like some other cars were.

I clambered up the stairs, not getting far before I slipped on one and went down to my hands and knees, this digging my keys into my palm so hard I cried out at the pain and dropped them through the slatted stairs.

I was pulling myself up when a light from above me came on.

I threw my head back and watched the door at the top of the stairs open slowly then it was thrown open, the storm was thrown open and Hixon was standing at the top of the stairs wearing nothing but a pair of simple, light-blue pajama bottoms, his hair a sleepy mess.

He looked down on me for not even a second before, for some reason, he bellowed, "*Shaw!*" and came down the stairs in great leaps, taking them three at a time.

I had one hand up on his railing, mostly hanging from it, knees to the slats, but then I wasn't hanging from it and my knees weren't on anything at all.

I was hauled up with his hands under my arms and then I was flying, my legs went careening, and finally I was caught snug in a hold at his chest as he ran (yes, *ran*) up the steps, taking them two at a time.

"Dad," I heard as Hix prowled into the dark room.

"Lights on. Get the icepack. And get dressed," Hix ordered.

"Holy shit, what happened?" the other male voice in the room asked just as a light went on and Hix carefully set me down in an armchair.

I saw a pullout bed open, covers mussed, and a cramped room.

Then I saw nothing but Hix's face.

"What happened, baby?" he asked.

"I...that guy...I...that creep..."

Greta, pull your shit together!

"Hix, that creepy guy from the Dew attacked me while I was coming into my kitchen tonight." I reached out, grabbed his neck on both sides and pushed out, "He's in my house. I got away but I left him *in my house*."

"Dad, what's going on?" a girl's voice asked.

Hix lifted away and then I saw nothing because I had the cold of an icepack in a dish towel held to my face.

"Get dressed," Hix ordered. I felt fingers wrap around my wrist and lift my hand to hold the icepack, all the while Hix kept issuing commands. "Girls, get dressed. Shaw, take her to the hospital. Have them check her out. The girls go with you."

"Dad, where are you going?" a younger girl's voice asked.

I pulled the icepack away to see Hix disappearing down the hall and his two daughters standing to the side of it, heads turned, watching him go.

Then I saw his son bent toward me. "Uh...Greta," he was gently lifting my hand then he disappeared behind the biggest icepack in history, "keep that on. Long's you can. 'Kay?"

"'Kay," I mumbled behind the pack.

"Hurry, Cor, Mamie, fast. Get dressed," Shaw took up the bossing.

For my part, I started shaking.

Like, *a lot*.

But I jumped when I heard Hix roar, "*Corinne!*"

My hand not holding the icepack was taken up in a firm, warm grip.

"Greta, sweetheart, you hold it together," Hix started bossing me.

"I'm here, Daddy," I heard.

"Corinne, come here, sit with her, talk to her while your brother and sister get dressed. She's going into shock. Make her talk. Keep her with you."

"Where are you going?" she asked.

"Sorry," he said, like it wasn't to his girl. "Greta was slippin' into shock. That's an affirmative, Hal. She's three-two-two Rosewater. Get there. Now." Then, definitely to his girl and not a guy named Hal, "I'll meet you at the hospital. I got my phone, honey. You call me you need anything. Okay?"

"Okay, Dad."

"Take care of her."

"'Kay."

His hand left me, another hand took mine, and then I felt Hix kiss the top of my head.

"Get this sorted, sweetheart, promise," he murmured to my hair and then I felt his presence leave.

There was silence before I heard a hesitant, shy, "Uh...hi, I'm Corinne."

I burst into hysterical laughter, leaning forward with the overpowering pull of it.

What pulled me out was feeling her hand squeeze mine again and again, her other hand behind the back of my neck doing the same, and her calling, "Hey. Hey. Hey, Greta. Heyheyhey."

I sat up abruptly, her hand at my neck falling away, icepack still held to my face.

I sucked in breath and said, "I'm here. I'm a little freaked out right now, darlin'." I held her hand tight and shook it. "But I'm here."

"I'll take over now, Cor. Go finish gettin' dressed," Shaw ordered, my hand was exchanged and I had Shaw. "Good job holdin' that icepack to your face," he encouraged.

I wanted to burst into hysterical laughter again but instead I held his hand in a vise-grip in an effort to hold it together.

"Okay, well, remind me not to arm wrestle you," he quipped.

I released my grip some.

"I just need to...uh...get over having my face slammed into my kitchen island...um, *twice*...and then it'll be all good," I shared.

Stupidly.

"Fucking *fucker*," he hissed.

Okay, apple doesn't fall far from the tree.

So noted.

"Shaw, Dad's gonna be mad you dropped the F-bomb *twice* and *in front of a lady*," the younger girl's voice declared in deep horror.

If I wasn't in pain, freaked out and skimming the edge of hysteria, it would strike me as not a good thing I was meeting Hixon's children this way.

Instead, before that thought could catch hold, Corinne came out, calling, "I'm dressed. I'm good. Let's get her to the hospital."

Shaw's hand got firm in mine in preparation to pull me up as he suggested, "You might wanna lower the icepack to get down the stairs."

I lowered it then and looked into his dad's eyes in Shaw's own version of a handsome face, murmuring, "Good call."

But his face was tight as it took in mine.

I didn't take that as a good sign.

Hixon's kids helped me out, Corinne locked the apartment, and they put me in the passenger seat of the silver car, the girls in the back, Shaw in the driver's seat, doing the manly-man-arm-behind-the-passenger-seat thing when he reversed out of the spot.

He had a girlfriend.

She probably thought that move was *amazing* since it kind of was.

Shaw drove swiftly but carefully to the hospital.

And it wouldn't be until the nurse's eyes grew huge when they walked me through the doors of the emergency room at McCook County Hospital that I would realize I was bleeding profusely from the nose, it was all down my chest, the front of my dress, with drips and smears on the awesome, lightweight, champagne-gold swing coat I always wore over my cocktail dresses when it was nippy in the spring and fall.

"WELL, anyone catch any good movies last summer?" I asked in a nasally voice (because my nostrils were packed with gauze), sitting on the end of an exam bed in the emergency room with a nose I could actually *feel* swelling since it was goddamned *broken*.

Hix's kids were standing around me as we waited for Hix, who had called Shaw and told him we were not to move until he came to get us.

Shaw grinned at me.

Mamie noted while staring at the big bandage of gauze and tape that covered my nose, "It's good they don't have big nose casts. That wouldn't be too fun."

"I hope when I grow up I still look pretty even after someone broke my nose," Corinne muttered like she wished she didn't have to but the laws that made me pretty enough for that to withstand having a broken nose forced her to do so.

Still, it was sweet.

I thought this until Shaw growled out, "No one is ever gonna break your nose, Cor."

She cut a glare to her brother. "I'm just sayin', in the unlikely event I get one, I hope I get through it lookin' pretty."

"In the unlikely event you get one, you'll have other things on your mind like hopin' your dad and brother don't get jail time for handing the man who did it his ass."

Oh boy.

Mamie looked to me.

Corinne looked to me.

"I'm quite certain your father will not hand the man who did this to me his ass seein' as he's the sheriff and all," I assured.

"I wouldn't bet on it," Shaw muttered.

"Shaw!" Corinne cried. "Dad can't go to jail!"

"Daddy's going to jail?" Mamie asked, confused.

I opened my mouth to reassure her but her father's deep voice came, doing it for me, and my eyes shot up to see him round the curtain to my bay.

"I'm not goin' to jail, baby. It's all cool."

She ran to him, throwing her arms around his middle, and his long body jolted slightly as he slid his arm around her shoulders.

But his eyes were locked to me.

"Did you get 'im?" Shaw asked.

"Hal and Larry are processing him," Hix answered his son, his focus still on me.

But at his words my shoulders slumped in relief, my head dropped and I looked to my knees.

"Good," Shaw muttered.

"Just a second, baby," I heard Hix say gently and then I felt an equally gentle fist under my chin tipping my head back and I saw Hix disengaged from his girl bent in front of me. "What we got?"

And yep, that was also gentle.

And sweet.

"Broken nose. No concussion," Shaw answered for me authoritatively.

I was okay with that.

But it was not good he carried on.

"Other than slammin' her face in her kitchen island twice, he didn't hurt her."

I watched from close, and I'll admit I did it with a fascination that was mildly grim and not as mildly titillated, as Hixon's eyes ignited with wrath.

"She can speak for herself, Shaw," Corinne pointed out.

Before his son could answer, Hixon took his fist from my chin, straightened and ordered, "Time to go home."

Oh no.

Nonono.

I wasn't going home.

A man attacked me in my kitchen.

Until I burned some sage, drank a ton of gin and had about four hundred hours of therapy, I was never going back there.

"Can I use your phone to call Lou?" I asked Hixon.

He looked down at me.

But it was Corinne who asked, "Why would you call Miss Lou at this hour?"

My eyes slid to her.

"Um..." I mumbled, partly because I was confused she had to ask that question and partly because I was getting a little panicky because I always just hit Lou's contact in my phone and I didn't have her number memorized.

"You're just gonna freak her out," Corinne informed me.

"Well—" I started.

"Cor," Hixon growled.

"Well, she is," Corinne told her dad then returned her attention to me. "You can call her tomorrow."

"I kinda don't wanna go home tonight, darlin'," I explained softly.

She looked at me like I'd lost my mind. "Well, of course not. You're stayin' with us." As my mouth fell open, her attention shifted to her brother and she asked, "Can I drive home?"

"No," both Shaw and Hix answered at the same time.

"Dad," she turned to her father, "I need to learn night driving."

"Not at four in the morning," he replied. "And you got a learner's permit, honey, but Shaw is still a minor and you need an official adult in the car with you."

She threw up her hands in an unexpected teenage-girl fit (the only kind there probably was, I didn't know, I hadn't had any teenage years even when I was in my teenage years). "I'm never gonna learn night driving!"

"Cor, we've hit October. Soon it's gonna be night more than day *every* day," Shaw pointed out.

She was screwing up for a retort but Hix had experience with this which he demonstrated immediately.

He did this by ordering by way of request, "Can you two discuss this in the car so we can all get home?"

Mamie moved to her father and grabbed his hand.

I watched as his fingers automatically curled around and held tight.

And if blue roses and him leaping down stairs didn't mean I was totally unblocking him (and I was), seeing that did.

"Can I ride with you, Dad?" she asked.

"Sure," he answered.

"Is Greta riding with us?" she asked.

Hix looked at me.

"Yes," he answered.

"Cool," she said, turning to me and grinning. "And guess what?" she said to me.

"What, sweetie?" I asked.

"It's not real nice you got your nose broke tonight but now you got a *killer* Halloween costume," she declared, her gaze dipping down to the front of my dress before it came back to my face.

I stared at Hix's little girl who had blue eyes and dark hair and his frame and didn't look a thing like Hope but looked like he'd created her himself from sheer will, flying in the face of the laws of nature.

She was gorgeous.

Once I'd taken her in, I burst out laughing.

But this time, it wasn't due to hysteria.

Chapter 16

Junk Sunday

Greta

My eyes opened the next morning and at first I was disoriented.

Then the grogginess I felt, the pain in my face, aches down my neck and back, and the warmth cocooning me reminded me where I was.

I was in Hixon's bed in Hixon's apartment.

I could feel he was no longer with me.

However he had been.

This astounding event occurred after we'd arrived back at his place from the hospital.

And it was astounding because his children had maneuvered it.

It went like this.

We walked in and Hix started issuing orders, these being, "Right, girls, back to bed. Greta's on the pullout. Shaw, I'm bunkin' on the floor in your room. Get your sleeping bag."

To which Corinne declared, "Greta can't sleep on the pullout. It isn't even cool *you're* sleepin' on the pullout. But she has to rest and it'll be uncomfortable for her to be in our living room. I know *I* wouldn't be able to get to sleep in someone's living room if I was thinkin' any second someone would have to get up and go to the bathroom, bein' noisy, or goin' to the kitchen to get a drink of water. Especially if I barely knew those people."

"Right, so Greta's in Shaw's bed and—" Hix started to amend only to be interrupted by Corinne again.

This time more forcefully.

"*Euw, Dad!*" she squealed. "Shaw's room smells like boy. No one should have to sleep in there without an oxygen mask, even Shaw. She needs to sleep in your bed. Mamie and me'll sleep on the pullout."

"Fine," Hix bit out and turned to Shaw. "You know where the sleeping bag is?"

It was Mamie who put her two cents in that time, calling out, "Uh, *Daaaaaaaad.*" Then stating like he was a dim bulb, "We're not like...*three.* I mean, isn't she your girlfriend?"

Everyone stared at her in astonishment, even Hix and me.

"What?" she asked looking around. "All the kids at school said you're seein' the pretty lady that works with Miss Lou at the salon." Her eyes stopped on me. "And you're Greta, the pretty lady who works with Miss Lou." Again she glanced around. "Am I missing something?"

Shaw made a noise that sounded like he was swallowing laughter but Corinne stated commandingly and a little snootily, "Uh, no, Mame. You aren't missing anything."

Even with this information confirmed, Mamie wasn't done speaking.

However she was only beginning to work herself up, doing this planting both her hands on her slim, not-so-little-girl-anymore-but-still-a-little-girl hips and screwing up her face.

"Boyfriends and girlfriends sleep together, Dad, like moms and dads sleep together. We're not *babies.* We know *that.* Like, you think that we think, when we're not around, you guys don't sleep together? *Sheesh.*"

She didn't expect an answer to what she clearly thought was a stupid question that didn't deserve one.

She threw out an exasperated hand in my direction and kept right on going.

"And she got her nose broke by some bad guy. It's kinda like me. If *I* got my nose broke by some bad guy, I'd want you to be close. She doesn't want you on the floor in Shaw's room. That's closer than wherever her kitchen is. But it isn't close enough. I mean, she ran *right to you*, Dad. Didn't wipe her nose or anything. Just came right to you."

"She's right, Dad," Shaw put in smoothly, then demonstrated he was either a young man with a one-track mind (that wasn't the usual track), or he was a son who knew his father very well and therefore how to manipulate him, for he used this opportunity to remind his dad, "She got her face slammed in a kitchen island *twice* and then got so shaky we had to hold her hand. You should be with her."

Hix opened his mouth.

I was a little embarrassed about the truth of the fact that I did indeed get so shaky they'd had to hold my hand, but I opened my mouth too.

But Corinne got hers in first.

"Great. That's settled. Come on, Mame." She reached a hand out to her little sister. "Let's go change the sheets real quick so Dad and Greta can get in there and we can all go to sleep."

Mamie moved to Corinne and they walked down the hall hand in hand.

"I'll get you some water, Greta," Shaw declared. "So you can take that pain pill they gave you at the hospital."

I watched him go to the kitchen.

Hix watched him go too.

Then Hix and I looked to each other.

"Don't worry about it, sweetheart. I'll talk with them after we get you settled. Make sure they're good with this," he assured me quietly.

"I...all right," I agreed.

He came to me, wrapped his hand around the back of my head, bent in and kissed the top of mine before he pulled back.

"Go on back with the girls. Ask Corinne to get you one of my tees. Settle in. Yeah?" he said.

I nodded.

Shaw returned with a glass of water and dug the small envelope with two pain pills in it out of his back jeans pocket that they'd given me at the hospital (that, incidentally, he'd slipped out of my fingers the second they'd done that, clearly feeling in my state I couldn't be trusted with the important task of looking after a tiny envelope).

I took the water and envelope with a smile at Hix's son, sent that smile Hix's way, marveled for a moment as I looked between the two of them that they could look so alike and so different at the same time, then I went back to Hix's bedroom.

It was like the living room, crammed with furniture too big for a room of that size, and I saw the girls were finishing up with the flat sheet. I took the pill, set the glass aside, slipped off my jacket and draped it over a bunch of other clothes on a club chair in the corner and helped them finish up.

Corinne got me a tee and they left after saying goodnight, closing the door behind them.

I changed, got in Hix's bed, liked it precisely as much as I thought I would (which was to say immensely, he had very comfy mattresses), turned out the lights and settled in, eyes open, staring into the dark, not thinking about some creepy creep who attacked me.

Thinking about how Hix held my hand against my thigh the whole way back from the hospital.

At first, Mamie had chattered a lot.

When it became clear she'd talked herself to sleep, Hix had squeezed my hand and said in a soft voice, "Got there, your neighbor was there with his pistol, so was Hal. Your neighbor said he heard you scream and it woke him up. When he heard the squeal of your tires, he was lookin' out his window, saw you peel out down the road and caught a good look at your face. He'd already called nine one one, but when he saw that, he grabbed his gun and headed out. Hal had already gotten a call. By the time I got there, Hal was there. Said he arrived, your neighbor was in the driveway, training his pistol on the guy. Neighbor reported he caught the guy stumbling out of your kitchen door and detained him. Hal took over then."

"Which neighbor?" I asked.

"Man named Ned Cheever."

I was totally baking Ned some cookies.

"Who you are to me, I gotta stay removed," Hix shared. "Called Larry to work with Hal. EMT came to look over the guy. He got his head conked and good, was holdin' himself delicate, but he was cleared for processing. So they took him to the department."

Holding himself delicate.

I couldn't stop my smirk.

Hix must have caught it because he squeezed my hand and asked, "How'd you get away?"

"Punched him in the throat and then kneed him in the..." I didn't finish that because Mamie was probably asleep, but just in case she wasn't.

"Good girl," Hix murmured on another hand squeeze. "Asked, they said they took pictures at the hospital."

"Yeah," I mumbled, and they did. Both of me bloodied before they cleaned me up and me taped and the blood wiped away.

I knew those photos would be useful in case that creepy creep did something stupid and tried to fight the charges I was oh-so-totally going to file, but I hoped I never saw them.

"We have him on breaking and entering, criminal trespass, criminal stalking and assault. State of you, witness hearing you scream and fleeing the scene, catching the guy comin' out of your house, none of that will go good for him, sweetheart," Hix informed me.

I didn't want to say what I said next but I had to say it because Hix was sheriff.

So I said it.

"I, uh...well, you need to know that I'd just come in. I didn't have a chance to lock the door. I'd closed it so he entered, but he didn't do any breaking."

"Can't enter any property, intent to do the occupant harm in any way, door is locked or not, baby," he replied gently, not ticked in the slightest, even after he'd repeatedly told me to keep my doors locked (and that was the first thing I'd do from then on for sure).

He'd also told me to keep my phone out, something else I didn't do (and was totally doing from that point on). Saying that, as it went down, it wouldn't have mattered.

"Even so, all the charges might not stick if he makes a deal," Hix continued. "And Hal told me first thing the asshole did when Hal showed was ask for his attorney. Not sure we got enough on him to pin criminal stalking, either. But we're gonna charge him with it."

"Okay," I whispered.

"That said, Greta, it's known from his attendance at the Dew he knew your schedule and it was clear he either followed you or was lyin' in wait," he told me. "This was premeditated. That's a very bad thing. He's dumb enough with all we got on this to fight it, deals will come off the table and he'll be screwed."

That sounded better so my next, "Okay," was a lot stronger.

After it, Hix's hand gave mine another squeeze.

He'd nabbed my purse when he was at my house. And Mamie had woken up close to Glossop, so when we arrived at Hix's, she offered to carry it up for me like my broken nose was two broken arms.

However, I had the feeling she offered because she felt left out in the variety of duties there'd been to look out for me and it was something she could do.

I was learning Hix's kids were good kids. Thoughtful. Sweet.

Not surprising.

Hope being their mother notwithstanding.

Up we went with Mamie carrying my purse, Hix holding my hand, and then his kids maneuvered me into his bed.

The pill was working and I was nearly asleep when I felt the bed move as Hix got in it and I felt his warmth shift into my back, melding with the curve that was me.

"Baby?" I mumbled just as his hand rounded my waist.

It found mine and he laced his fingers through.

"Right here," he replied.

That was it before I fell asleep.

Now I was awake, the effects of the pill hadn't quite left me, the pain was dull but there, and I was in Hix's apartment with Hix and his kids there too, somewhere.

I pushed up, looked around, noted the sun was coming through the windows, and from Hix's bedside clock, it was just after nine thirty.

I'd had under five hours of sleep.

Whatever.

I threw the covers back and looked to the club chair to see my sandals were still on the floor in front of it but my dress and jacket were gone.

Regardless, I couldn't exactly put on a bloody dress.

I also couldn't exactly walk out only in Hix's tee.

In fact, I didn't exactly know what the immediate future held for me.

The problem was, I also couldn't think on any of this because I had to go to the bathroom.

Really.

I went to the door, opened it a bit, peered through, heard a TV playing low and some quiet conversation that didn't seem close, but I didn't see anybody.

I did see the bathroom door open.

So I scooted out, hurried there and ducked in.

I closed the door behind me, did my business, washed my hands and was carefully pulling the bloody gauze out of my nostrils when a knock came at the door.

Tossing the gauze in the toilet, I turned to the door, and when the knock came again, I called, "Uh...yeah?"

"You decent?" Corinne called back.

"Yeah, darlin'."

The door opened, she scooted through and closed it behind her.

Her gaze glanced off my eyes before she walked past me at my back, closed the lid of the toilet and dumped a stack of folded clothes there.

She then passed me again, moved to the doors of the narrow cupboard just in from the closed bathroom door and did it talking.

"Those are mine. You're, um..." she turned to me and gestured awkwardly with her hands around her hips then up to her chest, "like, a little bigger than me but that's some of my loose stuff."

Her eyes skimmed through mine again, I saw her cheeks were flushed, it was pretty, and she opened one of the cupboard doors.

It was full of stacks of folded towels and washcloths in the odd color combination of the darkest of blues and bright pink (this, I realized, was boys and girls, of which there was an equal number in that household with the boy part of that probably not real hip on using pink towels and the girl part of that equally not hip on using the darkest of blue). There was also a shelf of such things as bottles of pain reliever, Band-Aids, ointments, cold medicine, and other health and first-aid supplies.

The rest of it was shoved full of girl stuff, some of it Corinne was collecting.

She turned to me with her hands full and didn't quite look at me when she stated, "This is my eye makeup remover. You can use these cotton wipes. And my all-around makeup remover. You can use a washcloth for that if you don't want to get your bandage wet rinsing it off. And my moisturizer, because sometimes my face feels all tight if I don't put on moisturizer after I cleanse. I also have a scrub in there, if you're feeling like a deep clean. You can use it if you want. I don't mind. And my comb. And my brush. And whatever you want."

She did this handing me bottles, tubes and a sleeve of cotton wipes, all of which I took.

"Thanks, sweetheart," I said softly.

There was another knock on the door and neither Corinne nor I said a word before it opened and Mamie scooted through, squeezing by her sister, who was blocking her entry, as she closed the door and grinned at me.

"Hey, Miss Greta."

I grinned back. "Hey, Mamie."

Her nose scrunched. "Does that hurt?"

I didn't have to ask what she was talking about. I'd seen myself in the mirror. And an elbow to the eye might buy you a shiner that took days to come up dark but a broken nose shadowed the skin under both eyes deep purple the day after.

My raccoon eyes from not taking my makeup off last night didn't help matters much.

"It isn't that bad," I told her.

"Cool," she replied then asked, "What kinda donuts do you like?"

"Uh..."

"Dad's gettin' 'em," she shared and looked to Corinne. "Says we're goin' with him."

"'Kay," Corinne agreed.

Mamie turned back to me. "I like chocolate-covered raised. And chocolate-covered cake with sprinkles. And cinnamon twists."

"I like glazed yeast," Corinne informed me. "And cinnamon swirls."

They both stared at me.

Apparently my immediate future included donuts with the Drake family.

"I like...well, donuts," I told them.

Mamie smiled big.

Corinne's lips twitched.

Then I jumped as Mamie shouted, doing it putting her hand to the wall, her other one out to her side and rounded, executing a graceful plié, "Miss Greta likes anything!"

She did another plié as we heard Hix shout back. "Great! Let's go!"

"We should go," Mamie told me but did it doing another plié.

Corinne turned to the cupboard and pulled out one of the approximately seventeen new toothbrushes in their packages that was stacked in a pile on the first-aid shelf and handed it to me.

I juggled the bottles and tubes to take it, noting, "It's good you all take care of your teeth."

I did this remembering how hard Hixon had kissed me after I gave him a toothbrush and wondering if this was a Drake family *thing*.

"Mom's weird about body stuff," Mamie shared with me and I felt awkwardness coming from Corinne at the mention of their mother, none coming from Mamie, but I still felt that awkwardness also start coming from me in sympathy with Corinne's. "Says we gotta take care of them. Even our teeth. Daddy and Mom aren't together anymore but she still gets on him a lot if we don't eat peas and brush day and night and floss and blah blah blah." Another plié. "And Dad's a dad, so he's not like," she faked a low voice that had me not quite suppressing a giggle, "'Do whatever, kids.' I mean, we have Junk Sundays, which today is, thankfully. But he'd make us eat peas even if Mom wasn't big on things like that. Fortunately we like peas."

"Girls!" Hixon shouted.

"We should go," Corinne stated instantly.

"Yeah," Mamie replied on another plié.

"Thanks for all this stuff, darlin'," I said to Corinne, lifting my hands filled with stuff. "And the clothes."

"Not a problem," she returned, closed the cupboard and shot out of the room, again closing the door behind her.

Mamie did another plié then declared, "Don't worry. Dad'll like you even with your face like that. Corinne took a header going for the volleyball last year during a game, *bam!* face-plant on the basketball court. It was all swollen and bruised, I mean, like, *for days*. And Daddy was all snuggly and kissy like he didn't notice *at all*."

Yep.

So.

Totally.

Unblocking Hixon Drake.

"Good to know," I murmured, grinning at her.

"Mamie!" Hix yelled.

"I better go," she said swiftly, executing another plié before she shot me a grin, turned, and took off, also closing the door behind her.

I looked to the mirror only to have another knock come at the door.

I turned again that way. "Yeah?"

It opened and only Hixon's head came in.

My stomach flipped.

"Hey, baby. Gonna get donuts. Girls take care of you? You good?"

I nodded. "Yeah."

He smiled and said, "Good. Make yourself at home. Shaw'll look after you, you need anything while we're gone."

I nodded.

He kept smiling as he murmured, "Be back."

"Okay, Hix."

He gave me a top to toe look I couldn't decipher but it left my toes curling into the fluffy rug he had in front of the sink before he caught my eyes, his went soft (or softer) then he disappeared behind the closed door.

I sighed.

Then I carefully cleaned off my makeup, brushed my teeth, moisturized and put on Corinne's clothes.

I returned her stuff to the cupboard and walked out the door.

I went back to Hix's room, dumped the tee on the clothes-covered chair, struggled my bra on under the shirt without fully taking it off and went to the bed.

I made it and walked back out in a pair of Corinne's loose-fitting, light-gray yoga pants and an equally loose-fitting pale-pink, cowl yoga top that had a long hem that came down over my hips and openings at the cuffs that hooked over my thumbs.

The pants fit a little snug at my butt but the whole outfit was cute.

I came out and found Shaw lounged on the couch.

He knifed up the second he saw me.

"Hey," he greeted, looking at me closely.

"Mornin', Shaw."

"How you doin'?" he asked.

"In need of coffee, but otherwise good."

He started moving in the direction of the kitchen. "I'll get you some."

"You just show me where things are," I replied, following him, "I can make it."

"I got it," he returned, and I halted at the edge of the counter, which abruptly stopped and opened to the small dining area that had a handsome table in it, but one I could see had leaves, just in that small space, they couldn't be in it.

Seeing that, I glanced into the living room with its huge, slouchy, impossible-to-be-anything-but-comfortable-looking couch that had already had the pullout pushed back in and matching armchair, a big denim-covered beanbag that hadn't been there the night before, all of it not fitting that space. All of it was also such I had no idea how they actually got it up those stairs and in that door.

And taking that in, the weight of Hix's need to get his kids out of there and the sadness of Hix's need to restart his life after Hope ended the one they'd led bore down on me.

"How do you take it?" Shaw asked, and I looked to him happy to have my mind turned.

"Little creamer."

"Gotcha." He went to the fridge and opened it offering, "You need to charge your phone, we got every charger known to man, so just let me know what kind you need and I'll set you up."

"Okay."

He sloshed in creamer, stirred my coffee, tossed the dripping spoon on the counter while I bit my lip at that act and came to hand it to me.

I took it.

He asked, "You need aspirin or Tylenol or anything?"

"You're sweet, and yeah, actually. Whatever you got."

"'Kay. Go get you some," he muttered, rounding me.

I took a sip of my coffee, turned, saw my purse on the table and went to it.

I sipped again and opened the clutch, pulling out my phone.

I looked to the screen, and outside some Facebook notices, there was nothing, and I found it weird I was attacked in my kitchen last night and this morning there was nothing.

Then again, it wasn't yet ten o'clock. Maybe news hadn't made the rounds.

But I should call Lou and share things with her before she heard anything from anyone else.

Shaw returned with some pills, two white ones (I didn't tell him four would be better, I didn't want to concern him).

I juggled phone and mug, he dropped them in my upturned hand, and I expressed my gratitude before I said, "I should probably call Lou. If she hears before I tell her, she might not like that much."

He nodded. "I get that. But just to say, I heard Dad talkin' to Hal last night and he said he wanted a lid on this. Lotta stuff got 'round about that Calloway thing and he knows his deputies talk to their husbands, wives, girlfriends, whatever. It's inevitable, but he wasn't a big fan of it."

I could guess that since he hadn't shared even a single detail with me.

"It's mostly Hal, who can be a douche," Shaw informed me. "But it can sometimes be Larry. He's a good guy. But that Calloway thing was big and he was, like, I don't know...I guess frustrated they haven't nailed him yet. Anyway, they had to ask for the public's help because they have to find him. I mean, everyone knows the guy was insane just shootin' somebody, but he's like a drifter, and they have to find him before he drifts away for, like, *ever*."

"Yeah," I said softly.

"Dad wasn't mean about Hal and Larry," Shaw assured me quickly. "He didn't bitch...I mean, complain or anything. I can just tell when he gets quiet and into his head, and his mouth gets tight when folks ask him about stuff they're not supposed to know. But he gets that this situation is, you know, extreme."

"It's definitely extreme, honey," I whispered.

He nodded. "Well, you should call Lou and I need to call Wendy. She was comin' over to hang with us today but Dad asked me if I could ask her if she wouldn't so, you know, you could be comfortable after what happened, and since you're gettin' to know us all at the same time."

"You don't have to do that," I told him. "I can...go to Lou's or something."

Shaw grinned big. "No way Dad'll let that happen. He didn't say anything but I can tell he's super-miffed some guy slammed your face into your kitchen island, but he's still real happy you're here and gettin' the chance to get to know all the Drakes. And anyway, Greta, he said I can go for a few hours over to Wendy's this afternoon so it's all cool."

He's still real happy you're here and gettin' the chance to get to know all the Drakes.

God.

Sweet.

"Just as long as you're not disappointed you don't get to spend a day with your girl," I replied.

"No. Totally. It's all cool."

It was then I grinned at him.

He grinned back and muttered, "Gonna go call Wendy. Be back," and with that, he rounded the corner beyond the kitchen and disappeared.

I threw back the pills then walked my phone and mug around the dining room table to stand at the big window that faced out to Hix's stairs to stand in the sun while I called Lou.

I took a sip of coffee, noting that it was good the owners of the apartment complex planted those trees because now that they were tall enough, they kinda hid how ugly the units were.

But I froze while doing that when I saw my Cherokee was now parked next to the silver car.

While I stared at it, it hit me that Sheriff Drake must have deduced I'd dropped my keys where I'd fallen on the stairs. He found them and he moved my car from its place butting the trees and parked crazily to the space closer to his apartment.

It was just a few feet closer.

But it was closer.

It probably didn't need to be moved.

But he'd moved it.

And this told me that Hixon Drake wanted the people he cared about to have the premier parking spots (such as they were, but still).

He also wanted comfortable furniture his kids could lounge on, even in a cramped, not-very-attractive apartment. Good mattresses for his daughters to sleep on. Washcloths in colors they liked. Fluffy rugs in front of the bathroom sink.

His life had imploded and it had taken his kids right along with it.

But he bought fluffy rugs for them to stand on when they brushed their teeth, and pink towels for his girls, stocked his first-aid shelf with anything they might need and let his daughter shove all her girl stuff in the remaining space.

I knew something about living the life you thought you'd be living for the rest of it, the life you *wanted* to be living, having that end and having to start from scratch, and I'd only had Andy to look after.

Not three growing kids.

I thought about Corinne finding out about us, Hix learning his son was done with his mother, knowing he had to find a way to do the right thing about their deteriorating relationship, even not having the desire to do that, these at the same time investigating a murder. All this happening while needing to build something stable for his children and rebuild his own life with the additional complication of meeting a woman he connected with in a way that couldn't be ignored but had to have been confusing.

None of this made Hix treating me the way he did okay.

But being in that apartment. Seeing my car where it was. Standing by a nice dining room table that Hix probably couldn't afford but he bought because he likely didn't want to spend a lot of money getting a place that cost a fortune that he thought he wouldn't be staying in long, but his kids would have to be there however long it took, and he was going to make it as nice as possible. And knowing all the rest...

It made me understand why he lost it.

I dropped my head to my phone, called Lou and put it to my ear.

"Yo, girlfriend," she answered. "What's up?"

"I need to tell you something and say first, I'm okay, totally okay, so when I tell you, I don't want you to freak out."

"Oh shit," she muttered.

I decided just to lay it out and brace for any fallout, so I launched right in, telling her about the night before, doing it with my eyes to my car and forgetting the fact she was a mother, a business owner and Bill's wife so, even if the news was extreme, she wasn't a freaking-out kind of chick.

Thus, when I was done talking, all she did was ask, "Oh God, babe, are you okay?"

"Yeah. I've learned a broken nose feels a lot worse than a black eye but I just took some pills and I'll be all right."

"Do you need me to cancel your clients tomorrow?"

I shook my head regardless she couldn't see it. "No. I think I'll be okay to go in. I have to go to the hospital in the afternoon to have the dressing changed, but I'll call those clients and switch them around."

"And you say Hixon got the guy?"

"Yeah, they caught him."

"Good," she murmured, then, "And you're there? With him? *And* his kids?"

It was casual, the way she asked it.

But I could tell it was a *forced* casual.

She was worried. Hix wasn't in her good graces. But she knew now was not the time to lecture me.

That didn't mean she didn't want to know where I was at.

"He leaped down the stairs," I whispered, glancing to the corner where Shaw had disappeared.

"What?"

"He heard me fall on his stairs when I was trying to get to him. He opened the door. Took one look at me. And, Lou, he *leaped* down the stairs to get to me. In his pajamas. And bare feet."

"Yowza," she breathed.

She was right.

That had been a *yowza*.

"The kids have been great," I said quietly. "Shaw is like his dad. A lot like him. Very protective. Very sweet. Mamie's cute and funny. Corinne is...well, I think she's struggling. She seems awkward sometimes, maybe hiding confusion behind being snippy sometimes, and sometimes shy, but mostly underneath it all she's being sweet too."

"Well, not the way most would pick to meet the kids of the new man in your life but at least you had something to focus on rather than sitting at dinner and making small talk," she remarked.

I laughed softly. "I guess you could look at it like that."

"And he's your new man isn't he? This is the universe's dramatic way to make that so," she noted, now sounding forced noncommittal.

She *so* wanted to lecture me.

"He leaped down the stairs, Lou," I reminded her.

"Yeah. Hixon Drake leaped down stairs in pajamas and bare feet to get to me, I'd get over him taking out some serious life frustrations on me by being a huge dick too."

I let out a breath.

No, she wasn't going to lecture me.

At least not now.

"You want me and the girls to go get Andy?" she offered and I grew still. "Take him out and do something with him today?"

Oh my God.

I hadn't thought of Andy.

I never missed our Sundays. Not since we'd moved to Nebraska. And before that, Keith and I never missed them except for me, once, when I'd had the flu. But back then, I'd had Keith, and so did Andy, so he'd gone to see him.

Not to mention, we'd only taken two vacations without Andy the whole time we were married. We might do long weekends so we weren't away from him for too long. But if we took time off and did it going out of town, we usually took Andy with us.

"I can't...he can't see me like this, Lou," I pointed out the obvious.

"I know, babe. So me and the girls'll go out there, get him, take him somewhere and have loads of fun, and it won't be the same as a visit from his big sis but he won't feel like he's missing out too much."

"I can't ask you to—"

"Girlfriend, Bill went out and tied one on last night. He's still sleeping. I've asked him two hundred times to fix the leaky faucet in our bathroom and fifty times to drag out the fall decorations and I know today will not be the day either of those will get done. If he wakes up when I'm here, the first thing I'm gonna do is punch him in the sternum. And Andy's *da bomb*. The girls will love it. Much more than their mother punching their father in the sternum."

"That's probably true."

"It's totally true," she returned. "So call Andy. Tell him to expect us in an hour or so. And don't worry, we'll take good care of him."

She said this last while I watched the Bronco swing into the non-spot of grass next to my Cherokee, but Hixon did it without running into the tree.

"I'll call Andy," I replied. "And I'll send you an over-the-phone hug for being so awesome."

I spoke while watching Hixon climb out, the girls climb out, but it was Hix who took the two bakery boxes from Corinne after he rounded the back of the Bronco.

Apparently, people he cared about didn't even carry donuts.

Also apparently, they didn't want for donuts.

Two boxes?

"Our pleasure, Greta. I'll text later to let you know we got there and after that to let you know it's all good."

"I love you, Lou," I whispered, moving quickly to round the dining room table to put my coffee mug to the kitchen counter because the wood of the table was too nice to rest a hot mug of liquid on.

"Love you too. Get some rest. Charm the pants off those kids. But don't worry about that. Just be you and that'll do it."

"Shut up," I ordered before she made me start to cry.

"*You* shut up."

"Whatever. Later, babe."

"Later, Greta."

We hung up as I turned the corner and saw Shaw coming out of his room.

I had to get back to Hixon's room because I had to talk to Andy, and I didn't want to do it with an audience or with noise in the background that might confuse my brother.

"Hey," I said quickly to Shaw. "Your dad and the girls are back and I have to call my brother. I usually visit him on Sundays and I can't today because, well..." I lifted a hand and pointed to my face. "It might freak him out."

"Visit him?" Shaw asked.

In my haste to get to Hix's bedroom, it hadn't occurred to me that Shaw didn't know about Andy.

"I gotta call him," was all I had time to say. "I'll explain after, okay?"

He nodded.

I scooted by him as the door opened and Mamie called, "We're here with donuts!"

I kept going, head to my phone as I found Sunnydown's number in my contact list. I hit it as I closed the door to Hixon's room behind me. And I did this wishing that Andy didn't lose and misplace cell phones all the time, doing this causing him to feel like crap he wasted money and sometimes get angry or upset, meaning we'd come to the decision he shouldn't have one and I had to call Sunnydown and go through that rigmarole to talk to my brother.

I went to the bed and sat on the end of it as I asked to speak to Andy.

The noises were muted behind the door, thankfully, when he came on.

"Hey, Ta-Ta."

"Hey, buddy. Listen," I went right into it. "I have good news and bad news. The good news is, Lou and the girls are gonna be there in around an hour to take you out for a day of fun. The bad news is that I'm not feeling really good so I can't come too."

"Not feeling good?" he asked.

"No, darlin'. I'm so sorry. You know Sundays are the best days of the week because I get to spend them with you, but I just can't today. But I'll be there Thursday, like always. And I'll call every night, like always too."

And maybe by Thursday the swelling and bruising will have gone down so I didn't look so scary and I'd be able to come up with a story that wouldn't freak Andy out.

"Okay, Ta-Ta. And it's football time."

I stared at the carpet of the floor in front of me at his words but lifted my head when I heard the bedroom door open.

Hix walked in, his eyes to me, and I saw from a lot closer what I'd seen from the window in his dining area that Sundays were faded jeans, boots and cream thermals that fit tight at his chest and biceps days.

However, I couldn't appreciate that like I would normally do.

"Yeah, buddy, it's football time," I said to my brother quietly.

Hix closed the door behind him while Andy replied, "Can we go to a game?"

These were the times I had to tread cautiously.

Either he wanted to go to another one.

Or he forgot he'd already been to one.

If it was the second, and I reminded him, he might get frustrated and that could be bad, especially with Lou and the girls heading out to see him.

"Uh...a Glossop Raiders game?" I asked the floor where I'd again aimed my eyes.

"Yeah, that'd be cool!" he exclaimed.

He'd forgotten.

My head dropped so now I was looking at my lap.

Hix sat beside me on the bed.

"I'll have to talk to Gemini," I told him. "I work Fridays, Andy."

And I'd already asked for a weekend off. Gemini would arrange another one for me if I explained or if I didn't, he knew Andy had these problems, but I couldn't do it frequently.

There was an act coming in but that was weeks away and it might not be during a home game.

"Yeah, I know," Andy said.

"And, well, he'll have to let me take a Friday off."

Hixon's hand took mine and then he did something strange.

Strange and tender and fascinating and wonderful and amazing.

He rested the back of my hand on my thigh, put the heel of his palm to mine and stroked the insides of my fingers with his fingertips in a sweet, soothing way.

I liked every way he touched me physically, and it might make me crazy, but I liked that way the best.

"Yeah, I know," Andy repeated.

Staring at Hix touching my fingers, I replied, "I'll talk to him, darlin', and we'll see."

"Okay, Ta-Ta. Gemini'll say yes. He always says yes. And it'll be great. We can ask Lou to come and the girls too."

"Yeah," I agreed because I knew it was great because it already had been.

I also made a mental note to text Lou and tell her to tell the girls not to mention the game.

"Feel better," he said. "So you can come on Thursday."

"I will for sure, buddy. Have fun with Lou and the girls, yeah?"

"For sure, Ta-Ta. 'Bye."

"'Bye, baby bro."

He hung up.

I dropped the phone to my other thigh and stared at Hix and my hands.

Topper: he had beautiful hands.

"What was that?" Hix asked.

I looked up at him to see him staring down at me.

"Andy wants to go to a Raiders game."

He nodded. "Okay."

"He's been to a Raiders game."

It came more cautious this time. "Okay."

"He forgot he's been," I whispered.

"Shit," he whispered back and he stopped touching my hand so he could wrap his arm around me and pull me into his side.

I liked the hand touch but being tucked close to his warm, strong body didn't stink.

I dropped my head on his shoulder.

"Should be used to it when he forgets," I muttered. "I just sometimes...last night and everything...it took me by surprise."

"Yeah."

"At least he didn't get upset that I couldn't come today. Sundays are our days."

"Sundays," he murmured strangely, like he'd just figured something out.

"Yeah, Sundays," I confirmed because I didn't know what else to say.

"Least it's good he didn't get upset," he kept murmuring.

"I'm not sure what I'm gonna tell him when he sees my nose this way."

"We'll come up with something."

I nodded, my head moving on his shoulder.

"Greta?" he called.

"Yeah," I answered.

"Baby, you're sittin' next to me on the edge of my bed, head on my shoulder, wearin' my daughter's clothes, and I know last night that shit was extreme but—"

I knew where he was going with this so I interrupted him on a soft, almost-not-there, "I'm unblocking you, Hixon."

I felt his body go rigid, the pads of his fingers digging into my flesh at my hip before he relaxed and murmured a deeper than normal, "Good."

I liked that deeper than normal and what it meant.

I liked it a whole lot.

He cleared his throat and asked, "Are you good hanging with us for Junk Sunday?"

I tipped my head back with it still on his shoulder and he dipped his chin and twisted his neck in a way that had to be uncomfortable but he still did it in order to look in my eyes.

"What are Junk Sundays?" I asked.

"They start with the TV on and donuts, sweetheart, and healthy-living-wise, it goes south from there."

Okay.

Here it was.

All right.

This was it.

It was time to make it official.

It was time to complicate things.

"That sounds awesome," I whispered.

Something came up from deep in his eyes, it was warm, it was beautiful, then he dipped in and touched his mouth to mine.

He pulled away a breath and said, "One bad part, Hal's comin' over soon to take your statement. Once we get that done, you just get to relax and eat and hang with me and my kids. No pressure. No one to impress."

"Uh, Hix, I think I need to impress your kids."

"Then just be you."

Okay.

Crap.

That was unbelievably sweet.

I pushed through that before I ignored my broken nose and his kids down the hall and let what he said and the thermal he was wearing overwhelm me, and I jumped him.

"Is Corinne okay with, well...having this show up on her doorstep in the middle of the night causing a huge drama?" I asked.

He turned his head but did it to tip it so he could rest it against the top of mine (also sweet) before he replied, "My daughter isn't stupid and she loves her dad. I think the situation is coming clearer to her. Helps that Shaw's bein' how Shaw's bein' and Mamie too. Can't say in the last few weeks that she's come around. She's been chilly. But she's a good girl. She knows better than not to be at least polite. Sayin' that, she'll get where she needs to be."

"I don't want to make her uncomfortable."

He gave me a squeeze. "Baby, she gave you her clothes. It was her idea. I grabbed your dress and coat because I didn't want you to see them when you woke up in case they brought up bad shit for you. And when I said I had your keys and would stop by your place on the way to get donuts to get you something, she said you could wear something of hers. I don't know for certain, bein' a guy, but my take for a teenage girl, letting someone borrow her stuff is a big thing. So she's already getting there." His arm gave me another squeeze. "So don't worry."

So that was where my dress and jacket had gone.

And as mentioned, I'd never really been a teenage girl. I'd been a teen mother to a kid I didn't get to have the fun of making beforehand.

I still knew letting someone borrow their clothes was a big thing.

So maybe he was right.

"Babe," he called when I fell silent.

"Yeah?" I replied.

"Greta," he said and raised his head when I pulled mine from his shoulder to look in his eyes.

"Right here, Hix."

He lifted his other hand and curved it around the side of my neck.

"Sweetheart, you okay?"

"About spending the day with your kids?" I asked.

He blinked kind of slow and answered, "No."

"About Andy?"

"No, baby."

Oh boy.

"About us?" I asked hesitantly.

His fingers slid down so his thumb could stroke the side of my neck and he noted gently, "Greta, sweetheart, you were attacked last night."

Oh.

Right.

"I...uh..."

What did I say?

I was attacked.

I went to him.

And he leaped down the stairs to get to me and then sprang into action, catching the guy (well, he didn't but he went out to do that), getting me to the hospital (he didn't do that either, but he arranged it), him and his kids looking after me, bringing me donuts.

"Greta," he prompted, again gentle.

"You leaped down the stairs to get to me," I whispered.

His brows drew together. "What?"

"I...I was...not okay when it happened," I shared.

"All right," he said slowly when I spoke no more.

"But then I came here and..." I pressed my lips together then unpressed them. "You made it all okay."

"Fuck," he growled.

"What?" I asked.

He stared at my bandage and I felt him holding himself very still, even his thumb had quit moving.

It was then I knew what.

"I think you can kiss me," I told him quietly.

"Not the way I wanna kiss you."

My nipples in the bra under his daughter's top started tingling.

"Maybe we should go get donuts," I suggested.

"Yeah," he grunted like donuts weren't as awesome as they totally were.

"Um, like *now*," I pressed.

It took him a second before he muttered, "Right," bent in, touched his mouth to mine again then let me go and got off the bed, taking my hand to pull me up with him.

He held it as he walked me to the door, but I tugged his when we got there so he stopped, turned and looked down at me.

"Thank you for making it all okay," I said on a really hard hand squeeze, hoping the squeeze would tell him just how much I meant those words.

"That was my line," he replied, squeezing my hand hard right back.

I felt my chest constrict, collapsing in on itself to the point my next breath was a wheeze.

Then I felt my eyes stinging.

"Don't make me cry, it might hurt," I snapped.

He grinned. "There's no crying when there are two dozen donuts in the house."

Holy crap.

"Two dozen?"

"Right, maybe one dozen. Shaw's had plenty of opportunity to dig in."

"Three kids, one dozen donuts, maybe ten minutes, Hixon, that's a little crazy."

He reached out a hand and opened his bedroom door, declaring, "That's Junk Sunday."

With that, he led me out and we barely made the mouth of the hall when Mamie announced, "Dad got you custard-filled, chocolate-buttercream-filled, jelly, and he bought a bunch of glazed and raised chocolate-covered just in case you didn't do fancy."

"Sounds perfect," I told her.

And it did.

But suddenly, everything was.

A cramped apartment. A broken nose. Three kids who barely knew me, one not knowing what to make of me. A future that was complicated.

With my hand in Hixon's, it was all suddenly just that.

Perfect.

The Drake Family

"GONNA GET HER IN BED," Hix murmured, and his kids watched as their dad didn't scoot out from under Greta, who was totally out, stretched on their couch, her head resting on his thigh.

Instead, he pulled her gently up into his arms before he got off the couch holding her to his chest.

She might have been out but she turned her face into the side of his neck and slid her arm around the other side to hold on.

"Be back in a minute," he kept murmuring.

His kids watched him round the coffee table and head down the hall.

When they heard their dad's bedroom door latch, Shaw, lounged in his beanbag from his room, whispered, "She's freakin' awesome."

And she was.

Even Corinne thought she fit right into Junk Sundays.

Mom would have a hemorrhage and get all mad or pout all day if they tried a Junk Sunday when Dad was with her. She did that when she wasn't even there.

But Greta got in the swing of it and didn't once complain when Mamie did an arabesque or a chassé along the area in front of the television (something she did a lot).

In fact, she watched her every time with a smile on her pretty face and she'd say things like, "Wow, Mamie, you're really good at that."

And it wasn't fake.

Not at all.

She totally meant it.

"She's real nice and she's super-pretty," Mamie whispered, coming up from lazing on the floor in front of the TV to sit cross-legged and look between her siblings. "Always thought that when we'd go see Miss Lou. She looks perfect with Daddy."

"Mom looks perfect with Dad," Corinne snapped quietly from her spot draped over the armchair.

"Mom isn't with Dad anymore, Cor," Shaw pointed out quiet and careful, like he always talked when he talked to Corinne about this stuff, which Corinne thought, especially these days, was way too much.

"And if she wanted to stay perfect, she shouldn't have made Daddy leave," Mamie stated resentfully, but still quietly.

This resentment was new from Mamie.

Then again, a lot of new things were coming from Mamie recently.

"There are things you don't know," Corinne told her little sister.

"Yeah, and there's things *you* don't know," Mamie shot back. "Like how I heard him talking to Mom and askin' her would she *please* just *tell him* where she was *at* so he could get there with her and sort everything out."

"You heard that?" Shaw asked.

"Yeah," Mamie answered. "And he was, like, bein' real serious about it. Mom barely said anything, and I could tell even though I couldn't see him it hurt him, like, *a lot.*"

That made Corinne feel funny but she admonished, "You shouldn't have listened to that."

"Why?" Mamie asked.

"Because it's none of your business," she answered.

Mamie's eyes got big and mad. "My mom and dad aren't my business?"

"That isn't. And anyway, that's not all there is to it. There's stuff you don't know. There's stuff *Dad* doesn't know."

"Well, you think, maybe the person who should know is *Dad*?" Mamie asked sarcastically.

"Hey, we should talk about this later," Shaw told them. "He's gonna be back any second."

"Yeah, like when?" Corinne asked her brother. "We barely see you anymore."

Shaw's face got soft when he reminded her, "I still pick you up for school, Cor, and take you home after we get done with our practices. I see you every day."

She looked to the TV. "Whatever."

"I like Greta," Mamie declared stubbornly. "He hasn't been...he hasn't been, well, *Dad.* Not since Mom made him leave. And today, with her around, he was Dad."

"I know what you mean," Shaw murmured.

Corinne did too.

There was a lot of talk about girls who weren't good if they didn't have a guy around.

But apparently there were guys who were better when they had a girl around.

And their dad was one of them.

Especially after what happened last night.

He was always at his best when something was going wrong. Like when Corinne hurt her face or when Shaw broke his arm or when Mamie had that competition and she had a cold so she got second place, and she was devastated.

That was why Mom always said he was in the only job he could ever do.

He was at his best when he had people he could take care of.

And Greta had been all awkward at first when he'd touch her or pull her close or kiss her on the forehead in front of them, but then she'd settled in.

But Dad was always settled in, like she'd been there for years, not just that day.

And the way she sometimes looked at him.

Like he was...

Like she couldn't believe he was real.

"It's cool you were cool with her, Cor," Shaw told his sister.

"Whatever. She's got great hair," Corinne muttered. *And great a lot of things*, she didn't say.

"Yeah, she does," Shaw muttered back.

Mamie giggled.

Corinne rolled her eyes.

"It's all gonna get better," Shaw assured them. "Next weekend, Dad and me and Toast and Tommy and Larry and Donna and Herb are gonna move us into that place on Lavender Lane and then you guys will be back with me and Dad, and we're finally gonna settle into a new normal."

And Shaw couldn't wait because he got the basement room and it had a bathroom down there so he didn't have to see to stuff with girl crap all around, as well as a family room just outside the bedroom so it was like he had his own apartment.

Mamie also loved that house on Lavender Lane. It was sweet! And the family room downstairs was *huge* and Dad said he'd install a barre down there.

Corinne didn't want a new normal. She wanted the old one back.

But she still liked that house and not just because it was better than that apartment (because anything was better than that apartment). But because, it sucked to admit it, it was pretty awesome.

And as mad as she was at her dad, she knew he needed a decent place to live, and this was absolutely not that and it hurt a little more every time she saw him there.

Shaw picked up the remote and turned the volume down a little on the TV.

None of them complained.

Greta had been through a lot.

She needed her sleep.

Chapter 17

Journey of Discovery

Hixon

Hix opened his eyes to a dark room and laid still.

Then he felt his lips curving up in a smile.

Christ, he totally wrapped himself around Greta.

Then again, she hadn't shared she wrapped herself around him too, front to front, arms around each other, legs tangled, her face tucked in his throat, his face in her hair.

He drew her in with a deep breath.

After that, he gave her a gentle squeeze and called, "Greta."

She shifted a little, pressed close, her arm over him flexed, and she murmured, "Mm?"

"Gotta get up and get the kids going. You can sleep but it's pandemonium and bathroom space is at a premium. For the next hour and a half, you won't have your shot if you don't take it now."

"Thans, bubby, bu' 'm goo'," she mumbled, ran her hand up his back but it dropped, and he knew she had slipped back to sleep.

Still smiling, he kissed her hair, carefully extricated his limbs from hers and slid out from under the covers, making sure they were over her before he moved out of the room.

She was in his bed again because last night, when it became obvious to all of them the pain wasn't being overcome by Tylenol, he'd urged her to take a pain pill and she'd passed out on the couch with her head on his thigh.

The kids hadn't blinked when he'd carried her to his bed, and Greta hadn't moved when he'd joined her in it hours later.

Even if that hadn't happened, she'd be there not only because that was where he wanted her but that was where she needed to be until they could both go to her house and he could see where she was at being back in a place that was her place but it had been violated in the way it had.

She seemed okay but she was also with him and his kids after they'd gotten back together at the same time she was those right after she got attacked in her kitchen. She had a lot going on.

Today might be a different story.

Hix did his thing in the bathroom, and on the way to the kitchen, he bent over his older girl and shook her gently awake.

"Up, honey. Time to get ready for school."

"Guh," she replied, turning her head away from him.

"Up, Cor, hit the shower so I can get everyone moving," he pressed, giving her shoulder a squeeze.

"All right, Daddy," she muttered, turning her head again then pushing up on a forearm and shoving aside the bedclothes.

Corinne was always up first because she took more time getting ready.

She was also always the one who rarely fought it.

The other two, the battle would soon commence. So even when he was with Hope, seeing as she worked for her dad and made her own hours, and he did not, he let her sleep in and it was him who got the kids moving in the morning.

Therefore, even in the days before Corinne's makeup and hair regime added forty-five minutes to her get-ready time, he always started with the easy one first.

Hix went to the kitchen to start coffee to fortify his upcoming efforts.

Then he began the process by informing both Shaw and Mamie in two different ways they had to get up soon so they could hit the Dad Snooze and mostly ignore him until he had to threaten them to get them to move their asses.

As usual, pandemonium struck when Mamie got up because she pushed it to the final moments, and then had to act like a crazy kid while getting ready to go to school. It didn't help matters that Hix had to take orders for what his girls wanted to wear that day so he could get it from his room, and Mamie changed her mind three times.

After she made her final decision, or more accurately Hix declared it was that, with Shaw horking down Cream of Wheat at the table and Corinne eating it between doing shit to her eyelids with some applicator, her makeup bag having exploded all over the dining room table, Corinne asked her mirror, "Is Greta coming to my volleyball game on Tuesday?"

Hix stood in the kitchen with his coffee mug held up, his bowl of hot cereal on the counter beside him and looked at his girl who did not look at him. He glanced to his son who was staring at him. When Shaw got Hix's attention, his son gave a slight shrug.

Hix looked back to Corinne. "You okay with that?"

She didn't look from her mirror when she replied unfathomably, "It's whatever."

Hix and Shaw exchanged glances again before he told his girl, "I think for Greta, and your mom, honey, that maybe we'll wait on that."

"Yeah, like I said. Whatever," Corinne returned, dropped her mirror in her makeup bag and started gathering her makeup and shoving it in.

When she got up to return it to the bathroom, he called her name.

She looked to him.

"I really appreciate you being cool with Greta this weekend."

"Greta didn't date some chick like, *right after* she divorced my mom," she returned and immediately commenced storming off.

Hix blew out a sigh.

Shaw called after his sister, "Uncool, Cor."

"Whatever, Shaw," she called back.

Shaw looked to his dad. "I'll talk to her again."

"Maybe we should let her get where she needs to go on her own, kid."

"And maybe I'll give her the shot to do that, say, she's got this week, and then I'll talk some sense into her," Shaw retorted.

"Son, we're all getting used to a lot of new things."

"And Dad, life is gonna throw a lot uglier things her way and she needs to learn to deal with it without bein' a pain in the butt," Shaw replied. "I mean, it isn't like it's lost on her that that woman's husband got dead helpin' some guy out and she was there right after Greta got attacked in her own kitchen. She needs to clue in. Stuff happens. You deal. Then you move on. The end."

"Gotta admit, it's freakin' me out how smart you are," Hix murmured, and Shaw shot him a big grin.

"Yeah. I'm like Yoda except taller, younger and hotter."

Hix started chuckling.

Mamie made an appearance on a sideways skid that didn't go too well on the carpet so Hix tensed to jump if she went down.

She didn't go down.

She declared, "I left my backpack in your room, Dad," like this was the end of the world.

"Then I'll go get it, baby," he told her, sipping his coffee, putting it down then moving out to do that.

His kids got themselves sorted out, and Hix stood outside at the top of the stairs watching them get into Shaw's car so he could take them to school.

Mamie waved at him through the back window.

Shaw gave him a wrist flick before he folded into the driver's seat.

Corinne kept her head bent to fiddling with her backpack in her lap, and she did this meticulously.

Hix watched them back out and take off and then he went inside.

To give Greta more time to sleep, he got his own shower in, got dressed and only then did he wake Greta.

Sitting in the bend of her hips, he watched her turn to her back, stretch and open her eyes to look up at him.

How she could look cute with that big bandage on her nose, he didn't know, but thank Christ she did or seeing it would remind him he'd very much like to murder somebody.

He had the light on in the hall but he switched the one on beside the bed, watching her blink against it even as he bent into her to block some of it out.

"I need to get you home and then get to work, baby," he said.

"Right," she mumbled, still looking sleepy but now adding unhappy.

"I'm gonna be there, Greta."

She pushed up on her elbows, looking down at her body in the bed. "Mm-hmm."

"Babe."

Her head turned to him.

"He's in a cell. I get you home. You're there with me. I leave when you settle and I know you're good. I do my thing. You do yours. I pick you up from work, take you to the hospital to get your dressing changed. And tonight is Monday Night Football. Shaw's with me full-time now so we make that night a thing. Tonight, you're gonna be our special guest."

Her eyes grew more alert as the sleep left her and she replied, "I can't horn in on your and Shaw's thing."

"If you don't, he'll probably go to your house and get you himself."

"Hixon—"

"Babe, you agreed to complicated. You might as well give it all it's worth."

Her pretty lips quirked under that big white bandage. "I have noted your son is much like his father when it comes to kicking in when a damsel is in distress."

"Don't say shit that might mean they'll have to reset your nose seein' as I'm wantin' to kiss you and do it hard," he warned and exited the bed before he did something else. "Get up, sweetheart. Let's get you home."

"All right," she said like she didn't want to and tossed the covers aside.

Hix looked away because he hadn't just carried her to bed the night before.

She'd woken up groggy in the middle of him trying to help her put on his tee before he'd put her in his bed.

And she looked way too good in it.

"I need my dress back, Hix," she told him as he moved toward the door to get her a travel mug of coffee.

"Just wear Cor's stuff again," he told the door.

"You know, you're depriving me of my Halloween costume," she joked.

He stopped at the door and looked back at her.

Standing by his bed, her hair a beautiful mess from sleep, her eyes still lazy from the same, wearing his shirt, outside deciding to start a family, Hix knew in that instant she was the best decision he'd made in his life.

"I'll give it back for trick or treat," he returned. "Now you want coffee?"

"Am I breathing?"

"Yup."

"Then yup."

He grinned.

She gave that back.

Then Hix went to get his woman coffee.

"It's a kitchen."

"Unh-hunh."

"It's *your* kitchen."

"Yep."

"With your stuff. Where you make great pancakes. And look amazing wearing a robe."

Greta was standing in his arms in her kitchen, now wearing his daughter's clothes and a pair of Corinne's flip-flops.

Greta's purse was on the island. Her Cherokee in the drive. His Bronco behind it where he'd parked it after following her there.

As he'd asked, without bitching, Hal had gone to her place the day before and cleaned up the blood drips that had fallen on the kitchen island and the flagstone floors. How he managed it, Hix didn't know. That porous stone would normally soak the blood and leave a stain.

But he'd done it.

Hix made a note to buy his deputy a bottle as Greta tipped her head back to look at him.

"What makes a man do something like that?" she asked.

He drew her deeper into his body and dipped his face closer to hers.

"I'm not that man so I don't know. I also don't care seein' as there's no excuse for it, no reason I'd believe that was even close to valid behind it. All I know is he did it and now he'll pay for it."

"He said I don't matter," she reminded him, because he'd heard her tell Hal that same thing while giving her statement at his dining room table the day before.

And yeah.

It was good she looked cute even with a broken nose or Hix would be fighting the urge to murder someone.

"If I don't matter, why go through the trouble?" she asked.

"I wish I had answers but I've seen a lot of shit people have done that have no answers, sweetheart, so I've learned not to wreck my head and my peace of mind trying to figure it out. It's their problem.

He made it yours doin' what he did. Don't make the rest of it yours tryin' to figure it out."

"Good advice," she muttered to his shoulder.

He gave her a careful shake and got her attention back.

"I need to know you're good before I get to the department, Greta," he told her quietly.

She looked from his eyes through the room then back to him.

"It's my kitchen," she replied.

He gave her a grin. "Yeah, it is."

She suddenly looked hesitant.

"I can...uh, call you if I get, well...tweaked?"

"I'd be pissed if you didn't."

She relaxed against him. "Okay."

"You're good?" he pushed.

She nodded. "At least I think I can take a shower and get to work, and then I'll tackle Monday Night Football with the two Drake men and after that, we'll see."

"Shaw won't mind you spending the night tonight, baby," he assured her.

"I don't think he will and he seems very mature for his age but he's still only seventeen, so as complicated as this is, darlin', maybe we should do what we can to make it less complicated for your kids."

When he opened his mouth to say something, she gave him a shake.

"I might not be able to do it, being here alone...uh, just now. So I might need to stay with you tonight. But I should also not let it go on too long." Her lips tipped up. "And anyway, I can call you, right?"

His lips tipped up too. "Anytime."

She moved her hands to bunch them in the fabric of his shirt at his sides and she swayed him, ordering, "Then get to work, Sheriff."

He moved his hands to either side of her neck, bent in and took her mouth with a touch that included a touch of his tongue against her lips.

She parted them so his tongue touched hers.

He gave it that and necessarily pulled away before he felt compelled to give more.

"I'll meet you at the salon at one to take you to the hospital."

"Okay, Hix."

"You want me to bring Harlequin?"

"Maybe we can go there later in the week when I don't look like I went a round with Muhammed Ali."

Fuck yes.

"I'd like that."

She smiled. "Me too."

He gave her neck a squeeze, kissed her forehead then let her go.

He felt her at his heels as he walked to the kitchen door.

Oh yeah.

That ass in a cell in his station without Greta around breathing and joking and being Greta, that urge he was fighting was going to get harder to hold back.

She had her hand on the door before he even cleared it.

He turned in it and looked deep in her eyes.

"You're safe, sweetheart."

She nodded and swallowed.

"One o'clock," he said.

"See you then, darlin'."

"Yeah, you will."

She forced a smile.

He started moving to his truck, hearing the door close and the lock go before he was two feet into that journey.

He idled at the side of the road two houses down with his phone in his hand just in case.

She didn't call.

So Hix went to work.

Hix walked into his department to see Reva in dispatch, Larry at the back at the copier, Bets at her desk and Hal at his.

He did not look to the cells at the back.

He would not look to the cells at the back.

That asshole existed but Hix didn't need to remind himself that he did or waste even the energy it would take to aim his gaze at him, because he wasn't worth it.

He walked right to Hal and stopped beside his desk.

"Weekend on call deputies get Monday off, Hal," he reminded him.

Hal's face got hard and he replied, "I wanna take that jackhole to his bail hearing."

"Larry and Bets can do that."

"I brought him in."

"Yeah, and I get why you'd wanna see that through. So you and me will sit in the gallery during the hearing."

Hal stared at him.

Hix ignored it.

"Greta was hesitant about bein' back at her place this morning. Think that's gonna take some time," he told Hal. "She didn't mention it because she probably didn't notice it because she's not there in her head but I know for a fact it helped, not seein' her own blood on her island and all over the floor. You mighta done that because I asked you to do it as my deputy, but mostly you did it because you're a good man. And I appreciate it. So, it's Macallan, right?"

Hal stared at him a second, lifted the side of his fist to his mouth and coughed in it and dropped his hand before he answered, "Yeah. It is. But you don't have to do that."

Hix felt his lips curl up. "I know. If you thought I did, I wouldn't drop a hundred bucks on a bottle of single malt."

"It's only fifty, Hix."

"You cleanin' blood from flagstone is worth the fifteen-year, man."

Hal smiled at him.

"We'll walk over to the courthouse together, drop by and get a coffee at Babycakes on the way back, and then you need to go home and take your day off, Hal."

"Right, boss."

Hix nodded.

Larry gave him a grin and a shake of his head as Hix walked by him on his way to his office.

Bets muttered under her breath, "You're the shit, boss," as he walked past her desk, but she did it with her eyes studiously fixed to her computer screen so he replied, "Mornin' to you too, Bets."

Her lips quirked.

Hix's cell beeped as he was walking through the door to his office.

He pulled it out of his breast pocket and felt the warm hit to his chest when he saw Greta's name above the text on the screen.

He stopped and took it.

It said, *Reporting in, I've survived the first fifteen minutes. I made coffee and everything. All good.*

Hix replied, *Great, babe. Keep it up. See you at one.*

He hit send and waited.

It sent immediately, no block, and he had only turned on his computer when he got back, *One, and until then, pray my next bandage isn't also the size of a mini diaper.*

Getting that, Hix didn't set the phone aside and tap in his password.

He busted out laughing.

"Bail set at two hundred and fifty thousand dollars," Judge Bereford announced.

The defense attorney jumped up, shouting, "Two hundred and fifty thousand? That's twenty-five thousand in bond!"

"I do understand the bond percentage, councilor," Bereford replied.

"Your honor, that's outrageous! My client has never been arrested in his life. He has a business in Sheridan County with clients who count on him and employees who need him on the job, so he's not a flight risk. He—" the defense attorney began.

Bereford cut him off. "I hazard to say those thoughts should have occurred to him before this weekend's events."

"Your honor—"

Sitting in the gallery beside Hal watching this, Hix tensed as, uncharacteristically, Bereford swiftly lost patience, lifted a finger and jabbed it at the attorney.

"Listen to me, councilor." His finger curled in, his thumb came out and he thrust it toward himself. "This is *my* county. And I'll share with you right now that in *my* county men don't shoot young fathers on the side of the road and they also don't attack women in their kitchens. If they do, the message will be relayed with a clarity that cannot be missed that they *should not*."

When the defense attorney was screwing up to say something, Bereford slapped his hand on his bench, lifted up a piece of paper and kept talking.

"Now, I've read the victim's statement." He slapped it down and lifted up another piece of paper. "And I've read the witness statement." Again with the slapping and the lifting, this time the blank side out. "And I've seen the pictures the hospital sent to our sheriff's deputy of the victim after the attack." Another slap down and lift. "And right here I have details of why this man has a protection order on him as lodged by his ex-wife." He also slapped that down. "Now, he may not have been arrested in the past, councilor, but I assume *you* have passed the bar. So I'll advise *you* to have a conversation with your client. Because, you see, if this court is forced to convene a jury to look into this matter, wasting time and county resources, during sentencing I'm going to be in a *very bad mood*."

"You've tried and convicted him yourself, Judge," the defense attorney spat.

"It's not my job to try and convict him, sir," Bereford returned.

"What I'm *trying* to communicate to you is that you'll have to wring miracles to come through with what I'm assuming with what's been laid before me this morning is a very foolhardy promise you've made your client."

"There are glaring issues with this case. He was held at gunpoint by a civilian, for God's sake," the attorney retorted.

Bereford leaned into his bench. "Son, if you think for one second a jury of Nebraskans is gonna have an issue with a neighbor hearin' their female neighbor screamin' and they see her racin' away with a face full of blood then that neighbor joggin' out with his pistol to see to things, you obviously come from somewhere else." He waved his hand to the prosecution table. "Talk. Be smart. Do right by your client. And just to make things even more clear, if this gentleman posts bond and he's within one hundred yards of the victim, he'll be accommodated by McCook County for some time seein' as he'll be held without bail until this matter is settled." Before the defense lawyer could say another word, Bereford stood while slamming down his gavel and shouting, "*Adjourned!*"

"All rise!" the bailiff called.

Hix had barely got his ass off the bench before Bereford disappeared through the side door, his robes flapping behind him.

Larry and Bets came forward to get the defendant while Gemini moved from his seat two rows back and approached Hix and Hal.

Gemini stopped and looked up at them.

"I'll just wait for you outside, Hix," Hal murmured and said, "Jones," as greeting to Gemini while he shifted by him.

"Deputy," Gemini replied.

They watched Hal go, and he was halfway down the aisle when Gemini turned back to Hix.

"It would seem I made you a promise I unintentionally didn't keep, Sheriff."

"You're about as much to blame for that asshole attacking Greta as I am," Hix returned, finishing with, "And it's Hix."

Gemini smiled but it died as his gaze shifted to the defense table.

"There are some who listen and learn and there are some who need to experience harder lessons."

"Yup," Hix agreed.

Gemini looked back to him. "He'll make bail."

That morning Hix had learned the man who attacked Greta was some rich muckity-muck who did something with construction over in Sheridan County. This, maybe, being why he thought his shit didn't stink enough to shovel a colossal amount of it his ex-wife's way during their divorce.

This also, maybe, why he thought he could sit in his car and face off against Gemini, his man and Hix in staking a claim to Greta he'd never have, thinking, maybe, if she knew who he was and how loaded, she'd feel flattered. Or thinking he had the money to elevate himself above any shit they piled on him, thus convincing himself he was untouchable.

He could just be psychotic.

He just *was* an asshole.

And until he made bail, he was now incarcerated and things would go worse for him if he approached Greta again.

It wasn't a guarantee.

But he'd have to be an asshole, a moron and a tool not to catch Bereford's message just now, and he didn't get as loaded as he was being the middle of those.

The other two were a given.

"She'll be all right," Hix assured.

Gemini's focus intensified. "Will she?"

That was when Hix's focus intensified. "Yes."

Gemini studied him a beat before he murmured, "I see."

Hix suspected Gemini saw a lot.

So he confirmed, "Yup."

Gemini smiled again but said, "I'm sorry you'll need to be keeping his company at your department until he posts bond and scurries back to Sheridan County."

"Not a lot of folk who take temporary residence in one of our cells are a bundle of laughs so me and my deputies will survive."

Still smiling, Gemini nodded.

The smile died again when he asked, "Is she okay?"

"You may need to find another act for a week or two, Gemini. She's okay but he did a number on her nose. I'm sure she'll call and talk to you about it."

"Call me and try to explain how she can still sing so she doesn't lose her weekly installments to her keep-Andy-settled pot."

"Sorry?" Hix asked.

"She looks after her brother," Gemini told him.

"I know."

"I mean financially as well. She's his guardian."

That wasn't a surprise, knowing what little he knew about her mother, but that little was enough.

"So she sings because she loves it and she sings because she has to," he murmured mostly to himself.

"I try to focus on the first part," Gemini said.

Hix wanted to as well.

He knew Sunnydown. It was a nice place. But any of those places cost a whack.

"She's a hairstylist," he noted.

"Yes, but before that, well before that, Hix, Greta is a loving sister."

"Shit," he whispered.

With all that was going on, none of this had occurred to him.

And right then, it occurring to him, it also occurred to him that had to be rough on Greta and she lived that. She had for years.

And he'd walked into her house, laying her out about a mother who put her brother right where he was, also putting Greta in the position to look out for him for the rest of his days.

Christ.

Christ.

"I'm not telling you any of this as a break in confidence," Gemini shared, pulling him from his thoughts. "Everyone in town knows, except, it would seem, you." He lifted his hand and gave Hix another smile before Hix could speak. "I know. It's complicated. But I also know it's not my business." He dropped his hand and the smile changed. "I further know, and am happy to do so, that you're about to embark on a fabulous journey of discovery. Enjoy, my friend, and while you do, take care of our girl."

Hix's mind full of all he'd learned, he could do nothing but lift his chin.

Gemini gave him a low wave, turned and walked away.

At one o'clock, Hix walked into the salon, his gaze on Greta who was folding something at her chair.

She looked wiped. Dead on her feet.

She should have taken the day off.

"Hey, sweetheart. Ready?" he asked.

"Yeah, let me grab my purse."

His eyes moved through the room and he dipped his head to the woman sitting in a dryer chair, the one in Lou's chair, and he murmured, "Ladies."

He got a "Hixon," and a "Sheriff," before his gaze hit Lou.

She tried to hide it but she looked uneasy.

He got why.

He was there getting Greta, but there might have been times since he last saw Lou that Lou, being a good friend who looked out for her girl, a girl Hix had asked to think about trying to make a go of it with him after what he'd done to her, had stated her case against Hix.

But it was more.

The last time he saw Lou she'd been out of line in a variety of ways and now that things had come around with Hix and Greta, she had a good friend who was seeing the man who she'd instigated him learning something about his ex-wife that another man might wrongfully lay blame on her just because she did it.

So it was his job to get them at least past that.

"Lou, you good?" he asked.

It seemed her entire body drooped with relief when she replied, "Yeah, Hix. Thanks."

He felt Greta come up to his side, her fingers start to touch his, and he turned his own to lace them through hers and looked down at her.

"Ready," she said.

"Right," he replied, bent in and touched his mouth to hers.

He could swear he heard a fluttering, female sigh coming from the dryer chairs.

So he was grinning when he pulled away.

She was grinning too and her fingers were tight in his.

"Do me a favor, lawman," Lou called out, and Hix turned his attention to her to see her jerk her head Greta's way. "Get that one to cancel her clients tomorrow. She might look like a Charlie's Angel but she's not, and even Charlie would let one of his angels sit out a day, she got her nose busted by an asswipe...sorry, ladies," she said to the women in the room.

"No apology necessary, Lou," the one in her chair declared.

"He *is* an a-wipe," the one at the dryer decreed.

Lou looked to Hix. "Seein' as I'm her Charlie, she should listen to me. But she's not. Now if I gotta get a speaker to talk to her through, I will. Though I'd rather someone else talk sense to her so I don't have to go through that effort."

"I rent my chair from you, Lou, you're not my boss," Greta chimed in.

"Girlfriend, I'm totally the boss of you when you're bein' plum nutty."

"I'm not being nutty. I'm totally fine," Greta returned, sounding like she was getting heated.

She also lied, because anyone looking at her could tell she wasn't fine, and not only due to the bandage covering her nose.

"You do know I'm the mother of two girls, don't you?" Lou asked sarcastically.

"Neither of them are thirty-eight years of age," Greta retorted.

"And when they're thirty-eight and bein' stubborn in a way that makes them stupid, I'll share my wisdom with them too."

Hix felt Greta's body tighten at his side, so instead of laughing his ass off at their exchange, he intervened.

"Maybe you two can make a mud pit and sell tickets for the football boosters while wrestling this out after Greta's nose sets. But now, I need to get her to the hospital so we can make sure her nose will set properly."

"That's disturbingly sexist, Sheriff Drake," Lou shot at him.

"And it would totally buy us a big screen, Lou, and don't argue, you know it would."

"It would. I'd buy tickets to that," the woman at the dryer put in.

"And I'd absolutely take you," Greta announced.

Lou's eyes grew huge. "You would not."

"It would be embarrassing," Greta taunted.

Hix fought chuckling as he started pulling her to do the door.

"Right! You're on!" Lou shouted as they moved.

Hix stopped chuckling.

"Don't think I won't do it," Greta retorted.

That was when Hix frowned.

"As soon as that bandage is off, the gloves are off," Lou returned.

He stopped at the door and turned back. "You're gonna both get over it and not in a mud pit. I was jokin', Lou. Greta's getting nowhere near a mud pit with an audience or without one, but definitely not *with* one."

Greta jumped right on that. "That's only because Hix doesn't want me to embarrass you."

Lou opened her mouth but Hix spoke.

"Say goodbye, Lou."

She snapped her mouth shut and narrowed her eyes at him.

He looked down at Greta, and not just to hold back the impending storm of him laying an order on a woman like Lou, to declare, "And you're takin' the day off tomorrow."

She glared up at him. "I am not."

He dipped close and said softly, "Baby, you're dead on your feet. Lou's right. You need to look after yourself."

"She is right, you know, and so is Hixon," the woman in Lou's chair called. "Hair usually won't wait for another day, but, Greta, honey, your girls will wait for you."

Greta kept glaring up at him as she ignored that and asked, "Can we go to the hospital?"

He grinned. "Sure."

She looked away with a roll of her eyes.

He looked over his shoulders and tipped down his chin.

They got goodbyes as he walked her out.

He took her right to his Bronco and helped her in the passenger side before he swung in the driver's seat.

He started her up, backed her out and had them on their way before he asked, "You get lunch?"

"Yes," she said shortly.

He grinned again and asked, "You pissed at me?"

It took her a second to reply and she did it after he heard her push out a breath. "No. I'm just tired and a little achy, so I'm also just annoyed you and Lou are right, but I'm not pissed."

He reached out, took her hand and rested both on her thigh. "Good. Now you want the good news or the good news?"

He felt her gaze so he glanced her way before he looked back at the road.

"If it's that way, I want all the news," she answered.

"Well, to say the judge was not a big fan of a woman being attacked in her kitchen in his county is an understatement. During the bail hearing, he laid that asshole out. Essentially told him to make a deal or, if it got to him having the chance to announce a sentencing, he'd give him the maximum."

"Ohmigod," she breathed.

He unconsciously adjusted his hand from lacing with hers to glide his fingertips along the insides of her fingers as he smiled and continued to give it to her.

"So his attorney smartened up and sat down with our prosecutor. Unfortunately for that asshole, the prosecutor was handed all he needed to drive a hard bargain, this being something he did. This means that guy signed a deal admitting he committed three felonies. They dropped the breaking and entering to focus on trespass and stalking, mostly because trespass is much the same crime and holds the same punishment as breaking and entering and stalking will mean he can't come near you even after he's out. Not to mention, the prosecutor wanted to push that the sentences would be served non-concurrently. This means the man is out on a twenty-five-thousand-dollar bond and has to a week to get his affairs in order before he turns himself in to serve non-concurrent terms of two and a half years each for trespass and assault, one year mandatory protection order after he's out, and in the meantime he's not allowed within one hundred yards of you."

She gasped and her fingers curled back into his hand.

"Five years?"

"He'll be due for parole a lot earlier, sweetheart, but criminal trespass and assault hold up to twenty years each, and if Judge Bereford was feeling any more ornery than he was today, something he said he would be if they forced a jury trial, he could have that."

"Ohmigod...I...ohmigod, that's..."

She trailed off in order to bust out laughing.

He twisted her hand in his and brought it to his thigh, giving himself the added gift of looking at her a couple of times while she laughed.

When her laughter died down, he noted, "I take it you like that."

"Not thinkin' I'll be scared of my kitchen anymore," she said as reply.

"Good," he muttered.

She grew silent but ended it to remark quietly, "It's Nat, isn't it?"

He drew in breath and let it out, thinking he'd never thought she was stupid but not knowing until then how smart she was.

"Yeah," he confirmed.

"That's sad," she said.

"It is. It's also a deterrent," he replied. "Two serious felonies committed in his county in a short period of time when that shit doesn't happen here, the judge is sending a message that anyone else thinks they can pull something like that, they should think again."

"Yeah," she agreed.

"A lot of the time the system is a mess, sweetheart. Twisted up with plea deals and cops screwing around, not doing their jobs right or havin' the need to prove who's got the biggest dick and judges worried about their next elections. It's not only good that it worked this time, it's good that it worked the time it needed to so you can move on. So that's it. You take tomorrow off, give yourself a day to start the process of healing, then you heal and move on. You with me on that?"

"Yeah, Hix."

He lifted her hand, touched it to his chest then put it back to his thigh relieved she'd agreed to take a day off.

Once he did that, and her fingers had tightened in his hold after he did, he told her, "You should know, Gemini was at the hearing."

"So word got out before I showed at Lou's with my nose like this," she murmured.

"Actually, no," he replied. "I asked Hal to call him yesterday."

He felt her eyes so he glanced at her before looking back to the road and he kept talking.

"Did that for a variety of reasons, baby," he said quietly. "First, it's about you and how I know Gemini is with you. Second, it's about Gemini and how he runs his business. This started in his club, and as a courtesy, not so much as the man in your life who holds the position I hold so I was in the position to make sure he knew, but more as the sheriff of this county who should extend a courtesy like that to a man like him who runs the business where this all began."

"That makes sense."

He was glad she thought so.

"You need to call him," he said. "He's worried about you."

"I need to call a lot of people," she muttered. "I cleared this afternoon but I have a full schedule tomorrow. Think I'll keep Mrs. Whitney's appointment tomorrow night, though. She'll freak at the bandage but she'll get over it and she needs the company."

"Mrs. Whitney?"

"My at-home client. I go see her every other Tuesday."

"You take at-home clients?"

Her hand moved in his as an extension of her shrug. "Just her."

"She sick or somethin'?" he asked.

"No. Her husband has zero brain function so he's essentially in a coma, dying a very sad, very slow death in their bedroom upstairs."

"Jesus," he muttered.

"I know. It's awful. She doesn't get out much. She'd be okay with me rescheduling but, you know, after a day and a half of rest, I should be good to do a wash, rinse and set so she'll have someone to talk to who can actually talk back for an hour or so."

Taking care of her brother.

Taking Lou up on a challenge of mud wrestling.

Going to the home of a lonely client to do her hair and give her a little company.

You're about to embark on a fabulous journey of discovery.

Gemini had been right.

And Hix had been a total moron, putting at risk a future that included having Greta's ass in his Bronco at his side.

"Hix?" she called when he fell silent.

His voice was gruff when he pushed out, "Yeah?"

"You okay?" she asked.

"Yup. All good," he said, squeezing her hand.

"Can I tell you something?" she asked.

He wanted to learn everything about her.

"Absolutely."

"If this doesn't work, you know, between you and me..." she began.

His chest got instantly tight.

"Just sayin', I'm totally stealing this Bronco, loading Andy up and we're heading to Mexico. I feel safe in telling you this because you'll never find us. But just so you know, we'll keep her safe so you'll at least have that," she finished.

"And, you know, just sayin', I lose this Bronco, sweetheart, I'll go to the ends of the earth to find her," he returned, the tightness disappearing from his chest.

He loved his Bronc, but he wouldn't be looking for his truck.

"Hmm," she mumbled.

"Seems it's best we work on gettin' along, baby," he suggested.

"Maybe you're right," she replied then asked, "Can I drive her?"

"My ass isn't in her, yes."

"Is that an alpha-male thing?"

He bit back a surprised bark of laughter and asked back, "Is it a what?"

"An alpha-male thing, you know," her voice dropped low, "me man, me drive, you woman, you ride."

He chuckled. "No, it's I own this beast so I drive it if I'm in it so she knows she always has my love, but I'm totally cool you wanna take her for a spin if I'm not around."

"Okay then," she said, sounding amused.

"Okay," he replied.

With that, he drove Greta to the hospital.

Hix also chuckled a lot as he drove Greta to the hospital.

She ended up with only a piece of tape across the top of the bridge of her nose.

Unfortunately, this highlighted just how deep the bruising was coming down the sides from her inner eyes.

Also unfortunately, but in the end it worked in his favor, she was in enough pain, halfway into Monday Night Football with him and Shaw, she took a pill from the prescription they got at the hospital that they filled and she passed out with her head on his thigh on his couch like she had the night before.

So she slept in his bed.

And he woke up with her there too.

So yeah.

It worked in his favor.

And even better, when he dropped her in her kitchen the next morning, she didn't even blink walking over the threshold.

So it was all good and Hix rode that high to the department not knowing it wouldn't last a full day.

But now there was Greta and Hix's journey of discovery.

So he would learn he was set up to deal with the hitches in goodness.

Because he was unblocked on her phone.

Chapter 18

Put Me to the Test

Hixon

The next night, while Greta was with her at-home client doing a wash, rinse and set (whatever that was), Hix was walking into the high school's basketball court in order to watch his daughter play volleyball.

The minute he walked in, his eyes went to the team benches to see his daughter in her red and black Raiders uniform with its long sleeves, too tight shorts, black knee pads at her knees, her dark hair pulled back in a ponytail, standing with her coach and the rest of the team.

He felt his lips form a grin.

A grin that died immediately when Hope materialized in front of him.

He stopped dead because she was blocking his way.

"Hix, we need to talk."

He blew out a sigh and asked a question he knew the answer to because they'd been in Hope's care for only a day and he'd seen one of them with his own eyes, "The girls okay?"

"Yes, but," she got closer and her expression changed to one that Hix had to work hard not to let annoy him, "they, well, they shared that...that...that *woman* spent the night at your apartment *while they were there.*"

Hix stared down at her.

"You know that isn't right, Hixon, *you know,*" she hissed under her breath.

He continued to stare down at her.

"The girls also told me the unfortunate event that took place that was the reason she was at your house, but it's not like the woman doesn't have friends," she carried on.

Hix said nothing and just kept staring down at her.

"If you must see her, don't shove her in the kids' faces," she ordered.

That was when Hix sidestepped her and walked right by her, along the front of the bleachers, knowing eyes were on him.

His were on the wall at the opposite end where Toast had his back to the cinderblock, the sole of his boot up against it, arms crossed on his chest.

This was the position he'd assumed when he came to watch his daughter play volleyball (that was how he and Hix had become friends, their daughters played sports together) shortly after his own ex made it impossible to sit in the bleachers without her finding opportunity from close proximity to harangue him.

When Hix's back hit the wall at Toast's side and he assumed the same position, Toast muttered, "Hate to say it, but welcome to my world, brother."

Hix just emitted an unintelligible grunt.

"Let me guess, she's pissed your woman stayed over," Toast deduced.

"While the kids were there," Hix confirmed.

"No, bro, she'd be pissed even if they weren't, just gives her more ammunition that they were."

Hix made no reply, just kept his attention on his daughter and her team.

"And heads up, they lose all rationality, they lose hold on your dick and some other woman is enjoying it. It doesn't matter to her your woman got attacked. But the looks she's gettin', it matters to everyone else," Toast told him.

That made Hix slide his eyes to the bleachers and it wasn't hard to read the censure Hope was getting as she made her way to a seat.

It also wasn't hard to read she didn't miss it either.

Fortunately, his attention was taken with his younger daughter skipping his way.

"Hey, Dad," she greeted, stopping toe to toe with him, bending forward so she hit him with her weight, resting the length of her along the length of him, her hands on his forearms, her head tipped back to grin up at him.

"Hey, baby," he murmured, uncrossing his arms to touch a finger to her nose.

"Can I have popcorn?"

Oh shit.

"You ask your mom that?" he asked.

Her expression told him the answer.

"Mamie," was all he said next.

She scrunched up her face then slid to the side, but twisted as she did, so she ended up with her shoulder tucked into his side.

He ran a hand around both and held her there.

"Your brother here yet?" he asked, again scanning the bleachers.

"He's goin' to pick up Wendy then he'll be here," she told him.

"Right," he muttered.

"Hey, Uncle Toast," she belatedly greeted.

"Hey there, gorgeous girl," Toast returned.

"You want some popcorn?" she asked and immediately offered, "I can get it for you."

"And eat half the box before it gets here?" Toast asked.

She gave him a sassy smile. "Sometimes they don't fill it full."

Toast pushed away from the wall to pull out his wallet. "Then I totally want popcorn."

"Toast," Hix warned.

"What?" Toast asked with sham innocence. "I had dinner all of fifteen minutes ago." He gave Hix's girl a bill. "I'm feelin' peckish."

She shot him a huge smile, grabbed the money and took off.

"More knowledge, brother," Toast began as he settled back in. "You got the opportunity to fuck with 'em or piss them off in any way, you take it."

"Hope doesn't exist outside being the woman who my daughters go live with every other week, man. But she likes to find every reason she can to remind me she does. I'm not a big fan of giving them to her."

"She doesn't exist?"

"Nope."

"Lookin' right at her, bro."

Hix took his attention from the court where the girls were heading out to look at Toast and then follow where his eyes were directed to see Hope sitting in the stands, watching them.

She no longer looked pissed.

She looked sad.

Christ.

Hix returned his attention to the players and said nothing.

"She wants you back, Hix, and *bad*," Toast shared.

Hix said something to that.

"If that's true, that's not gonna go well for her."

"This other one, you know..."

His voice died away so Hix looked to him. "I know what?"

Toast looked uncomfortable when he said, "It's been a while for you but you should know, you don't play with that kind."

"What kind?" Hix asked, wanting to know where this was going so he knew whether he was about to be pissed as shit or other.

"The good kind, Hix."

So it was other.

Toast wasn't done.

"Me bein' tight with you, everyone is opening wide about her. And I've learned she's like a second mom to Lou's daughters, which is good, seein' as half the time they don't have a dad. Hear she's got a brother whose brains were scrambled and she takes care of him. They go and play with the dogs at the shelter on the weekends, for Christ's sake. Walked into Babycakes a Sunday ago or so, right after her and her brother left, and I swear, Babycakes laid it out for me either I got your head out of your ass about this Greta woman or the rest of the town would."

Hix blew out another sigh and said, "They can relax. We're back together."

"You got a solid rep, bro, but this woman is—"

Hix cut him off. "We're back together, Toast, and I'm not gonna fuck that shit up. I know what I got. *I've* got it so I know. So they can relax and you can too."

Toast gave him a huge, goofy-assed smile. "Well, all right. When you bringin' her to the Outpost to meet your boys, then?"

"Soon's the broken nose that asshole gave her slammin' her face in her own goddamned kitchen island heals."

While Hix spoke, Toast's smile died.

"Fucker," he muttered.

"He's going away for a long time," Hix said, watching as play began and his daughter, a starter as a sophomore on the varsity team, sprang into action.

"How much effort it take for you not to kick his ass while he was in one of your cells?" Toast asked.

"So much, it's a wonder I can walk."

Toast chuckled and turned his attention to the game.

They watched and Hix uncrossed his arms from his chest and clapped, shouting out, "That's it, Corinne!" when she aced a serve.

Pissed at her dad, her head needing to be in the game, she still loved her old man and he knew it when her eyes slid to him briefly and a grin flirted with her mouth as she walked to the line with the ball before she regained focus to set up for her next serve.

"The kids like her?" Toast asked after the team blew it and lost Corinne's serve.

Hix knew what he was asking.

Did they like Greta?

"Nothin' not to like."

Toast left it a beat before he murmured, "Happy for you, bro. Way to land on your feet."

Hix glanced at him before looking back to the play. "You'll find someone, Toast."

"I need to get laid on a semi-regular basis and I need to stay single. Outside that bullshit getting me my kids, shoulda stayed single from the start."

"You'll get over that."

"I wouldn't bet on it," Toast muttered.

Hix shook his head and said no more.

Hope and his shit was ugly. Toast and his shit with his ex was Armageddon.

As the teams were switching sides, Mamie skipped up with half a box of popcorn she'd consumed the rest of and handed it to Toast.

She then dug back into her dad's side so Hix held her there.

He caught his son arriving and tried to stay loose even after he also caught the expression on his face.

And the set of his girl's.

Hix gave Shaw a sharp look.

Shaw shook his head at his dad and Hix knew the state of play with the way Shaw actually spotted his girl as she led them to some seats, like she was doing it with a broken foot.

Things weren't going good with her dad's treatments.

Shit.

He'd talk to his boy.

Now it was about Corinne.

So he turned back to the game.

After the game, while Shaw was finishing up his date with Wendy, which Hix assumed would take him to the very last minute of his weekday curfew, Hix pulled his Bronco into Greta's drive but he rounded the front seeing as he saw her on her porch as he pulled in.

He made it all the way to her with her watching his progress and bent to wrap his hand around the back of her head and touch his mouth to hers before she spoke.

"Hey, did she win?"

"No."

"Bummer," she muttered.

He grinned, let her go, shifted and rested his frame in the chair beside her.

"Want a beer?" she asked.

"I'll get it in a second."

"I have a broken nose, Hixon, not a broken leg."

He looked from her street to her and repeated, "I'll get it in a second."

She rolled her eyes but did it with her lips twitching.

Then she lifted a mug to her lips and took a sip.

"What's that?" he asked.

"Sleepytime," she answered.

"Say again," he ordered.

She took her eyes from her street and repeated, "Sleepytime. Sleepytime tea. Chamomile. Spearmint. And—"

He cut her off. "Babe."

"What?"

"Don't waste your breath. The concept of tea does not exist for a man who owns a Bronco."

He enjoyed the show as she busted out laughing.

When she was done, she noted, "Britannia ruled the waves, darlin', and those boys drank a lot of tea."

"The kind they drank didn't have spearmint in it."

"Good point," she muttered, her lips curved up as she took another sip.

He hated doing it but he had to so might as well get it out of the way.

"Hope was at the game."

Her gaze slid to him. "And?"

"She's in the know you've spent the night at my place while the kids were there."

"And she's not a big fan," she guessed.

"Not sure I care but just in case she gets up to something, you should know."

She nodded and added, "And we'll slow that down."

No, they wouldn't.

"I like you in my bed."

He also liked how her face got soft when he told her that.

"I like it there too, baby," she told him. "But your apartment isn't real big and it's kinda in their faces more than it would be in that space. Plus, this is very new to them."

"It's also very much happening so they might as well get used to it."

"Another good point," she muttered again.

"And Greta, we're movin' to a place on Lavender Lane on Saturday."

She stared at him. "Lavender Lane?"

He grinned at her.

And he did it because he liked the place they found but now he liked it even more because it was two blocks to the north of her place, on the same block.

"Wow, we're practically gonna be neighbors," she remarked and did it looking like she was trying hard not to laugh.

"Yup," he agreed the same way.

"You buy?" she asked.

He shook his head. "Nope. Everything on the market sucks and I can't keep the kids in that apartment any longer, and not just because I hate the freakin' place so much myself. Folks who own the house we picked are retired and movin' to Florida. But they're worried they're gonna hate Florida. So they're renting their place for a year to try it out. If they hate it, they'll come back and revisit where they wanna spend their golden years. If they like it, they'll sell to me and deduct the year's rent from the final sale."

She gave him a smile. "Great deal."

If they didn't come back, it was.

If they did, he had to find another place.

But they'd assured him they'd give him plenty of notice and his real estate agent was going to keep an eye out in the meantime.

It might mean moving twice in a year, which would suck.

It might mean settling in, but even if it didn't, it gave them more time to find what was right instead of them moving into another place that was going to be wrong.

"Three bedrooms, two full baths, one in the master, on the top floor," he shared. "Living room, dining room, half bath, big kitchen on the ground level. Refinished basement where Shaw will be with his own bathroom and a massive family room."

"Sounds like my place," she noted.

"Your basement refinished?" he asked.

She nodded.

"You need to give me a tour," he told her.

She tipped her head to the side. "You want that now?"

He shook his head, pushing up from his chair. "I want a beer now."

"Hix, I can get it."

He stopped and looked down at her.

"You got a problem with me in your house, baby?" he asked softly, with genuine interest.

"Of course not, but I like..." her teeth came out to score her lip before she finished, "looking after you."

And fuck, but he liked that.

"How about I get my beer tonight, and after tonight, we'll go from there."

She shot him a grin. "Works for me."

He gave himself a moment to fully take in her grin before he asked, "You need more of that?" and he tipped his head to her mug.

She shook her own.

"Right. Be back," he murmured, went in, got himself a beer and came out, doing it giving himself his first chance to really take in her space.

It wasn't only the kitchen that was nice. The rest of it was too. All redone. Big, old-fashioned, kickass table in the dining room with one side having a bench instead of chairs. Huge couch in the living room with lots of woodwork on it, scrolled arms and massive pillows for the back in a print of some fancy, subtle cream and beige swirls.

The couch was ornate but it still looked comfortable.

A lot of her stuff was his style. He liked it. Even if it wasn't, it worked and he liked that too. It was pretty phenomenal.

It was also confusing.

He knew women paid a lot of money to have their hair done. He knew how much it cost for Hope and the girls for theirs. They were in rural Nebraska, it might cost more in big cities, but even as it was, it wasn't anywhere near what Hix paid for him and Shaw to go to the barber.

But it wouldn't set Greta to rolling in it.

He went back out and saw her waving at something, so he looked that way as he moved to her and tipped up his chin at a woman who was walking her dog in front of Greta's house.

The woman threw him an enormous beam through the dark as he sat his ass back down with his beer.

He stretched out his legs out and crossed his ankles.

He did this as he tried to remember how to do the getting-to-know-you portion of being with a woman you're interested in.

It seemed strange, all that had gone down between them, like she'd been a part of his life a lot longer than she had.

But she hadn't and he barely knew anything about her.

He started it with, "How's your nose?"

"Better today, thanks, Hixon," she answered.

"Your brother?" he asked.

"Good, thanks, baby," she said softly, this how she talked whenever she spoke about her brother, when she wasn't laying shit out for him after he'd been a dick, that was.

Hix sucked back some beer and then asked, "You figure out what you're gonna tell him?"

"I think I'm gonna say I had a fall."

Hix was surprised she was going to lie so he looked from the dark night to her. "Yeah?"

She let out a big breath she aimed at the night and said, "Yeah. He..." she turned to him, "he can be unpredictable. Most of the time, he would be able to process what happened, understand it, understand the guy was caught and he was going to be punished and he'd be upset for me, but he'd see that I'm okay and he'd deal. Other times..."

She didn't finish.

"Other times what, sweetheart?" he prompted gently.

"Other times anything can happen. He could get so upset and frustrated at not being able to do anything, he could get violent. He could regress to the point he's like a little kid and stick in that zone for a while, which is harder to cope with for the staff because dealing with a young man with a brain injury is one thing. Dealing with a young boy who has tantrums or can turn sullen or uncommunicative is another." She shrugged. "So I think I have to lie. For him. There's nothing he can do anyway, it's over. To keep him safe, I'll give him an alternate version of events that doesn't harm anything. No one would tell him. He won't find out."

After she gave him all of that, he whispered, "I don't know how you do it."

She genuinely looked confused when she asked, "Do what?"

He lifted his beer in a circle to indicate everything. "All of it. Work. Look after him. Handle what happened. Keep on keepin' on."

"I have no choice."

He transferred the bottle to his other hand so he could reach out and take hers.

"If one of the kids—" he began.

"Don't," she said quickly. "Don't think about it. It happened to us. But it doesn't happen a lot so don't think about it. Not with one of your kids. Not with anybody."

"What I'm tryin' to do is get in your headspace so I can be in a place of understanding with you," he explained.

When he quit talking, she looked at him like she'd never seen him before.

So he gave her fingers a squeeze. "Greta?"

"I'm, like, really, *really* glad I unblocked you, Hixon," she declared.

And after she gave him that, Hix leaned into her and pulled her hand to his mouth to touch it to his lips so he wouldn't do something else, like pick her up and carry her into her house and touch his lips to other things.

He relaxed in his chair, put their hands back between them and remarked, "I still don't know how you do it. This is a nice house, sweetheart. And I'm in the position to know how nice it is, bein' in the market for my own. You work. You look after your brother. You dress great. You made this a great space. It's like you can make miracles."

He could have gone on but he didn't because she'd returned her gaze to the street and lifted her mug of tea up to her mouth, both in what he read as an attempt to hide her face.

"Did I say something wrong?" he asked, twisting their hands so their fingers were facing up and he could run the tips of his along the insides of hers.

Her head turned again so her eyes could light on their hands before they lifted to him.

"Keith gave us this."

His fingers quit moving.

"Keith?"

"My ex-husband. Keith. He's...um, very wealthy. I didn't, uh... want it, but he impressed on me that I needed to take it so the divorce settlement was exceptionally comfortable. For me. And for Andy."

Hix just stared at her.

"He was...we were...we were dating when Andy got hurt. They were close even before. He, well, he always took care of Andy," she shared. "He still does, kind of. And me. Well, just in the sense the settlement bought my house."

Shit.

"And my car."

Christ.

"And my furniture."

Fuck.

"And it pays for Andy's home and will for a good time, so I can, you know, not having a mortgage or a car payment or, um, other stuff, I'll be able to do it for, maybe, um...ever."

She stopped talking.

"That's *very* wealthy, Greta," Hix said low.

He watched her swallow.

Hix looked to the street and threw back some more beer.

He did this thinking he could never do that. Buy her a house outright. A car outright. Hell, he couldn't even help her take care of her brother, not with setting up his own house and what would be coming up with his kids as they finished high school and entered life. He'd already dipped into his uncle's inheritance to buy furniture and pay for the divorce and he'd need more.

He didn't get paid shit but he'd never be able to buy anyone a new car outright.

No way a house.

Not in his life.

"Hixon?" she called hesitantly.

"And he divorced you because of your mother?" Hix asked the street.

"He took care of Andy, and obviously gave me a really good life. I mean, I worked and sometimes I sang but, you know, we had a comfortable life mostly because of him."

He bet they did.

"But, well, I gave her money and he hated her and it bothered him that I did."

Uh.

What?

He looked again to her. "Sorry?"

She did another shrug. "He really hated her. Like I said, we were together when the accident happened. He knew Andy before and after. She hurt him. And she wasn't ever nice to me. So me giving her money—"

"She's your mother."

Greta shut her mouth.

She opened it right back up to say a loaded, "Yeah."

He didn't know what that was loaded with but he didn't ask after that.

He asked, "So that's it? He had you and gave you up because your mother is a parasitical bitch?"

"Well, that and I, um..."

She tried to slide her hand away.

Hix kept hold of it.

Her focus sharpened on him and she whispered, "I didn't want to have a family."

"And he did," Hix guessed.

"Yes."

"And you two didn't talk about that before you got married?"

Her head twitched. "No. We did. He knew."

That made Hix's brows draw together. "So what was his beef?"

"He thought he could change my mind."

"That's not a beef, Greta. That's bullshit."

Her fingers convulsed around his.

"Why didn't you want a family?" he asked.

"I had one."

He twisted her way. "I get your mom isn't great, Greta. And it goes without sayin' I hate that you and your brother gotta live with what she did to him. But I mean a family that's yours."

"I had one, Hix."

"The one you make," he explained.

"I raised Andy, Hixon," she told him. "He was mine. He was never hers. I took a bus to the hospital when she called me after she had him and the nurses got him for me and put me in a little room where I sat in a rocking chair and held him and that was it. He was mine. And I mean that in an emotional sense. But also in an everything sense, because she had nothing to do with him."

Uh.

What?

"Come again?"

"Nothing." She shook her head. "No bottles. No diapers. No forcing him out of bed for school in the morning. We weren't latchkey kids who had to look after ourselves while Mom was out making a living. She lived her life with two kids in her trailer she had to put up with and maybe throw some money at so we could eat, I could buy Andy diapers or go to Goodwill to get him clothes. I mean, in the beginning, I had to go to school and someone had to look after him. But if I couldn't get a neighbor to help out, I'd come home and he'd be bawling because he had a dirty diaper and she barely pulled it together to give him some food so she'd hand him off to me and then she'd vanish. Other than that, we didn't exist until I started making money and she could lean on me to give some of it to her."

He couldn't believe what he was hearing.

"You're joking," he growled.

She shook her head, again trying to slide her hand away but Hix held tight.

She gave up trying to get away and kept giving him her story.

"Normally, he would walk. But it was raining. So she was the one who picked him up from that party, because I was out with Keith and Andy didn't want to interrupt us so he called her for a ride. And unfortunately, she felt in the rare mood to give him one."

Hix looked back to the street and the amount of beer he threw back was a lot bigger.

"So now you get it," she noted in a strange voice that regained his attention.

"Get what?" he asked.

"Get how Keith felt about her. About me not wanting a family because I'd already raised a son and started doing that at fourteen so I wasn't feeling doing it again, this also because of her. How all that, being what she made, could..." she gave a tentative tug on her hand but when he didn't let go, she quit doing it, "make him divorce me," she finished.

"No, I don't get that."

She blinked several times before she asked, "You don't?"

"Hell no."

Her mouth got soft, her eyes went troubled, and she said quietly, "Hix, he lived with it for ten years."

"Sweetheart, maybe he feels okay about himself that he left you to your life puttin' you in a nice house in a nice car in a nice town with your brother in a good place where they take care of him, but you're still here and he's wherever he is and it isn't here with you, so no. I don't get it. I think he's an idiot."

Something lit in her eyes like humor with a whole load of something more before it faded and she said, "You haven't even met Andy yet."

"I've met your mom and I haven't led my life or my career in law enforcement all in this town, so I know women like her and I know they're bad news and I knew that, babe, before she even opened her mouth. I got more of it when she did. I get it. I get it would be frustrating. I don't think bad about the man because of that, because this shit is extreme and he obviously wanted to look out for you in a variety of ways. He just totally fell down on that job."

"But I was...I was weak about my mom," she declared. "It wasn't like she'd ingratiate herself or she was around all the time, being annoying. She'd come and she'd go. But when she'd come, she'd always have her hand out. And part of me giving her money was the fact that, if I did, she'd go without making a mess of things, because she'd make a mess of things if she didn't get what she wanted. But part of it was because, well, she's far from great, but she's the only mom I've got."

"Greta, baby, she's clearly even less of a peach than I expected, but I've seen kids take care of parents who beat them. Who sexually abused them. Who let men or women into their homes repeatedly, and it was them who would administer the abuse. I get that she'd manipulate shit to get what she wants, making it hard for you to say no. I also get it's just straight up hard to say no to a parent. It isn't that one person is stronger, being able to cut that shit out of their lives. It's maybe that your heart is larger that you'd look after her, but it's also not just that. It's like the chicken and the egg. No one can say what's the right answer in how to handle that. It's just one of life's things that we deal with the way our heart tells us to do it and there's never anything wrong with that."

She said nothing.

She just stared at him with those big eyes in that beautiful face that even a broken nose couldn't make any less beautiful, and taking that in, Hix knew even more the man who divorced her was an idiot.

But even with all she'd just laid on him, Hix felt fucking *great.*

Because he couldn't give her a house or a car or help out with her brother (much, this being financially) until after the girls were out of school.

But he could put up with her mother, and with the way her voice got when she talked about him, he had not the slightest hesitation of having her brother in his or his kids' lives.

So yeah.

If this worked out, he could give her that.

And he had a feeling that meant more to her than a top-of-the-line Cherokee ever would.

Or a diamond ring.

He threw back more beer and heard her cautious, "Hix?"

He looked to her. "Yeah?"

More caution when she muttered, "I just, uh...gave you a lot."

"Unh-hunh," he agreed.

She studied him.

He leaned to her and whispered, "Put me to the test."

"Sorry?"

"I'll pass."

He watched her eyes get bright with wet.

He did not want to make her cry. He liked she felt that much from what he said.

But he never wanted to be the man who made Greta cry.

"We're new," he stated. "Life has thrown me some curveballs lately so I have no idea how it's gonna go. It's obviously thrown more at you and has since birth. What I do know is how much I like bein' with you. How good it feels. And I wanna take care of that. I let your mother put that at risk once, that was stupid but I'm not stupid, so I learned that lesson and it won't happen again. And I think there's nothing in my life I've heard that's more beautiful than what you give your brother, before he got hurt and after. I also know I can say all that 'til I'm blue in the face, I still have to prove it. So put me to the test. Go for it. At least with all that, I'll pass. What I don't want is to make you cry about it, Greta. You laid it out and it is what it is and all you gotta do now is sit back and see."

"Okay, I really wanna have sex with you, like, right now," she announced.

His cock felt that.

But his lips only smiled.

"Baby, I'm not making love to you two days after you got your nose broke."

"It's been three."

His lips kept smiling. "Greta, sweetheart, I'm not making love with you three days after you got your nose broke."

"We won't kiss."

"The fuck we won't," he growled.

"We can—"

He gave her hand a firm shake and leaned to her. "Weekdays, Shaw's curfew is ten. He's gonna be home soon and I gotta be home with my boy. But Friday, Shaw plays ball and you won't be singing. I'll tell him to maneuver a sleepover with one of his buds. And after the game, we'll have all night."

Her eyes instantly rolled to the ceiling of her porch while her lips moved but no words came out.

"Babe?" he called.

"Hush," she shushed him.

He started chuckling. "Greta."

She rolled her eyes back. "Hush, Hix, I'm counting the hours so I can count them down."

He stopped chuckling and busted out laughing.

Then he leaned farther and took her mouth in a slow, gentle, wet kiss.

When he was done, he pulled back an inch. "Tide you over?"

"Not even close."

He touched his lips even more gently on the tip of her nose before he sat back, kept hold of her hand and lifted up his beer.

When he'd taken a tug and dropped it, he asked, "Okay, so what in the hell is a wash, rinse and set?"

That was when Greta laughed, he turned to watch, and when she quit, she explained a wash, rinse and set.

Having a dick, he discovered he really didn't need to know.

But he was glad he did.

Chapter 19

So We're Good

Hixon

The next night, Greta met him at the top of the steps to her porch, her feet in thick socks, a slouchy cardigan on, a big scarf wrapped around her neck, her head tipped back, the swelling nearly gone around her nose, the bruising still angry but receding.

"Beer?" she asked in a firm tone.

He smiled at her. "Yeah. But kiss first."

She leaned into him, put a hand on his chest, and they exchanged a short, wet kiss before she broke away and whispered, "Be back."

She went in and he went to his chair on her porch.

It was nippy. Dark. Mid-October weather in Nebraska was still nice during the day, but when the sun went down, the chill set in.

He turned his head and saw that she had her mug of tea sitting on the table by her chair. She also had a book and some catalogs.

He was eyes back to the street when Greta returned, handed him his beer and then adjusted her chair so it was set butted up to his. Then she settled in it so she was pressed to the side of the chair closest to him, her feet up on the pad in the seat, knees falling to his side, and her hand came out and ran down the inside of his forearm.

He transferred his beer from that hand to his left, thinking she wanted to hold hands, also thinking he was totally okay with that.

But she engaged her other hand, pressing his right hand flat between both of hers, her eyes watching.

It was an affectionate touch, but there was something poignant about it that concerned him.

"Everything okay, sweetheart?" he asked.

"You have really beautiful hands," she murmured, still pressing his between hers before she laced her fingers through his, dropping her other hand away, bending their linked ones toward them with elbows resting on the arm of the chair as she rested her head on his shoulder.

He liked she thought that about his hands.

He was still concerned.

"Greta, something happen today?"

"Nope, just...nope," she answered. But before he could prompt further she said, "I was..." She stopped and started again. "Having you for a spell, then things happened and I didn't have you..." He felt her head move on his shoulder like she was shaking it. "I like my house. I don't mind being alone. Or I didn't. Then I had you to sit on the porch with me and I minded. And I, well..." Her tone became hesitant. "I like having you back."

He twisted his neck so he could kiss her hair before he righted it and replied gruffly, "I'm glad you let me come back."

"Mm," she mumbled, digging her head into his shoulder for a beat then settling in.

He decided to move them beyond this or they wouldn't be sitting on her porch, getting to know each other in a way he could leave and get back to his house to make certain his son came home on time after his study date with Wendy at her house.

No. They'd be doing something else. Something they couldn't do for as long as he'd like, and after, he couldn't stay with her, sleep beside her, because he had to go home to his boy.

And he knew from experience the swelling could go down, the bruises recede, but it took weeks for a broken nose to heal, and the longer he gave her to do that, the less pain he might inadvertently cause making love to her.

So he had to give her as much time as they both could endure.

Which was two more days.

Therefore, he told her, "Shaw's at his girl's house, studying. Told you earlier in that text, babe, we were having dinner together tonight. That's because I needed time with him. There's stuff going down with Wendy's family. Shaw's feelin' the need to keep an eye on her. But apparently, her folks let them study in her room. So I needed to lay some things out about that. I also need to be home when he gets there so I can give him the eagle eye to make sure nothin' came of that."

"Risky business, letting a handsome, young man study in your daughter's bedroom," she observed.

"Yup."

Greta laughed softly.

"The stuff going down isn't good stuff, baby, so it's doubtful Shaw will go for anything."

And this, he hoped his son wouldn't do, knowing that her dad was growing sicker, weaker and depressed from his treatments, that depression also hitting the family since they had to watch it.

Hix had been wrong the night before. The doctors felt the treatments were working, but it was coming clear that road wasn't going to be easy.

"Shaw's a good guy, so you're probably right," she replied.

"I also shared I'd be disappointed if he took that road, even if it seemed Wendy needed that kind of closeness for whatever reason she would have."

"And you're a good dad," she murmured before she went on, "Not an easy chat, darlin'. I feel your pain. I remember having that conversation with Andy. He'd been young but he'd been popular with the girls. Keith had already had it but I found condoms in his room so I had to have it again."

"At least he had condoms," Hix muttered, doing it thinking something else.

Thinking he kind of hoped the kid got himself some before having the chance at any normal relationship swept away by his mother.

Also thinking it hadn't occurred to him how much of a parent Greta had been until she gave him that info.

She was right. It was not an easy conversation to have with your son, your brother or any kid. He knew that from past experience and some that was very recent.

And you didn't do it, in most cases, unless you were a parent.

"He didn't use them," she shared. "He didn't tell me that. He got ticked I talked to him about it because he was embarrassed. He complained to Keith and he told Keith that."

Hix had no response she'd likely want to hear.

"And now, I kinda wish that he'd...you know," she said.

He knew.

And he was beginning not to be surprised Greta's thoughts ran the same way his did.

"Yeah," he whispered.

Her fingers started fiddling with his fingers in a manner that he liked and Hix decided it was now time to take them out of this because it felt heavy, and she had to live that heavy every day. She didn't need it on her porch when she was unwinding at night.

So he asked, "You do your porch thing all year long?"

He felt her head move and he knew she was looking up at him. "My porch thing?"

He twisted his neck again to look down at her. "Sittin' out here to unwind at night."

She grinned and settled back in, aiming her eyes to the street, so he did too and took a sip of his beer while she spoke.

"I have to give it up around Thanksgiving. I can bundle up but then it gets too chilly. I thought about getting a space heater but I have a great house. I might as well use more of it than my bed, kitchen and porch for a few months a year."

He chuckled, replied, "Yeah," and started returning the fiddle of fingers as he asked, "Why do you do it?"

"Sit on the porch?" she asked back.

"Yup."

She flipped out her other hand toward the street. "Because of that."

He was confused. "Your street?"

"That and the fact that it's how it is. Quiet. Nice. People keep up their homes. Tend their yards. Plant flowers. Put out decorations. It's a good view and it's always changing. Plus they walk their dogs in front of my house and say hey, sometimes stop and chat." She tipped her head on his shoulder so he knew she was looking at him again so he twisted his neck to catch her eyes. "I grew up in a trailer park."

When she let that lie, he grinned at her and asked, "Am I supposed to take that as a dire admission?"

She laughed softly again and turned her attention back to the street.

He took in her hair, her smooth forehead, her taped nose, before he also turned back to the street while she was answering.

"Not really. But our park wasn't a very good one. Even so, there were a lot of nice people in it. Good people. They helped look after me. Then when Andy came, they helped me look after him. But there was always a lot happening. A lot of noise. Folks fighting. Coming and going at all hours because that was their work schedule or it was their play schedule. Parties. Loud music. Cops showing. This...a place like this is like heaven."

Hix stared at the street.

"I like the city," she informed him. "I like malls and Cineplexes and nice restaurants. But I like better going to the grocery store and running into someone I know and having a natter. I like getting a coffee and knowing the lady who runs the place and she knows me because that's the only coffee place in town. And it has good coffee, but it kinda feels like you're getting coffee at a friend's house. I like the fact that most people know most everyone else and they care. If someone dies, they make a casserole. Someone gets engaged, they buy a gift. I know there are bad seeds. I know bad stuff still happens. But it feels like...it kinda feels like the trailer park but without the bad parts. Like a big family. The good kind of family."

Hix stared at the street feeling something move deep in his chest.

And he knew what that something was.

It was the understanding that that was what Hope had wanted them to have. Not just their family, but her giving it to Hix too.

She'd never explained it that way, maybe didn't know how because it was what she grew up with. She just knew how good it was, and she wanted the people she loved to have it.

He'd just never understood it, the gift she'd wanted them to have.

Until now.

Greta must have felt his thoughts had turned because her head came off his shoulder and he felt her gaze.

He looked to her.

"Do you think I'm crazy?" she asked.

"Not even a little bit."

She studied him closely. "Then what is it, darlin'?"

He gave it to her without hesitation.

And he'd discover, he maybe shouldn't have hesitated, but he should have been more careful with how he gave what he gave.

"She didn't explain it that way, but I think that's why Hope wanted us to move here. What she wanted to give us. She grew up here. She knew how good of a place it was to do that and more, just have. Life in a small town where the mall might be a trek and the only movie theater is fifteen miles away and there are only two screens."

Something crossed her expression he wasn't a big fan of before she twisted away to grab her mug and let go of her hold on his hand.

"Greta," he called as she sipped, and when she looked at him, he noted, "It's what she wanted for us. I didn't get it then, but I'm getting it now. Think I was getting it before, after Nat was killed, what a shock that was because that kind of thing never happens here. I'm getting how folks look down on small towns, and maybe in my way, I did that too. How they think the people in them are hicks. How nothing much happens in a small town so folks think the people in them don't know much about life. But it isn't that. They just get more of the good without the shit leaking in. And now, getting that, I don't mind as much that my boy is goin' into the marines because he's gonna have learned all he needs to know about bein' a good man, a good person, leading a good life because of the goodness he grew up around that wasn't screwed up with big city shit."

"Yeah," she agreed.

She still had a look on her face he didn't like.

So he asked carefully, "Okay, sweetheart, you get it too, why do you look like I killed your puppy?"

Her expression turned startled then it softened with her smile as she put her mug back, twisted his way and leaned into him, getting close, her breasts brushing his arm, her smile not its usual luminous but kind of sad.

"It happens like this," she stated confusingly. "You get low. Ask yourself a lot of questions. What did you do? What could you have done? Then you get pissed. Why didn't they see what we had? Why didn't they fight for it with me? And then you come to understand. You come to understand a lot of things. And that's where you are right now, Hix. You're coming to understand."

He wasn't, not even close.

But he guessed, "Are you talking about Hope?"

She nodded.

"Babe—"

"It's okay, Hixon," she said quietly, her smile gone, her face still soft, but the sadness was not close to hidden in her eyes.

He didn't like that look.

And he still didn't understand.

"What's okay?"

"You said that night after the grocery store incident that it was an uncomfortable realization that she was a good mom but other than that..." She tipped her head to the side in a kind of shrug. "The truth is, you loved her. You don't see the reasons why right now because you're ticked at her. But they'll come back through. You'll remember them and the good times and—"

"Stop," he ordered.

She stopped.

He watched her closely as he asked, "Are you saying you think I'm gonna get back with Hope?"

"You loved her a lot, Hixon. Everyone saw it. Even me."

That was when he stared at her.

Before he started chuckling.

He didn't roar with laughter mostly because Greta wasn't looking sad anymore. She was looking miffed.

So he shared, "I'm not gonna get back with her."

The sad came back. "You don't know what the future will bring."

Now he got it.

And it was definitely funny.

But since she didn't think so, he had to take the time to explain.

"Right." He turned to her, transferred his beer again and lifted a hand to cup her jaw, moving in to bring their faces even closer. "Even if she didn't end our marriage not actually wanting to end our marriage but as a play to get an expensive ring, she never told me *why* she ended our marriage. Maybe it was dawning on her how I'd react to the real reason. Maybe she felt justified and truly thought I would get with her program. But regardless of all that, Greta, since then she's behaved in ways that, yeah, I loved her. There were reasons. I'm not feelin' 'em right now because I'm not feelin' real warm and fuzzy about Hope right now. And maybe some miracle will occur and she'll sort her shit out so I can remember some of that fondly so we have some kind of relationship that isn't bitter or difficult and we can carry on raising our kids and being their parents in a way that isn't ugly. But other than that, babe, believe me, it is well and truly done."

"I know you can think that, Hixon, but history has a strong pull."

What was she really telling him?

He withdrew a couple of inches and dropped his hand from her jaw.

"Are you still hung up on this Keith guy?" he asked.

Her eyes rounded, her lips tipped up and her body started shaking.

Her answer was shaky too. "Uh, no."

"So what are you saying?" he pressed.

Her humor died. "Hix, I saw you with her."

"Babe, you shared a decade with a man who," he jerked his head to the side to indicate her house, "if what he gave you when he divorced you is any indication, when he had you, he gave you and the brother you adore a pretty damned good life. I don't have to see you with him to know you're speaking from some kind of experience right now."

"Hix—"

"Everyone saw me with Hope. It's a small town. We got kids so we're always out and around, and I don't know why, maybe it's because I'm in an elected position, but they had more than a healthy interest in her and me, and I don't gotta say because you gotta know, now you and me."

"You don't know why?" she asked, her eyes big again.

"No. People gossip but I get they do it more about me. Hope and me. The kids and me. You and me."

"You don't know why," she repeated as a statement this time, her words again shaking.

"I'm not seein' anything funny."

"Hixon, you're hot."

"Greta—"

She put her fingers over his lips. "No, baby. Seriously. You're *hot*. You're like, movie star hot. You're like a twenty-four-seven reality program starring yourself. You don't even have to do anything interesting, but you wear that sheriff's shirt and it makes you *more* hot. You looked great with Hope. Your kids are gorgeous. You were like the royal family of Glossop."

He wrapped his hand around her wrist and pulled her fingers away but didn't let her go when he declared, "That's ridiculous."

"Apparently, our sheriff hasn't deduced the pull of a hot guy law enforcement officer," she muttered over his shoulder, not hiding she thought this was hilarious.

"Greta," he growled.

She grinned and looked back at him. "Get on Facebook sometime. Or Google. Or *anywhere*."

Fuck.

"There's pictures of me?"

She leaned into him. "No, Hix. There's pictures of random hot guys. Women are taking that action back. Men have spent years ogling calendars and magazines, objectifying women, reducing them to a pretty face, a head of hair and a hot bod. With social media, there's probably more pictures of shirtless hot guys with six-packs wearing cowboy hats or shrugging off police shirts than there are oiled-up hot chicks rolling around on Ferraris." She pulled back and finished with sham seriousness. "Of course, I frown on that entirely. Turnaround, in my book, is not fair play."

She was totally lying.

And she was very cute.

However.

"I'm not getting back together with Hope."

Her humor died.

Hix curled his hand around the back of her neck. "I'm getting, the life you led, you don't expect good things to come to you. What I hope is that you think I'm a good thing. And you got me. We work on this, you'll keep me, because I hope I've made it clear, I want you to. I won't stray. I won't go back to her. But I also get I have to prove that too."

"Hixon—"

"And I will."

"Okay," she whispered, her hand coming up between them to slide along his jaw and back into his hair. "And just to say, you know, Keith's already remarried, but even if he wasn't, he gave up on me. And I loved him. We had a good life. I missed it when it was gone. I missed him. But that's done, baby, because he did the one thing I can maybe understand due to the circumstances, but I can't forgive. He gave up on me."

Her eyes tipped down to his mouth then back to his and she kept whispering.

"And there is the aforementioned fact that you're hot. But I failed to note that I'm somewhat enamored with your creative uses of my headboard."

He was glad of that, almost more than he was pleased to hear her ex was remarried, and he was thrilled to get that news.

"So we're good," he murmured, moving closer, seeing her beautiful face but thinking about her headboard.

"We're *so* good," she breathed in reply, tilting her head.

Hix took her mouth.

It was necessarily gently. It was also wet. It lasted a long time. It was its usual spectacular. And he didn't care his dick started to get hard during it after Greta started nibbling his lips and mewing in his mouth.

It further didn't stop until they heard, "Greta. Sheriff."

He had his hand tangled in the back of her hair, she had hers wrapped tight around the side of his neck, when they both turned their heads to the street to see a man and woman (a different woman this time) out with a dog on a leash.

"Sheriff," the man grunted, clearly unamused that his wife had interrupted and trying to pull his woman along.

She was standing solid and staring up at them, smiling huge.

"How are you two?" she asked.

"Nancy," her man bit out.

"We *were* great," Hixon told her.

The woman's smile got even bigger.

"Hix," Greta hissed, but he could tell she was laughing.

"Sorry, sorry," the man called and put more force into it with his wife so she would actually start moving. "We'll let you get back to it. Have a good night."

"'Night, guys!" Greta called.

The man waved behind him, still dragging his woman and also his dog.

The woman called, "'Night, Greta!"

Greta turned to him, and when he felt her gaze, he tore his annoyed one from the departing couple.

"Well, that killed the mood," she noted.

It unfortunately did.

"What were you saying about good people in a small town?" he asked.

She busted out laughing but kissed him quickly in the middle of it.

When she sobered she looked deep into his eyes and announced, "I'm telling Andy about you tomorrow."

And he knew he'd at least passed one test.

Brilliant.

"That means a lot, baby," he said softly.

"Yeah," she agreed.

"When you're ready for me to meet him, I'm there," he promised.

She shot him a happy smile. "I kinda can't wait." Her hand still at his neck gave a squeeze. "He likes cop shows. He's gonna love you."

He grinned at her.

She moved in, brushed her lips against his jaw and moved out, murmuring, "Drink your beer, smokey."

"Ten-four, angel."

Greta laughed softly.

He glided his hand from her hair, settled in his chair and threw back some beer.

And then Hix stared into the quiet night, drinking beer and keeping it light as he got to know his woman, pushing it to the last minute until he had to go home and wait for his son.

Late the next morning in his office, after he did what he did every day since things cooled with the case, this being going over Nat Calloway's file hoping something would jump out at him, Hix was reading Donna's report on a bust-up she and Larry had waded into the night before at the Lasso, the country and western club outside Yucca, when he heard Hal call, "Boss?"

Hix looked up to see the man in his door.

"Yup?"

Hal walked in. "Just, uh..."

He stopped talking but didn't stop moving until he was standing between the chairs in front of Hix's desk.

He looked uneasy.

This could mean anything, coming from Hal.

Damn.

"Just what, Hal?" Hix prompted.

Hal moved his neck in an uncomfortable way before it seemed like he forced himself to look in Hix's eyes and he rushed out, "I got no plans on Saturday."

"Sorry?" Hix asked.

"I could..." Hal gave a short cough and started again. "Ashlee said she'd make sandwiches and bring 'em over. And I could, uh...help you all out, movin' you to your new place."

Hix stared at him a beat before he inquired, "You're volunteering to help me move?"

"Not, like, as a brownnose or any of that shit," Hal stated shortly.

"I didn't think that," Hix returned immediately. "I thought maybe I should call in the doc and have your head examined because you clearly forgot the stories of what a huge pain in the ass it was to get that sofa *in* my apartment, and I don't figure it'll be any less of a pain getting it *out*." He shrugged, his lips twitched and he concluded, "You're up for that torture, I'm not gonna say no. But I am gonna supply the pizza and beer at the end. And Ashlee can come and join us then, but she doesn't have to make sandwiches."

"She likes doin' stuff like that," Hal murmured.

"I figure around noon when everyone is plotting my murder, sandwiches will be appreciated." Hix smiled at him. "We're gonna start at eight, man, but anytime you get there would be good."

Hal smiled back. "I'll be there at eight."

"Right."

Hal looked like he didn't know what to do so his movements were awkward when he turned to walk away.

Hix called his name and he turned back.

"Just wanna say at this juncture that I'll be gettin' on writing those commendations for yours and Bets's files, and not because you're helpin' me move. Because you both went beyond the call, her lookin' for Nat, you ridin' that hunch that guy would toss the weapon and finding that gun. It was good work, Hal. Not just solid. It was smart and showed serious initiative. We ever find him, you tied that bow. And I'll make sure that's in your file."

Hal's voice sounded clogged when he said, "Thanks, Hix."

"Not sure why you're thankin' me, but you're welcome."

Hal nodded, moved out looking even more uncomfortable and that didn't change when Donna passed him walking in and she did it smiling at him.

She came right to his desk and her smile went strange as she said, "It sucks I gotta dim the glow of whatever you said to Hal leading him to tackle the herculean effort of proving he's a decent human being, but Jep's here."

Hix looked out the window to see Hope's father standing at reception.

"Jesus, shit," Hix muttered.

"You want me to tell him you're busy?" she offered.

He did.

But that wouldn't nip this in the bud like he had to do.

So he shook his head, coming up from his chair.

"I'll talk to him."

He followed her out but stopped at the back of the aisle between desks and called, "Jep, you wanna come on back?"

"Yeah, son," Jep returned, and then moved through the swinging half door.

Hix watched him and did it noting Jep, who was always sure of himself, looked even more awkward than Hal had.

They shook hands when Jep arrived at him but they said nothing until Hix walked him into his office and closed the door behind him.

He moved to the back of one of the chairs at his desk, stopped, turned to the man and crossed his arms on his chest.

"What can I do for you?" he asked.

"You got time to have lunch, Hixon?" Jep asked back.

"Not really," Hix lied.

"Son—"

"Jep, I got a phone. You got a phone. We need to talk about somethin', you can call me. You wanna have lunch, you can call me about that too. You showin' here, it tells me this is either official business or it's somethin' else. If it's official, you can talk to me here. If it's somethin' else, we gotta have another conversation."

Jep's hand started to move up to his collar, dropped, and he blew out a breath between pursed lips before he said, "I'm sorry, Hixon, but I'm here because I gotta urge you...strongly...to have a sit down with my daughter."

Hix didn't move a muscle. "Right. Since that's the case, I hate to do it but I'm gonna have to do it. This is my place of business, Jep. You don't pin me here because you know I'm gonna be here and Hope's activated you to deal with her shit. That isn't right, it isn't appropriate, and I'll end with it not bein' your style."

"It's important."

"I don't care."

"She's the mother of your children, Hix."

"We got a problem?" he asked.

His ex-father-in-law stared at him a beat before he shook his head once. "No. Nope." He lifted a hand palm out and again dropped it almost before he got it up. "I know you've moved on. Hear she's a great gal. None of my business. But Hope's got some things she wants to explain to you and she knows she's messed it up so she can't approach you. She's sent me as proxy. I'm her father." This time, he lifted both hands low to his sides. "What'm I supposed to do?"

Hix gave him the obvious answer, "Tell her no."

Jep looked to the wall beyond Hix's head.

Hix gave it a few moments before, quietly, he stated, "This can't happen again, Jep. It's not right how you went about this and it's not right how Hope asked you to intervene. She wants a chat, she can grow up, suck it up and ask me for one."

Jep's eyes came to him and his face was set to stubborn.

"You got two girls, you'll learn. They grow up but they never quit bein' your babies."

"Maybe you're right," he allowed. "Maybe one day I'll have cause to remember this and feel like an ass. But if I do, what I'm gonna say is gonna sound harsh, Jep, but it'll be in the middle of me already feelin' like an ass because I know I'm in the middle of a situation where I'm in the wrong for bein' where I am and doin' what I'm doin'."

Jep looked ticked for a second before that wore away and he muttered, "Damned if you ain't right. Knew it before I walked in here but..." He shook his head and finished at the same time Hix's cell rang. "I'll talk to her."

"Obliged," Hix muttered, walking to his phone that was sitting on his desk, saying, "I hope you get part of what she's done is possibly put important things we share, that I'm thinkin' mean something to the both of us, in a bad place."

"Nope, son, I did that not havin' the fortitude to tell my girl to do right."

But Hix didn't hear Jep's reply.

Because he saw his screen told him Greta was calling.

At that time she should be off to Sunnydown to take her brother out for lunch.

Why would she be calling?

"Gotta take this," he muttered, turned his side to Jep and took the call, acutely and irritatingly aware of the company he was in. "Hey."

"Hix, she's here."

Hix felt his spine snap straight at her tone.

"Who?" he asked.

But shit.

He knew.

"Mom!" she cried, giving him the answer he knew. "She's making a huge scene. She knows. She knows it's my day off and I come here to see Andy and she's here. Shouting and carrying on and demanding to see him, saying I'm keeping her away from her baby and—"

He snatched the keys to his Ram from the desk and cut her off. "You with Andy?"

"I can't get to him. She keeps shouting at me and getting in my space, shoving me off. I can't get in a catfight with my mother in Andy's home, Hix!" Her voice had been rising but it dropped with her next in her increasing panic. "I know he's hearing it. Everyone is but his room isn't far from the front. And it's probably *freaking him out*."

That was not good.

But no.

Hell no.

That bitch did not put her hands on Greta.

"Go sit in your car," he ordered, moving by Jep, dipping his chin, saying, "Gotta take this," and that was it.

He was out the door.

"Go sit in my car?" she asked, her voice pitching higher with her also increasing anxiety.

"Go sit in your car," he demanded and stopped between Donna

and Bets's desks. "Both of you," he looked between them, "in a Ram. Follow me."

"Hix," Greta called in his ear as he started moving again, feeling Donna and Bets move behind him.

"I'm coming. I'm bringing some deputies. She can either calm down and remove herself from the premises or she can be arrested for trespassing and disturbing the peace. But I'll be giving her that choice. You'll be sitting in your car while I'm doing it."

"It'll take you twenty minutes to get here and—"

"Not with my lights on."

"Oh," she mumbled.

"Get in your car, baby."

"Okay, Hix."

"I'll be there in ten."

"Right. Okay."

"Letting you go now."

"Okay, darlin'. Uh...see you."

"You will."

He hung up standing by his Ram with Donna and Bets standing with him, eyes to him.

"Greta's mom is at the home where her brother stays. Greta is his guardian. Her mother is a lot of things, including the woman who gave him the injuries he has that put him in the home by driving drunk and getting in an accident when he was a teenager."

That got him big eyes from Bets, narrowed ones from Donna, but he ignored both and kept going.

"Greta's denied her mother access to him. She's there, causing a scene. You heard what I said to Greta?"

"Yeah, boss," Bets replied.

"Yeah, Hixon," Donna said.

"Follow me," he commanded, went to his Ram, angled in and rolled out, the light on his dash and the two that blinked through the grill going as he raced to Sunnydown with Donna driving the Ram, Bets in the passenger seat, following him.

He got the call from Reva that Sunnydown had reported the disturbance on the way.

He swung in at the diagonal yellow lines that were at the front doors of Sunnydown, but he'd caught sight of Greta getting out of her Cherokee as he swung in.

Donna swung in beside him as he folded out of his Ram.

He lifted a hand his woman's way and ordered, "Stay by your car, Greta."

She stopped walking toward him and started walking backwards.

Hix prowled into the building to see a man in a security uniform, big guy, big stomach hanging over his belt, no baton or gun on that belt, not even a Taser, barring the way into a wide hall, staring unhappily down at the woman who was standing in front of him, her voice scratchy from continuous shrieking.

"*You can't keep me from my boy!*" She leaned beyond the guard, who bent that way to impede her should she make a break for it, and screeched, "*Andy! Andy, baby! Your momma is out here.*"

"*Quiet!*" Hix barked.

She jumped and whirled.

Then he watched her lip curl.

"Well if it isn't—" she began.

"I said quiet," he bit off.

"You can't muzzle me!" she shouted then swung an arm behind her, finger pointed. "My baby's back there!"

"You have two choices," Hix announced. "You settle down, get in your car and leave, not to return unless you've received word you've been approved as a visitor for Andrew Dare, or these deputies will be arresting you for trespassing and disturbing the peace."

"I can't trespass where my boy is kept," she spat.

"You aren't legal guardian of your boy so that'd be wrong."

"Just because you're fuckin' my—"

Hix turned and dipped his chin to Donna. "Arrest her."

"*You can't arrest me!*" she screamed and whirled again, making a break to run down the hall and colliding with the security guy who jumped in her way, screeching, "*Andy! Andy! Your momma's—*"

Donna took her forearm in one hand, stating, "You have the right—"

She whirled again and twisted her arm from Donna's hold. "Take your fuckin' hands off me!"

Bets moved in. "Ma'am, calm down."

Greta's mother shuffled back. "Fuck you."

"Ma'am, calm down, turn around and put your hands behind your back," Donna instructed.

"Kiss my ass," she bit out, turned again and shouted, "Andy!"

"Hon, no. No," Hix heard coming from down the hall and he looked that way to see a tall young man with dark hair and a serious scar marring handsome features shuffle sideways into the hall. "Andy, honey—" A woman was trying gently to push him back in the room.

Fuck.

Hix started to make his way there as Tawnee saw her son and shrieked, "*Andy! My boy!*"

Hix halted at Greta's mother, turned his back to her brother and whispered, "You make one more move to resist arrest, we're charging you with that too. Now, I've had occasion to sit in front of the judge recently and we'll just say, with current events, he's not in a good mood." He leaned closer. "But I think someone else will not be pleased you're makin' this play and I got a feelin' you should be more concerned about his reaction. So shut your mouth, Ms. Dare. Calm down. Walk with these deputies out of this building where you'll put your hands behind your back so they can cuff you and read you your rights without your boy seein' them do it, then allow them to take you to the station."

Suddenly, making his stomach turn, she smiled and exposed this was all a play to upset Greta when she threatened in a quiet voice, "Buckle up, baby. I'm just gettin' started."

"Whatever," he muttered and saw her face go slack in confusion before he jerked his head to Donna and she moved in.

She put a hand on Tawnee's biceps but Tawnee snatched her arm away, tossed her hair and didn't even glance at her son as she strutted out of the building, Bets and Donna following.

Hix looked at the security guy. "Could you please follow them and make sure all's well out there, then, when they got her in the back of their vehicle, tell Greta she can come in here?"

"Sure 'nuf, Sheriff," the man replied, then broke into a lumbering jog, following Donna and Bets.

Hix drew in breath, turned and walked down to where Greta's brother was standing outside his room, worrying his lip, staring down the hall where his mother disappeared.

"Andy," he called, and the man's eyes moved from the hall to Hix.

He didn't look a thing like his sister.

But he was a good-looking kid.

He lifted a hand to him. "I'm Hixon."

Andy looked from Hix's eyes to his hand to his badge back to his eyes.

"You're police."

"Yes, Andy, I'm the sheriff."

"Police," he repeated.

Hix dropped his hand and looked to the woman at Andy's side.

She gave him a shake of her head that Hix could not interpret before Andy stated, "Police took Mom."

"I'm sorry, Andy, but yes. Greta's outside and she—"

"Ta-Ta?"

Ta-Ta.

Sweet.

Hellaciously sad coming from a man his height, his age.

But sweet.

"Yeah, buddy. She's outside and she'll be in—"

"Police didn't take my mom."

"I'm sorry, bud, but we had to—"

"Ta-Ta's my mom."

Hix closed his mouth and looked again at the woman with Andy.

She gave him big eyes.

No freaking help at all.

"My sister, but my mom," Andy gave it to him and Hix looked at Greta's brother again.

"Yeah, bud. I get it."

"That lady, I don't care," Andy told him.

"Yeah, Andy," Hix said quietly. "I get it, man."

"Man," Andy said and then he grinned. "I coulda told her to go. I didn't mind tellin' her to go. She doesn't visit much and I don't miss her when she's gone."

"I can imagine."

Andy grinned again, his eyes shifted and his whole face lit up.

That was when Hix watched him lope down the hall and take Greta in his arms, doing it twisting his head to rest the side of it to Greta's shoulder like a little kid.

Hix's gut went tight as he watched Greta wrap her arms around her brother and close her eyes like she just hit heaven.

Andy jumped back, out of her arms, and Hix watched his frame string tight.

"Your face!" he yelled.

"I fell, bud," she said quickly. "That's why I couldn't come last Sunday. My hand slipped away and, *crunch*, busted my nose." She gave him that like it was nothing at all then didn't let Andy focus on it before she grabbed his hand, shook it and asked, "You good? You okay?"

"Police took Mom," he told her.

"I know," she said carefully. "I saw. Are you okay?"

"It was awesome."

Hix felt himself relax even as he watched Greta do the same.

Her mouth quirked as she said, "I'm not sure we should think it's awesome our mother got arrested, buddy."

"Maybe not. It was still awesome."

Hix watched as she drew in a deep breath she was trying to hide pulling in and let it out before she glanced at him and back to her brother. "Did you meet Hix?"

"Hix?" Andy asked, sounding confused. She took a step his way and Andy turned with her, caught sight of Hix and said, "That's the sheriff."

"Yeah, Andy," she confirmed. "Hix. Hixon Drake. The county sheriff."

She was guiding Andy to him by his hand.

"Trespassing and disturbing the peace," Andy said to him when they arrived.

"What?" Greta asked.

"Mom," he said to Hix then turned to his sister. "Trespassing and disturbing the peace." He looked back at Hix. "She's good at disturbing the peace."

"I got that impression."

Andy smiled big at him and repeated, "I got that impression."

He then started laughing.

But Greta was smiling so that was when Hix fully relaxed.

"Do you, uh...wanna, maybe, um..." she stammered then swallowed and finished, "Maybe ask the sheriff if he wants to come to lunch with us?"

Hix felt a burn in his gut like he'd just put back a good bourbon.

"Yeah!" Andy exclaimed. "Yeah, Sheriff. Wanna eat with us?" he asked.

"You can call me Hix, Andy, and yeah. That'd be good."

"We're gonna go to the Harlequin for chicken fingers," he shared.

Hix had been wanting to take Greta to the Harlequin for weeks.

But right then, he didn't give one shit that the first time they sat opposite each other in a booth there, her brother would be with them.

"Sounds good," Hix said.

"Can I ride in your cop car with you?" Andy asked.

"Andy—" Greta started.

"It's a cop truck, bud, and sure. Your sister thinks it's okay."

Andy's head swung to Greta.

"If Hix says okay, it's okay by me," she allowed.

Andy beamed at her then to Hix.

Hix grinned at him and then to Greta. "We'll meet you there?"

She nodded, biting her lip but it didn't quite hide her smile, a smile that was shining at him from her big eyes.

"Ready to go?" he asked Andy.

"Go," he said then he started into his room but looked back. "Jacket," he explained and he disappeared.

Greta got close and Hix looked down to her.

"Are you...I put you on the spot. Is this okay?" she asked.

"Hell yeah," he answered.

That was when she aimed the full force of her smile at him.

Hix fought back a blink.

"Ready!" Andy declared, jumping out of his room.

"Right, let's go, man," Hix invited, wanting to touch Greta, give her a kiss, but just giving her a look before he started down the hall, Andy walking beside him, Greta beside her brother.

"Whoa! Way cooler than a cop car!" Andy declared when he saw the Ram.

Hix bleeped the locks and Andy moved to the passenger side door.

Greta got close and skimmed the back of her fingers against his.

He looked down at her. "He'll be okay with me."

"I know," she whispered.

And more of that bourbon feel hit his gut.

She smiled, looked to her brother, waved and yelled, "See you there!"

"Yeah!" he yelled back from inside the truck.

She moved to her Cherokee.

Hix got behind the wheel.

"You can't do it, you know, 'cause this isn't official or anything, but later, when we get there, can you turn on the lights?" Andy asked when he'd started up the truck.

He looked to Greta's brother. "Absolutely."

"Cool," Andy whispered.

Hix backed out and idled, making a point that Greta caught.

So she pulled out in front of him and he and her brother followed her back to town, straight to the Harlequin.

For a variety of reasons, Hix was in a far better mood when he returned to his department than he was when he'd left it.

And it was so much better, Tawnee calling out to him as he walked down the aisle, "We can get a curtain, Sheriff, put it up, then I can give you the mother part of the mother-daughter experience all private-like," didn't shake it in the slightest.

He'd barely looked at her when Donna said loudly, "Perhaps due to the uncanny resemblance, they gave Greta to the wrong woman at the hospital."

Hix grinned at his deputy.

"You bein' a man-woman and all, just because you couldn't get any dick unless you paid for it doesn't mean you should be ugly to a sister," Tawnee sneered to Donna.

Donna looked over her shoulder at Greta's mother. "I'll tell my husband that after I give him his nightly blowjob."

Hal let out a bark of laughter.

Hix swallowed his.

"Tell him, he wants to feel how good it is when it's *really* done right, he should give me a call," Tawnee returned.

"Honey, if he ever gets the urge for aging skank, I'll send him right your way, and he gets that disgusting urge, you can have him," Donna fired back.

Tawnee shot hate from her eyes but fortunately shut up.

Hix went to his office to make a call he knew he was going to enjoy, not half as much as he enjoyed being let in over lunch on the sweet Greta had with her brother, but it would still feel good.

Allowing Andy to turn on his lights outside the Harlequin might have been a good call.

But Hix suspected he just loved his sister.

So when Greta pulled Hix into the booth beside her, making a point that Andy's damaged brain didn't miss, it just made him grin at them a lot during lunch, it made Hix feel like he'd downed a double shot of the finest bourbon there was.

"Yo, Hixon, how's it hangin', son?" Kavanagh Becker said as greeting when he picked up Hix's call.

"Courtesy call, Becker," Hix replied. "We got your woman down here, arrested for trespassing and disturbing the peace at her son's home."

"Her what?"

Oh yeah.

As he suspected.

Becker hadn't mentioned Tawnee's son in their previous conversations. Instead, he'd said that Greta was the only child Tawnee had. At the time, Hix didn't know Greta had a brother so he didn't cotton on to what Becker not knowing about Andy might mean.

Now he had a feeling he knew what it meant.

Yes.

Definitely.

He was going to enjoy this.

"Her son. At his home. Sunnydown."

Silence from Becker.

Hix didn't extend that further courtesy.

"She lost guardianship doin' time for puttin' him in a place like that after drivin' him home drunk from a party. Greta looks after him. And she wasn't feelin' a lotta love for her mom so she took her off the visitor list. Tawnee felt her next move was causin' a scene on the day she knew Greta came to spend time with him. This didn't go well, not because Greta's seein' me and I intervened, but because Andy doesn't really give much of a fuck his mother was arrested. But this is neither here nor there for you. These aren't serious charges, we'll just make a note of the arrest on her record and I'm happy to release her to you under her recognizance and her promise that she doesn't do that shit again."

Becker still said nothing.

"Did I lose you?" Hix asked.

"We got a problem because of this?"

"You mean a bigger one than the last one she caused?" Hix asked for clarity.

"Yeah," Becker bit out, not sounding happy.

The light went out of his voice when Hix ordered, "Come get her ass and impress upon her I don't want it in my department again. Be convincing, Becker. And for your efforts, I'll share you know I don't like what you do. You also know you bought me steppin' over the deal you had with Blatt. But I figure you further know I got dick on you or I'd have been up in your shit after you made your last bad play. So that's where we are. You trip up, I catch it, we'll go from there. You stay smart, I won't have any choice. In the meantime, you buy me not feelin' the need to get really fucking nosy for a good while, you get that woman to refocus on something other than her daughter and son."

"Not sure how you got the idea she means that much to me," Becker replied.

"Then she has a problem and so do you because right now I'm feelin' your connection more than you are, and everything she pulls, I'll read as shit comin' direct from you. And I can assume you'd understand it doesn't make me happy to walk into my department and have her offer up a taste so I can compare mother and daughter."

"Jesus," Becker muttered.

"Those blowjobs probably don't seem so awesome right about now, am I right?"

"I'll send a man to get her," Becker stated on a sigh.

"Obliged."

He gave it a beat before he said, "I didn't know about her boy, Hixon. That shit's fucked up."

Like him understanding the concept of a mother disabling her own son because she operated a vehicle inebriated made Hix think he was a better person.

"You're correct," was all he said.

"I'll deal with her for you then I'm scrapin' her off. Too much trouble," Becker declared.

"That's not my business. Just take her off my hands, and for now, we're good."

"My man is already on his way."

"Thrilled," Hix muttered, said, "Good luck," and he hung up.

"Please, God," Bets begged, walking in the second he put his phone down, "let me record five minutes of that woman and then let me shoot her. Judge Bereford won't arraign me, he listens to five minutes of her crap. He might pin a medal on me."

"Becker's sending a man to pick her up."

"Becker?" she asked.

"Ms. Dare likes to be multi-faceted in the ways she's a piece of work."

"Can I hide in here until he shows?" Bets asked.

He smiled at her and joked, "Where's badass Deputy Bets?"

"Badass Deputy Bets is badass enough to admit she can't spend another minute with the trash in our cell and she's okay with that, that trash is so trashy."

"Then go on patrol, don't bug me."

She grinned. "Good idea. I'll take Donna with me. And Larry. And Hal."

"Bring me a coffee from Babycakes."

"You got it, boss."

He looked down to the file he'd never finished reading but back up to her when she called his name.

Then he braced when he saw her face.

"It was uncool," she said hesitantly. "I was just bein' stupid. You're a good guy and there's not a lot to choose from around here, but you were—"

"It's okay, Bets," he said quietly. "Forgotten."

"Yeah?"

He nodded.

She shot him a relieved smile and disappeared.

Five minutes later, he got up and walked to the door she'd left open when Tawnee screamed, "*Where's everyone going? Fuck you! I didn't do dick! Let me out!*"

He shut it, shutting out her voice.

He did it thinking that Donna's suggestion had merit.

They looked alike.

But Hix had concerns when they handed Greta to her mother in the hospital, they'd given her to the wrong woman.

"So, HE LIKES YOU."

"Yeah?"

"Like, a lot."

"Good."

Hix and Greta were not on her porch that night.

They were making out, stretched on her couch.

As well as, apparently, talking about her brother.

Hix didn't want to talk about her brother.

"What we got?" Hix asked to change the subject, sliding his mouth up the side of her neck.

"What we got?" she asked back breathily, sliding her hands up either side of his spine.

He made it to her mouth and looked in her eyes. "Hours."

She knew exactly what he was talking about.

"Twenty-two."

He grinned against her lips.

She frowned against his.

"Shaw's gonna be home soon," she noted but did it with her arms closing around him.

"Yeah," he grunted, doing it rolling off her, to his side, and taking her to hers in front of him.

She shoved her face in his throat and held on to him.

He buried his face in her hair and held her back.

"Thanks for today," she whispered against his skin.

"My job in two ways."

He felt her press close.

It was a good response.

And all she had to say.

She tensed against him when she warned, "She's just warming up."

"We'll get through it."

"You've got kids."

"She sinks even lower, which it's clear she's capable of, I'll talk to them and then we'll all get through it."

She pulled her face out of his throat and he tipped his head down to look at her.

"If that guy dumps her—"

He'd told her about Becker.

"Baby," he gave her a squeeze, "we'll get through it."

"Just...batten down the hatches."

He grinned. "Consider them battened."

She frowned at him. "It sucks you can be cute and hot and you won't have sex with me."

"Twenty-two hours," he reminded her.

"My nose is not attached to my lady parts, Hixon."

He started laughing, gathering her closer. "It feel better?"

"Yep."

"Every day?"

"Yep."

"Then trust me."

She rolled her eyes.

When she was done doing that, he ordered, "Now kiss me. I gotta go home to my son."

"Just to say, after I'm done with my clients, I'm helping you move on Saturday. I'll be done at three."

"You can unpack boxes."

"My nose is also not attached to my arms or legs."

"You can unpack boxes," he repeated.

"Part of me thinks I should not find a protective man annoying, but I do," she informed him.

"Get over it."

"I also find a bossy man annoying," she shared.

"Get over that too."

"And a repetitive one."

"Greta?"

"What?"

"Kiss your man so he can get home to his son."

"Whatever," she muttered, but still, she kissed him, wet and sweet.

Then he pulled them both off the couch and walked her to her door, holding her hand.

It was Hix who kissed her, wet and sweet, at the door.

"Twenty-two hours," he whispered when they were done.

She shot him one of her blinding smiles. "Yeah."

He touched his lips to the tip of her nose, let her go and walked out.

He heard the lock go before he was halfway across her porch.

Twenty-two hours.

An eternity.

Chapter 20

Something Worth Fighting For

Greta

"You're really good."

"I don't suck."

"No. Really. You're really good."

"Thanks, man."

I stood beside Hix just outside the gates of Raider Field, watching a just-showered-after-the-game Shaw lift a hand and smack Andy on the biceps.

I'd just watch the Raiders lose (unfortunately).

But I'd done it with my brother sitting on one side of me, Hix on the other, Mamie wedged in between me and Hix.

This happening part of the game.

The rest of it, she'd wedged herself between me and Andy and they got in a competition to chatter each other's ears off, a competition that ran four ways with Maple and Snow.

It was a little bit of a surprise that Mamie hung with her father (and Andy and me) when her mother, uncles, aunts and grandparents were sitting in those same bleachers not too far away.

But we'd barely sat down before she was jumping down the seats to give her dad a hug, me a hug (which was sweet) and then shoot Andy a huge smile and cry, "Is this your brother, Greta?"

That started it and it didn't end. Lou had come with the girls and they sat on the bench behind us, so I got to chat with her and Andy got to hold court with Mamie and Maple (Snow took off with some of her friends).

He'd loved every second of it.

So had I.

I just hoped he remembered it.

For me, it was a night I'd never forget.

"Your dad's the sheriff," Andy informed Shaw, and I tensed, not thinking Shaw would be strange about Andy telling him something he very well knew for reasons he probably couldn't fathom, just understanding sometimes talking to Andy could be awkward until you got to know him and understood how he expressed things.

I didn't have to worry.

Shaw just smiled big and said, "Yeah, bud."

"He arrested my mother," Andy shared.

Shaw's smile faltered, he looked to his dad but looked back to Andy when he kept talking.

"It was *awesome*."

"Right," Shaw muttered, fully regaining his smile but Andy lost his attention when Wendy (Shaw's girlfriend was one of my clients, I now saw) walked up.

He lifted an arm her way and she slid under it so it was around her shoulders.

"Hey, babe," he said. "This is Andy, Greta's brother. Andy, this is my girl, Wendy."

"Hey," she said shyly to Andy.

"Hey," Andy greeted Wendy.

I studied Shaw and his girl.

Wendy was a good kid and I'd always thought she was pretty. Lots of ash-blonde hair she begged her mother to let me highlight (her mother hadn't yet given in but I hoped she would soon because it would be fabulous). She was long, slender, but not tall, just average height, so since Shaw was tall, she fit right into his side like she was meant to be there.

Very nice.

"Hey, Mr. Drake. Hey, Miss Greta," she called to us.

"Wendy," Hix replied from where we were standing five feet away, with me in the same hold as Shaw had Wendy.

"Hey, honey," I called in return.

"You gonna go get pizza?" Andy asked them and both Shaw and Wendy looked to him.

Shaw shuffled his feet a bit before he answered, "Yeah, Andy, do you wanna...uh...come with us? We can, well...take you back home after."

It seemed Wendy snuggled closer to Shaw when he offered that.

As for me, I did the same into his father but only so I wouldn't melt into a pool of gratitude that Hix's boy was such a good guy.

"Aren't you, um...goin' on a date?" Andy asked in confusion.

"Uh...yeah," Shaw answered.

"Then you don't want me there." Andy twisted at the waist and threw a hand Hix and my way. "Anyway, Ta-Ta and Hix gotta take me home so they can go on their date."

I loved my brother.

But we *so* did.

"Right," Shaw replied through a grin.

"We'll go to pizza some other time when you aren't on a date so Ta-Ta and Hix can have *another* date," Andy told him.

"Yeah, man, that'd be awesome," Shaw said, still grinning.

"Cool," Andy muttered.

"We should all probably get going," I called. "Shaw's undoubtedly hungry after that game and it's getting late."

"Yeah," Andy agreed, looking my way and then turning to Shaw and Wendy. "You did good tonight, sorry you didn't win." His attention turned to Wendy. "Cool to meet you."

"Cool to meet you too, Andy," she said.

"Thanks, bro," Shaw said. "See you later." But with that, he went on, "Uh...Sunday? That's your, uh...day with Greta. So, um..." He glanced Hix and my way before he looked back to Andy. "Well, she's with us on Sundays now so we get you too. Right?"

I didn't know the Drakes had claimed my Sundays.

But since I liked the Sunday I'd had with the Drakes, and they wanted Andy too (or at least Shaw did, but I seriously doubted Hix would argue), that worked for me.

Just as long as it worked for Andy.

It did and I knew that when my brother shot Shaw a bright smile. "Yeah. Yeah. Sunday." He moved toward Hix and me but did it still aimed toward Shaw and Wendy. "Have fun."

"Thanks, you too," Shaw replied.

"'Bye, Andy," Wendy said.

Hix's arm around my shoulders tightened as he turned us while we called our goodbyes to his son and his girl, and Andy fell into step beside us as we walked toward his Bronco.

There weren't many people left hanging around after the game. We'd said goodbye to Lou and the girls before Shaw came out and Mamie had taken off with her mother, who made it clear she was taking pains to ignore the fact that Hix and I existed, and she did this by leaving and not hanging to tell her son his team might have lost, but he'd done a good job.

That said, her parents both came right up to Hix, her dad shaking his hand and introducing himself and his wife to me in a surprisingly friendly way (though, I knew Hope's mom, Marie, she was a client of Lou's).

Marie gave Hix a brief hug before she smiled hesitantly at me and they both took off after Hope. Hope's brothers and their families didn't do the same, though one of the brothers gave Hix a wave, and both wives did (one, Jessie, was my client and she hadn't stopped being that even with all that was happening, the other one, Molly, was Lou's client and she'd been in two Thursdays ago so clearly they also weren't holding grudges, which was a relief).

I found all of that interesting.

I didn't pay it much mind because I found it concerning that Mamie stuck by our sides until the very last minute, trudged to her mother only when called as they were leaving, and she did this like she was dead ballerina walking.

Also concerning was the fact that Corinne popped by once during the game to give her father a pointedly dutiful hug and kiss, her greeting of me and meeting of Andy vast degrees warmer than the chill she gave her dad. I noticed she hung with friends most of the game, and left with them, but that didn't mean she didn't spend a whole quarter of the game sitting beside her mother and her family.

The dis to Hix was not veiled just as Mamie's dis to her mother wasn't either.

Yes, this was all concerning.

But these were the only things that dimmed the brilliance of the night, having Andy with us, but mostly having Hix make a statement to the entire town that he was with me. When the opportunity was afforded him, he did it with his arm thrown around my shoulders, holding my hand, dipping down to touch his mouth to mine. And he did it in a way no one could be in any question, what with Andy and Mamie with us, Corinne dropping by, Lou and Maple sitting close, and in the end, Shaw, that we were to the point we weren't together, we were *together*—merging families.

And although I was concerned about both Mamie and Corinne, I loved all that so much that the dim of that barely shadowed the brilliance of the rest.

Making things better, we were only T minus the trip to Sunnydown and back before I could connect with my man in the way I'd been wanting to connect with my man since the second he actually, officially became *my man*.

When we hit the Bronco Hix opened my door for me, and I

caught Andy's big smile that he did as my brother climbed into the back seat.

I settled in and was grabbing the seatbelt while Hix was closing the door, and that was when I caught the soft look on his face as he stared at my ass sitting in his passenger seat.

And that was when I knew.

Andy sitting in Hix's Bronco.

Me sitting there.

Andy being invited to Junk Sunday.

T minus less than an hour before I had Hixon Drake naked.

Yes, that was when I knew.

I knew this was it.

Having this, building it, keeping it...

I'd fight for it.

Finally, I'd found something to fight for.

Mom could pull her shit, and I'd battle her to the death.

Hope could pull her shit, and I'd go head to head to keep hold on my man, his kids, the promise of the life he was offering.

I'd take any lick they could offer, and if it meant having Hixon, I'd keep on ticking.

Hixon had barely closed the door after he'd folded himself in the driver's seat when Andy asked, "Are you comin' with Ta-Ta to get me on Sunday?"

Hix's eyes slid to me, his mouth twitching, his hand turning the key in the ignition, as he replied, "Yeah, bud. You up for early? We do donuts in the morning."

"Heck yeah!" Andy cried.

I felt my lips curl up as I looked out the windshield, the ignition caught and Hix slid her in reverse, thinking, yes.

Oh yes.

I'd finally found it.

Something worth fighting for.

And if I had to, I was going to fight for it.

Because I was falling in love with complicated.

Hix's head dropped so he could bury his face in my neck and I felt his heavy breathing against my skin just as I felt the weight and warmth of his body pressed to mine, his cock buried deep, fingers of one of my hands in his hair, the fingers of the other one laced in his, my legs curled around the backs of his thighs.

He'd just come.

He'd taken me there a few minutes before.

It had been like the first time. Fast and desperate, then slow and gentle and sweet. Kissing, nuzzling, touching, tasting, gliding, connecting like we had all the time in the world.

And like we'd have just that.

For the rest of our lives.

Hix's breath started to come easy and his mouth started to work my skin where he murmured, "You good?"

I'd never been better.

"Yes."

"Your nose?"

"It's fine, baby."

He lifted his face out of my neck and looked into my eyes before he touched his mouth to mine, to the tip of my nose, and then he slid his hand from where he had it curled around the back of my neck down to where his thumb came out and he stroked the side of my breast.

"Good night?" he whispered.

Yes, it had been good.

More than good.

I slid my hand from his hair to his cheek and whispered back, "No, Hixon, it was great."

His blue eyes registered that, openly gave me just how much it meant to him, before he dropped his head and kissed me, deep and wet and beautiful. All through it his fingers threaded through mine, as they'd been since the moment he'd slid inside me, squeezed.

He ended the kiss, his eyes roamed my face then he raised them to look over my head before he looked again at me.

"We neglected your headboard."

I grinned at him. "It's not going anywhere."

His return grin gave me a shiver when he replied, "Nope."

His face disappeared into my neck again where he slid his lips up from the junction of my shoulder to my ear, sliding his cock out as he did, and he said, "Sucks, but I gotta get back to the apartment early tomorrow, sweetheart." He again lifted his head and looked at me. "Shaw and I have packed approximately three boxes in the last week. We don't have a lot but I gotta get him outta bed and we gotta get some more shit boxed up. We have the unit until the end of the month but the sooner I can close the door on that place forever, the happier I'll be."

This made me frown, because in the last week when he wasn't working or with his kids, he'd been with me and it hadn't occurred to me once to go to him and help him get ready to move.

"I'm sorry, Hix, I didn't think. We should have been packing last night, not making out on my couch."

At that, he didn't grin but smiled huge like I was hilarious.

"Babe, if you think I mind rollin' out of your bed at oh dark thirty to start a day of packing boxes and lugging crap because I made the decision to make out with you on your couch and not pack boxes last night, you'd be wrong."

I smiled back. "I see."

"And tomorrow's gonna suck because moving sucks, but after tomorrow I'm gonna have my kids in a good place that's two blocks from you and that is *not* gonna suck."

I kept smiling. "I hear that."

He was still smiling too. "So what I'm sayin' is, I gotta deal with this condom and then we gotta settle in because I need some shuteye, seein' as I'm not twenty-three anymore and I can't go all night with a woman and roll outta bed and spend all day doin' somethin' physical without it kicking my ass."

I was enjoying gliding my free hand along the skin of his back, holding him anchored to me with my legs around his thighs and also still smiling when I asked, "When you were twenty-three, could you go all night with a woman?"

He looked to the pillow over my head and muttered, "Maybe we shouldn't talk about this."

I wrapped my arm around him and gave him a squeeze with it as well as my legs as I teased, "I thought tops for a guy was three times in one night...maybe."

He looked down at me, brows raised. "You read that in some woman's magazine?"

I quit smiling and stared at him.

Then I asked, this time seriously, "When you were twenty-three, could you go all night with a woman?"

"Greta—" he started hesitantly.

"No, really, I wanna know," I told him.

"I didn't have half a dozen people showin' at my house tomorrow at eight with only three boxes for them to move, I could go all night tonight."

I felt my eyes get wide right before they narrowed.

He was full of it.

"That's impossible," I declared.

He grinned. "And that sounded like a challenge."

"No, Hix, it's physically impossible."

He dipped his grinning face close. "No, baby. See, the key is, to go all night, I gotta make it so *you* got your mind on other things so the last thing on your mind is counting how many times anything happens for me."

My body experienced another shiver as I whispered, "Oh."

"Though I didn't know that when I was twenty-three, so to answer your question, yes. That three times is bullshit. But since then I learned how to play it so I can have all the fun doin' a lot of the work but not *all* of the work, if you catch my meaning."

I was still whispering when I replied, "I totally catch your meaning."

He touched the tip of his nose to mine before he continued, "You want me to have a go at doin' all the work, I'm up for that challenge too." He pulled half an inch away. "Just not the night before I gotta wedge that couch out the door of my apartment without sending it flying over the side of my stairs."

"I wondered how you got it in there," I shared.

"Brute force and a promise to God I wouldn't say 'fuck' for at least a week."

I started shaking under his big body with my laughter. "Did you keep your promise?"

"Barely."

I lifted up, brushed my lips against his and dropped back. "Go, darlin', so you can come back and we can get some sleep."

"All right, baby," he murmured, returned my lip brush then rolled off.

I turned out one of the lights on the nightstand before he came back and Hix turned off the other one before he slid back in beside me and curled me into him.

Once there, I curled in deeper.

"Hix," I called into the dark.

"Yeah?"

"I love it that you made a son who would ask my brother to go with him and his date to eat pizza."

His arm around me pulled me even closer and I felt him do a slight curl before his lips touched the top of my head.

He settled back in before he murmured, "I do too."

I turned my head, rubbing the point of my chin into his chest before I put my lips to it and whispered, "And I love it when you hold my hand when you're moving inside me."

His hand slid up my back, over my shoulder, so he could use the backs of his knuckles to stroke my cheek. "I'm glad, Greta, 'cause I love doin' that too."

I tilted my head back, rested my chin on his chest and looked at his shadowed face. "And I love it that your self-imposed, unnecessary ban on sex due to my broken nose, a ban you also imposed on me, is finally over."

"Greta?"

"Yes?"

"You're cute, you're funny and you're sweet, but you need to shut your mouth and go to sleep."

Since he sounded like he was smiling when he said that, I grinned through the dark, turned my head and rested my cheek to his chest.

He kept stroking my face for a while before he moved his hand to curl it around my waist and hold me tucked to his side.

I loved other things about that night, about Hix, about his kids.

But I'd tell them to him later.

Right then, naked with my man naked at my side, I fell asleep.

I WAS on my hands and knees, naked, scurrying to the side of the bed in order to get in a better position to attack with the intent to win because this had gone on *way* longer than I expected and something had to give, when Hix's fingers locked around my ankle.

He pulled it, which meant he pulled my knee out from under me. The other knee went as his hand left my ankle, both went to my hips, and he whipped me on my belly perpendicular on the bed, him between my spread legs.

He then yanked up my hips, putting me back on my knees.

And at this maneuver (not the first time it happened that session, but much stronger than all the others), the walls of my pussy convulsed.

I flipped my hair around so I could look over shoulder at him and they convulsed again when I saw the dark, hungry expression on his face as he stared down at my ass.

Right.

Naked bed wrestling with Hix was over.

It was time to get down to business.

"Fuck me," I whispered and his eyes sliced to mine. "Fuck me, Hix. Hurry."

One of his hands left my hip and dove between my legs, scoring a path of electricity from clit to nipples that made my hips jerk and would have made my mouth protest that was all he gave me, no matter how good it was, if he didn't lean away and I didn't hear the drawer of his nightstand opening.

I ground into his hand and he fingered me as I watched him tear into the condom packet with his teeth.

God.

That was hot.

"Baby, hurry," I breathed, rocking against the magic of his fingers.

His gaze came back to burn into mine as I felt him shift closer, his movements, the promise of what was about to come making the insides of my thighs quiver as I tried to brace.

And then he was there. The tip of him at my opening.

He removed his hand, both went to my hips, and I reared back as he thrust in.

I tossed my head, feeling my hair drifting over sensitive skin, as I moaned low, "Yes."

He curled over me, mounting me, one hand cupping my breast, fingers pulling at my nipple, the other arm slashing across my upper chest, fingers curling around my shoulder, hauling me back into his drives.

God, he was good at this.

"Yes," I whimpered it this time, moving with him, meeting his thrusts, the noises of our flesh slapping together sounding in the room mingled with his quiet grunts, my muffled mews.

My whole body quaked when his teeth sunk into my shoulder blade and he growled, "Who won?"

He wasn't serious.

"Just fuck me," I begged.

He pulled out so I only had the head.

I twisted my neck to spear him with my gaze. "Don't stop."

"Who won, Greta?"

"Fuck me, Hix."

He tugged hard on my nipple, grinned a grin that should be illegal it was so damned sexy, and repeated, "Who won, gum drop?"

I was going to kill him.

After he finished fucking me, of course.

"I want your cock back," I demanded, and him being a man who liked using his cock the way he'd been using it, I didn't think I'd have to say it twice.

"You'll get it, you declare me bed wrestling champion of the millennium."

All right.

Someone shoot me for waking Hixon Drake early on the Sunday morning after he'd moved into a new house and throwing down the gauntlet in a tease that I'd take him in the bed wrestling championship of the millennium, seeing as I thought I *could* take him considering he'd gotten up early the morning before, made love to me before he left at six thirty and then he'd been engaged in the strenuous activity of moving all day.

I had some moves in my arsenal. They mostly involved my hands, fingers, lips, tongue and teeth, but not strength, though I could be fast and I'd only stood on my feet for hours then unpacked boxes the day before.

I thought I was good to go.

Problem was, Hix was all that plus strong, and clearly moving hadn't taken anything out of him.

Not a thing.

But he'd just taken something out of *me* and I wanted it *back*.

"You," I bit out.

"Me what?" he pushed, still grinning that *fucking* grin that just made me want him back inside even more.

I tried to press back.

He moved with me and thus withheld.

"Hix!" I snapped.

"Me what?" he pressed.

I gave in. "You win."

"Which makes me what?"

I glared at him.

His fingers rolled my nipple.

My eyes slid nearly closed as my legs trembled.

"Which makes me what, baby?" he coaxed, gentle and sweet.

The gentle and sweet did it for me.

That and I wanted his cock and was in the mood to say just about anything to get it.

I opened my eyes. "It makes you the bed wrestling champion of the millennium."

Slowly, making my eyes go hooded again, but I still caught his grin melting to something that was even hotter, he slid back in as he murmured, "That's right, sweetheart, now take your fucking from the champ."

I felt his lips draw the curve of my shoulder blade and whispered, "Yes," as I commenced taking my fucking from the champ.

He kept me anchored with his arm across my chest but moved his hand from my breast to between my legs where he played with me as he fucked me. He did this unrelentingly, and amazingly, until I pressed my forehead into the mattress, reared back, my fingers fisted in his sheets. My cry was stifled when the force Hix was building between my legs exploded and tore through me, making me shudder uncontrollably under him.

I kept doing it as his arm around my chest left me and he pushed me to my belly in the bed with his hips, his cock planted inside. He braced his weight into his forearm beside me, his finger on his other hand still working at my clit, his mouth at my ear as he pounded me into the bed.

Oh my God.

How could I be coming and I was going to start coming again?

"Give it to me again," he growled.

"Yes," I gasped and pushed out, "Yes, baby."

"Dig your ass up, I want more, Greta," he ordered roughly.

I did and he might have gotten more, but I did too.

Oh yeah, I was going to come again.

"Hixon," I whispered.

"Fuck yeah, Greta," he rumbled.

My body started trembling, I whimpered, "Ohmigod," and bucked under his weight, my head slamming back so far it hit Hix's shoulder, and the second blistered through me, leaving me shuddering beneath him through the jolts as I kept taking his thrusts.

His finger left my clit so he could wrap his arm around my belly and hold me steady to take him before he slammed in and again, and again, and again, pressing his forehead into the side of my neck and grunting through his orgasm, each sound he made slithering over the skin of my back and ass, crazy-delicious.

His climax sounded *awesome.*

But both of mine had felt better.

I caught my breath and he caught his before he kissed my neck, slid a hand up my side, over my shoulder and up to tangle in my hair. He pulled it out of the way and nuzzled all of the back of my neck, flexing his hips into my ass, his still-hard cock inside me, and all this felt really freaking good, so I shivered under him.

He did this silently and I took it silently for a long time before he slid out, gliding his lips down my spine as he did.

They swept the small of my back to my ass before they disappeared and he murmured, "Be right back."

I felt him leave the bed but not leave me until he closed my legs and caught them at the knees, shifting them, and me, to the side, bending my legs up. I then watched as he leaned in, brushing his lips along the top of my hip before his eyes caught mine. He grinned a grin that wasn't wickedly sexy, just sweet, before he pushed up and away. I then kept watching as he disappeared into his bathroom.

I curled my knees up higher, and after some of the cloud of great sex coasted away, I took stock of a fact I'd taken stock of before I started my bed wrestling demise. This being that Hix's master was at the front of the house (like mine) and Shaw's bedroom was at the back of the basement, it was early, so as I suspected prior to foolishly instigating the bed wrestling championship of the millennium, we should be good in the sense there was no way Shaw could have heard anything.

Hix came back, strolling casually in his earth-shatteringly awesome nakedness, with his fabulous chest that had a smattering of dark hair that was thicker between his pecs, thinner but far more than a sprinkle outward from that. It climbed up but disappeared just under his collarbone and narrowed entirely in a thin but not dense line down his midriff and stomach.

He had boxed abs but they weren't cut, just lightly defined.

He also had thick, dark-furred thighs and great calves.

All of that was amazing.

But his cock was perfection. Perhaps slightly over average length, more than slightly over average in breadth, the formation was where it was at. It was absolutely flawless.

And watching it come my way, still somewhat hard, attached to the rest of all that was Hix, I was getting turned on again.

Yeesh.

I forced my attention to his face, caught a look at his expression, and felt my eyes get squinty as he entered the bed, doing it claiming my space and *me*, forcing my knee then my thigh over his hip as he forced his knee between my legs and pulled the rest of me into his body.

He rolled slightly into me, giving me some of his weight, and commenced doing verbally what his face had been doing inaudibly.

Gloating.

"I think I've decided my nickname should be 'champ.'"

"Don't be an annoying winner," I shot back.

A grin curled his lips. "Don't be a poor loser." He looked to my mouth, up and over my hair then leaned slightly away to look down at my body before his eyes came back to mine. "Though, not sure how you could be, you comin' that hard twice, doin' it after begging me to fuck you."

"I didn't beg," I bit out.

He pressed into me again and dipped his face to mine. "You totally begged."

"Did not."

"You so did."

Whatever.

"And I didn't come *that hard*," I lied (again).

He started chuckling and kept gloating, "You bucked so hard when I was fucking you into the bed, you nearly bucked me off."

I turned my eyes to the mattress, muttering, "Now you're being a dick."

He shoved his face in my neck and murmured, "You like my dick."

Yeah, I did.

Though I wasn't giving him that.

"Now you're being an ass."

He nipped my ear.

I didn't quite fight back the shiver that caused, and I definitely didn't fight back the irritation it caused when I felt him smile against the side of my neck before he challenged, "You wanna try to take my ass, we'll have the bed wrestling match of the millennium part two, which, by the way, sweetheart, you'll totally lose that too, which means I get to slide up *your* ass."

I shivered again.

Hix chuckled again before he slid the tip of his tongue down my neck.

I moved my hands to press against his chest, and I'll admit (only to myself), I did it feebly and not only because I didn't have the strength to put more oomph behind it, but because he smelled good just being Hix in the morning, but also being Hix after sex in the morning. Not to mention he felt good and he was all warm and strong and goddamned *Hix*.

"I like this," he whispered into my skin.

"Yes. You're making it *very* clear you like winning."

He pulled his face out of my neck to look at me and said, "Yeah, baby. I like that. I like the kind of trophy I got to claim winning. But I also like that you're a really shitty loser."

"I'm not a shitty loser," I retorted.

"You're totally pouting."

I felt my mouth form into a (deeper) pout. "I'm not pouting."

"Totally are."

"Hix—"

He cut me off by going in for a hard press of his lips against mine and then he pulled back.

And after that, with no warning, he changed my entire world.

"You're gorgeous. You're funny. You're loving and kind and hard-working. You like to take care of me and I like that you do. You listen. You give honestly. You make great breakfasts. You're fantastic with my kids. We're combustible in bed. I love making love to you. I love fucking you. But you're a shit loser and that's awesome because I was beginning to get a complex thinking I'd found the perfect woman and I'd never live up to that."

My insides had seized but he just gave me a big smile and kept talking.

"Good to know you got at least one flaw." His big smile got huge as he finished, "Two, seein' as you suck at wrestling."

"You think I'm perfect?" I whispered.

"*Thought*," he corrected. "You suck at wrestling, remember?"

I stared at him and the beautiful, teasing light in his pool-blue eyes shimmered away and became a tender, attentive light.

"Greta? Sweetheart?" he called.

"She can't have you," I blurted.

The tender, attentive light flickered out as his brows drew together and a perplexed look took over.

"What?"

"She can't have you," I repeated. It was stronger this time and included me scratching my nails through the hair at his pecs like I could latch on to him through the sinews in his flesh.

He leaned into me and I bore more of his weight as he brought his face closer to mine.

I knew he got me when he said, "Baby, you don't have anything to worry about."

"Okay," I stated curtly, fighting trembling for another reason as emotion started to take control of me. "But if she tries, if she makes a play, I'll fight her and I'll keep fighting and I won't let her win." When I noticed the intensity of his stare, I tried to take the intensity that was just plain me down about a dozen notches. "Like I just let you do."

He brought his face even closer before he declared, "You didn't let me win."

I opened my mouth.

"Shut it, Greta."

I shut my mouth and then it was me staring at him.

Because he was looking at me like no one had ever looked at me.

"You're not gonna have to fight anything," he proclaimed.

"If she—"

"Greta, sweetheart, quiet."

I went quiet.

Hix didn't.

"It's you. It was you from the first time you sat your ass across from me at that table at the Dew and you know it. I knew it. It freaked me and I bailed, that's how strong your pull was. All the shit I jacked up between us was because I couldn't deal. I couldn't adjust that fast to being given a shot at something so fucking beautiful when my life had turned to such shit. I couldn't believe in it. I wouldn't let myself believe. But in the end I didn't have to do dick because you turned out to be just as beautiful as you are and I had no choice but to let you make me believe."

Holy hell.

My bottom lip started quivering.

Holy hell.

"Ohmigod, you're gonna make me start crying."

His gaze grew soft on me. "You can't start crying, gum drop. You gotta get your ass up, showered and in my Bronc so we can go get your brother, some donuts, wake my boy and commence Junk Sunday."

Junk Sunday.

With Andy and Shaw.

And Hix.

"I think I'm falling in love with you," I whispered.

That didn't get me a soft look.

His face went harsh as his lips bit out, "Jesus, fuck."

Oh no.

Shit, no.

"Okay, I...okay, I get it. Too soon. It's way too—" I started to backtrack but was cut off when Hix totally leaned into me, giving me all his weight at the same time running a hand down the inside of my thigh that had been at his hip, pushing it open so his hips fell through when he got me on my back.

"Shut up," he growled while moving into me. "After you gave me that, I gotta fuck you again, do it quick, find a way to make you come again after I just got two hard ones outta you and do that in time that we don't make your brother worry or delay Junk Sunday and make my boy ticked."

His face disappeared in my neck as his hand delved between my legs, I gasped, but I also moved my hands to catch his head on either side and pull it up.

"Hixon—" I tried to start again but that was as far as I got.

"Yes," he clipped confusingly.

And then, joyously, he kept speaking.

"It started for me the second your eyes moved through that room and you looked right at me and didn't stop lookin' at me while you sang 'At Last.' You were singing those words to me but I was feelin' those words about you, Greta. So yes. Fuck yes. Get that look off your face, baby, because it's not too soon. It's where we are. So it's just right."

I stared up at him.

He stared down at me.

My eyes started to get wet.

He saw it because he again bit out, "Jesus, fuck."

And in the worst timing in history, his cell on the nightstand rang.

Both our eyes went to it and he repeated an even more terse, "Jesus, *fuck*," before he looked again to me and said, "My job, I gotta—"

"Get it, honey," I whispered.

He bent to touch his mouth swiftly to mine, but when he reached to the phone, he pulled me with him so we were diagonal on the bed with me still mostly under him when he caught sight of the screen.

My body strung tight as I watched his face turn to stone.

I forced my gaze to his phone and saw the back of it, his thumb moving on the front and he put it to his ear.

"I swear to Christ, Hope, if this isn't about one of the—"

My body had strung tighter at the name he spoke only for it to threaten to snap when I caught the look that hit his face before he rolled off me, knifing up to sitting, but yanking me up with him and plastering me with his arm around me to his side.

"How long?" he asked and there was barely time to take a breath before he went on, "Okay, I know, of course you don't know." He was now speaking in a calming tone, doing it taking his feet at the side of the bed and hauling me up with him. "You call your dad?" he inquired. "Okay, right. Get off with me, Hope, call him. Her girlfriends' parents. Madam DuBois. Anyone you can think of she'd go to. I'm goin' out to look for her." A pause while he pulled me to his closet, my heart racing at listening to his words and what they might mean. "Yeah, now. Goin' out now, Hope. You hear anything, you call me, okay?"

We were in his walk-in closet. I flipped the light switch on and went right back to him, pressing into him, one arm around him, one hand at his chest.

"Yeah. I'll do the same," he said. "We'll find her."

"Oh God," I mouthed, no sound coming out but it was like Hix felt it because he looked down at me.

"Right. Yeah. Gotta go look so lettin' you go. Okay?" He paused. "Okay. Later, Hope."

He listened for a split second then took his phone from his ear.

"Hope was gonna surprise the girls with a shopping trip today, takin' 'em to Scottsbluff. She went in to tell Mamie she had to get up and get ready and Mamie wasn't in her bed. She woke Corinne. Mamie isn't anywhere in the house. They looked everywhere, she's nowhere. Gone." He sucked in a deep breath through his nose and finished, "I gotta get on the road and find my girl."

"Oh God, Hix, of course, yes," I replied, rushing to the back of the closet where there were some as-yet-unpacked suitcases and boxes filled with clothes, dropping down to my knees in front of one to unzip it and flip it open.

That was as far as I got. I didn't even get a look in to see if any of his jeans were there before he wrapped his fingers around my biceps and pulled me up and around to face him.

"Get dressed, sweetheart. I need you to get dressed. I can find some clothes."

Of course, I was naked.

I was so stupid.

I needed to get dressed.

I nodded and ran out to the bedroom where he'd dumped the bag I'd brought over with me yesterday.

I had panties and bra on with my jeans up but undone when the doorbell rang.

I stilled in buttoning my fly and looked to the bedroom door, but then my eyes flew to the closet as Hix tore out of it wearing jeans, a thermal in his fisted hand, his phone in the other.

He sprinted out the door and I wasted only the time it took to bend and tag my top before I took off after him.

I was pulling the top down at the same time hiking my jeans up because they were still undone and sliding down my hips when I raced down the stairs to see Hix pull open the front door.

"Daddy," I heard and I halted on a sway, nearly slipping off the stair four steps from the bottom but not caring if I went down, my relief at hearing Mamie's voice was so intense.

"Jesus, Mamie, Jesus, baby," he rumbled and squatted.

Coming right back up, he carried her in, holding her tight to him, leaving the door open behind him.

I quickly did up my jeans and then hurried to the door to close it as he pushed his girl's face into his neck, still holding his thermal so her face was hidden from me, and he swayed her in his arms, muttering, "Jesus, God, baby. You scared the hell out of me."

"I'm sorry, Daddy." Her voice came muffled against his skin, and then I heard a sob and her arms locked around him but she pushed her head back to look at her dad's face before she wailed, "*I can't be there anymore! I wanna live here with you! I wanna live with you and Shaw. I wanna live with you, Daddy. You and Shaw and you...and...and...you!*"

After that, she shoved her own face in her father's neck and her slender, not-so-little-but-still-little girl's body bucked in his arms as she burst into loud, body-wracking sobs.

I moved into Hix's line of sight in an attempt to assess his state of mind only for him to catch my gaze and reach out with the hand he had still holding his phone.

"Call Hope," he mouthed.

I moved immediately to take his phone and he wrapped his arm back around his girl, moving to the couch and swinging out her legs as he sat in it with her in his lap.

She burrowed deeper, still bawling.

I'd taken his phone but my heart was hammering in my chest at the idea of calling Hope.

But she had to know, immediately, that her daughter was safe.

I looked down at the phone and started to rush out of the room toward the kitchen.

"Fourteen, nine, three," he called, and I looked back over my shoulder at him, nodded and then hurried into the kitchen, touching Hixon's code into the screen.

I went to recent calls, saw Hope at the top and touched her name.

I put it to my ear, it rang once, and she answered saying, "I called Dad. He's coming into town. I'm making calls to her friends. Corinne's helping me. I—"

"Hope, I'm so sorry to interrupt you but you've got Greta and you need to know that Mamie's here. She's with her dad. She's all right. I don't know what's happening but she rang the doorbell before Hix had the chance to go out to look for her, but she's here. She's fine. She's safe. She's with her dad."

"She's there?" Hope asked for confirmation.

"She's here. She's fine and she's here."

She wasn't fine. She was bawling and asking to live with her dad but at least she was safe and healthy and the people who needed to know where she was knew where she was.

"She's there, honey. She's at your dad's," I heard Hope say, probably to Corinne, her relief running so deep, it dribbled out of the phone into my ear.

I drew in a breath.

"I'll...I-I'll..." Hope started but said no more.

Okay, crisis over and I had Hix's ex on the phone.

Now what?

"I, um...why don't I get him to call you after he calms her down?" I suggested.

Wrong thing to say.

"Calms her down?" Hope asked.

"Well, she's wound up about something, and Hix was intent on you knowing she was safe so he just gave me his phone and I gave them privacy and came into the kitchen to call you."

"You're in Hix's kitchen at seven thirty on a Sunday morning?"

Without thinking, I looked around Hix's kickass kitchen that beat even my awesome kitchen by a mile.

First, it was bigger. It also had a showstopper recessed ceiling over the island that had been set in old, tamped tin. There was a copper hood over the stove. The many cupboards had different finishes, a mix of cream, distressed green and dark wood. The upper cabinets that had windows also had arched panes that were amazing. Further, there was a copper sink that had a faucet that looked kind of like an old-fashioned well pump. The floors were immaculately refinished wood. And the pièce de résistance was a recessed pantry that had latticework screen doors covering it that I'd give my eyeteeth for.

It was sublime.

The minute I saw it (and his porch, which was also a lot like mine, but wider and longer and it had a porch swing) I totally hoped the people who owned it *adored* Florida and never stepped foot in Nebraska again.

What it also had was a drawer microwave in the island in the middle, that microwave was the only thing in the room currently that had a clock on it that was programmed and I couldn't see it from where I stood so I had no idea what time it was.

But seven thirty sounded about right.

That said, in all that was happening, I had no idea why Hope would ask that question.

Then it hit me, and I might know why, but I still didn't.

I walked to the island and put my hand to it, saying, "Hope, why don't you let—?"

"My son is in that house," she declared.

"I'll get Hix to—"

"Unless he's at a sleepover. Is he at a sleepover?"

"Hope, please, if you'd let me—"

"I cannot fucking believe you," she hissed, her voice lowered like she was hiding what she was saying, likely from Corinne. "I cannot fucking believe *him*. But you, you're a woman. People say you raised that brother of yours. *You know better*."

"I—"

I said no more that time because the phone was no longer to my ear.

I whirled around and watched Hix put it to his.

He had his thermal on.

And he had a face filled with thunder.

Oh man.

"I asked Greta to phone you and tell you Mamie's okay and I can only guess why that conversation lasted longer than it needed to but I'm too pissed to get into that now. Mamie's here. Mamie's fine. She's upset and she needs some time," he declared into the phone and kept right on talking. "I'll call you when it's cool for you to come and get her. But before that, my girl, her brother and I need to have a chat. Then I'll need to have a chat with you. But I'll let you know when we're ready for you to come and do that."

He listened for a second. I watched him do it and his face didn't clear while he did.

Crap.

"No, you won't come now. I told you, I'd call you..." he trailed off, his eyes flashed, he scored them through me and I felt my own eyes get big at the fiery look in his. I bit my lip and he clipped into the phone, "Listen to me, Hope. She's done with your shit and she wants to move in with me. I do not think that's right. And all our kids have got to get where we're all at and get on the path to movin' on. Now she's at an age she needs her mother. But if you keep fuckin' with me and shovelin' your shit my way, *I swear to fuck*, I'll file for full custody of all of them and I'll use every goddamn dollar you wanted me to use for that fucking ring you wanted so damned bad to get them. Are you hearing me?"

He didn't listen for very long before he continued.

"We're not talkin' about that fucked-up shit now, Hope, and far's

I'm concerned, we're not talkin' about it ever. Yes, I know. I've known for a while. It's done. I've moved on. You need to pull your head outta your ass and move on too. Now, I'll phone when we're ready for you." He took in a sharp breath and finished, "Later."

With that, he rang off and stood there, completely still, staring at his phone like it was taking a superhuman effort not to hurtle it across the room.

"Baby," I whispered.

His eyes cut up to my face.

"Is she okay?" I asked.

"Hope?" he asked incredulously.

"Mamie," I answered.

He no longer looked incredulous but still, his mouth got tight before he said, "She knows about her mom wanting that ring. She hears her mom bitchin' to her friends about me. About you. Talkin' trash about you and Lou and Bill, Lou havin' a foul mouth and Bill bein' a drunk and both of them bein' bad influences she doesn't want around her kids. And about me movin' into this house, sayin' I did it because it's close to you. And she's done with her shit. She misses what we had. She's too young to understand all that's going on. It's too much for her. And it's simpler with me. It's more peaceful. It's not ugly. It's not negative and pissed off and bitchy. And she can't wrap her head around that ring. So she's pissed and she's hurt and the hurt is makin' her more pissed. So no. She's not okay."

"Okay," I said softly, moving into him.

He didn't hesitate to slide an arm around me, so I did the same to him with both of mine.

"I gotta get back to her and I also gotta wake up Shaw," he told me.

I nodded. "I'll go get Andy and we'll do something else—"

"No you won't."

I stared up at him.

"Will he freak, comin' here, bein' involved in a drama?" he asked.

"Um, did you block out the two times you met my mom?"

He stared at me back then his lips twitched and I felt some of the tension ebb from his body.

"If we need privacy, you guys can go somewhere, unpack some shit, sit on the porch, go out and get some food, whatever excuse you gotta make to make it cool with Andy," he said. "But with all the shit that just went down, I did not forget what happened in my bed right before it did so you're a part of this now, Greta. So is Andy. That means you need to swing with this. If he's got it in him and it doesn't harm him, he needs to swing with it. And my kids need to see that you and him aren't going anywhere."

"Oh crap, you're gonna make me cry again," I warned, pressing closer to him.

His hold tightened on me and he murmured, "We got even less time for that shit now."

"Right, yeah, of course," I muttered, drawing in breath to pull myself together.

"She's gonna start her period soon."

I stopped pulling myself together as I felt my head twitch at his comment.

"Sorry?" I asked.

"Corinne started at her age. She's gonna start developing. She'll need to go out and buy bras and shit. I can deal with that. You're around, you can help me deal with that. Corinne can help her deal with that. But she should do that with her mother."

I slid a hand around to press it to his chest and agreed, "Yeah."

"Hope needs to get her head out of her ass."

I nodded and repeated, "Yes."

He held my eyes for long moments before he blew out a breath.

Then he stated, "I promised Andy I'd go with you to get him. I need to get Shaw up, have a word with him so he's with the program then talk to him and Mamie, and then we'll head out."

"I can go get Andy while you look after your kids, Hix."

"I promised him I'd come with you."

"He'll understand."

He shook his head. "I'm not breaking the first promise I made to your brother, Greta. Big shit is happening here but that's important. I need him to know he can trust me and through that he can trust me with you, and I don't know how he processes things. Something little you think he'll understand might mean more to him than either of us know so I gotta handle that with care. It's forty minutes. You and Andy and Shaw can go out and grab donuts when we get back while I look after Mamie and we'll take it from there."

I was totally not listening.

I was stuck on, *I'm not breaking the first promise I made to your brother, Greta.* With a little bit of dealing with, *Something little you think he'll understand might mean more to him than either of us know so I gotta handle that with care.*

So he had to give me a little shake and ask, "Greta, babe, you with me?"

I nodded.

Because I absolutely was.

More than he knew and I suspected he knew I was definitely with him.

He nodded back and ordered, "You get a quick shower while I deal with my kids. Then call Andy and let him know we'll be there soon and give him whatever heads up you gotta give him so he knows what he's walking into. I'll shower while you do whatever else you gotta do and then we'll go. We got a plan?"

"We have a plan," I said quietly.

"Good," he muttered, bent to me, touched his mouth to mine and then moved us directly out of the kitchen.

I broke plan just a hint by checking in with Mamie, giving her a hug, assuring her it was all right and I wasn't mad she freaked her dad and me out, and then promising donuts were coming soon.

The last part didn't work as well as I'd hoped but it did get me a sliver of a smile.

After that, I went about instituting our plan.

It was in his shower, Hix's words hit me.

But with all the shit that just went down, I did not forget what happened in my bed right before it did so you're a part of this now, Greta. So is Andy. That means you need to swing with this. If he's got it in him and it doesn't harm him, he needs to swing with it. And my kids need to see that you and him aren't going anywhere.

I was worried about Mamie.

I was worried for Hix because he had a lot on his plate.

But for the life of me, as I showered, I couldn't stop smiling.

Chapter 21

Yup

Greta

It was late Sunday morning and we were hanging out on Hixon's furniture in his living room, watching TV.

Not surprisingly, considering his gender, Hix had shared with me he'd ordered the cable to be installed first thing after signing the rental agreement. So the guy had come to do it while he was moving in the day before.

In other words, we were watching the pre-game shows in clean, clear HD with the decimated remains of the plethora of donuts Shaw, Andy and I had gone out to get all over the coffee table.

I'd found the day before that Hix had a storage unit and his friends had emptied that as well as his apartment.

It included an old, beat-up desk that Hix had put down in the basement in a room that was just cement floor and unfinished walls that was meant for storage. But he put the desk there with the addition of boxes of his stuff from the unit (these being boxes of stuff from his life with Hope and before). Framed pictures of him and cop buddies, team pictures of him with his friends in baseball uniforms, old trophies, yearbooks and the like. This room was obviously going to be his man cave.

The stuff in the unit also included a big loveseat that matched his furniture, two big ottomans, one double-wide, to go in front of the loveseat and armchair, and another end table that hadn't fit in his apartment.

Upon seeing this the day before, it had given me pause for reflection because it stated, when Hix had outfitted his apartment, he'd done it with a mind to his future. If he was convinced he could fix things with Hope, he wouldn't have needed all that furniture for the house he'd eventually be setting up for his kids, because it certainly didn't fit in his apartment and it was the kind of furniture that didn't come cheap in a set.

With this in mind, I wasn't sure Hix thought there was something to save in his marriage before he even gave up trying to save it.

This was a conversation for another time and that morning was not that time and not simply because everyone was on tenterhooks waiting for Hope to show and pick up Mamie.

No, it wasn't that time because I was pissed and getting even *more* pissed.

By, like, *a lot.*

This was because I'd had time since the drama occurred with Mamie leaving her mom's house very early in the morning and *walking* two miles to get to her dad.

It wasn't that far in the grand scheme of things and it probably didn't take long.

What it did was veritably *scream* her desperation to get away from her mother so she could get to her father.

And Hope had created that. Hope had done it not only from the beginning, divorcing a man like Hix, a *father* like Hix, for a stupid, fucking ring, but also behaving like a bitch and not having the motherly chops to hide it from her daughters.

However, it was more.

Much more.

Since I called Andy and shared what I could share so he'd know what he was walking into, I was able to think (and Andy was sweet as pie, he just felt bad for Mamie, Shaw and Hix and said, "I don't have to come today if you think it wouldn't be good, Ta-Ta," to which I was happy I could reply, "Hix wants you with us, buddy.")

I was able to think about what I'd walked into the day before after I got done with my last client. Seeing Hix's house for the first time, being in it, seeing the big rooms and the fantastic wood floors and the great fireplace and the fabulous kitchen. Seeing how his furniture fit in it, it wasn't cramped and way too nice for the space. There were boxes around, and when I showed, they were in the middle of moving furniture in the living room this way and that to see where they'd settle it, but it still already looked like a home.

It was also seeing Hix with his buds but more *feeling* it.

I knew Donna and I dug Donna. She was a tell-it-like-it-is woman who was hilarious. I'd liked her from the first time she sat in my chair at the salon. But I'd met his other friends and they were great. They talked and they gave shit and they worked hard, all for their friend because they were good friends but also because it was a good day.

A happy day.

A new beginning that held promise because a person they cared about was setting the crap life had hit him with behind him and moving on.

There was a weird vibe with Hix's deputy Hal I didn't get, but he was nice and he worked as hard as the rest without complaint.

He also hung with his wife, Ashlee (one of Lou's clients, a sweet lady, though she had a strange sadness about her all the time that I'd always wondered about) and all of us for pizza and beer when all the big work was done.

We'd joked and laughed and chatted and shared stories, and it was clear they all loved Shaw to death and the same with Hix.

It felt good being around them. It felt good being a part of this new beginning that had such hope. It felt good that there was no tension, no worried looks, no caution, just friends hanging together after helping out a bud. It felt good being in that great house, the kind of house that Hix belonged in, where he could give his kids what he wanted them to have.

It felt real and natural and mellow and they'd all been welcoming to me at first, but that had melted into a feel like it wasn't the first time I met Larry and Tommy and Toast and Herb and Hal, but like I'd known them ages.

It had been awesome.

And part of that awesome was knowing that Hix was going to be taking the afternoon off on Monday because his girls' bunkbeds, dressers and desks were going to show, the sectional for the basement was as well, since he'd already bought them. I also knew that when the girls came back Monday night, they were going as a family to J&K's Electrics to buy a TV for downstairs. The girls had already bought new sheets and comforters for their beds, they got them online and they were in big boxes in their room, ready for the furniture to arrive (except the sheets, I put them in the washer to prepare for the girls' arrival the next day).

So it was all happening. They were all settling.

Sure, Hix needed some rugs and some stools for the island in the kitchen and things up on his walls. And he hadn't lied. He might have bought furniture and towels but he didn't go whole hog on anything else, had the bare minimum for his kitchen, so unpacking boxes didn't take hours.

But they were there, and all that would come whenever it came and it didn't matter when that would be.

They had the important stuff.

And another part of that awesome was knowing that Andy would be there that next day, as would I, sharing Junk Sunday with Hix and Shaw.

And the reason I was pissed, and getting more pissed, was the fact that, although that day had started great for Hix and me, Hope had screwed it all up.

She'd screwed everything up.

Hix and Shaw couldn't enjoy their first day in their new house kicking back, watching football, relaxing and eating a lot of garbage.

No, because Hope's crap had leaked in in the form of a desperate, sad, angry, sobbing young girl, who should be feeling none of those things, and they'd all been given no choice but to deal.

It didn't surprise me that it was Andy who kept the vibe as sweet and smooth as it could be. Mamie was withdrawn. Shaw was showing signs he might be even more pissed than his dad. And Hix was trying to hide it, but I could feel the struggle he was having in controlling his anger and frustration.

So Andy being jokey and playful and excited about donuts and enthusiastic about Hix's house and downright thrilled at how *cool* it was Shaw was going to be a marine (and so on) was semi-saving the day.

No one had forgotten the drama and everyone was on edge because Hix had called Hope to come get Mamie, and we were all waiting for her to show, but at least Andy got to be Andy. He might have sustained damage to his brain that forever challenged his abilities to live what was considered a normal life, but he'd never displayed any alteration in his functionality at being able to read a room and react to that, in this instance, being himself—loving and sweet.

So it was his eyes I caught first when the doorbell rang.

Shaw was cuddling his sister in the loveseat. Hix and I were in the corner of a couch. Andy was in the armchair. And when the bell rang, any smooth and sweet in the room vanished and Andy bit his lip then stretched out the lower one before his shoulders slunk up to his ears.

I gave him a careful smile as I felt Hix's arm around me give me a squeeze before he set me aside and pushed out of the couch.

I turned to look at Shaw and Mamie, who had been lounged together, but now Mamie was on her behind with her knees pulled all the way up to her chest, her arms around her calves, her chin to her knees and eyes to the door and Shaw was standing, facing the door.

"It's gonna be okay, guys," I tried to reassure them, but Shaw's lip just curled and Mamie only glanced at me before looking back toward the door so I figured it didn't work all that great.

Right.

For me and Andy, it was time to clear the donuts away and set about making French onion dip and whatever else we could do in order to stay in the kitchen and give the Drake family privacy.

I started to open my mouth Andy's way and fold out of the couch when I heard Hix mutter, "Hope, Jep."

But I froze when Shaw hissed, "Unbe-freaking-leivable."

I looked to Shaw then over my shoulder at the door where Hope was walking in, face a mask of fury as her eyes lighted on me and that fury didn't change when they took in Andy. It only minutely changed when her attention swung to Mamie.

Hope's father was walking in behind her.

He seemed to be feeling ill at ease, but I didn't know the man and I didn't get to take time to analyze his demeanor because Hope spoke.

"I love you. I love you more than you will ever know, until you have a child of your own. But Mamie, you scared me to death this morning and that is not okay."

"I can't believe you," Shaw clipped and didn't make anyone wait to find out what it was, precisely, that he couldn't believe. He shared it. "You brought *Gramps*? You're, like, forty-one years old and you got your butt in a sling and you bring *your dad*?"

"Shaw," Hix muttered warningly.

I shoved to the edge of the couch and said softly, "Andy and me will just—"

"Yeah, why don't you *just*," Hope spat and I froze again, looking over my shoulder at her hate-filled face aimed at me.

"Hope," her father murmured irritably.

Before I could snap myself out of it and get a move on, Mamie stopped me by speaking.

Or, more accurately, with what she said when she did.

"You're mean," she whispered then spoke louder. "You're just *mean*. Like, you're a grown-up mean girl. Like, so mean, they could make a movie out of you and everyone would hate you, that's how mean you are."

I decided not to look at Hope's reaction to that because I felt the sting of those words snapping in the air, it hurt something awful and it wasn't even directed at me.

I also decided not to speak again. I just pushed out of the couch and reached a hand out to Andy who was already getting up. He took my hand and we started to move toward the kitchen but stopped when Mamie spoke again.

"Greta, don't go."

Shit.

I turned to her. "Sweetie, I think it's best Andy and I hang in the kitchen while—"

"I want you to know, in front of her," she pointed to her mother, "that I like you. I like you with Daddy. You make him happy. And things have got better for him since you've been around. And if he got this house because it's close to you, then good. Because it's closer to Corinne and me too, when we're with Mom. And it's a pretty house. And it's the kind of house Daddy and Shaw should live in."

"Thank you, Mamie," I said softly. "I like you too, honey. And you're right about this house, though you should know, he didn't get it because it was close to me. He got it because it was right for his family. Now Andy and I should—"

"And I wanna live here, even if you live here too," Mamie declared. "Like Mom says you're gonna be moving in, because you make things happy."

I sucked in a huge breath and looked to Hix.

"Greta isn't moving in, baby," Hix said gently.

"Yet," Shaw put in.

I bit my lip, squeezed Andy's hand and he started tugging it, shuffling us to the kitchen.

"There are things you don't understand, Mamie," Hope shared.

"Yeah?" Mamie asked. "Well tell them to me."

"You're too young," Hope replied.

"I'm not too young to know that Shaw's right. I get it that Daddy hasn't been with Greta very long and he's got us so he can't move her in, like, right away. But I see how they are together and Daddy makes Greta happy too. So she might not be moving in now but she will and that's okay by me, and it doesn't matter what you think or all you have to say about it to Miss Julie, it has nothing to do with you because you threw him away."

"Baby..." Hix started, and Andy gave my hand a harder tug pulling me out of the room and into the kitchen.

He rolled the pocket doors closed behind us then crowded me back so we were at the opposite side of the kitchen.

We both stopped by the sink and turned to stare at the doors.

It was Andy who broke our silence.

"Jeez, Ta-Ta, I'd rather deal with Mom than that lady out there."

I looked to him to see his gaze still on the doors and stifled my giggle that came because my brother was funny but also might have been because I was slightly hysterical.

When I controlled my inappropriate mirth, I asked, "You wanna make onion dip?"

He looked to me and his mind wasn't on dip. "You okay?"

I nodded.

He stared at me.

Then he said, "Okay, Ta-Ta. Let's make dip."

We made dip. Then we grabbed chips. Then I found a pad of paper and a pen and I started to make a grocery list for Hix and his kids because, in unpacking the kitchen, I'd noted that Hix did not have many of the basics of cooking. I did this with Andy bent over the island with me, helping me. We figured out how to program the coffeepot. And then we just hung together uncomfortably, through that and all we'd done before, our eyes straying to the doors.

They finally opened and I was surprised to see not Hix or Shaw coming through, but instead, Hope's father.

He shut them behind him but did it facing us and saying, "Just gotta give that family some time."

I pressed my lips together and nodded, unpressing my lips to say, "Of course."

"You're mean to my sister, I won't like it," Andy declared, and I looked to him to see his chest puffed out and he was edging my way.

"I wouldn't dream of bein' mean to your sister, son," Hope's dad replied, moving to the opposite side of the island from where we were.

"Okay," Andy muttered and relaxed.

"Are they...how are they doing? Are they okay?" I asked.

But before I got my last word out, Shaw could be heard shouting, "*God, Mom! You're unbelievable!*"

"Not too good," Hope's father muttered.

I felt for him. He looked sad. So sad, he looked vulnerable and defeated, like his years were decades more than he'd actually lived.

There was nothing I could do about that except get even more pissed Hope was all Hope was.

"Andy, this is Mr. Schroeder. Mr. Schroeder, this is my brother, Andy," I introduced.

"Good to meet you, Andy. And please," his eyes moved from Andy to me, "both of you, call me Jep."

"You want onion dip?" Andy asked, reaching out to shove the bowl and bag of chips across the island toward Jep.

"Not feelin' hungry, son, but thanks," Jep murmured, but did it with his eyes trained on the dip and they didn't move.

I looked to Andy.

He looked to me.

The pocket doors opened and Hix strolled through.

"Jep, Hope's goin'. Mamie's stayin' with me. She's with me tomorrow anyway so no reason with the state of things for her to go back now. I'll have time to get some things straight with her and she'll go back to Hope after next week."

I examined Hix's face and saw he didn't look furious, but he didn't look any less angry and frustrated than he had been all morning.

"Right, son," Jep replied, turning. "I'll just get on with gettin' her home." He stopped next to Hix, lifted a hand and rested it on Hix's shoulder. "We'll just..." he patted Hix's shoulder and removed his hand, "get past this. All of us. Eventually." He turned to Andy and me. "Wish it was better circumstances. Maybe next time it will be."

"Yeah, Jep," I said. "Take care."

He lifted his chin, Andy mumbled a farewell and Jep took off.

Hix walked farther in. "We gotta change Junk Sunday to Going-to-Dansboro-to-Pick-Up-Beds Sunday. Mamie needs somewhere to sleep and she isn't sleeping her first night in this house on the couch. So I might need your Cherokee to get it all in. The place is in Dansboro. You up for that, babe?"

I nodded. "Absolutely."

"I'm good at carrying things," Andy proclaimed.

"That'd be great, bud, since Shaw and me'll need your help," Hix replied.

I turned to my brother. "Hix is under the mistaken impression that my broken nose means I can't lift things."

"Doesn't seem mistaken to me," Andy returned.

I rolled my eyes only to roll them back and see Andy grinning.

"Gotta call the store then we'll move out," Hix muttered and my attention went back to him.

He moved out before I could say anything and Andy moved out with him.

I moved to find some plastic wrap to cover the dip so I could put it in the fridge and join them.

It wasn't until we were all going through the (also awesome) mudroom at the back of the house that led to the garage, where Hix had parked both the Bronco and my Cherokee, that I could grab Hix's hand and waylay him.

Andy, and Hix's subdued kids, kept moving.

Hix stopped and looked down at me.

"You okay?" I asked softly.

"I'm gonna sit down with Hope next week and hear her out. It's what she wants and the woman goes all out until she gets what she wants. It shits me I gotta give her that, but if doin' that might bring some peace to my family, I'm gonna do it. I'm gonna freakin' hate it, but I'm gonna do it. So right now, I'm pissed and feel like I'm trapped in a corner, but if all I gotta do is listen to her shit to get outta that corner and buy some peace for my kids, I hope like hell I'll be better after it's over."

I nodded and squeezed his hand. "I'm sorry, baby."

"I'll get it done quick as I can and then, hope like fuck, this can be put behind all of us."

I nodded again.

"I'm gonna do that and Mamie's staying with us but I don't want her to get the impression she can pull crap like she pulled this morning and get her way. This situation is extreme but I gotta have faith Hope will get her shit together and be the mother her kids need so they can stop lickin' their wounds or tearin' 'em open wider and start healing. If not..."

He let that lie and I shifted closer. "How about we cross that bridge if we come to it?"

"Good plan," he muttered.

"We should go," I said.

"Yeah," he replied and gave my hand a tug.

And then we moved out.

The bunkbeds were set up and they were great. A double on the bottom set perpendicular to the single on the top, made of wood painted white, a ladder with a little wardrobe to the side and a cute shelf off the top bunk that could serve as a nightstand.

The girls had picked a pretty green and white comforter with flowers and leaves for the double bottom, a matching, gorgeous matelassé quilt for the top, shams to match the comforter, white sheets and green toss pillows, with the addition of a nice strike of blue with green trim for another toss pillow to make it interesting.

Mamie shared with me this vision was Corinne's and she had an eye.

We picked up the bed and mattresses from the store, but we could also fit in one of the desks (which was more like a vanity since it had a mirror) and a dresser so we put those in too and the guys set them all up. The rest of the furniture would be waiting for Corinne tomorrow.

While the guys were setting up, I offered Mamie a fifty dollar online gift card and we sat on our butts in the hall, going through Shaw's laptop and ordering a lamp and a cute picture to go in the room. I told her Corinne would have the same, Mamie could tell her she had it, and she could help pick out stuff and email it to me and I'd order it.

But now, we were both on our knees on the floor in front of her dresser, finishing up putting her stuff away from the only boxes that hadn't been unpacked, and although she'd gotten excited to buy her lamp and picture, she was quiet again.

I didn't know what to do. The times when Andy was around that age and he could listen and retain (maybe, he *had* been a teen) what I said were long ago.

That said, even then I didn't know what to do. I just went with my gut.

So right then, I had to go with my gut.

"She was frantic, your mom, when you took off," I said gently as I handed her a folded leotard.

Mamie ducked her head and shoved the leotard in a drawer.

"Mamie, I'm not saying that to make you feel bad," I told her. "Life stuff happens and sometimes it makes us feel so much, we don't think before we react. We just gotta do whatever we have to do because we hope it'll make us feel better. And then we learn and hopefully the next time we feel too much, we'll have it in us to take a second and think. I'm just saying this because your mom is in a bad place right now, but you need to know that she loves you very much."

She turned to me and declared, "See. Right there."

When she said nothing else, I replied, "I'm not sure I see, sweetie."

She gave it to me immediately. "You're bein' nice. About her. She's not nice about you."

"Well, I don't know your mom and I can't say why she does the things she does. All *you* need to know is, I speak truth. No matter all that's happening, she loves you."

"If she loved me she'd see it hurts me to watch her hurtin' Daddy and she'd stop doing it," she retorted.

She had a point.

So I just folded another leotard.

Her next came timid.

"Will you talk him into lettin' me live here with him and Shaw?"

I looked to her. "No."

Her face fell then it got hard.

I lifted a hand to the back of her head and gave her ponytail a little tug before I leaned close to her. "I want you to have what you want and I want you to be happy. And you don't know it now but you need your mom and your mom needs you."

"She doesn't need me. She's got Miss Julie to talk nasty to and help her stay angry."

Another point.

"Things are gonna be happening with you—" I started.

But she cut me off. "Yeah. I know. Boys and maxi pads and blah, blah, blah. Dad's lived with girls his whole life, I mean, he had a mom then he had *my* mom. When he went to the store, he bought her tampons like he'd buy a bag of potato chips and he didn't catch fire or anything."

I couldn't stop my chuckling. Her lips quirked and she took the leotard from me and put it in the drawer.

Her mood shifted back as she muttered through quivering lips, "I wanna live with him."

"And there'll be a day a long time from now when you'll look back and you'll understand a whole lot more what your mom is going through and you'll wish you had your share of time with her."

Mamie looked at me and I kept going.

"I promise you that, Mamie. I'll tell you straight, because I think you deserve it and I'm not sure you're getting a lot of that with what's going on around you because you're the baby and they want you to stay the baby even though you aren't a baby anymore, but I agree with you. Your mom is acting out because she's upset and scared and hurting, and maybe she isn't acting the right way. But just today, you took off and scared both your mom and dad like crazy. So if you think about all the things you were feeling that made you behave that way, maybe you'll understand a little about all the things your mom is feeling that are making her behave in ways that aren't right."

Her mouth set, she jerked up one shoulder and she reached past me to get another leotard.

I just grabbed my own and started folding it.

Mamie changed the subject.

"I like Andy."

"He likes you."

"If...when...you know, say you and Dad get married, am I not gonna be the baby anymore?"

I was confused.

"Why wouldn't you be?"

"Because you and Dad will have babies."

My hands stilled but my mind didn't.

I'd told him I didn't want to have a family and how that affected me and Keith. And Hix had already made a family.

But he hadn't said then if he'd want more.

We were both no longer young. We were also both not old.

Damn.

"Greta?"

I pulled it together and looked to Hix's girl.

"Do you understand that what your dad and I have is very young?" I asked.

She nodded.

"So we haven't gotten around to talking about that yet, and because of that, I have a feeling something about it is weighing on your mind. But do you get that if I haven't talked about it with your dad I shouldn't with you?"

Something lit in her eyes as she said, "Yes."

"So how about we not talk about any more heavy stuff now and get you settled in then go down and join the boys and eat more food that's really bad for us?"

That bought me a smile as she agreed, "Let's do that."

I smiled back, folded a scary amount of leotards and helped her clear the rest of her stuff. We had just begun breaking down boxes, an endeavor Hix must have heard because he joined us and ordered us out so he could do it (apparently, girls couldn't break down boxes either).

Since that wasn't my favorite task and there were only eight, we left him to it and went down to join the boys, the game and eat really bad food.

"I'M NOT sure this is the right thing to do."

"I am."

I sat on the side of Hix's bed and watched him walk into the bathroom.

He closed the door.

I stared at it.

It was late.

Andy was back at the home. Shaw was in the basement. Mamie was in bed across the hall.

And I was spending the night, according to Hix, but I wasn't sure that was the way to go.

He came out of the bathroom and I caught his eyes immediately.

"Hix, we need to slow this down."

He walked right up to me, stopped and stared down at me.

"What, baby, from our conversation this morning gives you the impression we should slow this down?" he asked gently.

"The drama with your daughter that happened right after it," I answered.

He bent to me and rested both hands on the sides of my neck. "Is this happening?"

"Yes, but—"

"Is it very much happening?"

"Yes, Hix, but—"

"Is there gonna be a day when you're makin' breakfast for more than just me in my kitchen?"

I nodded and whispered, "I hope so."

He nodded too. "So everyone has to get the message that's gonna happen, Greta. And I'm not usin' you to make a point to my ex-wife or my kids. In that everyone, I also mean you. If you have genuine reason that any delay in relating that message will be useful, I'll listen. But it is what it is and it's gonna be that for a long damned time. So why delay it?"

Another Drake with a good point.

"Mamie asked me if we got married, if we'd have kids," I divulged.

The pads of his fingers bit into my flesh momentarily before he let me go and straightened.

"What did you say?" he asked.

"I said I hadn't even talked to you about it so I didn't feel it was right discussing it with her."

"Good answer," he muttered.

"Hix—"

I said no more because he tagged my hand, pulled me up but he did it only to sit and tug me back down, right in his lap.

He wrapped his arms around me and only spoke when I looked into his eyes.

"You said you didn't want kids," he remarked carefully.

"I don't," I replied just as carefully.

"I got kids."

I smiled a small smile. "I know."

"Babe, you feel like changin' your mind, you wanna make a baby with me, we'll talk. But right now, that part of my life is behind me and I'm girding for losin' my babies to the lives they're gonna lead. I'm not feeling a hankering to go through that again." He lifted a hand and ran his fingers along my jaw, murmuring, "We'd make a beautiful baby so if you want that door open, we'll talk. But if you don't, I'm down with that too."

I stared at him and I did it not thinking about Mamie or Hope or our crazy day.

I did it thinking about all the times I'd had this very conversation with Keith, the crushing guilt that I so very much didn't want to give him something he so very much wanted, that guilt compounded by the fact that he already gave so much I felt I was being doubly selfish not giving it to him.

But it wasn't like he wanted an expensive new car that you could find a way to pay for or eventually sell and move on.

He wanted to make a child with me.

And I loved kids but the one I'd had had been work even before my mother hurt him in ways that would never heal. So in the end I'd just wanted Keith and Andy and calm and peace, because I'd never had the chance to live my life just how I might want it. I never would have that chance because I'd always have Andy, and I didn't want more.

But with Hix, it was if you want it, we'll talk and I'm leaving that door open, if you don't, we're good.

And I couldn't cope with it being that easy.

"Baby, have you changed your mind?"

Hix's question jolted me out of my reverie.

"Women are supposed to want to have kids," I shared.

"There are a lot of women out there so that all-encompassing statement might not be true, sweetheart."

"We...would..." I cleared my throat, the thoughts in my head tumbling. "We actually would make a beautiful baby."

Hix stroked my neck and watched me closely. "Yeah."

"If this...runs its course, we'll always have Andy, Hix."

He grinned at me. "If this *runs its course*," he said teasingly, "we'll also always have Shaw, Corinne and Mamie. It'll be in different ways, but they'll always be my kids and you'll get to share in that."

"I haven't changed my mind," I whispered.

"All right. But so I know where you're at, you want that door open?"

God.

He wasn't to be believed.

"Not right now but no door should ever be closed."

He grinned again, moved in to touch his mouth to mine and moved back. "Right. That's settled. Now are you gonna get ready for bed?"

"We can't have sex. Mamie's across the hall."

His gaze drifted to the door and he muttered, "Yeah."

"Quickie after the kids are off to school and before we go to work."

He looked back at me. "Deal."

That was when I grinned, pushed off his lap and went to my bag to get my nightie.

The lights were out and I was cuddled up to Hix who was on his back, stroking my arm, when he noted, "Andy's a capable guy."

I adjusted to put my chin to my hand that was flat on his chest in order to look at his shadowed face.

"Yeah," I agreed.

"Can't he be in a work program or something? A home where he has more independence?"

I shook my head but said, "The home. Yes. Though he can decide to roam which isn't good, so there has to be supervision. He also can't do things like cook on his own, because he forgets he's cooking and things can go south when he does. But regardless, they don't have a home like that around here."

"Right," Hix muttered.

I carried on, "But he helps with the staff and other residents who aren't as functional as he is. The work thing, we tried that in Denver. He got a job bagging groceries and he had another one where he cleaned up and had tasks in the stock room and putting stuff on shelves at a hardware store. But if he gets frustrated or flustered, the results can be a little frightening. And he had a really bad seizure at the hardware store. It freaked out the customers, and even though the owner knew it could happen, it didn't sit easy with him either. He'd been taught what to do but he felt pretty powerless, and for whatever reason, it wasn't long before he said he had to let Andy go."

"Think folks in a small town might have more patience and understanding, babe," Hix remarked, and I nodded my chin on his chest.

"Yeah. I've been thinking about it, talking to his therapists about it. They get work requests and he's been given a good deal of time to settle in and get used to the change. Maybe, if something comes in that fits, we can get him set up."

"I'll ask around," he murmured.

I settled back into him. "That'd be sweet. He likes making his own money and he's social. Stability is good but it's also good when he has more than the people he sees all the time to talk to."

"We'll find something for him. And Shaw wants to go out and get him and take him somewhere to watch Thursday night football. I know that's your day with him, sweetheart, but Shaw likes him and I think he gets what's going on and he definitely gets he's gonna be enlisting in the marines soon so he's not gonna be around and he's packing a lot in..."

He went on but I wasn't listening.

I'd closed my eyes to beat back the wet.

"Baby?" Hix called.

"Shaw can have Thursday night," I whispered.

His hand curled around my arm and held me there. "He'll be okay with Andy. If he's gotta keep his eye out for something, you just give him a brief but they'll be good to—"

"I'm sure Andy will be fine with Shaw."

Hix was silent a second before he asked, "Then what am I feeling coming from you, sweetheart?"

"I just...I just..." I moved my hand so when I turned my head to kiss his chest, I'd be able to go in direct. I settled back in on my cheek and gave his middle a squeeze. "I think you're just feeling me being happy."

He pulled me closer and his voice was gruff when he replied, "I'll take that."

He didn't take it.

He gave it.

But I didn't share that.

I whispered wondrously, "This is gonna work, isn't it?"

Hix answered instantly.

"Yup."

I shoved my face in his ribcage. "God, I'm gonna cry."

"Baby—"

"No really, this time I'm gonna cry."

Hix rolled into me so I was on my back. He was mostly pressed down my side and my face was held in one of his hands.

"You cry, I'm gonna have to take the time to comfort you and this will delay sleep so I'm not gonna have the energy to break in *my* headboard tomorrow morning during our quickie after the kids go to school."

I blinked up at him and took in a shuddering breath before I declared, "I'm good."

"Thought that would do it," he muttered.

I slapped his arm.

He came in and took my mouth but I could tell his was smiling.

When he was done kissing me gentle, wet and for a long time, he rolled us back to our previous position and held me close.

I said no more because, if Hix was given the opportunity to change my world again, I'd totally lose it and end up bawling and not get headboard sex in the morning.

So instead, cuddling closer, with Hix's fingers trailing soothingly on my arm, I just fell asleep against my man.

It was after morning pandemonium with Hix's kids getting ready for school (which, to be fair to Shaw, who was definitely a morning person, after he woke up of course, was entirely Mamie).

It was also after our headboard sex quickie.

So I was letting myself in my side door with bed hair *and* sex hair after I drove home from Hix's to get a shower and get ready for work, when I saw something come at me from the side.

Panic assailed me and I jumped back, my phone in my hand (I didn't get out of my car without my phone in my hand anymore), a scream clogged in my throat, as I saw Hope storming up my drive toward me.

However, her step faltered when she witnessed how she'd surprised me and the determined look on her face melted to something that could actually be read as chagrin.

"I didn't mean to scare you," she said when she arrived at me.

"Well, you did," I snapped.

"I wasn't..." She shook her head. "That wasn't my intent."

"Just for your education, after a woman is assaulted in her home, a sneak attack at any time, but mostly at said home, isn't your best lead in."

"I'm sorry, Greta."

God, she actually looked sorry.

This could mean she was sorry.

Or she wanted something.

I braced.

"I just...I need to have a word with you," she told me.

"I can't imagine why," I returned.

She stared at me. "You can't?"

"Hope—"

"You need to step aside," she stated quickly.

It was me now staring at her.

"It's the right thing to do and you know it," she went on.

"For who?" I asked.

Her brows shot together making her look both perplexed and annoyed. "For my family. For my kids. For Hix."

"I'm not sure any of that is true anymore," I shared honestly.

"Yes, because it's not *your* family, though you're trying to make it that way," she returned.

I drew in a calming breath, deciding arguing with Hope was not the way to carry on my day after it had started so well (I mean headboard sex with Hix?—forget about it) so I also decided to try not to do that.

"You have things to say to Hix and he's giving you time. Say them to him. Please keep me out of this," I requested.

"You've wormed your way right into it."

"Hope, I don't want to get angry—"

"*You* don't want to get angry?" she snapped.

"Stop it," I hissed, leaning into her, and when I did her eyes got big, sharing surprise that stated eloquently Hope didn't often have people call her on her shit. "Hix says you go all out until you get what you want but you're an adult now, Hope. You have to learn that life is about getting what you want and it's also about dealing appropriately when you don't."

"He talks about me to you?" she asked.

"Okay," I stated curtly. "It's clear you're in a space where you can't think of anyone but yourself, but if you manage to pull yourself out of that for a second, first, you're the mother of his children so that's gonna happen. Second, you're his ex-wife so that's gonna happen. And last, you've been pretty active lately in ways that don't make him real happy so *that's gonna happen*."

"You need to step aside," she bit out.

"*That* is *not* gonna happen," I shot back.

"He's my husband."

"He's not your husband, Hope. He's my man. I'm angry you forced this situation but I honestly don't intend to hurt you when I say that's where this is at. This is real. It's serious. It's going places. And you have to focus on yourself and your life and *your children* and not on the man who is no longer yours not because he's mine, which he is, but because he...is...*no longer yours*."

Her expression turned catty. "We'll see."

"No, we won't. *I* know how it is. *You'll* see. And Hope, honest to God, you need to prepare because what you'll see is not what you're thinking, and as much as you're obviously hurting now and trying to find ways to make it stop, if you don't prepare, it's only going to get worse."

"You think it's about the ring. He thinks it's about the ring." She leaned toward me. "But it's not about the ring." She leaned back. "And when he knows what it was about, he'll come back."

I stared at her and I thought about headboard sex.

I thought about the words to "At Last."

I thought about the way Hix stroked the insides of my fingers in that sweet way and didn't even know he was doing it.

I thought about Junk Sundays and having a broken nose and not being allowed to lift anything and slipping on a set of stairs and watching Hix leap down them to get to me.

I thought about the fact Hix had had a variety of opportunities to walk away from me and he didn't. Even when I tried to close that door, he put his boot in it, keeping it open.

I thought about the man I knew who knew all the crap that came with me, and he didn't go running.

I thought about that man and the man I knew him to be and knew he'd never tell me, not ever, that he was done with his ex-wife and he was intent to build something with me if he didn't mean that down to the bottom of his soul.

And after I thought all that, I said to my man's ex-wife, "Prepare, Hope."

"We'll see," she purred, grinning venomously at me, turning and sashaying down my drive.

I watched her go, now thinking about if I should tell Hix that happened or not.

I decided to give it time. Not too much, if he found out before I told him, he might think I was keeping it from him if only to protect him, but he wouldn't like that.

However, I had to shower and get to work.

I had a client.

"Right."

I bit my lip at the way Hix said that after I'd shared with him what had happened with me and Hope that morning over the phone in the back room of the salon I'd just opened up.

That one syllable didn't sound happy.

"She's phoned," he shared in return and my eyes went to the door as Lou walked through it.

Hope had been busy that morning.

"Yeah?" I asked.

"She wants to go to Jameson's tomorrow night to have dinner and talk."

Jameson's?

The swankiest, most romantic restaurant in the county?

That *bitch.*

I narrowed my eyes at Lou but mumbled, "Mm-hmm," to Hix.

"Babe, I'm goin' over to her place tonight. I'm not going to freaking Jameson's with her. Though," he said that last word reflectively, "we should make a reservation."

My eyes unnarrowed and I was pretty sure it was me who now had a smug grin.

Lou's eyes weren't narrowed. They were widened at me.

"I'd like that," I said.

"Right, when the girls are back with her next week, we'll go. And I'm not goin' over to hers until after the kids and I get a TV. You wanna come with us? We'll get a quick dinner after then you can hang at home with them and be there when I get back."

"Is that what you want?" I asked.

"Do you have to ask that?" he asked in return.

"Probably not," I muttered.

"When's your last client?"

"I'm done at six thirty."

"Right. We'll have the TV by then. Wanna meet us at Po-Jack's?"

"Yep."

"Okay. Let me know when you're on your way. You have time to hit the Harlequin for lunch?"

I grinned.

Hope was so going down.

"Yep."

"What time?"

"One."

"Pick you up or see you there?"

"It's a block away from me, Hixon."

"Okay, baby," he said through a chuckle. "See you there."

"Yeah, honey. See you there."

"Later, babe."

"Later, Hix."

We hung up and Lou declared, "Your client's here."

"Right, I'll go out and—"

She grabbed my arm. "Unh-unh. I just watched you go from looking like you wanted to commit murder to looking like a cat who got her cream. What's going on?"

I didn't have a lot of time so I laid it all out for her as best I could.

When I was done, she was grinning like a fool.

"What?" I asked.

"Yup," she said.

"What?" I repeated.

"First, you got something to fight for and you're finally freaking fighting for it, and since it's worth it that makes me all kinds of happy. And second, when you said to Hix that what you two have is gonna work, he said, 'yup.'" She leaned right into my space. "And I…fucking…*love that.*" She leaned back and cackled before she said, "Yup. That's it but that's all he had to say. *Yup*! That…is…*awesome*!"

She turned, nabbed an industrial-sized bottle of conditioner and turned back, strutting right by me and throwing open the door.

She shouted, "Yup!" into the salon as she walked through, and I noticed my client staring at her curiously.

The door swung closed.

And I burst out laughing.

Chapter 22

The Ride of Life

Hixon

That night, Hix parked at the curb of the house he'd once called home and walked up the front walk.

He did it staring at his old front porch thinking he needed to invest in some furniture to put on his for Greta.

Maybe some of those Adirondack chairs.

He was at the door with his hand lifted to ring the bell when the door opened.

Hope stood there made up like they were actually going to Jameson's, but without a nice dress. Instead she was wearing nice slacks and a pretty top, not like she normally made herself up in some jeans and a sweater, with just mascara and blush and whatever she did with her hair when she did it quick for when she had a day of running Mamie around and working for her dad.

Shit.

At least she had bare feet.

She reached to the storm door and Hix got out of the way as she pushed it open, greeting, "Hixon."

He caught the door and returned, "Hope."

She turned and walked in. He followed her and he did it thinking he'd forgotten to keep track of the time since he'd last been in his old house. She'd demanded he come get any of his stuff that he'd want, and after they'd gone around about it for weeks, he'd done it.

That had to have been four, maybe five months ago.

But it looked just the same. She hadn't changed a thing. It was still clean as a pin, like she liked it, tidy, like kids didn't live there, and well-decorated in a way they both had liked it.

Their divorce agreement meant he left her with the house and the furniture, and since she made enough money he didn't have to pay child support. Seeing as she made that money at a job she'd never lose, Hix's lawyer had told him to fight her for a settlement since she got everything and he walked away with the old desk his father had given him for his apartment in college and some boxes of other shit that had meaning but no value.

He hadn't fought for it. She didn't have it, her father would have to have given it to her, or she'd have had to sell the house or dip into accounts that were healthy because they'd fought to keep them that way and she'd already given him his share of that.

But regardless, anything she gave him would be put toward the kids' futures so there was no point. All they'd saved for that was in an account neither of them could touch except to do something for the kids.

In return, she'd signed away any rights to go after his pension or retirement accounts.

He hadn't wanted the divorce so he'd thought it was a decent enough deal.

Now he was glad. He didn't have pushing their situation to someplace ugly to get money out of her, which would have surely endangered his relationship with her family, something that meant something to him, but even if it didn't, he'd need to keep it copasetic for the kids. It left their house intact for the kids to live in it without at least that change to their lives. And he didn't have a single memory of her or the life they'd shared that he had to face daily.

Clean slate.

All good.

She turned to him in her living room and he stopped three steps in.

"You wanted to chat," he started when she didn't. "I'm here."

"Would you like a beer?" she asked.

"No," he answered.

"A bourbon?" she offered.

"No, Hope," he told her.

"Would you at least sit?" she requested, beginning to show impatience or nerves, he couldn't tell which.

He could do that so he went to one of the two couches that faced each other vertical to the fireplace and sat in the corner.

A fireplace where he noticed she had a fire going.

And there were candles lit.

Jesus.

Throw on some music, and with her made up, dressed like that and the room this way, he'd be smacked in the face where she wanted this to go instead of it being just in his face.

He didn't settle in. He sat close to the edge with his elbows to his knees, his hands hanging between them, and looked at her settling in across from him.

When she did, she tucked her legs under her like they'd be chatting all night, and Hix fought his mouth getting tight.

"I'm glad you finally agreed to talk to me," she said softly.

"I did and we're doin' that but I don't wanna do it for long. The kids are home, they got a new TV and—"

She interrupted him. "Shaw can watch over the girls and Shaw can also set up a TV."

He kept going like she didn't say anything. "Greta's with them."

She assumed a hurt expression and looked to the fire.

"Hope, I'm here, you wanted to talk, talk," he prompted.

She drew in a delicate breath and looked back at him, tears now shimmering in her eyes.

Christ.

"It wasn't about the ring," she said quietly.

"All right."

She stared at him a beat before she asked, "Don't you want to know what it was about?"

He felt his brows draw together. "Am I here to play games?"

"Of course not," she said swiftly.

"So let's get this done, Hope, be straight with me and say what you gotta say."

She again stared at him before she lifted her chin a touch and declared, "Cooking."

His brows did not unknit when he asked, "Say what?"

"Cooking."

"Hope," he growled, sliding to the edge of his seat.

"You let me cook, Hixon."

He went still.

"You expected it," she stated.

"Are you telling me you didn't divorce me because I didn't tell you I'd buy you a twenty-five thousand dollar ring but instead you did it because you did the cooking?"

"You expected it."

"I don't like to cook, and Hope, you know I'm shit at it."

"Because you never tried to learn."

"You're right, because I never *wanted* to learn."

"So it was down to me."

For fuck's sake.

"There's no point to this," he muttered, beginning to take his feet but he kept his seat when she spoke.

"It's about the cooking. And the cleaning. You also let me do most of that too."

He didn't get a chance to say anything, she carried on.

"You'd vacuum, Hix, but I asked you to do it more than once a week and you said it didn't need it when it did. We had Maynard for thirteen years and he shed crazy, all over the place, but we also have three kids. The floors needed vacuuming more than once a week."

Their dog Maynard died three years ago.

And he was getting this shit now?

"You're not giving me a point to this," he informed her.

"I dusted, you never dusted, not ever."

"Hope, that's bullshit."

"Right, okay, so maybe you did it a couple of times, but Hix," she threw up a hand, "we were married nineteen years."

"Together only eighteen since you kicked me out," he corrected her.

"Like that makes a difference," she returned.

"And you bitching about me not dusting and vacuuming and you cooking makes a difference at this point?" he fired back.

"You don't get it and I thought you got it and it hurt, Hixon, it hurt like you wouldn't believe when you didn't get it."

"Get what?" he asked.

"Get this." She threw both her hands out that time, doing it with arms wide, indicating her immaculate house. "I kept this house nice. I cooked. I cleaned. I did the dishes even, most of the time, when it was *me* who cooked. I'd get Mamie from dance and I did most of the running them around before Shaw could drive and you *let me.*"

"You have a job that's more flexible than mine but that's beside the point. You were my wife and you *are* their mother, Hope," he reminded her.

"I was and I am, and I thought maybe you might appreciate it a little bit."

That shut his mouth.

"But no, you *expected* it and when you got that money from your Uncle Jack, I asked for that ring because I thought you'd *want* to give it to me, I thought you'd *want* to show me you loved me, you appreciated what I did for you, for this family, but you *laughed at me.*"

"Hope—"

"And that *hurt*."

"I can see that," he said quietly, watching her.

Her chest moved out as she drew in a big breath and she looked to the fire when she let it out.

"It wasn't even like that ring was all the money Uncle Jack gave you. It wasn't even half. But that doesn't matter because that wasn't what it was about," she whispered to the fire.

"So you didn't want the ring," he noted.

Her eyes cut back to him. "Of course I wanted the ring. It was a beautiful ring. But what I really wanted was what it would *mean* if you gave it to me."

"So why didn't you tell me that?"

She bent slightly toward him. "Because you should *know*."

Okay, she had a point, a good one, and she'd made it.

But that pissed him off.

"And when I shared with you repeatedly I didn't know, why didn't you tell me then?"

"Because you should have figured it out."

"Are you joking?" he whispered.

"No," she snapped.

Yeah, he was pissed off.

"You didn't once mow the lawn, Hope."

"You don't have to mow the lawn every night, Hixon."

"You didn't once take the trash out, not even fucking once, not our whole marriage."

"And you don't have to take the trash out every night either," she retorted.

"You never took your car in to have the oil changed. I did that."

"And what?" she asked. "That happens every three months?"

"You also didn't get up with the kids *every morning*. I did."

"Hix—"

"What about shoveling the walks, Hope?" he pushed.

"Again, that didn't happen even *close* to every day," she returned.

"We're gettin' into the minutiae, you wanna talk about grocery shopping? Who did that?"

"We both did, Hix. But I'll admit, you took the kids and made a thing of it most the time, but only because you bought them junk and I didn't like it."

"So we both did things to take care of this house, our lives and our family," he pointed out.

"Yes, but—"

"And I didn't ask for a twenty-five-thousand-dollar anything because that was my job as your husband, their father. I just did it because it had to be done and because a part of me *liked* doin' it because I was looking after the ones I loved."

Now *she* shut her mouth.

"I'm not as clean as you and I know this because you dogged my ass for nearly two decades about it, but it's just the way it was. I didn't need every dog hair vacuumed up and every particle of dust swept away because I was living in a house with my wife and three kids and our dog and I actually *liked* the mess of my family around me."

She kept her mouth shut.

Hix did not.

"You wanted it like that and I didn't mind hanging my jacket on the hooks by the door so you wouldn't see it flung over the couch or puttin' up the towel folded like you liked it because who gives a shit? But I'd never consider it grounds to throw a tantrum or, say, end our marriage to get up in your face about the fact that it was a pain in my ass to do shit that meant nothing to me because it meant something to you. And since we're lettin' things fly, you never lettin' us have another dog because they shed fucking sucked, Hope. The kids were devastated when we lost Maynard, they wanted another pet, I did too, and you puttin' your foot down about that with the excuse of what a pain in the ass pet hair was blew. So, frankly, Hope, it sometimes bugged the crap outta me you were so damned neat and bitched about it when we weren't. And it definitely bugged me you were that way when we all wanted another dog."

"You never said anything," she stated quietly.

Was she serious?

"Now you're definitely joking," he bit out.

She got what she'd just said and how fucked up it was and tried to backpedal.

"I...what I meant was—"

Hix cut her off. "You meant what you said. And I hear you about the ring and about what it would signify to you and you actually had a point, fourteen months ago. Now you don't. You had plenty of time in between to stop tryin' to make me dance to your tune when I didn't even hear the record that was playing. And it shits me we're sittin' here now talking about all this crap, but take it as honest when I say I'm sorry I laughed when you asked for that ring. It was insensitive and that wasn't the right response. But Hope, you lost traction immediately not sharin' with me I hurt you then, and your response to mine was so outta whack, it's freaking insane. And now I'm thinkin' you got just a hint of bein' in the dark about something someone you give a shit about has a problem with and they never shared it with you. Magnify that to make it cause the end of a marriage and powerless to do anything but watch a shitload of garbage land on your kids because that happened, and maybe you'll get where I'm comin' from."

He watched her swallow. Then Hix held her eyes as she held his and he was about to put an end to this waste of time when she spoke again.

"So where does this take us now?"

"Sorry?" he asked.

"Where do we go from here?"

He felt his neck get tight.

But before he could figure out what to say, she uncurled her legs from under her and rushed across to him. Getting on her knees in front of him, she grabbed his hand and held it tight in both of hers.

"I'm sorry," she whispered urgently. "I'm so sorry. I knew I'd done wrong at the lawyer's office when we signed those papers but it had gone so far, I didn't know how to stop it. But then you wouldn't *talk to me* and I couldn't tell you I was sorry. I couldn't explain where I was at. I couldn't start fixing things between us. Then you found *her* and—"

"Stop."

She stopped.

He tugged his hand from hers.

The second he started doing that, her eyes dropped to his hand and she kept them there even as her hands fell to her sides.

"We're done, Hope."

Her gaze shot to his. "We're not done."

"We're done."

"You love me."

"I did. I don't anymore."

More tears hit her eyes and she scooted forward on her knees, pressing her stomach to his leg as she lifted a hand and rested it on his chest.

"You do. You love me. You totally love me, Hix, in a way you always will."

"Hope, *God*," he pulled in breath through his nose and finished, "I'm sorry. I don't. Not anymore."

"That's not true."

He wrapped his fingers around her wrist, pulled it away, let it go and slid down the couch from her.

She fell back to her calves and stared at him.

"I wanna get along with you, for the kids," he told her. "I want you to stop doin' the shit you're doin' that hurts them. I want to help repair your relationship with Shaw so you'll have him for the time we still have him before he goes off to live his life. But us, we're done. There's no turning back."

"We were good together," she reminded him.

"We were. Now that's over," he reminded her.

"We weren't good, honey. We were *great*. We were *happy*. We're talking now about this...this..." she shook her head in a fierce way and forced out, "*stuff*. The bad stuff. But it wasn't bad. It was good. We laughed a lot. *I* made *you* laugh a lot. I should have listened after we lost Maynard and I should have shared what I was feeling, but all this stuff...this stuff we're talking about...I see now it doesn't *mean anything*."

"You're right, Hope, and I'm sorry but now all of that is over in a way there's no going back," he said as gently as he could.

"I don't care about the cooking, Hix. It's not that." She flipped out her hands. "I mean, it is but it isn't. It's the significance—"

"I get it, Hope. It doesn't change things."

She leaned his way. "It *does*."

"You should have told me. I'd hurt you, you felt I was taking you for granted, that was something I needed to know."

She nodded repeatedly and quickly. "I should. I know that now. I should have told you. And from now on, I will, Hixon. You have my promise."

"Hope, you broke it. It can't be fixed. It's done."

"It's not."

"I'm sorry," he said again as gently as he could. "It is."

The tears started flowing over when she reminded him, "We vowed forever."

"Then you filed for divorce."

She slapped a hand against her chest. "This isn't just on me. You have your part in it."

"Maybe I did but then *it* got done and there was nothing left but our kids."

"That's not true. You promised me forever, so if it's broken, you have your part in fixing it."

"Hope—"

She surged to him, grabbing both sides of his neck and pressing between his legs. "I love you, Hix. You're the only man I ever loved, and I'll never love anyone else because I *shouldn't have to*."

Again, Hix wrapped his fingers around her wrists, both of them this time, and he pushed her back but held her not too far away with their hands between them as he dipped his face in hers.

"I tried to fix it," he reminded her quietly.

"I should have let you, but now—"

"You didn't," he told her. "And now, it's over. There's nothing to fix."

"We can get it back," she begged, tears still flowing.

Hix used his hold on her wrists to pull her gently to her feet as he stood but he held her in front of him and kept at her.

"I know you're hurting and that doesn't make me happy. I know what you want and I lived so long wanting to give you what you want, it's hard, even now, to say you can't have it. But you did what you did and then you acted the way you acted, and it sucks I gotta remind you, but that was even worse than what you did to put yourself where you are now. For me, Hope, it sucks to share this with you too, but I'm not where you are now. I'm somewhere else and I'm not turning back. I'm not because you threw away our lives the way you did. I'm not because you played the games you played and pulled the shit you pulled after you did that. And I'm not because I just don't love you anymore in a way I know I'll never do it again."

"*Her*," she spat.

"Yes, Greta. And also you, Hope. You let it die and now it's dead, and if you can't understand that, I'm sorry. But it's the God's honest truth."

She yanked her wrists from his hold, stepped away several paces, lifted a hand, dashed it on her cheek to wipe away the tears and hissed, "And you're blameless."

"Probably not. But what I'm trying to say is it doesn't matter now."

She squared her shoulders, tossed her pink champagne hair and sniffed. "Right. Then you can get out of my house now."

"You wanted this talk, I'm here and we should take it where we're at least good to raise our children healthy and happy and not runnin' away and walkin' across town at seven in the morning because that shit is whacked."

She opened her mouth and he knew it was about to come

spewing out.

But surprisingly she shut it and looked again to the fire.

She crossed her arms on her chest and declared, "I miss my son."

"I'm sure and we'll work on that."

She looked to him. "And I want that woman not staying the night when my children are with you."

"Don't go there," he growled.

"It isn't right."

"What it isn't is your business."

She dropped her arms but held them out to her sides. "They're my *children.*"

"They're mine too and Greta's gonna be in their lives, the way things are goin', for the rest of them, so no reason for her not to be in them now."

Her face froze in shock with her mouth open.

She unfroze to stammer, "You're go-go-gonna...you're gonna... you're gonna *marry her*?"

"I don't know. But I know if you take a second and think about it, you'd know that I wouldn't have a woman around them that I didn't have feelings for. You also know you can trust me to do the right thing by our kids. So we don't have to have this conversation not only because it's not your business but because I'm a good father who loves his kids so you shouldn't insult me by saying anything."

She crossed her arms on her chest, protectively this time, and stated, "You've got to know that hurts me, Hixon."

"I can imagine, Hope," he murmured. "But it is what it is, it's happening, and you're gonna have to get used to it too."

She looked to the fire and declared, "I think you should leave."

"Hope, you need to stop talkin' shit around Mamie."

She turned again to glare at him but he kept going before she could say anything.

"You can be pissed at me. You can hate me. You can hate Greta. You can do what you want, say what you want, talk all you want. That's your prerogative. But not in front of our daughter."

"I'm sure *Greta* went tattling to you about our conversation this morning," she spat.

"She called me when she got to work, yeah," he told her. "But you're an adult, she's an adult, I can't control you, and because of that, I can't protect her from you. Do I want you never to do that again? Hell yes. Can I stop you? Unfortunately no. Can we put up with your shit and carry on? Fortunately yes."

"My shit," she murmured, her lip curling.

Hix sighed and prompted, "Mamie?"

"Since the girls are both desperately in love with her because of her hair and her stupid heels, not to mention she's buying their love by giving them gift certificates to make their room in your house nice, I won't mess with that," she gave in ungracefully.

"Thanks," he muttered.

"But it'd be nice if you'd also have a few words with Shaw."

"I'll do that."

"And I'll curtail discussing on *my* phone in *my* house about how I feel about your new *slut* when the children are around."

"Now see," Hix whispered, holding his body perfectly in check, and Hope didn't miss it, he knew it when her face paled, "that's stepping over a line I'll state plain right now you just crossed and you better never fuckin' cross it again."

"I—"

He took one stride to her, getting in her space and dropping his head so they were nose to nose.

"Do not ever speak about her that way again, Hope. Not ever. Not fucking *ever*." He pulled his head back and bit out, "Now we had our talk and you got a choice. You get your head out of your ass and get with the program or you don't. I can't say what'll happen if you don't. I'll have to deal with it if it happens. What I will say is, right now, we got eight months with Shaw, two years with Corinne and five years with Mamie. Five years to make our kids happy, teach them what they gotta know to live their lives, take on the world and be decent human beings. If I gotta do all that on my own, I will. But it'd be nice to have your help."

Her head moved like he'd slapped her, but he was done.

And he communicated that by sidestepping her and walking right out of her house.

He was in his garage having just shut down the Bronco when she called him.

He sucked in a breath, grabbed the phone, hauled his ass out of his truck, slammed the door and leaned his back against it before he put the phone to his ear and greeted, "If this is ugly, I'm hanging up and blocking you until you have the girls again."

"I shouldn't have said that about her," Hope declared.

Hix went silent.

Hope, unfortunately, did too so Hix had to end it.

"Hope, it's late and I wanna—"

"I messed things up, didn't I?"

Hix fell silent again.

This time, she didn't.

"I won't say anything in front of Mamie, and I know Corinne's upset with you so I'll sit down with her and...and, I don't know. Share a few things."

"Make them the right things, Hope," he ordered.

"They will be, Hixon."

He sucked in another breath.

"It wasn't about the ring," she whispered in his ear. "I just... thought you knew me better."

"In eighteen years there's nothing I learned about you that you didn't tell me or show me, Hope. Marriage is not a guessing game. It requires constant communication to keep it strong. That said, I probably would never have bought you that ring. I'd want you to have it but with what we were facing financially, it couldn't happen. But if I got where you were, I would have done something big if you needed, or small every day so you'd get what you meant to me."

"I know." She was still whispering.

"We gotta settle this shit down for our kids."

"I know that too."

"I need you with me on that, Hope."

"I'm with you, Hix."

Christ, could this be the end?

"I really need to trust in that," he told her.

"You don't call me babe anymore."

He looked to his boots.

"Or peaches," she went on quietly, hurt in each word.

He said nothing.

Hope did.

"I did that too."

"We need to move on," he said gently.

"Mamie says she makes you happy."

He looked to the wall of the garage. "Let's not do that, Hope."

"I just...it's just gonna take some..." She paused for several long beats before she finished, "It hurts a lot and it's gonna take a long time to come to terms with the fact that I messed this up."

"That might go faster we can work together to get our kids to a place where they're good."

"Yeah."

"I'll work on Shaw this week, see if he's willin' to go back with the girls next week," he promised. "He's not, I'm not gonna push it now but I will if it starts takin' too long."

"I appreciate that, Hixon."

"Right. So we're here, good talk."

"Yeah."

He pushed from his truck, saying, "Later, Hope."

"Hixon?"

He didn't want to say it. He heard it in her voice.

But the truce was about two seconds old, he had to say it.

"Yeah?"

"I love you."

"Hope—"

"Just that. Just know that. Just know I always will and I'll always be so, so sorry I messed this up, you can't even...you are..." He actually heard her draw in breath before she said softly, "You're the best man I've ever met. You're a fantastic father. And I...I did this to us. I lost you. So you'll never imagine how sorry I am."

He didn't know what to say to that and it was lame but it was all he had when he replied, "Right."

"All right, I'll uh...maybe see you at Corinne's game?"

"I'll be there."

"Okay, Hixon. Tell the kids hi from their mom."

"I'll do that, Hope. Later."

"Okay, later, Hix."

He hung up.

He stared at his phone.

Then he walked to the wall, hit the garage door opener so it'd go down and went through the door into the mudroom, starting down the stairs to the basement.

He hesitated halfway down when he heard Greta shout, "Holy crap, Corinne! You got this! To your left! That's it. *Yes*! Now clear the perimeter!"

He was pretty sure he heard a slap of flesh that would herald a high five.

And therefore he was shocked as shit after all that had just happened that he walked into the basement with a smile on his face to see his three kids and his woman arrayed on his new couch, all of them on the edge of their seats as Corinne and Shaw played some war game on the Xbox.

"Hey, Dad!" Mamie cried, looking at him then looking back to the action on the new TV.

So Shaw could set up a TV and an Xbox and apparently a receiver because the surround sound Hix also bought was absolutely functional considering the grenade explosions and *rat-a-tat-tat* of machine gun fire were ear-splitting.

"Hey, Dad," Shaw said to the TV.

"Hey, Daddy," Corinne said, then stuck her tongue out and jabbed the controller at the TV like it wasn't her modified fake gun but she was hitting assailants with it.

Greta was just looking at him.

Or, more aptly, examining him.

"Hey," he said to them all, but his eyes were on Greta.

She tipped her head to the side and her face got soft.

That beautiful woman shouting encouragement to his daughter to do well in a violent videogame then staring at him with that look on her face was falling in love with him.

This was good.

Because Hix was all in for that ride.

"Your mom says hi," he told his kids.

That got him stares from all of them, though Shaw had the wherewithal to pause the game.

"She did?" he asked.

"She did," Hix confirmed.

Corinne was studying him and he figured with her mom also her best friend, she probably knew about the cooking and the vacuuming, which was most likely why he was getting hit with her attitude.

He didn't know what to do about that and figured he'd have to trust Hope would do something about it, so he just held her gaze and said, "It went good, honey."

"Should I, uh...call Mom?" she asked.

Hell no.

Hope in her state sharing with their daughter?

Shit.

"She always likes hearing from you. But now maybe it'd be good she got a call from her girl."

Corinne nodded, handed her controller to Greta and got up.

She left the room as Mamie asked, "Is Mommy okay?"

He looked to his youngest and moved to the sectional, sitting next to her and scrunching her as he did so she had to dig into him until she was nearly on his lap.

He held her there and said, "She's okay and things are gonna get better."

He felt her thin arms around him and he memorized that feel as she asked, "Yeah?"

"Yeah, baby," he murmured.

She dropped the side of her head to his shoulder.

"Greta, do you wanna learn how to play?" Shaw asked.

"Maybe you should save Corinne's score because she was killing it," Greta replied. "We can start a new game."

"Sounds good," Shaw muttered, looking edgy, like he didn't know what to think and he couldn't get a lock on how he was feeling.

Hix couldn't help with that either.

Time.

That was what they all needed.

And if Hope was finally with the program, it would start working.

Mamie scrambled out of his lap to crawl to Greta and sit on her knees behind her, hanging over her shoulder and pointing out things even as Shaw pointed out things on the controller, teaching her how to move her character in the game, shoot her gun.

Mamie kept hanging over Greta's shoulder as Shaw started a new game and Greta got shot to shit within five minutes, giggling herself sick the entire time, jabbing her controller at the screen just like Corinne had done.

"You're terrible at that!" Mamie yelled happily.

"Go again, Shaw. I'm gonna get this," Greta declared determinedly.

"Your funeral," Shaw replied but he wasn't done. "Videotastically literally."

Greta burst out laughing, Shaw joined her, Mamie collapsed on Greta's back and did it too, and for the first time in fourteen months, Hix sat back and watched, enjoying the fuck out of the ride of life.

Chapter 23

Well Done

Greta

The doorbell rang.

I tottered to it on my high heels, the girls moving in behind me.

I then hit the outside light switch that meant the porch went dark, but the revolving lights that Hix had put out that displayed dead trees and cats with their backs arched and witches flying across full moons could be seen, the images covering both sides of the porch along with hanging fairy lights with ghosts on them.

Everything at the ready, I opened Hix's front door for the umpteenth time that Halloween night.

I bent low, and in a ghoul's voice, said through my fake fangs, "Good *eeeeeeee*vening."

I then stepped aside.

That was when Mamie and three of her girlfriends, all in tattered tutus and leotards with blood dripping down their fronts from two fake holes in their necks, faces made up pale, eyes shadowed, hair in perfect ballerina chignons (makeup and hair courtesy of me), flitted out with arms gracefully held out to their sides.

They arrayed themselves, two by two on either side of the door. They then got up on pointe, arms curled in front of them, and did a pirouette. They stopped and raised their arms over their heads, but with heads drooping to the sides, staring down at the five trick-or-treaters (a Harry Potter, two Reys from *Star Wars*, an Elsa and a Captain America).

All five trick-or-treaters stared among the dancers in awe.

"Oh no! The sheriff and his deputy!" I cried, and all the ballerinas flitted back into the house as the kids whirled around and watched Hix and his deputy, Bets, walking up the front steps wearing jeans, boots and their sheriff shirts, both carrying big, orange jack-o'-lantern, handled buckets filled with candy.

"The *sheriff*," Captain America breathed.

"Hey, kids," Bets greeted, coming to the top of the steps.

She got a couple of waves (from both Reys) but the other three were staring at Hix.

"Candy after you promise to look both ways when you cross the street, always let your parents know where you are, brush your teeth morning and night and you never talk to strangers. You with me on all that?" Hix asked.

"Totally!" Harry Potter exclaimed, jumped toward Hix's bucket and Captain America followed him.

Elsa went to Hix (not surprising). Both Reys went to Bets staring up at her in wonder (also not surprising).

Hix looked at me.

I'd talked him into doing this. He'd only agreed when I'd allowed him to lecture the kids (slightly) prior to them getting candy. Bets was all in since she said giving out candy alone sucked.

"You're the awesomest vampire I've ever seen."

I turned my head to one of the moms (who was also one of Lou's clients, I thought her name was Georgina), and smiled.

My makeup was the bomb. I had pale skin, winged brows, dark

makeup around my eyes that gave way to a bright purple and dribbling blood coming down the sides of my mouth. My hair was fabulous and huge and sprayed black. And I was wearing my blood-stained cocktail dress from the night of real terror in my kitchen.

That night made for a far better memory in that dress than the last time I'd worn it, for certain.

"Thanks," I replied.

"Right, kids, say thanks to the vampire and the sheriff and his deputy and let's go," the other mom said.

The kids cried their enthusiastic thanks. Hix and Bets wandered toward me. And as they left, I heard one child say, "We're totally coming to this house *every year*."

That made me smile again.

I loved Halloween. It was my favorite holiday (not counting Christmas because Christmas was in a league of its own). Last year, I'd gone trick or treating with Lou and Maple and some of Maple's friends (Snow declared she was too old to go with us, she'd done something with friends). It had been great, but I missed handing out candy.

This was way better.

I felt Hix's lips at my ear. "I'm totally fucking you in that getup later, but you'll have to lose the fangs."

Oh yeah.

This was *way* better.

We moved in and I saw Andy standing with the girls, smiling at me.

"So...*awesome*," Andy said.

I smiled at my brother too.

He was also done up as a vampire. We were taking turns opening the door. And if there was ever a time his scar worked for him, this was it. Even he said so, declaring after I was done with his makeup, "I'm scaring even myself. I'm Scarface Vampire!"

"It's getting late, girls," Hix said to his daughter and her friends. "You wanna go out, the time is now."

They looked undecided.

I knew why. They were having a blast doing our thing with us.

It was Mamie's time with her mom but when I talked to Hix about doing this with him and Andy, she'd been around and said she'd wanted to join in. She'd then asked her mom if it was okay and Hope had said yes.

Mamie had been elated.

It had been only just under two weeks since Hix talked to Hope, during which nothing had happened, so it showed progress from Hope.

That made me elated.

Hix decided for the girls.

"Next year you'll be freshmen, too old for this, so pack it in. Get out on the sidewalks, and Mamie, like we talked about, two block radius and you're taking Greta's phone."

"We got great costumes and totally awesome makeup, we should," Mamie told her friends.

"Pointe shoes off," Hix ordered.

"Right, Dad," Mamie said. Then to her girls, "Let's go!"

They ran up the steps.

I slid my fangs out and looked to my brother.

"It's up to you and me now, bud," I told him.

"I'm in!" he replied.

The doorbell rang.

A cacophony of ballerinas instantly could be heard storming back down the stairs with Mamie screeching, "*One more time!*"

Hix gave me a look I liked a whole lot, full of sweetness and tenderness and hotness and promise, before he and Bets took off to go out the back and walk around the house.

So when I turned to the door as Andy rushed to it, I did it smiling.

I WAS RIDING Hix and getting close when his hands at my waist lifted me off.

He tossed me to the side, rolled me to my belly, pulled me up to my knees and drove back in.

I flipped my hair to the side (or, with all that black spray in it, it more like *shifted* to the side), looked back at him and breathed, "I can't suck your blood like this."

He kept thrusting inside me even as he grinned and said, "My blood is all in one area of my body now, baby. But you wanna suck that, I'm good to lie back and take it."

"No, no," I said hurriedly (or more like, *moaned* hurriedly). "Carry on."

His grin turned wicked and his hand slid from my hip down, around and in, and it was then I stuffed my face in his bed and got makeup all over his comforter.

I didn't think he minded.

"I DON'T KNOW. That's all Larry saw. But she's still with him."

It was Monday the week after Halloween. Hix had had his kids back, but that day, they'd gone again to Hope. All of them, including Shaw for the first time since he moved in exclusively with Hix.

Hope was doing her thing, Hix was doing his.

And it seemed to be working.

This meant he could resume Monday Night Football at the Outpost with his buds, Toast and Tommy. He'd brought me. Donna had showed. So had Hal and Ashlee.

And now he was telling me Larry had seen Mom with Kavanagh Becker getting a coffee at Babycakes.

I hadn't heard from her since the Sunnydown incident.

Maybe this was why.

"So, you think she got her meal ticket, you made your point you're not gonna take her crap or let me do it, she smartened up enough to take heed of your official position, and she's doing what she has to do to try to settle in with this guy for the long haul?" I asked.

"Been in the woman's company not even a handful of times, sweetheart," Hix replied. "Got no clue. You said she'd come and go. It's been a while. She ever go for this long?"

I looked to my beer and muttered, "She didn't keep a schedule." I looked back to Hix. "Sometimes it would be long enough I'd think that was the end. Then she'd come back."

He wrapped his hand around the back of my neck and dipped in close. "Just givin' you the info on what Larry saw. Keepin' you apprised. Didn't do it to bum you out. But just to repeat, she tries any more shit, we'll deal."

I held his gaze and nodded only to have my arm cuffed on the other side and hear Toast say, "It's Monday Night Football, people. Serious conversations are verboten."

"Her first Monday Night Football and the chick is breakin' all the rules," Tommy, on Toast's other side, teased.

"Shush," Toast hushed Tommy. "You might scare her off and she's a chick that doesn't glare at the plate of nachos like she can make it combust with her eyes or act like she doesn't want to shove her face in it and eat it all herself. Be gentle with this unknown entity, Tom, she might bolt."

"Right," Tommy said. "Sorry, Greta. You can get serious with Hix all you want. Don't glare at our nachos and make them combust."

Through my laughter I assured, "Your nachos are safe, boys."

"No they're not," Donna declared, pushing through Toast and me holding a salad plate and commencing scooping half the remains of the nachos on it.

"Hey! You're hoggin' it all!" Toast shouted.

"I told you to move it down my way," Donna reminded him, licking melted cheese from her fingers.

"Then it wouldn't be smack in front of me," Toast returned.

"Betty-Jean, another plate of nachos, yeah?" Hix ordered, and when I looked to him, I saw his eyes on the bartender.

"Got it, Hixon," Betty-Jean replied and shuffled to the electronic cash register to put our order in.

"Stop being logical, Sheriff, it kills the fun of gettin' up in Donna's shit," Toast demanded.

"Oh, don't you worry," Donna returned. "I'll do something else you feel you need to get up in my shit about. Like continuing to root for the Cardinals."

"Don't make me puke," Toast retorted. "The Cards? This is Broncos country."

"It is not. It's Chiefs country," Tommy fired back.

"Dude, give it up with the Chiefs," Toast advised, turning from me to Tommy. "The Broncs are *where it's at*."

"You grew up rooting for the Chiefs. You only switched to the Broncs like, four years ago. Where's your loyalty?" Tommy replied.

"It's Seahawks all the way," Hal put in from down the bar.

"Yeah!" Ashlee cried. "They have the best colors for their uniforms."

"Are you shittin' me?" Toast asked.

"No," Ashlee retorted. "That green is *amazing*."

"Someone shoot me," Tommy requested of the ceiling.

"Okay," Ashlee agreed. "Hal, give me your gun."

Hal started laughing.

Toast and Tommy dipped a shoulder hunched Hal and Ashlee's way and began to launch in.

"You're welcome," Donna said, and my eyes swung to her. She motioned between Hix and me with her plate. "Carry on."

She then went back to her seat on the other side of Tommy and tucked into her nachos.

I turned to Hix. "Your friends are *da bomb*."

His eyes lit. "Did you just say *da bomb*?"

"Yes, because they're *da bomb*."

He burst out laughing.

I watched, grinning at him the whole time.

And when he quit, he dug into the nachos. I did too.

That Wednesday night, I watched Hix walk up my front walk and I did it with more than my usual admiring eye, and not because there was more than usual to admire due to the fact that there was always a lot to admire about Hixon Drake.

I did it because I could tell by the line of his body and the look on his face that something was wrong.

I stayed where I was like I always stayed where I was when Hix came to me at night (these being the nights I didn't go to him, which was most of the time when his kids weren't with him).

I was under a blanket with a sweater and scarf on, my tea on a heating pad beside me, my book forgotten on my lap as he made his way to me.

He bent deep and took my mouth in a quick, wet kiss before he turned and did what I'd trained him to do. Sit and give me his order of what he needed.

But this time, instead of folding into the chair beside me and telling me he wanted beer, bourbon or food, he collapsed in it and stayed silent.

He was wearing his sheriff's shirt, a thermal under it, and a cool brown leather jacket with his badge pinned on the outside of it.

I approved of his winter sheriff's uniform.

I did not tell him this.

I noted softly, "It looks like a bourbon night."

He didn't turn his eyes from the street.

He stared at it for long enough for me to get more worried then lifted his hands and rubbed his face, which made me definitely worried.

"Hixon, darlin'," I murmured.

He dropped his hands but kept his eyes to the street when he said, "Faith came in today to ask if there was any progress with the case."

Oh boy.

I hadn't seen Faith since the murder. Her mom had called to cancel her appointment, which was every six weeks and would have fallen three weeks after Nat was killed.

It had been way longer than that and she hadn't been in. I also hadn't bugged her to reschedule.

And looking at Hix, I thought maybe I should have.

"Talk to me," I urged gently.

"She looks like hell. She's lost, I don't know, least twenty, thirty pounds. Eyes sunk in. Hair a mess." Finally, his head turned my way. "She needs answers. She needs closure."

"I'm sure," I murmured.

"That gun was registered. It was also reported stolen."

I said nothing because he'd never talked about any case to me, not in any depth, and definitely not Nat's, so I was surprised.

"Guy in Kansas reported it stolen the day he came home and found someone broke into his house, this being months before our guy showed in Grant County and did Nat."

"Okay," I said quietly to that when he didn't go on for a long time.

"Crazy shit, guy breaks into his house and what does he steal?"

When it was clear he was actually asking a question, I shook my head but answered, "His gun, obviously."

"His gun, all the leftover meatloaf and potato salad in his fridge, and far's the guy can remember, three candy bars."

"That's very weird," I murmured.

"Owner of the gun was cleanin' it. Left it out on the kitchen table."

"Not smart," I muttered.

"Nope."

"So if he was cleaning it, was it loaded? Or did your guy buy bullets somewhere?"

"He reports it wasn't loaded and he also reports his ammo was untouched, though that was in a locked cabinet where the gun should have been. Cops saw no indication the guy went anywhere but the kitchen, got in breakin' a window on the kitchen door to do it. So the guy broke in because he was hungry. Ate 'til he was full. Grabbed some snacks and the gun on the table and took off, leaving the Tupperware in the sink. Where the guy got the bullets, we don't know. Anywhere he could get them between here and there, we checked and no one remembers seeing him."

"Did anyone in this place in Kansas see him?"

"That gun turned out to be our murder weapon, the boys in Kansas asked around and even though it had been months, this guy is memorable, so yeah. Our drifter was seen by three people. A kid leavin' after his shift at a fast food restaurant, a man out walkin' his dog and a mom in the neighborhood where the robbery took place, goin' out to her car to pick her kid up from preschool."

"So you've got him there."

"Yep. Though they saw him around at the time of the robbery, no one had ever seen him before or after. So we got proof our drifter is a serious drifter, makin' his way from middle-Kansas, hundreds of miles to here. What we don't got is any understanding of the origins of where this guy started drifting. Outside Kansas and Grant County, no one has seen him. But now we got pictures and bulletins out to every homeless shelter in forty-eight states should this guy go lookin' for another meal or whatever else he might need, and we got everything to nail him. We just don't have him."

"Did they get prints in Kansas?"

Hix shook his head. "Like the truck here, wiped clean. Gracious guest. Put his Tupperware in the sink and wiped down his prints."

Damn.

I reached out and wrapped my hand around his forearm. "Even if you had him, you couldn't heal what's hurting in Faith."

"You're right and you're wrong, baby. Victims of this kind of thing benefit from a case being closed. An understanding of what happened. Knowing justice was served. It isn't a miracle cure. That wound will remain open a long time and the scar will never fade. But it helps."

I nodded because I figured that was right. He would definitely know.

Hix looked back to the street. "I need to get this done for Faith."

"You're doing everything you can do."

He gave me his attention again. "I know that. First thing I do every morning is open that case file and sift through it, hoping something will jump out at me, a new idea, a thread of a lead. Nothing ever does. But that doesn't change the fact I need to find this guy and at least put that to rest for Faith Calloway and her kids."

I leaned his way and offered what I could, as weak as it was, it was all I had.

"She hasn't been in. I'll call her. If she needs it, I'll go to her place, do her hair, have a chat, see where she is. Talk to Lou, some of the other ladies, start looking after her better. I didn't push things because I don't know what she's going through and I thought she'd need some time. Maybe it's time for us to start pushing things, help her pick up the tatters of life after Nat and find a way to carry on."

"Think that's a good idea, Greta."

I nodded. "I'll call her tomorrow."

He twisted his arm in a way he could catch my hand and he did just that, trapping it under his on the arm of his chair with the back of my hand up so he could run his fingers along he insides of mine.

He did this and he watched himself do it.

I let him and I let him do it in silence for some time, watching the preoccupation on his handsome face, knowing the thoughts behind that were troubled and frustrated, and thinking that the people of McCook County lucked out that someone who cared this much ran for their sheriff.

Finally, I spoke.

"I don't know what you need from me, Hix, but whatever it is, I'm here. I'll listen. I'll get you bourbon and sit with you. A beer. Make you some dinner. All you need to do is tell me."

His eyes drifted up to my face. "You're doin' it, sweetheart."

I gave him a small smile.

He looked to the street, still touching my hand.

I scooched my hip against the side of the chair, leaned into him and dropped my head to rest on his shoulder.

We both sat in the cold, one of the final days we'd have before it chased us inside, and studied my street, letting its peace envelope us.

Hix's voice was less tight, not less exhausted, when he murmured, "Bourbon and a warmup would be good about now, babe."

I nodded my head still on his shoulder, lifted it up and set my book aside. I grabbed my blanket and cup of tea, got up and threw the blanket over my arm so I could take Hix's hand.

He walked me into my house.

I threw the blanket over the back of the couch and he threw his jacket over it.

I got him some bourbon.

And we snuggled in my couch over mindless TV and warmed up before we went to bed, Hix took his time making love to me, and we fell asleep.

I ENTERED the auditorium feeling anxious.

It was the night of Mamie's recital.

I wasn't nervous because it was Friday and timing was tight. By my calculations, I'd have just enough of it to watch Mamie's recital, maybe be with Hixon after she was done as he gave her the big bouquet of flowers he'd brought with him, before I had to take off and get to the Dew Drop. There, I had to slap on some extra makeup, do something with my hair, pull on my dress and be onstage for the first of my sets, which thanks to Gemini being cool, started that night at nine thirty not my usual eight thirty.

No, I was nervous because I'd been able to talk Hix out of pressing me into going to see any of Corinne's volleyball games because I didn't want to be too in your face to Hope about my place in Hix's life so soon after they'd established their détente. Even if it made timing to get to the Dew tight, I went to all the home football games with Hix because Raider Field was larger, more open and seemed safer, for Hope and for me. The gymnasium seemed more closed in, smaller, with less opportunity to be able to put space between us.

I felt guilty about this because Corinne definitely wanted me to go see a game. She didn't come right out and say it but I could tell by her demeanor when the Drakes talked about the games around me that she was disappointed I didn't show. And the season was almost over. Not to mention, it hadn't been days since Hix and Hope sorted things out, it was now weeks. I needed to hit a game.

But Mamie's dance recitals didn't come around very often. The next one was a Christmas show that would heavily feature the younger dancers, with no solos, while this one was about the older girls, and specifically Mamie, who had a solo. The next big recital wasn't until spring and it wasn't a given she'd have a solo.

So I had to attend.

I wanted to attend.

However, the auditorium was even smaller than the gymnasium and Hope and her entire family would be there.

So I was nervous. I didn't want an incident. And Hope had proven to be like my mom in some respects, especially the ones where you couldn't predict when she might pull something.

This was why we hadn't brought Andy. It sucked because he'd wanted to come. But if some scene was to play out, I didn't want it to play out in front of him, especially in public. He had an excuse for his unpredictability, but he was still unpredictable, and if something should happen, I could deal. I didn't want Andy to have to deal too.

We'd promised he could go to the Christmas recital. I just hoped Hope would carry on as she was so he actually could.

"It's gonna be okay," Hix whispered in my ear as we walked down the aisle, the attention we were getting something we always got because Hix was Hix, I was with him, all that had gone on had gone on, and that came with the territory.

"Mm-hmm," I mumbled.

"Babe," he said as he stopped us beside a row but didn't start leading us in.

I looked up at him.

"It's been weeks. And this is Mamie's night. She's makin' an effort. I know her, Greta. Can't say I fully understood the games she played over the last year but the woman we're dealin' with now I know well. She loves her daughter. She's not gonna screw up this night for her."

Before I could reply, I heard, "Hix, son. Greta, darlin'. Good to see you both."

We turned to see Jep and his wife Marie standing close.

Jep had his hand raised.

Hix took it, shook it, offered a greeting to them both and let Jep go to move in and kiss Marie's cheek.

Jep then moved in to kiss mine before Marie moved in to give me an awkward hug.

We settled in our uncomfortable huddle with eyes all over the auditorium on us and Jep said, "Lookin' forward to watchin' our little girl wow us tonight."

"Yeah," Hix replied.

"Heard..." Marie started, stopped, and started again. "Heard that cute thing you did on Halloween, Greta. Mamie told us all about it. Reckon all the kids in town'll be goin' up Hixon's walk next October thirty-first."

I smiled at her and at the kind way she made it plain she thought I'd be with Hix next Halloween and she was (relatively) okay with that.

"Best buy more candy then," I replied.

She smiled back and I turned when a man's voice said, "Ma, Dad, we need to find our seats."

It was then I saw one of Hope's brothers standing not close but not far. But how he was standing was turned slightly to the side, his arm up behind him toward Hope, like he was holding her back because she faced some physical threat from Hix and me.

"Reed, have you met Greta?" Jep asked.

"Heard enough about the woman, don't need to meet her," Reed replied.

I stilled.

Hix turned fully to Reed, his frame set in a way that was more than a little alarming, but the vibe coming off him was beyond alarming.

"Reed!" Marie snapped like he wasn't whatever-age-he-was (I was guessing mid-forties) but instead about eight.

"Son, this is not—" Jep started.

"Reed, for crap's sake," Hope hissed, rounded her brother's arm and got closer to all of us in order to whisper irately, "Don't be a dick."

This time it was Hix who grew still.

I blinked.

"Hix, pretty flowers, Mamie'll love them," she said to Hixon and looked to me. "Hey, Greta. Sweet you can make it. Mamie was hoping you could."

My mind was tumbling with things to try to catch onto in order to push out a reply, but Hope kept talking before I got the chance to say a word.

"Now the curtain will be up soon and seats are filling so we should find some. Hix, Greta, enjoy," she bid us then started hustling along.

It was then I got over my surprise and noted how much that took out of her because she didn't do it for the audience of onlookers who were watching with avid interest. She did it for Hix. For Mamie. And maybe for me.

But it hurt her to do it.

It hurt a great deal.

"Hope's right, we best be gettin' on. Take care, you two," Jep said, and he led Marie after Hope.

Her brother Reed glared at us as he stomped past but her other brother stopped, said hello to Hixon and so did Jessie, his wife. Molly, Reed's wife, who looked fit to be tied, also stopped, forcing a smile at me in between glaring at her husband's back.

They left.

Hix guided me into the row, right in the middle, where we could see everything. It was also four rows back from where Hope and her family settled, also right in the middle.

Hix took my hand.

I pulled in a deep breath.

"That cost her," I whispered trying not to stare at the back of Hope's head.

"Yeah," Hix whispered back.

I turned eyes up to him. "You okay?"

He looked down at me. "Sure. You?"

I nodded.

He bent in and touched his mouth to mine.

When he pulled back a couple of inches, he grinned gently and said softly, "This is gonna work."

I grinned back and nodded.

"You think we'll miss complicated?" I asked.

He settled in, eyes to the stage, muttering, "It'll come back, sweetheart. So let's enjoy this while it lasts."

I knew he was not wrong.

What I didn't know was how heartbreaking it would be when he was proved right.

I WAS up in my bathroom putting the final touches on when the doorbell rang.

I turned and stared at the opened doorway to my bathroom, frowning and wondering who that could be.

It couldn't be Hix. I'd given him a key. He'd come right in the side kitchen door and shout, "Babe!" to let me know he was there seeing as that's what he always did when he showed and I wasn't on my porch.

But I was expecting Hix. We had a reservation for Jameson's that night. It was Tuesday, a kickoff to a big week that included Thanksgiving Thursday.

And I couldn't wait to have what was really our first, official, just-him-and-me romantic date (we'd been to the Harlequin together repeatedly, we went out with the kids and/or Andy also repeatedly, we met his friends at the Outpost often, and once we went to a movie together, but that was just a date, not a *romantic* one).

I was totally looking forward to it.

But what I really couldn't wait for was Thanksgiving.

The kids were spending the morning and early afternoon with Hope and her family at her mom and dad's ranch, and then they were coming to my place for pie and more football. In the meantime, Andy, Toast, Tommy, Lou, Maple, Snow and Bill were coming over, and obviously Hix would be there, and we were doing dinner together with the added goodness of the kids being there in the evening.

This was a bigger occasion than just our first family holiday together, because in all this time, the kids had never been to my house. Hix and I had talked about me making them dinner but with them at their mom's half the time, games, dates, practices, me singing at the Dew Drop, we could never get anything scheduled (ditto that for our date at Jameson's).

As much as I'd wanted that to happen, things worked out the way they should and I loved it that the first time they'd be in my house, at my table, was Thanksgiving. A family day. When Andy and Hix's friends, and Lou and her family would be there.

But right at that moment, I loved that Hix had made reservations at Jameson's for a special date for just him and me where I could wow him with my new dress (forest-green, chunky cable-knit, slinky, clingy sweater dress with a cowl neck).

I'd ordered an amazing pair of fawn suede booties to go with it. I had big hair and smoky eyes. I knew Hixon was a sure thing, but I also knew that he thought I was beautiful and loved the way I dressed, so I was hoping that sure thing would get (even more than usually) inspired after sitting through dinner that night with me wearing that dress.

What I didn't love was having an unknown caller when Hix was due any minute and I hadn't put on the finishing touches.

Since they were unknown and Hix was due, I decided to go through those finishing touches, hoping it was someone who wanted to guide my path to Jesus or something like that, and who would take a hint when I didn't open the door. But I did it in a hurry just in case it was something else.

So when the doorbell rang again, I was putting my gold hoop earrings in at the same time zipping up my booties, going back and forth between each.

I finished with the last earring after I got the second bootie on and hurried down the stairs toward the door.

When I hit the bottom, I became confused. Through the sheer curtain, silhouetted by the outside light, I could see a hulking frame that could be Hix's but also couldn't because he'd come right in.

Maybe he'd lost his keys.

Though if he did that, he'd phone me.

I hastened to the door, pulled the curtain aside and stared in shock up at Keith who had noticed me and was staring down at me.

What in *the* hell?

In that moment of surprise, I took him in. His brown hair. His beautiful straight nose. His big, brown eyes. His square, clean-shaven jaw. His broad shoulders.

He was maybe an inch taller than Hix, but though his build was strong and could not be described as lean, it was somehow less substantial than Hix's. Hix had slightly more bulk, but since it was all muscle, it gave his frame that nuance of added power.

Keith had the body of a tight end.

Hix had the body of a linebacker.

"Greta," I heard him clip, and it was then I saw he was not only surprisingly there, standing on my porch, unexpected, at six twenty-seven at night, two days before Thanksgiving, he was doing it pissed.

What in *the hell*?

I quickly unlocked the door, pulled it open and only noticed then he'd already opened my storm door and was standing in it.

I then immediately scuttled back because he was forcing his way in.

"Keith, what...I...hey. What are you doing here?"

He looked me up and down and he did it seeming strange, like he was holding himself in check and the effort to do that was immense.

Suddenly, he lost that battle and reached out with both hands, yanking me to him and wrapping his arms around me tight as I stood in them, my hands held slightly out to the sides because I didn't know what to do with them and I had no clue what was going on.

"God, God, *God*, honey," he whispered into the top of my hair. "God. Okay. I'm here. It'll be okay. I'll make you safe."

I stared at his jacket in my face and it took a few seconds before I pushed out, "What?"

"He won't hurt you again. I'll get you safe. I'll get Andy safe. We're going home."

Safe?

Home?

I *was* home.

I blinked at his jacket and repeated, "What?"

He transferred his hands to either side of my face, tipping it back and coming right in.

I stiffened entirely as his mouth brushed mine and I hadn't recovered from the shock as he pulled back, and that shock deepened when he spoke.

"I fucked up. I knew it then," he whispered. "I just couldn't see past it. It tore me apart but I couldn't see past it. Then Tawnee called me. Told me what was happening. *Showed* me what was happening. And I saw past it. Now I'm here. I'm here to make it all better. I'm here to get us back to where we're supposed to be."

Oh no.

What had my mother done?

I carefully tried to pull back, starting, "Keith—"

And then it happened.

Coming from the direction of the kitchen, we both heard, "What the fuck?"

It was Hix.

I tore myself from Keith's hold and turned to Hix, watching him prowl down the hall from the kitchen, past the dining room, his eyes darting from me to Keith, his face carved from granite, his gait beyond aggressive straight to hostile.

I began to move to him, opening my mouth to speak.

But Keith hadn't needed a chance to recover.

He was approaching Hix in the same manner and doing it talking.

"You are no longer welcome here."

That jolted me out of my inactivity, that and the fact that Hix's face changed to incredulous fury, not to mention they were about to connect in a way it looked like both of them would be thrilled to start brawling in my living room.

I ran directly to them, shouting, "No!"

They had fists raised, torsos twisted to put power behind whatever they were going to do, but I shoved in between them, hands to Hix's chest, pushing him back (he wouldn't budge), so I twisted my torso and kept one hand in Hix's chest and added a hand to Keith's chest and shrieked, "*Stop it!*"

"Greta, step aside," Hix ordered, his hand to my waist trying to make that so.

But I held steady even if I wanted to scream or stamp my foot or at least glare at him, because he was ready to throw down and not only did he not know what was happening (as, I will point out, neither did I), he didn't even know who Keith was (though, he was the sheriff, he probably could guess).

"Calm down, Hix," I hissed and looked to Keith. "Step back, Keith."

"Greta, move," Keith growled.

"No!" I snapped then shouted, "*Step back, Keith! Right now!*"

His eyes cut down to mine. "Do not protect this man. I know what he is. I know he's got you twisted up. And I know I'm gonna get you free."

"Okay, that. That right there," I stated, shoving into Keith's chest (who also didn't budge) standing firm between them, my other hand still to Hix's chest, "needs to be explained because I don't know what the hell you're talking about."

"You do," Keith retorted.

"I do not," I asserted.

"Then you're twisted up more than Tawnee said you were."

God!

My mother!

"Keith, you realize you're spouting shit Mom told you, and first, you know anything she says is suspect, and second, you know anything she says that's suspect is also bullshit. So putting that together, pretty much everything out of her mouth is pure bullshit."

"I have pictures," he declared.

"Pictures of what?" I asked.

At that, thankfully, he stepped back (though unfortunately not very far), his gaze slicing to Hix's face as he pulled his phone out of his back pocket.

He engaged it not looking at it but eventually looked down only to lift it up and turn it our way.

I was pretty certain I gasped but I was too busy staring in complete and utter disbelief with a healthy mingling of being creeped right the fuck out at the picture on the screen.

It was of me with the shiner Andy gave me. I was walking from my Cherokee toward the salon.

"Not enough?" Keith asked snidely, but I didn't take my eyes from the screen when his finger came up and he swiped the picture to the side.

My stomach dropped at what I saw next, and Hix growled, "Jesus Christ," from behind me as we were treated to a picture of Hix pinning me up against the shelves at the grocery store, the photo taken during the part where he had his hand locked on my neck and his face right in mine.

"Want more?" Keith asked antagonistically, and another swipe showed a photo of me with my nose completely taped up after the kitchen incident, the photo taken while Hix was escorting me to his Bronco that Monday in order to take me to the hospital to have my dressing changed.

"More?" Keith went on, swiping again, and we had a photo of me, again walking into the salon, but this time with only tape on my nose, however the bruising under my eyes was horrendous. "I don't know what hold this asshole has on you, Greta, but it ends now."

I looked from the phone to him, feeling Hix pressing into my hand in his chest so I removed it but moved in a way his chest was now pressing into my back and I was returning that, leaning into him.

"Keith, Hix didn't do those things to me."

"Yeah, your mother said you'd say that. Small town, fucked-up, shady sheriff gettin' away with fucking with women. He's got power. He's got authority. He's got ways to fuck with your life and make bad shit turn nasty, so you can't get away." His gaze lifted beyond me to Hix. "Wife got fed up, yeah? Took years of it then finally kicked your ass out? So you had to go lookin' for fresh meat."

"Greta, sort this guy out," Hix growled from behind me.

"Keith, look at me," I ordered.

He didn't look at me.

He kept his eyes on Hix and stated, "You got ten seconds to move out, motherfucker. You don't, I'll move you out, and if I have any problems with you and your deputies, trust me, my lawyers will make mincemeat of you and these pictures will hit every paper from Iowa to Nevada."

"Greta," Hix warned.

"Keith, *look at me.*"

It took him a second before he did, his face held its wrath but then softened a little before he said, "Honey, it's okay. It's over. Please come here."

"Andy gave me that black eye."

He shook his head. "Don't do that. Don't cover for him. He may have power here, baby, but he can't abuse it this way and I'll see he learns that."

"I had Andy for the weekend. It rained."

Keith's frame visibly tightened.

He knew about Andy and rain.

"That broken nose, I'm sorry, I hate to share it with you this way, but I had an admirer from the club, he turned out to be a creep and he attacked me in my kitchen. He broke my nose. I got away. I went to Hix. His kids took care of me as he and his deputy arrested the guy and now that guy is serving five years in the Nebraska State Penitentiary. That's on record so it'd be easy for you to validate, not to mention, it was reported in the local paper. As for the black eye, you'd have to ask Andy. If he remembers, he'll tell you. But it upset him he did it so I'd rather him not be reminded of it if he's forgotten." I licked my lips and hurried on, "Mom lied, Keith. We've had some run-ins since she's come here and she's upping her game. She's screwing with me, with Hix, with Andy and now...with you."

He stared at me.

"It's true and I'm sorry," I carried on. "I'm so, so sorry she fed you those terrible stories but they aren't true. That picture of me and Hix in the grocery store was the first time he saw me with the black eye. Mom's seeing the local meth cooker and Hix was worried they'd worked me over. He was a little distressed. But it isn't what it looks like. He was just really concerned for me."

Keith just stared at me some more.

So I kept explaining. "She...well, she clearly has it out for Hix, probably because he arrested her when she was making a scene at Sunnydown, and you know Mom. She's not a big fan of not getting her way and obviously, pulling her crap and it being a misdemeanor means the local sheriff can intervene and she won't get her way. So he was already in her sights, us, um...being together. But obviously he's now a target and that's just...that."

Keith said nothing and kept staring at me.

"I'm telling the truth, honey," I said softly. "And I think you know that. She can get ugly, and you know that as well as me. But lately, she's ratcheted that up to unprecedented levels as, obviously," I threw a hand lamely his way, "you're seeing."

It took a second of him staring at me some more before his jaw went hard(er). He looked to the side, lifted his hand like he was going to do what he did when he got frustrated and tear it through his hair. Instead it dropped and his gaze scored through Hix before coming back to me.

"You got attacked in your kitchen?" Keith asked.

"I'm okay now."

"You got attacked in your kitchen." It was a statement this time, anger warring with not a small amount of pain I heard threading through it, but also saw on his face.

I knew that pain.

He was worried about me. He hated that that happened to me.

But maybe most of all, he hated that I'd gone to Hix, he'd taken care of it and Keith was hearing about it for the first time now when it had always been Keith who had taken care of things for me.

"I'm okay," I whispered.

He stared at me again, doing it hard, his eyes finally flicking up to Hix before coming back to me.

"I didn't take her calls," he said, sounding calmer, still angry, also, upsettingly, still feeling pain.

"Keith—" I started.

"Then she sent the pictures and I took her calls."

"I'm so sorry," I whispered.

"You deal with this," Hixon said close to my ear from behind me. "I'll be in the kitchen."

I turned to him to nod, but he wasn't looking at me, his eyes were locked on Keith.

"I'll be wanting those pictures."

"Why?" I asked.

He looked down at me and he was not feeling pain. He was just feeling anger.

A lot of it.

"*That*, Greta," he jabbed a finger Keith's way, and from what he said next I knew this movement indicated Keith's phone and the photos, "is criminal stalking. I want that evidence. I want it in front of the judge. I want that fuckin' bitch to have a protection order slapped on her so she can't get near you. And I want this on her record so the next time that woman pulls her nasty shit, I got as much as I can get to land her ass in jail."

"I'll get the photos, baby," I murmured soothingly.

He just scowled at me before he looked again to Keith and declared, "I'm just down the hall and I hope you get me when I say I'm gonna be fuckin' listening."

"Darlin'—" I began.

His gaze sliced down to mine and I shut up.

He speared Keith with a look then he turned and stalked out, and that was the first I noticed he was wearing a beautiful, tailored, dark-blue suit, a sky-blue shirt and a pair of awesome brown dress shoes, all of it making him look like a linebacker-sized, male model.

It wasn't what I'd met him in.

But it was just as hot.

Right.

I absolutely, totally *hated* my mother.

Doing this to Keith?

Then making me miss my dinner with Hix looking that hot?

I turned to Keith.

"Janice knows I'm here," he announced.

I felt my shoulders fall and my heart lurch.

Janice, better known as Lawyer Barbie, Keith's new wife.

"Keith," I whispered.

"She knows why. It was her opinion it was none of my business. Not that she wanted harm to come to you, just that she wanted me to find a way to intervene without me actually doing the intervening. I got in my car to drive to you while she was putting suitcases in hers to leave me."

I closed my eyes, opened them and started to him but stopped when he leaned away from my movement.

"Darlin'." I was still whispering.

"She was right to go. Not fair on her. Me coming here to visit you and Andy and not letting her come with me and her knowing exactly why. Me racing here when I thought you were in a bad situation and her knowing exactly why that is too, seein' as I'm still in love with my ex-wife. And that's seein' as I knew, just like Janice knew I knew, that I never should have let her go."

My heart didn't lurch at that.

It started bleeding.

"I don't...I honestly don't know what to say," I told him.

He studied me a second before his gaze flicked toward the kitchen then came back to me.

"And I honestly didn't think that's what you would say after I shared that."

Oh my God.

Keith.

I took a step to him, trying again, "Keith—"

He took a step back, forcing out a rough, tortured, "Don't, honey."

I stopped and swallowed in order to soothe the burn in my throat.

But nothing could soothe the burn in my eyes except, maybe, the tears I felt trembling at my lower lashes before I felt them begin to glide down my cheeks.

He watched me cry then whispered, "Fuck me, I fuckin' blew it."

"Now *you* don't, Keith," I urged huskily.

"She reminded me of you," he told me.

"Stop it," I whispered.

"Didn't even know I was doin' that shit to her, until she threw it in my face."

"Keith, please."

"Married my rebound, lost my shot at reconciliation, doin' that dickin' around."

"I can't—"

"I did, didn't I?" he asked. "If I didn't move on fast to prove to myself I was right to let you go, get on with my life, draw that line in the sand between us, I could have won you back."

"It doesn't matter now," I shared honestly.

"Guess it doesn't," he bit out, jerking his chin to the kitchen.

I took another step to him, begging, "Keith, please—"

"Don't come closer, Greta," he warned.

I stopped again.

"I see I gotta let you go but I can't do that to Andy so I'll go visit him tomorrow and then I'll leave, but he's not part of this fucked-up shit so he shouldn't pay for it. I'll email you when I'm comin' to see my guy. But I won't bother you."

I hated that.

I hated it so much, I didn't think it was possible, but it made me hate my mother more.

"Maybe we can someday get to the point where—" I began to attempt to lessen the damage.

He again didn't let me finish. "That's not gonna happen. Not ever."

"Don't say that."

"I shoulda known, I divorced you, you changed your name back to hers. The name a woman you hated gave you, not keepin' the name of the man who loved you."

"I did that for you," I told him quietly. "For Janice. And for Andy. He shares that name too, Keith."

"Right," he stated dubiously.

"I did," I asserted.

He jerked his head toward the kitchen this time. "You gonna give him a kid?"

My body locked at being confronted with this version of a familiar refrain, but I forced my lips to push out, "He has kids."

"Right," he clipped that word this time. "Greta gets to spread her abundance of love wide but do it removed so the shit of life can't deliver another blow that will rip her apart. You orchestrated that good. Well done, baby."

Now my heart was aching.

"Don't do that."

I lost his attention in a way that he was looking beyond me and it made me pivot. When I did, I saw that Hixon was indeed listening, and now he was sharing he didn't like how the conversation had turned because he was leaning against the newel post of my stairs, arms crossed on his chest, deep in a staredown with Keith.

Keith ended the staredown by announcing, "Think that's my cue to get the fuck out."

I turned back to Keith to see him sauntering to the door.

For a split second, I didn't move.

Then I found my feet rushing to follow him.

"Keith, please, God, darlin', don't leave it this way."

He pulled open the door when I made it to him and he turned to me.

I halted and froze when he lifted his hand to cup my jaw.

"Fuck me," he whispered, his aching eyes roaming my face. "But I blew it."

A tear slid into the side of his palm and he didn't do what he'd done time and again when he'd had a crying Greta on his hands—sweep it away with thumb, fingers or lips.

It wasn't his right. Not anymore. He knew it. So did I.

And even though I'd moved on to something beautiful, that didn't mean I didn't feel, right then, like I'd lost him all over again.

He dropped his hand, shoved through the storm door, strolled across my porch, down my steps, right to his slate-gray Range Rover parked at the curb, his tall, striking body at his command, even if there was a stiffness to the loose agility he usually always carried himself with.

The storm whooshed closed as I stood in the open door and watched him round the hood of his truck, the lights flashing as he unlocked it.

I continued standing there as he folded in, started up the truck, the headlights illuminated the street and then he drove away.

I felt an arm wrap around my chest, another one around my belly, and the hard heat of Hix pressed into my back.

The tears just kept coming and I didn't pull my eyes away from the now-empty, dark, peaceful street.

"Come away from the door," Hix murmured into my hair.

I stayed where I was, silently weeping.

He put slight pressure on, not too much, but stopped when I refused to move.

"Baby, come inside," he urged.

"What makes her this way?" I asked the sleepy street.

Hix settled in behind me and answered, "I don't know."

"Does she enjoy knowing that she causes this pain?"

"I wish I had answers for you, but I just don't, sweetheart."

"Now she's destroyed one young man's life and two marriages. That young man her son, one of those marriages her daughter's. How can she even sleep?"

"Don't know," he whispered.

"I hate her," I whispered back.

His arms gave me a squeeze. "I know."

"I *hate* her, Hix," I decreed, my voice breaking.

"I know, baby," he said, and forced me to turn into his arms, but he didn't move us from the door as he held me close and I sobbed into his sky-blue shirt, standing at the front door to the house that the man I'd just lost forever in a way I never thought I'd lose him had bought for me.

It took time but I pulled myself together, pulled an arm from around him and shoved it up between us to wipe my face.

Only then did I tip my head back to look up to him.

"He'll email me those pictures," I told him.

He nodded. "I know."

"Do you think we can still make our reservation?"

He put a hand to my face and it was Hix's thumb that drew away the wet still there, one side, then the other, as he answered, "Think I should get you a gin and tonic and we should order a pizza."

I shook my head. "I'll fix my makeup and I wanna go."

"Greta—"

It came out suddenly harsh when I stated, "She won't beat me."

Hix's thumb stilled on the apple of my cheek and he stared into my eyes.

"So I have puffy eyes and it'll take until glass of wine number three for me to wash away a little bit of what just happened so I can maybe taste my steak, but I had romantic dinner date plans with my man and we're gonna keep those plans. We're gonna spend too much on dinner. I'm gonna get tipsy. And then we're gonna come home and I'm gonna fuck your brains out. And she can go fuck herself, living in her nasty world doing nasty shit to people she should treat with respect and love and..." I lost the urge to rail on about a woman who didn't deserve my time or my anger, so I finished, "Fuck her. Just *fuck her*. I want steak."

I didn't want steak. I was pretty sure if I ate steak, I'd throw up.

But damn it, I was going to take this licking and keep on ticking, and Tawnee Dare could go jump in a lake.

"That's what you want, I'll call the restaurant and tell them we're gonna be a little late. It's Tuesday in McCook County before Thanksgiving and they're a restaurant where you can't get out without payin' at least fifty bucks a plate. They won't give our table to someone else."

"Good," I bit off.

He grinned a small, careful grin, dipped in and touched his mouth to mine.

When he pulled back he murmured, "Go fix your face so we can head out. I'll make the call while you're doin' that."

I nodded, got on my toes, brushed my lips to his and when I was rolling back, he let me go.

I rounded him and headed to the stairs only to stop with my foot on the first step when he called my name.

"Yes?" I asked, looking back at him.

"*Really* like that dress, baby."

That bought him a small, not-careful grin before I took my time and maybe swayed my hips more than normal as I walked up the stairs to go fix my face in order to go out and have a romantic date with my man, county sheriff, father of three, excellent lover, all-around good guy, Hixon Drake.

One thing Keith had been right about, as heartbreaking and terrible as he'd meant it to be when he'd said it, it made it no less true.

Landing Hixon Drake was a job well done.

And I could live with that.

Easily.

Chapter 24

Hollow

Hixon

She didn't take her eyes from him, not from the moment Elvan touched his fingers to the keys, not a second as the room suspended, the others melted away, and her lips sang Pink's "Glitter in the Air" straight at him.

He'd been wrong. Gum drop wasn't it.

He should have been calling her sugar.

Because he thought it could never get better than that first night.

But every one since, she'd made better and better.

And in that moment, sitting at a table with an empty chair across from him, her sparkling water there waiting for her to return, Hix knew the ride he was taking to fall in love was over.

At the same time it never was and never would be.

That was what love was, he knew right then.

An endless night of beauty that didn't include making plans to retire to your RV.

Just sitting back and seeing what came next in your never-ending journey of discovery.

He was in love with Greta Kate Dare.

It was too bad he couldn't afford to buy her a twenty-five thousand dollar engagement ring.

But he'd get her one on their twentieth anniversary.

Hix walked in through the kitchen door of Greta's house to see Shaw and Wendy at her island hunched over the books and papers spread all over it, studying. Corinne was nowhere to be seen (probably in the living room on the phone with her new boyfriend, a recent development that didn't make Hix happy). And Mamie and Greta were bending over pots at the stove.

They'd started to do this after Thanksgiving, come to her home for dinner, because Greta liked having them all there. He didn't know exactly why, since she had all of them at his house, except for the fact it was part of who she was, having a bent to take care of people she cared about, and there was something in it for her to do it in her own space. So now, a couple of times in a way Hix knew there'd be more, the kids and Hix came to her.

Then again, the kids liked her house. Greta had made them comfortable there from the moment they'd walked in the door Thanksgiving night. Not to mention there was a fully-stocked kitchen in all the ways that could be and Greta made more than just great breakfasts, so his kids knew they'd get a good meal that wasn't takeout, delivery or its origins were mostly from a box.

But that wasn't the only reason they did it.

"Hey, Dad," Shaw greeted.

"Hey, Mr. Drake," Wendy called.

Greta looked over her shoulder at him and smiled.

Mamie whirled and cried, "Hey, Daddy!"

"Hey, guys," Hix said, coming in, shrugging off his jacket and moving around the room to lift a hand and squeeze the back of Shaw's neck, get Mamie's hug when she danced to him and bend in to touch his lips to Greta's mouth. "We need a second," he told her quietly when he'd pulled away.

She stared into his eyes and nodded.

He retraced his steps to go to the living room and jerked up his chin to Corinne before he threw his jacket on the back of the couch. Curled in Greta's armchair, his daughter grinned at him and gave him a little wave before she went back to her conversation, curling a lock of her hair around her finger.

He unbuckled his gun belt and started up the steps, going to Greta's room where he hung it on hook inside her closet, coming out of that closet to see her walking into the room, eyes on him.

"Is everything okay?" she asked.

He moved into her space, putting his hands to her hips.

"Right, you filed for that protection order on your mom and the judge granted a fourteen-day order, *ex parte*. Yeah?"

"I know," she told him, looking like she spoke even while holding her breath.

"Yeah, you know. What you need to know now is that we haven't been able to find her to serve the order. I called Becker, he told me he scraped her off and has no idea where she is. He didn't sound happy to be talking about her, so my guess is, she finally did some shit that made him find his way free of whatever hold she had on him and he's done with her."

"Not great news for Mom but I'm not in the mood to care that my mother lost her meth-cooking boyfriend so..." She didn't finish that but did lift her brows in request he get to the point.

"If she isn't served, sweetheart, the order is ineffective. She needs to be aware that the order has been issued, if she isn't, it hasn't officially been processed. And she needs to have that order served so that fourteen days can play out so you can return to the judge and request a permanent one."

"Do you...want me to call Mom? Ask her to come around?" she asked.

"Hell no," he answered.

"Then what are you saying?"

"I'm just saying, she pulls shit, gets near you, takes pictures after she's been served by a protection order, that pushes her into felony territory. But if she hasn't been served, she can still do whatever the hell she wants."

"Awesome," she muttered sarcastically.

"She doesn't have a job, she's not at home, she lost her sugar daddy. Maybe she took off," Hix suggested hopefully.

"Maybe," Greta replied skeptically.

He bent in and touched his lips to her forehead before moving back. "Seein' as the process servers for McCook County are me and my deputies, not thinkin' we'll give up on this one."

That made her grin.

Hix grinned back.

She watched his mouth a beat before she looked again to his eyes.

"We have kids to feed," she reminded him.

"Yeah," he murmured.

She lifted a hand to his neck, rolled up on her toes and kissed the bottom of his jaw.

She then rolled back and they held hands to the top of the stairs.

He let her go so Greta could walk down before him.

They managed to pry Corinne's phone from her ear to sit down to eat.

Then they sat at Greta's awesome table and had a family dinner.

"You need to call Hope. We need to know what she's buying them from these lists. We shouldn't double up."

Greta was sitting across from him at his desk at the department, her head bent as she shuffled through the papers in her hands—his kids' Christmas gift wish lists—doing this bossing him.

"I'll get on that right away," he muttered and her eyes shot to his.

"This is serious, Hixon."

"Of course it is," he assured.

She gave him a hard stare to assess if he found her amusing (which he did) but he figured he'd managed to hide that when she raised the lists and shook them in the air. "We also need to be careful to go equal. It wouldn't be cool to make it bigger than what she gives them since there are two of us."

"Babe, they're gonna be at their grandparents' house Christmas Eve night, gettin' spoiled rotten, dropped at my place at the end of that to wake up and get spoiled rotten on Christmas morning, then heading to Hope's to get spoiled rotten Christmas night. With all that, I don't think anyone is gonna be able to keep track of who spoils them *more* rotten."

"It'll be noted," she returned.

He leaned into his folded arms on his desk and reminded her, "Hope's lettin' that kinda shit go."

"I know she is," Greta replied. "And I know it has to be hard on her, the holiday is going to make it harder, so we shouldn't do even the littlest thing to make it even *harder*."

He stared at the woman he loved, having reason once again to love her more before he sat back and said quietly, "I'll call Hope and we'll get it straight."

"Thank you, Hix," she replied quietly.

It was time to move on to something else.

"I'm settin' up the guest room," he declared.

"I...okay," she returned, sounding confused.

"My folks come visit every once in a while, they don't have plans to hit town until the weather shifts since they're not big fans of snow, which is why they now live in Florida. But Andy can't sleep on the sectional anymore when he's over. I know he doesn't mind and that just means he's closer to the TV and Shaw so they can play videogames every waking moment they're together. But the man should have his own space when he's at home so we'll set it up for him. I'm sure it'll be cool with him that we use it as a guest room when he's not around."

It was Greta staring at Hixon when he got done talking, and the way she was doing it he felt in a number of areas of his body, his gut and chest the most prominent.

"What?" he whispered when she didn't speak.

"Can we shut the blinds to that window and do something probably very illegal on your desk?"

That he felt in his dick.

"No," he unfortunately had to answer.

"Shame," she murmured.

"But the minute the kids are back with Hope, you can do something not illegal to me in my bed and I'll return that favor."

She gave him a look he also felt in his dick.

"It's gonna be so good it'll feel illegal, smokey."

"Then I'll look forward to that, sugar."

She smiled at him.

He smiled back and decided it was time to move them on to something else again or he'd be sitting behind his desk at work with a raging hard-on.

"You wanna cook for the kids tonight or go out and—?"

He didn't finish because a sharp rap sounded on his window.

His head jerked that way and the warmth in his chest and gut vanished when he saw Bets standing there, her back to the window, her hand to the butt of her firearm in its unclipped holster, her eyes glued toward the front of the department.

Hix's gaze immediately moved there and he went entirely still for half a beat before he was out of his chair, his voice low and abrasive as he ordered, "You do not move from that seat, Greta."

"Hixon," she whispered but she didn't move and he knew this even though he didn't pry his eyes from the window as he quickly walked across the room.

He shut the door behind him and just as quickly moved down the hall.

He slowed his gait when he hit the mouth of it and swiftly assessed the situation.

Donna was five feet from the left of her desk, clearly having been stopped by what was happening in the process of walking in from the back. Her hand was on her firearm also in its holster, eyes locked on reception.

Hal was up and to one side, behind the reception desk, legs braced apart, one in front of the other in a modified squat, firearm out, up and aimed at reception.

Larry was the same, behind his desk, and he was ordering, "Drop the duffle and put your hands where we can see them!"

And just inside the door stood a very large, very tall man with straggling, wild, light-brown hair, a weathered face, wearing a canvas jacket with a big duffle slanted across his back.

He was unmoving and his eyes were not at the guns pointed at him or the further threats from the deputies who were ready to unholster their weapons.

They were on him.

"*Drop the duffle and put your hands where we can see them!*" Larry shouted.

"Larry," Hix called loudly, but calmly, moving in front of Bets slowly, making his way to the aisle, his arms down by his sides, his right elbow hitched up slightly but his hand was not on his gun.

"Boss—" Larry started.

"Lower your weapons," Hix ordered.

Hal's "Boss?" was terse.

"Do it, Hal," Hix commanded as he made his way deliberately down the center aisle, not taking his attention from the man just inside the door who still had not moved.

He didn't check to see if Larry and Hal had obeyed his order, he just kept walking with his attention locked on the man at the front until he was standing two feet from the swinging, half door.

He braced and heard Hal's clipped, "Fuckin' *shit*," and Larry's, "*Goddammit*," that came when the man moved.

But the guy just walked directly to the reception desk, lifted his hand and lowered it to the desk. He engaged his other hand when a balled piece of paper fell out of the first.

He smoothed it out, spreading it open, then he took a step back, leaving it there.

It was one of the artist's sketched pictures of him they'd sent out as a notice to homeless shelters.

"Is that you?" Hix asked him.

The man didn't speak.

"Are you here to turn yourself in?" Hix asked.

The man said nothing.

"Did you kill Nat Calloway?" Hix pressed.

The man stood still and stared into Hix's eyes.

An unpleasant thrill chased down his spine when Hix saw the man's eyes were empty. Void. Hollow.

"He had a wife and two children," Hix told him quietly.

Nothing came from the man. Not a movement. Not a sound. Not a change in expression.

Except one thing.

A tear fell from his left eye.

Shit.

"We need to take your duffle. We need to take your jacket. We need to pat you down. We need to cuff you. And then we'll need to arrest you," Hix told him, voice calm and still quiet.

The man moved, the room tensed, the duffle dropped.

Hix let out a breath and then another one when the jacket dropped.

The guy lifted his long arms and put his hands behind his head, his gaze never leaving Hix's.

"Careful and gentle, men," he ordered as Hal and Larry moved around him.

Hix followed them, going through the swinging, half door to stand with his hand now on his firearm as Larry got behind the guy and Hal took his brother's back with his hand also on his holstered gun.

"Read him his rights, Deputy. Go slow," he instructed then called, "Donna."

"Here, boss," she said from close.

"Get the defense attorney here and call the court psychologist," he ordered, not losing eye contact with Nathan Calloway's killer.

"Do we have a court psychologist?" Donna asked.

"Find one," Hix bit out.

"Right," he heard her mutter as Larry finished with reading the man his Miranda rights.

"Do you understand your rights?" Larry asked.

Hix butted in. "You can just nod."

The man took two beats then jerked up his chin.

Hix nodded. "Take him back." He moved out of their way as they carefully pushed the guy forward. "Process him."

Hal held open the door, Larry guided him through, Hal fell in behind Larry as they took him to the back.

Hix followed them until he got to Bets.

"You monitor that, every second, every move, holster clipped, Bets," he commanded in a low tone. "That guy is big and that guy is unpredictable and Hal and Larry need you as backup. He gets loose and gets the jump on you, I don't want him to have a clear shot to your gun. You need to use it, you can unclip it."

"Yeah, boss," she murmured, moving directly toward where Hal and Larry rounded the corner to get to where they did their fingerprints and mugshots in the back corner of the department.

"I get these calls done," Donna started, standing with the phone to her ear but her eyes to Hix, "I on that too?"

"Absolutely. But you and Bets give him space. I do not want that man to feel crowded or threatened beyond what I'm guessing he knew was gonna happen."

Donna nodded, looked toward the back and Hix moved straight to his office.

Greta was getting up slowly as he opened the door and her face was white as a sheet. "Is that the guy who—?"

"I need you out of here. I need you to keep this quiet. But I need you somewhere safe and right now, that is not here."

She immediately started gathering her jacket and purse even as her face got even paler. "Is it not safe for—?"

"Baby, no questions. I gotta escort you out then I gotta do a lot of other shit."

She nodded and didn't delay. She got her jacket on, her purse over her shoulder, and she scooted out with Hix dogging her heels.

He got her out the front door and around the side of the building where he stopped her, bent in, pressed his mouth hard against hers and pulled back, muttering, "I'll call you later."

"I love you, Hix."

He froze.

They hadn't said it. He'd been waiting for the right moment. He felt it from her and guessed she was waiting for the same.

Then again, she sang "Glitter in The Air" to him so she'd already said it.

"Best man I've ever met," she whispered, rolled up on her toes, pressed her lips hard against his and rolled back.

She then walked swiftly in her high-heeled boots down the sidewalk cleared of the snow they got yesterday.

"He's mute, due to a medical condition or a trauma, I don't know. He'll have to be examined," the psychologist told Hix and Donna outside the interrogation room. "He's also suffering a variety of other conditions, none of which I can accurately diagnosis, considering he's mute, he's big, and he scares the beejeezus out of me."

"Doc—" Hix began but stopped speaking when the psychologist lifted her hands and shook them.

"He needs a full medical evaluation and a full psychiatric evaluation. However, the one thing he's given me, his attorney and your deputy is that he killed Nathan Calloway. He jerks up his chin every time it's mentioned. He jerks up his chin when he's asked if he understands the meaning of that. He jerks up his chin every time he's asked if he understands why he's been arrested. I've asked him to write down what he wants to say if he has anything to say and he's refused. For whatever reason, physical, psychological or some of both, that man is deeply disturbed. However, in my professional opinion, he understands completely that he's done wrong. He saw that picture of himself and knew you knew who he was and you were looking for him. But my sense is, he's not here because he thought you'd find him. If that man doesn't want to be found, he could get lost forever. He's here to atone for it."

This was not news to them, except the last. They'd watched it all in the observation room, with Hix watching from inside the room while Larry asked the questions.

Hix turned to Donna. "Set up a supervised physical. The psych eval can happen here."

"On it," Donna muttered and took off.

He looked back to the psychologist. "Your professional opinion, we ever gonna know why he did what he did?"

She shrugged. It wasn't casual. She was taking this seriously. She simply didn't know.

"I honestly can't say. He doesn't trust me to open up to me, which isn't a surprise, I haven't had enough time with him and I've never done this. I did my best but the man frightens me and I'm afraid I couldn't completely hide it in a way he surely read it. It may be you'll need to do the psych eval somewhere else so he doesn't feel trapped or cornered and he might open up. But he may never open up. He might not even know how. Again, I can't say for certain."

"He's arrested, an unknown who's committed a violent act and a flight risk," Hix pointed out. "Not feelin' good about takin' him to a doctor so I'm not feelin' good about doublin' up on that to take him to see a shrink."

"Yes. But this man is not one who spends much time surrounded by four walls. Just being inside, my hunch, is costing him. It being a sheriff's department isn't helping matters."

"He essentially turned himself in."

"That's the atonement I told you about. This isn't easy for him. But he's doing it. If someone can get him to a place he'll find some way to communicate in the presence of someone he can trust," she shook her head, "I just don't know."

"I can't let you be alone with that man even observed and even with his attorney present and even as he is now, chained to a table. When I say that, not you or anyone," Hix told her. "We have some idea of what he's capable of. His size, I'm not testing that."

"I know. And I appreciate that. And I don't know even if he was lounging unencumbered out under the sky if he'd share. My suggestion is, the hospital will have psychiatrists on staff. Get one, another suggestion, a male one, to do the eval there. One visit, double duty. But every indication he's giving is that you're correct. He turned himself in for the crime of murdering Nathan Calloway and he's here to let justice take its course." She got closer. "You might never have answers, Sheriff, but you have your man."

Without her able to give him much more, he nodded.

"You want me to hang around or—?" she began.

"You can go but I'd like to be open to give you a call if we need to," he told her.

"Anytime."

"Obliged," he muttered.

She gave him a close look, a small, forlorn smile then she turned and walked out.

Hix turned to the window to interrogation, one of two one-way windows that looked inside, and saw the man staring at his hands cuffed to the steel ring in the middle of the table.

He'd allowed them also to shackle his legs.

The defense attorney was leaning toward him, speaking.

Larry was against the wall, giving them space but watching.

Hal and Bets were in the observation room monitoring with the recording equipment on.

Nat's killer was right there.

Right in his interrogation room chained to a table.

The man with the answers.

The end of it.

And studying him, Hix didn't feel the relief he thought he'd feel.

Mostly because all he could think about when his mind had opportunity to let anything else in was that tear sliding down his craggy cheek.

On that thought, he pushed through the door.

Larry and the attorney looked at him.

So did their guy.

Hix took the chair the psychologist had been sitting in across the table from their perp.

He looked him in his eyes and saw right down to an empty soul.

He then put his hands on the table, but other than that, didn't move in his direction at all.

"In order to do right by you and by Nat's wife, we need to be thorough, sir," he said quietly. "This means my deputies are going to have to take you to a medical doctor to be examined."

That got him nothing.

"A psychiatrist will either be coming to this department to speak with you or you'll be seeing one at the hospital," he continued.

More nothing.

"Do you understand these things?' Hix asked.

Finally, he got a chin jerk.

"Good," Hix muttered and held his gaze before he whispered, "There's a woman who's now raising two kids alone who needs answers. You can find it in you to—"

The guy thumped the side of his fist lightly on the table, the chains rattled, and Hix grew tense, as did the room. But he looked down at the man's hands and saw one long finger pointed at the legal-sized pad of paper there.

Hix shoved it his way.

The man put his opened hand on top of the pad then turned it palm up, and since they didn't leave a pen that could be used as a weapon lying close to him, Hix looked to his attorney.

"I think we should get this gentleman's evals out of the way before—" the attorney tried.

The man thumped his fist on the table, harder this time, then opened his hand.

The attorney sighed then leaned in and put a pen in his hand.

Hix didn't look to the attorney, to Larry, to the observation window.

He looked right at the pad of paper.

The guy wrote on it, set the pen down, then flipped it around to Hix.

On it, he'd scratched in shaky but careful capital letters, I DID IT.

It took no time to read that but Hix barely got that job done before the guy was flipping the pad around again and writing.

He set the pen aside one more time and turned the paper Hix's way.

Hix read it.

I'M SORRY.

A prickle slid over his scalp.

Hix looked to his face and whispered, "Why?"

The man's blank eyes stared into his.

"I'd like to be able to tell her why," Hix shared.

The man continued to stare in his eyes before he slumped in his seat, tucked his chin in his throat and stared at his bound hands.

"You got your confession, Sheriff, now get this man his evaluations," his attorney demanded. "It's clear where this is leading and we should get there as soon as we can because this man needs help. Not a stay in a penitentiary."

Hix looked to him then to their guy.

He was still staring at his hands.

"You didn't want to, did you?" Hix guessed quietly.

The man stared at his hands.

"He gave you a ride and you were grateful. You were tired. It was hot. You wanted to ride a while. You wanted out from under the sun. He gave you that ride and you were grateful."

The man stared at his hands but his shoulders pressed into his ears slightly.

He'd been grateful.

"What came next?" Hix asked.

The man said nothing.

"Sheriff," the attorney butted in.

"What came next?" Hix pushed.

"Sheriff," the attorney clipped. "This gentleman needs evaluated before you ask another question."

"What came next?" Hix repeated.

The guy didn't speak.

"Sheriff, I really must ask you—" the attorney tried.

"Why did you kill Nat Calloway?" Hix pressed.

The guy suddenly moved, making Hix's body go tight. But he just grabbed the pen, pulled the paper to him, and wrote in a diagonal scrawl that was nothing like the careful, block letters he'd written before.

He set the pen aside and shoved the pad at Hix, not turning it like he'd done the other two times he'd shared.

Hix reached out and turned it himself.

I don't know. Can you tell me?

Hix's eyes cut to his face.

There was nothing there.

Hollow.

"No," Hix said quietly. "But if you let the doctors see to you, maybe we can find out."

The man jerked up his chin.

"Can this be done now?" the attorney asked impatiently.

"It can be done," Hix murmured, about to get up but the guy grabbed the pen and reached for the pad.

He scrawled, set the pen aside and shoved the paper to Hix.

Hix stood and turned the pad his way again.

It's never done.

Hix looked at him and replied, "No, man, it isn't. And the way it goes, it never will be." He turned his attention to Larry. "Let's get him in a cell and get him a meal."

Larry nodded.

Hix looked to the attorney, to the empty soul who wandered alone in order to protect the world from the unknown, inexplicable urges that lie within, the man who killed Nat Calloway, and then he walked out the door.

GRETA AND SHAW hung back when he walked through the back door that night.

But Mamie was on him in a way he knew they'd been watching for him to return home, and Corinne was on him two seconds later.

He held his girls to him but his eyes were on Shaw and Greta who were standing in the mouth to the mudroom, Shaw's arm around Hix's woman.

Shaw gave his sisters some time before he called, "Guys, let Dad take his jacket off. Dad, you want a beer?"

"Yeah, kid," Hix answered as Corinne slid away but Mamie held on.

"You okay, Daddy?" Corinne asked.

"Yeah, honey," Hix answered gently.

Mamie leaned into him, arms still around him, just arching her back and looking up at him.

"Yeah?" she asked for confirmation.

He glided his hand over her hair. "Yeah, baby. Now let me get my jacket off, okay? You can keep on huggin' me after that."

"'Kay," she agreed and did just that, unclamping her hold on him for just long enough for him to shed his jacket and put it on a hook, then clamping on to him again so he didn't bother to take his gun belt off and he had to shuffle from the mudroom down the short hall and into the kitchen with his baby girl attached to him.

The smells he was experiencing hit him before he hit the kitchen though, and he was reminded that Greta had been in his office to meet him for lunch, something he didn't have, he'd only had the coffee that Ida had brought in from Babycakes.

"What's that?" he asked, his eyes to the stove.

"Greta showed us how to make Mexican skillet casserole," Corinne told him.

"Excellent," Hix muttered.

"We'll go set the table, help me, Mame, Cor," Shaw said, handing Hix a beer.

"Sure," Corinne replied, moving to a cupboard.

"Mame, babe," Shaw urged gently, holding his hand out to his little sister.

She hesitated before she let her dad go, took her brother's hand and held it even while Shaw went to the drawer and got out the cutlery.

The kids left.

Greta, standing at the stove sprinkling cheese on a skillet filled with what looked like heaven in ground beef form, turned her head his way.

He set his beer aside and moved right into her space.

Bag of cheese still in hand, she wrapped her arms around him.

"You good?" she whispered in his ear.

"Better," he whispered back.

"You tell Faith?"

He nodded, her hair catching on his whiskers as he did it with his jaw pressed to the side of her head. "Her hair looks great."

She gave him a squeeze and held on.

Hix held her back, and after a time, he tipped his chin down to put his lips to her ear.

"That man is broken."

"He gave that impression."

"But whatever snapped in him to make him kill Nat annihilated him."

She just held him tighter.

"It's the only time a murder was solved where the answer makes sense," he shared.

"How's that?" she asked softly.

"My guess, even he can't control the demons that moved him to do it, he's just got 'em. And if he was holding them back before, when they took over in that moment, whatever he had left, they took it with them. Only thing he's got is the will to survive and the remorse he feels for taking a man's life. In other words, there is no answer, there is no reason. It's incomprehensible, just like it always is."

She started stroking his back.

After a time, she said, "I need to feed my man and his kids. They insisted on waiting. But it's late and I heard Shaw's stomach rumbling so we should get down to that."

What she meant was, *I need to give my man normal with his woman and kids around, fill his belly and be in a position to assess where his head is at so I can do something about it if I need to and we should get down to that.*

"Yeah," he replied but didn't let go.

She didn't shift or move an inch.

In other words, she didn't let go either.

The Drake Family

"Hey," Shaw whispered urgently, catching Mamie, who had her mind on other things and was heading into the kitchen.

Corinne was already pressed to her brother's back.

The three of them stood, frozen in the open doorway to the kitchen, watching their dad holding Greta.

No, watching Greta hold their dad.

"Let's give them time," Corinne whispered.

As one, they all slunk backwards on silent feet.

Mamie leaned against Shaw as Corinne adjusted the place settings so they were all just so and they waited patiently until their dad walked in with his gun belt gone, an open beer in his hand and an oven glove on the other hand that was holding the big, cast-iron skillet Greta had brought over to cook in.

"Get drinks, kids. Let's get this grub in our stomachs," he ordered.

They moved out as Greta moved in, carrying a big wooden bowl (that she'd also brought over) of salad.

"Corinne, can you grab the salad dressings from the fridge? And Shaw, can you get the cornbread out of the oven? Just put it on the hot pad by the stove. I'll come in and deal with it."

"You got it," Shaw muttered.

"No problem," Corinne said.

"I'll get drinks, what does everyone want?" Mamie asked as she entered the kitchen.

Shaw and Corinne did as Greta asked and Mamie got the drinks.

They sat down at the family table.

They all watched closely as their father tried to make it normal while they ate Greta's amazing food, but they did what they could to take their dad's mind off things, talking about school, telling stories, anything.

It never got normal.

But they gave it their best shot.

And their dad, being the kind of dad he was, didn't bother to hide he appreciated it.

Hixon

THE CALL CAME when they were all cleaning up.

He saw who it was on the screen and muttered he had to take it as he walked out of the room, through the living room, out to the front porch, doing it sliding his thumb on the screen, taking the call, putting the phone to his ear.

His storm door closed behind him as he answered, "Hey, Hope."

"Hey, Hixon," she replied gently.

"You okay?" he asked.

"That was my question, honey."

He looked to his boots.

There was the woman he'd married.

"It's good it's over, yeah?" she asked.

"Yeah."

"Greta and the kids taking care of you?"

He looked to the street, the snow covering his lawn, his walk and driveway clear.

"They are, Hope. Thanks."

"How'd the wife take it?" she inquired.

"Confusion. The guy is...off. But there was also some relief. Blatt's semi-related to her. I called him, he was there when Larry and I visited. He took over when we left. He can be an arrogant ass but I think he's got this."

"That's good," she murmured.

"Yeah," he agreed.

"Okay, I didn't want to take up too much of your time or anything. I just...heard and I've been thinking of you."

"That's appreciated, honey."

She was silent for a few beats before she rushed out, "Okay. You probably need a bourbon about now so I'll let you go. Just...take care of yourself, yeah, Hix?"

"I will. You too."

"I will. Tell everyone I said hey."

"I'll do that."

"'Night, Hix."

"'Night."

She hung up.

He dropped his hand with the phone in it and stared at the street.

When he noticed his breath come out in a visible puff, he cleared his throat, shoved his phone in his back pocket and went inside.

He was up, his knees were up, but Greta was straddling him, riding him, her fingers in his hair, her lips attached to his so the noises she made were muted since they sounded down his throat.

Her rhythm was gentle, but he could tell she was working to keep it that way, so he put his hands to her waist, lifted his hips and took her to her back before he threaded the fingers of one hand through hers and he stopped going gentle.

"You're...too good at this," she breathed against his lips.

He could not believe it in that moment for a variety of reasons but what she said made him smile.

"What?" he asked.

"It's...hard to...stay quiet," she pushed out.

He slanted his head and took her mouth to help with that even as he ran a hand down her chest, snagging her nipple hard with his thumb, forcing a gasp into his mouth, thus making it harder.

She lifted her knees high at his sides and he went deeper, which felt so fucking good it made him go faster.

He slid his lips to her ear.

"You love me?" he whispered.

"Yes," she panted.

"You know I love you?"

She tilted her hips up and held his hand laced in hers so tight, he felt pain at the webbing.

"Yes," she repeated breathlessly.

He lifted his head and looked down at her indistinct face, the shadows of her sunshine and honey hair somehow bright even in the dark. "Good, baby, because I love you a lot."

"You can't..." she tipped her knees back farther, he slid in deeper, and she lifted her head to put her mouth to his when that caused a low groan to rumble out of him, "imagine how awesome...that is, baby. But can we have this conversation when I'm not...about...to...?"

She didn't finish.

Her neck arched, her mouth opened, and her pussy seized his pulsing cock as she climaxed under him.

He watched. He enjoyed it. Then he kissed her so when his world exploded, the grunt it forced from him was quietened by her mouth.

Hix came down slow, made sure she came down slow, and kept his fingers wound through hers long after, kissing her, working her neck, feeling her work his, her free hand moving on him, his doing the same.

Finally, he found her ear with his lips and whispered, "At last."

Again, her fingers convulsed in his hand before she repeated, "At last, Hixon."

He kissed her throat, pulled out and rolled them both out of bed.

He got rid of the condom, cleaned up, pulled on some pajama bottoms. She pulled on panties and her nightie.

They slid into bed together and she curled into his side.

"Love you, Greta," he murmured to the ceiling.

He felt her kiss his chest before she settled back in. "Love you too, Hix."

She burrowed deeper into him and after some time, he felt her weight fall into him with sleep.

Hix closed his eyes and saw hollow.

But he felt Greta.

So eventually, he followed her.

Chapter 25

Seventh Circle

Hixon

"Come around," Hix rumbled.

"Mm," Greta mumbled to his back before she took a nip of the flesh at his lat.

His hips pulsed into her hand.

"*Come around,*" he growled.

She slid her lips up to the side of his neck, pressing her tits in his back, and bossed, "Keep your hands to the headboard, Hixon."

"Greta," he warned, fucking her fist that she kept wrapped tight around his cock, her other hand cupping and squeezing his balls, the whole of her pressed to his back, her lips on his neck—it was too hot, he couldn't take more.

"This feel illegal?" she asked.

No.

It felt phenomenal.

Fuck it.

He took his hands from where they were, curled around his headboard where he'd promised to keep them, and twisted, his movement making her lose hold and throwing her back.

He caught her at the waist, hauled her around to his front, then up. His other hand going to his dick, he pulled her down, the head of his cock slid through her wet as she wound her legs around his hips, and he found her.

He surged up as he yanked her down and her head flew back with her, "*Yes.*"

He walked on his knees until he had her back tight to the headboard and then he hammered her.

"This feel illegal, gum drop?" he asked.

"Yes, baby," she gasped.

"Tit, Greta," he ordered.

She took a hand from clenching his ass to put it to her breast and lift it to him. He kept pounding inside her as he bowed his back and sucked it hard into his mouth.

She jolted in his arms, he felt that jolt in his cock and not because her pussy spasmed around it, and she started shifting her hips to meet his thrusts.

He circled her nipple and muttered, "Other one," against it.

She exchanged hands, one now in his hair, one to her other breast, and lifted it for him.

He took it with his mouth.

She ground into his drives.

"Baby," she whimpered.

He let her nipple go, quickly slid his middle finger between his lips and out, wetting it. He then put his lips to hers and kept hold of her with one arm, the other hand he slid down her spine, over her ass, through the cleft, and he dug that middle finger up her ass to the second knuckle.

That did it.

"*Hixon,*" she breathed, bucked, cried out, and her pussy throbbed around him.

Her reaction took him over the edge and he drilled her against the headboard, shoving his finger all the way in at the back only to hear her moan and feel her legs wrap tighter around him as he exploded, thankfully now able to do it ungloved since she'd got her ass on the Pill, shooting deep inside.

Hix came down with his face in her neck, sliding his finger gently out but keeping her planted on his dick.

"No fair," she muttered hazily into the skin of his neck.

"No fair?" he asked, grinning into the skin of hers.

"You hadn't won the bed wrestling match of the millennium part two to earn your right to take my ass."

He lifted his head, looked down at her beautiful, sated face and asked an unnecessary question, "You didn't like it?"

She rolled her eyes and didn't bother to answer his unnecessary question.

He pressed her into the headboard, tightening his hold on her with his arms, getting her complete attention.

"That wasn't taking your ass, sweetheart. That wasn't even fingering your ass. That was staking a future claim when I win our bed wrestling match of millennium part two."

"I'm totally buying lube," she declared.

"Good idea." He grinned at her.

Her eyes narrowed. "For *you*."

He busted out laughing.

"I'm so gonna win, Hix."

"Right," he snickered through his continuing laughter.

"You'll see."

He did his best to sober, was shit at it, so was still chuckling when he said, "You're right. We'll definitely see."

"I should have spanked you when I had your hands to the headboard," she snapped.

He put his mouth to hers and held her eyes, "Now we're totally havin' our rematch 'cause that's a good idea, and you got a great ass, baby, but it'll be pretty, takin' my cock, all pink."

Her eyes got big right before she nipped his lip and did it hard.

He took her mouth.

She smacked his ass.

He pulled her off his cock, tossed her to her belly on the bed and covered her, shoving both hands beneath her, each going separate directions, all this while burying his face in her neck.

And from there, Hix commenced proving to his woman he could still go all night.

They both had work the next day.

They both dragged their asses all day that next day.

And they both thought it was totally worth it.

"Okay, I got the stocking stuffer candy and the stocking stuffers are all bagged in different bags to make it easy to stuff them tomorrow night after the kids go to sleep, but they're not wrapped. Andy wants to help me do that. We'll do it tomorrow while the kids are with Hope at Jep and Marie's. But I got the tissue paper. Christmas plaid for Shaw, snowflakes for Corinne, candy canes for Mamie. I already wrapped Andy's in star paper. Your paper, I'm not gonna say, you'll see on the day, but that's also done," Greta prattled.

Hix was sitting at a stool at his kitchen island (Corinne, Mamie and Greta had chosen his new stools, Shaw, Andy and Hix had approved them, but it was Hix who bought them) watching his woman pace around the island.

She had a pen in one hand and a huge legal pad in her other that she was flipping through, back and forth, in what Hix would suspect Santa would do with his list if he used a pad and not a huge-ass scroll.

"Babe—" he tried to cut in to find a gentle way to tell her he didn't give a shit what kind of tissue paper his kids' stocking stuffers were wrapped in and they should also get a move on because the sun was setting and they needed to go get her brother.

"Nuts in their shells, check. Always have to have nuts with shells so you can use the nutcracker," she declared. "We're having Coke-glazed ham." She opened the fridge. "Ham in fridge, check. Two-liter of Coke, check. Four more two-liters of Coke for you, Shaw and Andy. Check. Diet for us girls, check. Hash brown casserole." She closed the fridge and opened the freezer. "Hash browns, check." She shuffled to the pantry, tapping the end of her pen to the pad as she called it down. "Cookie stuff. Check. Roll mix. Check. Stuff to make Chex mix. Check."

"Sweetheart—"

Still tapping her pad with each "check," she went on like she hadn't heard him, which she probably hadn't. "Crackers. Check. Chips. Check." Back across the room to the fridge she opened. "Deli meat. Check. Blocks of cheese for crackers. Check. Cheese *slices* for sandwiches. Check. Grated cheese. Check. Makings for cheese *ball*. Check. Philadelphia cheese. Check. Three types of bread—"

Christ.

There was more cheese in his house than all of Wisconsin.

"Greta," he pushed out through laughter.

She whirled on him and abruptly changed subjects. "Where's Mamie's barre?"

"Like I told you three times, Tommy's bringing it over Christmas morning, early. He's gonna put it up when he gets here. If we're still asleep, he's got a key."

"We won't be asleep. It's the law you don't get up past five o'clock Christmas day. Will he be able to get here before five?" she asked.

"I know the law pretty well, baby, and I'm not sure that's the law," he told her through a smile he knew was immense because it was hurting his face.

"It's a *Christmas* law, smokey, and only Santa gets to be sheriff of that."

That was when his gut hurt from stopping himself from busting out laughing.

"Can Tommy show at, say, four?" she requested.

"Tommy's a forty-three-year-old, never-married, single guy who took a single's cruise last Christmas, and by his report, nailed four broads during this cruise. Do you think a man like that is gettin' up at three-thirty in the morning to drag a ballet barre across town and install it in his friend's basement?"

"It's Christmas, so yes," she sniffed.

"I wouldn't get your hopes up on that, gum drop," he warned.

"I wouldn't call women broads again, Hixon," she returned. "I'd take you to task for that but I'm in a Christmas mood."

Hix could say for definite he hadn't missed her Christmas mood.

"I didn't think bitches was the way to go," he teased, and she assumed a severe expression.

"You were right," she shared.

"Or pieces of ass," he went on.

"You're right about that too."

"Or asses he tapped," he kept at her.

"Hix...the *barre*," she pushed.

"He'll get here when he gets here, but he said early and the man owns a farm. His early will be *early*."

"If it isn't *early*-early, she'll hear the drill, Hix."

"You can't muffle a drill, Greta."

Suddenly, she threw up her hand with the pen, her other hand with the pad, and declared loudly, "There has to be a big Christmas surprise! Corinne only wanted clothes, hair stuff and makeup, nothing big enough to make a huge to-do over, except her new phone, which we agreed with Hope that she could give her. Shaw wanted videogames and money, so ditto with the to-do. Andy never gives a crap what anyone gives him because he's too excited for them to open what he got them. Your Christmas surprise is gonna be a Boxing Day surprise after the kids and Andy are gone because I don't think I'll be able to be quiet after you do what you do to me when you see me in it. Mamie's barre is our only surprise!"

Hix wasn't feeling amused anymore.

"Let's go back to my Boxing Day surprise," he suggested in a growl.

He had no clue what Boxing Day even was.

He still wanted to know about his surprise.

She looked smug, a look he felt tighten in his crotch.

She also sounded smug when she announced, "We'll just say Santa has a variety of little helpers and you're gonna be glad one of them is sleeping in your bedroom."

"Sneak peek now," he decreed.

She shook her head. "We have to go get Andy."

"He can wait an hour...or two."

"He always comes to me Christmas Eve's Eve, Hix. Homemade pizza and viewings of *Lethal Weapon* to start the festivities. It's tradition. And it's getting late. So if we're missing something, we have to drop by the store on the way home with Andy."

"Babe—"

She interrupted him. "We need to make sure we have everything. The Christmas feeding orgy starts tonight and I'm not going to the grocery store if we're missing something after we get home and you aren't either."

And thank Christ for that since she'd sent him on four runs the last three days to prepare.

He opened his mouth to say something, whatever that had to be to get him a sneak peek of whatever his present was going to be, when the doorbell rang.

He got off the stool, ordering, "I'll get that. You get your ass upstairs and get in my surprise."

She shook her head. "Not gonna happen, darlin'."

So it was lingerie.

Please, Christ, make it a teddy.

She had three teddies. He'd seen them all. He liked them all. Enough he wanted another one.

He stopped in the doorway to the kitchen. "Thirty minutes."

"Oh no," she said softly, her eyes flaring. "That would be an impossibility."

Fuck.

She smiled a wicked smile. "Maybe I shouldn't have said anything."

The doorbell rang again.

So Hix muttered, "You knew exactly what you were doin'." And he heard her equally wicked chuckle as he stalked to the door.

The lead glass panes in the door obscured who was behind it except for the fact whoever it was had big hair.

Hix didn't have a good feeling about that.

His feeling was correct when he opened the door and saw Tawnee Dare standing on his porch.

She didn't waste any time.

"I wanna see my daughter."

Shit, he had her, they hadn't yet served her, and he didn't have the papers.

All his deputies had volunteered to find her in order to serve her but it was Donna who won that job in an epic scissors-paper-rock battle that took fifteen minutes.

This meant Donna had the papers.

Shit.

Before he could think of what to say, she kept speaking.

"I know she probably doesn't wanna see me but it's Christmas and I wanna see my boy."

Probably?

"We're not doin' this," he told her, beginning to close the door at the same time scanning his street, his hand going to his back pocket to get his phone.

"No!" she shouted, and his eyes sliced back to her as she opened the storm, stepped in it and put a hand up to press on his door.

"Stand back, Ms. Dare," he warned.

"I get it. She's done with me. But I wanna see my boy."

"Take your hand off my door, Ms. Dare, and remove yourself from my property."

"I got him a present. It's in the car. I wanna see him. I wanna give it to him."

"Do you honestly think she gives one shit what you want?" he asked and went on, "And trust me, your boy wants nothing from you either. Since birth, Greta's given him everything he's needed, you didn't damage his brain so much he doesn't understands that, so he won't give a shit he gets anything from you now."

He couldn't credit the wince his words got him, but before she could say anything or he could push the door closed, her eyes went over his shoulder.

"Greta. Greta, girl, I'm not here to cause problems," she said quickly. "I just wanna see Andy."

"Greta, move outta sight," Hix demanded. "Call Donna, tell her Ms. Dare is here and tell her, she leaves before Donna gets here, the woman is driving a late model, blue Honda Accord. Colorado plates. Plates that are expired."

Tawnee's eyes shot to him. "What're you talkin' about?"

He didn't answer her.

He ordered, "Step back, Ms. Dare."

"Okay, just let me give you his present and I...I..." Her eyes went over his shoulder again. "I got something for you too, girl."

"I'll say it once more, step *back*," Hix clipped.

Greta obviously wasn't doing as he asked because Tawnee kept her attention over his shoulder and something came over her face. Something strange. Impossible to achieve. Pugilistic but defeated. Entreating yet stubborn. Sad but hopeful.

"I know you're done," she said quietly, all those things in her tone too. "You haven't unblocked me, they haven't put me back on the visitor list. But I got nothin', Greta. Kavanagh ousted me. Got nothin' and it's Christmas. Not askin' for much. Just to give you and Andy a little somethin'." She tried an unpracticed smile. "And you love Christmas. Always did."

"You're wrong. I hated it," Greta said coldly. "Until Andy was two and he could grasp a little bit what it meant."

Tawnee's face fell but she pushed, "Just let me drop your presents. You can give Andy's to him."

"Though," Greta went on like Tawnee hadn't spoken, "only way I could give him anything was to steal from you. But it's miraculous how a three-dollar, beat-up teddy bear from the Salvation Army can light up a two-year-old kid."

"I knew that was you," her mother muttered.

"Yep, didn't remember to buy us presents but you sure missed that three dollars from your purse," Greta returned.

"It wasn't just one year you did that, Greta," Tawnee fired back. "And I never said shit. Did I? I never got in your face about stealin' from me so you could give Andy a Christmas."

"Are you serious?" Greta whispered.

Hix had the same question.

He just didn't give a fuck about the bitch's answer.

"This isn't gonna happen," Hix growled, pushing on the door, and Tawnee's boots actually slid his welcome mat (Greta and the girls got it online so he didn't have to buy that) across the porch as she put her weight into keeping it open.

"I wanna...I wanna explain. I wanna...I want you to understand why," she stated urgently.

"Greta, call Donna," Hix ordered.

"No, honey. I wanna know," Greta said.

He looked over his shoulder at her.

Her eyes were pinned on her mother but she kept talking to him.

"She wants to explain, I wanna hear it."

"Right, sweetheart, but *I* don't want this woman in my house," he shared honestly.

She looked to him and nodded. "I get that. So I'll get my jacket." Her attention returned to her mom. "Stand out there, I'll be out in a minute."

"Greta, it's cold and—" Tawnee began.

"Mom, do that or spend Christmas in one of Hix's cells. You're trespassing. You have another arrest for that in this county. You also have a record. And you have a protection order as granted by a judge that you haven't yet been served, but he knows you've been stalking me and taking pictures. And we'll just say, you haven't made a friend of local law enforcement. Stand on the porch. I'll be out in a minute."

Greta's mom looked shocked. "A protection order?"

"You can't follow anyone around and take photos of them with malicious intent, Mom. You did that. When you're served, if you continue to do anything to harm me in any way you can, it'll be handled as a felony."

The woman's face paled.

"You wanna explain, I'll give you time," Greta granted. "You have this. Then it's over. No more chances. No more time. No more anything. If you don't leave me and Andy alone, I'll take it as far as I have to take it to make certain that you do."

Tawnee's hand came off the door so fast, the pressure Hix was putting on it meant it closed right in her face.

He didn't think of that.

He turned to Greta to watch her moving quickly toward the kitchen to get to her coat in the mudroom.

"Baby," he called after her, his hand at his back pocket to get out his phone as he followed her.

"I wasn't kidding, she gets this, then it's over," Greta said, not looking back at him.

"Not sure this is a good idea," he told her.

"There's half a chance I'll get back out there and she'll be gone," Greta replied, hitting the mudroom and grabbing her coat.

Time to call Donna.

This he did at the same time he grabbed his jacket and shrugged it on, following her.

Donna answered, he gave her the details and he was doing this as he saw Tawnee hadn't left.

Greta moved out. Hix moved out after her.

"Gotta go now," Hix said into his phone.

"Be there in ten, max, Hix," Donna replied, reading the urgency in his tone.

"Right," he muttered and hung up.

Tawnee had her gaze to him.

"Reckon I'm about to be served, right, Sheriff?" she asked snidely.

"Is that more important at this juncture than speaking to your daughter?" Hix returned.

She glared at him then looked to Greta.

"You got me, Mom. Last chance, after thirty-eight years, to finally give me the answers for why you broke Andy, why you broke Keith and me, why you tried to break Hix and me, eventually broke Keith and never faltered in your quest to do just that to me."

"If I could take back what happened to Andy, I would," Greta's mother said softly.

"Well, that makes you about one-sixteenth of a decent person, but nothing *happened* to Andy except *you*. *You* happened to Andy," Greta told her. "*You* did that to him so the appropriate words are, 'if I could take back what *I did to Andy*, I would.'"

The soft disappeared.

"I paid for that, girl," she hissed.

Greta shook her head and turned to Hix who was standing just outside the closed door, murmuring, "This is meaningless."

He began to move to open the door for her but Tawnee cried, "No! Don't! I don't got nothin', girl. I don't got *nothin'*. 'Cept the two of you."

Greta gave her mother her attention. "Now give me one reason, one even *infinitesimal* reason that would make me feel you earned me giving that first crap."

She swayed forward like she was going to move toward Greta, and Hix coming forward to stand close to Greta's back wasn't what stopped her.

She stopped herself, her gaze never leaving her daughter.

"I'm your momma."

"You are. And?" Greta prompted.

Tawnee shook her head. Fast, short, little shakes like she was trying to pry something loose to keep a hold on a daughter she'd never actually had.

"I was supposed to have a different life," she said. "Not be knocked up at seventeen and thrown out on my ass by your grandparents."

"Were you raped?" Greta asked unemotionally.

"No," Tawnee snapped.

"So you had consensual, unprotected sex with someone, decided not to abort the baby, but instead, do your best to make the whole of her life a misery," Greta deduced.

"Look at me," Tawnee exclaimed, suddenly angry, lifting a hand, finger pointed to her face. "The life I led wasn't the life meant for me. I was supposed to have more. Be a model. Be a movie star. Be a singer, like you. You got that from me too, Greta. I got chops. Choir director at school said I had more talent than any student he'd seen. I coulda gone the distance. Maybe found a man who'd look after me, the real way, hold me close and not let me go. Then I got *you* and all my chances were shot to *shit*."

"So because you were attractive, you were supposed to live the big life, not work for it, not earn it, not find a way to be happy with whatever you worked for or earned, but what? Be handed it because you aren't hard on the eyes? Then when I came along and ruined that, *I* had to pay for the fact you're literally *criminally* conceited?"

"It's hard to bounce back from your dreams dyin'," Tawnee bit out.

"Sorry. I wouldn't know about dreams, Mom. The way I grew up, I knew from early never to have any," Greta retorted.

At hearing that knowledge, Hix couldn't beat back his snarl.

"Well, it's hard," Tawnee shot back.

"You had fourteen years before Andy came along to accomplish that," Greta noted.

"And Andy was supposed to do that," Tawnee spat.

"Yeah? How?" Greta asked.

"His daddy was loaded. His daddy also wouldn't leave his fuckin' wife to make an honest woman outta me."

"Andy's father is wealthy?" Greta whispered, and Hix put a hand to her hip as he felt a different energy coming from her.

"Don't get excited like I did, girl," Tawnee advised, now sounding world-weary. "He was. He was also twenty-seven years older than me. And now he's very dead and he gave half his money to that cow he called a wife, and since the bitch couldn't give him kids, when *I* could, he gave the other half to some museum or somethin' so you won't get blood from that stone. Believe me, I tried."

"Did he...did he want something to do with Andy?" Greta asked.

"He wasn't gettin' his shot at havin' a son without puttin' a ring on it, Greta. God, did I never teach you nothin'?"

Hix didn't snarl at that.

He stared at the woman in shock.

"So he did," Greta whispered.

"In the end, I told him Andy wasn't his. Asshole believed that fast enough."

"What, after you did that, did his wife want DNA and you couldn't assure he was the daddy?" Greta asked.

Now the woman was offended. "You take me for a slut, girl?"

"Yes."

"Jesus," Tawnee hissed. "*No.* 'Cause lawyers like to get paid even before the big payout actually happens, least the good ones do. The other kind are shit and can't get nothin' done."

"So you actually harassed this poor woman whose husband you slept with in order to take his money, harassing her after the fact in order to take another shot at getting her husband's money?"

"Didn't work," Tawnee muttered.

"You do know, Mom, that this isn't making me feel real good about standing out in the cold listening to your crap."

"I was tryin' to do right by you both," Tawnee retorted.

"That wasn't the way to go about it," Greta informed her.

"It was the only way I knew how," Tawnee snapped.

Greta let that ludicrousness go and asked, "And my father?"

"Your father what?" Tawnee asked back.

"This is the first I've ever heard about Andy's dad. So what about my dad? Who was he? Did you know him? Should *I* know him?"

"He was a waste of space," Tawnee answered. "A punk ass gettin' his rocks off with an underage girl, and when that had consequences, he scraped me off. I was seventeen, Greta. He was twenty-two. I needed help. He didn't have a lot but he coulda helped me. He wanted nothin' to do with you and the fifteen thousand times I asked him to help after I had you, he *still* wanted nothin' to do with you. Eventually got himself a wife. Made himself a family. I even showed at their place with you standin' at my side, holding my hand, and *that bitch* shut the door in our faces. So fuck him. And fuck her. Because never, not once, did he show, askin' after his girl. He knew where I was. Where *you* were. And he didn't give a single shit. I'd even see their asses out in Denver and he'd look right through me. You were with me, he didn't even look at you."

Greta had no response to that, she just turned her head away and Hix pressed closer to her back.

"Greta, girl." Tawnee leaned in and his woman looked back to her mother. "*I got nothin'*. I got some clothes. That car. Kicked out of my mobile home. Sold all my shit I can sell and I got three hundred and twenty-two bucks in my purse and *that's it.* That won't even get me back to Denver."

"So you're here to give Andy and me presents and ask for gas money," Greta guessed.

"I'm here to see my boy, and yes," she bit off the last word, "my girl for Christmas."

"Mom, although you've never used this tactic, I'll warn you now, pretending to be nice won't work."

Tawnee's voice was rising. "You broke my life."

"You broke your own life," Greta shot back.

"*Then I broke his!*" Tawnee screeched.

Greta went still.

Hix went still.

Tawnee stood before them, panting.

"Do you have any clue...any *clue*...?" Greta's mother's head jerked to the side, her hands came up in fists, her head jerked back, and she whispered, "He was so beautiful."

"Yes he was," Greta whispered back. "He still is."

"I would...I would... Sometimes I'd look at the two of you and think God got it wrong. God wouldn't saddle me with that. God wouldn't give me the ability to make somethin' that beautiful and then weigh me down with it. The biggest diamond in the world could be the size of a boulder and you might want it, but you couldn't wear it on your finger 'cause you couldn't do nothin' but that seein' as it was weighin' you down."

"So we were nothing but a weight," Greta said quietly.

"You had babies, you'd get me," Tawnee replied.

"I did have a baby, Mom, and the only time in my life growing up with you I felt light was when I was with Andy."

Hix got closer to her and slid his hand to her belly.

"You took him," Tawnee accused. "You took him and made him yours. You two were so close, even if I tried, I couldn't get in. It was like I wasn't even there. Put a roof over your heads, food in your bellies, and both 'a you acted like I was a piece of furniture."

"It's odd to know right now that you felt the same as you made us feel," Greta remarked coolly.

"You aren't gettin' me. You took my life then you took my boy," Tawnee stated.

"You *gave me* life, Mom, and it was your responsibility to do everything in your power to make it a good one."

"You never went hungry, you had clothes on your backs and where's the thanks for that?" Tawnee sneered.

"That isn't even half of it," Greta retorted. "If you watched me with Andy like you said you did, you'd know."

"By then, it was too late. You two had each other and I was the outsider in my own home and there was no turnin' back."

"How can you know? You didn't even try," Greta pointed out.

Tawnee's focus became acute. "And if I'd tried, would it have made a difference?"

"We'll never know since you didn't," Greta responded. "You did something entirely different. Do you even have a clue how much pain you've caused?"

"What happened to Andy was an accident," Tawnee spat.

"What happened to Andy was an *avoidable* accident," Greta returned.

"You don't think I live with that every day?" Tawnee asked. "You don't think that doesn't eat away at me? You don't think that's why it was tough to get up the nerve to go see him, because goin' to see him meant seein' right in front of my face what happened to him?"

"You know, no," Greta told her. "Until right now, the way you've behaved my whole life, Mom, that never occurred to me. But you're standing here talking to *me*. You're standing here trying to explain to *me*. We both know what you did to Andy was hideous and tragic. What I want to know is why you felt the need to torture *me*."

"You coulda been somethin' too," Tawnee fired at her. "You coulda used the looks I gave you, that voice I gave you to go places. You didn't. But you did manage to hook yourself a man who was rollin' in it. And what? Every time I came to you for help, you acted like I was a huge pain in your ass. And *he* was worse. He treated me like a snake in the grass. You ever been treated like that, Greta, you'd know. You'd get it. You'd get pissed about it. So if you think I should feel bad for playin' with that asshole, you're wrong. You say your momma didn't give you dick, but I did, you just never paid attention. But I taught you that too, girl. People treat you like shit, you don't let that lie. You treat 'em like shit right back and you do it ten times better."

"I think you might just be crazy," Greta whispered.

Tawnee studied her daughter a beat before she said, "You don't understand me."

"No, I don't," Greta confirmed.

"You'll never understand me," Tawnee stated.

"No, I won't," Greta agreed.

"You don't want my present," Tawnee went on.

"No, I don't," Greta repeated.

"Andy won't want his either."

"No, he won't."

"So we know. We know what I always knew. I'm standin' here in front of you, tryin', and you're throwin' it in my face," she kept at Greta.

Greta didn't flinch or hesitate.

"Yes, I am."

Tawnee's focus intensified on her daughter's face and her shoulders straightened before she decreed, "You also don't understand I made you what you are. All you are, Greta. From your looks right down to your grit. I gave you *all 'a that*, girl."

"You're forced through the seven circles of hell, you get to the other side, you don't turn and thank the seven circles of hell for making you pull up the fortitude to endure. You take hold of what you earned after you got free and you get as far away from them as you can. Unfortunately, my seven circles live and breathe and can drive a car, so they keep following me."

"Well, that'll be done now, Greta," Tawnee spat.

"Finally, something from you that I actually want."

Tawnee's head jerked, her mane of fake, golden curls jerking with it.

Before either of them could say more, Hix cut in.

He did it because it was time.

He also did it because Donna's Ram had parked at the curb and she was out, making her way up his walk.

"I think this has run its course," he stated. "Now, Ms. Dare, you're about to be served. If you break the protection order you're about to receive, I'll charge you with criminal harassment and I'll talk with our prosecutor to see you serve time. The maximum is five years. The good part of that is, it won't matter you only have three hundred and twenty-two dollars since your accommodation will be courtesy of the state. The bad part of that is, your accommodation will be courtesy of the state."

Donna had arrived while he spoke and she lifted up the envelope with the order in it that Tawnee automatically accepted when he stopped.

"This protection order lasts fourteen days," Hix continued. "The minute it expires, we'll be requesting a permanent one from the judge. I can't speak for him, but he's not been feeling beneficent these days, especially about the fact that people keep fucking with Greta. So my guess is, he'll grant it. You can't be within one hundred yards of her. If you are, I'll do everything I can to put you in prison. If you harass Andy, we'll get a protection order for him too. And after your scene at Sunnydown, the photos the judge saw that you took of Greta, the effort you clearly put into that, and the statement he read from Greta's ex-husband as to how you used those, I doubt Judge Bereford will deny that request. So my suggestion is, get out of Glossop, get out of McCook and don't come back."

Slowly, Tawnee's gaze went from studying the envelope to Hix.

Then it went to Greta.

Hix waited. He felt Greta waiting. Donna didn't know what was happening but she also waited.

He didn't know what he expected. He didn't expect much. The woman was what she was. She was also a mother.

So he expected something.

Greta probably expected nothing.

And that was what she got when Tawnee turned to his steps, walked down them, right to her car. She got in, slammed the door, started it up, pulled out into the street and drove away.

She didn't even say goodbye.

"Okay, that woman is, well...that woman," Donna started after the silence of Tawnee's departure stretched long. "But I'm not feelin' even a low hum of Christmas spirit on this porch. What'd she do now?"

"She gave me the only thing of value she's ever given me," Greta answered.

Donna looked to his woman. "What's that?"

"She left," Greta answered, pulled from his hold, walked around him and into his house.

Hix looked to the door she closed behind her and then to his friend.

"It wasn't even half as much fun to serve her as I thought it would be," she quipped worriedly, watching him closely.

"Thanks for comin' out, Donna."

"Think you best get in there and look after your woman, Hixon," she replied quietly.

He nodded.

She turned to leave.

He went into his house.

Greta was standing in the doorway to the kitchen pulling the strap of her purse over her shoulder.

"I have my coat on, might as well go get Andy," she announced. "If we missed anything, I'll go get it. Andy likes going to the store."

"Just a minute," he replied, moved to her and got in her space, putting his hands to either side of her neck and bowing his back so he could set his face in hers. "You okay?"

"Yep."

"That was rough," he noted.

"No it wasn't. It's just her."

Carefully, he reminded her, "Can't believe it, we never talked about it, but it's clear that's the first time she spoke to you about your dad."

"I don't have a dad, Hixon. Just a swimming bunch of cells that came out of some random guy I never met and never want to meet. It isn't a loss, darlin'. Honestly. You can't lose something you've never had."

"Babe—"

"It's done. To rejoice would give her time and emotion, which she doesn't deserve. To be sad or angry would be the same. She clearly kept the trump of knowledge of our fathers close at hand, ready to use when she needed it, but that backfired because they gave us less than even she did, which is saying something. They gave up on us so easily, it's clearly no loss." Her shoulders shrugged. "And now, it's over. I suppose when you finally swat the annoying fly that's been bugging you for hours, you take a moment to feel the satisfaction of it being gone. Then you get on with shit. I'm getting on with shit. It's Christmas Eve's Eve. I'm gonna go get my baby brother."

"I'll come with you," he said gently.

She made a move to pull from his hold but he pressed his thumbs under her jaw and she halted.

"I love you," he told her.

"I love you too. And I love my brother. And we got it down to a tag-team art to make hella-good homemade pizza. So get a move on, smokey."

He examined her face and saw she'd gotten over it after what her mother did to her ex.

She wasn't in a place where Tawnee Dare could harm her anymore. The fact that Tawnee Dare wouldn't be physically in a location she could try to harm her was irrelevant.

Greta had made it through the seventh circle.

And now she was free.

"We have another Christmas surprise, sugar," he reminded her.

Her expression turned curious. "We do?"

"Andy's bedroom."

She melted into him, her arms finally going around him. "He knows you're setting that up for him, Hixon."

"He knows, but it's now set up and he hasn't seen it yet."

She grinned and gave him a squeeze. "You're right. We do have a surprise. Because he's gonna love the comforter Mamie and Corinne chose for him."

That surprised Hix because Andy might have a TBI but he was still very much a guy.

"He will?"

"He won't care even a little bit, until we tell him Mamie and Corinne picked it. Then he'll make a big deal out of loving it."

That, Hix had learned, was undoubtedly true.

Hix had no idea about Greta and Andy's fathers, he knew too much about their mother, so he figured it was down to that grit Tawnee Dare mentioned that Greta had that made her brother fall not far from his sister's tree.

He dug his fingers into her neck gently and said, "Let's go get your brother."

She blinded him with a smile and replied, "Yeah, let's go get Andy."

He kissed her. He walked her out to his Bronco.

And even if she didn't want to rejoice, that bitch was gone, so he did.

Thus as a celebration, for the first time in his life with his ass in his Bronc, he let someone else drive her.

And he was in no doubt Greta was the one.

But how much she loved driving his baby proved it beyond a shadow of a doubt.

"I WAS CLOSE."

"Mm," he mumbled, sliding a hand over the curve of her ass.

The scary thing was, she had been.

Close to winning.

Then again, he'd been dazzled by his Boxing Day present, a skintight, red lace teddy with fluffy, white feather trim at hips and chest, little straps over the shoulders, crisscross ribbons between her tits and even a thin, red-velvet belt with a tiny rhinestone buckle.

Watching her walk into his bedroom wearing that, he hadn't even paid attention when she tossed a tube of lube on the bed.

His attention didn't come back seeing as she tossed it then

crawled to him in that getup with her tits almost hanging out and he had to devote his attention to all of that.

So she'd laid down the gauntlet for their rematch, immediately got the upper hand and it took a while for her to lose it.

This was why they were both covered in a sheen of sweat, on their stomachs, flat out across his bed, and he'd just slid out of her ass after making her come taking it then coming himself really fucking hard giving it.

She was hot up there. Unbelievably tight. And she'd gone wild with his hands on her, his mouth on her, drilling her into the bed with his cock up her ass.

It was Hix's best Christmas present ever, bar none.

Starting with the teddy.

He slid two fingers through her crevice and held her there, murmuring, "You good?"

She turned her head on her arms, her mass of curls shifting with it, and gave him her big, blue eyes.

"You up for a bath?"

He grinned at the look on her face that gave him his answer as well as her question. "Yup."

She grinned back and he slid his hand up and over, smoothing it on her hip.

"After a recovery bath, loser gives winner a colossal blowjob," he informed her.

She frowned even if her eyes flared. "That wasn't the deal."

"Winner gets to say the deal after he wins."

She started pouting. "You're a terrible sport, Hix."

"How's that?"

"It's not how you lose that tells the tale, it's the class you show when you win," she educated him.

He leaned in and kissed her shoulder, saying there, "Maybe you can show me that if you win someday."

"It's good I love you," she groused.

He lifted his lips from her shoulder, looked her dead in the eye, and there was no teasing in his voice when he said, "I know."

The pique went out of her face and her eyes got bright. "Don't make me cry."

He shifted so he could pull her slightly under his body, but keep his place on his stomach and put his face in hers.

"I'll never make you cry," he vowed.

"Happy tears," she told him.

"Never," he whispered, moved in and touched his mouth to hers.

Hers opened so he took the touch into a full-blown kiss.

When he pulled away, she didn't look like she was going to cry anymore.

There.

All better.

"Did you like your present, baby?" she whispered.

"Are you in doubt, baby?" he whispered back.

"No."

He touched his nose to hers and held her gaze.

"Hated hearin' you never had a dream, sweetheart," he shared gently.

She tightened. "Hix, don't bring her—"

"But I figure," he cut her off, "when you're a walking, talking, singing dream come true, you don't get it the other way around."

Her eyes got bright again. "Shit, totally gonna cry."

He grinned again and moved his hand to cup her ass and give it a squeeze. "None of that."

"Boss," she muttered, pulling it together.

"I'll run the bath," he murmured in return.

"I'll lounge here and let you run the bath."

He pulled back an inch, thinking how hard she'd come.

"Don't fall asleep," he ordered.

Her brows shot together in insult. "Would I fall asleep?"

"Not with the promise of sucking me off on our agenda."

"You like that more than me, Hixon."

"Considering you'll be sittin' on my face doin' it, I'm not sure that's true."

That got him another eye flare.

"Bath," she ordered.

"Boss," he muttered, kissed her nose and moved out of the bed.

He ran their bath. He made it nice and hot.

Then he walked out and smiled to himself when Greta let out a surprised scream as he grabbed her ankle, dragged her off the bed and threw her over his shoulder.

"You fell asleep," he accused, his woman's ass in the air, her body draped over his shoulder, walking to the bathroom.

"Whatever," she replied to his back.

They entered the bathroom with Hix still smiling.

Epilogue

I Win

Greta

"Babe!"

"Coming!" I shouted, sitting on the side of my bed, slipping up the zip on my boot.

I dashed into the closet, grabbed a black pashmina, my black leather gloves, then I dashed out, through the room and down the stairs.

I found Hix in the kitchen, fridge open, bent with his face in it, wearing a dark gray suit, his overcoat thrown on my kitchen island.

"Hey," I greeted.

He straightened as he closed the fridge door and turned to me.

Dark-green shirt, green and gray patterned tie.

Handsome.

I walked to him, asking, "Are you hungry?"

He looked to the fridge then back to me, putting his hands to my waist when I arrived at him.

"Habit," he muttered.

"Ah," I replied.

He studied my face.

"You okay?" he asked gently.

"I didn't know the man, Hix," I reminded him, resting my hands still holding my scarf and gloves to his chest.

"I know, but you know his wife and all funerals are rough. This one…" He didn't finish that, but I got him.

Three nights before, Mrs. Whitney's husband had slid into the eternal sleep that was far more eternal than the eternal sleep he was in already.

It was odd to think of the death of someone as a relief. However, Mr. Whitney had died long ago, so as odd as it was, it was still true, which made it difficult in a different way because, even if that might be logical to have that feeling, it still didn't seem right.

"I'll feel better when I see her and how she's handling it," I told him. "We spoke on the phone but she sounded understandably preoccupied. It'll be good to get a handle on where she's at."

He nodded.

I gave him a small smile and started to move out of his hold, but stopped when his fingers tightened.

"We got a few minutes, and after this goes down, I gotta get changed and back to work, so need to tell you something now," he shared.

I nodded and it was my turn to study him.

It was mid-February but something had been bothering Hixon and that something started bothering him right after Christmas.

It became more pronounced around January fourteenth, Corinne's birthday, her sweet sixteen.

I got the idea that a father had issues with his daughter becoming more of a woman, especially since that daughter now had a boyfriend. I also understood that, this being the first event where the families had to officially merge—Andy, Lou, her brood and me going to the party because Corinne wanted us there, a party that had Hope and all her brood there—that this would cause everyone, especially Hix, some unease.

I couldn't say it'd gone great. Hope, Lou, Jessie, Molly and I hadn't stood in a corner and cackled like the sisterhood we were.

I couldn't say it was a bust. I'd been nice but distant, as Hope made it clear she wished me to be, even though she too had been nice but distant. And Molly had clearly gotten Reed's head out of his ass about things so he'd been civil.

It still was awkward. But it didn't appear Corinne felt it at all.

I thought once that occasion was done, Hix would relax.

He hadn't.

February third had rolled around, Shaw's eighteenth (we'd just say it was a one, two, three punch with the Drakes: Christmas, Corinne's birthday, then Shaw's—fortunately Mamie's birthday was June third so there was a breather).

Again, it was a momentous occasion, his son officially becoming, for all intents and purposes, a man.

Hix showed pride, affection and obvious emotion at that birthday party that, at Shaw's request, had been split. His dad, Andy, his sisters and me for dinner. His mom and her family for a big weekend do, with Shaw and the girls going to Hope's house for a few hours before we had dinner and cake at Hix's in order to share some time with his mom on his big day.

But two weeks had passed since then and Hix's manner hadn't changed.

And it was beginning to dawn on me that it was Corinne becoming a woman, with the unavoidable threat of Mamie not being too far behind (she'd started her period, another hit for Hix that he couldn't ignore that his kids were growing up).

However, it was mostly Shaw.

It wasn't about him being officially a man.

It was about him intending to be the man he intended to be and *that* being official.

Shaw had an appointment to go to the marine recruiting office with Hix in a couple of weeks.

And that was where it was at.

Every day that passed was a day closer to him losing his boy, him losing his boy to the marines and the marines taking over the process of making Shaw into the man he'd become.

I had no idea how to make things better for Hix, and in wracking my brain, it was becoming apparent that there was no way to make things better.

He had to ride this out. It was inevitable. He had to see it through, support his son. In the meantime, I just had to be there for him, keep a finger on his pulse and do what I could to see Hix through.

So this could be anything. Hix didn't hide the fact he was aware his kids were getting older and going about their own lives and he wanted them to do that responsibly, but he also wanted them to know they'd always be his kids and he'd be there for them. Alternately, he did hide (from all of them but me, though he didn't tell me outright) that he was struggling with it.

I wanted him to open up to me. I also didn't want to open up a dialogue about it with him if he was dealing or he just didn't want to talk about it yet.

Hix was communicative. He shared. You didn't have to guess about stuff with Hix. If it meant something to him, you knew.

But if he wasn't ready to talk, you waited.

"Owners of my house got in touch with my real estate agent," he announced.

That I wasn't expecting.

"Yeah?" I prompted when that was all he said.

"Their son got a transfer. He's moving from Virginia to Florida. They have a kid, the wife is pregnant again. They'll be living about an hour away."

I arched into him, getting excited. "Really?"

He grinned down at me. "They're asking for an offer."

"They haven't even experienced a full Florida summer yet with its attendant humidity," I pointed out, some of my excitement melting away.

"That's not my concern, babe. They *have* experienced most a Florida winter and I'm thinkin' they dig it. I'm thinkin' they dig more the idea of close proximity with their son and his growing family so I'd guess they'll learn to put up with humidity. But if they're ready to let go of the house, I'm jumpin' on that."

"Totally," I agreed.

"And I want you there."

"Of course. That house is perfect for you. Close to work. Close to Hope for the kids. Lots of space for everybody. Why would I not—?"

"No, babe," his hands slid from my waist to the small of my back, pulling me closer to him, "I want you *there.* We come to terms, I buy that house, I want you to move in with us."

I stared up at him.

He wasn't done speaking.

"And Greta, I want you to think on it, it's your choice, but when you do that, I want you sellin' this place. We'll talk about furniture because I prefer your dining room table to mine. You got some other great stuff that'd fit. But the rest you can let go and invest all the money you make on it so you can breathe easy about Andy permanently."

Throughout this, I didn't stop staring at him.

However, it didn't matter.

Hix still wasn't finished.

"And I'll state plain I got more than the obvious reasons for askin' you to think about that. But I'll point out the obvious just to make sure you know. I love you. I'm sure about how I feel about having a future with you, and by that I mean I'm sure I want a future with you. And this two-house stuff is gettin' old. I like this place. The kids do. But I want you in my bed every night and I don't want you to have to lug your Crockpot or griddle or whatever over every time you're cookin' up something that you need them. Most important, it's time we got serious about this. It's time to take that next step, because that step's gonna lead to the next one and I wanna move on through all of them with you. But the reason that might not be obvious I want you to let go of this place is your ex gave you this house and I'm down with him providing for Andy because of who he is to your brother. But where we're at, you're mine. So I'm not down with him providing for you."

"Hix—" I forced out, having to force it because I was dealing with all he'd said, all it made me feel, how awesome all that was, but I got no further.

"That's where I'm at. You'll call it alpha-male behavior and I'm okay with that. It is. And that's who I am. You need to know how I feel and I gotta share that honesty. That said, if you think on it and you love this place and you wanna open up the possibility of me and my kids movin' here, we'll talk. I'll listen, sweetheart. I swear it. You love your porch. Your street. You want it, I'll see if I have it in me to give it to you. But to do that, I might have to let go of my place so the owners can sell it and I still want us takin' the next step, wherever that step will lead us."

When I had my shot, I responded immediately.

"You buy your place, I'll sell this place, Hix."

His chin jerked into his throat. "Really?"

"Really."

His brows drew together. "That easy?" he asked.

"Your street is the same as my street in all the ways that are important. And I love this house, but your kitchen is bigger, it's nicer. And the kids are settled in."

"Your bathrooms are nicer."

"Your bathrooms aren't awful, but you can gut a bathroom and make it pretty. We have room to put Mamie's barre in my basement, but the floors in yours are wood so she can dance there and mine are carpeted. There also isn't a bedroom down there for Shaw or a man cave for you." I pressed my scarf and gloves into his chest and grinned up at him. "And if it bothers the alpha, I don't wanna prod that beast."

His eyes warmed, his face going soft. "You wanna stay here, baby, honest, you make that case, I'll find a way to be cool with it."

God, but I loved him.

"I failed to mention your mudroom and attached garage," I noted.

"Babe—"

"It's a house," I whispered. "And yes, it's the house that Keith bought me. And after what happened, where he is, how he's made it clear he's not gonna go back on what he said and find some way to make things all right between us again, for us or for us to share our love for Andy, I'm where you're at in a way. It's a reminder of that. And that isn't a pleasant reminder. But more, if it bugs you, I can't have that. So it's a house, Hixon." I pressed even closer and lowered my voice so he'd understand how much I meant what I said next. "I'm all in for taking the next step. I'm also all in, doing that, leaving behind what needs to be left behind so we can move forward through the rest of them."

I transferred my gloves to my scarf hand, slid my free hand up to the knot in his tie and unnecessarily straightened it before I finished.

"Put an offer in, honey. We'll tell the kids. You guys make a deal, you close, I'll put my place on the market. When it sells, I'll move in. That gives the kids time to come to terms with it happening and us time to deal with merging houses. Is that a plan?"

He took an arm from around me to put his hand on my jaw and sweep his thumb across the apple of my cheek.

He didn't confirm we had a plan.

He still did.

He managed this by saying, "Love you, gum drop."

"Love you too, snuggle bug."

He grinned down at me.

Then he bent and kissed me.

When he lifted his head, the warmth was still in his eyes but it was tempered and I'd know why when he murmured, "We best get to Mrs. Whitney."

I nodded.

Hix let me go.

He put on his coat while I draped my pashmina around my neck. He went to get my coat and helped me on with it.

I pulled my gloves on as we walked out to the Bronco.

And then Hix drove me to Mr. Whitney's funeral so we could support Mrs. Whitney in her even more difficult effort to leave behind what needed to be left behind.

So she could take her next step.

I WAS SITTING NEXT to Lou watching Snow and Corinne play soccer at the same time glancing frequently to the side where Hix was standing having what appeared to be a serious conversation with Shaw.

Most high schools played soccer in the fall. But with most of the girls on the volleyball team also playing soccer, not softball, in a decision that divided the county and caused rifts between family and friends that were still healing to that day, Lou had reported that five years ago, they'd shifted seasons so all the girls' soccer and/or volleyball teams weren't terrible.

God, I loved a small town where the only thing that could upset you was the high school girls' soccer schedule.

"You know what that's about?" Lou said under her breath as she leaned into me.

"Wendy broke it off with Shaw," I said under my breath back.

Lou's voice rose. "Is she crazy?"

"Shh, Lou," I hissed, slapping her on the leg.

"Is she crazy?" Lou whispered.

"Her dad's treatments are over, things look promising, but that was harrowing. She's a junior. She's looking at going to University of

Nebraska in a year. What she's not looking forward to is having to go through that with her dad then having to deal with her boyfriend being wherever he's gonna be, becoming a marine, thus not free to come visit her on weekends and the like. So she pushed the option of Shaw giving that up and going to work for his granddad so he can be close. He signed on. That didn't go over great with her. There's no turning back now but she didn't stop pushing. He wasn't liking that much."

"Oh boy," Lou muttered.

"A couple of days ago, she gave him an ultimatum. He made his choice. She ended it," I concluded.

"Oh boy," Lou sighed.

"He's tried to get her to understand. She's digging in her heels." I glanced at father and son. "It appears she's still digging in her heels."

"Some stay. Some go. So many go, the pool gets less populated. So I'll pull out my crystal ball to confirm when I get home, but right now I can say with some authority in a year or three or five, or for the rest of her life, Hixon and you hang around Glossop, Shaw comes home to see you guys, and Wendy stays here, she'll see him and she'll be kickin' her own ass. Especially after he lands a babe who's smart enough not to give a man an ultimatum about something like that."

"Mm," I mumbled my agreement.

The conversation ended and both father and son walked up to sit with Lou and me.

Hix gave me a look and a short shake of his head.

I returned his look but gave a smile to Shaw.

He gave one back but it was one he didn't commit to.

They sat.

Hix curved an arm around me.

We watched Corinne and Snow help the team beat the crap out of Yucca.

We then went home.

Shaw was barely in the back door when he muttered, "I'm gonna go out to Sunnydown and hang with Andy."

Mamie had spent the game dancing under the bleachers with her friends. She'd already danced into the house. Corinne gave her brother a look, me a look, her dad a look but kept quiet and moved into the house.

Hix murmured, "That's cool, kid. Call when you're on your way back."

I stood there allowing the glow of how much Shaw liked my brother to warm me.

Then I followed him out to the garage.

"Hey," I called.

Standing at the door to get outside to his car parked in the drive, Shaw turned to me.

I got close. "She's not the one."

His mouth got tight. "I know, we're young, it's not the end of the world." He looked away, mumbling, "Whatever."

"It's not that you're young," I stated and he looked back to me. "And it might not be the end of the world, but that doesn't negate the fact that it feels like it right now. It's that she's not the one."

I had his attention and since he didn't say anything or cut the conversation off, I got closer and brushed my fingers along the back of his hand.

"She either believes in you and your dreams or she doesn't. If she doesn't, Shaw, honey, she's not the one. She can be seventeen or she can be thirty-five. The woman you pick has to understand what you want out of life and she has to support that one hundred percent. It's your job to give that back. What is not your job is to settle for anything less. You don't make a man what he's not. You find the man you want and stand beside him no matter what."

"Yeah," he whispered.

"Yeah," I decreed.

"I liked her a lot," he confided in me.

"I know that, sweetheart."

"But you're right. What you said. She's not the one."

I gave him a gentle smile. "You'll find her, Shaw."

He stared at me and he did it hard.

Then he said, "Yeah."

I liked how he said that and what he didn't hide he meant by it so my smile got less gentle and a lot bigger.

"Go see Andy," I ordered.

"Should I take him candy bars?" he asked.

"If you want. Do you need money?" I asked back.

He shook his head. "I got it."

"All right. Be safe, yes?"

"I will, Greta. Later."

"Later, Shaw."

He walked out the door.

I walked in the one that led to the mudroom only to see my man leaning a shoulder against the jamb of the doorway to the hall with his arms and ankles crossed, waiting for my return.

Seriously.

My man was hot.

"You sort him out?" he asked.

And seriously.

My man was a good dad.

"I gave him a few things to think about."

"Good," he murmured. Then asked, "You gonna make dinner or am I takin' my girls out to eat?"

"Mamie's on a cooking binge. When she's not pirouetting, she all about spices. I promised to demonstrate the art of making tacos tonight, this art including not worrying about spices too much since McCormick does it for you. She's looking forward to it."

"Tacos sound good."

He said that but he didn't move.

"You gonna get out of my way so I can get your girl and convene my lesson at the Drake Culinary School?" I asked.

He lifted one shoulder. "Sure, you earn passage with a kiss."

I could totally do that.

So I did it.

Then I taught Mamie how to make tacos.

And at the dining room table we were selling when I closed on my house in two weeks, Hix's girls with Hix ate them.

I WALKED INTO OUR BEDROOM.

Hix, sitting on the edge of the bed, elbows to his knees, one hand clamped on the back of his neck, didn't move.

This was not a pose that alarmed me.

Shaw had graduated three hours before.

My heart lurched, I closed the door, went and sat next to my man.

I pressed up against his side, wrapping my arm around his back and resting my forehead to his shoulder.

He cleared his throat but didn't lift his head when he said gruffly, "Kid's smarter than me and I'm a forty-two year old man."

I wasn't sure that was true but I didn't disagree verbally.

I just hummed, "Mm."

"He'll be okay."

I agreed with that. "He will."

"He'll do good."

"Yes, he will."

"Find a good woman. Build a good life."

"Yes."

"Hear him cryin'."

That confused me. Shaw was out partying with his friends. He was amped. Hix had hidden all of this as best he could, Hope had done her part with that too, so it was all good for Shaw.

"What?"

He lifted up, turned to me, and I saw the red rimming his eyes.

Oh, my Hix.

"Came out bawling. Didn't even have to induce it. He let it be known he was a part of this world the minute he slipped out. Keep hearin' that. Hearin' the memory of that moment my boy became mine."

I pressed closer to him and rounded him with both arms.

"What happened to my baby boy?" he whispered.

I'd barely got my arms around him, but at that, I put both hands to his cheeks and my face in his.

"He grew up, Hixon," I whispered back. "And you did good, baby. You and Hope did so good with him. He's amazing. Simply amazing."

He sniffed and sat straight.

My hands fell away.

"Andy's a mess," he declared.

I nodded.

It was far from lost on Andy that his new best friend was soon to enter the marines. He loved Hix. He adored Mamie and Corinne. But he'd bonded with Shaw.

"I know. I'll go to him in a second, see if he's okay. Just wanted to make sure you're okay."

"He goes to basic in three weeks."

"Yes," I said.

"We're gonna make that a great fuckin' three weeks."

I smiled weakly at him.

He took my hand and stood, pulling me up with him.

He let me go instantly and I let him do it when he stated toward the door, "I'll go to Andy."

"Okay, darlin'."

He looked down at me.

"Love you," I whispered.

He bent and touched his lips to mine.

Then, while Shaw partied with his friends, the girls were with their mom looking after her, my man went to my brother so they could commiserate about the upcoming loss of their boy.

At the Dew, I slid on the barstool next to Hix, murmuring, "Thanks, baby," as he handed me my sparkling water.

It was packed that night, but Hix had arrived early, bringing me in to sing. There had been tables available. Why he was at the bar, I had no clue.

Before I could ask, he said, "It's totally corny."

I took a sip from my straw but did it with my eyes to him.

When I finished, I asked, "What?"

"Wanted to do it before, but wanted things to be about Shaw during his graduation and before he left. I struggled with it. He'll be upset he wasn't around when it happened. But it'll get his ass home when he can come home so we can have a delayed celebration."

I stared at him as he spoke, not having any idea what he was talking about.

"I'm not following, darlin'," I shared.

"Met you here. Started the ride when you sang 'At Last' to me. Tried to deny it when you sang 'Stay' to me. Knew I was gone when you sang 'Cold' to me. And knew you were gone when you sang 'Glitter in the Air' to me. So it had to be here. And here is where it's gonna be."

I was kind of following, but not exactly.

And I couldn't find it in me to figure it out because I was dealing with him sharing he remembered all the important songs I'd sang to him.

His eyes dropped to my drink but all he said was, "Corny."

I felt my brows draw together then I looked down to my drink.

Sparkling water. Ice glittering. Blue straw with those ridges that you could bend so—

Oh my God.

My hand started shaking.

Oh my God!

I felt Hix's hand span the top of my thigh, his lips to my ear, where he whispered, "Time for the next step, Greta."

I turned my head, he pulled back, and I caught his eyes.

"Is that—?" I started.

"Marry me."

Tears filled my eyes and he saw them instantly.

So just as instantly, he lifted both hands to my face and put his in mine. "Baby, no tears."

"No...no...no damned way I'm not crying right now, Hixon Drake."

His thumbs went under my eyes and he warned, "Sweetheart, no—"

Too late.

One slid over and hit his thumb.

His gaze came to mine.

"I love you," I whispered.

His eyes flashed with humor. "Does that mean yes?"

"Do you have to ask?" I retorted.

"Kinda important for this question I get an answer, gum drop."

"Then yes."

No humor for that.

Just intensity.

He also didn't move.

"Yes, Hixon." I lifted my free hand and wrapped it tight around his wrist. "Yes. Yes. Yesyesyesyes. *Yes*," I stated fiercely.

I said it but Hix still didn't move.

He just sat there, holding my face, his pool-blue eyes staring into mine.

I was going to get to swim in those eyes forever.

Another tear slid into his thumb.

"Glass, bro, put that bling on her finger before she combusts," we heard from beside us, and I looked to Danny, the bartender, who'd set an empty glass on the bar between Hix and me.

He was also grinning like a maniac.

Hix took my glass, poured out the water, but sifted it through his fingers in the end so he could catch the ring.

Danny threw a bunch of napkins on the bar for Hix to dry his hand but Hix didn't touch them.

He took my hand and slid the cold metal of the ring on my finger.

It was very simple, not large, not tiny, set in white gold or platinum, and it had five little diamonds embedded in each side of the band.

Keith had given me a two and a half carat, cushion-cut diamond surrounded by a band embedded with two rows of them.

This was not that.

What it was, was the most beautiful thing I'd ever seen.

I felt another tear fall.

"Baby," Hix warned, his hand closing around mine, taking the view of my ring from me, his other hand sweeping away the tear. "Stop it."

I looked to him. "You're right, it was corny."

He grinned.

"Totally corny," I declared.

He kept grinning.

"And I'm so happy, if you don't kiss me, I'm gonna scream," I shared.

He continued grinning even as he stood from his stool, got in my space in a way I had to twist my legs to the side and wrapped a hand around the back of my neck.

I tilted my head way back, curving my arms around his middle.

And it was then, he kissed me.

I heard the tinkling of something against a glass but I was so lost in Hixon, I didn't take it in.

I still didn't take it in when I heard Gemini shout, "She said yes! Raise a glass! We're toasting to the soon-to-be Mr. and Mrs. Hixon Drake!"

I only surfaced when Hix lifted his mouth from mine and I suspected he only did this because everyone was cheering and shouting.

We looked to the club to see everyone on their feet, everyone looking our way, everyone clapping and everyone smiling.

Hix slid an arm around my shoulders and tucked me into his side.

"Danny, champagne for all!" Gemini announced.

More clapping and cheering and I settled my wet gaze on Gemini.

He moved to us, smiling even bigger than Danny had been doing.

Hix lifted his hand to shake Gemini's and accept his murmured congratulations then Gemini moved in and touched his cheek to mine.

He moved back and caught my gaze. "Happy for you, beautiful."

"Me too."

He gave me a soft smile. "You need the rest of the night off?"

I shook my head. "If you don't think I'm gonna give the performance of a lifetime crooning to my new fiancé, you're crazy."

That got me a bigger smile.

He moved away and clapped Hix on the arm before he walked away.

I looked up to my man.

No.

My fiancé.

My future husband.

No.

Just my future *everything*.

"I should have taken the rest of the night off."

He dipped close to me. "You want that, Greta, have a feeling Gemini would give you anything."

"Do you want me to grab him?" I asked.

"I want you to do what you want."

"Okay, but what do you want?"

"I want what you want."

I looked into his eyes.

And doing it, I knew that was what he wanted.

That was all Hixon Drake actually *was*.

He was a man who wanted what those he loved wanted.

After the life I'd lived, how had I gotten so lucky?

I lifted my hand, pressed it against his shoulder, watching myself do that, seeing my new ring wink at me. Then I slid it to his neck and curled it around, looking back at him.

"I want to sing 'At Last' to you. And 'Stay.' And 'Cold.' And 'Glitter in the Air.' And then I'll cut the set short because I wanna go home and make love with my fiancé. Does that work for you?"

"Absolutely."

I tipped my head back and swayed closer to him.

"You've made me very happy, Hixon Drake."

"That makes me happy, Greta, but just to say, sweetheart, even before that you returned the favor." He touched his nose to mine and finished, "In spades."

"No," I replied and saw his eyes smile.

"Uh, baby, I'd know."

"No you wouldn't. Because you didn't grow up like me. You didn't live a life like mine. You got kicked in the teeth at forty-two, then you found me. So this match, smokey, no doubt about it, *I win*."

Both his hands cupped my jaws before he growled, "I'll give you that win, angel."

I smiled at him.

He kissed me.

People around us started whooping and cheering again.

And for the first time in my life, with not one thing dragging on it, weighing it heavy, I was happy.

Oh, I'd won.

Yeah, I'd won.

Spectacularly.

Mrs. Swanson was in my chair and I was sectioning a piece of her hair to put a roller in, doing this wearing a She Told Me So T-shirt with an arrow pointed in a way that, where I usually stood by my chair, always pointed to Lou.

Lou had given it to me in the back room the day before.

I'd laughed my butt off.

This being after we'd hugged for a long time because my bestest bud had given it to me and then promptly burst out crying.

Needless to say, Lou was happy that Hix asked me to marry him.

Lou had told me the shirt was a joke. I didn't have to wear it.

I totally wore it.

I looked up from Mrs. Swanson's hair to see Joyce standing close to me.

"Told you," she said softly, "that man never struck me as stupid. He knew, the good that dropped in his lap, he'd be fool to let it go. He knew, Greta."

"Yeah," I whispered, staring in her eyes.

"I cannot say how happy I am," she shared with me, still talking quietly. "Don't know if I'm happier for Hixon, he got a good girl like you, or you, that you got what you deserved. But I'm happy. Whole town's happy, darlin'. Watchin' you two find each other through all that garbage was like watchin' a dream come true."

"You're gonna make me cry, Joyce," I warned.

"None a' that," she dismissed, stared at me some more then nodded her head sharply. "Right," she stated briskly. "I'm off. Six weeks, Lou?"

Lou had to clear her throat before she replied, "You're in my schedule, Joyce."

Joyce said nothing.

She just took off.

I looked to Lou.

She grinned at me.

Mrs. Swanson sniffled before she asked, "Greta, sweetie, I forgot my hankie. You got a tissue?"

I looked at her in the mirror to see she had tears brimming in her eyes.

I gave her a gentle smile and went for the tissue box. "Right here, Mrs. Swanson."

"You're a dear," she murmured, taking the tissue I offered.

I sectioned more hair thinking how odd it was, a girl who didn't dream, living a dream come true.

Then I rolled Mrs. Swanson's hair and tried to do it well, even if my engagement ring kept taking my attention.

"I CANNOT BE-FREAKIN'-BELIEVE this day," Hix groused as we walked into the mudroom from the garage.

I tried not to burst out laughing.

Instead, I murmured, "Hey, boy. How's your day been, boy?" to Rocky, Andy and the girls' dog that we rescued from the shelter, a mature pup, eight years old when we got him last summer, part lab, part they didn't know what. A dog we said was Andy and the girls' but he was Hix and mine and not only because we were the ones around the most to take care of him.

"And I cannot freakin' tell you how much I need a bourbon," he went on.

I could imagine.

I still found it funny.

I let Hix help me off with my coat. He took it and hooked it on the hooks by the door before he shrugged off his own.

I wandered into the kitchen to get him his bourbon with Rocky doing what Rocky did whenever Hix and I separated.

He stood there uncertain whether to hang with one or follow the other.

I'd thrown my beaded clutch on the island and was in the process of walking to the cupboard where we kept the liquor when Hix and Rocky joined me.

"Porch?" I asked, raising a brow at him.

"Gin?" he asked back, glaring at me.

I kept trying not to laugh. "For me, it's not a gin night, darlin'. I didn't deliver a baby on a dance floor. It's a wine night though."

He went to the wine rack in the pantry and decreed, "Donna's fired on Monday."

I barely suppressed my giggle.

"Greta, this shit isn't funny."

I pulled down his bottle of bourbon and looked to him.

"Ashlee gave birth on the dance floor during the reception at Bets's wedding," he told me something I knew.

My body jolted as I chased the laughter back into it, which wanted so desperately to bust out of it.

He recounted the whole thing. "Hal lost his mind. Donna couldn't stop laughing long enough to help. And I think Larry went somewhere and puked."

I couldn't help it, I started sniggering.

"I've never seen a baby come that fast," he declared.

"She'd told me earlier she was feeling strange. I think she was in labor," I shared.

"That's insane."

I shrugged, smiling hugely at him.

"What woman dances while she's in labor?" he asked me irritably.

"Well, obviously, Ashlee," I answered.

His eyes narrowed. "You didn't help either."

"I was busy holding her hand," I pointed out.

"Thank God for Andy or I think Hal would have passed out," he muttered, turning back to the pantry.

I smiled, turning back to his bourbon, and I finished with it thinking he was right. Hal had descended into panic and Andy had jumped right in and calmed him right down.

I waited until he opened a bottle and poured my wine.

He handed it to me, murmuring, "Go on out. I'll get your sweater and be out in a minute."

I nodded. "Thanks, baby."

Rocky and I went out with my wine and Hix's bourbon (Rocky was never uncertain about porch time, he always came right out with me). I settled myself in an Adirondack chair and Rocky explored the front yard long enough to do his business before he came back and laid down on my high-heeled feet.

Hix joined me carrying my sweater, but he'd changed into jeans and a thermal, which I thought was a good call, considering his trousers, shirt and tie had newborn baby all over them.

I pulled on the cardigan as Hix sat down beside me, tipping up his chin toward the street at the same time Rocky's head came up and also turned toward the street.

I shifted my attention that way and called, "Hey, Nicki."

"Hey there, Greta. Hix."

Rocky woofed softly.

Nicki's dog strained at the leash to get to Rocky.

Hix said nothing but he adjusted his scowl long enough for Nicki to pass with her dog.

"Uh, you know, since you're in a bad mood..." I began.

Hix's scowl returned full force as he turned his eyes to me.

I beat back my smile. "Corinne and I chatted at the wedding. She's broken up with Jake."

Hix looked back at the street. "Good. That kid's a tool. Never liked him."

Since the boyfriend she got her sophomore year, and with Corinne now into her senior one, she'd been through three, Jake being four.

Hix never liked any of them.

"Okay, well, that wasn't bad, as such, but...uh, Donna shared a little bit about Becker talking to the Feds about a deal."

He threw back some bourbon then declared to the street. "Woman's totally fired on Monday."

"Hix—"

He looked to me. "She shouldn't be talking to you about that stuff, Greta."

"She didn't say much. But she's worried because you've been moody."

"And again, I'm moody at work, she doesn't talk to my wife about it."

"I'm her stylist, darlin', except for talking about stuff with you, it's very close to the sanctity of the confessional even if she's not in my chair but instead at a wedding where a woman gave birth on a dance floor."

"Babe, you rat out people all the time, which, I'll note, you just did, sharin' that shit Donna gave to you."

I grinned. "If they share with the sheriff's wife, they deserve me being a snitch."

Hix didn't grin.

He looked back to the street but at least he did it with his mouth quirking.

"Are you okay with this Becker stuff?" I asked.

"Him makin' a deal, ratting on bigger players in order to get his ass in WITSEC after we finally shut down his shit in this county? No. Do I want that house of cards to collapse? Yes. Do I want Becker to live cush after he's gotten away with his crap for decades? No." He took another sip and muttered, "But I got no choice. It's outta my hands."

I reached out and wrapped my fingers around his forearm. "Sorry, baby."

He pulled out of my hold but only to take over, placing the back of my hand on the arm of the chair and then running his fingers along the insides of mine. He did it automatically, his eyes were still aimed at the street, but he did it having so much practice, he didn't have to watch to do it expertly.

"I'm glad Hal finally got his head out of his ass," he whispered eventually.

I was in the know about the fact that Hal had not been a very good husband, until for some reason things broke loose after Hix gave him a talking to during the investigation of Nat Calloway's murder.

Or maybe it had just been Nat dying, leaving Faith to face a life without her husband.

Whatever it was, he'd gotten rid of his women and recommitted to his marriage.

Now they had a baby.

And when Ashlee came and got her hair done, she didn't look sad anymore.

"Me too," I whispered back.

"Hope called," he shared.

"Yeah?" I asked.

"Jep and Marie want us at Thanksgiving. Andy's invited too, of course. Your call, sweetheart. It's a big day and important to you and Andy just like it is to everybody." I felt his eyes so I stopped looking at our hands and looked to him. "I know you and Hope manage to keep it good. I also know you two aren't the best of friends. So if you'll be uncomfortable, we'll say no."

"Shaw'll be home and it'd be good we don't make him split too much of his time. So maybe we can meet them there for pie at the end but maybe go over to Lou's or have Tommy and Toast over here and do our own thing before we go."

"That'll work."

I smiled at him.

He stopped stroking my fingers, threaded his through mine and held on.

"Sheriff," I heard and looked to the street. "Hey, Greta. Nice night."

"Year's getting old. We need to enjoy them while they last, Joe," I called.

"I hear that," our neighbor replied, nodding to us both and continuing to walk his dog.

I sipped my wine.

My husband held my hand and sipped his bourbon.

We let the peace of our street melt away the craziness of the day.

"I want more bourbon. I'll get you more wine. I do that, you get upstairs. I'll bring up the drinks. But I wanna fuck my wife."

My lady parts spasmed and my gaze shot to Hix to watch him down the rest of his drink.

When his gaze came to mine, I didn't hesitate offering him my still half-full glass.

He didn't take it.

He pulled me up and then he pulled me into the house.

Rocky followed.

Our dog and I stopped with Hix as he let me go to close and lock the door.

"Headboard?" I asked when I got his attention.

"We'll see," he answered and took my glass.

I grinned a lazy grin.

He watched me then growled a low growl.

Once I heard that, still in my heels and dress from the wedding, I sashayed across the living room and up the stairs, knowing my husband's eyes were on my ass, even under my cardie.

I eventually got headboard.

I got a bunch of other stuff too.

It was magnificent.

It would be.

Because I got it all from Hix.

Hixon

Hix stood by the mantle of his fireplace, looking at one of the many framed pictures resting there.

The one that had his attention was the biggest of the lot.

Greta was wearing a long-sleeved, drop-waist, filmy, ivory gown. The sleeves where see-through. There was an elegant drape at the neckline, not low, but wide, exposing her chest and collarbone all the way to the points of her shoulders.

No beads. No pearls. No bling.

Just that.

Her wedding dress.

He was standing beside her wearing a suit, his arm around her, but his other arm was around Corinne who was pressed to his other side and he had his head turned and bent, kissing his daughter's hair.

Andy was at Greta's other side but she didn't have her arm around him. She had one around Hix and her other hand was holding her bouquet of blue roses and white calla lilies. Andy was just standing close to his sister, but bent over the back of Mamie standing in front of him. A Mamie who'd been caught by the camera, laughing uncontrollably, Andy's arms wrapped around her in what looked like an embrace, but what memory served as him tickling her.

Shaw stood next to Andy with his hand on Andy's shoulder, he was bent slightly with his own laughter toward his sister and a man he treated as a brother.

Greta, however, was looking at the camera with a look on her beautiful face Hix had seen only three times from her in his life.

The first was the first time he saw her brother wrap his arms around her that day her mother was making a scene at Sunnydown.

The second was when he looked back to her face after he'd slid her wedding ring on her finger during their wedding.

And that picture was the last.

Her expression was sublime.

As it would be.

She looked like she'd just hit heaven.

"Ready," she said from behind him and he turned to see her coming in the room in a gorgeous, tight dress, her usual heels on her feet.

He suspected with one look at her that he looked like she did in their wedding photo.

Then again, Hix suspected most times he looked at his wife, he looked like that.

She was rummaging through her bag, doing it talking.

"We gotta go. With everyone coming in to see her, hair ran long and I didn't get back in enough time. We're running late."

He knew this, she didn't have to tell him.

He didn't share that info.

He walked her out the door, managed to keep Rocky from following them to the garage as he got her in his Bronco and they took off.

"I talked with her and Mamie's driving Andy back to Sunnydown after he's done at work. So we don't have to leave early."

"Right," Hix muttered.

Andy had started about a month after Shaw left for the marines at J&K's Electrics. He did cleanup and stock work.

That was, he did that until he'd been caught talking to some customers about a TV and he'd surprised the owners with his knowledge and enthusiasm. It surprised the owners further when the customers took Andy's recommendations and bought the expensive TV Andy recommended.

That had earned him a polo shirt with the store name stitched on it and a salesperson's position. He had heavy supervision. But he even surprised Greta with the fact that he was a savant at all things with a plug.

The owners used what made Andy special to their advantage.

Andy didn't mind so Greta didn't mind, which meant Hix didn't mind.

He'd had three seizures there and got flustered once, enough to bump into a display of thumb drives, knocking it over and making a mess, which flustered him even more.

They'd just called Hix, he'd come, calmed him down, took him home and they said no more. They just called "hey" when Hix walked him in the next day.

He didn't remember a quarter of the sales he made but he didn't have to remember what he'd done to sell more.

It worked and it might not have changed Andy, but it made him happy.

Hix drove them to the church, helped his wife out of the Bronco and got her ass to a pew.

It was when he was sitting next to her, staring at the front when he felt her fingers curl around his.

"Hey," she called.

He turned to her.

"You okay?" she asked.

"Yeah," he lied.

Her smile was soft and her head tipped to the side.

"Don't lie to me, smokey," she said quietly.

"Not sure I should be here," he told her.

"She asked you as well as me."

"I'm a remin—"

Greta squeezed his hand, got close and whispered, "She asked you. It means something you're here. And you're you. You know that. So you're here."

He swallowed.

He then nodded.

She gave him another soft smile, turned to face forward but did it dropping her head to rest it on his shoulder.

Only then did Hix relax.

He watched the groom come in with his groomsmen.

Then, with Greta and the rest of the congregation, he twisted in his seat to watch the bridesmaids walk down the aisle.

The wedding party was small.

The attendance at the wedding wasn't.

So when the wedding march started, there was a lot of noise of shuffling feet when they all stood to watch the bride walk in.

Her kids walked in front of her.

Her father was at her side.

And after she arrived at the front and they all sat down, Hix allowed his wife to cry for the third time since they got together.

The first was when he asked her to marry him.

The second was while she was getting married to him.

And that was the third and he hoped the last.

Then they sat in a church and watched Faith Calloway standing with her kids, her hair perfect, her dress pretty, the smile on her face luminous, as she married a man named Owen.

The End

Read more Kristen Ashley Standalones

Play It Safe

No connections. Play it safe. These were the rules Ivey lived her life by.

Until she hit Mustang, Colorado, a perfectly imperfect town where the citizens were welcoming and one of them included the tall, beautiful, macho man rancher cowboy, Grayson Cody.

On the run for a decade, Ivey knew she was supposed to play it safe. But she was tired of being on the run. She wanted normal. She wanted real. She wanted a home.

And she wanted Grayson Cody.

And Grayson Cody wanted Ivey.

Everyone who saw them could see they belonged together. There was one man in this world for Ivey and one woman in this world for Grayson Cody.

So they fell in love.

But just as quickly as they fell together, they were betrayed and torn apart. Separated for years, Ivey was certain her life would not include her rancher cowboy.

Until the town of Mustang reached out to her when Gray was in trouble. Even though she thought he broke her heart, she charged in to help. Then Gray and Ivey discovered they were betrayed and not only that, Gray had an enemy who would stop at nothing to defeat him.

Keep reading for more of Play It Safe.

Play It Safe

Chapter One

No Connections. Play It Safe.

It was time to get back to the hotel, I knew it.

But I didn't want to go.

Because he was still sitting at the bar, drinking beer from a bottle, chatting and smiling at the bartender, nice, friendly. She was very pretty but older than him, five years, maybe ten. They knew each other, they liked each other, both well. But not like that. Just friends. Maybe good friends. He came in a lot or in this small town they ran into each other a lot.

Whatever.

It was just friends.

Which was good.

Not that I was going to do anything about it. I couldn't.

No connections.

Play it safe.

Still, if I could connect, if I could let go, if I could take a risk, I'd do it with him. In all my wandering, all I'd seen, all the people I'd met, he would be the one I'd smile at and do it without a guard up.

He'd be the one I'd want to smile back at me.

Time to go.

I sucked back the last of my beer, set it on the table in front of me, shrugged on my jacket, buttoned it up and wound my scarf around my neck. Then I pulled the long strap of my bag over my head, hooking it around my neck so it slanted across the front of me. Then, eyes to the door, I slid out of the booth and left.

I didn't look at him.

Couldn't.

So out I went without even a glance.

The cold hit me like a slap. It was late January. We should be in the south. What we were doing up here, I didn't know. But Casey led and I followed. That was always the way.

Always.

Half a block down, cross the street, two blocks up, I went through the parking lot to the cement walkway, then down to our door.

I stopped at it and stared.

I didn't need the Do Not Disturb sign to tell me not to disturb. I heard the giggling moans, the chuckling grunts.

Hells bells.

I sighed, lifted my hand and looked at my wrist.

It was eleven oh two. Nothing open in this burg except that bar.

And he was there.

I couldn't go back.

It was also cold.

I sucked in breath, lifted a fist and pounded on the door.

The giggling, moaning, grunting and chuckling stopped abruptly and I shouted, "Fifteen minutes to wrap it up!"

Then I turned and walked through the parking lot, checked both ways even though in this tiny town at this hour, traffic was light as in, non-existent.

Still, I hadn't survived my life to get run over on a deserted road in a nowhere town at twenty-two years old.

I crossed the street and headed into the park I'd spied there. Even in this weather, I'd noticed kids playing in the playground, folks walking their dogs, men jogging, women jog-walking. Active community. Safe community.

If I let myself think about it, I knew I'd like it. It would intrigue me. It would make me feel things I couldn't feel, want things I couldn't want.

So I didn't think about it.

I headed to the playground, sat down in a swing, wrapped my hands around the cold chains and started swinging.

I needed gloves.

We didn't have the money and I didn't spend a lot of time outside. So I didn't really *need* them except right now.

So no gloves.

I was lucky I had a scarf.

I kicked my feet out then shoved them back and again until I was swinging, not high, just back and forth, gentle, soothing. Something to keep my mind on while I waited. Something to keep my mind off other stuff while I waited.

Surprisingly, I heard the rattle of a car and not a good one. My eyes went down the street and I saw a beat-up pickup truck heading my way. It kept going. Streetlights showed it was light blue. Lots of rust. Not just old, *old*. It looked it and it sounded it. I kept swinging as it passed right on by.

I stopped watching and kept swinging.

Then, my heart beating a little faster, I kept swinging as it came back in my eyesight, this time reversing.

Not good.

It stopped opposite the park, opposite me and it idled.

I counted. One, two, three...I got to twelve and it shut down, the lights going out.

Really not good.

I heard the creaking, loud squeak of a door that seriously needed some WD-40 then the same sound ending with a slam.

But I saw him over the roof of the car and my heart beat even faster. I kept swinging slow and gentle as the man from the bar rounded the hood of his truck and walked toward me.

Faded jeans. Leather jacket. Scarf. Hands shoved in the pockets of his leather jacket. But I knew he had gloves.

I saw all that hours earlier when he walked into the bar. Scarf and gloves said he had someone who cared about him or he worked outside. Men like him didn't buy scarves, women bought them for them. The leather jacket was a nice one, expensive, but it wasn't new. It hung down over his hips, had flannel lining I'd noticed when he swung it off in the bar. It was beat up but not worn out. Fit him well.

Too well.

Like the jeans.

He headed my way, and in the dark without streetlights close I couldn't see his eyes on me.

I could feel them.

I dropped my feet and my heels thudded into the frozen dirt mixed with packed snow under them. My body kept swaying and my feet brought me to a halt about a half a second before he came to a halt six feet away.

"Park's closed at nine."

That wasn't good. Not that I was in the park well past closing hours but that he had a nice voice, deep, resonant, rich. It was attractive. Very much so.

Also not good.

My guess, he was in his twenties, not as young as me but not much older. Still, his voice and manner—both held authority, confidence. Lots of it. More than his age would give him in normal circumstances. Men that age, they were still boys.

Unless life made them men.

Play It Safe is available everywhere.

About the Author

Kristen Ashley is the *New York Times* bestselling author of over eighty romance novels including the *Rock Chick, Colorado Mountain, Dream Man, Chaos, Unfinished Heroes, The 'Burg, Magdalene, Fantasyland, The Three, Ghost and Reincarnation, The Rising, Dream Team, Moonlight and Motor Oil, River Rain, Wild West MC, Misted Pines* and *Honey* series along with several standalone novels. She's a hybrid author, publishing titles both independently and traditionally, her books have been translated in fourteen languages and she's sold over five million books.

Kristen's novel, *Law Man*, won the *RT Book Reviews* Reviewer's Choice Award for best Romantic Suspense, her independently published title *Hold On* was nominated for *RT Book Reviews* best Independent Contemporary Romance and her traditionally published title *Breathe* was nominated for best Contemporary Romance. Kristen's titles *Motorcycle Man, The Will*, and *Ride Steady* (which won the Reader's Choice award from *Romance Reviews*) all made the final rounds for Goodreads Choice Awards in the Romance category.

Kristen, born in Gary and raised in Brownsburg, Indiana, is a fourth-generation graduate of Purdue University. Since, she's lived in Denver, the West Country of England, and she now resides in Phoenix. She worked as a charity executive for eighteen years prior to beginning her independent publishing career. She now writes full-time.

Although romance is her genre, the prevailing themes running through all of Kristen's novels are friendship, family and a strong sisterhood. To this end, and as a way to thank her readers for their support, Kristen has created the Rock Chick Nation, a series of programs that are designed to give back to her readers and promote a strong female community.

The mission of the Rock Chick Nation is to live your best life, be true to your true self, recognize your beauty, and take your sister's back whether they're at your side as friends and family or if they're thousands of miles away and you don't know who they are.

The programs of the RC Nation include Rock Chick Rendezvous, weekends Kristen organizes full of parties and get-togethers to bring the sisterhood together, Rock Chick Recharges, evenings Kristen arranges for women who have been nominated to receive a special night, and Rock Chick Rewards, an ongoing program that raises funds for nonprofit women's organizations Kristen's readers nominate. Kristen's Rock Chick Rewards have donated hundreds of thousands of dollars to charity and this number continues to rise.

You can read more about Kristen, her titles and the Rock Chick Nation at KristenAshley.net.

facebook.com/kristenashleybooks

instagram.com/kristenashleybooks

pinterest.com/KristenAshleyBooks

bookbub.com/authors/kristen-ashley

tiktok.com/@kristenashleybooks

Also by Kristen Ashley

Rock Chick Series:

Rock Chick

Rock Chick Rescue

Rock Chick Redemption

Rock Chick Renegade

Rock Chick Revenge

Rock Chick Reckoning

Rock Chick Regret

Rock Chick Revolution

Rock Chick Reawakening

Rock Chick Reborn

The 'Burg Series:

For You

At Peace

Golden Trail

Games of the Heart

The Promise

Hold On

The Chaos Series:

Own the Wind

Fire Inside

Ride Steady

Walk Through Fire

A Christmas to Remember

Rough Ride

Wild Like the Wind

Free

Wild Fire

Wild Wind

The Colorado Mountain Series:

The Gamble

Sweet Dreams

Lady Luck

Breathe

Jagged

Kaleidoscope

Bounty

Dream Man Series:

Mystery Man

Wild Man

Law Man

Motorcycle Man

Quiet Man

Dream Team Series:

Dream Maker

Dream Chaser

Dream Bites Cookbook

Dream Spinner

Dream Keeper

The Fantasyland Series:

Wildest Dreams

The Golden Dynasty

Fantastical

Broken Dove

Midnight Soul

Gossamer in the Darkness

Ghosts and Reincarnation Series:

Sommersgate House

Lacybourne Manor

Penmort Castle

Fairytale Come Alive

Lucky Stars

The Honey Series:

The Deep End

The Farthest Edge

The Greatest Risk

The Magdalene Series:

The Will

Soaring

The Time in Between

Mathilda, SuperWitch:

Mathilda's Book of Shadows

Mathilda The Rise of the Dark Lord

Misted Pines Series

The Girl in the Mist

The Girl in the Woods

Moonlight and Motor Oil Series:

The Hookup

The Slow Burn

The Rising Series:

The Beginning of Everything

The Plan Commences

The Dawn of the End

The Rising

The River Rain Series:

After the Climb

After the Climb Special Edition

Chasing Serenity

Taking the Leap

Making the Match

Fighting the Pull

The Three Series:

Until the Sun Falls from the Sky

With Everything I Am

Wild and Free

The Unfinished Hero Series:

Knight

Creed

Raid

Deacon

Sebring

Wild West MC Series:

Still Standing

Smoke and Steel

Other Titles by Kristen Ashley:

Heaven and Hell

Play It Safe

Three Wishes

Complicated

Loose Ends

Fast Lane

Perfect Together

Too Good To Be True

Printed in the USA
CPSIA information can be obtained
at www.ICGtesting.com
CBHW032339020524
7993CB00008B/58